Annette Kinnear

I0526271

On the Bit
Catherine

Romantic Thriller

Translated from the German original by the author -
Rappenschwarz © 2012 Annette Kinnear

10 9 8 7 6 5 4 3

Editing:	Dr Peter Merrington, www.petermerrington.com
Cover Design:	Kirsty Macfie, www.mac2design.carbonmade.com
Cover Pictures:	Young Couple:© Shutterstock 47723926 / Serg Zastavkin
	Horse's Eye:© Shutterstock 2954226 / Yusef El-Mansouri

ISBN:	978-0-620-61601-0

www.on-the-bit-thriller.com

Books by Annette Kinnear

2009 Your Career, Your Life, Penguin Group
2012 Rappenschwarz, Annette Kinnear
2013 Headhunting. Bitte husten Sie, falls Ihr Chef gerade
mithört, Schwarzkopf & Schwarzkopf
2013 Rappenschwarz 2, Annette Kinnear
2014 On the Bit. Catherine, Annette Kinnear

Part I

Catherine

"Strength does not grow from physical power, but from an unbending will."

Mahatma Ghandi

1.
South Africa, May 5

"My decision is final." Catherine drummed her fingers on the desk top while she waited for Alexander's reaction. On the desk lay the dismissal letter that she'd just slammed down in front of him.

Alexander weighed up his next move: Denial? No chance! This fiasco had gone way beyond that. There was no plausible explanation. The only thing to do now was to show remorse. "Okay, I messed up. Once! Do you have to fire me for that? I've always done a good job, come on!"

"I'm sorry. I can't work with you anymore."

"Look, I understand what you must be thinking right now, Catherine, but you know my background. I need my job. Make an exception. It won't happen again." Alexander forced a smile onto his face.

"You abused our trust and used your privileges to access my personal database, Alexander. You had no right to snoop around in there and," she swallowed, "yesterday you lied to me without batting an eyelid. Had you really regretted this, you would have come clean then."

"I never harmed the company!"

"Because I stopped you just in time!"

Catherine showed no sympathy.

Alexander didn't know her like this. She had a temper, yes, over small stuff, but one could always reason with her. The bigger the problem, the more level headed her typical response. Her rigor surprised him, although he never did trust her entirely. Don't mess with her; a colleague had warned him right from the start, describing her as an unpredictable spoiled brat, who'd accomplished nothing on her own. The highlight of her career, he'd claimed, was to take over the headhunting business from her late father.

Other employees, especially those who worked closely with her, loved their charismatic boss. Catherine was undeniably unconventional. This trait worked for some, others hated it. She had a strange enigmatic flair about her – which was why he'd snooped around in that mysterious database in the first place.

Alexander resolved to regain her trust and then prove to her that she'd made the right decision. "Catherine, I'll fix this! Give me another chance." He would not let those dubious foreigners get to him again. From now on he would be the best IT guy that Firm Commitments ever had.

"Fetch your papers from HR on Monday. If you need a reference, give them my number. I'll keep it to your work and won't mention this little debacle. More than this - I can't do for you, Alex." Catherine stood up.

He didn't move from his chair. Her final verdict invoked a look of shame and his eyes drilled an imaginary hole into the table top. He wanted to follow her example and get up. The meeting was over. He understood this but his body was doing its own thing. Short of breath, his mouth dried up and while he was gasping for air, a spongy powerlessness flooded through his veins. It was unbelievable: no second chance. No reconciliation. No warning. Not even a disciplinary hearing which he was after all entitled to, or at the very least an offer to part on mutual terms. This isn't how it's going to end, you witch from hell! Internally he hissed obscenities about the female anatomy. Rational thinking was out the window — he felt like he was on a medieval battlefield facing the enemy. As his consternation ebbed off, his anger welled up. The adrenalin rush caused his muscular body to become rock-hard, now steering his energy towards self-justification in order to restore his cracked self-image. Gradually, the blame for his mess-up shifted to her "injustice".

Catherine began to sense the silent anger and started to feel unsafe. Slowly she slid along the edge of the table back into her chair. Alex now stared straight at her and it was Catherine who looked down. It was Friday, shortly after 6 pm, the offices were nearly deserted. "All right then," she gave in, "we'll talk about it on Monday."

"I want an answer now!"

"Give me some time to think, okay, Alexander? I'll try to solve our problem and we'll talk again on Monday. Let's say at 9 am?"

Her voice sounded too soft, her tone too sweet — surely she was feeling intimidated and only pretending to be ready for a compromise, he surmised, silently celebrating his upper hand. "Our problem? A few minutes ago I was the cheat and you the judge. And you can keep your stupid reference!" Catherine, usually quick-witted, didn't utter a syllable. He'd never seen her unsure of herself, and now she was scared. Of him! Gripped by a sudden attack of bad conscience, he reminded himself that after his release from Waterberg Correctional Services after two years of incarceration, Catherine had financed a Network Administrator course for him and given him a job. With a sweeping motion over his forehead he wiped away the guilt and re-organized his mind: one mistake and gone was her grace and goodness. Typical capitalist employer! No sense of community and solidarity.

"Alexander, we must finish off now. I'll see you on Monday."

Her attempt to regain control infuriated him. His anger compelled him "to teach the bitch a lesson". At lightning speed he shot up, bent over the table, grabbed her right arm with his left hand to hold her down, and with his right hand he gripped her neck. He knocked her head into the table top, held down her face for a New-York-second, lifted it up and slammed it on the surface again. Then he jumped around the table, pulled her from her chair and dragged her singlehandedly to the corner where he pressed her against the wall.

"Alex, Alex," she pleaded, flailing about and fighting for air.

The power was thrilling. Reveling in his superiority, he held her against the wall by her neck. "Alex, please," she croaked again and dug her nails into his hand around her throat, which resulted in him using even more force and pushing her higher up the wall. Her feet were no longer touching the ground and this gave her space to move. She managed to hit his shin with the sharp tip of her stiletto shoe. In his adrenaline rush he felt no pain but in reflex, Alexander let go of her neck and Catherine fell to the floor. Bending over her, he now pummeled her body with his fists. She threw her hands over her head and twirled around, but was now trapped between the corner and the desk. His blows pounded into her back. Every one of her defensive moves was surpassed by masculine strength, but her throat was free. Her lungs filled with air again. With all her remaining strength she screamed for help as loudly as demon, which frightened the living daylights out of Alexander.

"Okay, okay, I'm sorry."

He let her go.

The door flew open. Tom, Catherine's 2 IC burst into the room. "Hey, what's going on here?" He pounced on her attacker and pulled him off her. "Are you nuts?" thundered Tom and shoved him aside. He took Catherine's face in his hands. "Are you alright?" Catherine nodded weakly. "Hey, where do you think you're going?" Tom jumped up to chase after Alexander who was bolting out the door but Catherine held Tom back.

"Let him go."

"Let him go? We have to call the police! What's going on here, dammit?"

"It's okay Tom. I just fired him. He'll fetch his papers on Monday and we'll never see him again." She buried her head in her shaking hands and wondered about how strenuous it was to think and talk. Tom tried to help her up and muttered words such as "unstable", "jail" and "you never listen to me", but she brushed him off. She also declined Tom's offer to drive her home. Still lying on the floor, she curled up and started to cry.

Two hours later, she was home. Her phone rang.
Tom: "How are you feeling now?"
She: "Fine."
He: "Should I come over?"
She: "No."

Shortly afterwards she called him back. "Sorry I was so cranky earlier. It's just that nothing like this has ever happened to me. When I couldn't breathe anymore, you know, I thought I was going to die. It was awful. But I'm okay now, really. Thanks for everything. It's over now."

--- oOo ---

At the same time in Spain - a man, whom Alexander knew as Javier answered his call from South Africa. After hanging up, Javier dialed a number in Buenos Aires. There, a housekeeper answered and put through the call. As Sophia eavesdropped for a moment, she heard that "the man from South Africa was off the job and no longer had access". Before she put the receiver down, she heard the words "Miami" and "May 13".

2.
South Africa, May 12

The day of her trip to the States turned out to be a huge challenge for Catherine's diary. It was 5 pm by the time that she turned on her out-of-office-text. "I am currently abroad and will be back on May 19. Please get in touch with my assistant Gaby Harris. She will assist you until I return."

On her way out of the office, chewing on an apple, her hand- and laptop bags over her shoulder, she issued last minute instructions to Gaby.

Her bookkeeper, Dora, chased her down the passage.

Eyeing the signature blotter which seemed to burst at the seams, Catherine stomped back into her office in a huff, put down her bags and took the pen that Dora held out to her. She sat down at the small conference table next to her desk and with an irritated sigh turned to her industrious colleague. "Dora, why do you come at the last minute? You know I have to get to the airport!"

"Oh, it's fine Catherine, I'll ask Tom. I just thought, since you are still here, I'd quickly catch you."

"Dora, how long have we known each other?"

"Since I joined Firm Commitments. Uh, two and a half years I think."

"Two and a half years?"

"That's right."

"Will you allow me to give you some advice? I mean, since we've known each other for two and a half years?" Catherine's cynicism was hurtful.

"Of course."

"My advice is: be more economical with your communication." Dora's puzzled look revealed, she didn't get it. Catherine clarified, "Next time, say nothing, except that you need the signatures."

Catherine was clearly overstrained. She'd been in the office since 5 am and was nearing the end of a taxing day. Her schedule had been mapped out in detail, including scores of unexpected tasks, but she had to be at the airport by 6 pm – and now she faced a brutal encounter with the rush hour traffic. Despite her hurry, she studied each invoice carefully before signing it.

Gaby stuck her head through the open door. "I have Albert on the line. I told him you just left, but I'd try to catch you. Do you want to talk to him?"

"Put him through." "Hi Albert. How are you doing?" While talking to the client, she reluctantly signed an EFT for a mobile projector screen, which she found unnecessary, but Tom insisted on buying.

"I would be better if I heard from you once in a while."

She closed the blotter and nodded her dismissal. "Albert, I'm sorry. We should have kept you in the loop but we're onto it. Promise."

"Well? How is my search coming along?"

"Susan is putting together a shortlist as we speak. She'll be in touch with you later to give you a quick overview, okay?"

"Thanks Catherine. Sounds good, but we're running out of time. You press me for an exclusive mandate and a juicy retainer and then you don't deliver!"

"We'll deliver, Albert! Don't you worry about it. I'm on my way to the airport, but I'll only be away for a week. As soon as I get back, we'll do lunch, okay? In the meantime Susan will set up the first interviews for you."

"She can reach me on my cell. Where are you going?"

"To Florida, on a search conference."

"Have a good trip, Catherine."

She called Susan via her office shortcut. When she didn't reply, she pressed Gaby's. "Gaby, where can I find Susan? She's not answering."

"She left early today because her baby is sick."

"Oh right, I forgot. Please call her at home and ask her to ring Albert. He paid us a huge retainer. He wants to see some results, or at least hear from us. She must tell him about a few of the candidates, definitely about the one from

Freestreme. That résumé looked the most promising. Find out how little George is and tell her I hope he gets well soon." After pausing for a moment, she added, "Tell her, the profiles of the process engineers *must* be on his desk before the end of the week. And she must call him tonight still!"

"Will do. Should I let Tom know that you're running late?"

"Where is he anyway? And where is my suitcase?"

"In the parking garage. He took your stuff down already. Will you be a while still? Should I call him?"

"No, I'm on my way." Tom had offered to take her to the airport. They traditionally used this time to discuss last minute hand-over issues. "Keep well, Gaby. Look after everything for me. Oh, one more thing. Did you arrange for roaming? I forgot to ask you for this."

"Your cell is unrestricted."

"You're the best."

"*Please* hit the road now. The traffic! And as soon as you're out the door, I can get to my own mess that's been piling up."

"Bye now. See you in a week."

Catherine took the elevator down to Level P4 where Tom was waiting in his ridiculously luxurious Range Rover. With a sigh of relief she sank into the cream leather seat. "What a day. I picked a really bad time for this trip. We've got so much on the go."

"Don't worry about us. We're quite capable of getting on without you, you know." He winked at her. "Every now and then!"

"Glad to hear it, but you really need to keep an eye on this Jesstron Works assignment. Susan seems so distracted at the moment. Albert is getting nervous, and frankly, so am I!"

"Yeah, yeah, we went through this yesterday, remember? We'll be fine. Stop control-freaking. I've got this!"

"Your words in God's ear."

"When should I fetch you?"

"Already organized. Gaby will take care of it. What can I get you from Florida?"

"A Nascar model. Ford Fusion."

"Sounds complicated. Can't I get you a toy dolphin or a fridge magnet? Do they even have car models in Miami? I'm not going to Detroit, you know."

"Nascar's big in the South. Best you order it straight after your arrival from Nascar Merchandising and have them deliver it to your hotel. Otherwise, a Chevy Impala."

"Oh come on. Can't you ask Gaby to do this? She knows where I'm staying and she's got my card number."

"First you offer to bring me something and then it's too much trouble!"

"Nonsense! It's only about the logistics. Of course I don't mind and you're right, I'll handle this myself. In the States, Alexander said the other day, they deliver within hours. Wouldn't hurt Susan to try to do the same for a change," she muttered under her breath.

"Leave her alone, she's got a lot on her plate right now. But speaking of Alexander. We have to talk about what happened on Friday."

"What about it?"

"Catherine, he attacked you! Nearly killed you! You don't let me take you to the doctor, don't even let me drive you home. How did you even manage to get home in the state you were in? You don't call the police, a week later, you're off to the States! As if none of this happened!"

"No use crying over spilled milk. What happened is what happened. If I gave up after every setback, where would I be today?"

"Set-back? What are you trying to prove? That you're Superwoman?"

"We're in a tough business, Tom. No work no pay!"

"You have to lay charges. If you don't, I will."

"Don't you dare interfere! I want to forget the whole thing."

"Fine! It's your life! But then you'll at least tell me what triggered it off."

"He hacked into my database."

"How did he manage that?"

"No clue. You know how IT people are! Always one step ahead of us. Damn nuisances! Anyway, it's irrelevant. The data is encoded, there's nothing he can do with it."

"How did you find out?"

"Coincidence. I unexpectedly showed up at his doorstep on Wednesday evening to press him on the new format of the billing reports we asked for, because he was two weeks behind."

"Typical!"

"He was just finishing a phone call and acted strangely after he'd hung up. The more I dug, the more evasive he got. I smelled a rat and called Jan the next day."

"Jan from Neflics? The security guy?"

"Yeah. He confirmed my suspicions and I confronted Alexander with the facts. He denied everything, but on Friday late afternoon Jan's official report came through and so, proof in hand, I grabbed Alex that same evening. You know what happened after that."

"Why are you refusing to lay charges?"

"Um, didn't we just kill this one? The deal was, I tell you what happened and you stop getting on my case about involving the police!"

"Catherine you can't just pretend nothing happened."

"Tom, Alexander has a previous conviction. He'll end up straight back in Waterberg if I report him. How is he ever going to find another job?"

"So?"

"Tom!"

"You feel sorry for him?" Tom lifted his eyebrows in disbelief.

"Kind of."

"I'm not buying that. Has your resistance to the police anything to do with the contents of your database?" Tom didn't wait for her answer. "Why all this secrecy? All our data is confidential, why are you making such a song and dance about your personal database?" Catherine sulked in silence. "Sorry, I didn't mean that, but people are talking. Rumor has it that your father had some dubious dealings going on. And that this database has a lot to do with it."

"Oh is that right? Rumors! Well how about this? During the economic crisis in the early nineties my father saved the company from bankruptcy. He did so with one single placement from this 'dubious' database that kept the company going for a whole year. Why don't they rumor about that!"

"Catherine, come on, I'm not stupid. What records are you keeping in that database? Hostage negotiators? Pirates?"

"Pirates? Who recruits pirates? Have you lost your mind?"

"Why not? Crime is rife everywhere."

"Who said anything about crime?"

"Alright then, what are you worried about? Why all these phone calls to Brussels, the disguised invoices, the huge fees? What's going on?"

"Okay Tom, listen. My father placed scientists. Special scientists."

"How 'special'?"

"Do you remember the trials of the Truth and Reconciliation Commission in the mid-nineties?"

"Sure. They were part of history at school."

"Did the name Dr Werner Van der Sonsen come up?"

"The guy who invented that poisonous necklace? He refused to testify, giving up his chance of amnesty."

"Precisely. The necklace story was fodder for the rainbow press. I mean – move over James Bond! Desmond Tutu appealed personally to Van der Sonsen but he preferred to take his secrets to jail with him."

"I suppose that's where he's still 'residing'."

"Yes he is. He invented a lot of other stuff, too. Much of it was never made public."

"And?"

"And what?"

"Catherine, come on. Do you have Van der Sonsen in your database?"

"Maybe. I haven't been able to decode all of the info but his team is there and many others of his kind. Almost all of them made use of the amnesty offer and were not prosecuted for their apartheid atrocities. Okay, some are retired now but many of them are still well connected. And a lot of them are playing around in the private sector."

"Are you telling me that you're placing these guys?"

"Not them, our industry here is too small, but my contacts have extended to a large network. These people attend congresses and make international connections. Besides which, I'm not talking about just these kind of scientists."

"I can't believe that you would get mixed up with a crowd like that."

"What's that supposed to mean? Where do you think I get these fantastic referrals to be able to work these intricate job orders? Do you think I enjoy playing cat and mouse games at the institutions for weeks on end? This way I make one or two calls and bingo! You can imagine how distrustful this target group is. No unknown headhunter can get to them. But they trusted my father, and now they know me, too. They see me as one of them and meet with me without reservation and give me tips on where to look. Tom, apart from private contacts I have no competition. In Europe, Asia and Africa I am the only source for such professionals. Wouldn't you protect such a treasure? Just because something isn't common knowledge, that doesn't make it wrong. Anyway, I only place these scientists into reputable positions."

"We're here."

"Thanks for driving me."

"Catherine?"

"Yeah?"

"How have you secured this database now?"

"Like I said, it's encoded. Only I can decipher it. There's no formal system. My father took details of my childhood, memories of my mother, school, friends, and so on and reworked the information. He used literature I liked, movies, vacations, relatives, music, everything that was of interest to me when I was growing up. The database gives me clues and I take it from there. To decode a name can take hours but following the logic I get there eventually. And I'm getting faster."

"I don't get it."

"Do you promise not to google around if I give you a name?"

"Do I have to promise that? Come on Catherine, you're asking too much of me!"

She laughed. "Oh well, it doesn't matter. I wanted to fill you in one of these days anyway. It's like this: A candidate's name is for example Natalie Flemming. He recorded her name as 'Greek Affair'. It sounds crazy but I get what he means almost every time. The word 'affair' stems from one of my favorite books from my teenage years, *The Natalie Affair*. I couldn't put it down!" The thought of past reading pleasure distracted her for a moment. "After that he always teased me about my affair with books. So, let's stay with our example. This was his way of telling me that the next word was about books. With 'Greek' he was referring to a book that I read while we were on vacation in Greece – *The Spy who Loved me* by Ian Flemming. So, I deduce that Greek Affair means that the target person's name is either Natalie Ian, Ian Natalie, Natalie Flemming, Natalie James, James Natalie or Natalie Bond. There are no contact details. I only get the encoded names and the appropriate fields of specialty. Then I run the names that surfaced against related areas of expertise until I get a match."

"The perfect security system because no one can crack the code, except you."

"Correct. Some are simple. Others are hard work, as I said. It's still relatively easy though because the people have been so perfectly pre-selected. After this, all I have to do is to carry on as usual and contact the person or someone from their professional environment."

"Is the database still on our system?"

She shook her head. "Jan removed it after the incident with Alex and now I take it with me everywhere. Here on this little hard drive." She reached into her bag and pulled out a handy little back-up device. "This way I'm not office bound and I always have access. The office copy is gone, as I said, but I keep one in my safe at home."

"Be careful, Catherine. This doesn't seem kosher to me."

"Tom, as soon as I'm back, we'll talk about everything, okay? I confided in you because I believe it's time to expand this aspect of Firm Commitments and to include you in the scientific branch. Yesterday I got a call from the Pentagon. The US market would be an absolute breakthrough. I could use your help."

"The Pentagon? Delusions of grandeur?"

"It's a natural progression! I have a flawless reputation in a unique niche market."

"What does the Pentagon want from you?"

"I'm not sure. Somehow they got wind of my trip to Miami and suggested a meeting. The client is a Mr Brower. I haven't had the opportunity to research him but a conversation never does any harm. I'll get to meet him in the hotel lobby on my departure day. What do you say? Are you keen?"

"Take care of yourself, Catherine. Have a good trip."

While he was unloading her luggage from the trunk, Catherine pondered on his cool good-bye. She would have preferred not to have opened these issues in a rushed conversation on the airport highway, but she was sure that she'd be able to convince him after a few more talks.

She hugged him and blew a kiss, and then – pulling her suitcase behind her – she disappeared through the door of International Departures.

In the departure hall several Muslim women, covered head to toe in black robes, walked past her. Catherine assumed from their way of dressing that they were allowing themselves to be dominated due to a lack of willpower and shook her head.

Had Catherine only had a glimpse of what tyranny she herself was about to be subjected to, she would have abandoned her plans.

3.
South Africa, May 12

"I need an aisle seat," said Catherine. "I get airsick." But the young clerk on the other side of the check-in desk shook his head. Gaby had made the seat reservation for her, but something had gone wrong. The Delta Air employee, overwhelmed by the last-minute rush, couldn't confirm her seating position. In her own hurry, Catherine hadn't checked her ticket and she realized too late that the seat reservation was missing.

Catherine wasn't lying – she really did suffer from airsickness. They'd have to do something – even if it meant giving her one of the front row seats that were kept open for special cases. A vomiter on board was the last thing anybody wanted, and the airline would have to get this right.

The overwhelmed young man behind the counter stared back at her: "You have to mention this when you make the booking."

"I did!" she protested.

"I'll see what I can do." While he hacked around on this keyboard she made a good study of his features – a habit she'd picked up as a recruiter. She admired the high cheekbones that offset his jet-black eyes. A set of short dreads framed his picture-perfect face. Her thoughts wandered off to the warm Caribbean and the friendly tones of reggae. She resolved to have long girl-dreads woven into her hair for her next beach vacation. Then she returned to the present moment, with rising apprehension. He was still searching on his computer, for what seemed like an eternity. She wasn't a frequent flyer, she never flew business class, she made few demands, but an aisle seat was imperative.

In the end she did get her seat in the exit row. Now she wouldn't be penned in between people, and she was near the toilet in case she got nauseous. Freedom was important to her. She hated restrictions. Of any sort!

The flight was uninteresting, like most. To make matters worse, her inflight entertainment center threw an erratic temper tantrum every time she'd progressed a few minutes into a movie. She figured that the defective console was the check-in clerk's revenge for her nagging. She resigned herself to a dull and boring flight and used the opportunity to think. Her thoughts ran for a while on the work that lay ahead, and then they drifted into daydreams. As usual, the image came to mind of her two horses – Make Me, and Illusion of Love.

Catherine was mostly immersed in her career, and at twenty-four she already carried a lot of responsibility – with little natural talent for the line of work in which she found herself. She had to fight for every small success, and she was used to that. She had one particular talent, however – the ability to fight, to struggle, to assert herself. She felt no qualms at wrestling with the world – her violent encounter with Alexander was a case in point. But being out in the country with her horses gave Catherine stillness of mind and restored her balance. Riding, riding, riding. She always made time for horseback riding. Catherine reflected on her riding lesson yesterday evening, and on her patient riding instructor Claudia. Claudia had coached her through all the ups and downs of horse riding since her seventeenth birthday. Oh to be a good rider! A constant battle, but it was worth it - she told herself.

Since the death of her father, Catherine lived alone. She had no family and only a small circle of friends, and one year ago she'd dissolved her engagement to Warner. Engagement! Absurd. Who still gets engaged? Truly a moment of madness! This is how she saw it today.

Her house was old, her garden large. She loved everything old and classical - and everything big. Perhaps this was because of her small frame. Short and very slim, but not fragile. Catherine was the female answer to small-man syndrome. Healthy, top fit from all the riding, and equipped with a fierce temperament – these qualities made up for her lack of natural talent and academic qualifications. That's why she stepped onto the battlefield daily. She enjoyed taking people on. 'My way or the highway' was her motto.

Her long red hair, highlighted blond, reached down to her hips when it was fully teased out. Her eyes were large and emerald green, framed by freckles that gave her a cute appearance. In business, she believed that this, along with her youthfulness, stopped people from taking her seriously in what was a cutthroat industry. As a result, she spent a lot of time on her appearance. She was always made up and well-dressed – as far as her budget allowed. Only at night, alone, or sometimes with her horses, she wore her face naturally. Her horses loved her as she was. And, when she was made up, with all her freckles covered, she liked her face, too.

Catherine was not aware just how her appearance affected others. It was striking, and yet girlish. Her petite frame, which she viewed as a disadvantage, triggered infantile erotic fantasies in men and her physical presence tended at first to disarm men and women alike. In business, they underestimated her – until they got to know her. This only enhanced the mystery surrounding Catherine Zitgow. With a fierce retort, she could sweep people off their pedestals in an instant – and reel them in again a moment later with her natural charm. She was authentic and puzzling at the same time. Underneath this unpredictability lurked a romantic moodiness, but she masked this so successfully with her sharp tongue that her opponent was drawn into a battle of wits before he or she could blink twice. Her enigmatic aura coupled with her unusual looks made her magnetically attractive.

It came down to an intuitive spiritual intelligence, which compensated for her lack of academic skill. But most of all it was her ability to fight like a she-bear that secured the deals. Clients and candidates felt safe in the knowledge that she would not surrender until she got them what they wanted. But the high energy levels needed to keep up the constant fighting came at a cost, even at her young age. She had a strange relationship with her body. She didn't know it well, and she felt irritated by it when a scratchy throat or a headache started to bother her. And tiredness, hunger and thirst she viewed as an unnecessary interruption to a busy schedule.

Two flight attendants pushed their cumbersome trolley down the narrow aisle, and she was invited to order a drink.

"Sprite Zero, please," she replied.

"Sorry, we've only got regular Sprite."

"Coke Light?"

"Sure. With ice?"

Catherine drank hardly any alcohol, ate almost nothing sweet and had never smoked a cigarette in her entire life.

She sipped her Coke and her thoughts wandered back to Tom.

Tom. He was discreet and creative. She didn't regret having confided in him about her special assignments, and she looked forward to working with him more closely. She wouldn't have trusted anyone else with this.

The first time that she had dug into that secret database was to secure a head of research for a power station in East Africa. This assignment came from one of her late father's contacts. It appeared to be a harmless requirement: a top caliber turbine engineer was wanted, with highly developed commercial skills. She didn't stop to wonder why an ability at intricate financial negotiations was necessary for a post in rotation technology. The thought of corruption and bribery in the African power generation industry didn't enter her mind. And sure enough, this placement resulted in a subsequent (and important) recommendation: she received her first government contract with a North African state. Concerned about her fee she demanded seventy-five percent of it upfront. To her surprise, they paid this and the final invoice without delay. Another mandate closely followed this one, and then that particular demand tailed off. Then, on Monday, she received the call from Washington. She was to meet them after her Miami conference, in order to discuss what appeared to be a lucrative deal.

The cabin lights were switched off and passengers pushed back their seats, preparing for sleep. Catherine, though, was kept awake by her active mind. Her thoughts moved to Alexander.

Alexander was supposed to come and see her to pick up his letter of summary dismissal, but he hadn't arrived for his appointment. The South African labor law granted him thirty days to respond to the instant dismissal. She hadn't followed the correct procedure, which would have been mandatory despite his gross misconduct. If he took any steps in that direction, Catherine thought to herself, she would of course answer by simply laying criminal charges for assault. Then again Alexander's situation in the job market was pretty poor and he had little to lose – so he might take that route in desperation. These uneasy reflections stripped her of any further chance of sleep. She propped herself up in her cramped seat and sat, wide awake, throughout the long haul. How uncomfortable planes are! The distance between the seats reminded her of the millimeter markings on her school ruler.

When she finally landed in Miami, after a short stopover in Atlanta, she felt like a bus had run over her.

4.
USA, May 13

Shortly after her arrival, Catherine received confirmation of her appointment with the Washington contact – a Mr Brower, at 10.30 am on May 17, in her hotel lobby.

The days of the conference passed quickly. She eagerly absorbed the new material outlining the latest recruitment methods for experts in the scientific field. By day Catherine rushed from seminar to seminar, took notes, met some of the speakers and networked with her North American counterparts. In the evenings she shopped and shopped and shopped.

At 10.20 am on her departure day she enquired about her Nascar parcel, the present for Tom. She'd been promised that it would be delivered to the hotel before her check-out date, but it hadn't yet arrived. She sat down in the lobby, ordered a skinny cappuccino and waited for Brower.

She was dressed to make a strong impression – a combination of urban fashion with a hint of traditional Africa. For this effect she chose her only Blumarine dress. She had purchased it in an attack of lavish overspending: a white, frilled tube dress with a pale leopard pattern in a hint of pink. She wore it underneath a soft pink goat-leather jacket. She had complimented the outfit with an oversized, playful fringed handbag crafted of goat leather, but this morning she left that in her room. To distract from her short height she chose radically high-heeled pink plateau sandals with ankle thongs. She wore her hair loose and – as always in public - she was dramatically made-up.

She dialed Tom's number but had to make do with his mailbox.

"Hi Tom. It's Catherine. I'll be leaving in a few hours. Your model car hasn't arrived yet. Please call me right back and tell me whether I can get you something else, in case it doesn't work out. I'm just about to meet with the Pentagon people and I must go through my presentation again. If I don't hear from you, I'll see you tomorrow."

She leaned back in her chair and opened the folder that she'd put together for her potential new client. She'd kept its contents brief: a few words about Firm Commitment's history, a couple of remarks about her team and the usual search strategy. She'd also included a discreet paragraph about her placement successes in the scientific field.

At 10.30 she put down her document and looked around for the waiter who still hadn't brought her coffee. Instead of the waiter, her view was filled by three well-groomed men who approached her across the lobby. Two of them slowed down and held back while one man stepped directly towards her.

"Catherine Zitgow?"

"Yes?" She stretched out her hand. "Mr Brower?"

Without taking her hand, the man replied curtly, "Mr Brower is expecting you. Please follow us."

"Um, I just ordered a coffee. Mr Brower is welcome to join me."

"He never conducts initial meetings in public."

The man motioned her to accompany him. She rose, frowning, and immediately all three formed a frame around her and urged her forward.

They left the lobby via the main doors and walked towards a black Chrysler 300C which was double-parked in the street outside the entrance. Catherine was irritated but she held no suspicions. The strange style of meeting seemed to her part and parcel of a top secret affair, and beneath her irritation rose a flutter of excitement.

The men spoke English to her, with an accent which she found hard to define. By their looks and speech she guessed them to be Latin American, but she wasn't sure. She didn't dwell on the matter. The driver, waiting at the wheel, had taken her attention. Unlike the others, he was not well presented. He was unshaven, and he wore neither a chauffeur's uniform nor a suit. Instead he was dressed in a faded pair of jeans and a washed-out T-Shirt which could have been yellow in color about fifty years back.

She was ushered into the rear of the Chrysler, where she found herself flanked by two of the strangers. The third one sat down in front alongside the driver.

"Have you packed?"

"Yes."

"Where is your baggage?"

"In my room."

"Do you have any bills to settle, other than the coffee?"

"No, I always pay my extras cash, but I have to check out nevertheless. Why do you ask?"

"Give me your key card."

"That's not necessary. I'll take care of that later, thank you," she replied. She spoke crisply, but with a rising inflection of uncertainty in her voice, like a teenager who didn't quite know what questions to ask but still desired clarification.

"Your card, please." The man repeated his request, this time with a gesture of impatience and a hardened tone. Catherine turned to him and stared. "We'll take care of your baggage and the check-out," he elaborated, "and then we'll take you to Washington."

"Washington? That's over a thousand miles! That's impossible. I have to be at the airport in four hours. The arrangement was that I meet with Mr Brower here in Miami. If he can't keep his appointment, he has my full sympathy. I want to get out now!" She moved to reach the door handle, across the legs of her escort seated on the right.

"Ms Zitgow, your key please!"

"Look, I'm not going to give you access to my room. My things stay where they are and I'm leaving now. Hey! What are you doing?"

The man poked around in her tiny jacket pocket for her key card, found it and handed it to his colleague in the front passenger seat. He removed her cell phone from her other pocket, which was barely big enough for it, switched the phone off and slipped it into his own pocket. Catherine clung to her presentation as though it was of immense value, and in a way it was – that document now constituted her only possession; everything else was in the room or had just been confiscated.

"Room number?"

Catherine stared stubbornly through the windscreen and didn't answer. Until she felt something hard drill into her waist and she heard the release of a gun's safety catch. She only knew this threatening sound from movies, but it was unmistakable.

"1187."

"Which floor?"

"Eleventh."

The man on the passenger seat got out and took quick long steps towards the hotel entrance. While they waited for him to return, it was so silent in the car that she thought she could hear her heart beat. When the man put the gun away she started to protest again: "Maybe what you're doing here is normal when one does business with the Pentagon, but before we drive to Washington now and I miss my plane, I would like to speak to Mr Brower on the phone."

Her objection bounced off a wall of silence, and she was forced to diagnose her dilemma. Influenced by Hollywood drama, she connected the strange behavior of the men, whom she believed to be Central Intelligence Agents, with the standard conduct of Pentagon employees. She would turn down the assignment, that's for sure! But she resigned herself to the fact that she would have to be driven to Washington in order to tell Mr Brower personally. And she'd miss her return flight. Even though she felt uneasy about having been threatened at gun point, she wasn't really afraid. Tom was surely right, she thought, when he said this was all a number too big for her. Many numbers too big.

The man reappeared with her luggage and loaded it into the trunk. Before he could get back in the car, Catherine asked for her handbag.

"You won't need it," replied the man on her right, while the chauffeur steered the Chrysler out of the city in a southerly direction.

This was too much. The rude refusal shook her. The blood rushed to her head and her hands started to shake. She had to gasp for air several times in order to stay calm. "Okay," she spluttered, "you know what? You're going to take me back to the hotel now, or straight to the airport, or you'll at least stop the car and let me get out here. I have no intention of accompanying you to Washington. Please tell Mr Brower that his offer is declined until his employees learn some manners."

"You're going nowhere but where we tell you," the man on her right said curtly. Then he added: "We're almost there."

"So Mr Brower is in Miami after all? We're not going to Washington?"

The driver headed for the yacht basin and once there, she was told, "We're boarding a boat now. Please stay calm and don't make a scene."

"Why shouldn't I be calm? Just tell me what you're planning. Is Mr Brower waiting for me on the boat?"

"Let's go."

When she got out, rough harbor air filled her lungs, that universal mixture of sea and marine oil. The sun already stood high up in the sky and she became intensely aware of her surroundings.

Not far out were two cruise ships whose vast hulls seemed to block out the sky. Seagulls cried loudly overhead, and a steamboat blew its horn. Somehow this is all very adventurous, she thought.

Hemmed in again by her escorts, she was led onto a luxurious Bertram yacht and taken directly below deck. Going down the companionway she felt the vibration and surge as the boat's engines came to life. She was shown into a windowless cabin, but she felt the movement as the boat maneuvered from the quayside. Two twelve-liter Cummins diesels effortlessly pushed the hull out, and into the waters of the yacht basin. The engines throbbed, and the motor yacht gained seaway with a surge as it exited the basin.

Catherine struggled between a sense of adventure, and rising panic. She didn't want to overreact, so she engaged herself with looking around. The bulkheads and the few pieces of furniture were all upholstered with soft white pleated leather, and the fanciful thought came into her mind of a padded cell in a sanatorium. A half-open curtain revealed a tiny bathroom facility consisting only of a sink and a very low toilet, both evidently made of some kind of plastic. She was still reflecting on psychiatric clinics and the abolition of straightjackets when she heard the unmistakable sound of the door being locked from the outside.

This she hadn't expected. She dashed over to the upholstered door and rattled on the handle. There was no response. She hammered in vain against the soft upholstery and shouted "Open the door! Open the door immediately!"

Her voice sounded muffled, deadened, in the cabin, and she realized that the bulkheads were sound-proof. She stopped shouting and applied her mind to the situation.

You fool. The Pentagon? An official contract? You never checked it out in advance, did you?

The self-reproach was the first of many such bouts to come, but she still didn't feel any fear. Her strong nerves had served her well, up to now. Her natural sense of the unorthodox still led her to believe that this exotic way of arranging things was only Mr Brower's eccentric habit. Wherever did he want to meet to discuss his mysterious search assignment? She thought of the Cayman Islands. Even Cuba came to mind. CIA drama, just like in the movies.

Her eyes fell on two fashion magazines, both latest editions. But her unease grew considerably when she saw a horse riding and a managerial magazine. How thoroughly had she been researched? She didn't touch the equestrian or business literature. That would have been too diverting. But she briefly flipped through the meaningless fashion magazines before she lost concentration. An hour passed, and she found herself motionless at the edge of her chair, doubled over, hands in her lap, shocked.

You even got into the car voluntarily. How could you have been so stupid? It's unbelievable, I mean, how naïve can you be?

She could no longer negate the threat of the pistol. Her stomach felt like it was churning gravel. Thin, hot saliva formed in her mouth in order to dissolve the stones in her gut and her rebelling stomach caused her to retch uncontrollably. But it wasn't just the rising anxiety and self-reproach that had upset her stomach; the increasing swells were making her seasick. She managed to dash to the dwarf toilet just in time. And, barely back in her chair, had to get up again and throw up once more. And again.

After half an hour, she was shivering feverishly and her reserves of strength were ebbing. He entire focus was reduced to one thing only: her seasickness. There was not an ounce of energy left for anything else. Again and again she vomited, and in the end she remained on her knees hanging over the toilet bowl.

Two hours passed. She was on fire with feverish sickness, and even though her stomach was completely empty, her body continued to be seized by violent gagging reflexes. Her throat burned and her temperature seemed out of control. She tried to imagine having land under her feet, but she could not fool her inner sense of balance which was hopelessly off kilter.

A hand, seemingly from nowhere, stroked the hair back from her face. A gentle hand. She was startled out of her misery. She hadn't heard anyone enter, and when she turned her head she was surprised to see a man in such close proximity. He wasn't one of the men from before. This man was overweight and much older. He had thin, light brown hair and a scruffy beard. He looked like he had jumped straight off a warrant-for-arrest poster. "Take this, Catherine. You'll soon feel better." He spoke in a matter-of-fact tone, while handing her a tiny white pill. Reluctantly she swallowed it, after a brief attempt at inspection. He helped her off the toilet bowl and onto the bunk. "Everything alright?" he asked. "Are you feeling better now?"

Of course I'm not alright, was her immediate response, but instead of speaking she merely nodded. As miserable as she felt, the seasickness was also a blessing because it was a distraction and a wake-up call at the same time. This is what it must feel like to die, she told herself – nothing else can be this terrible. Surely she'd be able to extract herself from this mess as soon as she felt better.

Think like a man. Don't scream. Stay cool. Men have testosterone to help them in such situations. Women also have a little testosterone.

With mantras such as these she implored her body to produce more testosterone. But instead of the strengthening hormone, her body seemed to push out only melatonin, because now she was feeling sleepy. Then it dawned on her that it wasn't the hormones that were responsible for her tiredness but the tablet that she'd swallowed. The man must have given her a sleeping pill. Sleep! A tried and trusted way of containing sea sickness.

At some point she dozed off and only awoke the next day. Although the sunrise was invisible to her in her windowless cabin, she guessed it must be early morning, because the man from the day before stepped into her cabin again and brought her breakfast on a tray. There was a glass of orange juice, a plate with a sliced apple and a hard boiled, quartered egg, as well as a small bowl of oat porridge. He put down a plastic bag and deposited the tray on her bedside table. Catherine sat up and glanced at the breakfast and then at him. "Eat, Catherine."

"What am I supposed to do with this 'balanced' prison meal? Is this the best the Pentagon has to offer its guests?"

"We're not from the Pentagon, Catherine."

"Yeah, yeah, the CIA then."

"We're not from the CIA either. We've got orders to take you to a secret location. Please eat. Your stomach is empty."

"If you treat me like this, how do you expect me to be positive about the assignment?"

"That's not our problem. We're only responsible for your transport."

"Okay, but why are you locking me up? Do you honestly think that I'd jump overboard? In the middle of the ocean? I know I was stupid to get into the car with your buddies, but come on!"

"Please eat now. You'll need it."

With a big frown she squinted at the meagre meal and moaned, "I can't! I'll have to throw up again. From which company are you?"

"Just eat now. And get changed." He picked up the plastic packet and emptied its contents onto the floor. A set of combat-type clothes fell onto the lush white carpet. The pile of the carpet was so thick that even the pair of boots failed to make a noise as it landed the floor. "Listen to me. I mean well." With this advice he left and locked the door.

Not from the Pentagon? A secret location?

For the first time Catherine sensed serious danger. She didn't touch the food. She slowed down her perception of time until it seemed to stand still. This way, her brain could process events more efficiently in order to make critical decisions. Nevertheless, she had absolutely no idea what to do next. All she could think of was "too little testosterone", which made her burst into a fit of laughter.

The desperate giggles made way for the first stream of tears and through the watery veil she finally inspected the clothing. They smelled of fresh sea air and looked unused. Her new wardrobe consisted of an olive green old-fashioned warm sweater, khaki colored cotton pants with laces at the bottom, and a pair of light brown laced hiking boots with uppers that reached just over the ankles. The boots were solid but pliable, and they seemed to be top quality. The clothes appeared to be military issue or heavy duty working kit.

She swallowed her pride and forced herself to act rationally. And so, in lonely surrender, she took off her beautiful dress and put on the new issue. The arms of the jersey were too long, the pants too wide at the waist but the boots fitted like they were made for her. Because she had no belt, she pulled up the waistband and folded it down and over twice to stop the pants from slipping off. She was grateful for the boots - her high-heeled shoes were a total mismatch for the situation.

Shortly after she'd changed, two of the original kidnappers from Miami brought her on deck, without saying a word. There, instead of spotting the expected harbor, she saw herself surrounded by ocean.

"Where are you taking me now?" Her voice was harsh and edgy.

No answer.

Pulling herself together, and without further word, she followed the two men to the railing. A quick glimpse revealed that a high-powered cigar boat was waiting to take her on board. These boats, commonly referred to as "fast boats", were the preferred method of transport for Caribbean drug dealers due to their speed and superior maneuverability. She clambered down into the boat, on which a tall burly man was busying himself with two massive Mercury 250 hp outboard motors. The two men on the deck of the Bertram left her in his care, and quickly disappeared from view.

The fancy yacht drew away slowly from the smaller boat at first, in consideration of the anticipated wake. However, as soon as they were some distance away, the motor yacht suddenly pulled off at an enormous speed. The little cigar boat bobbed up and down in the strong wake of the disappearing vessel.

Catherine's heart fell when she realized that she was at sea alone, with only this stranger and no idea where the journey would end. Without money, papers or provisions she was dependent on the giant in the boat. His weight seemed liable to capsize the small craft at any time, so she merely stood where she found herself, legs slightly bowed to keep her balance.

There was hardly any room on the narrow boat - almost half of the stern was taken up by petrol tanks underneath a tattered tarpaulin. The man motioned her to sit next to him and handed her a swim vest, even though he was not wearing one himself. Catherine approached him gingerly, put it on, sat down and kept quiet. He opened up the engines, and the boat surged forward.

She was afraid of the surly stranger and the open sea, and she was worried about getting seasick again. Every time they hit a swell, she felt as if her stomach and back were compressed to the density of a block of concrete. She couldn't believe how fast they were going. It felt worse than any amusement park ride she'd ever been on. And sure enough, after a few minutes of banging over swells at breakneck speed, she got sick again. Throwing up, the best she could do was turn her face to the side for fear of unbalancing the boat. What a disaster. How bad could things get? The man handed her a dirty cloth, which she took from him but didn't use, it was so disgusting.

"Please tell me where you're taking me!" she shouted over the noise of the engines and the sea.

He responded with not a word nor gesture.   No encouraging eye contact. Just deadly silence. Eventually, on account of her constant nagging, she forced out a response – and he replied in broken English, "To land."

"Which *land*?"

"Stay quiet and you'll be fine."

The Pentagon story no longer made any sense at all. This performance had nothing to do with the CIA. "Are you a terrorist?" she asked, even though she had to admit that none of the men looked like political or fundamentalist fanatics, least of all this giant. The man's facial expression showed no emotion and again he was not lured into a reply. "You don't look like a terrorist," she shouted with her eyes closed. They were stinging from the salt spray that was lashing them. Animated by the undoubtedly unusual sight of his blind but rambling hostage, he unexpectedly broke into such loud laughter that Catherine flinched and opened her eyes. The volume of his voice matched his size. Even the sea could not dampen it.

"How do terrorists look?"

"Terrorist kidnappers usually cover their faces, their heads are covered, they often have beards," she rattled off her clichés. "You look more like a South American drug dealer to me." That was the end of the brief dialogue. The skipper laughed once more about her drug dealer diagnosis but no longer responded to her.

For the remainder of the day not another word was said. The skipper reduced speed, the sea became calmer and her back no longer hurt so much. Evening descended and the sun spread less and less warmth and light over the ocean. When her guard noticed she was cold, he motioned to a man's jacket under the tarpaulin, which she held over the front of her body like a shield. "Thanks." In her gratitude she interpreted the gesture as an invitation for another attempt at conversation: "Why am I being abducted? What are you planning? Where are we going? Where are the others?" she shouted above the engine noise. "Okay, you're not talking to me, I get it, but what's your name? I'm Catherine."

The man nodded. "*Catarina, sí.*"

"Yes, Katharina, my German name. Where I live now, they call me Catherine. What's your name?" The conversation was over and every new attempt brought the same reaction: none.

During the night she asked for water several times, didn't receive any, and found a few hours' sleep despite her nagging thirst and nausea.

When she woke up at sunrise she felt so weak and desperate that she thought she couldn't live much longer. Her head hurt from the dehydration and she had no interest in her surroundings. She was completely taken up how to convince the man to give her some water.

If I catch some spray of the sea water with my hands and drink a mouthful, it will prompt him to give me some drinking water – dead I'm of no use, sick I'm a burden. But if this plan doesn't work, I have an even bigger problem.

She thought back and forth, but couldn't decide what to do. Still deep in thought, she noticed a reduction in the roar of the engines. She realized that the man had indeed throttled back, and up ahead she could make out a cove.

They came "off the plane" and water entered the open stern of the boat as it sank back. There were three men waiting in the sheltered cove, and the skipper steered the boat towards this group until they beached on the sand. They pulled the boat farther up the beach and the skipper got out. Catherine remained seated, dazed with thirst and unsure what to do.

Someone handed her a plastic container with water from which she drank until the greedy gulps started to hurt her gullet. He took the container from her and held out his hand to help her out of the boat. Her feet thudded into the sand as she took her first step. Since the night on the Bertram and this hell ride, her typical need for independence had flown out the window and she welcomed any small helpful gesture. One of the men put the container into a rucksack which he fastened to her back. The handcuffs dangling from his pocket made her hope that they were not for her. The rest of the team was busy with the boat where they were unloading and reloading various tanks and containers. They finished their work and, with Catherine in tow, they departed. The skipper and his cigar boat stayed behind.

--- oOo ---

At this moment an e-mail arrived in Tom's inbox. Catherine's writing style was unmistakable:

Dear Tom

They awarded me the Pentagon contract, provided that I start working on the assignment immediately. It's a huge deal and totally exciting, but it means my return will be delayed somewhat. Don't tell Gaby or anyone else about the Pentagon. Just say that I decided to stay a while longer in the States. Please take over all my appointments and Gaby must pay my bills from my private account regularly until I come back. It should only take a few weeks. Tom, don't call me, I've been isolated here day and night and have to keep my cell phone switched off. This also applies to e-mail. The colleagues that have been assigned to my project are super and I'm having a lot of fun. I'll explain everything when I'm back. What I'm doing here is top secret. Just decide on anything important and urgent and all the other stuff will just have to wait till I return. You'll hear from me from time to time, but I'll definitely let you know my arrival time, just before I fly home. I can't wait to tell you everything.

Hugs to you and the entire team,
Catherine

5.
Venezuela and Columbia, May 18

They marched away from the beach over stony terrain for about six hours, until they reached a road. Catherine had no idea in which country she was.

At the roadside, in front of an old MACK truck, there was another swift change of crew. It surprised her how many people were involved in her abduction. The loading area of the timeworn truck looked like an animal transporter - it was planked in and covered with a tattered olive green tarpaulin. They hoisted Catherine up into the back and chained her against the wooden framework. The old truck roared into life and laboriously began its journey. Through gaps in the planking, Catherine watched the truck swallow mile after mile of deserted landscape. The 380 hp engine rattled its load through the countryside reluctantly, not because its cargo was too heavy but because the truck was so old. She wondered about its mileage, and whether it would keep going. Trucks and boats, like everything powerful, had always been of interest to Catherine, and focusing on the condition of the truck diverted her from greater anxieties.

It was a long and hard journey, but nothing compared to the pounding that she'd got at sea. Swaying in the rear, she kept her travel nausea under control. Every now and again the engine's monotonous roar made her doze off until, after many hours, the truck came to a halt. She looked at her Rolex: 6 pm. They hadn't taken her valuable watch away from her, nor her notably large diamond ring, an engagement present from Warner, which he refused to take back after they broke up.

She expressed profuse gratitude for a short toilet break at 10 pm and one of her guards said, "*de nada,*" which she took to mean "no problem". He led her back to the truck where he took a packet of biscuits out of her rucksack and handed it to her. Her shaking hands ripped at the packaging, and she stuffed three into her mouth at one go. These biscuits were her first meal in over thirty-six hours. And they tasted really good!

As a child, Catherine had lived in the Rhineland in Germany for a few years. One dull afternoon, when she had nothing to do, she stumbled across a US Army unit which was out on a maneuver. The GIs invited her into their tent and she followed them in. Her father had strictly forbidden her to make any contact with strangers, but curiosity overcame her conscience. She wanted to see the army set-up. Any sense of danger merely increased her interest. Strangers in US Army uniform - what a thrill!

The soldiers welcomed the inquisitive little girl warmly. They were also bored with their own routine on that rainy Thursday afternoon, and the unusual visitor was a pleasant distraction. They shared the same kind of biscuits with her. Thick and dry, but not crispy. More crunchy. They tasted neither sweet nor salty, but weren't bland either.

Now, more than a decade later, in the darkness, in an unknown place, Catherine devoured one dry biscuit after another. She ate like a starving orphan. Quickly, quickly, before they tie you up again, she urged herself on, but the man allowed her ample time. Then he handed her the water container and let her drink before chaining her again – but not as tightly - to the truck's frame. In a rush of gratitude she imagined him being a family man, and that she had nothing to fear from him. Even though it was nonsense to make up stories like that, it occupied her mind with pleasant thoughts.

They drove through the night till sunrise. The scenery changed from flatland to hilly terrain and back again. The road was scantily tarred, and the surface deteriorated to pure dirt at times. But everywhere, on tar and sand, the wheels labored through potholes and over rough gravel. The width of the road accommodated only one vehicle at a time. If they had encountered another vehicle, one of them would have had to pull off the road to let the other come through. This wasn't necessary - for the entire route they encountered no vehicles other than a few shabby donkey carts. Catherine no longer doubted that she'd become the victim of an abduction. Her fears grew but she kept herself from becoming too emotional in the hope that she was moving towards a destination where she'd find rational answers – or a way out.

The second night they spent at a remote old farm house, and then continued their journey at 7 in the morning. On this day, after about two hours, the truck turned off the road and rattled directly across a stretch of dusty landscape before coming to a halt in the middle of nowhere. One of the men untied her and told her to get out.

Fearing the worst, she climbed out slowly and warily. Gradually, unawares, Catherine had become entrapped in a common psychological phenomenon: the notion that consistency implied safety. Thus, she sensed danger in each little change of events, any occurrence that deviated from what she perceived to be the ordinary. Taking into account the time of day and the deserted landscape she saw no apparent reason for stopping there. Her "family man" stayed in the cabin while his companion shoved her on foot farther and farther away from the truck. She stumbled along in front of him, and her unease turned to fear. He would rape her in the bushes or cut her throat, she surmised. Maybe both.

Her fear gave her new focus, and she began to resist. In a sudden panic attack she tried to tear herself away. She managed a few paces, yelling out for help. The intensity of her scream woke her from the daze into which she'd fallen from many hours of rough travel. It would have been deafening, had it not been swallowed up by the desolate landscape. It was utterly futile. Seconds later she was again in the power of her guard.

"Quiet! Sitting! Here!" he ordered her in angry, broken English. He shook her like a rag doll, and shoved her down onto the sand. For the first time, she was handcuffed. This was the worst of all, much worse than being chained to the truck. The wall of the MACK created the illusion of some protection and the vehicle was moving towards a goal. To a point, it was understandable to be tied up in the truck, but what was happening here made no sense at all.

"Please don't hurt me," she heard herself whimper as though she was standing outside of herself.

A cell phone rang. The man snapped open an old fashioned Motorola. "*Sí, Señor. Sí.*"

While she was still wondering how it was possible to get a signal in this wasteland, the man held the phone to her ear.

"Catherine?" asked a sovereign male voice.

"Yes?"

"Are you okay? More or less?"

"Yes," she replied without thinking about it.

"That's because you've been a really good girl up to now. You're doing well."

Was that a compliment?

She swallowed it like honey and was ashamed of herself for it.

Catherine, that wasn't a compliment, he's belittling you!

Unable to voice her insight, she remained captured by the words of the caller.

"Listen to me carefully. If you utter one word, I'll interpret this as you not desiring any information and I'll put the phone down."

Despite the content, the message sounded like a declaration of love to her. The timbre of the voice. The clear English, the sense of real contact after days of unknowing.

The voice.

"You're in the hands of our organization. We've taken you from Miami to Venezuela and from there over the interior to Columbia where you are right now. In order to shorten your journey, the driver will now change from the back roads to the toll roads. This new route will make your trip a lot more bearable. Other than the toll gates you may also pass some police road blocks. This is why we'll seat you in the cabin from now on. Should the truck get stopped, leave the talking to the driver, best you pretend to be sleeping. Don't try to explain your situation. It's unlikely they'll pay any attention to you, being a woman. Should I be wrong in this regard it will merely result in a short negotiation about a bribe. The worst that can happen is a shoot-out with you as its first victim. Here I'm not wrong, because these are my orders to your escorts. Catherine, the alternative is to cuff and gag you and place you into a crate. I want to spare you this, so stay reasonable.

"Shortly before the Amazon basin you'll reach a prison camp deep inside the woods. You'll spend a few days there until we have secured the route for your further transportation on foot. You may encounter other hostages there. They have nothing to do with you or us. Don't talk to these prisoners. Obey all orders. Don't waste your time with useless attempts to resist or flee. You have a long and arduous road ahead of you and there's absolutely no chance of escape. If you need anything from your Columbian guards that is essential to your survival, politely state your request and don't bother them unnecessarily for anything else. The less you inconvenience them, the more pleasant will be your stay. At the slightest resistance they will kill you. Without hesitation. The level of tolerance of the guerilleros in these camps is zero. Stay cooperative and nobody there or for the rest of your journey will hurt you. I give you my word."

I give you my word.

"If this is how you want things to be, listen to me. Catherine, I'm going to repeat the most important points now:

"1. There's no chance of obtaining freedom through a third party or escape.

"2. Avoid any unnecessary form of contact.

"3. Nobody will harm you, if you follow all orders. Answer me now, Catherine. Have you understood everything?"

"Yes."

"I must be sure that you'll do what I instructed. Will you do that for me, Catherine?"

Will you do that for me, Catherine? Who speaks like this to a stranger? Who is that?

"Yes," she breathed into the phone, barely audibly.

Yes? Why do you say yes? Protest, negotiate, demand something in return!

"Very smart. I'll make sure you'll be safe. Don't give up. Not much longer now and everything will be alright, okay?"

"Yes."

Why do you keep saying yes?

Click. Disconnected.

It was like waking from a spell. She followed her escort apathetically back to the truck. She let him remove the cuffs, climbed in the front and sat in the middle, hemmed in left and right by the two men. After they'd reached the toll road, they made faster progress, apart from a few severe traffic jams. It felt good not to be isolated anymore, to not be tied up any longer and to be able to sit in the driver's cabin protected against the bumps and shocks of the road. Whenever she didn't think about "the voice" – and that was very rarely over the next few hours – she observed the busy roadside activities and marveled at how drastically the scenery and conditions kept changing. The brown of the Andes turned into tropical green and the cold and dry mountain air warmed to a humid broth that was barely breathable. After the highway ended, the truck again chugged along slowly over ever worsening road surfaces. Eventually they were forced to leave the truck behind and continue on foot.

On the trip they'd paused at the predicted toll gates and she'd also spotted several cops leaning against their motorcycles on the side of the road, but they weren't stopped. She was more relieved than disappointed about that, because she asked herself without ceasing how she should respond to an encounter with the police. In the end, this decision was spared her.

Just before sunset, drenched with sweat, footsore, they reached a compound. Undoubtedly this was the camp which the man on the phone had told her about. They entered the inner court and from there they took her to her skimpy accommodation, pointing to an old dirty mattress as her bed. But finally she could have a wash, and she was given food. A meagre amount, but it was as good as a feast. Inside the building and the inner court she was free to move around.

Days passed. The next step on her journey was delayed. There was a lot going on inside the camp but none of it had to do with her. Her two guards had been replaced by innumerable armed men who all wore military uniform. One was particularly nice to Catherine and because he saw to her several times a day, they developed an almost friendly relationship, even though the caller had told her not to get involved with anyone. Sometimes this guard brought her some indefinable root vegetable or a piece of fruit. Once even a piece of chocolate, whatever he could lay his hands on. At these occasions he rattled on in Spanish, of which Catherine understood practically nothing. She found the conversations laborious and absurd. Because it was mostly meaningless small talk, she got used to replying "*Sí*", without knowing what she'd just agreed to. She waved off the thought that this Mr Brower even existed, and she assumed instead that the motive for her kidnapping was a ransom payment. Trevor would have to organize the money. Every day she hoped for further instructions on the telephone. Only direct contact with "the voice" would enable her to progress, but she didn't hear from that man again.

On the fourth day, after breakfast which consisted of apples, she strolled to the well in the center of the courtyard. She pulled up a bucket of water and began to scrub her few clothes with the tiny lump of soap that they had given her. They'd also supplied her with another set of kit: a second long pair of cotton pants and a long sleeved shirt made of light material. While she was busy with her laundry, the man who seemed to like her kept her company. After a while he started staring intently down the shaft of the well. Then he stood up and left with the words, "*Adiós Señorita. Buena suerte.*"

It was clear the man was trying to tell her something. She looked first at him and then into the well. She puzzled at the thing, and then she noticed that there were a few loose bricks in the wall of the well, halfway down to the surface of the water.

Could the space behind those loose bricks be hollow?

She was tempted to check out the shaft.

Has this man just pointed me to an escape route?

It wouldn't be hard to climb down the inside of the wall of the well, she realized. There was an iron ladder to hold on to and she would be strong enough – but the real danger lay in not getting caught. She looked around: a few guerilleros sat at a long table in the distance playing cards.

Wasting no time, she lifted herself over the lip of the well and gingerly took hold of the ladder. She descended towards the surface of the water, and then turned to face the loose bricks that she'd spied in the wall. She pulled at them and they came away easily, falling down into the water. An opening! A horizontal shaft! Without a second thought, she crept into the shaft and leopard-crawled inch by inch towards freedom.

She eventually emerged and found herself in the yard of a burnt-out ruin. Plant-growth sprouted out of the derelict structures. There was no fence or guard in sight. She didn't pause to think or to catch her breath, just glanced up at the sky to get her bearings. To the south was thick tropical forest. She settled on the north, the direction from which she'd come. She crossed deserted fields and untamed meadows, tussling with the unfamiliar thick vegetation. It grew thicker and she became entangled in bushes. It was no longer open ground. The bushes were now trees, and she found herself circling around lost and aimless in the fringes of the Andean cloud forest. Until she fell down from absolute exhaustion. Her body felt as heavy as a ten ton truck, her heart pounded in wild exhilaration, but emotionally she felt as if she had wings. She was free!

6.
Columbia, May 24

Catherine nestled down among the gigantic roots of a huge Ceiba tree, its climbing orchids providing an almost idyllic shelter, and waited for the night to arrive. She was hungry, thirsty, tired and very lonely. With the dusk came a cool breeze that chilled her. Sitting among the roots, leaves and low-hanging branches, she noticed the many exotic insects – beetles, and industrious ants – but she was too weak to take any interest in them. She'd lost her orientation completely. All she knew was that she was in the middle of a tropical forest, and somewhere outside the mass of trees was the open landscape.

Getting out of the well, she had scratched her hands and legs. Now, confronted by the unknown and without any kind of medication, she was more worried about the possibility of an infection than by the discomfort of the scratches. And she had other, more immediate concerns: no water, nothing to eat, no warm clothing. All she had was the optimism that came from being free again. This was enough to keep up her spirits and her strength for a few more hours, despite the abysmal facts of her situation. Surely, she thought, in the morning she'd discover a river or a pond to drink from. *Ekuseni*, Zulu for tomorrow – a fresh day, new hope – would surely bring something good. *Ekuseni*. Her father had often spoken of that to give her courage when she was down.

But Catherine's new-found liberty also had its downsides. For the first time since her abduction, she was truly on her own – and it surprised her how much she missed human company. She couldn't understand why she felt so lost without her kidnappers, until she gathered her mind and dissected the recent events rationally: they'd looked after her relatively well; they'd provided for her basic needs and had never been really mean to her. Emotions, however, threatened to swamp her reasoning, and she contemplated surrendering and returning to her captors. At that, she pulled herself together again and despised such cowardice. Governed by these contrary thoughts and feelings, she finally fell asleep.

The day was just dawning when noises awakened her. An armed troop was headed for her hideout. Through bloodshot eyes, she could make out their figures among the trees at a distance.

With infinite caution, without a sound, she covered herself with leaves and fallen branches and cowered under these behind the trunk of a large tree. She didn't see or hear any sniffer dogs and the vegetation was thick. If they didn't look straight in her direction, they'd miss her. She held her breath, and the trackers moved passed her. Then one of them turned around, and evidently spotted something. He made a quick sound, and a gesture, and within seconds the whole gang was storming towards her. There was no sense in trying to run away. Dejected, she emerged from her hiding place. She stood up and was dusting the leaves and dirt off her clothes when one of the men smashed his fist into her face.

The force of the blow was cruel. Catherine fell back under it, banged her head against a tree, and fell into the decomposing leaf mold beneath it. She lay there dazed for a moment, and then one of them pulled her up and sank his fist into her stomach. She went down again, slowly rising onto her knees before throwing up. She was horrified to see that her empty stomach was bringing up mostly blood. The men circled around her, but nobody helped her to her feet. With great difficulty she managed to rise, stood up for a moment and suddenly felt dizzy, as though leaves were falling down on her head. Then she passed out.

When she came round, her hands were tied behind her back.

Cooperate and nobody will hurt you.

She'd not cooperated and now they'd hurt her.

Fear develops from the anticipation of loss and pain, not necessarily through actual pain itself, she knew that, and this, she figured, was why she didn't feel afraid. Her fighting spirit resurfaced and she made an important decision: the caller had admonished her not to give up. She would persevere. They obviously didn't want to kill her, otherwise they would have done it already.

A dead hostage brings no ransom.

Coming to terms with the pain and dizziness, she wrestled with another (internal) drama – freedom, capture, the words of the "voice" – "cooperate, Catherine, and you'll come to no harm". Mustering all of her independent character she resolved to endure whatever lay ahead. A journey on foot, the "voice" had said. Fine. So be it. When they reached their destination she would face the "voice" in person, negotiate with it, and win her release.

7.
Columbia and Peru, May 27

For three unbearably long days Catherine marched on with her new group of abductors. These men were cold and unapproachable and purposely excluded her from any human companionship. The twelve-hour marches caused blisters on her feet, aching limbs and severe exhaustion.

On the fourth day they arrived at the banks of a wide muddy river where a small boat awaited them. For six hours they drifted downstream on this tiny vessel before landing on a beach of fine river sand.

Facing them, pushing its rank growth up to the riverfront, rose to view a rainforest like something out of National Geographic. It was thicker, greener and yet more soaking damp than the tropical forest through which they had marched over the past few days. Into this primeval forest her captors headed, deeper and deeper, with silent determination. She had no view of the outside world. Even the sky was blocked out by the dense canopy. The jungle was, itself, a foreign and hostile prison. Running away was not only impossible, it was suicide. She would never find her way through or out of it. The rain of condensation never ceased. She stumbled over, or shrugged from her face, outsized and hideous insects and creatures whose existence she'd never even imagined. Even the dark and steaming flora seemed to threaten her.

Catherine's hands were tied, and she stumbled after her kidnappers – mile after mile further into an ever-deepening nightmare. There was no path and progress was hard. Sometimes they waded through deep water, but the permanent dripping moisture was the biggest plague of all. Each of the three guards had a machete. They used it to hack open a small area through which to pass - step by step by step. But often the undergrowth was so dense that they couldn't even penetrate it like that. Then, they turned back a few feet and tried again from another direction. Because of her tied hands she could not protect herself from the many branches that sprang back at her and mercilessly scratched her face. Often the party crawled on all fours through low gaps in the undergrowth, or slid down banks of mud. When she had to climb a muddy slope, the kidnappers untied her as it would have been impossible to pull herself up without clinging on to branches or lianas.

The man that had beaten her was evidently there to keep her intimidated. Often he glared round at her evilly but to her relief didn't raise his hand to her again – at least not yet. His unsightly moon face was framed by a curly beard. His upper body was well proportioned but the distance between his knees and ankles was tremendously short, even for a short man. Under his faded shirt bulged a big round stomach.

She fell once again to fanciful speculations. He looked more like a low-class trader or merchant than a kidnapper. To get through the many hours of silence, she conjured up images of a Hamburg tea trader from another century. She smiled grimly to herself and invented an internal narrative of a stormy family saga. This was her entertainment, to distract herself from the harsh journey. She built up a private drama about seafaring spice merchants, rough sailors and crooked first mates, and visions of a glorious sun that shone onto the open blue sea. These things were her antidote to the unbroken mass of black and green that engulfed the small party every hour of every day.

Her "tea trader" tied the rope around her wrists so hard that her blood flow was almost cut off, and when this happened she imagined that she'd been captured by pirates. The pirate crew took her to Port Royal, Jamaica on a battered old schooner. There, in her fevered thoughts, she'd settle down on a plantation and make her fortune as a sugar baroness. For hours at a time she drifted off into these fantasies of a romantic future. It was ironic, and she realized that such crazy thoughts served her mind to retain a little bit of sanity. It was much easier to dwell on (or within) these fantasies than to bear the reality. When she did bring her mind back, the pattern was always the same: I have to free myself, it droned under her skull, without ceasing, until she embarked in her head on her next Caribbean adventure.

Disregarding the caller's warning, she eventually did start to forge plans to escape. She did this mainly in the evenings before falling asleep - but no opportunity came, by day or by night. The exhausting marches robbed her of any clear thought or spare strength. In the evenings they untied her hands, allowed her to go to the toilet in the bushes and then chained her to a tree – always well away from the men's camp. They placed her rucksack with water, raw cabbage and army biscuits onto her lap so she could help herself. Until late at night the men listened to the radio, from which emanated mostly Latin American sounds – with one exception. One evening the melody of a song in English came to her through the undergrowth: "Me and Mrs Jones". For days she couldn't get it out of her head. It was her only connection to a civilization that had once existed. Every day they rose before sunrise and the new day dawning presented her with renewed optimism, new hope, which the remainder of the day destroyed. Like the proverb says, "Hope is a good breakfast but a bad dinner".

One lunchtime they reached a deserted camp. Catherine had once watched a TV documentary about the Fuerzas Armadas Revolucionarias de Columbia, the FARC guerilla movement, and the footage had included something very similar. Here, in a clearing in the forest, was a forecourt, a wall of reeds, and a poorly-roofed and rickety timber barracks. In the court there was a well from which water flowed freely from six thin pipes into a stone basin. Here, her captors took off her rucksack and the moon-faced "tea trader" tried to blindfold her. This frightened her and she fought him off with all her might. The more she resisted, the stronger she felt. It seemed to her that she'd grown to six feet and weighed two hundred pounds of pure muscle. Another man rushed in but she'd already managed to struggle away. Spurred on by her unexpected victory she scrambled back into the forest, but they easily caught up with her and dragged her, kicking and screaming, back to the well.

Two men held her while the short guy again tried to blindfold her. And again she lashed out wildly with her tied hands and kicked at him with her legs. Dodging her blows, he lost his balance and slipped in the mud in front of the well. He stumbled to his feet, pulled a stick from his tool belt, and laid into her while he was still getting up. He knocked her down and she too fell on her back into the mud. She crawled away to one side, trying to avoid the rain of blows, but the man landed a final vicious hit on her right hip bone. Most of the force was absorbed by her left thigh, but the blow rendered her immobile. The struggle was over. She lay in the puddle and mud, doubled over and screaming from pain. Now helpless, she was blindfolded and left to lie in the mud. Nobody came to her. Nobody urged her up, or took hold of her. They just abandoned her. Surrounded by darkness, she started to cry. She cried until the tumult around her had completely subsided. She couldn't move an inch. She searched for strength and courage but every attempt to crawl out of the mud was prevented by the shattering pain of her injuries. The slightest movement and every lungful of air delivered more pain. Her right hip bone burned as if a dragon had breathed fire onto it, and her thigh felt as if every few seconds it was struck by a concentrated bolt of lightning. It was as though a gigantic thunderstorm was raging inside her. Apart from that, she was sopping wet, with her head and back resting in deep mud. Would they just leave her alone now to die? She was convinced that they would. But although these three men were no longer around, they had not left her.

And she did not die.

Silently someone bent over her. She felt how a man slipped one hand under her knees and another under her back. The fact that it was a man's touch made her flinch, but she stifled her scream. He carried her for a few feet as if she was light as feather and put her down carefully on a hard wooden bench. She assumed she was now inside the timber building.

The man unzipped her pants and carefully loosened her clothes, lifting her body to enable him to do so.

"Please help me," she whimpered. She didn't want her helper to think that she'd resist again so she desperately tried to lift herself to make things easier. He stripped her skillfully, drawing her clinging pants down to her knees and with evident medical know-how he explored the injuries on her hips and thigh. His hands were reassuring, Catherine felt calmer, and as her heart stopped racing she felt her adrenaline levels drop - which increased her sense of pain. The fire inside her bruised hip blazed more wildly than before. Then she felt the sharp prick of a needle in her upper leg. Within seconds, the pain dissipated. She was gripped by a brief bout of nausea followed by a blissful euphoria. Fully conscious, she lay on the bench feeling neither fear nor pain. She felt lucid and present, almost enlightened. She recognized the effect as that of morphine; there was no doubt about it. Once before she'd received a morphine injection – in the emergency room after a bad fall from her horse. The blindfold and the hand ties still restricted her but she was now completely free from any physical discomfort. The man, not speaking a word, washed the mud off her body as best as he could. In doing so, he always lifted only as much clothing as was necessary to get to each part of her body in turn. He then wrapped her in a soft blanket – it felt and smelled new, not like the rough blankets from the earlier prison compound – and then he sat down next to her. She could sense his presence. A kind of calm descended on her and she fell into a deep sleep.

At daybreak the kind stranger, as she called him from then on, helped her to sit up. He held fresh pieces of pineapple to her mouth which she gulped down hungrily. Then followed a piece of corn bread, and again she ate from his hands like a tame animal.

More days passed, though she lost all track of time. Every morning he put two tablets in her mouth and gave her some water to wash them down. When she needed the toilet, he untied her hands and took her into the bushes. She made an attempt to count the passing days, despite the permanent semi-darkness of her blindfold, by recording in her mind the taking of the tablets. Then there were no more pills, and she gave up the attempt. Perhaps three or four days had passed. Then, out of the blue, she felt him fiddling with the strap of her watch.

"Please leave me the watch," she begged. "Take the diamond ring, it's more valuable."

Unrelenting, he untied her again and helped her to put on fresh clothes, a long-sleeved man's shirt and a pair of pants which he tied with string around her waist. He tucked the pants into thick men's socks, and helped her to put on her boots. She assumed that he was equipping her to protect her from the bites of mosquitos and ants. But it was more than that – her journey was about to continue. He led her out of the building. She heard voices and sensed that he was handing her over again to her escort party. She realized that her time with him, the Kind Stranger, was up. It was foolish to imagine that she could stay with him any longer. However, her depth of feeling – her wondering sense of closeness to the Kind Stranger – served to focus her mind. It motivated her, and she pulled herself together. Even though she was gutted by all that had happened, she would keep her composure.

Her captors led her back into the forest for about a mile, and then they removed her blindfold. As her eyes adjusted, she saw herself completely surrounded yet again by the dense rainforest. For a further two days they marched through the jungle and bivouacked in tiny clearings. The kidnappers no longer made proper camps. Instead, they slept directly on the wet forest floor, with Catherine again tied against a tree a little distance away from them. She still received her apples, cabbage and water, but they now spared her the burden of carrying her rucksack. Her wrecked body was no longer up to the task.

One day they started early, as usual, but had not been underway for long when they stopped at what seemed to be another clearing. It was no clearing, however. It was the end of the jungle. While they rested there, a thin fog rose up among the now-thinning trees. Catherine saw how the men became alert, looking through the fog in one direction, with what seemed to be great anticipation.

8.
Peru, 04 June

Through the thick mist burst the Third Horseman of the Apocalypse on his black horse, or so it seemed to Catherine. She stared in disbelief. A magnificent stallion and his rider were cantering directly towards her. The horse's thick mane flowed dramatically down his massive neck. His chest was broad, indicating the capacity of his lungs and heart. His legs were long and noble, and his coat gleamed through the fog. Deeply engaged, his poll perfectly raised, he was a picture of moving power and glory. Into her mind leaped one of those energetic paintings by the French Romantic School. Horace Vernet, *The Start of the Race of the Riderless Horses*. Imperious, bursting with power, the stallion was so collected that he seemed to canter on the spot. Never before had Catherine seen such a magnificent creature.

His bridle was masterfully crafted of fine black leather and from its brow band a classical mosquero swung to the rhythm of his gait. There were at least thirty horsehair tassels and they swayed from side to side, amplifying the dramatic effect. His rider wore a Spanish caballero hat. The saddle was a flawless *Doma Vaquera* covered with thick cream sheepskin. He neck-reined the horse with his left hand, as was customary for Spanish cattle work.

Within an inch of Catherine, the stallion performed an exemplary halt. Like a dragon he blew his hot breath directly into her face and the steam from his flanks mingled with the mist. Catherine breathed in the familiar aroma of the horse, and it gave her strength. She wanted to go up to it, but her captors crowded around the horse and rider excitedly, and she was ignored. Then, to her astonishment, the rider pointed to her and called out in Spanish. She was expected to join him in the saddle! One of the men gave her a leg-up. The pain of the jolt shot through her injured hip and she grasped the cantle as the rider immediately spurred his mount. She understood the haste. The stallion had to be kept warm. With a masterful turn on the haunches, horse and rider faced the way they'd come, and she was swiftly carried away – on a fairy-tale horse ridden by a chevalier from another epoch.

She found it unnecessary to cling. Even though she was sitting behind, instead of in the saddle, the horse's strong round back pulled her into a deep, secure seat. It was impossible to lose her balance - the Andalusian's gait was so perfectly even. The primeval forest receded behind them and Catherine's world was now the reassuring rhythm of hooves, creak of leather, and the horse's breath. The smell of horse filled her senses, and the rhythmic beat enfolded Catherine in a blanket of delight. She had no idea what lay ahead, but with each canter stride she felt more liberated. No sound came from the rider; he didn't even seem to breathe. He was in complete unison with his horse. Catherine yielded to the ride. She felt like she was being born into a new, better world.

The rain stopped and it got warmer. The terrain opened up, and the stallion increased his pace. He seemed to need no break.

They changed direction, slowed down to a walk and ascended a steep mountain range. The Andalusian now started to breathe heavily – the long stretches of cantering, the double weight on his back and the steep incline began to take their toll even to him.

She peered forward round the rider's back to watch the action of the horse's great neck and forequarters. It seemed to her a breathtaking privilege. The days of pain and beatings, hunger and dehydration, fell away. All that she now felt was a delirious exultation. A sign of madness, she wondered. Soon she would start hallucinating – or was she already in the process?

The climb got harder. The horse panted so heavily that Catherine became concerned, but his rider seemed to take no notice. He just looked straight ahead and concentrated on the path. And that was good, because it now seemed impassable. A sheer wall of mountain restricted them on the right; on their left gaped a deep ravine. But the horse was surefooted and the rider skilled. Nevertheless, Catherine sat dead still, avoiding any movement that might distract the balance of horseman or mount.

She estimated that they had been travelling for about seven hours, when she announced her thirst. "I need a drink," she demanded in English.

The rider halted the stallion and let her get off, while he stayed mounted. Without a word, he passed her a water bottle from his shoulder bag, and she drained it. After so many hours in the saddle, her legs betrayed her and she staggered unsteadily. She then threw up the entire liter of water. Immediately she felt better and she tested her legs, wandering for a little way along the path. After a short distance the man whistled her back, like one would call one's dog and she obeyed. Running away was of no use; there was no getting away from this horse, which would probably climb trees if asked to do so. She asked for more water but this time the man gave her a yellow soda. The label said "Inca Kola".

Inca? Was she in Peru? The man on the phone had mentioned only Venezuela and Columbia. She drank slowly this time in order not to get sick again. She asked for some food and was given a small meat pie. She took a bite and was overwhelmed at how good it tasted.

"What is this?" she asked.

"*Empanada Chilena.*"

She swallowed it greedily and asked for another one which she devoured just as quickly. The man now gestured for her to mount. She stroked the horse's great neck and then allowed its rider to pull her up again. They moved forward, at a careful walk, up the serpentine and narrow mountain path.

Another hour passed, and they reached a plateau. She thought she saw a lake in the distance, and she was right - they walked straight towards a small mountain lake. Its water was crystal clear, not like the muddy brown broth she was used to in the jungle.

The rider guided the horse into the water, to let it cool down after the long slow climb. It was important, Catherine knew, that a rider should keep his horse's temperature stable. She, too, wanted to go into the water. She, too, needed cooling and a wash. She tapped the rider on his shoulder and pointed. He nodded and she sank directly from the horse's back into the lake. And took her first bath in weeks! She opened her mouth and let the clear water flow into and around her entire body. It tasted metallic and slightly sour.

The stallion drank very carefully. How smart he was! He first pawed the water with his forefoot and then ducked his head under. He seemed to take pleasure in blowing bubbles up to the surface. Then, he motioned back and forth with his head as though pushing at the water. What a character! Even though the water was cold, Catherine also dived under. With exaggerated vigor she washed away all the frustration and pain of the last few weeks.

The stallion became frisky and kicked out with his hind leg, splashing the rider who remained in the saddle. The rider laughed, but obviously didn't want to let him roll over in the water. He lifted the horse's head and nudged him forward. Catherine moved back, out of the way of the hooves. Horse and rider turned towards her again and the man reached out his hand to help her up. Catherine was soaking wet but it didn't seem to bother the man – and the stallion took in his stride whatever was presented to him. The party rode on, across the high plateau.

After another hour, Catherine saw paddocks. Then a ranch. And then the first grazing horses. The path widened and led through pasturage directly to the *finca*.

The horse now broke into a trot, for the first time on their long ride, and she was worried that this gait would hurt her injured limbs but it was so smooth that it caused her no discomfort. They came up to a paddock gate that led into a fenced yard, and a young man accompanied by two German Shepherds appeared and opened it for them. They carried on to a second gate which, without dismounting, the rider leaned down to and opened by himself.

The yard consisted of many old buildings and barns laid out in an oval. In the distance she spotted further barns and stable blocks and on her left was a huge old house, fronted by a generous wooden porch in Spanish colonial style. On the right of the entrance was a small herb garden. Other than that, the growth around the house was left idyllically wild. Catherine noticed a garden bench half-hidden inside the shrubbery, and again she felt as if she'd been swept up and dropped into the middle of a fairy tale.

At the ornate veranda, two new men awaited her. Catherine asked herself if she would ever again see another woman. The rider turned to her and motioned her to dismount. She stiffly swung her right leg over, supported herself on the horse's back and slipped to the ground. Catherine gingerly tested her sore legs, and then the two directed her towards the entrance of the house, while the rider, now on foot, led the stallion away.

Suddenly, seemingly out of nowhere, there appeared a staggeringly handsome man. She guessed he was in his mid-thirties, tall and slender but with a muscular build. His presence took her breath away. It seemed to eclipse everything else. It surpassed even the charisma of the black stallion.

Somehow he appeared to be a human version of that horse. A strand of his jet black hair fell over his eyes. In a careless motion he brushed it back, stepping up to meet the rider as he led the horse away. He was dressed in expensively cut dark blue jeans and wore a tight-fitting sleeveless white T-shirt. He wore fine leather calf-length boots with fashionable mock spur straps. There was no doubt in her mind: he was the one – the leader. Compared with him, all the men thus far on her strange journey were mere oafs, or peasants. Without hearing him speak, she recognized him as the man who had telephoned her in Venezuela. It had to be him!

He seemed not to notice her as he went up to the horse whose rider was now loosening the girth. Catherine watched him as he expertly ran his hands over the horse's legs to check their condition. Next, he hugged the stallion who answered his affection by rubbing his head against his chest. In doing so he soiled the man's white T-shirt which didn't seem to bother him in the least. He exchanged words with the horse and his rider, and laughed at whatever they were telling him. She was sorry that she could not watch them longer – the two men by her side were shoving her impatiently up the steps towards the front door.

Then she crossed the porch and took her first step over the threshold into the mysterious house. A step into a house that would become a home - a home that would change her life forever.

Part II

Rivas & Andalus

"And if you're not willing,
My force I'll employ."

From 'Erlkönig'
Johann Wolfgang von Goethe

9.
Peru 04 June

Catherine was completely under the spell of the man and his horse. Leaving aside for the moment the magnificent *Pura Raza Española*, Catherine realized that its owner was the rare kind of figure that – in a crowd – would have caused her to turn her head, to stand on tiptoe to seek out, even to shadow. She was hooked. She was taken. A hostage now to something far deeper than mere physical abduction.

Her two guards urged her across the threshold, and the interior of the handsome *estancia* brought her back to her immediate surroundings. The entrance hall was like something from the set of a Humphrey Bogart movie – Spanish-American décor from another era. Catherine slipped into the role of a Hollywood diva. What was the name of the movie? "Panama" perhaps? She'd always loved playing the heroine.

Two broad ceiling fans whisked elegantly above her head, stirring the air that carried a fragrant masculine blend of oiled wood, tobacco, and leather. Left and right of the entrance, solid doors led to various rooms and at the end of the passage on the right a broad winding staircase led to the upper floor. Her instincts told her that this was her destination – and she felt relief that it was such a mellow and civilized house. Surely this was the end of her torment? Her courage returned, and she silently resolved that she would overcome all enemies, whatever it took. But her valor evaporated the moment she arrived on the top level, where they marched her down a dark and narrow corridor – a stark contrast to the bright and inviting ground floor.

When she saw the closed shutters of the chamber she was taken into, her mood became as dark as the room. It was warm, and here also, a ceiling fan was cooling the air. Alone now, she pushed aside her indignation at the iron bars that barricaded the windows. At least the room was clean and had a pleasant smell. Against the left wall was a bed, covered with crisp white sheets. On it lay lady's underwear. Her injured leg and hip acted up again as soon as she spotted the bed. Her sore body begged her to lie down and, just like during the last work week before a vacation, she suddenly felt she could not go on another minute without resting. Beside the door was a small table and a wooden chair and next to it a solid free-standing shelf packed tightly with books. In the corner, an old chair promised long nights of cozy reading and between it and the bedside table stood a locker. The door of the locker was open and she saw two dozen hangers, which were of course useless to her since she didn't have one dress she could have hung up on them. The image flitted into her mind of her cupboard at home, filled to the brim with dresses and suits. The hectic business at Firm Commitments appeared to be light-years away, and seemingly pointless. From now on she would tackle life day by day, hour by hour, and put aside any thoughts about the future.

Without knocking, and without saying a word, a man brought a tray into her room, put it down on the table and disappeared. She heard him lock the door, but this neither surprised nor worried her. He had left on the tray a portion of *Queso Blanco,* a small bowl of green olives and four thick slices of freshly baked white bread. Also a jug of iced water and a glass, again the Inca Kola, and an opened bottle of *Cusqueña.* She sniffed at the bottle neck and read the label: Peruvian beer.

Cheese and beer? Books and female undergarments? She shrugged and dug into the meal. Undoubtedly, it was the most delicious food she'd ever tasted. It even surpassed the pineapple in the FARC camp. She emptied almost the entire jug of water, then drank the Inca Kola and finished off with the beer.

Underneath the clothes on the bed she now spotted a small cosmetic bag. It contained a tooth brush, a miniature tube of toothpaste and cardboard nail-file. When she saw the file she inspected the state of her nails. She would not need a manicure for a long time – there were no nails! Who put together this strange collection of items? What she urgently needed were soap, face cream, sun protection, makeup, a comb, and soon, tampons. Her skin was hard like that of an elephant and probably looked like it, too. She hoped that she would find a mirror somewhere, but for the time being she had a bed.

A bed!

She realized that she hadn't looked behind the door to an adjacent room, so distracted she had been by the food and by her first impressions. She turned the doorknob and entered a bathroom.

A bathroom!

With a mirror! She was shocked by what it revealed. Thanks to the brief dip in the lake earlier her face wasn't dirty, just a little dusty – but how scratched and burnt it was, and the red marks from insect bites and lots of little red veins and broken capillaries revealed just how much strain her body had taken over the past few weeks. The worst was the condition of her hair. The dreadlocks she'd fantasized about at the airport were taking shape by their own accord.

She inspected the bathtub – clean. And the rudimentary showerhead in the corner – old. She turned on the tap and tested if there was hot water. When the water warmed up, she plugged the drain and ran a bath. In the meantime, the toilet caught her attention. Next to it hung a roll of toilet paper.

Toilet paper!

What luxury. On the search for a bar of soap she opened the mirror cupboard above the sink, which extended down to the floor on the left and right side of the sink. Her eyes widened and she struggled to take it in: the cupboard was filled from top to bottom with personal hygiene products and cosmetics. Was the little sponge bag on her bed a mean joke? In this cupboard she found exactly the same products she had at home. Impatiently she ripped open one of La Source's blue bath tablets and watched as it dissolved in the water, bubbling refreshingly. She breathed in the unusual fragrance and paused a little to savor it. After turning off the tap, she turned her attention again to the contents of the cupboard. And there she saw it: the complete, wickedly expensive range of La Prairie products – items that she'd denied herself at home. On other shelves she discovered makeup and perfumes, mostly from Chanel. The selection could have competed with the stock of an upmarket department store. Next to things such as soap, shavers, cotton wool, nail brushes, deodorant, ear buds and tampons she found a small first aid kit including some prescription-free drugs such as Tylenol. Furthermore they'd stocked the cupboard with exquisite hair care products by Carita, a brand specializing in blonde hair. With it came brushes, combs, hairclips, hairbands, a hair dryer and a GHD iron. A hair iron! What were they planning? Catherine sensed danger. And a long stay.

In one of the bottom shelves were fresh towels. She couldn't find any scissors, but there was always… the nail-file from the little bag she'd found on her bed. Focusing again on the cosmetic products, she discovered a card on top of one of the Le Prairie boxes. On it was written in classically elegant handwriting:

With compliments
Maria Santa Cruz

She turned the card over:

Follow our orders!

Was she in a psychiatric clinic and the patients had taken over the wards? Was someone with a warped sense of humor playing a dirty trick on her? And who the devil was Maria Santa Cruz?

She brushed her teeth and stepped into the tub. Afterwards she wrapped herself in one of the large soft towels and returned to her room. She kept herself covered, since the door could be unlocked and fly open at any moment.

The clothes on the bed consisted of two T-shirts, underwear and feminine white satin pajamas as well as a light, soft pair of jeans with fashionably rolled up ends. The material felt so outrageously regal that she inspected the label and read that it was a Skinny Jeans from Balmain. On the floor she found dark blue suede stable shoes from Mountain Horse in her size with matching riding socks by Pikeur. These comfortable slip-on shoes she also wore almost permanently around home. Although she was concerned that someone would enter to fetch her, the bed was calling her, so she grabbed a couple of books from the shelf and crawled under the cozy duvet. Outside, a donkey called, answered by the neigh of a horse, but other than that the silence was unbroken save for the quiet hum of the ceiling fan.

A leaden tiredness overcame her and as she dozed she reviewed the events of the day. She was lying in a soft bed, locked up in a dark room in a strange house full of men, who provided for her needs but held her against her will. She wore clothes that didn't belong to her, but fitted as if they were her own. She had groomed herself with brands of the highest order, provided by a mysterious woman with exquisite taste.

For the first time she wondered if Alex had anything to do with her situation. Her last thoughts were about her throbbing leg and then she fell asleep.

The next morning the same man brought her breakfast. Black coffee, fresh juice and fruit. She ate a giant banana, almost as large as the lower arm of a child, and an orange. One more banana and two apples she decided to save for later. She drank the coffee, but missed the milk and sugar even though it wasn't very strong, which surprised her, not knowing that coffee in South America was traditionally (and against all foreign expectations) brewed weak.

Again her thoughts circled around what they wanted from her. Surely negotiations were underway and that's why they treated her better now, she reflected to herself, in anticipation of a solution around the corner.

However, to her dismay, she saw nobody the entire day, except to bring her dinner. She read *The Pit and the Pendulum* by Edgar Allan Poe, cover to cover. Every now and then she refilled her jug with water from the tap, did her hair, put on makeup and pampered her body. Time passed, she managed to endure the boredom, but even the following day there was no sign of any progress about her release. The only interruption of the tedium was that they brought her several used, but perfectly ironed men's shirts of leading brands. One of these shirts, much too large for her, she put on and it gave her a peculiar sense of comfort. The waiting, however, became pure torture. She longed to be free and to be back home, but also for the black horse that had carried her out of her jungle hell. She wanted to stroke his coat, feel his strength and warmth and breathe in his scent. She wanted to see the rider again and to meet the horse's owner. Why was nothing moving forward? Yes – she was in a civilized environment now. But they still isolated her.

Without any success, she clung to the men who brought her meals. But she never received an answer to her questions.

In the late afternoon, they released her from her prison. A guard took her to the ground floor and left her at the open door of a huge study. Its walls were lined with shelves that were filled with books from top to bottom. Beneath a large window stood a dark green leather couch and in the middle of the room there was a table with a laptop and printer. A gigantic classical wooden desk with dark green leather inserts dominated the left side of the room.

He stood in front of it.

Facing the door, he grabbed a packet of cigarettes, took one out and lit it. As he inhaled, he stared intently at her – rendering her motionless. Then he stubbed out the cigarette in the ashtray and walked towards the threshold where she stood. Catherine could hardly breathe, and it wasn't due to the cigarette smoke. He reached her, and there was a strange momentary standoff between the two, which seemed to chill the air. His eyes fixed on hers. He stroked her cheek with the back of his hand and said, "Catherine Zitgow." She showed no response, at least no conscious response, to his impertinent gesture. What signals did I send to invite him to touch me like this? she pondered. And what do I mean to them, that causes these men to make such a fuss of me?

He lowered his hand and spoke in perfect English: "Don't stand in the doorway. Why don't you come in?" He returned to his desk and lit another cigarette.

Catherine followed him. "Thanks," she opened up the conversation.

"For what?"

"You said you'd see to it that I won't be harmed. Sometimes I didn't think I'd survive, but now I'm here."

"How are you feeling, Catherine?"

Good question. How was she feeling? She didn't know how to answer. Was she feeling good? Bad? Under the circumstances not too bad, but she decided to spare them both the cliché. Instead, she changed the subject. "On the phone you said that you were taking me to Columbia, but I'm in Peru, aren't I?"

"Yes."

"That was you on the phone, right?"

"Yes."

"It was your encouragement, not your threats, that enabled me to get through it all."

"Why are you telling me this?"

"I want to ask you for a non-violent negotiation."

"We're negotiation partners? I wasn't aware of that."

"Are you making fun of me?"

"I do apologize! But that was really cute. I couldn't help myself."

His clear and expressive voice sounded so rational, so authentic, that she mistook his sarcasm for a compliment. In her confusion, she interpreted his tone as good humor and urbane manners. Her needy mind insisted that she could have a cultured conversation with him. Decent, balanced communication would bring a quick resolution to her ordeal. But his next comment instantly dashed her illusions: "Chica, we're not at a board meeting. There'll be no negotiation! I tell you what to do and you do it. If you don't cooperate, you'll regret it. That's it."

Catherine guessed what Chica meant but she wanted to know what he meant by cooperation. She felt so beaten by his sudden frosty tone that she couldn't even ask that simple question. His attractive face, his lithe but imposing body, and his magnetic aura forced her to lower her head. He put his finger beneath her chin and lifted her face again, and at the contact her knees weakened. She found it hard to look him in the eyes, but only because she so badly wanted to do so. There was a tension that emanated from him, which she could not fathom. The way he spoke and behaved threw her emotionally back and forth, up and down, like ice cubes in a blender, seconds before being crushed. A cocktail of fear, anger, curiosity and hope churned in her mind. In order to regain her poise, she focused on studying his physical appearance. Over a tight-fitting long-sleeved grey T-shirt, he wore a short-sleeved open black shirt. His hipster jeans ended in elite black riding boots with spur straps. Jimmy Choo, she reckoned. Everything about him was perfectly coordinated and looked hellishly expensive. Perhaps he was the mysterious Mr Brower after all? She had to know. She mustered all her courage and asked forthrightly, "What's your name?"

"Tell me how you are. You haven't answered my question yet. Are you still hurt?" He sounded polite and gentle again.

"No," she lied, without knowing why. He blew a last puff of smoke and put out his cigarette. She dared a quick look in his eyes, gaining in confidence. "What's with this farm? What am I doing here? How exactly must I cooperate? If you don't tell me what you want from me, how can I meet your expectations?"

"You'll find out soon enough. Don't worry, Catherine. You won't get hurt if you just do as I say."

The danger of his implied threat passed her by because she believed she was finally in the company of a man who meant her no harm. What else could explain the warm touch of his hand and the reassuring tone of his voice? And, at last, she had someone she could talk to in English. He was the first person on her whole horror trip with whom she could actually communicate in entire sentences. She was sure she would be able to influence him, as long as she stayed calm and alert. "Are you taking me home?" For a brief moment she even hoped that these people were her rescuers. She forgot the hearty welcome the uniformed men in the jungle had bestowed upon the rider when he took her over from them. In her desperation, she pushed aside any hint of reason.

The man didn't reply. Instead, he instructed her: "Go back to your room now, Catherine. Your dinner is waiting. Don't let it get cold."

Catherine didn't want to go. She hadn't achieved anything yet. Her temper flared up. "Whether I have my dinner hot or cold is the least of my worries. Actually I find it really hard to process these weird contrasts. I am held here against my will while you play the courteous host. You know what! You can keep your crummy meals, Mr … oh, whatever you call yourself. You are one sick human being!"

She suddenly took fright at her boldness and hoped he would not now refuse her the meals she had just scorned.

"For someone who's recovering from a recent abduction you're in surprisingly good shape."

"I assure you I've never been in worse shape. And this will not change until I'm free again. No matter how many cosmetics and good books you pile up in my room. Do you really think you can manipulate me with this nonsense? That I'll be eternally grateful because you let me sleep in a bed, allow me to use a bathroom and give me a warm meal to eat? You're crazy! But fine, be that as it may. I'll tell you the truth. I'm not wealthy and I have no relatives, but whatever money is available or can be made liquid, my lawyer will organize. This shouldn't take longer than a few days and then you can lavish your stuff on your next victim. How much do you want?"

"If I was after a ransom, Catherine, I would have it already. And I certainly didn't bring you here because of your bank balance. Your cash position and all your investments combined wouldn't nearly cover the cost of your abduction." He laughed.

"Oh? So I'm small fry? This fish isn't big enough for you? Tough luck! Well then, I suppose I can go now!"

"The question is where will you go. How long do you think you'd survive here in the mountains? And the fish in question, Catherine, is gigantic and you will land him."

"What are you saying?"

"It'll soon all make sense. I just want you to rest a while and get back your strength. Trust me a little, okay?"

"Trust you? You're even weirder than I thought. You refuse me any clarification, don't give me your name and then you say, *trust me a little, okay*?" She mocked him by pursing her lips, mimicking his tone and shaking her head side to side to the beat of each word. "I've never had respect for people that hide behind anonymity. And you won't be my first exception, that's for sure!"

"No respect, huh?"

Quickly she tried to appease him. "Names are important. Imagine if you didn't know mine. To withhold yours is not fair."

"Catherine, come here," he demanded matter-of-factly without any emotion.

She became aware of her tense and stooped posture, and headed as upright and proud as she could towards him. Not under any circumstances would she show him how scared she was. Because he stayed silent for so long, her determination started to wane. Why did he scrutinize her like this? What was going through his mind?

Then, out of the blue he hit her hard in the face.

The force of the blow made her stagger. It hurt and she felt disorientated. She touched her burning cheek in absolute disbelief. The fiery pain ran across her cheek to her nose. Her eyes watered and her ears were ringing. Shocked by the burning pain and his unexpected change of mood, she instinctively placed her hand over her mouth and nose and drew back a few steps. The wheels she'd set in motion to influence him were coming apart.

"Do you want to know why I did that?"

Catherine, completely humbled, clamped up. Then she said meekly, "Because I provoked you with my comment about respect. I'm sorry."

"No. Your rebuttal was justified. I hit you because I felt like it."

He lit another cigarette. Without noticeably blowing out the smoke, he added, "You'll learn a lot here. Fairness is not part of the curriculum." He watched her as she nervously pulled back further. "And if I didn't know your name, Catherine, I would simply invent one for you. Why are you so far away? Come here. Come on."

"You said I wouldn't be hurt if I did what you say and when I complied, you hit me. Because you *felt like it*."

"I changed my mind."

"So your assurances are completely meaningless!"

"You may be right about that. Still, I want you to come closer now." She walked up to him, but stayed out of reach. "Closer."

She realized that she was chewing on her lower lip, and she forced herself to stop it. She had to avoid biting into it when he dealt her his next blow. And this time she would hit him back. She stood right in front of him now and waited.

But he merely stroked her face with the back of his index and middle fingers, from the cheek to her mouth. Then he ran his fingers over her lips and opened his hand. Now it was his palm that slid over her chin and onto her neck. He gripped her neck gently and she didn't dare move her face away from him. Anger and courage were both out the window, and pure fear streamed forth from all her pores. He would be able to sense it, smell it, see it and her heart beat so loudly against her chest that she dearly hoped it wasn't audible to him.

How could a man that radiated such charisma have such a pitch-black soul? She asked herself how such a thing could come about. What sort of life had he led? What strange circumstances had shaped such a dark character? Had he been a bully from his youth? He seemed educated and wealthy, and clearly able to differentiate right from wrong. This made him all the more dangerous.

"What are you thinking?" He blew the cigarette smoke sideways past her face.

She heard him as if from a distance, as if she were looking down on herself: standing there, in front of this refined and elegant being, one of God's masterpieces - that was ridden by the devil.

"You want to know what's going on inside me?" he asked again.

"I am asking myself what I'm in for. Carrot and stick; sugar and whip?"

"An accurate deduction. This is more or less what I had in mind."

"That wasn't hard. And what exactly is the whip that awaits me?"

"I am."

"And the sugar?"

"Also I. Dear Catherine, I'm the only good thing you'll encounter here."

"And the bad thing."

"Let's say the worst thing. Bad surrounds you as it is. It lurks behind every corner, always ready to pounce on you."

"May I go to my room now?"

"Yes."

She turned around and headed for the door. With her back to him, she breathed a sigh of relief. I will master every day, one at a time. I will meet every challenge. I will not surrender. I will get through this. As she was still reeling off her mantras, she heard him call her name.

"Catherine?"

She turned around. "Yes?"

"My name is Rivas."

Strange creature. Puzzling name.

"Is that supposed to be your first or your last name?"

"First, in my case." She turned towards the door again and he called her back one last time. "You look delightful in my shirt."

Fear again gripped the room. Silently it fell over her, like the first snowflakes in winter.

"As long as you wear my shirts, Catherine, you'll be safe here. But watch out for one thing: I'll break your heart."

"I'm already broken in pieces. Body, soul, spirit — everything kaput!"

"I was talking about your heart."

Catherine was caught off guard by his unexpected pedantic tone. He didn't talk about broken hearts like an idiotic womanizer in a night club. He spoke with the scientific authority of a physics professor who was outlining a law of nature to his students. She had to rebut this immediately, or else she would come off the loser.

"Nobody... *Rivas*... will break my heart - especially not you. I know you can take anything you want - you just demonstrated it - but for as long as I live you will *never* win *my heart*."

"Go now, before the thought of what's underneath that shirt gets too much for me."

She returned to her room and assumed rightly that the door would stay unlocked that night. A plate of tasty *Patasca* waited for her there. That was a thick soup made of potatoes, beans and various types of meat, always including rabbit meat, which she didn't know at the time. They'd served it with a thick slice of corn bread accompanied as usual by *Cusqueña* and Inca Kola.

She ate hungrily, even though the soup (as Rivas predicted) was now only lukewarm. Afterwards she showered and went to bed early, but she couldn't sleep because once again her mind was wide awake. She wasn't locked in her room anymore but she was now at the mercy of a crazy guy. She quickly wiped away any tempting fantasies of trying to escape again, despite the open door. The man was right. She first had to get back her orientation and her strength. It was unthinkable what revenge he would take on her if her plan failed. Apart from that, she was convinced that this Rivas, as unpredictable as he was, would be the key to her freedom. She had to find a way of getting along with him. He was her only shot at leaving this place alive.

The next morning they brought her breakfast but paid no attention to her for the rest of the day. Driven by hunger and boredom, she opened her door and looked down the deserted passage, but she closed it again. She was tempted to go downstairs in search of food from the kitchen. In the end, she chose to avoid giving further provocation to this Rivas character.

Around 8 in the evening they came to fetch her. She quickly slipped into her chic stable shoes and followed her escort downstairs. When she entered the study, Rivas, smoking again, was engaged in talk with two other men. One of them was the rider who'd brought her out of the jungle. Her arrival interrupted their conversation and the others left the room, leaving her alone again with Rivas. Once again she felt deeply insecure. She tried to compensate for this by stepping into the room with an air of grit and determination.

"Sit down."

Pugnacious by nature, she remained standing. How would he react? He seemed used to always getting his way. The needs, wants and rights of others didn't seem to concern him.

Once again, he worked his voodoo on her, that he did so well. And once again, it had a hypnotic effect. His hair! His hands! His face! His body and his dress sense! Top quality jeans, one of those classy shirts, this time in a pale yellow and again the same tasteful boots. Conquered by his aura she could only stammer when he asked her, as he'd done the day before, how she was. He seemed to have overlooked the fact that she'd disobeyed his order to sit down. On purpose?

She briefly answered that she was fine, and then she pulled herself together and got to the point: "Why are you keeping me here, Rivas? And for how long? Please let me go."

"Don't bombard me with the same questions whenever we meet, otherwise I'll send you back to your room every time. That prolongs your stay with us and delays my project. You'll have to stay a while longer. Do as I say and everything will work out fine."

"That's what you said yesterday and then you didn't keep to it. Just tell me what you want from me. And anyway, why can't I ask questions? I actually have a couple of burning ones right now. For starters: who the hell gave you my bra size and how do you know my bank balance?"

"See you tomorrow. Be ready by 8."

"I don't have a watch anymore!" she retorted in a huff.

"Then get ready now and stay up all night. Sooner or later it'll be 8." He went to the door, opened it and called a name.

"Rivas, please don't send me to my room yet. Please tell me how long I must stay here and why. Please."

"Good night, Señorita."

Rivas gave his helper an instruction in Spanish and paid no further heed to Catherine. The man wanted to take her to her room but she stubbornly waved him off. "I'll find my own way!"

Back in her room, she went to her window and stared at the closed shutters. She started to cry. A tray with olives, cheese and bread waited for her. The beer and the Inca Kola stood next to the tray and, with streaming tears, she consumed it all. Then she lay down and fell asleep, overcome by the emotional turmoil.

Sometime during the night, a rooster crowed and woke her up. Shortly afterwards she heard the sound of something being dragged directly underneath her window. She couldn't work it out. Then she overheard a conversation between two men, in whispered Spanish. She didn't understand a word, and she lay down again.

Perhaps, after she'd "cooperated", they wouldn't let her go but planned to kill her instead. Nothing made sense. First, strangers abducted and beat her, then she was taken to this farm on a breathtaking Andalusian. Here they didn't harm her – not yet. But they wanted something from her without telling her what it was. And who is this captivating Rivas?

She only fell back to sleep in the early hours of the morning. It seemed as though she'd barely dozed off when the door opened and she woke up again. They brought her coffee, black as usual, and a slice of buttered bread. The man said she should hurry, as someone would fetch her in a few minutes.

Catherine quickly brushed her teeth, washed her face and got dressed at lightning speed. She drank the coffee, ate the bread and waited. Then there was a knock on the door. A knock? It was the first time someone knocked before entering. It was the rider who had fetched her from the rain forest. He greeted her with a friendly smile and took her out to the yard.

Finally, finally, she could leave the house – but where were they taking her this time?

10.
Peru, June 7

Catherine followed the man across the courtyard to the stable. The sight of the contented horses soothed her anxiety. Horse lovers are good people, she reassured herself.

The stable was cool and the fragrance of straw, hay and livestock was an unbeatable combination as far as Catherine was concerned. For her, the symphony of snorting and grinding noises emanating from the stalls eclipsed even a symphony at Carnegie Hall. The stable was a converted barn with a center passage. On both sides of the passage, large stalls accommodated no less than sixteen horses. Wooden side poles separated them from each other and an iron chain kept them from getting out the front.

The man motioned her to wait and disappeared out the stable door. She gestured into the air after him and went to stand at the first stall, in which that magnificent Andalusian was being groomed by a stable hand. The horse clearly enjoyed the vigorous strokes and occupied himself by pulling big tufts of grass from his hay net. The groom disappeared briefly and returned with bridle and saddle, paying no attention to Catherine, not even answering her tentative "hello".

"Morrrnen Rrrivass," the man suddenly called towards the entrance of the stable. He spoke English, with a Scottish accent! Catherine turned towards Rivas and the sight of him sparked an involuntary admiration that was so intense that she felt the blood rush to her face.

Please don't blush. Don't blush!

The grown woman inside her pointed out that she was standing face to face with an unscrupulous criminal. The girl inside her adored him like a groupie worshipping her pop idol.

Not only does the stallion belong to him, he also rides him.

He was dressed for riding, and how! The Spanish riding outfit hugged his impeccable body and an absurd, infantile wish overcame Catherine:

Oh to be his shirt!

"Good morning, Sam." He returned the groom's greeting and turned to Catherine with a subtle smile.

The faint gesture spoke louder than words. A shimmer of hope warmed her heart. *Ekuseni!* A new morning. New strength. New plans. She sensed that she was on the point of falling in love. Her head reminded her quickly of his malicious slap the other day. She recalled how hard he'd hit her and how undeserved it had been. Immediately her heart rushed in to defend him: "How could he not set boundaries after you insulted him the way you did? Why do you always have to be so cocky?"

Catherine clasped her hands behind her neck and exhaled audibly.

Please not him. Please Catherine, don't fall in love with this bad guy. Not with him!

But how could she stop it? Her stomach was fluttering and her temperature had gone up by two degrees. She'd barely exchanged a dozen sentences with him, she hardly knew him, but what he'd predicted had now been set in motion. With just one smile!

She was still engaged in this futile inner dialogue when Rivas turned to his stallion and embraced his neck. She'd never seen a man unleash such unbridled passion on a horse before. The black beauty shamelessly exploited his owner's affection and subjected him to a body search in an effort to sniff out a treat in one of his pockets. Rivas excused himself and returned with a handful of molasses, which the horse licked from his hand with much gusto. "He prefers butter cookies," explained Rivas, "but we're all out."

"Cookies?" Catherine laughed self-consciously and gave the horse a bashful pat. He clearly basked in his status as an object of human veneration.

"And coconuts and jam sandwiches."

"You're kidding! That's not at all good for him!"

"You tell him! I tried, but he won't listen. He knows everything better!"

"Shall I tack up Metodista?" the Scotsman asked and handed Rivas a supersize Peruvian banana.

"Thanks." He peeled it and seconds later the Andalusian sucked it into his mouth in one go. "No, get Pichon ready, Sam." The smell of crushed banana spread across the barn, tantalizing the other horses. They nickered enviously and a big grey pawed the ground to assert its presence. The banana peel landed in the dustbin by the barn door, and Rivas asked the fateful question: "Want to come for a ride?"

It was a fine morning for an outride but Catherine couldn't believe her ears. Had he really just invited her to accompany him? "You know that I ride?"

"He needs to be exercised otherwise he'll sulk. How about it? Are you coming with us or not? It's up to you."

It was the first time she'd been invited to make a choice since that coffee she'd ordered in Miami and never received. "Not without a riding hat." For Catherine, riding without a hat was like driving without a seat belt, or sitting down at a boardroom table without a jacket.

"You'll find riding gear back in the tack room." He pointed his head in that direction. "Get changed. Nobody will bother you there."

In the tack room she did indeed find ample riding equipment, and then some! The hat, which naturally again fitted like a cast, a pair of fine dark-blue jods, riding socks, soft leather riding gloves and a brand new pair of long, beautiful riding boots made of fine Spanish leather. The boots didn't have a brand name; they looked handmade. Next to the chest lay a dressage whip and a jumping crop for the country. The pants were slightly baggy because Catherine had become so thin, and she couldn't pull on the boots because they were new and stiff. She rummaged about for boot pulls, couldn't find any and had to fight long and hard to get them on. When she did, she was astonished that the shaft height matched her legs so perfectly. Normally, riding boots always had to be altered for her.

When she re-emerged, everyone had disappeared. She walked along a path towards the paddocks, ogling the many fine horses, some together on the big meadows and others in their own smaller paddocks.

She spotted Rivas, mounted on the Andalusian, walking the horse on a loose rein along the paddock path. The herd enthusiastically greeted the imposing Spaniard, who strutted around with head held high and without neighing back. Rivas turned round and rode back to Sam who was waiting for Catherine in front of the paddocks with a bay in hand. Catherine strode nervously towards the bay, who paled in comparison to the stallion.

The Scot addressed her for the first time. As it turned out, he was not fond of using many words. "This is Pichon. Thorrroughbrrred. Polohorrrse. Rrretirrred. Verrry quiet."

'A quiet horse is good! My riding isn't up to much, you know."

"That's not what Ey hearrrd."

They talked about her? About whether she was a good or a bad rider?

In the glaring absence of a mounting block, she stood around helplessly wondering how on earth she was going to get on. Sam noticed her distress, took a quizzical look at her short build and offered her a leg up. She declined and took Pichon to a small rock instead, led him to the right of it and mounted from there. Sam re-tightened the girth and adjusted the length of her stirrup leathers while she leant over Pichon's neck, stroking him and whispering words of endearment in his cute ears.

In the meantime, the black horse pranced impatiently on the spot. It didn't faze his rider. He kept the reins loose, just sat straight and deep and stayed relaxed. Rivas seemed wholly at one with the powerful creature beneath him. Catherine saw herself standing face to face with a centaur. Her admiration turned into worship. Followed by timidity. What kind of a ride was she in for? She was no match for this pair and already saw herself being catapulted across the countryside at a full-speed bolt. The humiliation!

Rivas seemed to guess what was going in her mind. "Don't worry, Catherine. I'll keep an eye on you. I still need you."

From this she took courage. There was no question that he wouldn't easily lose control of his mount, if at all. And as long as the lead horse was kept in check, she should be safe. She nodded in agreement, glancing again at the black horse. He was so full of vitality that the base of his tail almost touched the ground in anticipation of the imminent use of his haunches. It was a wonderful privilege to go riding with these two. She could surely only gain in self-confidence.

"Are you good to go?"

"Mhm," she nodded and took a deep breath. How heavenly it felt to be in the saddle again.

They crossed the yard to the first gate at a walk. That is to say, Pichon walked, the stallion piaffed in impatient indignation. He showed off his immensely powerful hindquarters through this highly collected trot, almost on the spot! Rivas just followed his movements discreetly with his lower back and seat. Catherine marveled at the paradox of so much excited impulsion being contained with the subtlest of aids, resulting in a calm and relaxed movement, despite the animal's urgent desire to get going. It was a natural display, no force at play anywhere, and strikingly beautiful to behold.

Catherine's bay horse, however, seemed unmoved by the stallion's display of supremacy and marched calmly on behind them. What a sight in front of her. Dreamily she observed rider and horse from the rear. The rider seemed glued to the saddle, undeterred by the stallion's strong movement. Rivas startled her out of her rapturous daydream by calling her to catch up. His horse, resentful of the pending conversation causing yet another delay, now raised his front hooves in a mild, disobedient attempt at a rear, but Rivas refused to become involved in a dispute. He ignored the protests as if he was not even aware of them, which only infuriated the stallion further. Eventually his horse resigned himself to the fact that this newcomer to the yard seemed to be in charge of the pace and gave in after clearing his lungs and airways with a loud endearing snort. The reins still hung loose, the horse's neck was rolled up - it was incomprehensible to her. In terms of horsemanship, Rivas was far beyond anything she had ever seen.

"Come on," he urged her. His horse snorted once more for all he was worth, likewise encouraging her to get a move on. She put Pichon into a light trot until she'd caught up, then they continued side by side. "He's not normally such a show off. He can actually be charmingly humble. You'll see when you get to know him better. It's just that he doesn't often get the chance to ride out with a woman."

Catherine knew that some stallions tended to act up in response to a whiff of human estrogen. It closely resembled the equine version of the substance and this was also why the estrogen of mares was commonly used in human hormone replacement therapy. She was embarrassed by the hint and noticing it, Rivas said: "Sorry, that was said in bad taste. Are you okay? Can we trot?"

"Yes." She shortened the reins to the trotting length to which she was accustomed.

"Don't take him too short. The horses here aren't used to it." She lengthened the rein by an inch. "Better." They trotted on and, mindful of his nervous companion, Rivas kept a modest pace. Every now and again they were stopped by a gate and Rivas opened and closed it without dismounting. The Andalusian naturally performed exemplary turns on the forehand to enable him to do so. The surroundings were so tranquil that neither said a word. Silently they trotted next to each other along the path until the pace became brisker as they crossed a meadow. "A little gallop?" he broke the silence.

"I don't know. I mean of course I want to. But what if he gets away from me?"

"Stay behind me. I'll keep my horse checked until you feel okay. If he gets too strong, just shout. I promise you, my horse comes straight back."

"You won't hear me," she argued hesitantly.

"Aim at his hind quarters. Let Pichon run into him if necessary. My friend here won't kick, he'll stop him." Catherine was not convinced, and her facial expression testified to this. "Catherine, I can get him from a bull charge to a full halt in a microsecond. He's a fully trained PRE!"

"If you feel like it."

He let her dig pass. "No. It's because he likes showing off his strength."

"And I should rely on that?"

"You've been through a lot. I don't blame you for being skeptical. Do you want to go back?" Rivas ended the tiresome debate with a shrug of the shoulders.

Turn back? No. No.

She gave in. "I witnessed his spectacular canter-halt transition in the jungle. I trust him." His smile settled it and an unfathomable lightness set in. Horses were the best cure for any woe. She said aloud in German: "All the happiness on earth rests on the back of horses."

"What did you say?"

"Oh nothing, a German saying. It's lost in translation and doesn't rhyme in English."

"Try."

She did.

"Very true," said Rivas. "That's completely true. That's why I put you on that horse today. I want you to feel happy."

"How can I believe you?" she sighed.

"Believe me," he said, cantering on while watching her closely. Pichon kindly and calmly struck into canter without her having given him the aid. Rivas saw this and scolded Pichon for not waiting for his rider's timing. By addressing the horse, he was of course tactfully reprimanding Catherine.

She liked it. She had no idea why.

Catherine had no difficulty with the pace, even when it increased, and she surrendered to a long, exhilarating gallop across the meadow. The anguish of her peculiar captivity was gone with the wind. When they reached the end of the fields they returned to a walk and rode side by side again.

"This stallion you are riding seems very valuable. Do you own him?"

"Yeah, I've brought him on myself."

"He's incredibly well schooled and so powerful. He brought me all this way here without flinging."

"I lent him to Pedro because he is the only one who can manage the journey with two people in such a short time."

So Pedro was the name of the rider, Catherine noted. "What is your horse called?"

"El Andaluz."

"El Andaluz? Isn't that the Arabic word for Spain?"

"A corruption, but in principle yes. There is only one *Pura Raza Española* like him, that's why we call him El Andaluz or *the Spaniard*. He's registered as César VIII. He was given to me seven years ago when he was two."

"So he must be eight or nine now. Who gave you such an unusual present?"

"A good friend of the family."

Intuitively she enquired, "What's the name of this good friend?"

"Maria Santa Cruz."

She was tempted to dig further into her captor's past but thought it wiser to carry on talking about the horses for now. "And this gelding, Pichon?"

"He is eighteen, a passionate polo player."

Polo player.

Catherine giggled ecstatically. "I like thoroughbreds. I have one myself: Illusion. And your name? I've never heard the name 'Rivas' before."

"Rivas is actually a surname and the name of the place where I was born. Rivas is a district in Nicaragua. My mother and her best friend were staying there when I came into this world unexpectedly early."

"And so your mother called you 'Rivas'. She also just invented a name."

"No that idea came from ..."

"Maria Santa Cruz," she finished his sentence.

"You're very smart, Catherine. We'll soon be finished here and then I'll let you go."

Rivas cantered off again and Pichon followed of his own accord. The eucalyptus trees they passed swayed in the rising wind and the horses, animated by the breeze, picked up the pace. The thoroughbred threw himself on the forehand and pulled her out of her seat. Instead of straightening up and bracing against him, she yielded and went into light seat. This way she stayed in balance but increased the tempo further without meaning to. The English saddle offered little support but she avoided pulling on the reins and stayed fairly relaxed. Rivas sat upright in an Iberian saddle on his stallion, whose movements went upwards and forwards naturally. To allow himself a weakness of the hindquarters and throw himself onto the forehand was clearly below his dignity.

At the next trot phase, she asked Rivas: "Where are we?"

"In the Andes."

"Yes, I get that, but where exactly?"

"In the Peruvian highlands, northeast of the Pacific coast."

"And why are we here in the Peruvian highlands, northeast of the Pacific coast?"

Without answering, Rivas cantered off again with Pichon and Catherine flying off behind him. The Andalusian flaunted his power and sense of urgency and Catherine could not fathom how Rivas succeeded, without any visible influence, in keeping his stallion's Iberian zest in check. She became conscious of her limited riding ability and grew scared. Her anxiety unsettled Pichon, and he lengthened his stride. "Rivas!" she called hesitantly, but loudly enough for him to hear. She was reluctant to ask for help, she found it embarrassing, but Pichon's gallop had become too strong for her.

Rivas pulled up to a trot instantly, as promised. "Everything okay?"

Pichon calmed down nicely, but El Andaluz pushed out an impressive Passage, a highly elevated version of a trot. If we can't go forward then let's at least go upwards, he must have decided to himself. He really seemed to be tireless.

"Yes, everything's fine. Sorry, Rivas, that was a little too fast for me."

"I shouldn't have let him storm off like that. Come on, we'll trot back quietly now. I planned to do that at the next fork anyway."

She was mortified about her limited riding skills because there was no question of Rivas having let his horse storm off. She'd lost her nerve and he was merely courteous, she concluded. As if in a fever she fantasized about this wonderful man and cast aside the bitter reality, as if she was on her first date with the most heavenly male creature on God's earth. Rivas kept to his word and did not canter anymore no matter how often El Andaluz urged him to do so. When they arrived at the stable she felt like a spoilsport, and she apologized.

Rivas waved it aside: "I didn't expect anything else. You'll get used to our pace. We don't usually ride out just for fun but because we want to get somewhere and as a rule we need to get there fast. The horses aren't used to anything else. You did well."

You did well!

His compliment transported Catherine into an unexplained state of bliss. Had his opinion become so important to her, so fast, she pondered.

They untacked and took El Andaluz and Pichon to their paddocks. They went back to the house like two old friends, as if they'd known each other for years. Catherine was amazed how strongly a love for horses could unite two people, even when those two people were a kidnapper and his hostage.

The reality check descended on her hours later. How arrogant of him to decree "then I'll let you go".

Then I'll let you go!

And why had Rivas confided their whereabouts to her? Certainly not due to a slip of the tongue! She hadn't believed that Maria Santa Cruz's name was her real one from the start, and the nonsense about his weird Nicaraguan name, she dismissed as well - but he'd revealed the Andalusian's pedigree. The purchase of a registered horse could be traced. Why didn't he care that she would be able to testify in this regard? Either he was lying or she was truly not meant to come out of this alive. Still, she couldn't imagine that this appealing man could ever commit murder or order an assassination. It didn't suit him. He was so nice. So nice! No, she told herself, he'll keep his word. I'll soon be free...

11.
Peru, June 8

In the days that followed, Catherine went out riding or watched Rivas work with Andalus, which is what they called him for short. Not having been assigned any tasks, she began to suffer from boredom. She offered to help with the horses and finally Rivas and Sam agreed. She grew closer to the horses, found her way around the stables and adjusted to the routine on the farm. In the mornings, she groomed the horses and led them to their paddocks, and she fetched them again in the evenings while Sam looked after their food and mucked out. They let her ride as often as she wanted to and she exercised the horses as much as she could. Sometimes she rode up to eight horses a day and greatly improved her skills. Her self-confidence grew. As did her trust in Rivas. She often thought of Claudia's saying "You only learn riding from riding" and she changed it to "You only learn riding from watching Rivas and Andalus". She wondered how Claudia was - and the others at home. While in the saddle she often thought about escaping, simply riding away from all this madness and not stopping until she was free, but always abandoned the idea when she recalled her last attempt in Columbia. Pedro and Joe, Rivas's helpers, took care of the house and everything else that needed doing. Pedro cooked every evening for the four of them and sometimes also for Sam. Pedro's skills at the stove were limited. He served exclusively Spanish, Peruvian or Columbian dishes, some of which were not really to her taste – but it wasn't much of an issue. The ranch had its own vegetable patch and big reserves of groceries. They baked bread on the premises and kept a large supply of meat in oversized American freezers. Every now and then Joe got fresh supplies from the valley using his horse and a donkey. The valley was about a day's ride away. For this reason, he always returned from these trips after midnight. Sam explained that horse supplies were delivered up to the mountains twice a year, but during her entire stay at the *finca* she never saw one such delivery. She observed many men on the farm who came and went. Only the core around Rivas stayed on permanently. Pedro treated Catherine like a chum, Rivas kept his distance, and Joe was reserved towards her, almost suspicious of her. Despite his nickname he could hardly speak English. Perhaps this was why they called him Joe in the first place. And as far as

Sam was concerned, although he of course spoke English fluently, being Scottish, she didn't manage to build any kind of relationship with him at all. Rivas was often away, or held lengthy telephone conversations in Spanish or French. Most of the time though, he occupied himself with some or other project in his study. Since she lacked close human companionship she made friends with the books in her room. She had a choice of Dickens, Hesse, Tolstoy, Twain and many other classics. In addition, the shelf offered her a complete selection of horse-riding classics such as Podhajsky, Müseler, Seunig and Steinbrecht. Even the ancient works of Xenophon were among them. And, a little different in its theme, was a book on *Doma Vaquera* riding. Her favorite book of the lot was Clemens Laar's novel *"My father's horses"*, a classic about military-style German riding, packed into a romantic Irish setting. It moved her to tears every night. She much preferred the riding literature to the contemporary works that were available to her. Especially the many non-fiction books about management or recruitment – these failed to ignite her interest. Just a few weeks back they'd have been her first choice, but Catherine was now living in another universe. She was fast unravelling the thread that once bound her to the outside world. Her journey inwards connected her more to the suffering of Anna Karenina than to the management theories of Collins or Drucker. Catherine tried to integrate herself into her new social structure and willingly completed her trivial tasks but she longed for a more meaningful role. In particular, she hungered for more attention from Rivas. The less approachable he seemed, the more drawn towards him she felt. She wanted him to involve her more deeply, and let her into his interests and concerns, but he left her completely in the dark on anything that mattered to him. Rivas now played a paramount role in Catherine's life. He was her only source of hope, the only way to freedom, and ironically, he made her feel safe. She was not only physically out of touch with the people at home but also emotionally. Her longing for Rivas shoved everything else aside. Her previous relationships, her fondness for thriving cities and tough business deals, had lost their meaning. It was plain to all on the farm that she had a crush on Rivas, even though she tried hard not to show it. Then, just at the point where her yearning for Rivas reached its peak, he decided to fill her in on his mission. It changed everything.

12.
Peru, June 13

Rivas had summoned Catherine to his study. The long time she had now spent on the farm, working and living closely with the men, didn't mitigate his hold over her. It was nothing less than a summons, and yet again she was intimidated by his strong personality. She entered the book-lined room with great apprehension.

"Come in, sit down. What you're having?"

"What are you drinking?"

"Bourbon."

"Me, too."

"Are you sure? Aren't you going to get nauseous from that?" Everyone on the *finca* knew that she easily felt sick.

"Yes. Bourbon."

"How do you want it?"

"You?"

"Without anything."

She giggled at how he put it. "Me, too. Without anything."

"As you wish." He poured her whiskey. She nipped tentatively at the masculine beverage, put it down immediately and fanned her right hand melodramatically up and down her open mouth in order to cool her burning throat. "How are you Catherine?"

"So so."

"Don't you like it here anymore?"

"Rivas, what can I say to that? Of course I don't like it here. I want to go home. What am I doing here? I feel like I'm on a riding vacation at 'Camp World Peace'."

"World peace, huh?"

"Huh what?"

"That's great, isn't it?"

"What's great?"

"Vacation and world peace."

"What would be great, is real peace and a voluntary vacation. I just don't understand why you're keeping me here. I'm a burden to all of you. When can I go home?"

"Would you prefer it if I sent you back into the forest? I can easily arrange that."

"Actually, what *was* that all about? Why didn't you bring me here an easier way?"

"How do you imagine we would have gotten you across the border? With a helicopter, or what? That's the route from Miami and you had to take it."

"Route? What strange camp was that anyway?"

"The camp you tried to run away from via the old well?"

"Yeah. The one with all the soldiers or *guerilleros* or whatever they believe themselves to be."

"That's a compound for the temporary housing of hostages en route to other destinations. There's an untold number of kidnappings in South America every year. Some victims spend years in captivity. Each hideout is eventually discovered. They have to stay mobile. See it as a hotel for hostages."

"Ha ha!"

"It's true."

"Don't they storm these camps?"

"They do. But the barracks are well guarded and as soon as there is any sign of discovery, they clear out the hostages at lightning speed. It's imperative to always be a step ahead of the government forces. That takes skill, equipment and money. This particular camp is run by a financially strong organisation called OLHPA."

"OLHPA?"

"Organisation for the Liberation of the Hispanic Peoples of the Americas."

"When you called me in Venezuela you said there would be other hostages, but there weren't any."

"Then you happened to be their only 'transfer guest' at the time."

"Is that supposed to be funny?"

"It's a fact. You didn't have such a bad time there. Or did they treat you badly?"

"What do I have to do with this OLHPA?" she asked crankily.

"Nothing. We can hire their facilities when we want to hide hostages during transportation." She was about to ask her next question, but he anticipated it. "You've been kidnapped by a group of activists called WICED – Western Initiative Countering Eastern

Dominion. I'm a kidnapper within this initiative and Maria Santa Cruz is one of its leaders."

"What kind of activism are we talking about?"

"We are an anti-terror movement."

"ANTI-terror? You're not serious!"

"From your perspective I would also wonder, but we don't foster terrorism. We fight it. Our aim is to protect the Western world from imminent takeover. Be it by North Korean despots or Islamic fanatics. Right now we're working on fighting off an Islamic invasion. Everywhere in the world, they are indoctrinating peoples with their rigid dogma. The smaller the country or the less educated its population, the more vulnerable they are. Even big, emancipated states are increasingly becoming exposed to Middle Eastern value systems."

"What would be so bad about exposure to other cultures' value systems? It increases personal choice. What's wrong with that? If I believe strongly in something I also like to talk about it to others and hope they'll see my point of view."

"It's not about talking. If the fundamentalists we are up against meet with any resistance, they plan to subject that country by force. Be it through viral warfare internally or a military attack from outside the borders."

"How do you know that?"

"We know it."

"Do you honestly think that I'm going to buy this insane conspiracy theory of yours?"

"What you believe is irrelevant. And so is your opinion on this matter. Your value lies solely in you completing your assignment, which forms part of our resistance strategy."

"It can only be a headhunting assignment you have in mind. My riding skills won't get you very far. Or have I been brought here as some kind of Joan of Arc?"

Rivas laughed. In his mind's eye he must have imagined Catherine leading a charge of soldiers in full medieval armor, her brows contracted in a look of fierce determination. "You've made good progress with your riding, but you're a long way off a crusade on horseback. And I'm sure you're no virgin either?"

"Neither was she after you men were finished with her."

"What's that now? A campaign against the male gender as a whole?"

"What she suffered strikes a nerve in me. Surely you can understand that."

"Nobody abused you sexually, Catherine. Don't hype yourself into a state of martyrdom."

"Why didn't you just pay me off if you think I can help you to recruit someone? Did you want to save yourself a fee?"

"Your life is your fee!"

She swallowed audibly. "Alex! My database! You tried to steal it, didn't you? But you could do nothing with it, without my help! Alright then, what are you looking for? A mediator between East and West? A top-level negotiator with superior political savvy? It'll be hard, but I can try."

"The world's gone way beyond mediation or negotiation. Look around! No! We are going to end this five-thousand-year war between the descendants of Isaac and Ishmael, actually between Sarah and Hagar, to be exact. We will wipe out every single opponent of our Western values. Only a complete annihilation can secure peace at this stage. You weren't that far off with your remark about Camp World Peace."

Catherine gasped for air. "You are asking me to recruit someone who will assist you in committing genocide?"

"Unless you want to end up like Jeanne d'Arc. Do you want to sacrifice yourself for these fanatics? Do you think they would do the same for you? Would they bat an eyelid if you and all other women were oppressed for the rest of your lives?"

"You're the one that's oppressing me!"

"Only temporarily – and only for a good cause."

"Rivas, you don't have to try to coerce me. It won't work. And I also won't you let you force me into this. I'll never take part in such a plan. Ever."

"You're right in the middle of it, Catherine. Whoever sets up such a database…."

"That was my father!" she defended herself.

"Whoever keeps such a database must expect that this data is also going to be put to good use some day."

"Why did you fill me in? I wouldn't have to know all these gory details. Perhaps I would have agreed if you'd given me the search criteria but kept the purpose to yourself."

"The qualities we seek are intrinsically connected to the purpose of the mission. It couldn't be avoided. And, your work is not confined to the release of data, but extends over the entire recruitment and placement process. You can only fulfil our requirements if you understand the ideals involved. There are other reasons why we need your personal participation. I'll get to those another day."

"Give me a moment to think." She took the glass of bourbon and emptied it in one go. Not only did she feel sick from it, as he predicted, but also dizzy. Rivas used the short break to light a cigarette. The fact that he thrashed this out with her, instead of putting a gun to her head, deceived her into the assumption that there was cause for hope. If she refused, he would demand the code from her, which he could nothing with anyway. And then he would surely let her go as soon as he realized that she was not to be convinced. He would warn her that if she tried to blow the whistle on WICED, they would find her and kill her, but he was no barbarian. He wouldn't go through with it. The slap at their first meeting had been a ruse, a game. He was crazy but he was also educated and he behaved in a cultured manner. He would never seriously harm her. She was convinced of it.

"Forget what you are thinking, Catherine. You will cooperate. Willingly, I hope. But, if not, you *will* work on this assignment, one way or another!"

Or would he?

"What now?"

"Come down at 8 am tomorrow and I'll brief you."

"Good night, Rivas."

"Good night, see you in the morning."

"Rivas," she said as she was leaving. "You said you could send me back to the jungle any time. But you wouldn't hand me back to this bunch of thugs now, would you?"

"That's up to you."

"You would do it?"

"If I had to."

"I wouldn't survive it a second time."

"That's why I'd kill you instead. Less effort, same result."

"You'd be capable of that?"

"Without a doubt."

"You're bluffing."

"It wouldn't be the first time."

At that, she knew she had to flee. This very night.

13.
Peru, June 13

On the way back to her room her injured hip and leg reminded her to consider the consequences of her last escape attempt, but her options were limited: Become an accomplice or die. She settled on running away.

With trembling hands, she rummaged through her things. She put on both T-shirts with one of the men's shirts over these. She tied a second shirt around the waist of her jeans. Instead of her riding boots, she dug out the laced jungle boots. Although her plan was to escape on horseback, she reckoned she may be forced to continue on foot at some point. Since she didn't have a bag, every useful item was packed into the pockets of her jeans and the shirts. There were only a few things of use in the room anyway: two apples, one for the horse and the other for her, tablets and Band-Aids. With no water bottle at her disposal, she'd have to drink from rivers and lakes.

She switched off the lights to make it look like she'd gone to bed. In the dark, she paced the room restlessly two dozen times, sat on the edge of the bed, stood up once more, went to the bathroom, came back. She repeatedly went to the door which was slightly ajar, listening to the sounds in the house. When she was sure that everyone had turned in, she waited for another half an hour as a precaution. Not having a watch had forced her to develop a good sense of time. It must have been around two o'clock in the morning when she slipped out of the house across the yard towards the barn. She looked up at the sky. Yes, the moon gave off adequate light.

On Andalus she would have the best chance of escape, she figured. She needed to get to the valley. He surely knew the path – she'd only have to point the horse in the right direction and he'd follow it. Horses always preferred a path that was familiar to them. There, she would seek out a village or perhaps a remote farmhouse. She guessed it would not take longer than five or six hours at trot and canter since the journey at a walk took a whole day. Andalus would have enough stamina to sustain the fast pace for a long time. She also hoped that he of all the horses would manage the longest without food and water if they were to get lost – Andalusians were robust by nature. She was optimistic that she would be able to manage his temperament with no problems and as soon as she found help, she would hand Andalus over to the authorities. She reckoned the police would take him into their care and Rivas and Andalus would never see each other again. To abandon him and to rob Rivas of his beloved horse had worried her a lot as she forged her escape plan, but she justified her decision with the fact that Rivas had left her with no other option.

She fetched his bridle and saddle from the tack room and quietly made her way to his stall. Her hands were full and she left the whip behind, but she did make certain of the riding hat, crammed onto her head.

Excited by the prospect of an early feed, the horses began to neigh - only Andalus failed to honor her with a greeting. "Easy, easy," she whispered to them. "You'll soon get your breakfast."

Her hands were unsteady but she forced herself to move about as calmly as possible in the darkness. If Andalus sensed her jitters, he would get nervous and the last thing she needed was a jumpy stallion to deal with.

As she led him across the yard, his hooves clopped sharply on the ground and she broke into a sweat, but there was no other way past the buildings. "Please don't neigh," she whispered to him imploringly. Once in the saddle she put him into a gallop. Andalus obeyed but did not offer the rhythmic motion that she had experienced when riding him together with Pedro. He refused to soften, and was wooden and sully.

Some distance from the yard, Catherine eased Andalus to a canter. But the stallion was annoyed. He went forward, but his reluctance was expressed by his rigid motion. She'd fetched him in the middle of the night from the hush of his stable, had allowed him no brief orientation before giving him the canter aid and even denied him a few obligatory warm-up strides. He decided to cooperate for the moment, at least until he could make sense of this folly. Reluctantly, he cantered for a good hour in the direction of the valley before he began demanding that they now turn back.

Catherine was so preoccupied with her escape that she let the protests of the irritable stallion pass, and in the way of things this led him to believe that her riding skills were better than they actually were. And so, for now, they made quick progress.

The eerie surroundings, the fast ride through the night, soaked up her attention. The words of *Erlkönig*, a poem by Johann Wolfgang von Goethe, came to mind. She'd hated learning the poem at school. As a child she'd found it irrelevant and outdated, and it had made no sense to her. It was pure torture and she hadn't thought of it again until this day. It was a mystery to her how and why she could recall it now. But truly, verse by verse the drama unfolded, here and now. And this time, she understood. And it made her shiver:

Who rides there so late through the night dark and drear? The father it is, with his infant so dear; He holds the boy tightly clasped in his arm, he holds him safely, he keeps him warm.

They'd put quite some distance between themselves and the farm when they approached the rocky escarpment that marked the beginning of the descent into the valley. Andalus started to act up, was not on the aids and demanded increasing amounts of leg in order to stay in canter. This tired her out. More and more often she had to let him trot. After riding for about two hours, Catherine started to doubt. What if she failed? The landscape was not as she'd imagined it – was she already lost in the wilderness? A fog drifted in. In her mind's eye she was seeing things.

My son, wherefore seek you your face thus to hide? Look, father, the Erl-King is close by our side! Do you see not the Erl-King, with crown and with train? My son, it's the mist rising over the plain.

At a fork, Andalus decided he'd had enough. Catherine wanted to take the path to the right that led downhill, but Andalus broke out to the left, intending to turn back. He used the strength of his enormous neck to resist her rein hand. She tried to block him with her left reign and leg and then to drive him forward energetically with both legs. In vain. The stallion lifted his forelegs off the ground while pushing further to the left. She turned him sharply to the left in a circle until they were again facing the direction she wanted to take. After a few steps, Andalus again sabotaged her plans. He ran backwards and rolled up behind the reins, thus robbing her of any control. She forced herself to drive him forward without pulling on the reins to get his head back up. She expected that in his disobedient state her leg pressure would temporarily drive him backwards even faster and she was right. But she knew she would have to keep her leg on to regain control, despite how frightening it felt. When his backhand tired, he let her drive him forward for a few steps, but he soon broke out to the left again, where he napped once more.

When a horse "naps" it refuses to move into either direction, waiting for a release into the direction it is aiming for. And Andalus was making a meal of it. He'd seen through her trick with the 180 degree turn. Next time he wouldn't let her catch him out. Not him! And anyway - where was Rivas whenever you needed him?

Catherine lost her temper and used the solid heel of her boot to deposit a firm kick into his left flank. Andalus yielded. They rode on. Catherine sensed it was only a matter of time until Andalus would resist again. Tears welled up. She would have to turn back - she wouldn't make it. Perhaps she was lucky and her departure hadn't yet been noticed. She would return the horse to his paddock to cool off and say that she'd risen early and he'd wanted to go out. There he'd let off steam and that's why he was so sweaty. She invented one story after the next while she proceeded further and further away from the *finca*. And, if they had noticed her escape already she would have come back voluntarily and she would say she'd taken him on an outride. She wasn't allowed to do that, but they wouldn't kill her for it.

Ride on? Turn back?

It was getting light and still they headed downhill in the direction of where she suspected the valley to be, when her indecisiveness finally sealed her fate. Andalus relieved her of the decision. Out of the blue, he balked at the progress. He'd had enough. He wanted to go home. He turned on his haunches – a powerful, sudden and irrevocable movement – and bolted home.

A determined Andalus was headed back through the rocky escarpment and Catherine decided to abandon her mission for today and return home saying she'd been riding out. Then - in front of them appeared a cloud of dust. A posse of mounted riders charging downhill towards them. It was too late to pretend. However, she had one trump left: nobody would be able to catch Andalus. He was just so much faster. She gave him another sharp kick and pulled him so strongly on the right rein that he reared up on his hind legs in an angry demonstration of willfulness.

A rear is the ultimate disobedience of a horse, its most decisive form of resistance, for which it will face any punishment. Pleasure horses that expose their riders to this danger on a regular basis are usually destroyed. She knew that as a novice she would do well to jump off now because if she pulled him off balance he could flip over and crush her underneath his heavy weight.

But time was of the essence. If she leaped off, how would she be able to get back on in time? She released the reins, as one should when on a rearing horse and gripped his mane to have something to hold on to. Andalus landed back on the ground and she drove him forward but, after two, three steps he reared again. This time she was caught off guard, pulled on the reins and hauled him off balance - Andalus flipped over. He dragged her with him to the ground and she managed, just in time, to roll away sideways. The impact winded her and all she could do was painfully drag herself off the path and into the bushes. There, she raised her head and watched.

Andalus had got up and bolted towards the approaching horses. She saw that he'd been slightly lamed in the fall. She saw the stirrups and reins flapping in the wind. But when she saw how quickly he'd reached the posse, she gave up. She crept back to the path, sat down in the sand and began to pray.

Dear God, if you exist, please let me survive this.

The posse approached, with Andalus now part of it. Without a rider, and in a much better mood, he expectantly looked in her direction. Why didn't she get back on? His leg was hurting and he really wanted to get home now.

Catherine stared wildly at the scene. Her mind was in turmoil. She felt for Andalus, but most of all she feared for herself. What story should she give? What excuse for her actions?

The men dismounted. They tied her hands with a length of rope and left her sitting there. Then they all inspected the stallion's right hock and conversed excitedly in Spanish. One brought out a mobile phone and made a call. She recognized some of the riders but neither Joe nor Pedro or Sam was among them. This surprised her. What didn't surprise her, though, was that Rivas hadn't lowered himself to ride after her. That was to be expected.

"I was just about to turn around," she lied dully, without the slightest hope of sympathy or understanding. "Please let me go," she added, illogically. "He'll kill me if you take me back to him."

Her pleas went unanswered. Two of the riders remounted and spurred their horses back to the ranch. The others tied her hands to the black stallion's saddle. They too remounted and made off at a walk, for home. Right from the start she found it hard to keep up. "Won't you at least let me get on?" she begged.

"The *azabache* is lame," came the brief retort. By *azabache* the man meant Andalus. It was the word that Peruvians used to describe a black horse. This she knew from Sam. As the point sank in to her mind, she grew cold with fear – the consequences of their fall – the runaway and the prized stallion, now lame, returning to her kidnapper and the horse's owner. What awaited her seemed unthinkable.

Right now though, the pressing question was how to cope with the journey. Stumbling on foot, tied with her arms lashed to the stallion's saddle, would she manage the distance ahead? Due to the marches through the rain forest, she was top fit, and her stay at Andes height had acclimatized her to the thin air, but to be able to keep up with the group on horseback, uphill, on this stony ground, seemed impossible. If she fell back, the stallion could get irritated and either kick out at her or bolt off and drag her with him. The return to the farm at walking pace was about six to seven hours. Why didn't they at least let her double-donkey with one of the riders?

Cruel bastards!

With the rising sun, the air warmed up. The troop didn't even halt once for a short break. Because they kept the pace at a walk and the horses were used to long distances in the Andes, they could get away with it, but Catherine's physical resources were coming to an end. Her legs carried her mechanically but her heart was taking serious strain. She was overheated. She gasped for air and her head ached. Dragging at his side, pulling on the rope to the saddle, she became a burden to the stallion. If Andalus had been a skittish horse, he would have made it far more difficult. But he towed her patiently along, despite his lameness.

Twice they offered her water but since her hands were restricted by the tight rope, she struggled to drink. Thirsty and exhausted, she let her feet drag along the dusty path. When she stumbled for the first time, nearly slipping against his legs, Andalus jumped forward in fright – but he was firmly gripped with a lead rein. And a clever horse always tries to avoid any creature that gets under his feet. And Andalus was a clever horse, a very clever one.

"*Señores, por favor!*" she cried out with the last of her remaining strength. "I really can't go on."

The man who was leading Andalus finally stopped the troop. He got off and untied her so that she could drink some water. After this she rubbed her aching arms as the blood flowed back painfully into her hands. Some riders dismounted, others stayed seated. She sat down on the path and rested her elbows on her knees. Then she buried her head in her hands in a gesture of absolute despair. Once more she pleaded with the men to let her get on one of the horses with one of them. Her legs felt like cotton wool. Even an experienced jogger would be taking strain against the thin Andes air at over ten thousand feet above sea level.

After the break, it got worse. Her legs kept caving in. Andalus who'd started to understand pulled her along willingly, as well as he could.

Good, wonderful, kind Andalus!

With his help, she managed to keep herself upright, putting one foot in front of the other.

It was well into the afternoon when the house came into sight. Catherine's sense of reality returned. How would Rivas react to her behavior? Sure, a beating was undoubtedly on the cards but Rivas liked her by now, she figured. She would apologize and then she would cooperate. At first. As a pretense. She was no longer worried about being killed, because Rivas could easily have had her murdered in the mountains. And, after all, he still needed her. For his mission of madness. Of course he would be fuming, because she'd abused his trust and stolen his horse. Nevertheless she was optimistic that whatever was to follow would not be nearly as awful as the strenuous journey she'd just mastered.

When they untied her from the saddle, she took a deep breath of relief and collapsed on the steps of the porch. She would now have to face the confrontation with Rivas and then she could have a good long sleep and the next morning, fresh and rested, she would continue searching for solutions.

What happened next was not at all what she had expected.

14.
Peru, June 14

With unnecessary force, someone pushed her into the house through a side entrance. This alarmed her. Up to now, throughout the long trek back up the mountain, the men had acted quite indifferently towards her. Now, instead of taking her up to her room, they dragged her down some stairs into a cellar. There was a single bulb, giving just enough light to look around. The cellar was empty save for a chair, a blue tarpaulin, and a few heaps of chopped wood. Catherine was overheated, and she shivered in the sudden cold of the room. She pulled herself together and decided to say yes and amen to everything they might demand of her. Once she was back upstairs in her own room, she could think about new tactics. Shaking from cold and unease, she speculated on what would happen – who would hit her first, how long they would keep her down here in the dark and cold, and would she have the guts to take the punishment? What took place, in fact, turned out to be most harrowing experience of her entire life.

Two men pushed her to the floor and pressed her onto her back on the hard concrete floor. The others formed a loose half circle and watched. She didn't resist. That, she knew from previous experience, was of no use. One tied up her feet, while another ripped her shirt off and pulled the T-shirts up over her head, covering her face and robbing her of her sight. Only her bra remained in place. While one man stretched her arms out above her head and tied her wrists together, she felt two rough hands pull away the spare shirt that she'd tied around her waist. Then they unzipped her jeans and pulled them down to her ankles. With almost inhumane strength, Catherine resisted the temptation to struggle. She bit her lip and stayed calm. To kick around with tied legs was useless, as was screaming for help in a dungeon. She was outnumbered. She had no chance against them. Any defensive action would only increase their brutality. They turned her on her right side, bent her legs at the knees, trussed her calves to her thighs and left her like that. Then all sounds of activity subsided. She heard them switch off the light and close the door.

Visualizing the position in which she was trussed, she felt her horror climax to a peak. The side position, stripped down to

her underwear, and the method by which her face had been
covered, bore the hallmarks of execution – the preliminaries that
the captives of South American bandits or rebels went through
before they were murdered. She knew this from a biography she'd
read, about a Latin American rebel. At some point, these men
would return and kill her. There were details that didn't make sense,
however. Why had they tied her calves to her thighs? Why had they
stretched her arms above her head? And why did they go away
without finishing her off? Not even the worst of enemies had to
suffer like this. They were shot quickly - one by one - after being
tied up. She assumed that these men were not equipped or trained
to kill and that the assassin would turn up shortly to finish the job.
Her stomach rumbled, and she was so cold that she shook
uncontrollably. The next moment she was so hot that she believed
she would die from a fever. Her arms and underarms ached from
the strain and as the time ticked past the cramps in her bent knees
became unbearable. She didn't whimper or cry. That was too
strenuous. She just waited silently for her imminent death.

It was as if hours had passed when she heard the door
open, followed by voices. Then she heard footsteps approaching.
She listened for the sound of a gun's safety catch being released, a
sound which she now knew from her own experience. But it never
came. No shot rang through the cellar. No bullet penetrated her
neck. She was still breathing, thinking, suffering. What was going
on?

*I love thee, I'm charmed by your beauty, dear boy! And if you're
unwilling, then force I'll employ. My father, my father, he seizes me fast, for
sorely the Erl-King has hurt me at last.*

She'd resigned herself to the prospect of dying but the
ordeal that she was about to experience was beyond anything she
could have been mentally prepared for.

The footsteps went away. She heard them shut the door
shut once more. Then she realized that there was still someone in
the room! Shortly afterwards she felt a man's hands untie her wrists.
He turned her onto her stomach and now she felt her hands
fastened behind her back. He left her ankles tied, but he cut
through the cord under her knees and pressed them flat against the
floor. The resulting rush of blood coming back into circulation was
extremely painful, but even before the throbbing and tingling had
subsided he lifted her legs, again bent her knees and tied an

additional rope around her ankles. He fixed a nylon cord around her neck and tied it to the rope around her feet. The short length of the thin cord between her ankles and neck made it necessary for Catherine to hold her lower legs upright with the mere strength of her muscles. Her knees were weakened from the previous position in which she'd been immobilized. The new refinement of cruelty increased the pressure on her back and thigh muscles. But each time she lowered her calves, the nylon contracted around her throat, cut into her flesh and restricted her air supply.

The man moved away from her and she heard him pull up the chair, and light a cigarette. She knew it wasn't Rivas - she would have felt that. She addressed the man in English. He replied by shoving a piece of her T-shirt in her mouth.

It was not a quick and painless death through shooting that awaited her but a slow and cruel death by suffocation.

Her limbs tired quickly, but something else kicked in – Catherine's will to survive. She surprised herself at the depth of it. It gave her enormous strength, the source of which was an enigma to her. She found a strange new mastery over her own limbs and muscles, holding them still without undue strain or effort, resisting the natural temptation to kick and struggle. In any event, the vicious web of ropes and cords prevented any drastic movements, which was a blessing in disguise.

This garrote, which trapped Catherine so cruelly, rendering her motionless, was an improvised version of an old Spanish method of public execution. Spanish and Latin American society used it for centuries before it was banned in 1977. Today it remained a popular and cruel method among killers, by which a victim was caused to die while allowing full control of the process. The murderer had his hands free and could watch and regulate the pace and severity of the suffering at will.

As terrible as it was, it forced Catherine to reduce any movement to a minimum and suppress her panic reflexes. This gave her some control of the situation.

But not for long.

Her thighs had gone numb but she still held her legs upright as if fastened by an anchor. Eventually it was her back that let her down. Without any warning, it succumbed to a violent spasm and forced her into a cruel choice: the unbearable pain in her spine that felt like an ongoing electric shock, or strangulation.

The decision was made for her. She had no strength left. In her first and terrifying fight against total suffocation, she lost consciousness. She came round because the man had lifted her legs and by so doing released the pressure of the cord around her neck and restored the air flow. She wanted to cry for mercy, beg and plead, promise whatsoever obedience they might demand. Not just for show, as had been her stupid plan, but for real, and forever and eternity. However, since he'd also gagged her, she could not even whimper her assurances of submission.

To cut off verbal communication, to rob the victim of eye contact and to prevent arm and leg movements, made torture easier for the perpetrator. This she also knew from books. The man on the chair did not sit beside a human, but a non-person, a thing.

Three more times she fainted, three more times the man loosened the string to bring her back. With each wakening she felt intense pain and was completely clear in the head. The most frightening thing of all was to know that this sadist, who didn't seem to care if she was closer to life or death, watched her in her agony. Who was this? Where was Rivas? He wouldn't approve of such a deed. She had to stay strong until he came into the cellar. He would free her, take her in his arms and comfort her. He would apologize for losing control over the situation and explain that the man had acted of his own accord. Every now and then, when painful doubts interrupted her fantasies, she succumbed to hopelessness. Was Rivas really not informed? Or was he a coward who escaped his responsibility by giving the dirty work to others? Catherine's confusion grew.

After the fourth loss of consciousness her will to survive was spent. The upcoming apathy opened the gate to a strange garden of peace and contentment. Catherine pronounced her own death sentence. In a last effort, she pushed her legs down against the fixture and against the arms of the man who was once again readjusting the cords. She wanted the string to finish its work – to strangle her to death. Lucidity reared up for one final time and she recited to herself the last verse of *Erlkönig*. Goethe's words were the last she mouthed before she felt the life drain out of her.

The father now gallops, with terror half wild, he grasps in his arms the poor shuddering child; He reaches his courtyard with toil and with dread, – The child in his arms finds he motionless, dead.

At that precise moment, with a single thrust, the man cut through the string around her ankles and throat and removed it. He pulled her jeans back up and untied her hands. With her hands free, she removed the T-shirts from her face and slipped her arms sluggishly back into their sleeves. She tried to rise but before she could, the man picked her up and carried her almost lifeless body back to her room. He dumped her down on her bed like a parcel, left and locked the door behind him.

After a few minutes on her bed, she was gripped by a violent attack of tears. She curled up into a fetal position. With her arms hugging her stomach, she sobbed and trembled in complete disbelief at what had taken place. Her shock was so great, that the fact that she'd survived passed her by at first. It was the deed that occupied her mind. No accident. Pure malice! No apology from Rivas. Not a sadistic act by a wayward pervert of an underling, but Rivas's own coldhearted plan to make her suffer. Black thoughts clouded her mind and she even yearned for the return of blissful lack of consciousness. She was now caught in a new nightmare – and fully awake to face the awful reality of it!

She needed the toilet. And she also had to wash up and attend to the cut around her throat. She dragged herself to the bathroom door only to find it locked. Only now did she comprehend the purpose of the empty bucket in the middle of the room. She took a closer look around. On the table were a plastic jug and a plastic mug. That was all. Even her few pieces of clothing they had taken away from her. Her beloved books were also gone. The desolation caused her to burst into tears again. She couldn't believe what was happening to her in this house - a place where she'd come to feel safe, where she'd spent a few relatively carefree days. Surely no crime justified such harsh punishment. She was completely at the mercy of this unjust brute. Wasn't it normal to want to flee?

For hours, she wept. She wept in turn from depression and frustrated anger. Then, as time passed, she turned her energy once again towards getting out of this hellhole.

The bitterest disappointment was Rivas. Her bubble of fantasy about him had burst. She had nothing left to hold on to.

The long night came and went.

15.
Peru, June 15

The next day, around lunch time, Catherine was sitting at her table when the door was unlocked and Rivas entered. He'd never come into her room before, at least not while she was there. Immediately she was overwhelmed by him again, this time from fear rather than admiration. Everything that had happened in the last few hours was on his account. How closely he'd brought her to death's door! How she had mistaken him - underestimated his cold-hearted cruelty! Yes, he'd kept her from death – but not out of sympathy. He was capable of the worst.

She got up and took a trembling step in his direction. To move towards people, especially when she felt fearful, was one of Catherine's instinctive defense mechanisms. Others drew back, but she rarely did that. Catherine usually moved towards the source of her fear and this flight forward, disguised as a confrontation, often helped her out of a tight spot because it confused her opponent. She also carried a flicker of hope that she might appease him – after all, she'd already suffered so much. She stuttered out a tentative apology: "Rivas, I'm so sorry about Andalus…" But she got no further because he'd already struck her. Now she fled, not forward, but into the closest corner. There he hit her so many times in the face that she fell down. On hands and knees, she scrambled to the table, crawled underneath it, curled up, making herself as small as possible, and held her hands protectively over her head. And she screamed like a madwoman. He pulled her out of her refuge and tossed her against the bookshelf. The contact with the solid wood smashed her mind into fresh clarity and she started to plead: "No! Stop, please stop! I'm so sorry! Please stop!"
"What are you so sorry about, Catherine?"
"That I ran away! That Andalus got hurt! That, that I…"
"Where were you going with him?"
"To the valley."
"And what would have happened to him there?"
"I'm so sorry," she sobbed.
"A strand of his mane is worth more than you will be in a life time."
"I'm so sorry."

After her third abject apology, he nailed her against the wall with a piercing look. Alongside his cold brutality, he showed staggering composure. "Don't ever steal my horse again. Don't touch him, don't ever dare come near him again, or I'll kill you. Be sure of it!" He left the room and she heard him lock the door.

Catherine only saw Rivas again the next morning. She was still in bed when he unlocked the door. He put down a tray with a fresh jug of water and a few apples and strolled over to her. He pulled her up from her bed and slapped her in the face a few times. Without uttering a word, he left. In the evening he returned, put down another tray with water and a plastic dog bowl with a few junks of cheese and slices of tomato. He hit her again, removed the tray from the morning, and disappeared. He repeated this drill for days. At noon each day, a man silently exchanged the bucket. The procedure was always the same.

Once she was standing right next to the door when Rivas paid her one of his visits. He left the door ajar and put down the tray. Against his usual habit, he sat down at the table and lit a cigarette while watching her closely. She was aware of the open door and suspected that he was just waiting for her to try to run through it. "How long do you still want to lock me up? I made a mistake. Please forgive me. I know I don't deserve it, but please trust me. I won't run away again." Silently, he carried on smoking. She had no idea what was going through his mind. Then she realized his intention and she pressed away from the door into a corner, shaking her head in horror. "Rivas, you can't do that! Please!"

He got up and moved towards her, but halfway he paused to toss the burning cigarette into the bucket. Her relief didn't last long for he closed in on her and again pounded her with blows.

In the days to follow she no longer attempted to address him but let him mistreat her without tears or protests or pleas. She never saw Pedro or Joe. She responded to the treatment with the classical symptoms of the Pavlovian reflex. Like Pavlov's dogs that salivated after conditioning by the sound of a bell that announced their feeding time, she now expected to be beaten before every meal.

Her fear of mealtimes grew into the most arduous of psychological torture.

--- oOo ---

All the while, Rivas kept an eye on Catherine's condition. He took careful note that she was still eating the meagre meals that he provided. Due to her experience in the jungle she was realistic enough to know that eating was crucial if she was to continue functioning properly. She would eat anything - even choke it down somehow if necessary. At this stage of the torture it was customary to reduce the victim's diet to leftovers or dog food, but Rivas didn't want to overdo it. Soon, when conditions were beyond bearing, she'd stop eating altogether. Then the work could begin.

As far as Rivas could judge, Catherine responded to everything as if programmed. She was much stronger than expected, but he was still within the time frame. He had no doubt that she would soon submit, despite her robust constitution.

Two milestones had been laid: the physical dependence was complete. The second objective was to make the hostage believe that she was worthless and didn't deserve better. The third part of the control strategy was to frighten the victim so much that she started to accept mistreatment as the status quo and viewed non-violent phases as a demonstration of mercy and grace. This state she had not yet reached. His only problem with the prolonged punitive phase was the danger of injury. The task that awaited Catherine necessitated that her body remain in perfect condition. He could not risk any broken bones which would limit his options.

He didn't want to punch her in the stomach because he wanted to spare the tender female organs as a matter of principle. The chest area was also off limits because her collar bones were so delicate. And anyway, he found her much too pretty. It would have been a shame to damage her breasts. So the only areas left were her face down to her neckline, her legs and her back.

His colleagues would have tied their victim face down onto a bench and worked from there. But then he would have had to use his fists or a belt or another type of object. He found that too unrefined. And it had been years since he personally last tied up a victim, especially a woman. Such an overdose of force would also bring about a different effect from the one he intended. So he limited himself to her face while taking great care not to injure her seriously or risk the possibility of unsightly scars. Her attractive appearance had to stay intact, and the danger of visible bruises to be avoided at all costs.

Therefore he only hit her with the back of his ring-less hand. Even the toss against the bookshelf had not been an arbitrary act but meted out with care. With male hostages, it was different. There, you could move with less precision and you had many more methods at your disposal: electric shocks, baseball bats, cuts or burns. Much too rough for this enchanting little lamb. The intensity of the beating was never the critical thing; it was about terrorizing her until her will was broken.

The next afternoon he would reach his goal.

--- oOo ---

Rivas put down the tray of cheese and tomato and noticed that she hadn't touched her apples from breakfast. She was still cowering in the same corner that he'd beaten her into in the morning. Her face showed no expression, her eyes were glassy. Something was going on inside her, but not one word passed her lips. One more day, he reckoned, and he was just about to strike her.

"Don't," she whispered. "I'll do it."

Catherine dragged herself up to the corner of the bed. He sat down next to her. "I can't go on," she groaned, and lent against him. "Please don't beat me anymore." He put his arms around her and she nestled up against him, dissolving into his embrace. Rivas was wearing a black leather jacket and her face pressed against the cool, soft leather. "Please hold me." He did so, and he stroked her head. She let him comfort her as if he'd just rescued her from some other bad guy. She longed for the tenderness to continue, but Rivas stood up and unlocked the bathroom door. He ran her a bath and poured antiseptic liquid into the water.

The escape attempt, the cellar and the many days of confinement without any means of personal hygiene had left her badly soiled. He led her into the bathroom, positioned her next to the tub and turned on the tap. Then he took off the T-shirts that she'd worn for six full days and undid her bra. Offering no resistance, she let him undress her and help her into the tub - like a chronically ill patient. He took a towel out of the cupboard and put it down next to her. "Come down to the kitchen when you're finished," he said, and left her.

Catherine washed herself, shampooed her hair, combed it out and brushed her teeth. She put on fresh underwear, a new pair of jeans and one of the men's shirts – the items that they had locked away and that she now found in her bathroom.

With her hair still wet, she made her way downstairs to the kitchen, where Joe, Pedro and Rivas were just finishing their dinner. Sam was not present. He didn't always eat with them. Neither Joe nor Pedro showed any emotion. Clearly they wanted to avoid humiliating her yet more by any sign of expression. They kept their heads bent down to their plates, Rivas, on the other hand, stood up and fetched a plate, cutlery and a glass. She sat down at the table and asked, in a hushed voice, "How is Andalus?"

"Better than you," replied Rivas.

Pedro poured her water and started to serve her dinner. She waved him off and just took small sips of water. The men talked in Spanish until Pedro cleared the table and he and Joe left for the night. Instead of washing up, they left the dishes in the sink. She was alone with Rivas. She glanced at him, and then offered him an apathetic look: "You've won, Rivas."

"Come here." She walked around the table and stood in front of him. Rivas took her hand: "You can only win when you have an opponent who has a chance of competing, no matter how small."

"Thanks for the lecture," she replied flatly, and pulled her hand away.

"You're right. That was unnecessary. I'm sorry."

"For this you apologize? For what you did to me in the room, you don't? And in the cellar!"

"That was your own fault."

"You know what? You're right. You didn't win, you dominated. But I can see now that it was necessary." Her voice remained flat and dispirited.

Good girl, thought Rivas. He then turned the screw on her with the redundant question: "What was necessary?"

"To use such a heavy hand on me."

"To tell you the truth, that's hard work and not at all economical. I would prefer it if you worked along voluntarily, instead of making things difficult for all concerned. When are you going to get this, Catherine?"

"I got it, Rivas!"

"Don't you want to have a bite to eat? You must be hungry."

"No appetite. Just tell me what I must do."

"Tomorrow. Get some rest now." He got up.

Catherine studied him intently. He was so self-sufficient. And she so dependent. She longed for his embrace. He was the only person of importance in this surreal world.

Rivas put his hands around Catherine's waist and pulled her towards him. She didn't resist. She wanted that. She no longer wanted to fight, perform verbal pyrotechnics, or scheme up plans. She no longer wanted to be strong. For once in her life she wanted to allow herself to be weak, and she surrendered to this need without guilt. She yearned to be protected by a man. Like these "weak" women whom she'd always despised. And of all men, it had to be Rivas! It made no sense. How could he protect her from himself? She really did want that and she couldn't grasp it. An unconditional capitulation.

A horse whinnied, and then another one.

Rivas bent over her face and touched her lips with his. He did that with tantalizingly slowness. His arm still held her tight, the other hand he put on the nape of her neck. His grip was so animalistic and demanding, and yet so gentle. She wanted to sling her arms around him but she felt too weak to lift them. His lips urged her for an answer until she slowly opened her mouth. And then, just when she thought she couldn't stand up straight anymore, he reeled in the passion.

Her lips implored him not to bring her back to reality. How could he stop now? Surely he wanted her also? The air was electric with desire. Why didn't he want to have all of her? Where did he find so much self-control? Could he just turn the tap on and off — at will?

Her knees softened and started to cave in under her. Only his hands around her back kept her from sinking to the floor. She wished he would unbutton her shirt, or to tear it off her – she was literally offering herself to him. Surely he must have sensed her passion? Why then did he only stroke her hair? She pressed her head into his chest and breathed him in. She had her arms around him now, but he brushed them off. "Go and lie down," he said. "Tomorrow after breakfast, come straight to the study. Okay?"

Catherine returned to her room like a sleepwalker. Did he really not want her, or was this brush-off just another humiliation? At some point she crawled under her duvet and fell asleep. She slept through till the next morning.

--- oOo ---

Rivas went to his bedroom and sent an SMS to a mobile number in Argentina. "Phase One – completed."

Within seconds his cell phone rang.

"Two days before deadline. Congratulations."

"Hello. How are you?"

"Excellent. Since I read your text."

Rivas reported Catherine's behavior in the kitchen.

"It couldn't have been easy to send her back to her room untouched," remarked the caller.

"True. Even in her desperate state she's almost irresistible." He hesitated for a moment. "Emaciated but still incredibly beautiful. The thing is, if I'd lost control of the situation, it would've been no more than rape."

"You wouldn't want that."

"I'll seduce her soon, but not in this state. Her offer had nothing to do with me. In her condition she would have thrown herself at anyone in my role. When the time comes to sleep with her, I want her to fall for me unconditionally, not because she's been subjected to violence or as a result of fresh trauma. On that day - and it will come soon - I don't want a victim but - a woman."

His caller chuckled. "Good night, my angel."

"Good night Maria."

16.
Peru, June 20

The following day Catherine rose early and did her make-up with new-found enthusiasm, back to her usual "work mask". The exquisite products that she again had access to quickly created the illusion of a beautiful and unmarred complexion. The scratches from the jungle had almost healed and the Chanel base covered the remaining signs of sunburn and her ever present freckles, as well as the dark rings under her eyes. She planned, when evening came, to try out the hair coloring products to turn her natural red back to blond. In the meantime she blow-dried and ironed her hair. The nails that had grown back slightly were thirsting for a coat of polish and she decided on vampire red. The aggressive color matched her mood.

Purposefully she marched into the kitchen and prepared herself an opulent breakfast: coffee with lots of milk and sugar, three eggs, a big portion of bacon, two grilled tomatoes, two thick slices of buttered farm bread, followed by more bread with jam. She had an enormous appetite, but even so she still only managed to eat half of everything. She added her dishes to the ones from last night's dinner and washed them up.

The house was still quiet and for the first time she entered Rivas's study without his presence. Unhindered and unsupervised, she had a good look round. She went up to the bookshelves that lined the walls and studied the titles. All his literature was about psychology or psychiatry. She reached out but could not decide between Scott Peck's *"The People of the Lie"* and Erich Fromm's *"The Fear of Freedom"*. According the cover, the former dealt with the evil of humankind. She put it back on the shelf – she didn't need any theory about this topic; she was having daily hands-on practical experience of this. She hoped that Fromm's work would give her some kind of clue regarding the inexplicable passions of last night. She sat down on the green leather couch and read until Rivas arrived. With pleasure she noticed his astonished gaze.

I do look damn good this morning!

Catherine was back in her element, and Rivas was just as courteous as he'd been before her escape attempt – polite and distant. She didn't receive the compliment she hoped for, but she was also relieved that he didn't greet her more intimately. She was ashamed of her behavior in the kitchen the night before, but she had to get through this now. She also had the feeling that he understood what went on inside her and didn't seem to judge her for it. He appeared to be an expert, a man who's seen everything. Sometimes he seemed to her like a medical doctor. It was all so bizarre.

Rivas opened the safe in the wall and, to her astonishment, took out her hard drive. He flipped open a laptop, typed in a password and gave the computer time to boot up. Then he connected the hard drive to the laptop via a USB cable, in order to transfer the data. The hard drive demanded a password. Rivas pointed to the screen. She typed it in and said audibly, *578 Tashab.* He'd want to know it anyway. The small device buzzed and whirred importantly while it revealed its secret contents. Catherine felt obliged to explain her eager cooperation: "I want to get all this behind me, so you can blow up half the world, or the whole one, if you like. I don't care, I just want to get out of here."

"You won't be looking for an explosives specialist."

"A nuclear physicist?"

"No. Biological."

"Toxicology? Bacteriology?" She pretended to appear nonchalant, as if she'd seen and heard it all – as if she really were the best possible expert in these matters.

"Virology and genetics," said Rivas curtly, interrupting her performance.

"Whatever. A geneticist then. And the virologist – what field of expertise?"

"Equine. And, I need one person for the job."

She could no longer hide her surprise. She hadn't expected this. "Why horses? What have they got to do with it?"

"They will spread a virus that will first wipe out the entire Arabian horse population."

It dawned on her – an attack to the heart! Everyone knew how much Arabs appreciated and needed their horses. She thought of the wonderful, gracious Andalus. How she despised Rivas, the two-faced horse lover! The hypocrite! She'd given him the credit, at least, of truly caring about horses.

"And then," Rivas continued, "the virus will extend to humans through a mutation. First to the stable workers, carriage drivers and riders, and then the entire population. A virus, like I said."

Utter madness, she thought. She was about to make a sharp retort but she bit her lip. Why raise rational objections to such nonsense? It'll come to nothing of its own accord. This ethnic group and their horses were spread all over the world - they couldn't just be wiped out. Soon this whole madness would be uncovered. In her mind she already heard the clatter of special-forces helicopters hovering above the roof. How could she have subjected herself to such torture for such unworkable insanity? It would have been smarter to just agree from the start. She was done with heroism. Joan of Arc was dead. Why put your life on the line fending off the crazy plans of a madman? However, she couldn't avoid asking a technical question: "Okay, the deal with the horses and the cross-over virus, I can sort of understand, but when and where do genetics come in?"

"The tribe of Ishmael," was his brief response.

She burst into laughter.

"What's so funny?"

"You hate Arabs but you give your horse an Arabic name!"

"That's exactly the point. Their influence is everywhere! But not for much longer. The same goes for their traditions and mosques – soon to be no more!"

"That's their faith. Why don't you leave them alone?"

"They shouldn't force their beliefs onto the whole world. We'll put an end to this, once and for all."

"Do you also want to abolish mathematics, no longer drink coffee, and censor guitar playing? If you don't see the injustice and evil, don't you at least recognize how nonsensical your plan is?"

"What is nonsensical is this discussion."

"I'll need internet access. That database alone is not enough." She couldn't see any cables connected to the laptop and wondered how the wireless communication on the farm could possibly work, because on none of her outrides had she ever seen a satellite tower. She asked, "Don't you need a modem?"

"It's built into the laptop, the SIM card is already inserted."

The browser opened its default page. "And from where in this wilderness do you get the signal?" she dug further.

"Organized by WICED, huge effort, very costly."

Rivas's explanation was incomplete but she left it at that. "I will need a telephone line. I can't headhunt without a phone."

"Of course."

He gave her back her cell phone and an additional one. She caught her breath when she saw her own phone, but she asked no questions. "I need someone to help with the research, someone who follows up leads. This can take weeks - I won't be able to go this alone."

"You'll have to think of something. You're not getting an assistant."

"I need proper clothes," she pushed further. "No headhunter in jeans and supersized shirts can get on the phone and convince high caliber professionals. I need this for my psyche. I need to feel good about myself, otherwise my candidates feel my lack of confidence and run away."

"Already taken care of. When you return to your room this afternoon you'll find everything you need. But first there's an important task waiting for you. Catherine, this won't be easy, but it has to be done." He took her own cell phone and placed it firmly in her hand. "You have to call Tom." Rivas put down in front of her a set of printouts. They were copies of e-mails that he'd sent to Tom in the last few weeks, written and addressed as if from her.

She read them and her world collapsed again. During her entire captivity nobody had come looking for her, and now she had to pretend that her disappearance had a logical reason. "Rivas, I know I haven't even started yet, but please give me a quick break." Tears ran down her cheeks while she went into the entrance hall and gasped for air. Then she took a deep breath, wiped back her tears and disappeared into the guest bathroom. She checked her make-up in the little mirror: still intact. With brave composure she strode back into the study. "What must I tell Tom?" He told her. "Please write it down for me." She opened one of the drawers, found pen and paper and pushed them across to him.

"I want you to speak freely. It must sound credible."

"My cell is not on roaming from here."

"It's open."

Of course.

He didn't warn her not to give anything away. That wasn't necessary, and she wouldn't have risked it. She typed in the password, again saying it out loud, and pressed Tom's shortcut. After a few minutes his mailbox answered. "He's not answering."

"Leave a message."

"Hi Tom. It's me," she warbled in fake cheerfulness. "Pity that we're missing each other now. I'm still in the States. It's going to take a few months before I'm finished here." Her phone beeped while she spoke into his mailbox, and she saw that Tom was trying to call her back. She glanced enquiringly at Rivas but he shook his head. She kept up the charade: "Tell Claudia she must carry on exercising my horses and ask Gaby to pay Claudia regularly and to look after my personal bills and keep the house sitter happy. I have to go now, we have to hand in our phones again, but I'll be in touch again soon. Look after everything, you hear? That's what you get when you tell me you don't need me. Serves you right. Give my regards to all – and thanks for everything, Tom." Rivas took back the mobile phone and Catherine, without revealing any emotion, returned to the agenda. "What else?" She picked up a pen and a writing pad in order to take notes. Together they thrashed out the profile of the person for about an hour, until Catherine fully understood the technical aspects of her assignment. "I know of a man who's a specialist in biological warfare." After hesitating for a moment, she added, "He's not a virus expert and he won't be right for this job, but you always have to start somewhere. In South Africa in the eighties he pulled some strings in Dr Werner Van der Sonsen's genetic warfare program. The guy has an unusual background, but I know he dealt with race research among other things. At the time that surprised me because, from a humanitarian standpoint, there is of course no such thing as race. But the apartheid regime thought differently, and they did conduct this type of research, undercover. I read somewhere that they wanted to systematically reduce the black population through genetically targeted birth control chemicals that would be administered involuntarily. I know for sure that he was also involved in torture and human experiments on the enemies of the regime. At the TRC hearings he made a full disclosure of his personal involvement and he received amnesty as a result."

She reflected on her father, who lived in South Africa at the time, and did business with people such as Van der Sonsen and his shadowy colleagues. Except for the years between 91 and 93 when he lived in the Rhineland in Germany, he spent his most of his significant working life in South Africa. Even during his time in Cologne, he carried on running Firm Commitments in South Africa with the help of his business partner Trevor Torrente. And after the death of her father, she had taken over his work! The dawning implications pained her, and she felt an onrush of shame. She was woven tightly into this dark network, out of her own accord, and now she was faced with the direct and terrible consequences.

"Okay then, look him up and find out his name."

"I don't need to. I know him personally. His name is Dr Piet Van Wyk. A year ago we met at a coffee shop. He'd been one of my father's more influential appointees and he was very helpful with his referrals. I was working on a government contract for an African state and I needed insights into the manufacture of chemical weapons. Of course, that search assignment was not for someone to develop weapons, but to protect that country against them."

"And you believed that?" She blushed. He was right. How gullible she'd been and what damage she'd done, driven by her addiction to success and need for recognition. "Don't be too hard on yourself, Catherine. You have very little life experience. The next few weeks will accelerate your personal growth. You are in the process of getting to know what the world is really about."

"You can say that again! In any case, he lives and works in Pretoria. I can't imagine that he would have moved. A consistent and cowardly type, I think."

"Cowardly is good."

"May I remark that if you force your ideals on people, you are exactly like the ones you claim to be fighting?"

"We hardly ever have to resort to force. We convince with rhetorical arguments and we pay well. Cowardice and greed are good starting points for influencing people in this way. And if use of force or even murder becomes necessary, as in your case, then the end justifies the means."

"That brings us to the personality profile. Okay, so cowardice and greed are preferred traits." She shook her head but made no comment on his means-to-an-end credo. "What else is important?" Rivas described the desired psychological profile. When he was finished, she groaned: "Rivas, there is no such person on earth. The technical aspects are a contradiction in themselves:

equine genetics, human genetics, virology, chemical weapons. All this combined with hatred for extremists, or fear of them or whatever. And how am I supposed to find a criminal like this, who, even if he meets all the requirements, isn't going to shrink back from following through with such madness at the last minute?"

"All you have to do is find us a candidate who meets the criteria and leave the negotiations to us."

"How should I pique his or her interest?"

"With money."

"How much money?"

"Eighteen million US dollars." Catherine gasped. He added, "That is only his or her personal compensation. The entire project flows into the billions. Scientist crave being able to research with unlimited resources."

"I don't even know how to deploy all these resources. Will I even get this far? The data isn't mine, you know. My late father collected the information and encoded it heavily. I'll try, Rivas, but it's really hard to get behind the code, especially under so much pressure. I'm not sure how to explain this to you."

Rivas gave her a quizzical look. "Tell me, Catherine, are you actually aware of all the information contained in your database?"

"The records of scientists?"

"Yes, dodgy scientists and wheelers and dealers, document forgers, dubious plastic surgeons, professional killers, drug barons, economic criminals and confidence tricksters, crooked lawyers and undercover hostage negotiators."

And Pirates.

She swallowed hard, and finally became fully aware of what she'd suspected, but suppressed for a long time.

"Just get started. Once the first step has been taken, every project gets rolling and develops its own dynamics. We'll take each day as it comes. And you will have resources at your disposal that you wouldn't even have dared dream about. Or give me the code and I'll work with you."

"That's the thing, Rivas. I can't. Please believe me. I'd love to hand over this whole damn database to you, complete with the key needed to decipher it. I want nothing but to get home and be done with this, but my father made the information so personal. The criteria are inconsistent and extremely encoded. Only I can solve this puzzle and even I have immense problems with it." She wrung her hands. "Do you believe me?"

"I told you that we need you. That's why we're here now."

"How come you know so much about the contents of this database?"

"From Maria. And she learned about it from her contact."

"Tell me more about this Maria. How did she become involved with WICED?"

"She was a good friend of Freya Dahlberg. For personal reasons Maria was very interested in her theories."

"Dahlberg? Do you mean that radical Swedish journalist who died recently? The one with the strange views on Islamic extremism? She never gave interviews, only communicated through her blog. Are you talking about this Dahlberg?"

"Yes, she was a recluse, but she and Maria were very close. Dahlberg was a founding member of WICED. Come on, get a move on now."

"Rivas, I need a phone number for people returning my calls. How is that supposed to work? I need an email address, a company logo. I need a brand, and a presence in the market, otherwise the target group won't take me seriously. How do you see all this?"

"The name Zitgow speaks for itself. You are your own brand. You don't need a company name or a logo. That would hinder you more than it would help. In the environment that you're entering now, everyone understands the need for discreet research. An email address is in place, directed to my inbox."

"I won't mail a lot, that takes too long and there's limited control over the conversation. Headhunting is best conducted on the phone. But as I said, I'll need a number for call-backs. I can't always reach the people first time."

He scribbled a number with an Argentinian dialing code on a piece of scrap paper and handed it to her while pointing at the second cell phone he'd given her earlier. "This is your work phone. You can make and receive calls but the SMS function has been deactivated. All internet search engines are available to you, but access to the free-mail offers, social networks and forums is blocked."

"And I suppose you'll watch me day and night from now on?"

"Will I have to?"
"No," she replied with a grim expression on her face.
"That's my girl."
Stupid idiot!

Because Catherine had never saved Van Wyk's phone number in her cell's address book, she looked for him on the internet. Her father had only left names and fields of specialization in his coded legacy, knowing that she'd be smart enough to find the relevant contact details herself.

She couldn't reach Van Wyk, so she left a message on his voice mail: "Hello Piet. This is Catherine Zitgow. Do you remember me? A year ago you helped me with a few referrals. I'm working on a new assignment and I want to ask for your help again. Please call me back, but not at the office. This is strictly confidential. Please dial this number." She mentioned it and put the phone down. Then she turned to the database and started her work.

Pedro brought her lunch which she devoured, despite her big breakfast. In the late afternoon she ended her work for the day and went to her room.

On her bed she found a bulging trunk-sized Louis Vuitton suitcase. With a muffled click it opened and revealed its treasures:

Atop the clothes lay various jewelry boxes out of which she drew a valuable broad bracelet made of white gold, studded with black diamonds, a Wempe diamond ring, white gold chandelier earrings studded with thirteen onyx stones and diamonds, and a Joallerie watch, also made of white gold. The watch was covered in hundreds of baguette diamonds.

Next to the jewelry boxes lay a Dolce & Gabbana handbag made of white leather and Sicilian lace, embroidered with chains of Swarovski crystals.

Catherine unpacked some sheets of black tissue paper that covered the rest of the contents of the suitcase and pulled out Italian Tiny Cuts from La Perla, arguably the producer of the most elegant lingerie in the world. From garters to wafer-thin petticoats and bras with decorative stitching. In addition, delicate G-strings and panties with high waistbands made of the finest lace and silk, with silk ribbons and tulle in various colors. She also found corsets with tight-fitting waistbands and bras with lace cups from Jean Paul

Gautier, and if that wasn't enough, lace corsages and panties with seductive straps as well as silk and chiffon boob tubes from Agent Provocateur. Catherine began to feel uneasy. She knew this brand was the undisputed symbol of sex and eroticism. She had said she needed to feel good in her clothes in order to be able to work properly, but this selection frightened her. What sort of a headhunting assignment was this supposed to be? Inspecting the next layer, she decided to confront Rivas at dinner about the astonishing and decadent luxury of it all.

It wasn't over yet. Next she unwrapped a neon green silk organza with a submarine neckline by Oscar de la Renta. It was breathtaking. She removed another layer of tissue paper and took out a scarlet Guy Laroche dress made of shiny satin, accentuating a slim waist – totally made in the style of the latest Paris chic with an oversized shiny crimson belt. This piece was accompanied by matching red patent leather pumps with stiletto heels.

About twenty more pieces followed, all supplemented by perfectly matched accessories. Each item was so exclusively unique that she inspected it closely before laying it out on the bed in absolute awe.

There were also some casual clothes among the selection: a Capri hipster with a matching super-short double-breasted jacket that barely reached under the bust. It was made by Francois Girbaud. Complementing this were sneakers made from fine canvas in jungle green shades. She also discovered two more pairs of jeans, similar to the one she'd already been issued with. But this time, there was no man's shirt to go with it. No! Instead, the jeans came with a low-cut white lace tube top and a black leather belt with silver studs. That was followed by mini denim shorts, extremely short and frayed at the ends, with a soft brown leather belt and a white, low-cut tank top made of netting material.

Hidden in the last layer were a black leather bolero and several pairs of shoes of various exclusive brands. And beneath all these was a card made from that unmistakable paper that she'd also found in her mirror cupboard shortly after her arrival at the farm:

With compliments
Maria Santa Cruz

And, at the back:

We have big plans for you!

Catherine was overwhelmed. She loved fashion but even one of these items would have burst her budget by a long way. Apart from the valuable jewelry, the contents of the case must have been worth several hundreds of thousands of dollars. What were their plans? "Big ones", Maria had revealed in her message, but just how big? She could not wait till dinner time. She sprinted down the stairs and knocked on Rivas's door.

"*¡Adelante!*" he invited her in.

"Rivas, what's with the suitcase?" she demanded. "Was it your idea to lend me these exquisite clothes?"

"We're not lending them to you. You may keep them." Until the day, you die, which won't be long from now, he thought to himself.

"And the jewelry also?"

"Yes."

"Are you trying to bribe me?"

"If you don't want it, throw the stuff away when you're finished with it. What use would it be to me?"

"Finished with it? What are these clothes for?"

"Didn't you say you had to be dressed well in order to your job?"

"Yes, but not like this!"

"You're working on a much higher level now. Besides, I want you to look elegant in public."

"What?"

"Your work is not confined to the telephone, Catherine. We want you to get to the best scientists in the world. Some of them you'll find in the upper echelons. Surely you know that you have to mingle among them at some point?"

"With you behind me with a gun pointing at my back, or what?"

"Wait and see."

"And the lingerie?"

"What lingerie?"

"Well the absolutely unaffordable sexy underwear."

"Every classy outfit needs decent underwear to go with it."

"Have you seen it?"

"No," he grinned, "but I can imagine it. Maria has great taste, don't you think?"

"The question is for whom these things are really intended."

"What are you saying?"

Catherine was embarrassed. Rivas answered for her: "You think I'm going to molest you and force you to wear them for me?"

She couldn't utter a word.

"Hm, let's see what Maria has packed there for us. Come, show me your suitcase." He pushed her out the door.

"It's fine," she waved him off. She regretted having confronted him with this.

"No no, I want to see this now. Come on."

She followed him reluctantly to her room, where he made a casual glance over the selection. He couldn't stop himself from teasing her. "Maria knows exactly what I like."

She stared into the floorboards and felt herself blushing. Her lapse in the kitchen the day before was a far cry from what she now imagined.

"Stop worrying," he calmed her down and turned to leave. "I'm not going to hurt you."

"Really? You won't touch me?"

"Let's just say, I am going to uphold your right to sexual self-determination."

"What the heck is that supposed to mean?"

"You know what that means."

"Really? And nobody else will bother me either and ask anything indecent of me?"

Rivas was indignant at the thought that third parties would interfere with *his* hostage. "You can count on it. I won't let anything like that happen to you, Catherine." He gave her a friendly pat on the shoulder. "Don't wrack your brains over this. Just concentrate on doing your job."

"Do you promise?"

"Yes."

She still doubted him. He saw it and reassured her again. "I can understand your fears, but you don't have to worry about sexual abuse, Catherine. That won't happen, okay?"

She nodded.

"Come, let's go down. Do you feel like visiting the horses before dinner? Joe's given us cookies for Andalus again." He knew that he'd unnerved her with his teasing, and he now planned – by means of the horse – to regain her trust.

"You said that I'm not allowed near Andalus anymore."

"And now I'm saying, you may feed him some cookies."

"Am I only allowed to do what you decree, depending on what mood you're in?"

"Yes."

He ended the dialogue with his compelling smile. It made her tingle and her heart skipped a beat.

I am at his mercy. In every respect. There's no doubt about it.

With the visit to her beloved Andalus, Catherine's first day at work ended on an idyllic note.

The following day she worked like crazy. Van Wyk's referrals took her into in a dead end. She had to tackle the decoding of her father's database.

For a while the search progressed nicely, but then came some serious setbacks. Successes and disappointments came on each other's heels like relay racers and she reached the point where, sooner or later, every tricky headhunting assignment ends - at zero.

This is why specialized search was often such a long and tedious process. She was marking time on the spot, getting no further. Some days she was so exhausted from the long hours that her head was completely blocked.

When she absolutely couldn't go on, she would grab Pichon, Metodista or Evangelista and work on her seat. Concentrating on the horse, nature and the fresh air released the tension and renewed her creativity. She returned from the riding arena with fresh ideas and took up her work again.

One day she plucked up the courage to ask Rivas if she could ride out into the country. To her surprise, he agreed to let her do so without supervision. She cantered over fields and meadows and felt the bliss of it. There was no better place on earth to recharge her batteries than the back of a horse. Every rider knew that, and Rivas was no exception. He didn't bother to implore her not to try to run away again. Somehow this made the point even more clearly. She didn't even think about escaping. There was no need for any discussion about the matter.

Since the day that Rivas had allowed her to feed Andalus with cookies, she spent more time with him again. She just couldn't resist him. In the beginning, she stroked him over the fence or the chain of his stall, but eventually she spent hours with him in his box, sometimes just to dream and sometimes with her notebook on her lap. She did this with Rivas's approval, and he seemed totally acquiescent. It struck her how he always took every circumstance into account when making a decision – how he handled each situation on its own merits. He never clung to stubborn principles. He would have been a top manager in any industry. With such extraordinary talent, why was he resorting to crime?

Every now and then, they sent a casual e-mail to Tom to reinforce the original story that Rivas had made her tell him. The weeks passed by harmoniously until one evening, out of the blue, she dove headfirst into another conflict with Rivas.

17.
Peru, July 15

That night, after dinner, Catherine went back to her work in the study while Pedro washed the dishes in the kitchen. Rivas had poured himself a drink and was also immersed in his laptop. Catherine's eye fell on the cell phone that Rivas had provided for her and she toyed with the idea of dialing Tom's number, and leaving the phone lying by her side while she involved Rivas in a conversation about her abduction. Tom would be able to hear them. Even if he didn't answer, his mailbox would record some of their dialogue. She knew Tom's number off by heart. While she was still thinking about her plan, her finger not yet on the dial, Rivas closed his notebook, got up and casually strolled across to her. He had a full glass of whiskey in his hand. He leant against her table and drilled right through her with his eyes.

"Yes?" she enquired, trying to sound as innocent as possible. She permitted herself a strained smile. "What's up?"

"Yeah, what's up, Catherine?"

It was hopeless. This man missed nothing! He had the extrasensory perception of a superior being, an alien. He could always read her thoughts. Her first instinct was to appease him by confessing. "Rivas, if you mean the cell phone, I'm sorry. I don't know what possessed me. The temptation… I couldn't resist. Surely you understand? If you were in my position, you'd also be tempted…"

He interrupted her, ignoring her pleading look. "From now you'll follow my orders. When I tell you to make a call, you'll do so. If I tell you to bake a cake and throw it into a bonfire afterwards, you'll do so. You'll only think about your damn database and nothing else. You'll make no more decisions of your own and from now on you'll spare me your irrelevant commentary. He opened his hand and let the glass fall to the floor. It shattered into fragments in a pool of brown liquid. "If I tell you to wipe this up with your tongue and swallow it, you will do that also. To the last fragment. I've had enough of your antics!" He went to the door and called Pedro who rushed in instantly. "I dropped my glass. Please clean it up." Without taking his eyes off Catherine, he pointed to the mess on the floor. Then he turned and left. Pedro did likewise, to fetch a pan and a brush.

Catherine sat motionless until Pedro came back. She knelt down next to him and helped him to clean up. "You're pale,' he said. "What happened?"

No answer.

"Did he hit you?"

Silently, she placed a piece of glass on the dustpan.

"For crying out loud, Catherine! Just do what he says! Is it that so difficult?"

"He didn't hit me. He threatened me with suicide on command. Imagine that!" Pedro gave her a look of sympathy. Pedro loved animals, a sign of empathy with lesser creatures. This is how he's looking at me - like I'm some suffering animal, Catherine noted sadly. "Pedro, what can I do? What's going to happen to me?"

"Catherine, just do what he tells you. Stop fighting with reality."

Catherine whispered, "You'll lose every time."

"What?"

"Oh, nothing. Just something I picked up somewhere."

"Drop your combative attitude and learn to adapt. Do you really think you can beat him at his own game? He's not Maria's 2 IC for nothing."

"Yeah, the Balkan butcher reinvented as the Iberian slaughterer!"

"Catherine, I've known him for seven years. Work with him, don't make life so hard for yourself. If you want to get out of here, you'll have to comply with his demands. How many times have we told you that now? Soon it'll all be over and you'll be home safe and sound."

She sighed in disbelief and wiped aimlessly around the floor, making things worse. She followed Pedro to the kitchen and made *Mate de Coca*, a Peruvian tea. They sat down and drank it in uneasy silence, before Catherine lamented anew, "He'd probably stuff the glass down my throat himself or whatever else he can think of and you'd all stand by and watch. What should I do? I'm not even allowed to think about freedom anymore!"

"Be nice to him, and he'll be nice to you. All WICED hostages get the point. You're the only one who can't seem to face up to reality."

"Oh yeah? Where are those hostages now, Pedro?" Trapped, he looked away. "You see! But I'm not like your other hostages. I've never submitted to those in power without ever standing up for myself." She thought of Dora, her subservient bookkeeper. "Submission only brings out the worst in them." She thought of herself. "You have to face authority head on and voice your opinion. If you don't, you only provoke them more and they treat you like a doormat. I have to stay true to myself. I can't function without my chutzpa." She remained in thought for a moment, and then continued: "Rivas can only go so far with his threats. There was nothing I could do in the jungle. There I had no chance of asserting myself verbally. They avoided speaking to me altogether. I mean you also hardly said a word to me on the ride to the farm. You know why?" Pedro didn't answer, so she closed the loop herself. "Because silence kills the seed before it can germinate. Because when thoughts become words, they verbalize the possibility of action. He can threaten me with the jungle and its silence, but he can't expose me to it anymore. This whole damn ordeal was nothing but one big orchestrated show to intimidate me, otherwise…"

"What is *wrong* with you? A show? Intimidation? Have you forgotten what he did to you in the cellar, and in your room? Catherine, he *will* kill you if you keep trying to sabotage him like this."

"Let me finish. … Otherwise, I wouldn't be alive after trying to run away *three* times. He needs my spirit. He has to keep it intact. Only with my wits about me, can I complete my task. He knows it. He's trapped."

"The only one who's trapped is you."

"Yes, up to a point. He knows how far he can push me. There are limits and he can't go beyond them. I've been watching him closely. He thinks he's inscrutable, but he isn't. He's got no choice but to dispense his power over me in such a way that I can still operate. He can try to control me but he can't hector me into oblivion. He has to put the brakes on every now and then and let me keep my personality. Like he does with Andalus. If he robs me of all my energy, he's finished, or at least he suffers a huge setback. He can't kill me. Then he's got nothing. He even assumes that I'm going to strut around in public one day, decked out with the bribes in Maria's suitcase, but he's got another thing coming!"

"Too much information!" Pedro scowled. "I don't want to know all this and you shouldn't be so cocky, Catherine. Be careful. Nobody here is on your side. I like you. You held up remarkably on your ride with Andalus up the mountains, but…."

"He made it easy for me."

"You're a nice girl, Catherine, but don't try to turn me into your accomplice."

"Sorry." Catherine responded. "You'll get into trouble.".

"It's a matter of loyalty."

"And yours lies with Rivas. I get it. Are you afraid of him?"

"Of Rivas?" Pedro laughed out loud. "I told you it's about loyalty. And friendship. And the mission."

"And you don't want to be *my* friend?"

"Don't force me to choose."

"I don't give a damn about your mission. Or your friendship!" At those words from Catherine, Pedro got up abruptly and placed the cups into the sink. "Wait, Pedro. I'm sorry. Please don't go. I didn't mean it. Your friendship *is* important to me. You're the only one I trust."

"Catherine, you shouldn't do that."

She ignored his warning. Instead, she launched into a lecture. "You don't have to choose like that, Pedro. We think that our options are limited and we have to choose from those, but it's not true. We can have everything. All we need is the courage to see new options."

"Huh. Look how far this attitude's got you up to now. And so what? Rivas doesn't deserve that I'm sitting here with you, gossiping about him."

"And I? What do I deserve? Please be my friend, Pedro." She pushed her palm across to him. "Please?"

He didn't take it. "I can't, Catherine. I'm sorry."

She wouldn't give up this easily. Through her professional work over the past few weeks she'd regained confidence in her own strength. Her attempt to make friends with Pedro had failed - it was clear that there was no way past Rivas. But perhaps she could persuade Pedro to influence Rivas to treat her more kindly. She had nothing to lose. "Pedro, have you ever been married?"

"I am."

"Where's your wife? Why aren't you together?"

"Come on, Catherine. Isn't that obvious? Because right now I'm here.

"You know what I mean. Do you have children?"

"Two sons. Sixteen and fourteen, Juan and Esteban."

"Does your wife work?"

"She works as a PA at the same mining house where I worked before Rivas recruited me for WICED."

"What was your role there?"

"I'm a mining engineer."

"What did you extract?"

"Gold."

"Underground. Deep Level," she affirmed, nodding.

"How do you know that?"

"Our little Miss-know-it-all places such professionals," she heard Rivas interject sarcastically. He'd just entered the kitchen. "Officially. When she's not recruiting criminally inclined race scientists from her database."

Catherine was furious.

Unknowingly. Unlike you. You nasty hypocrite!

Rivas addressed Pedro. "I'm hungry. Will you please fix me a bite to eat?"

"We just finished dinner. You hardly touched it!"

"That's why I'm hungry now."

"Yeah, in a moment. I'm just having a chat."

Rivas stared hard at Pedro, muttered something in Spanish, and vanished.

"Why does he let you speak to him like that?" Catherine asked Pedro.

"Am I also his prisoner now?"

Perhaps there was a small chance of getting at Rivas through Pedro after all - if she could draw the man out further. "Okay, so you're a mining engineer. Where does your family live?"

"In Bogotá."

"How did you get involved with WICED?"

"Rivas and I met through a mutual acquaintance."

"And then he hired you to cook and clean for him," she remarked in a factual tone. Her comment seemed to have thrown Pedro somewhat, so she apologized. "Sorry, I didn't mean that. I respect all types of work. I just mean if you're an engineer, surely the work here can't be very satisfying."

"Everyone does their share and I'm well paid."

"I don't believe you. I mean that you're well paid, yes, but not that you're in it for the money."

"We all have to make sacrifices for the cause."

"So you're an idealist?"

"Life has handed me a task. It's my duty to complete it."

"And your family also have to make sacrifices? I get it. And where do you draw the line? I mean let's assume Rivas kidnaps your wife, keeps her locked up, forces her to work on a project against her will. How would that strike you, Pedro? Are you up to that?"

Pedro arose. "Are you also hungry?"

"No, man, we just ate!"

"Okay then, leave me alone now."

"May I help you?"

"No."

"Then I'll just keep you company."

"Not necessary."

"Does your wife know about WICED?"

Pedro no longer answered her questions. She stayed with him a little while longer but sensed that she couldn't expect any concrete help from him. He was too deeply woven into the WICED-net himself.

In order to avoid another confrontation with Rivas, she wished Pedro a good night and made her way to the staircase.

Too late. They crossed paths in the passage. He was just coming out of his room in the lousiest of moods. She tried to sneak past him, but he grabbed her ponytail and pulled her head back. "Don't get your hopes up, Catherine. Apart from me, nobody here can help you."

"What do you mean? Aren't I even allowed to sit in the kitchen and have a chat over a cup of tea? Ouch, you're hurting me! I can't talk like that."

He loosened his grip. "Didn't I just tell you? No more talking! Just listening and following orders!"

He spoke to her like she was an idiot. It made her angry, but the fear pushed the anger aside. "I *am* listening to you, honest! Please don't treat me like a stupid servant. I really didn't do anything bad then. How was I to know that you don't want me to talk to Pedro about his family?" She pretended to be stupid after all.

"Catherine, if you ever find yourself in that cellar again, you won't leave it alive. Is that clear?"

"*Yeees!* Let go of my hair now. Please!" He let her go and she retreated into the comparative safety of her room.

For the rest of the evening she immersed herself in *Madame Bovary* and commiserated with Gustave Flaubert's thorny protagonist.

The next morning she woke up to a new idea.

18.
Peru, July 16

Hunger strike. She would stop eating and thus rob him of his power over her. She kept up her food boycott for two days. It didn't take longer than this for Rivas to see through her plan. He filled in Pedro and Joe and told them to cook something special. When Catherine didn't appear for the evening meal, he sent Joe to fetch her, but he promptly returned without Catherine. "She said, she wasn't hungry."

"Come on Joe! Wake up, man! Go back upstairs and tell her I want her seated at the table this instant."

A second time, he arrived without Catherine. He shrugged his shoulders. "She refuses."

"She *whaaat?*

"She said to tell you, she's feeling sick and she's not hungry."

Every man at the table stared at Joe. Hostages were supposed to behave as such, not assert their likes and dislikes by regularly uttering personal preferences. Then, in unison, all four burst into laughter, dissolving the tension. "It's unbelievable!" Rivas shook his head. Pedro's delicious Peruvian dish *Arroz con Pollo* - chicken with rice - was cooling down and Joe took his knife and fork and started digging in. Rivas cut short the laughter and brought back the tension: "Stop eating and bring this woman to me now! Even if you have to drag her down the stairs by her flame-haired ponytail. How difficult can it be with that shrimp?"

After a few minutes, Joe appeared with Catherine in tow. She sat down at her place but didn't touch her food. She found it hard to resist, but she held out: "Mm, that smells nice, but please don't be offended. I'm just not hungry."

"Catherine, this hunger strike isn't going to work. Eat now and we'll forget the whole thing. And next time I call you, you'll come immediately. Is that clear?"

"Rivas, I think I am suffering from depression. I just haven't got any appetite at all. I'm homesick."

Surely he's already feeling helpless and concerned about my condition? Like with a useful horse that refuses its food?

Rivas said something to Pedro in Spanish, after which Pedro promptly busied himself at the stove.

"May I go now?"

"No. You're staying right here."

"Alright then, I'll stay here, but I can't eat anything. It's not what's on the menu - I just feel sick. I can't help it."

"Yeah, we wouldn't want you to have to force down this meal. You may choke on a bone, feeling as sick as you are, you poor thing. Pedro's making you a wholesome maize porridge. You'll soon get your strength back."

"Bah! I'd feel even sicker. You know that I don't like that mush."

"No no, you need some sustenance now. You know how much we need you. We can't risk having you collapse from weakness. And because you're feeling so sick, we're going to help you, okay? We'll help you with the porridge today and then three times a day, every day. You'll soon get your appetite back." Rivas took her plate and scraped the chicken and rice into the disposal bin.

A loud ding-dong went off in Catherine's head. She woke up to the fact that she had to terminate that wretched hunger strike, but she was so tired of having to beg for mercy. She jumped up and ran out of the house to the front porch.

What now?

She sat down on the bench that she called her "magical bench" among the shrubs and waited for "wisdom from above". After a few minutes, he stuck his head through the front door and called her, with an angelic voice: "Catherine, your porridge is ready! Pedro's just letting it cool down a bit."

She racked her brain. What could she do? "Rivas?"

"Yes?" He came across and sat down next to her.

"I'm sorry. Please don't force me to eat that. I'll eat again, but not that. Please give me something else. Please Rivas."

"I'm also sorry. You know Pedro has other things to do than to serve up one dish after the next for you. That's why we are going to force this maize down your throat, today and every day until you've completed your mission or 'til your dying day – it's up to you. Either you eat it voluntarily or I'll have a few men tie you up and force-feed you – like a Polish goose. We've all had enough of your escapades."

"You said, other than the captivity you would uphold my right to self- determination. And whether one eats or doesn't eat is part of that right."

Rivas laughed. "I said I would not violate your *sexual* rights but now I can't help thinking that was a bad idea. You're obviously too stupid to appreciate what you're up against here. Perhaps it would help you to get a better understanding if a few of the guys strip you down and shake you up a couple of times a day."

Catherine was horrified. "You'd never do that!"

"Not I, that's true. I wouldn't dream of touching a brittle skeleton like you, but there are enough hungry men around this farm who can't wait to sink their teeth into this tasty little rebel. She sneaks out the house, she steals horses, she runs away, she's angry, she's moody, she backchats, and nothing is done about it. This is starting to get embarrassing." Rivas seemed for the moment more amused than angry, and this led her to believe that he didn't really mean it.

"I don't believe that you'd let them hurt me like that."

"Don't test me, Catherine. Not only would I let them - I'd even watch how you squirmed around like a beetle on its back."

"How can you think up something so wicked?"

"I can think up whatever I want. So please stop jabbering about rights. Rights are not the same as justice. I tried to make it clear from the start that you're not to expect fairness around here, but you just don't get it, do you?"

"I'm well aware of your superiority. But I believed that I found a trace of honor and humanity in you over the last few weeks. Do you have no sympathy at all?"

"I never have sympathy with silly geese."

"I admit the hunger strike was a foolish idea. I should have known better, but a 'silly goose'? Is that what you think of me? Really? Wouldn't you also try every possible way to get out of this predicament?"

"You're no goose, that's true. They have a functioning survival instinct. Do you want to know what you are to me, Catherine? You're a means to an end. A thing. A thing that makes trouble. No matter whether I treat you kindly or harshly, you don't stop irritating me. You tire me out. That'll stop now. From now on, you'll get only what you need to survive. And you'll need this grub. In the camp, you also had to eat it and the same diet awaits you here from now on. We'll pack away your pretty clothes, there'll be no more dawdling at work, and no more horse riding. We'll take your makeup away and everything else that isn't absolutely essential."

She put her hand on his. "Please give me another chance."

"Better still, I'll have you tied up in the dog kennel outside the men's unit next door and have them bring your laptop and stationery there."

"One last chance. I'm begging you, Rivas."

He got up. "Come." Hanging her head low, she traipsed after him. Despite her hunger, her stomach revolted at the thought of the disgusting maize muck that awaited her. "Throw the porridge away, Pedro. The hunger strike is over. Catherine's going to make herself a sandwich now."

She looked at him sadly and whispered, "Thank you."

That night she lay awake for many hours. Rivas had hit the nail on the head. She was a thing. She was deeply hurt by his words, totally crushed. As soon as he didn't need her anymore he would finish this "thing" off. Everyone on the farm knew that she wouldn't leave it alive. Probably not even as a corpse. Pedro was right. Every attempt to regain her freedom had failed, and every new try only worsened her plight. Now he'd even threatened to hand her over as loot to these debauched bandits. He despised her, even though she tried so hard to endear herself to him by making herself look pretty and working so hard at his brainless plan. She considered her options. One was to follow Pedro's advice to be "nice", she pondered. She could give in and submit wholly to Rivas's dictatorship. Possibly that would keep him from killing her in the end. But this was really a theoretical solution. Unthinkable in practice. To rape her own soul like that? Never!

Running away again was also out of the question. If she got caught, she wouldn't survive the torture in the cellar a second time. And it would be a slow and painful death. That opened up option three: to at least, in some way, keep control over death. To determine the time and method herself. She would die one way or another, sooner or later. Why should she still foster these criminals by helping them with their insane and evil plan? Taking her own life was the only solution.

Days passed, and she fantasized about suicide. The "what" was settled - death, oblivion, the ultimate way to thwart Rivas. But the vexing question was the "how". She may have had the courage to leap, in a moment of Sturm und Drang, into a quick and painless death. But she couldn't jump off a building. She couldn't throw herself in front of a train, like her heroine Anna Karenina. She had no access to strong pharmaceuticals or a gun. The thought of the electric hair-iron with her in the bathtub sent shivers down her spine, besides which it would probably only trip the circuit breaker. A knife wouldn't work – she wouldn't know where to start. Death by hanging was out of the question. She would never muster up the courage for such a barbaric method. Her situation seemed hopeless.

19.
Peru, July 18

In deep apathy, Catherine got on with her job. Rivas treated her with nonchalant indifference. Pedro, not wishing to get ensnared in another uncomfortable discussion, avoided her as much as possible.

One late afternoon she was busy with Andalus's bridle in the lounge, while Rivas watched the news on TV. She'd taken the bridle apart and spread the pieces across the floor in order to clean and oil the leather. Minding her own business she sat in the lotus position and was peacefully absorbed in her task, even enjoying the deceptively homely atmosphere.

When the TV program was over, she noticed Rivas staring at her intently. She saw how he bent down to pick up one of the reins and how he contemplatively wrapped it around his fist. The curb bit was still attached to the rein.

Catherine saw a look of pure evil in his eyes. She got up, stunned by what she saw. Then her rising anger chased away her fear. "What's with the rein? Do you want to beat me up with it?"

"Yes."

"Why?"

"Because I feel like it."

"That's all?"

"Can't think of another reason." He shrugged.

"You really are something else! I bet you were cruel to animals when you were little. Squashed worms and pulled the wings and the little legs off beetles, didn't you?" she hissed with all the contempt she could muster. "How many birds did you shoot with pellets from your toy gun, Rivas? How many dogs did you kick into submission when they ran up to greet you when you came home from school? Did they not adore you enough? Were you only satisfied when they crawled along the ground, whimpering and howling in pain and disbelief? Did your mother never teach you…?"

"Shut up!"

"Of course you did," she carried on arguing, spitting out the words. You enjoy tormenting everything that's helpless and dependent on the grace of one of your rare good moods. I'm no different. Everything I need to survive, I get from you, or I don't, depending on your whim. You've cut my wings, too, and there's not much left of my legs either. When you fed me from the dog bowl in the room, Rivas, if I'd had a tail, you'd have seen it wag at the mere sight of you. Yes, even during that terrible time, I couldn't wait to see you again until I became so petrified that I almost lost my mind. And since then my tail, if I had one, would have been permanently clamped between my legs. Does that give you a kick, huh? Do like me best when I'm crushed and shaking from fear?"

"Tell me, Catherine, how do you manage to invent so much melodramatic trash? It runs off your tongue again and again and again!"

"I get it from living with you. Whenever you're finished with me, I can barely crawl on all fours. It's easy enough for you, you're probably twice my weight by now. You're *so* strong and still you find it necessary to attack me with Andalus's bridle. That's new, though. You're about to outdo your own wickedness. You're a ghastly coward."

The curb bit swung hard, and rebounded off her body. It hurt so much that she screamed. Surely Pedro heard her from the kitchen? Why didn't he help her? Physically she wasn't strong enough to defend herself so she lunged into a verbal counter attack. "You hurt me and enjoy it – for now. But in the long run, you're only bashing yourself around. You'll never again hold Andalus's reins in your hands without thinking about me. One day, Rivas, you'll crawl into a corner, riddled with guilt and shame, and you'll be the one that won't be able to get up. It'll be your turn to grow a tail and clench it so painfully between your buttocks that it'll cut off your blood supply. It'll be *so* awful when your past catches up with you one day! To be afraid is one thing, Rivas, but to be afraid of yourself is the deepest pit of all."

"Catherine! I'll beat the living daylights out of you if you don't quit now!"

"I'll always be present in your mind, when you're working, eating or sleeping., Revenge, my father always said, doesn't need human intervention. Life itself restores justice and punishes bad people like you. Have you any idea what bad karma you're loading on yourself?"

"I warned you!"

He beat her until her only defense, her presence of mind, was also whipped into submission by his colossal brutality. All that remained was a technique, which she'd acquired during her room arrest. It helped her to manage the pain. She closed her eyes, pulled her lower lip deeply under her upper row of teeth, bit down on it and put her hand in front of her mouth, in order to cut off her oxygen supply. Until she could stand it no more. Then she screamed again.

"Go now. And don't show your face around here for a while," he interrupted her ear-piecing cries. His tone was calm and contemplative, as it always was, after he'd become violent. Unable to get up, she let him help her, but she doubled over in pain and collapsed again as soon as he let go of her. So he picked her up and carried her to her room. To be carried gave her a false sense of comfort and she clung to his neck.

I belong in the loony bin.

He put her down on her bed and was about to leave.

"Rivas?

He turned round. "Yeah?"

"Why do you hate me so much?"

He sat down next to her and tenderly tidied the loose strands of hair in her sweaty, teary face. "When I find out, I'll tell you."

"Will you give me some painkillers, please?"

"Help yourself."

"There are only a couple of aspirins left in my bathroom chest. I need anti-inflammatories."

"I'm not your chemist, Catherine," he replied and left.

For almost an hour she lay crying on her bed, then she wiped her tears away and made a new decision. She would run away again. They would catch her and drag her off into the cellar and put the sling around her neck and ankles again and watch her suffocate. Or whatever. She wouldn't resist. This time she knew the drill and could make it go much faster, she rationalized. And then she would finally, through death, be free. There was no other way.

After midnight she crept out of the house.

For what might have been hours she dragged her aching body along the path down to the valley. Then exhaustion overcame her and she sank down and fell asleep by the side of the path. It didn't matter. She wanted them to seize her again, in any case. It was still dark when she woke up from the desperate cold. Nobody had discovered her disappearance, so she remained there and waited for her captors. And waited.

And waited.

When nobody came, she lost her resolve. It was unbelievable. Nothing was working out. She was freezing and she was confused. Wearily, she trudged back along the dusty path to the farm. When she arrived at the yard, she passed the garbage pit. She stared into it and thought of Edgar Allan Poe. And then: trash! - that fits. She leapt into the pit, lay down on the refuse and fell asleep again.

At first light Pedro arrived, carrying a refuse bag, and discovered Catherine in the pit. "*¡Santo cielo!* Catherine!" He climbed down and lifted her out of the ditch. While he swung her up, her sweater caught in his hands and her body was exposed, revealing her injuries. "Did Rivas throw you into the pit?"

"I jumped into it myself. I'm also trash. You can kill me right here and then you just have to set fire to the whole lot and get rid of my body at the same time."

"You're not trash and nobody wants to get rid of you."

--- oOo ---

Pedro wasn't speaking the full truth. His assurance that they didn't want to get rid of her wasn't true. He knew that. But – Catherine voluntarily in the garbage pit! What a triumph for Rivas! The abducted person must reach the point at which she considers herself absolutely worthless, Rivas had taught him. The end was in sight. In the last few weeks he'd begun to have serious doubts about the success of this venture. But now he was happy. He'd grown to like Catherine, and he was glad that her suffering was nearing its end. Soon they would reach their goal, Rivas would take her out, her suffering would be over, and they could turn their attention to their next project.

--- oOo ---

"I prefer to think of myself as worthless rather than thinking how much he hates me," said Catherine. "Pedro, what does he have against me?"

"I don't understand it either." This part was true. Pedro had noticed that Rivas behaved with untypical subjectivity towards Catherine. "What caused these injuries?"

"Andalus's bridle."

"What were you up to this time?"

"Nothing. He just beat me up with it. Because he hates me."

"These are more than lacerations. You've got heavy bruises."

"The bit was still dangling on the rein when he grabbed it and laid into me."

"He attacked you with an iron curb bit? I don't believe it. Rivas never hits a woman with a heavy item."

"But he did it to me. He despises me."

"He doesn't despise you, Catherine."

"I asked him why he hates me, and he didn't deny it."

"Don't believe everything he says."

"I cried for help, but you didn't come. Didn't you hear me?"

"I heard you, Catherine, but I can't get involved with things like that."

"I understand."

"No you don't understand. Come, let's go back to the house. You're going to take a shower and wash off this filth. Are you hungry?" She nodded. "I'll make you breakfast, okay?"

She nodded again. And she broke down at last. "Pedro! I wanted one of his minions to find me and take me to him, so that he could kill me!" She sobbed, with her arms around the man.

"I know, Catherine," he replied and held her in his arms. "I know."

"But instead, you found me and again it's not working out!. I want to die, Pedro! I can't live in this hell anymore. It's getting worse and worse!"

"I know," Pedro repeated helplessly. "I'll talk to him, Catherine. But we won't mention this incident for now. I promise you, at the next opportunity, I'll have a word with him."

"Speak to him now!"

"Catherine, he'll punish you and lock you up again, if he finds out that you sneaked out of the house again. That won't help you."

"Alright, but you'll talk to him? Persuade him to kill me?"

"Yeah, yeah, right." Pedro couldn't bring himself to offer Catherine any more courage. What was the point in helping her to persevere?

After a few days, when she'd recovered, Catherine again started to think up ways of killing herself. And again. And again. But there seemed to be no solution. No opportunity.

Then a simple discovery paved the way.

20.
Peru, July 19

In Rivas's all-male household, it was up to Pedro and Joe to keep the place clean. They did their best, but it wasn't great. That morning she was alone, listlessly carrying on with decoding the database, when she was distracted by the urge to give the house a good spring clean. First, she attacked the lounge, tidied up and dusted. There were no carpets in the house, but there was a vacuum cleaner. She used it on the upholstery. Then she polished the wood-and leather furniture. She did the same in the library, as they often referred to Rivas's study. Next, she mopped the kitchen floor and wiped the shelves and sink; followed by the bathrooms, and after hesitating at first, Rivas's bedroom, which was situated on the ground floor. There was little to do, however. Everything in his room was impeccably clean. She decided to tidy up the cupboards and if necessary wipe the shelves. She opened the cupboard doors, and she found herself frozen in a rush of contradictory emotions.

In her face were dozens of immaculately ironed shirts. On the other side of the cupboard hung a black casual linen jacket by Prada. She took it off the hanger, held it up and imagined Rivas in it. It was cut exactly to his masculine body shape. She put it back and inspected a Ralph Lauren jacket, the arms of which were still casually folded up from the last time he'd worn it. She nestled her face against it. It smelled nice, so much like him. The material was soft, but the style was manly.

I hate him. Why am I so fascinated with this stuff?

The belts were mainly by Dior and the shoes and boots ranged from Jimmy Choo to Yves Saint Laurent. On the side shelves he kept carefully-folded T-shirts and jeans from the Armani Collezione in classic blue, white and black. Catherine wondered if Rivas had ever been shopping himself - it seemed that Maria's taste strongly permeated the entire collection.

Catherine lingered over the cupboards as if hypnotized by their contents. Then she gathered her wits and was about to leave. She turned, but found herself magnetically drawn to his bed. She took one of his two pillows and pressed it against her chest.

What's wrong with me? Has he bewitched me?

She took a deep breath and sighed. Shaking her head like a swimmer emerging out of water, she left his room.

After finishing downstairs, she went one floor up and scrubbed there. Her excess energy then drove her to inspect the men's cottage next door. Finding this house also deserted, she started in the bathroom. They'll get a pleasant surprise, she told herself happily. Then she spotted her opportunity: an old fashioned razor had carelessly been left lying in the sink! After searching the bathroom and the bedrooms for a packet of blades and not finding any, she decided to take the used blade with her. Somebody would notice its absence, which left her no time to think. She had to act now. Quickly she unscrewed the razor, slid out the blade and dashed back to her room. For a brief moment she considered writing Rivas a letter, but having nothing to say, she dismissed the idea. The thought of Andalus made her chest contract, but it was a brief pang. She had no time for indulging in sentiment.

She determined that her bed would make the perfect place for her plan of action. It would make the ideal scene – a huge mess of blood (martyr's blood) among the pure white linen. Why should she give them the convenience of killing herself in a bathtub, like she'd seen people do on TV? They'd have to cope with the mass of sticky blood - the more the better! And if anyone ever did bother to look for her after her death, the remaining microscopic particles would leave a forensic trail for the investigators.

Deducing from what she'd seen on TV, she believed the cutting would not hurt. From the same source she'd learned that she'd have to cut the wrists lengthwise, not across, otherwise the blood would trickle out too slowly. Probing with the blade on her skin, she was surprised that it actually did hurt a lot. But then, summoning her courage, she inflicted a deep cut to her left wrist. With her bleeding hand she halfheartedly attacked the other wrist and took a bit longer to make the decisive incision. Her adrenalin-charged heart was pumping like crazy by then, forcing the blood out of the left wrist and more and more also out of the right, even though the second cut wasn't nearly as deep. It squirted spasmodically – like out of a malfunctioning fountain. The erratic stinging pain settled into a rhythmic throb, which she submitted to with increasing lethargy – and a vague sadness. She watched her blood as it ran to the floor. Confusing thoughts whirled around her head: She didn't want to die; she wanted to be free. But she was too useless to live. She'd threatened Rivas with bad karma, but, she, too, had to face the consequences of dabbling around in her father's wicked database. That's why she had to die. Just like her father had always preached - Lady Justice needs help from nobody!

She wanted to switch off her thoughts which threatened to become unbearably depressing. She wanted to hasten the process of dying. She got up and wandered around, spreading her blood across the entire room. Good! Growing weaker, she lay down on her bed, where the blood ran through the snow-white sheets into the mattress. Very good! She felt dizzy and nauseous and slowly her soul sank into darkness. That's how easy it was to escape this sadist. And that's how easy it was to die.

But she hadn't died. She awoke with bandaged wrists, in Rivas's room. A thin plastic tube was attached to her left hand, leading to an improvised drip suspended from the ceiling. She saw Pedro next to her bed and tried to sit up. Pedro pushed her gently back onto her pillow and said, "Hey you." He wanted to encourage her but he could think of absolutely nothing to say. She mumbled something and he thought he heard her ask for goose liver. She feels like something unusual to eat, he pondered. That often happens when one is sick, but where was he supposed to get a tin of *foie gras* up here in the mountains? "What did you say, Catherine? What do you mean?"

"These stupid, ugly geese."

"What about them?"

She muttered unintelligible words about overfeeding on broken glass and then she said, loud and clear, "They'd better be nice Pedro, as you said - otherwise the men will pounce on them, because they're too thin."

She fell asleep again.

The next day she woke up to sunshine and birdsong. The window was wide open, the air crisp. Rivas, Pedro and Joe sat next to her bed. The atmosphere was peaceful – but this lasted only a few moments. She realized where she was, and a chill ran through her. She was still bandaged, but the drip had been removed. Joe and Pedro patted her on the arm and said goodbye. Now she was alone with Rivas. Undoubtedly, as soon as they'd closed the door behind them, he would fly into a rage. But she felt beyond caring. She was cold and felt infinitely flat and sad. She'd failed again.

"Catherine, how are you?"

"I have to go to the bathroom," she heard herself croak. He helped her up. She swayed, she let him support her, and they walked to the bathroom together. "I can manage from here," she brushed him off in front of the door. He let her go and waited until she staggered back into bed.

"How are you feeling?" When she didn't answer, he stroked her face with incomprehensible tenderness.

This loving gesture re-awakened her spirit. "I've been thinking…"

"Everything will be alright. Stop talking now."

Unflustered, she carried on. "We're back to the broken glass and the cellar."

Rivas closed his eyes for a moment, then, reaching his arms down, he lifted her up and held her against his chest. "Everything will be alright," he repeated.

"Just give me the glass splinters. I'll swallow them. It's okay."

She's still not doing what I tell her, Rivas remarked to himself, while Catherine drifted off again.

--- oOo ---

This Catherine was turning out to be the biggest challenge of his career as a kidnapper. Never before had he encountered a hostage such as her. She contradicted every case study in the textbooks on abduction and all of his personal experience. He would have preferred another of her insurrections rather than this suicidal psychodrama. He couldn't let her die now. He'd invested far too much in her already and they were still light-years away from their goal; and he was mere inches away from his first failure. That, it seemed, became clearer by the day.

In the morning of the day of her suicide attempt, he'd felt the irrational impulse to give her a break from her work. Soon after sunrise, a flock of hummingbirds had descended on a meadow near the farm. He'd spotted the birds on his early outride, and he knew that having settled, they'd remain there for a while. He was sure that the rare spectacle would have a motivating effect on her. He spurred his horse homewards, sprinted up to her room to fetch her, and came face to face with shambles. He was stunned by what he saw. Her room looked like an abattoir, with Catherine barely conscious and no longer responsive. He quickly stopped the bleeding. She had to be revitalized. The smell of near death permeated his clothes and penetrated his skin. It invoked painful childhood memories, and it made him retch. He had to get out of that chamber of horrors as quickly as possible – with her. He lifted up the bloodied body and carried her down to his room.

There was something else that bothered Rivas, over and above the unfamiliar sense of failure. Catherine's attempt at suicide had stolen away his control of events, but beyond that he was concerned about her apathy in general. He wanted her to submit, not to lose her mind. She was governed, he realized, by a death wish while he'd been aiming to instill in her the will to *live* - assuming that she was prepared to pay his price for it. He didn't want her to give up. He wanted her to give *in*. She'd settled on the former and reasserted herself in this way. Again. He had to change tactics.

Rivas was on the way to the little guest chamber, which he'd moved into while Catherine occupied his bed, when a sullen looking Pedro passed him in the passage. That face was all he needed.

"Rivas, can we talk?"

Please not now, he sighed to himself. But he gestured Pedro into the small chamber. He'd decided on this sparsely furnished room, instead of one of the better equipped ones on the first floor, in order to be closer to Catherine. Pedro sat down on the only chair, Rivas on the bed. "What's up?"

"I'm leaving tomorrow. For a couple of weeks." Pedro's voice was terse and somber.

"Two weeks? You can't just make off now! In the middle of the project!"

"I have to get out of here for a while."

"Is something the matter with Carolina or the kids? Is there a problem at home?"

"Not at home. Right here."

"What do you mean? Here?"

"I have a problem with you."

"With me? Why?"

"You really don't get it, do you? Take a look next door, at what's lying on your bed. Yesterday she mumbled something about stupid, ugly geese which are fattened up with pieces of broken glass because they're too skinny and that they would be assaulted for it. You're going too far with your threats, Rivas."

Rivas waved Pedro's concerns aside. "She's confused in the head. Hallucinations, Pedro. She's got the wrong end of the stick."

"Maybe, but the stick can only come from you. The other morning I found her sleeping in the garbage pit. She'd run away again because you found it necessary to beat her up with a curb bit. She wanted you to find her so you could kill her and we could burn her with the trash. How could you beat her up so badly, Rivas? That's just sick."

"She ran away again? That little menace! Why didn't you tell me? I have to know things like that. The garbage, you say? We're making progress, Pedro."

"Progress? You've lost your grip. Just kill her then, if you can't handle her, but don't let her suffer like that. She's finished, man. I can't look at this living corpse anymore."

"Pedro, your whining over this hostage is starting to get on my nerves. You're welcome to take her over. I'd be interested to see how far you get with this irritating ant."

"I'm not questioning your methods. I'm merely distancing myself from them. What you're pulling off here is getting to me. I need a break."

"Day after day I grapple with this mental teenager and now you're also freaking out, just because she fails to get the picture."

"She tries to please you, but you don't give her slightest chance. Look at this mess we're in. The more you lose control, the more violent you become. And it's not working, Rivas."

"Pedro, I always use force. *We* always use force. We're not in a kindergarten. As for pleasing me, you must be joking!"

"I'm not talking about the occasional slap. It's this excess that's getting to me. This slow and sadistic destruction. I've never seen you with kid gloves, Rivas, but this time you've gone too far. And what for? It's not necessary. A blind man can tell that she's got a massive crush on you. Why don't you use that? Or have you lost your touch?"

"Not my type, that skinny rake," lied Rivas. He had no intention of sharing with Pedro his intimate plans for Catherine.

"Feed her up. Put a bit of fat on the right places. This skeleton is off-putting."

"You see! That's exactly what I mean. Is it her fault that they brought her here in such a scrawny state?"

Rivas clenched his fists in anger. "Is it my fault that they couldn't drag sacks of mademoiselle's favorite foods through the Amazon basin? And you know very well, Pedro, that starvation is necessary in order to wear down the victim. Has she wrapped you around her little finger so much that you've forgotten the basics? Come on, get real!"

"That's exactly what I'm doing. I'm leaving so that I can 'get real' again."

"*Lo siento amigo*, I can't let you go now. You've picked the worst time to bail out."

"So? Are you going to lock me up as well now? You're even further gone than I thought."

"Of course not, Pedro. But surely you don't expect me to take care of her all by myself while she's sick? When she's better, okay?"

"Joe can help you."

"Joe and Catherine can't communicate. I'd have even more work."

"Teach her a few words in Spanish."

"Do you think I've got nothing better to do than to teach that stupid girl Spanish?"

"I haven't noticed that she's stupid. I actually find her quite smart. So clever in fact that she's got you completely rattled." Pedro put on an impudent grin.

Rivas didn't let Pedro provoke him. "I don't mean *not intelligent*. I mean she is so childishly stubborn, like a schoolgirl who's going through a phase of self-assertion. How old is a fourth grader again?"

"Nine or ten."

"That's exactly how she seems to me. As if something in her got stuck between the ages of five and nine."

"I've never heard such nonsense in my life."

"Pedro, I'm telling you, that's an important age and there's a gap in her development, I'm sure of it. But I'm not her therapist. She'll have to pull herself together for these last few weeks. And yes, you're right, I have to try another angle, that's become perfectly clear. I'll deal with it, okay?"

"Alright."

"Does that mean you're staying?"

"How long have we known each other?"

"Seven or eight years."

"Seven."

"Why are you asking me then?"

"Have I ever interfered with your methods in these seven years?"

"No."

"Let you down?"

"Never."

"Then I won't do it now either, but ease off a bit, okay?"

"Yeah alright. By the way, what I said about better food for Catherine wouldn't do any of us any harm."

"What am I supposed to cook for her then, dammit? I don't know what'll make her gain weight. Nothing's working."

"Try cooking something German or South African."

"German? I can't cook German. What do they eat in South Africa?"

"Maize porridge."

"She doesn't like that. And neither do we. What else?"

"No idea, probably English or Flemish or who knows what. I think South Africans like to barbecue."

"Barbecue? That's not a bad idea. We could do that. It would do her good to sit outside by a fire, with some nice company. Joe can play the guitar, and…"

Rivas stiffened. "Are you pulling my leg?"

"No! I mean it."

"And how is Joe supposed to drag up here, up the mountain, all the meat that you'll need for Catherine's cozy barbecue socials?"

"We can grill chicken. There's plenty of them around here. Joe won't have to trek down to the valley."

Rivas snorted. "Next thing Catherine complains that the chickens are disappearing. Then you'll be the bad guy hereabouts." But the idea appealed to him. It could work. He stood up, laughing. "I have to make a call now and afterwards I have to look in on my patient."

Rivas dialed Maria's number. He preferred to solve his own problems, but this was a sizeable glitch and he had to inform her about it. And he needed to talk to someone that he trusted. An intelligent person. An equal.

It was exactly 5 pm in Argentina. Sophia answered the home phone. "*Hola?*"

"Good afternoon Sophia. This is Rivas. Please call the Señora to the phone." Rivas's communication was always a blunt directive, polite or rude depending on the situation.

"*Un momento, Señor.*"

"Rivas! How are you?" Maria was pleased to hear from her protégé. He told her what had transpired. "This foolish girl is becoming most tedious. She's not worth it. You should have let her bleed to death. All that unnecessary drama. No, this is never going to work. Get rid of her. I'll find another way."

"Maria, wait. It was my mistake. I was too tough on her. I stripped her of all hope and I have to find a way of restoring that in her. I have to steer her in a different direction." As often in life, a way opened up during the conversation – he had an idea.

"We're cantering around in circles, Rivas."

"That's not true. And I can't go back now."

"Is this about your honor as well?"

"Yes, about that, too."

"Please get a grip on yourself!"

"I know what I'm doing, Maria."

"Well then. Dispose of her. I'm through playing games with that silly goose. Burn the clothes and makeup with her body, and for goodness sake, get rid of every trace of blood! If you have to set the whole farm ablaze! I want no vestige to remain of her. What a botched operation!"

"Maria, if this is what you really want, I'll do it, but please listen to me first. I'll get her so addicted to life, that she'll do anything to avoid the danger of losing it. Not from the will to survive like in the jungle but from the sheer joy of being alive. I have to show her an indescribably beautiful world and combine it with just enough fear of losing it again."

"How do you plan to accomplish this? Do you need help?"

"Freud will help me. She once said something about carrot and stick, sugar and whip."

"What about it? Are you talking about her subconscious?"

"Yes. Our conscious mind guards our secrets well but our subconscious lets us down, usually at exactly what we perceive to be the worst moment. But the subconscious knows the inner needs of the soul and overrides the conscious mind by sending concealed signals."

"The Freudian Slip."

"Yes, but it's not a slip. It's the hidden truth."

"You mean she has secret longings without being aware of them?"

"I mean mixing the right dose of sugar with a pinch of whip is the perfect recipe for taking over a soul."

"I see."

"I'll let you know how it' goings. We've still got time."

"Alright then. But don't take yourself too seriously. This nonsense about honor is beneath you. Keep well now. I love you."

"I love you, too."

"Rivas? Botched or not, I love you," she repeated. "Do you hear? None of this matters - it's all in a days' work."

"Thank you. I know. Stuff happens." He played down his dilemma so that she wouldn't worry about him, but inside, for a fleeting moment, he sensed that his own subconscious was sending him signals, too: Catherine had become so much more than a hostage.

Due in no small part to the sudden kindness Rivas extended to her, Catherine recovered quickly. For two days Rivas cared for her with utmost dedication. During the day everything revolved around her and in the evenings he removed her file from the safe and delved ever deeper into it. He poured himself a drink, lit up a cigarette and studied her dossier over and over, leafing through it from A to Z. He looked into her taste for books, music and movies and everything else that he'd collected on her. From this, he improvised a personality profile using a simple process of elimination. It was possible to sketch a rough outline fairly easily, but he was running out of time and Catherine's personality patterns were pretty complex, laced with many contradictions.

In two days his plan was ready. It was time to bring Andalus onto the stage. And it was time to seduce her.

To finally tame that shrew.

21.
Peru, July 24

Catherine's daily highlight was when Rivas came to change her bandages. The undivided attention that went with being patched up by him revived her spirit and rekindled her hope. His tender care increased her desire to get well. Due to her immobile wrists she couldn't work on the keyboard for long and riding was out of the question. Sam had carpentered a heavenly reading stool for her, with a tilted book board at eye level. She read a lot, put on her makeup as far as her wrists allowed, wore a different perfume every day and showed off her extravagant wardrobe. She strutted around the house in her fancy high heels and radiated a femininity that nobody seemed to mind. In fact, the renaissance of her womanhood, the pleasant scents and the apparent end of the violence gave the masculine old mansion a new and warm feeling. It started to feel deceptively like a family dwelling, rather than a location where hostages waited out the end of their days amid terror and fear. Catherine thrived in the peaceful ambiance and her male companions also benefited from the new atmosphere. Despite his poor command of English, Joe taught Catherine how to play poker and with great enthusiasm she faced Pedro and Joe at a game almost every evening. When Rivas joined in every now and again, lighthearted laughter rang through the house, because he helped her to put on a real challenge against Joe and Pedro at their own game. On other evenings Rivas told anecdotes about Andalus, of which he had many in store. And when Joe played sentimental Spanish love songs on his guitar, Catherine sat down beside him and listened with delight. This prompted Joe to teach her a few chords, as far as her healing wrists allowed, and since Pedro had started to teach her a little Spanish, she felt more and more included within the macho group of foreigners. All three, and even Sam, the brusque stable hand, spoiled her like a princess and she behaved accordingly. She didn't even have to clean her own room anymore.

Joe had granted her a long list of culinary wishes on his last trip to the valley, that is to say, those which he could obtain. She'd craved a fresh yogurt and asked for one with pineapple pieces. Since he could only get his hands on one with a vague artificial flavor, he surprised her with a natural yogurt complemented by a fresh pineapple. She mixed together her own pineapple yogurt and found it tasted much better than a ready-made one. From then on, natural yogurt and pineapple were regular items on Joe's shopping list. They also barbecued regularly and their gatherings in the open air set off a chain reaction on the ranch. Inspired by Rivas's involuntary suggestion, fires outside the men's accommodation flickered up night after night, except when it rained.

Most of all, Catherine thrived on Rivas's new apparent affection for her. She was beguiled by his tenderness. She assumed that he was sorry for his cruelty towards her and that he no longer saw her only as a means to an end. Rivas didn't push her to take up her work again and it was she, in fact, who offered to continue. She knuckled down and soon began to make some major breakthroughs. Rivas rewarded her with lavish praise, in the same way that a rider makes much of his horse. His evident pleasure at her progress spurred her on to work even harder and she continued to pick up momentum. The first carrot, a significant part of his seduction strategy, was due to be offered.

"Don't you want to get back on a horse, now that you're feeling a little better? It'll do you good." Rivas made the suggestion out of the blue.

"I don't know. My hands aren't strong enough yet."

"Soft hands make willing horses."

"And the emergency brake?"

"Get on Andalus. With him you won't need that."

Catherine frowned. She remembered her escape attempt on Andalus. "That's not how I know him."

"You didn't handle him correctly, Catherine. There's no horse on earth that is easier to get on the aids than Andalus."

"I know. I can see this when you're on him, but I'm just not the right rider for him."

"Do you want me to come with you?"

"Do you mean it?"

"Give me an hour. I have to finish up here."

"Okay, I'll also wrap up," she replied, but her concentration had flown out of the window. Minutes later, she scurried upstairs and slipped into her luxurious riding gear.

They arrived at the stable. Sam had got Andalus ready and the energetic stallion didn't take kindly to being kept waiting when he was all tacked-up. When Andalus saw Rivas approaching, he nickered happily and greeted him with one of his unique little grunts. It was an atypical equine sound, especially for a horse at rest, but Andalus always grunted whenever he felt really good about life. The cute sound never ceased to enrapture Catherine. "Hello sweetheart," she greeted him and held out her hand. His soft mouth nuzzled the treat from her open palm.

They made their way to the arena, and Rivas said "Give him to me." He took Andalus to a corner. She observed how Rivas patted his neck before bringing him back to her. "Get on and start warming up. I forgot my cigarettes." On his return he found a puzzled Andalus and a grim looking Catherine on exactly the same spot where he'd left them. "What's wrong?"

"Rivas, I can't ride Andalus. He'll dump me straight back on the ground."

"No he won't. At least not today."

"How can you be so sure?"

"Because I asked him nicely."

She giggled. "What did you say?"

"That we belong together and that you're valuable to me. And because of this, he must look after you carefully."

That we belong together, that you're valuable to me. Oh my goodness!

Catherine was in seventh heaven. But, in order not to show it, she snarled, "And I'm supposed to rely on your little deal with him?"

"He always does what I ask of him."

"Well, apparently we all have to comply with what you say." Rivas's gaze remained steadfast, so she carried on accusing him. "And when he doesn't listen, you beat him up."

"I haven't beaten any horse for over eight years – and never Andalus!" Catherine threw him a skeptical look in reply, compelling him to elaborate. "I once hurt a difficult gelding really badly. After that I swore never to use a crop on a horse again. I learned that whips are completely unnecessary in any case. I found horses actually go better without any artificial aids. Andalus has never seen a whip in all his life. He would have no idea what the funny looking thing was for, if he saw one."

Catherine regretted not having taken her crop along when she ran away with Andalus. He would have probably thrown her off straight after getting on, and thereby spared her the nightmare in the cellar. "You really always ride without a crop? Not even with those Spanish olive sticks?" She was lost for the right term for the thin crops that Iberian riders broke off olive trees.

"Always."

"Did you train him with a serreta?" Catherine hated the jagged steel nose bands with which many young Spanish horses were trained.

"I told you, I don't hurt horses."

"Of course you don't," she muttered inaudibly. "You just exterminate them altogether." Then she spoke up again: "So how did you school him? Surely that's not possible. Every rider uses a whip at some point. How do you get around it?" She realized that she'd indeed never seen Rivas ride with a crop or spurs or any other artificial aid.

"A horse is sensitive and intelligent. It knows what you want from it without using excessive force. If it's bothered by a mere fly sitting on it, how much more must it feel a smack with a whip? If it doesn't accept the rider's aids, it's not about the horse. It's about the rider."

"But when I use my crop, you don't mind. You've even told me to use it on occasion." She was honestly confused.

"Yes. Because with your ineffective leg aid, nothing would be moving forward at all. But let's not do that to Andalus, okay? He interprets the slightest touch as an invitation to work. He's very responsive, you'll see. In fact he thinks along so fast that my only problem is to keep him from anticipating what I want next. You'll love working with him. Anyway, if you used a crop on him he'd get such a fright, he'd even tell me to go to hell."

She didn't find that funny. She pulled a face. "I'm a bad rider."

"You're a good rider. You just don't always use your leg and seat correctly.

"Will you teach me?"

"Yes, if you finally get on!"

"Not on Andalus. Can't we start with Evangelista or Pichon?"

"Look, you can take a hundred riding lessons on those two, but Andalus can teach you the correct timing of the aids in no time at all."

"I'm scared."

"Catherine, please don't waste my time. Do you want to get on, or don't you?"

"I'm too scared." In her mind she saw Andalus rear with her again, dreading even the thought of it.

"Alright, let's go." Rivas shrugged and led Andalus away, and she heard him whisper to the stallion: "Seems like you got away with it today, but your promise is good for next time - do you hear?"

On the way back to the stable, Catherine assured Rivas, "I do want to learn how to ride the beautiful classical way. I so wish I could ride in the Iberian style. Do you really think you can teach me?"

"I told you, you can learn it."

"Really? Like a Spaniard?"

He laughed. "Yes, really. Like a Spaniard."

Catherine had now spent several weeks on the farm. The days flew by and her source lists grew, but apart from the occasional helpful lead there was no significant progress with her research. Rivas was, however, never reproachful - it was clear that she left no stone unturned. Too much pressure would only have slowed her down. And all the while, Rivas tricked her more and more into believing that he was fond of her.

And himself into believing he was not.

Catherine's inner transformation ran its course.

So did Rivas's.

22.
Peru, July 29

Rivas offered Andalus to Catherine again. On this occasion, she plucked up the courage to mount him, but she remained tense. Anticipating that, Rivas had replaced Andalus's curb bit with a snaffle as a precaution. He let her ride in walk for a while and then said, "I want to show you something. Listen carefully. Whenever you ride, have a plan in mind. Don't ever just ride around the arena aimlessly. If you run out of ideas, or get tired of the same figures, rather stop." This advice was not new to Catherine. She'd read Wilhelm Müseler's *Riding Logic* seven times in a row and almost knew its contents off by heart. However, theory was one thing, and practical application was another. "So," continued Rivas, "are you riding with a goal in mind?"

"Yes."

"Which figure?"

"I'm going into a twenty meter circle around you."

"Are you fully concentrated?"

"Yes," she assured him, and tried to disperse the many distractions buzzing in her head.

"Tie the reins into a knot and rest them on his neck."

"Rivas! You don't have me on the longe!"

"That would be defeating the object. Come on, Catherine, I want to show you something." She sighed in surrender and Andalus stayed calmly in walk. She had framed him between outside and inside leg, looked in the direction she wanted to go, and, to her surprise, this was indeed sufficient to keep him in circle. "In a moment you're going to halt him. Just think 'halt' and breathe out deeply. Don't do anything else. No other aid, do you understand?"

"Yes, just thinking and breathing." And already Andalus had beautifully transitioned to a square halt.

"Ride on again. Just think 'upward transition' and take a deep breath as you do it. No exaggerated leg, just think 'forward' and breathe in." She complied and Andalus walked on. It was unbelievable. "Go large. Find a point to ride towards. Do you have it?"

"Yes, I'm looking at that pole on the ground. How am I supposed to ride him there with no rein or leg?"

"A good horse does not need reins or leg pressure to turn and you *have* leg. I just don't want you to overdo it. I want you to turn him mainly through the use of your weight aids."

"Easier said than done!"

"It *is* easy! It happens naturally if you move your center of gravity, for instance by putting more weight over your inside hip. Don't lean with your upper body, just push your inner heel down a little more and look at the pole. This way your weight will shift slightly to the inside seat bone. Andalus will feel that his own center of gravity now lies outside his four legs. He will try to regain his lost balance by stepping into the space underneath you where he will feel in balance again. And this way you will guide him very gently into the desired direction without even touching the reins. Do this now please. Stop halfway, again only through thinking about it and breathing out deeply." She did as instructed and Andalus rewarded her with a dream halt facing the pole. "Breathe in again and think 'forward'."

Andalus walked on. When she got to the pole, she bent forward and clung to the neck of her miracle horse. "Oh my goodness! How is this possible?"

"Take up the contact now and ride back to me. Do exactly the same at the trot. Think about wanting to trot on, breathe in, with both legs on the girth and give him a gentle driving aid." Andalus presented her with a soft, cloudy trot, which she had no trouble sitting to. Halfway back to Rivas he said, "Halt him now and listen to me. Imagine you're holding a chick in your hand. You don't want to let it escape, but you're holding it gently, so that you don't squash it. Trot on again, keeping this feeling in mind. Good. Nice trot. Now apply the feeling of the chick particularly to your outside rein. Oops, the chick in the outside hand wants to escape! Quick! A momentary gentle grip!" She giggled, delighted about Rivas's analogy, and was too distracted by it to carry out his instructions. "I'm not joking. That's enough of a half-halt for a thinking horse like him. At the same time, sit up, put your weight deeper in the saddle and slightly brace your lower back. Not as much as in the German way of riding, okay? Pretend that you want to slightly push the chick forward with your lower back muscles."

"Is it wrong to ride the German way?"

"No, it's just different. Andalus isn't used to it. He wouldn't understand you - he'd over-react."

"Okay."

"Come on now. Drive him 'forward' from trot into walk. I'm still not seeing my downward transition."

"That's what Claudia always says, forward into walk."

"There you go. Breathe out and think about your half-halt." Andalus majestically arched his neck and lowered his head while chewing industriously on his bit during a series of trot-walk transitions. Rivas was pleased with his horse and his pupil. "Good, you're doing well. He's starting to accept your aids and coming on the bit. The next exercise is child's play, you'll see. Take up a little more contact with his mouth. If you now put your outside leg behind the girth and breathe in, he'll strike from walk into a super-soft, relaxed canter for you."

"We call this *Losgelassenheit*," Catherine announced, bragging about her German riding expertise.

"I know. That's exactly what I mean. Okay, come on." She swallowed, and in blind faith dived into unknown riding waters. Andalus immediately struck into a mild, considerate canter - every rider's dream. His strong back muscles pulled her hips forward and sucked them down into a firm, deep seat. The feeling was sensational. "Keep your shoulders stiller by loosening your hips a little. Just go with him. Push your hips towards your hands in time with his forward movement. Do you know the dressage markers off by heart?"

"*Sí, claro.*"

"Lead him with your inner hip into a circle where you would find E. Remembering the chick, knead the inside rein slightly and keep a firm outside rein. Complete two circles and then place your leg back onto the girth while sitting up a bit more. Think about halting. You don't need more downward aid than that. Be careful now and don't overdo it, otherwise he'll stop too abruptly and destroy the harmony between you two. By thinking about your downward transition, you'll block the forward movement of your inside hip automatically. He'll feel it and respond. Breathe out at the same time. That helps, but no more than that." She'd never been able to halt from canter without tipping forward, but Andalus executed the halt perfectly, keeping his back supple and rounded, and this kept her upright. Catherine was thrilled and Rivas patted his stallion gently on the shoulder.

Catherine had just had her first glimpses into how sensitive and supple a horse could be, how little influence it needed to produce the desired result. She was overwhelmed by Andalus's *Durchlässigkeit*. It was the first time she'd experienced this mysterious feeling of "letting through" that she'd heard and read so much about. Andalus gave her confidence by reacting to "breath aids" and responding to almost telepathic communication. Her imagination ran wild: Andalus became Pegasus and she a mythological Amazon straight out of Homer's *Iliad*.

The bliss endured for half an hour. Rivas was about to initiate the cool-down phase on a long rein when Catherine lost her nerve. In the adjacent paddock some mares started to gallop around and distracted the stallion. Andalus kept glancing over to them and Catherine reacted by using too much hand, leg and weight aids. The rougher she became, the more disobedient were the responses of her horse. "He's not listening to me anymore. He's constantly looking at the horses over there," she complained about the spoiled end of the lesson.

"He's been sidetracked by *your* loss of concentration. Get his attention back. He must focus on you, not on his testosterone levels."

"Yeah – but how?"

"Straighten up by half an inch, brace your lower back slightly and drive him gently forward. That'll nudge him out of his dreams and will encourage him to work again." Rivas lit a cigarette.

Catherine tried to comply but Andalus kicked out against her leg aid with his right hindquarter and dashed towards the exit in a remarkable display of bad temper. His tantrum didn't unseat her, however, and she managed to get back to Rivas at a walk. Confused and mad at each other, horse and rider came to a halt before him. "Do you see how he carries on? I can't do this."

Andalus snorted impatiently in protest of the constant back and forth. The resulting shower from his nostrils nearly extinguished Rivas's cigarette. Couldn't his owner admonish this inept riding pupil to become a little more focused? First too hesitant, then unnecessarily rough. Which horse would put up with this? Certainly not one like him! What did she want from him?

"You *can* do this. You just used an ounce too much leg."

"Half an inch here, an ounce there. I don't get this. I want to get off."

"You can't give up every time you hit a little snag. You'll teach him the wrong lesson by putting him away now."

"What if he bolts? And jumps over the fence?"

Rivas laughed. "He won't bolt. Too much effort. And jump over the fence? Andalus? You've got to be kidding! The worst he'd do is to canter comfortably over to the mares and stop in front of the paddock fence."

"Yeah and then he'll hit the brakes and I'm the one that will land among the mares, not him."

"Well if you're that convinced, it's bound to happen sooner or later." Andalus pawed the ground. "Come now. You're teaching him bad manners."

"You do it," she replied in a huff.

"Catherine, that's not a solution."

"Not for me, but for him." He looked at her sullen expression and burst out laughing.

"What's so funny?"

"'The pout is actually the demonstration of the female artillery. He who has been shot at before, is tempted to hoist the white flag at the mere sight of it'."

Catherine burst into tears.

Finally he sees the woman in me.

"Why are you crying?"

"Oh, it's nothing."

"Nothing?"

"It's just that it almost sounded as if you liked me." Catherine cast out her net, in the hope of finally pulling in a compliment.

Rivas grabbed the opportunity. Perfect timing. Not too soon and not too late. Not too much and not too little. "Of course I like you. Would I stand here and watch you ride if I didn't? We've all grown fond of you, Catherine."

"Really, Rivas?"

"Yes."

She wiped away her tears and put on a broad smile. "That quote is really funny. Who said it?"

"A Swiss statesman from the nineteenth century. Count von Benzel-Sternau."

"Alright then. Are you going to help me now or must I get my artillery out again?"

"Get off," he sighed. With the tip of his boot he ground his cigarette into the sand. He mounted his horse and rode on without bothering to slip his feet in the stirrups. Then he bent forward and playfully pulled his horse's ears. Andalus shook his head and gave a little buck at the indignity. Rivas, amused, asked him, "How can you act like such a barbarian? You really want to say hello to the mares, huh?" He turned to Catherine. "Come with me to the paddock, Catherine. Open the gate for me."

At the gate, Catherine grabbed one of the dangling stirrup leathers to lengthen it, but Rivas found this superfluous. "Let me at least pull them up," she insisted.

"He'll have to cope with that little bit of dangling. It's not bad for the horses when something flutters about or pinches a little bit every now and then. If you ever find yourself in an emergency situation, they won't immediately freak out." Catherine took the opportunity to tell him about how wonderfully Andalus had tolerated her pulling on his side while the caballeros dragged her back to the farm after she'd run away. "Yes, they told me, but they shouldn't have done that."

"You mean they should have let me get on?"

No, that's not what I mean, thought Rivas, but he kept this to himself. For now, he was to be mister nice guy. Pretending not to have heard her, he trotted off into the paddock, straight into the commotion of the herd, and started to work on a circle. Andalus paid no more attention to the mares, who were now charging around out of control. The imposing stallion in their midst was a huge stimulant.

Andalus, however, had more important things to do. Fully committed to Rivas, he paid him undivided attention. It was as though the horse performed in front of fifty thousand spectators, intent on winning first prize in a FEI dressage final.

Catherine's respect for Rivas as a horseman drowned out any contempt she'd felt for him in the past. The way he handled the black PRE stallion impressed her so much that she envied Andalus for his intimate relationship with Rivas. She was in love with Andalus through and through – and her longing for his owner took on painful dimensions.

23.
Peru, August 01

The pace of Catherine's work increased, and with it her frustration - she was still unable to produce any substantial results. If she found a geneticist, he showed no background in veterinary science. When she finally dug up a few criminally inclined veterinarians, they were either specialized in the extraction of ivory or rhino horn or in the treatment of illegally-kept exotic reptiles or predatory felines. The chemical weapons experts that showed interest didn't have a clue about genetics – or horses. And her virologists all stemmed from irrelevant branches. Rivas had declined her suggestion to split up the money and appoint three different scientists. He gave no explanations and she pressed on with her mission in silent capitulation.

After a particularly hard day, Catherine walked around by the paddocks and watched the sun dip behind the mountains. She felt drawn to the stables, hoping to find solace there. Grouchily she lamented about the madness that life had catapulted her into. "If only I could impress Rivas with a small sign of progress," she bemoaned her plight, as though Andalus understood every word. Rivas had followed her to the stables and saw her talking to Andalus while she energetically massaged his withers. "Hello," she greeted him with a scowl.

"What are you doing here so late? It's getting dark."

"Don't worry," she snapped. "I won't run away."

"*¡Está bien* Catherine! What's wrong?"

Catherine flew into a rage. "I've had enough! That's what's wrong." Even the stable floor got the blaze of her anger. "Can't Sam sweep up properly? Just look at this mess!" She grabbed a broom and swooshed it aimlessly around the floor of the barn, enveloping Rivas, the horses and herself in a whirlwind of stable dust.

"Put the broom down." She refused and swept even more vigorously, accomplishing nothing other than more clouds of dust. He gently took it from her and said, "Please stop complaining. Everyone is doing what they can."

"Everyone is doing what they can? I'm also doing what I can! But I don't have to *sweep*! Every day I have to half-kill myself for this insane scheme. *That's* not appreciated!" The dust settled, but Catherine's fumes continued to fill the barn.

"Do you want a raise?"

"If I refuse or fail I'll be 'eliminated'. Would you like to lead a life like this, huh?"

"Come, let's go eat. Pedro's made fried eggs and potatoes – again. They're getting cold!" Rivas pulled her lightly on the arm.

"A raise! What a stupid joke!" Incensed, she shook his hand off her arm.

"You're right, that was a stupid joke. And now let's go." Once more he touched her elbow with respectful subtlety, to encourage her to accompany him back inside.

"Don't touch me! Just get your hands off me! You're an insufferable, obnoxious brute! Sometimes I think I'm dreaming this. When am I going to wake up?" Catherine amplified her words with wild gestures of frustration. "You disgust me! " she added, although she secretly meant the opposite. She pulled away from him and made to storm off in a defiant sulk. In two strides Rivas caught up with her at the stable door and pulled her back.

Next to the tack room was a feed room where Sam kept a small amount of hay bales, alfalfa, straw, shavings and concentrate, in order to avoid having to fetch supplies from the big barn every day. Rivas manhandled Catherine into this room and pushed her onto a small stack of hay. He threw himself on her, stretched her arms up over her head and pressed her into the prickly grass. He was so strong. Resistance was futile. But this wasn't why she didn't fight him off. Catherine suddenly found herself in an erotic frenzy which was completely new to her. She was overcome by the glowing lust. She half-heartedly searched for strength to stop the burning desire, but it rampaged on regardless. Rivas slipped his leg between hers to keep her pinned against the floor and kept his hold on her wrists. His face hovered above hers. He smelled of man, smoky and wild, and he looked like a god.

"What was that about? What do you want from me, huh?"

Please kiss me.

"You want appreciation? How can I show you my gratitude, Catherine? Tell me."

You! I want you!

He pinned her harder into the hay and grabbed her hair, tilting her head back. "What do you want?" he asked again, a daring look in his eyes.

Exactly that! Take what you want.

Suddenly Rivas let go of her. He stood up and in a consolatory gesture held out his hand to help her. Catherine took it and pulled herself to her feet. She regained her composure, determined to show panache, rather than admit how piqued she was feeling. She absolutely didn't want to appear ordinary in front of Rivas, but she had no doubt about what she really wanted. In order to prolong his attention, she launched a new missile. "Congratulations. Another demonstration of your power. Can you see how scared I am? That turns you on, right? Look how I'm shaking." She stretched out her trembling hand. She really did feel shaky, but it was from sexual arousal - she'd lied when she said she was scared. She wasn't afraid. She wanted to feel his weight on her again and to ignite his desire, like he'd kindled hers.

"You're wrong Catherine. That doesn't turn me on. It's easy to invoke fear in someone who happens to be in an inferior position. I know, I do sometimes frighten you but I find that ...," he scanned his vocabulary for the right expression, "... primitive and boring."

"I'm boring you?"

"You're twisting my words. I said, creating fear bores me, but come to think of it, you're not altogether wrong. When you carry on like that, it really does make me sleepy." Rivas put his hand over his mouth in a demonstrative yawn before continuing. "I loathe these little revolts of yours, which are constantly on the verge of tipping over into hysteria." Rivas casually pulled bits of hay off his clothing and then off hers.

"Do you have any idea how I feel right now?" She turned around so that he could remove the blades of dry grass from her back.

"How *are* you feeling?"

"Definitely not hysterical. I feel ...like an outcast."

"Such dramatic rhetoric? I mean considering you're the center of my attention every day! And didn't you just tell me not to touch you because I repulse you?"

"Rivas, you know exactly what I mean. And I know what you're trying to do here. You're hurting me on purpose by accusing me of boring you."

"Catherine, let's stick with the truth, shall we? You're angry with yourself because you're making no progress with your search. So you tried to force me into giving you recognition elsewhere and when I thwarted your plans by not indulging you, you feigned 'feeling like an outcast'."

"What a cheek! Are you crazy or what?" She was overcome with embarrassment, and the urge to deny everything. "I just don't want to be pushed around by you. Is that so hard to understand?" She hexed a look of innocence into her eyes.

"Okay, let's add up what you don't want. You don't want me to push you into a stack of hay and you don't want me to find you boring, right?"

"And I don't want you to make fun of me."

"Got it. Everything you dislike I've noted and now please tell me what you do want, except to get away from here. I know that already. So, what else would you like to get off your chest?"

"Are you my therapist now as well?"

He smiled.

"Oh well, at least I managed to amuse you. I can't be completely boring after all," she remarked happily in a sudden turn of mood. What an arousing experience it had been to roll in the hay with him. Well, almost.

Their arms touching, they left the barn together. As they passed Andalus, he nickered, snorted and flapped his lips – begging for a favor. Touched by his theatrics, they stopped to pat him.

"Will you ever sell him?"

"That wouldn't be possible."

"Why not?"

"He's priceless. If anything, I'd have to give him away."

"To whom?"

"Someone I love."

"Can you love, Rivas?"

"Can you?"

"Yes."

"Whom do you love, Catherine?"

Catherine gave no answer and so the three of them stood together in silence, enjoying a rare Selah moment. Each one with their own history and yet inextricably connected to the other.

What they didn't know was that the decisive breakthrough was just around the corner.

24.
Peru, August 04

Catherine had a conversation with a virologist from San Francisco who'd worked with a researcher at the Institute for Brain and Nervous Center Diseases in Chicago some years before. He recalled that this man was a leading authority in the field of Venezuelan Equine Encephalitis, VEE in short. This was a specialist area that Catherine had identified while trying to find an equine virus with the rare quality of being able to cross over to humans. The expert from whom she learned this was not from her father's database. Catherine had been unable to unearth a suitable researcher among her father's records of biological warfare experts. Therefore, she'd set these aside and poked around in official scientific circles. Among the criminals on the database she'd managed to isolate some pox specialists and pathologists as well as several hemorrhagic fever experts, but none who was an equine scientist at the same time. Her new contact referred her to a former colleague, with whom he'd lost touch fifteen years ago. Catherine ferreted out her new target person in Tel Aviv, and he in turn knew of the existence of a professional whom he'd never met personally. He claimed this scientist practiced human medicine but also had vast knowledge in the field of VEE, in particular its effect on the human immune system. He recollected some kind of connection to Germany, but couldn't recall more than that. She took her database to task again and once more worked herself through every entry to do with virology, targeting records with a link to Germany. Among the apparently useless clues was the number 1248. For days she brooded over this figure, but failed to get behind its meaning.

One day Pedro accompanied Joe down to the valley for a particularly large grocery order with the result that she and Rivas were alone in the house that evening. She'd prepared toasted cheese sandwiches and put them out with two bottles of beer for dinner. She was fixated on the idea that 1248 was a street number, or the digits of a telephone number, and ruminated about the mysterious entry while she chewed listlessly on her sandwich. Search engines seemed only to bring up duds. The web interpreted the number among other things as the year 1248 AD, but Catherine dismissed the notion that there was a historical link. Crusades had taken place. Kings had been born, others had died, and medieval masons had started the construction of Cologne Cathedral. It made no sense, especially not in connection with the second clue that her father had tied to the number: "The big dog likes his beer". After she'd washed the dishes, she joined Rivas in the lounge and sank into the cushions, letting out a deep groan.

"Now, now, what's that big sigh about?" Rivas asked sociably.

Catherine explained about her lead to Germany and that she could not crack the number 1248. She added that her father had combined this clue with a riddle in German about a big dog liking beer.

"Wasn't that the year in which they started building the *Dom*? The Cathedral?"

"How do you know that?"

"I told you, I researched where you come from," he dismissed her curious enquiry. "Well, is it or isn't it? I mean, aren't you from there originally?"

"Yes, but I didn't know that. You're right. The search engines confirm it. But what's that got to do with me?" She'd no sooner asked the question when she remembered an incident from her childhood. "My father once took me to Cologne on holiday after we'd already moved to South Africa. We came out of the train station and there stood the *Dom*, right in front of our eyes." Catherine began to gush as the memory flooded back. "It was very imposing. From the outside, it looked mysterious. I was fascinated, and I nagged him to let me see inside. However, my father insisted on first drinking a *Kölsch*. That's a fine beer from the region served in very thin small glasses. He couldn't wait to have one again. So we first went into a street café and he ordered the beer. I got an ice cream but I was bored and I pestered him to drink up. He threatened to not let me visit the *Dom* if I didn't pull myself together and stopped being so impatient."

"And?"

"I assume that there's a virologist in Cologne whose name is Bier, the German word for beer, or Kölsch."

"And the dog? The 'big dog'?"

"No idea."

"It could be a figure of speech. Maybe he means the 'boss man'?"

"Not in German. A big dog is a big dog. Basta."

"What dogs did you have growing up?"

"I was allowed two hamsters and a cat, but my dad didn't let me keep dogs."

"Who in his circle of family and friends had big dogs?"

"Nobody."

"Let's think. What big dogs are there, even if there's no connection to you directly?" Together they listed the large dog breeds: Great Danes, Rottweilers, Saint Bernards, German Shepherds.

"Speaking of German Shepherds, Rivas. What happened to the two Alsatians that were running around the farm on the day I arrived?"

"Max and Moritz? They belong to an Austrian. He left shortly after you arrived and took them with him."

"Wilhelm Busch!"

"The owner's name wasn't Wilhelm."

"No, I just thought of a German painter turned poet. He created a timeless children's picture book called *Max und Moritz*. It's about two naughty boys, set in Germany in the mid-nineteenth century."

"We're getting off topic. Come on. Focus."

"Sorry, but I just remembered that my aunt, my father's sister, often told me stories by Wilhelm Busch. She had a really cute Saint Bernard puppy. I made a huge scene because I also wanted a puppy – but I didn't get one, of course. Rivas, I've got it! The man's name is Bernard Bier and he lives, works or hails from Cologne." She ran into the library and reappeared, ten minutes later, with a triumphant grin on her face. "There's no Bernard Bier."

"Then why are you grinning from ear to ear?"

"The man's name is Bernhard Ruckebier!" She jumped up and down on the spot. "The German phrase my father always used to pull myself together was *Gib dir einen Ruck*. That's it, Rivas - Bernard, Ruck, Bier and Cologne. Only, he doesn't work in Cologne, but maybe he's from there - I'll find out. At the moment he lives in Appleton, Wisconsin. There's a research center in this town, the Institute for Viral and Infectious Diseases. They legally research defensive biological weapons. His title is 'Chief of Virology Research and Head of Genetic Engineering'. Rivas, he's a virologist and a geneticist! And from the man in Tel Aviv I know that he's a VEE Specialist. And the fact that he's mentioned on my father's database, is a clue that he may be criminally inclined."

The next day Catherine called the Institute. Ruckebier was not available, so she left a message. "My name is Catherine Zitgow. He can reach me on this number. Please tell him it's urgent and important that he calls me back."

The receptionist slipped into the role of a caustic gatekeeper. "And which *important* matter would that be?"

"A personal one. Please give him my name, then he'll know what this call is about."

An hour later she had him on the line. "Hello, Ms Zitgow. You called?"

"Dr Ruckebier! Thank you for returning my call. Can you speak freely?"

"Sure. Are you the wife of Rainer Zitgow?"

"His daughter."

"Please send him my regards. We haven't seen each other in years. How's he doing?"

"He passed away two years ago."

"My condolences. I respected him very much. What can I do for you, Ms Zitgow?" Without engaging in the clandestine nature of her assignment, she briefly outlined the reason for her call. "You caught me at a bad time. I'll be retiring in three months and I'm am busy with a comprehensive hand-over to my successor. However, I'll be glad to help you out with a few referrals. I'll compile a small list of names for you. Just send me an e-mail and I'll reply with the document attached. It's no big deal."

"That's very kind of you, Dr Ruckebier. Apart from your e-mail address, please also give me your home and cell numbers. I'd like to keep in touch with you in any case, even after your retirement." Catherine was back in her routine and overjoyed. Ruckebier gave her his full contact details and hung up.

Rivas, who'd followed the conversation, protested. "Why weren't you more assertive? You shouldn't have given up so soon."

"I'm not giving up. In a couple of weeks, I'll call him again and convince him to meet with me."

"That'll take too long."

"Rivas, here's my plan: During the delay he'll think about the opportunity and become curious. I'll reappear at exactly the right time under the pretext that there's no capacity that comes even close to him. Please give me some time, Rivas. If I do it too soon, I won't seem credible because I have to sift through his referrals. In any case, who knows who else may turn up this way? If I do it too late, his interest will have waned. I know how to time this. Trust me, okay? I'm really good at this."

In the following days she worked through Ruckebier's referrals, but the VEE know-how of his contacts didn't nearly match his. Not to mention the dubious aspects of her brief.

As planned, she contacted the scientist again after eight days, thanked him for his list and lamented about the shortage of skilled experts. They talked further but Catherine still kept the purpose of the mission to herself.

"Ms Zitgow, I just don't have time for you right now, but in three weeks' time, I'll be giving a lecture at a congress in Chicago. If you haven't found anybody by then and you can see me there, I'll pencil you into my diary now. Can you come to Chicago?"

"I'll make the time. Please send me an appointment and the meeting place and I'll be there."

"You'll hear from me."

She was extremely pleased with her success. Rivas on the other hand showed himself unimpressed. "You're wasting time. You lean on him to help you, but you can't get to the point."

"His interest is peaked, believe me. Do you think someone of his caliber is only going to take time out just to have a chat? And why does he insist on seeing me away from home? He's already sensing that this is no regular job."

"Fine. We'll fly to Chicago. But you'll need to interview three to four other candidates. Make sure you get your hands on at least two alternative prospects in the next two weeks."

"Rivas, it doesn't work like this! Are you playing HR Manager now, or what? We're not in the open economy with this deal. And anyway, the better the headhunter, the smaller the selection of candidates because he's already evaluated every potential contender out there. A brilliant headhunter only presents the top candidate to his client. It has to be Ruckebier!" Her sulky protest swung over into a tearful moan. "Are you actually aware of what I've achieved here? I'm finished! I'm completely exhausted. What do you want from me? Ruckebier is your man! My hunches are never wrong."

"Maybe, but we need backup candidates." Dismissing her protests, he insisted that she continue the search without delay. Angry about his lack of recognition, she took up her work again, complaining bitterly under her breath.

--- oOo ---

Rivas transmitted the information about the expert to Maria for a thorough investigation of his background, while continuing to motivate his little recruiter not to lose her thread. It was time to give her what she'd been longing for. So, with unambiguous sexual innuendos, Rivas prepared her for his next move. He paid her compliments, showed himself to be softer and even more attentive, and touched her casually whenever an opportunity presented itself. He made her laugh and he created the illusion of friendship between them - until the last of her mistrust had been erased and she felt completely safe in his presence.

He waited for a sunny day and took Catherine on horseback to a picturesque place that he'd never shown her before.

25.
Peru, August 14

It was shortly after midday. For about an hour, they rode up a steep mountain pass and then through a deserted stretch of land until they reached a meadow, which they crossed at a brisk but controlled canter. At the end of the green expanse, a quaint mountain stream bordered an enchanting eucalyptus forest. This is where they stopped for a break. Rivas let Andalus go and Catherine was astonished that he didn't run home. Because Andalus stayed with them, Catherine's horse also began gracing peacefully nearby.

On this day Catherine rode a horse that she'd grown to like tremendously - a Paso Peruano named Protestante. This gaited horse was almost as comfortable to ride as Andalus. Rivas had spent a lot of time on improving Catherine's riding ability. Patiently he and Andalus taught her flying changes and even her attempts at Piaffe and Passage progressed nicely. Frequently, too, Andalus grabbed the opportunity to impress her with his Spanish Walk. When he did, she was particularly enthralled and the more his bravado amused her, the more dramatically he alternately raised his forelegs up and pushed them forward. And now, on Protestante, she also learned to "pace", because he performed this comfortable two-beat gait to absolute perfection.

Rivas sat smoking in the grass next to Catherine, and silently observed the grazing horses. Catherine stretched out and, while gazing up at the blue sky, reflected on the outride. Captivity or not, all this would have been so much more romantic if he would only show more interest in her as a woman. While she was caught up in her amorous longings, Rivas turned to her and asked, "Do you know what type of clothes men deem to be the most attractive on a woman? According to studies?"

Catherine pricked her ears and sat up. "None?"

"That's what I thought, but that's not what the study revealed."

"Lingerie?"

"Wrong again."

"Miniskirt and leather boots?"

"Nope."

"Maria's lingerie?" she joked.

He shook his head, smiling. "A man finds it most tantalizing when the woman wears one of his shirts, but nothing else."

"Because he wrapped her up in his personal packaging?"

"Correct."

"So that's why I'm always running around in your shirts."

"That's right. I wanted to see if it was true."

"And? Is it?"

"I don't know."

"Hello! Look at me! I'm wearing one of your shirts right now." She pulled it out of her jods and let it hang over her pants.

"The theory implies that the woman wears nothing but the shirt. And you never only wear the shirt." Rivas looked at her as intently as he'd done on their first encounter in his study. This time Catherine didn't look at the ground but boldly locked eyes with him. For an imagined eternity. Then he gently pulled her closer and she felt the warmth of his lips on hers. She put her arms around him in complete surrender. Fantasy and reality melted into a happiness so entrancing that it dissolved into an exquisite pain. It was so intense that she could hardly bear it. He rose and pulled her up. Once on her feet, he started to unzip her jods.

"Rivas, you can't put this theory to the test *now*! Here in the open." Her humorous protest was a desperate attempt to try to hide her tension. She'd become nervous and wasn't in a joking mood at all.

"You're right." Apparently ending the romantic interlude, he whistled for Andalus, who briefly looked up and then carried on grazing. He looked gravely insulted at the summons. He was a horse, not a dog.

"Are you mad at me? Are we going back?"

"No. I get that you wouldn't be comfortable with that. Approximately a quarter of an hour's ride from here is a shepherd's hut where we store material for the patrol riders."

"This area is guarded?"

"Only when danger looms."

They fetched the horses and trotted on. It didn't take long before Andalus carried his beloved rider into an upward transition and so they continued at quite a swift canter with the result that they reached the stone cottage unexpectedly soon. The experiment with the man's shirt was moving closer.

In the hut were two chairs, a small table and a rudimentary plank bed. Mounted on one of the walls were four saddle racks complete with bridle holders, on each of which hung one *Doma Vaquera* saddle and one bridle. Spread across the floor lay bits of wire mesh, some tools and rusty nails as well as a few horse shoes. Rivas pulled the sheepskins off each of the saddles and covered the bench with them. Then he sat down on it and lit a cigarette. Catherine had taken a seat on one of the chairs and stared apprehensively into the air.

"Well?"

"Well what?"

"I want to see what you look like wearing only my shirt."

She was so embarrassed. "Riiiiivas!"

"*Por amor de Dios*. What's wrong now? Do you think I carried you off all way up here just to ride home again? This time, my little hostage, there'll be no getting away from me," he teased the shy young woman who fought very hard with herself right now. Her brain sent out a thousand warnings per second to be on guard, and her heart rapidly transmitted just as many contrary impulses back.

Her brain quickly invented a fitting excuse. "I don't have a boot jack." Rivas got up and positioned himself with his back to her chair, bending down. She pushed her legs between his one by one and he pulled her boots off. All the while, she felt a lightheaded laughter welling up in her - she could think of no further reasons to delay the outcome.

--- oOo ---

Rivas watched her squirm. He could have kissed her and undressed her with his own hands, but he wanted to summon her unconditional free will. This first step had to be initiated by her alone.

--- oOo ---

"Okay, but you must turn around."

He turned his back towards her.

"And close your eyes."

"Closed."

"No, rather wait outside, then you can finish smoking, while I get undressed."

"You're sending me outside?"

"Please."

"Okay." Leaning against the cottage wall, he took a last few drags, before stepping back inside. Catherine stood barefooted and wearing only the shirt, which she'd buttoned up to the top in a last desperate gesture at modesty. It reached well below her knees.

"And?"

"It's true. Take it off." She unbuttoned the shirt but kept it on, now holding it closed with her hands. "The whole thing, Catherine."

"I can't. I can't get undressed in front of you."

"Allow me?"

She nodded.

--- oOo ---

Her nonverbal affirmation was sufficient proof that she was ready to give herself up to him. She was of sound mind, she was healthy, happy, not subjected to overt dominance or undue external stress. She could have said no, but she had said yes.

Phase Two – complete.

Phase Three was now in progress.

--- oOo ---

He stood behind her and slipped the shirt off her shoulders, kissed her shoulder blades and then her neck, and gently touched her breasts. She felt a pulling sensation in her abdomen, which extended to her groin. His lips slid down her back and his hands moved around her tiny waist. A sweet faintness gripped Catherine, but then he turned her around and took a step back to look at her from the front. Catherine now writhed with shame. Rivas nudged her to the bed. To be eyed up and down while on the bed was a bit easier to bear. Catherine thought of herself as pretty, as long as she was dressed, but had a split relationship with her body - especially since his comments about her figure after her failed hunger strike.

Once again he guessed her thoughts. "I want you to know that I find you exceptionally beautiful."

Her syrupy submission returned. His words anointed her body, turning it into a pliable, tingling mass of feminine lust. "Rivas? Is it true? Since when?"

"Always, Catherine. Ever since I saw you for the very first time."

"In your study. In your shirt."

"No, since the day you arrived on Andalus."

"But you didn't pay any attention to me."

"Oh, but I did! I just didn't show it. I thought you looked adorable with your unkempt flame-haired dreads and dusty face. And extremely gorgeous in your wrecked jungle outfit. A late French writer with a very long name once said, 'perfection is achieved, not when there is nothing more to add, but when there is nothing left to take away'. We had robbed you of everything. What remained was perfection. Femininity - raw and pure and incredibly enticing. That was - is – you."

"Who was this wise writer?"

"Antoine Marie Roger Vicomte de Saint-Exupéry."

Oh how he pronounces these French words! Je t'aime, je t'aime, je t'aime.

A flight of butterflies fluttered around in her stomach. "Rivas, that's the nicest compliment I've ever heard. Are you really paying this to *me*?"

"Only you."

--- oOo ---

Catherine was completely emaciated from the strain of the last few weeks. She was mere skin and bone. Rivas would have to take Pedro and Joe to task. They seriously had to come up with a plan on how to pep her up. Enough of these silly barbecues! An extreme high-calorie diet was on the cards now. He needed a functioning worker. Besides which, her whole body was still covered in bruises and cuts. Why did these injuries not heal faster? He kissed each scar, each bruise, and especially her injured hip. "I'll make everything alright again, Catherine," he assured her without looking up, all the while showering her with kisses.

He'd stripped her naked twice before, once in her bathroom after he'd locked her into her room for six days, and once lying in the blood bath she'd caused when trying to kill herself. Since she was in a deep sleep after the last incident, he'd used the opportunity to examine the extent of her injuries. The thigh, even though it still hurt, was not seriously damaged, but the hipbone needed orthopedic therapy in order to avoid long-term problems. It would, however, be fine for the next few weeks, hence he decided to do nothing about it. After the mission, the problem would take care of itself - that is to say, he would take care of it.

--- oOo ---

Meanwhile, Catherine had become self-conscious again. When he kissed her breasts, she fidgeted at first. Then she froze up totally. "Please don't hurt me."

"Don't be afraid, Catherine." He tried very hard to relax her body, but she stayed as stiff as a board. "Don't you feel like it? Would you like to get dressed again?"

"Rivas, I don't have much experience. I've only ever had one boyfriend...."

"Warner Bentley," Rivas interjected.

She stared at him but then carried on, "And I always avoided loose relationships. I haven't slept with a man for almost a year. I feel insecure and I don't have much to offer. You'll be disappointed."

"You don't have to impress me. Did your boyfriend expect you to 'offer' him something?"

"Not sure, but he always seemed to have a good time."

"What then? Didn't you enjoy having sex?"

"Not really. I mean, of course I want to... with you... feel...well... but if... oh! I don't know what's wrong with me! To tell you the truth, I never really understood what all the fuss is about."

"Do you want me to show you what it's all about?"

She nodded. "Mhm."

"Okay then, just relax. You have no responsibility, you need not feel any pressure, you don't have to prove anything. Alright?"

She melted away again. Like a wax angel that got too close to the fireplace. The reassurance. He was so loving. Then she became aware that she made him treat her like she was a virgin, and she was overcome with a feeling of guilt about it. "Rivas, I'm so sorry. I'm making such a scene."

"I don't think you're worried about disappointing me. I think you just don't want to be let down yourself again. I can understand that. It must be like getting dressed up for a date and never being picked up." At that, she laughed. "Let go, Catherine and I'll take you where you want to go. Where you can go."

Rivas, who had begun to understand her inhibitions, didn't let her distract him anymore. He focused on touching all her senses.

Every cell of her body was under his spell and she let him lead her into completely unknown territory. She discovered nerves and muscles that she didn't even know she had. She'd never been as stimulated or ever felt as loved as on that day in the shepherd's cottage on those rough old sheepskins. Her expectations were not met - they were exceeded by far. And she finally understood "what all the fuss was about". At twenty-four years old she'd just experienced her first orgasm. She was so overcome by it that she clung to him and didn't let him go for a long time afterwards.

--- oOo ---

Rivas was satisfied with his progress, but a long journey still lay ahead of them. Soon they would leave the farm and re-enter civilization. This next phase would unfold in a much less controlled environment. He had to ensure that her psyche was completely dependent on him. If she didn't participate in the mission willingly, she would stumble upon many opportunities to escape in the weeks to come. Soon he would have to gauge the extent of his control over her. He planned to keep showering her with affection until her infatuated loss of mind led her into some or other careless mistake. The plan would be to use this mistake as a pretext to be mean to her again, and then probe her reaction. At this stage he expected absolute submission from his prey - driven by passion and longing, not fear or force. Sooner or later she'd trip up.
The victim always did. Catherine would be no different.
Especially not Catherine.

26.
Peru, August 14

Shortly before dusk, they returned to the ranch. They took care of the horses themselves as Sam was already at dinner with Joe and Pedro. Rivas joined them but Catherine first rushed upstairs, showered and changed. After they'd eaten, Rivas, Joe and Pedro settled down in the lounge. Catherine offered to wash the dishes, while the men were waiting for a weekly quiz show to come on TV. From the kitchen, she heard Rivas laughing and telling stories. She was troubled by the thought of him reporting on how they'd spent their afternoon together and that the whole gang were amusing themselves at her expense.

Catherine was deep in these thoughts when Rivas returned to the kitchen. She didn't hear him enter, but as always he infused the room with his presence and she sensed it. She had both hands in the sink, but she froze. She trembled with anticipation. Then his hands went around her thin waist, and he hugged her from behind. He lifted her hair and kissed her neck, and Catherine felt her temperature rising. She turned to look at him but an uncontrollable urge compelled her to close her eyes.

This fresh romance, that indescribable feeling of being utterly in love, swept her up and carried her off to a different cosmos. In that new universe, earthly conventions didn't apply. Nothing of importance on earth mattered *there*. Everything was turned upside down: surrender was not a sign of defeat, but a quality to be cherished - there was nothing to prove or fight for. She didn't have to *think*, just give herself up to her feelings. She didn't have to *do*. She could just *be*. Whatever Rivas wanted, needed and demanded, was what she wanted, needed and demanded. She was in union with another human being, on a level that she never experienced before. A union with a man. Oh what perfect design! Was it possible to be so at one with someone else? So *not alone* anymore?

He led her to the kitchen table and she followed like a lamb, not knowing what to expect. Whatever it was, it was fine for her. After their sexual encounter in the hut, she sensed another erotic moment; but whatever he wanted from her – in her complete enslavement she would gladly go along. And so she did – paying no attention to the hard edge of the table when he bent her over it, pinning her stomach against its surface. Even the loud voices of the men in the room next door faded as Rivas took control, rapturing her mind and body.

Neither of them spoke.

The green mini dress by Oscar de la Renta which she'd put on after her shower, made her feel feminine and sexy. Rivas slipped it up, pulled down her panties and entered her from behind. Catherine gave a sigh, a moan, of pleasure. As her soft cries increased, he used his body weight and his imagination to vary the force and tempo of his movements inside her. Sometimes gently and slowly, then unexpectedly fast and hard. Unpredictably, he changed the depth and direction of his thrusts until he completed the ritual with a rhythmic and unchanging beat that made her gasp. The sheer helplessness of her impalement caused an overwhelming ache deep inside her womb. To be his, totally defenseless and vulnerable, was intoxicating. In harmony with his movements, she rose and sank into unknown heights and depths of bliss, ripped upwards yet again only to implode in carnal ecstasy.

Rivas withdrew, gave her a slap on her butt, pulled her delicate La Perla slip up and her dress down. "Good girl," he said, like he'd done during their first encounter on the phone, back in Venezuela. Then he returned to the lounge. As if drunk, Catherine staggered back to her room. Sobering up with a second shower, she reeled off what had taken place.

"Good girl"? A pat on the ass? Is this for real? Not only that you let him, you even like it! What is wrong with you? How can you let him treat you this way?

Utterly bewildered, she found her way back to the kitchen and, by some kind of instinct, finished washing the dishes. When Rivas saw her hovering at the door to the lounge, he stretched out his arm and smiled at her. "Come," he beckoned, and Catherine was smitten once more. She leaned against his shoulder and he put his arm around her. Pedro and Joe were still there, and they smiled and glanced away. She found it thrilling to be Rivas's girl before their eyes. "Good girl." That's all she needed him to say. She craved his condescension. It went beyond any possible analysis. If she could have examined her feelings, she'd have found them incomprehensible. Her heart had crossed so many boundaries that there were no lines left to draw. An untenable condition, and she gladly endured it.

The thought that Rivas was systematically conditioning her, this time non-violently, didn't even enter Catherine's mind.

The Spanish TV quiz show started, and it seemed to be highly entertaining because the men followed it with interest. They took part actively, shouting their answers and competing fiercely with each other. Catherine sat beside Rivas, floating on her private pool of new-found happiness. Rivas smiled at her – subtly, like he'd done on their first outride together. And again she felt her heart melt, longing to be even closer to him. She wanted to dissolve into all his being. Spontaneously she demanded, "Give me a cigarette."

"You don't smoke!"

"I do now."

"Catherine, don't be silly."

Cleaving to him, she whispered in his ear: "I want your adult pleasures – all of them. I'm growing up – show me, please."

Rivas was unmoved. He replied dryly, quietly: "Catherine, any personal growth you claim to have achieved, you've just negated with that infantile request. If you have to smoke, take one of Joe's fags. French cigarettes are too strong. You'll only feel sick."

Catherine wasn't put off. She grasped his pack and lighter. With an exaggerated gesture and an officious expression on her face, she extracted a cigarette. Like an actor on stage, she held it up before lighting it. To her surprise (and the surprise of the amused men), she managed at the first attempt to inhale, and to draw the strong smoke into her lungs. She didn't choke or cough. But her head began to spin. And at the second inhalation she felt as giddy and nauseous as a child on a whirling roundabout. After her third drag, she awkwardly put out the cigarette, got up and staggered towards the door. Her face was pale.

"Where are you going?"

"To the toilet," she confessed, and vanished.

From this moment she was addicted – to "Rivas Cigarettes". She would never smoke another brand.

27.
Peru, August 17

Two days of bliss went by. Catherine, in love as never before, showed little interest in her assignment. She suffered from loss of concentration and she dawdled at her work. Instead of pressing on with her research, she hung around in the house or the stables like a teenage girl, her head filled with romantic fantasies. Her whims took her again and again to the horses, the stables, and what she saw as the center of Rivas's heart. She began to work again, this time not at her laptop and her professional task, but at the heart of things – Andalus and the other horses, the erotic heat and life of the stables.

On the third day the pattern became evident. Rivas was in the lounge, poring over documents with Pedro. Catherine dashed in and, with a tomboyish embrace, she interrupted the two men. Rivas freed himself and exclaimed, "Catherine! Where on earth have you been? Just look at yourself."

She was covered from head to toe in dust and hay. "I helped Sam to bring alfalfa from the barn to the stables," she reported proudly – like a teenager seeking approval.

"How did you manage that? The bales are much too heavy for you."

"I put them one by one onto the wheelbarrow," she replied, "and wheeled them to the storeroom." She pointed to her upper arm: "I'm getting quite muscular! Feel here."

One hand holding a document, Rivas reached out and touched her arm with the other. "I don't feel anything."

"You must press! Here, look! Where the muscle is." She braced her arm as hard as she could, and he prodded again.

"Sorry, but there's nothing there. Maybe that'll change when you start eating something other than yogurt and pineapple. What's that terrible smell?"

"What smell?"

"Stable smell."

"I also helped with mucking out and grooming."

Pedro was about to leave, but Rivas held him back. "We aren't finished."

"Yes, you are," decreed Catherine, and she recklessly snatched Rivas's paper away from him. Rivas said something to Pedro in Spanish and he left the two alone.

She threw herself around his neck again, but he fended her off for the second time. "Have a shower and get changed."

"Come with me now to the barn! I came to fetch you. It's so good there and I wished you were with me. Please come, just for a little while."

"Only if you shower first."

"Why? What's wrong with me?"

'You smell, Catherine."

"But it's horse. There's nothing better than horse."

"On a horse, not on a woman."

"You also smell of horses sometimes and I like it."

"That's different. A woman should smell like a lady."

"That's discrimination!"

"*Vive la différence!*"

"Are you coming now, or not?"

"To do what exactly?" he asked. He was both amused and irritated.

"We could go up to the loft and lie in the hay and dream and be nice to each other. I don't mean sex, just to cuddle."

"Come on, Catherine. I'm not a teenager. I'm not into canoodling. It gets nowhere."

"What do you mean?"

"There's no goal, no climax. It's pointless."

"Gee, you're weird. Have your sex then, if it's that important to you. Have I ever stopped you?"

"I want something else from you." Rivas put the documents into their file cover and turned to look at her.

"Candidates?"

"That would be nice, but it's not what I mean. Not today."

"What *are* you talking about?"

"You're going to let Pichon take you over the landing strip at a stretch gallop. If you manage that, I'll play in the hay with you as long as you want."

Catherine could ride fairly well by now, but due to two serious falls in the past she couldn't shed her fear of a long, fast gallop, no matter how hard she tried. Approximately four hundred meters north of the last farm gate, there was a grassed landing strip for light aircraft. The men kept it immaculately mowed even though she'd never seen an airplane land there. "A full-on racing gallop on a thoroughbred? You do know that if I break my neck, it'll be the end of the headhunting."

"I haven't seen much headhunting going on lately! But seriously, if I thought you'd fall off, I wouldn't suggest it. I know you can do it. A clean straight with lots of space, not a single obstacle, no holes, no trees, and you know what to do if Pichon throws himself on the forehand."

"And if I don't get him back on the hindquarters and he bolts? Let me at least use a stronger bit. Please."

"He loves his snaffle. He mastered all his polo matches in nothing more than that. A curb would only upset him. If you pulled him in the mouth, that would be dangerous. And you know how to get a horse back - you just lack confidence. Go on, tell me. How do you do it?"

"I lead him into a large circle and reduce it gradually, like an inward spiral. A snail shell. Compelled by the bend, he'll reduce his speed in order not to lose his balance." She recited the rule like a schoolgirl recites a poem. And was hoping to be praised like one.

Say "good girl". Please.

"Correct. Now you can apply all that spiraling in and out that you've been practicing in the arena. As long as you initiate the bend with your outer leg and rein and don't pull him on the inside rein, it'll only take a few seconds for him to slow down. And if not…"

"I'll bridge the reins…"

"Not necessary with him, Catherine. Just stay in light seat and don't yank on the reins. Sooner or later he'll stop pulling - he's not a steam train. Just let him have a bit of fun on the landing strip. There's no need to get into a fight with him there. It's really safe and I want you to experience what it feels like. You've got to stop panicking every time your horse wants to come out of its shell."

"Okay."

"Well then, off you go. Don your riding gear, Señorita."

"Aren't you coming with me?"

"I'll come with you to the stables and I'll wait for you there. The rest you'll have to master on your own."

"And if he bucks? I wouldn't be able to sit that."

"He won't. I know him."

A short while later she found herself at the start of the track, sitting on an alarmingly fresh Pichon.

How do horses always sense what's coming?

"Come, my Pegasus. Lend me your wings," she whispered, and she put him into a canter on the left lead. The bay responded immediately and (with her heart in her mouth) she urged him into the gallop. Together, without incident, they flew across the landing strip. At the end of the track, she had no trouble bringing him back to walk and so they turned and charged home at the same breakneck speed. Rivas disliked his horses rushing home. He'd told her always to trot or walk home because as soon as they faced their stable, the horses were naturally inclined to charge back to their herd. But the gallop was exhilarating and she reckoned that he'd forgive her. Pichon flew homewards like an angel, and she arrived back at the yard bursting with joy.

She found Rivas alone in the tack room, digging around in his equine medicine chest. "And? How was it, my darling?"

*My darling. My darling. **My** darling.*

Rivas, you're wonderful! You persuaded me because you knew how I'd enjoy it. I almost wish I never had to leave."

His plan was coming together.

They set off to the big barn, and here Rivas kept his promise and showered her with the kind of affection she had in mind. Under the roof they discovered a bird's nest with a few newly-hatched chicks, and Catherine felt like she'd died and gone to heaven from sheer happiness. For about an hour they lingered there, embracing each other, nestled in the loose hay, high up in the loft. Rivas complied with everything she desired, kissed her lovingly, held her tight, stroked her and spoiled her with compliments. He didn't push her for more. Eventually, it was Catherine who went further. She leant over him and her kisses became more passionate. He reciprocated, but she grasped his hands and declared boldly, "Today it's your turn." Then she blushed at her boldness, and became self-conscious. "Okay?" she added, tentatively.

"Okay."

She unbuttoned his shirt, pulled it off him and tossed it into the hay. She kissed his chest all over, then she plucked up her courage and undid his belt. His pants joined the shirt in the hay, and so did his shoes and socks. There was one more obstacle in her path – she removed his underpants. She took off her own top. The effect it had on Rivas made her even more nervous. Up 'til now, Catherine had always been passive when it came to sex - with Rivas, and certainly in the past with Warner. Rivas had changed everything. He'd taken her across new thresholds of intimacy, and she wanted to give back. She had to overcome her inhibitions, but nothing ever came easily to Catherine. Not even love. She feared rejection, or making a fool of herself. At the same time, she wanted to please him, so she summoned up her courage and she carried on. She was able, for the first time, to inspect his body thoroughly, and she discovered a gigantic scar on his leg. It looked like a series of deep, wide tears that ran down his upper leg from thigh to knee. The scar was at least ten inches long, uneven and jagged, and at no point was it less than half an inch wide. In her infatuation she found this flaw made his otherwise perfect body even more attractive. She was curious, but she made no comment. Instead, she lowered her face to his groin and gave herself to working gently, nervously, on his sex.

She *tried* her best to pleasure him with her mouth, but her clumsiness spoiled everything.

It was done, after a fashion, and she felt the need to apologize. "Next time I'll do better. I've never done that before." He made no comment, and in her awkwardness she rambled on: "You see, you got your climax after all." He gave her no encouragement, no reply, and her relief that it was all over turned into apprehension.

"Yes, I did," he eventually conceded. Inwardly, he groaned: this woman is a disaster.

"I'm a disaster, an absolute loser." No use pretending that all had gone well.

It's not her fault, he reminded himself. Be patient with her. It's new to her. "It's not your fault. It's new to you."

"I'm sorry. I don't know how."

Grab her by the neck and show her, shot through his head. "Do you want me to teach you?"

"Yes! Yes, next time definitely."

"Now."

"Now? But you just…?"

"If you do it again right away, it'll be easier for you."

"But how? Rivas, I can't. You can't."

"I can and you will. Now. And if you don't like it, I'll shove a bit into your mouth. Maybe you'll prefer to suck on that?"

Catherine winced. It wasn't his tone or the chance that he might hurt her, but the possibility that she could lose him if he wasn't satisfied. That thought made her so afraid that she stared wide-eyed at him, frozen in fear.

One look into her terrorized eyes and he regained his erection. "This time you're not going to make such a spluttering scene, otherwise you'll know all about it. Is that clear?" Don't overdo it, he cautioned himself. She's not ready for too much of this.

Again she flinched and held her trembling hand against her upper chest.

Rivas told her what he wanted by rapping out sharp orders like a sergeant to a new recruit.

Catherine, far from being intimidated by his tone or his tight grip on her head, found the explicit commands titillating. Her body tingled with sensual responses and her shame and inhibition dissolved. She was so eroticized by the experience that she wanted nothing more than for him to force her to satisfy him again and again. "I love you," she confessed afterwards.

Rivas showed no reaction. He was thinking about how and when he would introduce Catherine to other sexual fancies. That would take some time and patience. He didn't want to scare off this shy little doe.

"What are you thinking about?" she asked.

Rivas replied with a lie. "I'm thinking about love. Catherine, the whole world speaks of love, desires love, returns love sometimes, but do you know what true love is founded on?"

"Tell me."

"Trust."

"Yes! Love and trust go together. You can't have one without the other."

"Maybe it's possible to trust without loving, but you cannot love without trusting."

"Some people," ventured Catherine, "might argue the opposite."

"But what do you say, Catherine?"

"I agree! It's natural! It makes perfect sense." She looked at him with admiration. It seemed to her, in her state of absolute surrender to Rivas, that he in his genius had just invented this very ordinary idea. Both remained silent for a while. Then she happily spoke up: "So that's what you were thinking about?"

"How much do you trust me, Catherine?"

"With my life, Rivas."

"Not constrained by circumstances. I mean how much do you trust me really?"

"I trust you Rivas. Truly. With my life. I've fallen in love with you." But even as her heart spoke, her brain transmitted warning signals.

Don't do it, Catherine! Don't hand yourself over to this criminal!

Somehow, she took note of the warning. After a short silence, she voiced her counter-feelings: "You'll disappoint me, won't you?"

"Yes."

"When?"

"Soon."

"I know that Rivas, but it doesn't dampen my love for you. It makes it stronger. There's nothing I can do about it. I don't understand it. May I ask you an indiscreet question?" Catherine wanted to shake off the heavy mood that had descended. And she wanted to satisfy her curiosity.

"The right to ask is yours and the right not to answer belongs to me. What do you want to know?"

"Where did you get the scar on your leg?"

"You won't believe it, but I had an encounter with a crocodile."

"Seriously? Never! Tell me what happened."

"It *was* a crocodile."

"You expect me to believe that you survived a crocodile attack?"

"Not without help. I was no match for it, Catherine. I've never felt such immense power in my entire life. Compared to that, even a fifteen hundred pound stallion in full rebellion feels as light as a feather. It happened five years ago at the Rio Putumayo. That's at the boundary between Columbia and Peru."

"Was that the river where I drifted downstream in a boat?"

"Yes. We came across some FARC members who were on the run from the Columbian paramilitary. They decided to slip into Peru by crossing the river and then regrouping in Iquitos. Do you remember what I told you about OLHPA?"

"Sure."

"Due to our association with them, the Guerillas help us out sometimes. But on that day the roles were reversed. They called on us for assistance. Apart from that, we've got no ties."

"Aren't they all left-extremists?"

"Yes. As I said, we've got nothing in common."

"WICED is orientated right of center, correct?"

"Not really. We're completely neutral. We merely fight for freedom and the right to choose. Whatever that personal choice may mean."

What a contradiction! What a ridiculous farce, thought Catherine, but felt that would have been one remark too many on her part. "I think it was in a FARC camp where I got my hip and thigh injuries. You must have heard about that."

"Yes, that was a deserted FARC camp. So what happened was, they joined us because the enemy was hot on their heels. The partisans asked us to lend them our boat. Their party consisted of seven men and two women. I was travelling with two male hostages, our leader, a guard and Pedro. We were fifteen altogether, too many to fit into the boat. We split into four groups and sent the first lot across the Rio. The FARC people went first. One man returned the boat and the next team crossed over. What none of us knew was that at the other side of the river the Peruvian forces had already dispatched a search party. Those that had made it across into Peru had to abandon the boat and flee from the approaching troops. As banal as it sounds, we were left sitting on the wrong side of the water, without any means of transport. In fact, our party was now trapped on both sides.

We separated from the two remaining FARC members and we struggled on through the jungle, heading west, for a few days. The hostages became a burden. We had no option but to abort the mission and kill them or release them. We decided to set them free and leave them behind in the forest, but the four of us still had to get across this damn river. Our provisions were running short, and the way back was now also blocked. Eventually we were forced to swim across the Putomayo, two of us at a time. Our leader and I were to go first. Pedro and the other guy were armed and they waited on the bank to give us cover.

I had barely stepped into the water when I felt something grab me from below and swing me viciously around."

"The crocodile!"

"Yup. It thrashed around and flung me in circles, trying to force me onto the river bottom and drown me there. Because it had got my leg, not my torso, I managed to keep bringing my head up to the surface to breathe. It was insane. It was almost impossible to get air, even above the surface. Pedro couldn't find a clear line of fire, so he waded into the river, moved closer and shot at random into the churned-up water. He figured that if he hit me by mistake it really wouldn't matter if I was killed by one of his bullets or drowned by that monster.

He got us both. The croc was dead and Pedro's bullet put a flesh wound in my arm, but that was the least of my worries. The blood loss from my torn leg was the real problem. They literally pulled me out of the mouth of the crocodile and they dragged me somehow to the opposite bank even though it was farther away. At least we were now on the right side of the border. I was conscious the whole time. They patched me up and dragged me to a temporary camp. There I got basic treatment, and then they brought me back east to a hospital in Iquitos."

"Wow. A dog bite's painful enough! And you were shot on top of it! Did it hurt a lot?"

Poor Rivas, brave Rivas. Rivas, the hero.

"The shot actually didn't hurt at all and my leg only ached once it was bandaged, but even that was a piece of cake compared to the panic under water. I once heard about a man who managed to get away from a Nile crocodile all by himself. I don't know how he managed. I didn't have the slightest chance. It was as fast as lightening. And it just didn't let go."

"Pedro had the courage to risk killing you. And he saved your life."

"None of them stood around watching. They all risked their lives by getting into the water. They saved me from certain death."

"What happened to your other two friends?"

"They're well. One of them was at the ranch the other day."

"What became of the hostages?"

"No idea. I didn't care about them. Our leader had botched the operation - they were his responsibility."

"Would you have acted differently if you'd been in charge?"

"It's always easy to criticize in hindsight."

"Do you think if you'd died, I'd still have been kidnapped? Maybe by this other guy?" Catherine's thoughts had returned to her own fate. Rivas's account had ripped her jungle wounds open again. She shuddered at the thought of being in the hands of someone other than him.

"Sure, someone else would have done it. Perhaps even that guy. Who knows?"

"Would you wade into a jungle river again?"

"Only if it absolutely couldn't be avoided," laughed Rivas. "But you also don't give up horse riding just because you might end up in hospital once in a while."

After Rivas's narrative, Catherine felt even closer to him. Now they had something in common: a terrible experience in the primal forests of Columbia. That in fact was why he'd confided in her. It served him well. He could have brushed her off, but the opportunity to buy her sympathy, to reveal himself as vulnerable, served him well.

The illusion of being his equal (after all, hadn't he referred to her as "my darling"?) re-ignited Catherine's sense of self. However, this renewed self-confidence made her resist all the more strongly the research that he still demanded from her. In her opinion it was a futile exercise, now that she'd excavated Ruckebier. She was confident, but she was also moody – from lack of interest in the research, and from boredom as a result.

Rivas decided to use her apathy towards the work as a pretext to assess the depth of her submission to himself. The more outrageous the order he should give, the more effective the experiment.

28.
Peru, August 22

It was shortly after lunch. Everyone was assembled in the lounge, even Sam. Rivas seized the opportunity. How would Catherine react to being humiliated in front of the whole group? It was time to find out.

"Catherine. Your cranky mood's been getting on our nerves for days. I want you to stop this and apologize."

"You're right, Rivas," Catherine answered, taken by surprise. "I can't stand it much myself. I'm sorry. I'll pull myself together." She spoke with sincerity, and she turned to Pedro, Joe and Sam with an apologetic smile: "*Lo siento mucho, Señores.*"

"Get on your knees."

"Are you kidding?" The question came like a cold shock.

"I mean it. Kneel down."

"Now? Here?"

"Do as I say."

"I said I'm sorry for my bad mood. Please spare me yours."

"I said kneel, Catherine."

"Have you lost your mind? I already told you I was sorry. You're being unfair!"

"We're going round in circles. Do you really want to experience 'fairness' again?"

"You're perverted!"

"I'm not going to say it a fourth time."

"But I will. No, no, no! And one last time: No! I refuse! It's insane, Rivas! I apologized for my attitude and I assured you that I'll change it. There's no reason to bully me like this."

"I'm waiting."

"You can wait till hell freezes over! I won't kneel in front of you or anyone else. I'll never do that. Never!"

The atmosphere in the room was unbearable. Pedro's stomach churned and he got up to leave. Joe and Sam jumped up to follow him. "You'll stay right here!" bellowed Rivas. Pedro stared at him, but went back to his seat. The others did the same. "Sam, fetch a bucket of water."

"Rivas, please!" Catherine pleaded.

"Well then?"

"I can't. How can you ask me to do that? Why do you want to degrade me like this? And for no reason! In front of the others!" Catherine was utterly crushed, and bewildered.

Sam got up to fetch the bucket of water. "No, leave it Sam. We'll go outside with her. She'll just mess up the lounge."

"Rivas, please let me go to my room until you've calmed down! Then we can talk."

"Are you giving the orders now?"

"No, I'm asking you. I don't know why you're so angry. Just let me go to my room and be out of your way." She got up and crept, in abjection, for the door.

"Where do you think you're going? And don't carry on so pitifully. What sort of a pathetic exit is that supposed to be? Do you take me for a fool?"

He grabbed her by the arm and dragged her out of the room into the yard. He pulled her towards a zinc water-trough that stood alongside the nearest paddock. She resisted lightly at first, but when she realized that he was about to immerse her head in the water she fought back with all her might. In the struggle, her head banged against the edge of the trough and her right eyebrow was split open. The blood flowed freely down her face, strangely accentuating the sex appeal of her features. Glancing up, half-blinded by the flow of blood, she managed to catch his eye and saw something flicker through his mind. "Rivas, please don't! Lock me up or starve me if you want to punish me, but not this!" He seemed to be listening to her but he didn't loosen his grip. She carried on pleading. "I know you don't intend to drown me – but I'm going to panic! I don't want you to see me like this, fighting for my life. Please don't reduce me to this! Please, Rivas! Don't do it!"

He let go of her and shoved her away. She sank to the ground. "Alright then! It's your last chance."

"I'm in the dirt in front of you. I'm bleeding. What else do you want?"

"I told you, I wouldn't repeat myself."

She slowly shook her bleeding head. She looked up at him and whispered, "Go ahead then. If you really believe that I deserve it, then hold my head under water – but don't stop until I'm dead. I can't go on like this. It just doesn't end." Her voice regained strength and she added, "So I'm lying in a muddy pool of water again, just like it was in front of the well in the camp in Columbia. What else must I endure? What have I done to deserve this? Just like an unwanted puppy!"

"A disobedient, messy puppy."

"It's insane! You're going in the wrong direction, Rivas! Entirely! It's nothing less than torture – and with no justification at all. I don't hold back any information from you. I'm not rebelling. I don't refuse to cooperate. It's true I'm not a robot, but I said I was sorry. Hell, Rivas, I'm even sleeping with you!"

"Very sacrificial of you."

"What did you just say?" She stared up at him in disbelief. "You're without a doubt the most heartless man that God's ever made. No, I won't say that. That's unfair." Catherine began to rant, beside herself. "God created you uncorrupted, intelligent and healthy! He gave you everything that is good and useful to lead a successful and full life. He equipped you better than most of us. You clearly had a privileged upbringing. But you rejected virtue and you chose wickedness. Nobody forced you. Out of your own accord you developed your cruel, sadistic character. You alone are responsible for that." She began to weary. She felt weak and emotionally exhausted. "You know what?" she added, "I don't understand what's going on between us, and I don't really want to understand it anymore. I see now how much you despise me. You never give me a chance. You deny me any dignity. You grant me a few moments of happiness and then you take a sledge hammer and beat it out of me again."

"Go back to the house and wash the blood off your face. You look terrible." He punished her with a condescending final glance and left her crouching in the mud.

Despite the humiliation, Catherine believed that she'd scored a small victory. Getting to her feet, she reflected on her illusory success. It was the first time that she'd manage to dissuade him from carrying out his intention. Yes, she'd pleaded wildly, and yes she'd knelt and groveled before him, but only because he'd forced her onto the ground. She had stood up to him! Feeling lightheaded, she made her way back to house. The other men were of course a different matter. She was embarrassed that they should see her like this, and she crept past the lounge to avoid them.

In her bathroom mirror she inspected the cut that gaped above her right eyelid. It still bled, but she felt no pain. Head injuries always bleed profusely but she couldn't yet assess the full extent of it because of the blood and mud. She turned on the tap and gently washed her face. The damage was made clear. The upper half of her lid hung down like a shred of cloth. She blenched, and then looked again. She estimated that it would need at least three to four stiches. She tried to do her best with bandages and cold water, but after half an hour, her last bandage was drenched in blood. She reluctantly went downstairs for help, hoping not to come across Rivas on her way. The house was empty so she looked for Pedro in the cottage next door. Joe was sitting in their lounge, massaging leather oil into a Spanish halter. She must have looked odd with her improvised eye patch, and she still felt ashamed that Joe and the others had witnessed her humiliation. Self-consciously, she asked where she could find Pedro. "¿*Dónde está Pedro*?" Joe shrugged his shoulders so Catherine went directly to his bedroom.

There was a suitcase on top of the bed. Pedro was busy packing. "What have you been up to now?" he asked when he saw the bandage. He was angry with everybody – Catherine, Rivas, and himself.

"I banged my head on the water-trough," she answered truthfully.

"Just like that? By accident?"

"Don't you think it's normal to resist? Would you let someone drown you?"

"Every other captive would give in! If you only obeyed Rivas we wouldn't have to deal with these constant escalations!"

"I'm sick of being called a captive! Don't refer to me as a captive anymore!"

Pedro put his things down and stared at her in disbelief.

Catherine began to cry. "I thought I was more to him than that, Pedro! I thought I mean something to him."

"You don't know your place, Catherine."

"I don't want to know this 'place'."

"How bad is it? Are you okay?"

"No, I'm not okay." Catherine wiped away her tears. "Pedro, I wanted to ask you to take me to a hospital."

"Have you lost your mind? I can't take you away from here!"

"Pedro, I swear, if you take me to a hospital, I won't say a word and I'll return with you to the farm."

"Even if I wanted to, how would we get down to the valley at this late hour? Let alone the next town? Anyway, I assume you're covered in bruises. Even at the smallest of village clinics they'd ask question. They'd try to lay charges. Medical staff in this country are obliged to report abuse of women and children."

"Nothing else happened. He didn't hit me. We could say that I had a riding accident. Please! If I don't get this stitched up, my face will be ruined forever."

"You'll have to ask Rivas."

"I can't! Just look at what he did to me. I didn't even provoke him in the lounge. I said I was sorry. You were there, Pedro. You saw the whole thing. He's completely unpredictable! I still don't understand how it all happened."

"Didn't you tell me, the other day, that you knew exactly what goes on inside him?"

"Yes. But now I'm afraid he'll carry on where he left off. Out of spite!"

"Rivas never does anything out of spite. If you ask him to help you, he might refuse but he'll see no reason to beat you because of it. In any case, I'm sure he'll patch you up." He looked at her bandage and added, "And a whole lot better than you've done it."

"That's not funny. But what you said makes sense. You really think he'll help me?"

"Yes, but he definitely won't take you to a hospital. He'll have to think of something else."

"But I need stitches."

"Then he'll sow you up himself."

"He won't know how! I need a sterile environment and an anti-tetanus shot."

"Do you honestly think we're not equipped to deal with a simple cut?"

She recalled how the man in the FARC camp had fixed her up and remembered Rivas's first aid after she'd tried to commit suicide, and the drip. "Where is he anyway?"

"No idea. If he's not in the house, look in the barn."

"What are you doing with the suitcase?"

"I'm leaving tomorrow, Catherine."

"What? For how long?"

"I don't know."

"But why? Aren't you needed here anymore? And if you go, where does that leave me?" Alarm bells rang in Catherine's head.

"It's a personal matter, Catherine. Rivas isn't finished with you yet. When are you going to make some progress with your scientists? Why don't you just try a bit harder?"

"I *am* trying hard! How do you think I found Ruckebier? But, Pedro, how can Rivas do without you all of a sudden?"

"He doesn't know yet."

"You're leaving tomorrow and he's not aware of it? I see. And when do you intend telling him?"

"Tonight."

"What personal matter is it? Are you sick?"

"Don't be nosy, Catherine."

"Sorry. Will he agree?"

"Probably not, but he'll have to deal with it."

"Who else knows about this?"

"Joe. He'll ride down to the valley with me tomorrow and he'll bring Pistolero back to the *finca*. The next day I'll take the bus to Chachapoyas and from there I'll fly to Bogotá."

"Pedro, please don't leave! How can you leave me here, at his mercy? Now that he's being so mean to me? I don't have anyone else I can talk to. Please stay or take me with you."

Pedro looked at her sadly. "Sorry, Catherine. I can't help you. But it'll soon be over. Persevere a little longer, okay?"

"Peeedro! Please!"

"Go now and get your face fixed. Don't be scared. Earlier, that was just a test. He wasn't mad at you. He just wants you to submit unconditionally and if you had, none of this would have happened. But you had to get your own way as usual."

"You knew of a *test*?"

"I worked it out."

"I don't understand any of you! You're all insane. The lot of you!" She returned in anger and vexation to the main house, and up to her room, where she took off the bandage. She only had a few plasters left and she stuck them over her eyebrow while she reflected. She was upset about Pedro's decision and she couldn't face the consequences. What did he mean when he said "it'll be over soon"?

She found Rivas in front of Andalus's stable, leaning against the wall. He was reading an SMS and he glanced up at her. If he found her plaster construction silly, he didn't let on. He turned back to his phone and when he was finished, he asked, "What do you want?"

"How's Andalus?" She patted him.

"Ask him yourself."

"Rivas, can I talk to you?"

"Aren't you doing that already?"

"I still don't get why you tried to force me onto my knees. You wouldn't let anyone do that to you!" Rivas showed no expression. "But I want to assure you, how sorry I am that I was so lazy and moody over the last few days. It won't happen again."

"Apology accepted. Are you finished? I'm busy."

"May I help you?"

"No."

"Rivas, I have a cut above my eyelid. If I don't get this stitched, it'll affect the symmetry of my face. The eyebrow could grow together unevenly and leave an ugly scar. I want to ask you to take me to a hospital. We'll tell the doctor I fell from my horse."

"So that's what this is about?"

"Please help me."

"Let me see." He pulled her plaster away. "I can patch it up, but sooner or later you'll have to consult a plastic surgeon. Wait for me in the kitchen."

"You want to do this yourself? But you'll give me a local anesthetic, won't you?"

"We don't have stuff like that here. You'll have to grin and bear it."

"But it'll hurt!"

"I don't care how you look," lied Rivas. "You decide how important your face is to you."

"See you in the kitchen," she replied and left.

Shortly afterwards, they met there. Catherine's face showed her relief when she saw him prepare a syringe for an injection. "So you do have anesthetic after all?"

"Yes."

"Are you sure you know the correct dose?" Rivas's hand holding the syringe went limp. He looked at her in utter incredulity. "Sorry," she said quickly. "Please carry on. But remember I also need an anti-tetanus shot."

"We took care of that at the camp, Catherine."

"You mean, the man in the hut did? But why? I didn't have any open cuts."

"Just a precaution."

"I don't believe what I'm hearing! I'm injected in the jungle with some or other substance without my knowledge or consent. I could have an allergy! And besides, what on earth were you planning to do to me that I needed a tetanus jab as a 'precaution'?"

"A wild animal could have bitten you."

"I don't believe you! Fussing around with needles in that hostile, unsterile environment! In the middle of the jungle! I hope at least they found a clean one. Who knows what drugs they were abusing with it." Catherine was babbling out of nerves and relief.

Rivas silenced her with a warning look, and then he patched up her brow and lid. With a curt thank-you she disappeared to her room.

Later that evening all the company had again assembled in the lounge. Rivas was enjoying a drink and reading. Joe, Pedro and Sam watched TV and Catherine peeled herself an orange. She sat down next to him on the floor and offered him a segment. When he declined, she got up to her knees, pressed her cheek against his knee and stroked his jeans. "Can you see what I'm doing?"

"Yes."

"I'm kneeling," she remarked anyway.

"I see that."

"Don't you want to know why?"

"No."

"May I tell you a story that my father once told me?"

"No."

"Please?"

"No."

Pedro looked up from the TV and listened intently.

Ignoring Rivas's prohibition, she launched into her narrative nevertheless. "Little Johnny was sitting in class. He got bored and decided to stand up. The teacher admonished him, 'What are you doing Johnny? Sit down'. When he didn't listen, she warned him a second time, 'If you don't sit down this instant, you'll have to stay behind after school.' Again he refused. 'If you don't sit down right now, I'll take you to the principal and he'll call your parents.' Johnny complied and the teacher, satisfied, carried on teaching her class. After class was dismissed, his pals asked him, 'Why did you give in?' He replied, 'On the inside, I'm still standing.' Catherine is lying at your feet, because she wants to. Outside and inside."

She snuggled his head back against his leg and rested in that position until Joe and Sam left for the night. She looked up and saw that Pedro was giving her an intense look – a signal for her to leave the room as well, no doubt so that he could talk to Rivas about his departure. Catherine got up, kissed Rivas goodnight on the cheek and beamed at him. "Thank you," she said before leaving.

"Did you really think I wouldn't give you an anesthetic?"

"Yes, but I'm thanking your for something else. You said I'll have to consult a plastic surgeon. That means you always spoke the truth when you said you'd let me go." Rivas remained in contemplative silence. "What's going through your mind, Rivas?"

"Freud."

"You're thinking about Freud? Now?"

"And about you."

"What do I have to do with Freud?"

"More than I care to admit."

Somehow Rivas must have persuaded Pedro to stay, but in the days to follow Catherine's dependence on Rivas deepened. She could no longer count on Pedro. He might get up and go, at any moment. She clung to Rivas day and night, increasingly losing her self-determination.

--- oOo ---

Rivas was uncomfortable with this development, even though it had been his goal. He missed her spark, her courage. Without this last flicker of assertion from her inner self, which up to now she had clung to with determination, without her charme and temperament, she was just a pretty shell. Apart from that, it frustrated him that she wasn't progressing with the search for alternative candidates. Her pattern of switching from one extreme to the other was an irritation. His abuse got worse, partly to prevent the next rebellion and partly out of sheer dislike. Her endless self-sacrifice began to exhaust him. Her inconsistency gnawed at his patience.

One evening Rivas received a call from Maria.

"How are you getting along?" she enquired.

"Everything's running as planned. More or less."

"More or less?"

"Pedro wanted to throw in the towel a couple of times because he disagrees with the way I handle Catherine, but I convinced him to stay. If he does take off, I'll manage these last few weeks without him."

"I never liked Pedro. I'm only tolerating him because of you. I'll sort him out."

"Maria, that's a matter between him and me. Right now I'm more concerned about our little headhunter. The woman's turned into a time-consuming sponge. She's sapping all my energy."

"How far are you with her? I mean, she should have started to sympathize with us long ago. What's wrong with this girl?"

"I haven't been able to win her over to our cause. I can't fill her in completely, yet. But as far as her relationship with me is concerned, she's programmed."

"She's submissive?"

"Completely."

"Out of love?"

"Yes. She's in love with me. In fact, crazy about me."

"Excellent. You've fixated her on you. What are we waiting for?"

"Something's not right. I'm worried I won't get her ready on time. She's still much too skinny, she looks ill, she doesn't radiate any confidence and professionalism. This could interfere with our plans when the time comes."

"Perhaps Pedro's food doesn't suit her," teased Maria.

Rivas ignored her stab at his friend. "If I don't mess her around too much, she has a good appetite. That's not the problem."

"Well then? Is she ill? You tried hard, didn't you, to avoid excessive physical damage?"

Rivas took an extended drag of his cigarette and, deep in thought, disposed of the ash. "She managed the march through the jungle without getting sick, despite the early rains. We've never had such a strong girl before. The weight problem is psychological."

"You can't expect her body to just to put it all away."

"I told you, that's not it, Maria. She's given up her body long ago. It functions like a robot. She can withstand the physical strain, but she's completely focused on me. And it's irrelevant whether I treat her kindly or roughly. When I'm good to her she's cheerful and she seems unconcerned about captivity. When I beat her, to keep her under control, she becomes quiet and internalizes her pain. It doesn't matter how brutal I am – and lately I've been pushing her, often without any reason at all. But I just can't get to her last boundaries."

"So far, so good, Rivas. This is the tactic we've been counting on. The classical Stockholm Syndrome: you subdue her physically and manipulate her emotionally. She submits, first from fear and then from affection, until she identifies with her kidnappers and actively supports their cause. You're not doing this for the first time! You know very well what's what."

"She's intensely under my spell, yes. But it's making her look haggard and weak, and there's still no sign of her sympathizing with us. We're getting close to the interview phase, and I'm worried. And I injured her face the other day, which upset me. I should have been more careful."

"Nonsense. Stuff happens! At least she knows we're serious. The more unsettled she remains, the more easily we can steer her."

"She's too fragile. She could bail out in front of a key candidate at the wrong moment. She's still difficult to predict."

"Give her something to stabilize her." Maria was starting to sound annoyed. "Surely you can find something that'll work.

Antidepressants, amphetamines? You know more about it than I do."

"Maria, she's losing her personality. She's distancing herself more and more from reality. Nobody can do real work like that. She's completely caught up with her affection towards me. It's made her confused and dependent. It's about Rivas, Rivas, and nothing else. That was what I wanted, of course, but I've never witnessed anything this extreme. I'm her lover, her father, her mother, her brother, her son, her boss, her teacher, her horse. You name it. There's no medication without side effects. The obsession's only going to dissolve by a therapeutic process and that takes time. If we want her to come across as credible when the first interviews commence, I need more time with her. It'll take a few extra weeks."

"That's out of the question! The first appointment's around the corner."

"Maria, give me one additional month with her. We'll have to let the Chicago trip slide and fly to Wisconsin or wherever Ruckebier happens to be at the time. What's the big deal?"

"The big deal is that it'll upset our project plan, and that'll have a massive domino effect. Do you know what I'm beginning to suspect?"

"What?"

"I guess this isn't about our hostage. It's about you. You're taking on these roles that you've just spoken of, and you're making the problem worse. Instead of merely acting like her kidnapper, you're playing along to compensate for the fact that you find it difficult to mistreat her, right?"

Rivas exhaled in a deep, affirmative sigh.

"I understand that, Rivas. She's vulnerable and helpless. She's got nobody to protect her. And, as I know from the photos, you've got a beautiful young woman on your hands, which I'm sure doesn't make your task any easier. But it's not your job to see to it that she has a pleasant life with invented fathers, mothers and goodness knows who, catering to her every need. Her suffering is a critical part of breaking her down. If she feels lonely, she must feel lonely. If she feels lost, she must feel lost. So what? And you, too, must make sacrifices for the goals of WICED."

"I know that!"

"You also know, Rivas, that this treatment cannot be avoided if the hostage is to remain devoted. You said earlier that you sometimes hurt her 'without a reason' – but there is a reason. It's to compel her into utter and complete submission. She mustn't be able to gauge what'll happen to her next. You mustn't let her manipulate you into acting out the roles that she's assigned to you. Stay in command! The less unpredictable your behavior towards her, the better. To dominate her constantly, to always be miles ahead of her, that's your task. You as a psychology expert…"

"Psychiatry," Rivas corrected her.

"You as a psychiatry expert know this better than any of us. Why is this tried and trusted method creating so many problems now? Is this the first time, or have you had scruples mistreating a female hostage before?"

"No."

"This sentiment is new to you?" Maria continued to dig, making Rivas more and more uncomfortable. "During the operation with that American, what kind of emotions did you experience then?"

"None."

"No compassion? Even at the end?"

"None. But Maria, that wasn't the same. That was a job. Kelly was a means to an end. But Catherine - she's complex. I don't know how to explain this to you."

"Rivas, Catherine is also a means to an end," she said, a little too firmly. "What is it with this hostage? First Pedro falls over and now you're going weak, too."

Rivas understood Maria's reaction. From her perspective, none of this made any sense. "Okay," she conceded. "Four more weeks. Then she functions! Is that clear?"

"Yes."

"Rivas, mark my words: by the first of October you'll have her ready, so we can count on her, or she dies. The same day. That's the plan for Catherine. We have no alternative with her. If necessary we'll have to rethink this and go on without her at all, and we must go on – the sooner the better. Can you deal with it or must I replace you?"

"I hear you."

"Good. I'll handle the postponement with Carlos's team. You see to it that the girl moves the appointment with Ruckebier and gets a grip on herself. For goodness sake!" Then she added in conciliatory fashion, "If you weren't my godchild, and I was twenty years younger, I'd also let you seduce me and fall head over heels in love with you. You're irresistible."

"Yes, I must be," sighed Rivas, reflecting on Catherine's words about his character.

"How is she in bed?"

"Awful."

"Poor Rivas," remarked Maria dryly.

Rivas cheered up. Enough, he thought to himself, about conscience.

"I love you, my angel. Like I loved your mother. Bring this Catherine deal to its conclusion. We have a world to save. We need you. You can do it, Rivas."

"You can count on me."

"Don't I always?" she whispered.

29.
Peru, August 27

The next day, Rivas announced to Catherine that the meeting in Chicago was off. "Why?" she asked blankly.

"A change in WICED's planning," he fibbed.

"Does this mean I have to stay here even longer?"

"We have to postpone by four weeks. It'll give you a chance to come up with some more candidates. Call him now, then you can take the rest of the day off."

Instead of making the call, she changed the subject. She spoke quietly, not knowing how Rivas would respond: "This morning a military helicopter hovered over the farm. I'm sure they saw me."

"I thought I heard something. Where were you at the time?"

"Outside, hanging up my washing."

"Americans. They regularly carry out reconnaissance flights – looking for cocaine plantations. The local authorities call them in. If they're after a gang on the run, they sometimes end up here in the highlands. They wouldn't be suspicious of a farm girl hanging up laundry!"

She felt disappointment at his response. She'd hoped to be praised for her allegiance to him and he hadn't even asked how she'd reacted. She followed up, digging for some emotion from Rivas: "The sound was very tempting, but I didn't wave them down to the landing strip."

"Good."

"Good? Don't you want to know why? I mean, after all - I mean, hello?" She shook her head.

"Catherine, I didn't expect anything different from you."

"Do you think I like it here?"

"Alright then. Why didn't you signal them?"

"I don't know," she replied truthfully.

He got up. "But I do."

"Enlighten me."

"Some other time. Call Ruckebier now and we'll make it a day. Are you in the mood for a riding lesson?" He felt that this was a fitting reward for her good behavior but he made it sound like a casual suggestion.

She couldn't help but admire him. The nerve! Nothing seemed to throw him off track. How could he be so sure of her loyalty? She dialed Ruckebier's cell number and explained that she wouldn't be able to meet him in Chicago after all. "May I visit you a month later? In Wisconsin."

"Sorry, Ms Zitgow, but I'll be in Paris then."

"Paris, huh?" she repeated so that Rivas could hear it. He nodded. "No problem. At which hotel will you be staying?"

"I'm not sure right now. I'll e-mail you an appointment and the venue. You can send me a confirmation."

"Super. I look forward to meeting you, Dr Ruckebier."

She sprinted upstairs to change into her riding clothes. At last! Another riding lesson with Rivas!

She enjoyed the afternoon with Rivas, indulging in his attention. Later, though, he withdrew on his own, to his office. It was after dinner and Pedro and Joe had returned to their quarters. Behind the closed door Rivas conducted endless telephone calls into various time zones. Left out of it, she plucked some leaves from Pedro's carefully-groomed herb garden to brew herself a cup of fresh coca tea. She sat down at the rough kitchen table, drank her *mate* and indulged her deep longing for the man in the next room. She compared Rivas to Warner. Her ex was no match whatsoever: gray, boring, lacking in just about every virile quality; no substance at all. It simply wasn't a fair comparison, especially when it came to matters of intimacy. She'd never cared for sex with Warner. The first time her sensuality had ever peaked was during that teasing event in the feed room – followed by the orgasmic high in the shepherd's hut. She would never - she realized as the incident by the water-trough came to mind - be able to win Rivas over completely. Soon, their relationship would end, and that made it even more exhilarating. For Catherine, every encounter with Rivas was a sexual act. His mere presence kindled the fire in her.

He held her captive. He freed her.

He was her tormentor. He was her savior.

His sudden appearance at the door ripped her out of her thoughts. She felt herself blush.

"What are you thinking about?" he asked. He sat down next to her.

"Oh – nothing."

"I know what it is."

"You couldn't possibly! Okay, guess."

"You're thinking about me."

"Warm."

"You're thinking about sex with me."

"Warmer."

"You're thinking about captivity and freedom."

"Okay, stop!" she terminated the quiz. "Guessing games aren't any fun with you at all. You caught me imagining sleeping with another man when I've got back my freedom. He won't be able to give me anything. I'll despise him. Compared to you, all other guys are losers. I'll never be satisfied with any other man. I may as well join a convent."

"You must tell the man what you like. Believe me, he'll do anything you want."

"I don't want to talk about that. It's embarrassing. And I don't have to tell you anything. You play me like a guitar! You pull one string and achieve a certain note, pluck the next and I'm singing another tune. I can't imagine how you do it, but the symphonies you create always harmonize with what's going on deep inside me. I don't have to think or talk about it."

"You communicate all the time when I make love to you."

"Exactly. You hear me without words. Other men can't do that."

"Other men can do that, too, if you let them. Give the man you're with the time and the opportunity to interpret your wishes. I've also got to think, sometimes, about what you'd like next."

"That's the difference! You think about me. Other men just want to satisfy themselves."

"I also satisfy myself. Don't overestimate me," he *said*. You've got no idea how much I hold myself back, he *thought*.

"But not like that."

"I know what you mean, but be fair. Give the man a chance to get to know you. Open up to him. You'll see, he'll make you happy."

She laughed. "You really do know a lot about the secret desires of women. Are you a sexologist, or what?"

"Goodness no!"

"What are you actually, other than a terrorist?"

"Anti-terrorist," he corrected her.

"Anti-terrorist," she repeated, bored. She wanted to talk about him. not his ideology. Rivas was the most exciting topic of her life, apart from horses. And she was right in the middle of exploring him. "So, what did you study?"

"Psychology. In Buenos Aires. Maria helped me to get into a really good university straight after school. She insisted that no time or money would be spared when it came to my education. The first year was not uninteresting, but I was drawn to medicine. I became fascinated by the interaction between body and soul, so I changed to psychiatry. I found the power and possibility of medical treatment alluring, but I had to change faculties for this. Maria was adamant that I study under the best professors the world had to offer and they were situated in Paris at the time, much to her chagrin."

"And there you learned what women want. So that's what one learns when one studies psychiatry in Paris."

He laughed. "Let's say I learned how to influence both sexes in the most effective way. As far as sexuality is concerned, the patterns are always the same. If, for instance, a woman can't reach an orgasm it's not that there's something wrong with her. The same goes for men. The basic physiology is always in order – in almost all men and women, apart from very few exceptions. Sexual intercourse is a mechanical-chemical process and it functions as perfectly in humans as it does with every other creature."

"So what's the problem?"

"Primitive creatures follow their instincts. The human brain is highly developed and it hinges less on hormonal and instinctive drivers than is the case with animals. The orgasm is a reaction of the nervous system and plays out in the physical realm, but in *man*, what precedes the orgasm in the headspace is the decisive factor. What brings it about eventually, or not, depends on what's happening in the head, not in the body. A woman mustn't think about her sewing kit or which pudding she should cook tomorrow, or in your case, which sales deal she may or may not close the next day. She has to release herself, give *in* to the moment and give herself *up* to the man."

"She must submit to him?"

"Not in the way you think. The woman submits to her physical 'inferiority'. Her partner supplements this natural characteristic with his superior physical strength and this turns both on. To get there she has to switch off the desire for control. She can't think about how she looks during the sexual act, how her facial expressions are being judged by her lover. Whether it's light or dark, whether she's too loud or too quiet, if he will manage to hold himself back long enough. Only the moment counts."

"What you're saying sounds old-fashioned and politically incorrect."

Rivas laughed. "As old-fashioned as mankind itself."

"And it seems to me your theory is rather one-sided. The man does everything, she does nothing."

"There're many ways to kill a cat. But we're talking about you, now. In the abstract, yes – the third person – but it's about principles that apply to you specifically." Catherine giggled self-consciously, while he carried on: "So, she must trust the man and place herself into his hands. This way he can focus on her and give her what she wants."

"Most women need clitoral stimulation to get off. Don't men know that?"

"They do, Catherine. But the woman must come along in her head."

"But you just said, she must act like an animal and think about nothing at all."

"Her thoughts *are* important. It's *reasoning* she must switch off. The gods of love are irrational. You can only experience their magic if you get onto the same level as Aphrodite, Venus or Eros."

Catherine soaked up every word.

"Get undressed."

"What? Here? What if someone comes in?"

"Nobody's coming. Take your clothes off."

She slipped out of her shirt and placed it over the back of the chair. She found this stimulating, but she became aware of her surroundings again and she hesitated.

"Carry on."

She took off her bra. "Rivas, what if someone comes in?"

"Carry on."

She took off her shoes and socks, unbuttoned her jeans and pulled them off, and finally removed her slip. She felt embarrassed at standing stark-naked in the middle of the kitchen. She didn't find it erotic. She merely felt exposed and ridiculous. She told him so, and she reminded him again that someone could enter at any moment. "If we have to do it here, at least let me keep the shirt on."

"Do you see what's happening in your head right now?"

"Yeah, I get it. But isn't that normal?"

"Lie down on the floor."

"What? In the nude? Here on the cold floor?"

"That's why."

"Let's go upstairs. Please." She grabbed her clothes.

"The other day you didn't object to having sex in the kitchen."

"I was dressed then! Well, as good as."

"Lie down!" he commanded. She responded self-consciously, taking little childish steps as if mimicking his authority, and in that way went to lie down behind the table.

"No! Move round to the other side. By the door." She obeyed and lay down on the cold floor between the door and the kitchen table. She felt cold and utterly uncomfortable. Without getting undressed, Rivas lay down next to her. One arm he supported with his elbow and with his free hand he stroked her neck. "Close your eyes." He kissed her neck and her mouth and touched her whole body. His hand slid down her abdomen, lower and lower. Captivated by his touch, she finally forgot the environment and submitted to his hypnotizing power over her senses.

Then she felt him penetrate her, hard and deep with passionate brutality. She wanted that and she floated away underneath him to the point where she screamed internally, do with me what you like! Anything you like! Then she heard her audible screams.

Rivas continued. She was now in a state of absolute ecstasy, hardly able to bare the pressure. Then an indefinable wave flooded through her body, upwards from down below, down again and up again. Then he raptured her away. He pulled her with him, further and further away, again and again. Then the ocean in her subsided and she awoke from her sweet trance, her tension turning into a delirium of joy. She stammered, "I love you, I love you, I love you!" and held him tight, as though she never wanted to let him go.

He stroked her face. "Everything that happens is good, Catherine. If nobody enters, it's good. If someone happens to come in, it's also good. You can, and you may, turn everything into lust - each thought, sound and sight. Every event. Whether the bed is warm or the floor cold, clean or dirty, it's good. Whether you find yourself too fat or too skinny, it's good. If you take long, it's okay. If it happens quickly, it's also okay."

"I love you," she repeated. He'd got up and fetched a tea towel from the sink. She was still lying on the floor and was unable to think anything other than how much she loved that man. He threw the tea towel between her legs and she clasped it between her thighs. How indecent he was, she noted. She'd have to throw it away, or better, secretly keep it forever. Such an unconventional man, she thought admiringly, and was grateful and happy to be his prisoner. He helped her up, fetched the shirt from the stool and put it over her shoulders. She slipped into it, stood on her toes and clung to him again. "Rivas?"

"Yes?"

"You wouldn't really let someone watch, would you?"

"Of course not. That was just a game," he replied – truthfully for once. "Good night, Catherine. Sweet dreams," he added, auspiciously.

"I love you," she said again and went to bed.

The next morning Pedro, Joe, Rivas and Catherine happened for once to be at breakfast at the same time. Rivas ate little. Instead, he smoked ceaselessly. He appeared to be in a brown study, remote and absent minded, unlike Pedro and Joe who were scrutinizing her with unabashed thoroughness. Joe's face wore an amused grin and he exchanged knowing looks with Pedro, who also seemed to have something to smirk about. Rivas must have noticed, but he paid no attention to them. She felt like she had to face this alone. She made a show of taking Rivas's cigarette out of his hand. She inhaled the aromatic tobacco with an exaggerated look of pleasure, and she elaborated her theory: Pedro and Joe must have heard her screaming the evening before. The kitchen door and the front door had stood wide open. The whole ranch must have been party to her sensual cries. But, instead of being embarrassed, she felt liberated, and even proud. She took a last drag on his cigarette and handed it back to him. Then she looked directly at Pedro and Joe, got up and left.

Up until yesterday she'd been held captive by her inhibitions. Today she was an emancipated woman, liberated by the man that held her captive.

Rivas glanced up at her as she was leaving. "Wait, Catherine. I want to ask you something. Will you come for a walk with me?"

"*Claro.*" They were strolling peacefully between the paddocks, when she asked him, "Is this about last night?"

"Yes. Who was the man you imagined last night?"

"What do you mean?"

"Yesterday you fantasized that someone was watching us from the threshold."

"What gives you the idea that I fantasized?"

"It was obvious. Who was it?"

"You," she fibbed.

Who knows what he'll get up to if I tell him the truth.

"That's not true. Who was it?"

"I don't have to tell you."

"I want to know. Please tell me."

"I don't know his name."

"So he exists?"

"Yes, but I know nothing about him. I only saw him walk across the yard once or twice."

"He is *here*?" Rivas swallowed markedly.

"Not at the moment. I haven't seen him around for a while."

"You're looking out for him?"

"Rivas, he just popped into my mind. I really don't know why."

"Do you want to meet him?"

"Why? So you can put us in a cage together and give you a performance?"

"On the contrary. If he touches you, I'll kill him."

"First you lecture me on letting go, and when I play along, I get reproached."

"Catherine I'm not reproaching you. I'm just curious."

"Are you jealous or what?"

"A little."

"Really?" She beamed at him. "And I was worried *you* were planning to share me with someone."

"You're forgetting my Spanish roots. My woman doesn't get shared."

My woman.

Those words exceeded even the quote about perfection by Exupéry, which she'd written down and pinned up in her room. She snuggled against him and he put his arms around her.

"Come, let's go over to Andalus. He's already spotted us. If he feels excluded he'll also become jealous. That's all we need."

The next day panned out romantically, but there was something that burdened Catherine. Paradoxically, it also heightened her mood. In the last few weeks, she'd hardly menstruated and she seemed to have no cycle at all anymore. She started to wonder about a possible pregnancy, because Rivas never used precautions and she had no means to take any herself. Secretly Catherine delighted in the thought of expecting Rivas's child. She hoped it would turn her fate to the positive. Practically speaking, he'd no longer be able to cast her away – and he'd certainly not kill her. On the emotional side was the happy feeling of having a baby by her dream man, and the overwhelming sense of worth that came with a desired pregnancy. And Catherine desired. She *wanted*. But how would he react to this news? She decided to probe his responses by first pretending concern on her part. Even if he'd be displeased, she hoped that due to his medical background he would be understanding. "Rivas," she announced, "I haven't had a period for weeks now. I'm worried. That's not normal."

"It's because you've lost so much weight. When there aren't any fat reserves left, the female body reduces its hormone production. Eat properly and forget about it."

"Maybe I'm pregnant?"

"You're not."

"How do you know that? Are you sterile?"

"Just believe me, okay?"

"No, I have to know. How can you be so sure?"

"Because you were given something."

"I was what?"

"A long-term contraceptive, in the jungle."

"Excuse me? How come I know nothing about that?" She jumped up, outraged. And disappointed! "First the tetanus shot and now this! What on earth did you do to my body, you pigs?"

"Calm down, and – please – a little more respect!"

"Respect? You want respect? I don't believe this. I must calm down when you were going to have me raped! Don't you stop short of anything?"

"I assure you, Catherine, at no point did I expose you to the danger of being raped. Don't take it personally. It's a standard procedure with all female hostages." Rivas quickly invented an excuse in an attempt to diffuse the explosive situation.

"But why? If you say that nobody would have abused me?"

"It's routine, a precaution."

"Precaution against what - if there's no danger? That means there can only be one reason for preventing a pregnancy: did you expect all along that I would sleep with you? Is our relationship part of your brain-amputated plan?"

"Catherine, I told you, it's a routine procedure during a long-term hostage operation. It has nothing to do with you or me personally."

"What did they do to me?"

"Someone injected you with a contraceptive. It's 100 % safe. It's got no side effects and won't lead to permanent infertility."

"Who injected what exactly, when and where? Why wasn't I aware of it? Was it when I passed out after escaping through the well? Or did it happen in the FARC camp? There, they blindfolded me and they gave me a jab. Why?"

"Yes. In the camp. The man who treated you is a doctor employed by OHLPA. Perhaps he didn't want to be recognized - I don't know why he proceeded the way he did. That's up to each organization and whoever happens to be responsible for the hostage. You were actually very lucky that you got hurt at that place and at that time. That's why he had to keep you longer than intended. I'm sure they'd have only blindfolded you for a limited time. He was tasked with examining you at the halfway point to see if you'd manage the last stretch or if you needed a break. The heavy rains had arrived unexpectedly early, and the wet conditions increase the danger of exhaustion and disease. That's why I ordered them to stop there. They would have administered this contraceptive, the anti-tetanus injection and whatever else you needed, and then sent you on your way. But as usual you had to make a scene."

"I thought the man gave me morphine."

"He also gave you codeine which the body metabolizes into morphine. Since you needed a hefty dose, he called me first."

"Oh – and in your endless mercy you were gracious enough to grant me pain relief?"

"Yes," he answered aridly.

"I cannot fathom how you can sit there and talk about these remote violations of my body, as if we are chatting about trivia!"

"Restricted mobility due to pain or medical complications, especially pregnancies, during a long haul kidnapping, causes unnecessary delays. All of that's easily avoided by taking a few simple precautions. Just in case."

"Now we're back to the beginning. In which 'case'?"

"You know Catherine, it's not uncommon for a hostage to initiate an intimate relationship with one of her abductors in the hope of receiving better treatment. That's why it's a standard precaution. Don't take it personally. It didn't happen in your case, and you're no worse off."

"To think that I'd sleep with one of those disgusting guys! What do you think of me?"

"I'm in no mood to carry on arguing with you. Quit it now, it's really no big deal."

She shook her head – as much in sadness as in anger. As if Rivas was a schoolboy who'd failed to grasp an important point. "You're wrong, Rivas. This is the biggest deal of all!"

He got up and turned to leave. "Let me know when you've come to terms with it. Until then stay out of my way. I'm sick of your griping."

"What else? What else do I have to endure? Is there any human rights violation out there that you haven't yet dealt me?"

"Didn't you hear me?"

"Yes, I heard you," she replied. Crushed, she returned to her room.

Despite every betrayal of trust, she remained immeasurably in love with Rivas. Soon enough she was able to repress the horrible reality of the contraceptive. She became even more clingy, and she was particularly upset about not being able to spend the nights with Rivas in his own room.

One night, aching with longing, she took matters into her own hands.

Rivas, alone in his bedroom, heard the door creak open. An alarm went off in his head. That could only be Catherine, he surmised. For a moment, he was gripped by the notion that she'd fetched a knife from the kitchen and was about to stab him with it. He welcomed the interlude, anticipating an amusing little adventure. However, instead of a knife she'd armed herself with a blanket and a pillow, as far as he could make out her frame in the half light. When Catherine spread out her camping equipment on the floor, he switched on the bedside lamp. "Catherine, what are you doing?" he asked, even though it was obvious.

"I'm lying down here so that I can be near you. I won't disturb you at all."

"Catherine, go back to your room! What's this nonsense?"

"I miss you too much. It's not natural that we always sleep apart after we have sex. I need to feel loved and secure."

"What's not natural, actually, is that we spend every minute of every day together. Even married couples separate during the day to go to work and I told you before that I don't like this clingy business. Let me at least have this bit of privacy."

Ha! Interesting. You swept away even the slightest vestige of my own privacy, and now you can't get rid of the spirits that you've summoned up! You sorcerer's apprentice!

Of course this went unsaid. Audibly, she asserted, "I'm staying here on the floor. You won't even know that I'm here."

"Whatever." Rivas switched off the lamp and turned his back, while Catherine laboriously made her nest on the floor. After two minutes, the light went back on. "Catherine, how can I sleep, while you lie on the hard floor like a bedside rug? And it gets really cold here at night, as you know. You'll freeze. Come on now." He bent down to encourage her to get up and return to her own room. Mistaking this as an invitation, she crawled into bed with him.

"I'll be quiet like a little mouse and stick to my side of the bed. I'm so small and thin, you won't even notice me."

"Yeah, alright," sighed Rivas. "But this is the first and the last time, you hear?"

"Yes," she agreed happily.

The next evening, she repeated the procedure with her blanket and pillow and, gradually, she made a habit of spending the nights with Rivas in his bed.

Not long after this new habit began, on a fine day – a day of Indian summer - Catherine went outdoors at lunch. She roved around the garden, gathering together a bunch of the local flowers. Pedro was leaning against the garden fence, smoking. "Tell me, Catherine," he asked, "have you started making your own bed again?" Ever since her suicide attempt, Joe and Pedro took turns to clean her room as a pretext for keeping an eye on her.

"I sleep in Rivas's room now," she announced, not without pride, as they returned inside together. They went to the kitchen for a cup of *Mate de Coca*. Pedro looked at her in surprise and shook his head. "You disapprove?" she asked.

"Don't you think you're taking too many liberties? I happen to know that Rivas doesn't like women getting close to him."

"And I happen to know that he likes getting close to *me* very much."

"Catherine sit down for a moment, will you?" Pedro's voice was quiet, and earnest. "I'll give you some really useful advice, okay?"

"Okay." She switched off the kettle, poured the tea and sat down at the table, listening attentively.

"Take it easy with him. Rivas is a ticking time bomb, about to go off at any moment. Just think about the incident at the water-trough. It wouldn't surprise me if the next disaster was around the corner. Keep your distance, do your work, be courteous, do as he says and hold back this crushing affection of yours. What you interpret as a 'relationship' is a job for him. If you take it too far, you'll start irritating him. And believe me, that will put a quick end to your illusion of romance."

Pedro's well-meant attempt to illuminate Catherine about Rivas's charade bounced right off her. "Things are different now. He loves me."

"Did he say that?"

"No," she admitted, "but he's so affectionate. I can feel it."

"Believe what you will. I've said too much already."

She was about to fling a juicy retort at him, when Rivas entered. "What are you two gossiping about?" he asked amicably.

"We're not gossiping," retaliated Catherine. "We're chatting."

She was about to make up some sort of evasive explanation when Pedro interrupted: "We were talking about you."

"So? I hope I make for an interesting chat! Do tell. What are the latest reports about Rivas?"

"I cautioned Catherine to give you a bit of space, because her affection for you could backfire at any moment. At least from what I can see. Or am I mistaken?"

Rivas looked at Catherine. "That's good advice, Catherine. You should listen to Pedro."

Catherine shot back, "Why are you suddenly so mean to me? Is it because there's a third party in the room and you want to look cool? Or is all this staged again? If you have something to say, at least have the decency to tell me yourself. Oh, what's the use? You're all so nasty!"

At this point Joe came into the kitchen. Joe glanced questioningly at Pedro who replied with an uneasy grin. "What are you two grinning about?" rapped Catherine. From flowers and sunshine she was suddenly thrown into a foul temper.

"Don't be so rude, Catherine. Sometimes your manners are appalling!"

"You're appalling all the time!"

"That's true. You know, I have this strong urge right now to be really appalling and to beat the hell out of you again."

"Of course! You solve all your conflicts by using force! Sorry, I forgot."

"The only one creating conflict is you, Catherine. There's no reason to be so crabby, especially not with Pedro and Joe who wait on you hand and foot, all day long."

"Come on, hit me then! Or show me what else you've got in store. I'm quite familiar with your repertoire of atrocities by now. Nothing can scare me anymore."

Rivas said something in Spanish to Joe and Pedro and both men dashed towards her. She fled from the kitchen into the hall, where of course they caught up with her and blocked her flight. "Strip her," said Rivas in English, so that Catherine could understand.

She was startled. "What?" she asked. Then she relaxed and added, "You're bluffing."

"Whether or not I'm bluffing you're about to find out." Rivas turned to Pedro and Joe: "Take off all her clothes and get her outside into the courtyard."

"Rivas! Have you lost your mind completely?"

"Whether I have or not makes little difference. There's nothing you can do about it."

While she struggled fiercely under Pedro's tight grip, Joe plucked around at her back, trying to open the zip of her airy off-white Dolce & Gabbana dress. Pedro addressed Rivas in Spanish. Rivas nodded and Pedro let go of Catherine, and left. Joe continued to hold her and tugged clumsily at her upmarket dress, almost ripping the delicate lace to pieces. "You can't mean this, Rivas! Will you really let Joe drag me out into the farmyard with nothing on?"

"Sure. I'll have you tied against the fence and then everyone can have a good look at what the deal is with this little chica, who gets away with murder every freakin' day on this darn ranch. They all think you must be Wonder-Woman in bed, the way I rotate like a turbine around you twenty-four hours a day!"

"How can you speak so disrespectfully of me?"

"What do you think *they* think, huh? That I like your cooking?"

"Rivas, please don't," she asked, restraining her voice, trying to sound reasonable and calm.

"Why not? They can decide for themselves whether you're pretty enough to justify all this fuss. That'll stop the gossip around here and I'll have killed two birds with one stone. As a consolation to you, Catherine, I expect they'll find you really hot and the worst that'll happen is that they'll give me a few tips on how to get a grip on this little monster. I can do with the help, because to be honest, I'm at my wit's end with you."

"Rivas! You promised me more than once that nobody would abuse me!"

"See, you don't listen, do you?" he replied casually. "Nobody will touch you. It'll be nothing more to be endured than a 'visual examination'. "And I'll get a few fresh ideas for when next you fall out of line. These guys tend to be a lot more resourceful than I am when it comes to the treatment of insubordinate hostages. And rebellious womenfolk."

"That really is abominable! You know very well how hard it is for me to get undressed even in front of you!"

"I have no choice. I'm all out of ideas on getting you to understand that you can't carry on around here like a diva. I'm hoping this little display will bring back a few 'hostage manners'." Joe, meanwhile, had managed to peel her out of her dress. The dainty garment slid down her narrow hips to the floor. Catherine was ashamed of standing in the hall in her underwear and she dreaded the horrors she was about to face. As always when she was out of options, she began to cry. "Save your crocodile tears. They won't you help you today." Rivas nodded at Joe, who proceeded to fiddle with the clasp of her bra.

"Alright, alright, I'm sorry about my bad manners. I'll pull myself together. I'll always be polite from now on, I promise," she whimpered. She wiped her nose with the back of her hand. Joe didn't seem very experienced with bra clips. In the end Rivas stepped towards Catherine, motioned Joe away and opened her bra himself. Nobody restrained her now, but she needed both hands to keep herself covered with the loose bra and she couldn't run away with Rivas standing right beside her.

She braced herself for the worst and gave him a tortured look, but Rivas instead bent down, picked up her dress and held it out to her. "Here, get dressed again."

"Thanks!" She closed her bra and gathered up her designer gown. "Would you really have gone through with this?" She recovered from the shock quicker than he'd thought likely. She stood with her back to Rivas, inviting him to help her with the long zip.

"Of course not. I'd never do that to a woman. I just wanted to give you a wakeup call," he replied while pulling up her zip.

"What a sick joke!"

"It wasn't meant to be a joke. It was meant as a lesson."

"You know what? You make me puke!"

"You don't learn, do you?"

She didn't reply. Instead, she stormed towards the staircase, mad as a hornet.

"Hang on! That way!" At his voice, she turned around. He gave her a condescending look as though she was a simpleton, and he pointed to the study.

"I'm changing now," she responded. "And then I'm going riding."

"No, you're not going riding. You're going back to your desk to carry on with your work."

"The hell I will. I need some fresh air."

"Do you enjoy being beaten up or do you just lack intelligence?"

"Neither nor!" Catherine was ablaze with rage. She couldn't abide his presence for one more second. She turned around and stalked off to her room with her head held high.

"It's un-freakin-believable!" exclaimed Rivas, now also at boiling point. He caught up with her, pulled her back and slapped her full in the face. In her reflex, she hit him back and when he struck her again, she assumed a pugilistic stance and then drummed against his chest with her fists. Strengthened by her enormous anger, she struggled bravely for a while, but then he beat her to the ground so violently that she was reduced to tears again. He let her lie there and intended to let her go up to her room after all, but to his surprise she got up, returned to the study and took up her work.

"I don't know what got into me," she said, after a short silence. "I'm sorry." The nonchalance in her voice was staggering.

So Pedro was right, and she'd gauged Rivas wrongly throughout! Catherine was immeasurably disappointed, but this time she bore the brunt of it with remarkable composure. That evening, despite her disappointment, she found a new resolve. Her despondence fell from her like a rag. A new sanguine sense welled up in her and she resolved to bring things to a conclusion. This time she wouldn't try to kill herself. She'd kill *him*. If she failed, she would die, but that would happen anyway. Rivas didn't care about her. Recent events couldn't have made it any clearer. She felt strangely at peace. This was drastic, but it was her last shot.

Now it was all or nothing.

One of them had to die.

30.
Peru September 06

She'd never seen Rivas with a firearm but she reckoned that he must have one. She couldn't gain access to the safe but Pedro certainly had a gun. So much was apparent from the story of the encounter with the crocodile. In the following days, whenever the men were gone from their quarters, she searched around in Pedro's room, among his clothing, everywhere. But she couldn't find any trace of a weapon. Sam came into her mind. On this remote farm they would shoot sick or injured horses. She was sure they wouldn't call in a vet just to destroy an animal. Sam regularly rose early, fed the horses, returned to his room and had breakfast before leading the horses to their paddocks an hour later when his official working day began. She had a window of about thirty minutes while he was busy with the feeding. She hoped that he'd leave his gun in his room during that time.

The next morning early, she crept into Sam's room. If they caught her, she would say she was looking for him. Who would think that she was snooping around for a gun?

She got into his bedroom undiscovered and didn't have to look for long. On a counter lay… a gun. Without inspecting it properly, she tucked it under her shirt. Sam would soon discover that his weapon was gone and of course they would immediately suspect their hostage of having taken it. Thirty minutes was too short to lure Rivas into a trap, so she had to gain some time and hide the firearm until the opportunity arose. She was absolutely sure that she'd be able to pull the trigger. And with the gun pointed at him, she'd have to go through with it and fire a fatal shot. He'd never let her get away with something like this unpunished. But she had to plan it so that his death wouldn't be discovered straight away – she'd need time to make her escape. This time, she had to succeed!

She buried Sam's pistol in the garbage pit and went to have her breakfast. In the kitchen, she expected that at any minute there'd be a commotion around the missing the gun, and she was determined to deny everything. In vain. Even the next day nobody confronted her about a weapon having disappeared from one of the rooms. Perhaps they were not missing it? Perhaps it had been found in the garbage pit? But even then – why did nobody say anything? Demand an explanation? The next morning, she climbed down into the pit and dug out the gun. It was lying there, untouched. Catherine concluded that Sam hadn't reported it missing because he was worried about getting into trouble. Perfect! Carefully, she tucked the pistol into her waistband and drew Rivas's long shirt over it. On her way back to the house, she crossed paths with the man himself. Why wait any longer?

"Good morning, Rivas. Is it okay if I start work later today? I'd like to sit by the pond for a while."

"Why?"

"I feel like a bit of nature. It's a beautiful morning."

"Don't take Andalus. It's his day off."

"That's fine. I wanted to walk. To stretch my legs. That's why it could take a bit longer. Is it okay?"

"Whatever."

She strolled to the pond, which was about half a mile south of the farm. She surveyed the terrain carefully, mentally prepared herself by playing things out in her mind, and then returned quickly to the house. She decided to haul Rivas's dead body into the pond and to escape straight from there, on foot.

When she got to the *finca*, she stormed into the house, feigning excitement. "Rivas! At the pond! There's an injured animal!" She pretended to be out of breath.

"*What* animal?"

"I'm not sure. Some sort of wild cat. I feel sorry for it. Will you come and help me? I can't leave it like that."

"What's wrong with it?"

"I don't know! I think it's dying."

"Let it die. Don't get mixed up with nature's ways, Catherine."

"Rivas, please! You know that I can't just leave it to suffer on its own. I'll have to rescue it myself," she bluffed. "I'm sure I'll manage."

"Catherine, it'll bite you. You could get badly hurt or infected."

"Please help me!"

"*Por amor de Dios*, Catherine!"

"Please!"

"*¡Está bien!* Let's go." Rivas sighed in exasperation.

They approached the pond, and Rivas immediately sensed that something was amiss. "There's no injured animal here, Catherine. What's this really about? Another romantic game?"

"There is! Over there, by the bank."

He stared in the direction of the little lake while Catherine, standing behind him, drew the gun from her waistband. "There's nothing, Catherine. Why did you bring me here?" He turned around and found himself looking at the barrel of the gun. "Are you crazy? Do you think nobody will notice if you steal Sam's pistol and shoot me with it, just like that?"

For a few seconds Catherine held the gun in her trembling hands, without uttering a sound. "I love you," she said eventually, "but you destroy me."

She pulled the trigger.

Bang.

Rivas stood and shook his head in utter disbelief. Catherine, motionless, dropped the gun. Like in a bad dream, she wanted to run but stayed rooted to the ground. Rivas said, in a wondering tone, almost admiring her, "You really pulled the trigger."

"Rivas...."

"That's a blank gun, Catherine. Sam uses it to scare away predators. I underestimated you, Catherine. We all wondered when you were planning to use it, but if I'd thought for one moment that you'd fire at me, and from such close range, I'd never have followed you to the pond."

"What do you mean?"

"Unlike dummy cartridges, blanks fired from point-blank range can cause injury. They can even be fatal, from the explosive gases and the wad used to seal the gun powder. Believe me, I'm more surprised than you that I don't even have a bruise on my chest."

"Do I have to go back to the cellar now?"

"You can count on it."

"Okay, let's go then."

"Yes, let's."

She picked up the gun and handed it to him, and they walked home in silence. Catherine was utterly numb. Mechanically she set one foot in front of the other. I won't cry, beg or talk, she resolved. She felt no emotions whatsoever. Like the last chip at a roulette table, she'd just gambled away her life.

When they arrived at the mansion they went straight to the cellar door. Rivas unlocked it and they descended the stairs. She sat down on the only stool and waited for him to pull out his own gun. *This* is a gun, Catherine, he would brag, he the invincible kidnapper, her nemesis. The victor. Again. But she saw no pistol in his hand. Instead of triumphing, he merely gave her a cold instruction, "Under the chair you'll find a plastic sheet. Pull it out and spread it on the floor." At this, her numbness left and she was gripped by panic. Whenever Rivas issued level-headed commands, things got serious. She got up, bent down, took out the painter's drop-sheet and spread it out. She nearly threw up, and tears burned under her eyelids. "Get undressed. And put your clothes on the first step of the staircase." She stripped down to her underwear. "Your bra also." She took it off and wanted to pull down her panties. "You can leave those on."

"Why?"

"Standard procedure."

"Why?"

"Stop asking questions. Kneel on the sheet in front of the chair with your back to me and your arms on the seat. Put your head between your arms with your forehead resting on the seat." She did as told and waited for his next instruction – or the sound of the safety catch of the pistol that she was sure he had. Instead, she heard him light a cigarette. He seemed to take forever to smoke it. Then she heard him close in on her. She felt him draw her hair aside and lay it over her left shoulder. She grabbed his hand and pressed it against her wet cheek, because by now tears were streaming down her face in floods. "Stop that. Put your arm back on the chair."

She let go of his hand and whimpered pitifully, "Rivas, I need the toilet."

"That's not unusual. That's why I said you can leave your slip on."

"Rivas, please! That's not dignified! I can't... I can't hold it back anymore."

"If you can still discuss it, you can hold it back. Then I haven't scared you to death yet, Catherine."

I will not beg for mercy she implored herself; and the next second she heard herself plead, drowned in tears, "Rivas, I don't want to die! I thought I was prepared for it but now I'm scared! Please don't kill me! I'll do anything you ask. I'll never refuse again. I give you my word, from now on I'll do exactly as you say. I'd never promise something and not keep it."

"Under the circumstances you'd swear to anything and nobody would expect you to keep your promise. It's no use. Don't waste your remaining breath on senseless pleas."

"Rivas, I'm different! If I promise something, I keep it. I swear, you won't have a minute's trouble with me from now on. I'll bring this assignment to its successful conclusion. It'll be much easier for you when you start negotiating with Ruckebier. He could even bail out if he loses contact with me. You always said you need me. And you need more candidates. I'll carry on. I won't quit now! I'll find them. Please let me live! One last chance, please. I can still be very useful to you."

"We'll be fine without you from here on."

"Oh dear God! Rivas, surely you can't be this heartless? Are you really going to shoot me? Here? Half naked, on my knees on a plastic sheet?"

"Catherine, I could have killed you a hundred times, and you certainly provided me with enough provocation to do so. I've even been instructed to do that and yet I spared you. Whereas you tried to trap me in the cheapest way and pulled the trigger without hesitation. You made my blood curdle from disbelief. Now tell me Catherine, who's the heartless one among us?"

Catherine screamed out in absolute panic. "Rivas, please!"

"There, there. Now, now." He stroked her gently and continued to torture her emotionally by kissing her head like a father who caresses a dying child.

"What I did was wrong, but it wasn't heartless," she sobbed. "I acted in self-defense!"

"There was no reason at the pond for self-defense. And I've assured you several times that I wouldn't hurt you as long as you merely complied."

"I did believe you, Rivas, But then a few days ago I was just picking a few flowers and having a conversation with Pedro about whether I should sleep in your room or mine. Moments later I was stripped down to my underwear, humiliated in front of your accomplices and then beaten to a pulp on the floor. I had no choice but to apologize. *I* had to apologize to *you*! Because I didn't know what you'd do to me next. I couldn't go on, Rivas! I'd lost hope! I *had* to try to free myself." Rivas displayed zero emotions. "And the trap, Rivas - how else could I do it? That's why women poison men when they want to kill them. Few women can just walk up to a man and kill him. Please consider also that I didn't simply pick a hapless victim from pure bloodlust. I'd done nothing wrong. Okay, I dabbled around in that database, but it was an ignorant mistake. Do I deserve to die for that? Can't you see that I'm innocent? How can you execute an innocent person? I can't believe you'd do that. How could you do that?"

"You know very well that's not what this is about."

"Please forgive me for being deceitful, Rivas! And for trapping you. Rivas, I was scared. Don't judge me for that. That's not fair! If I was a man I would have stood up to you and fought with you. If nothing else, believe this!"

"Okay. Cut the sermon. I've listened to you long enough."

"I love you."

"Shut up."

"I do!"

"I told you to be quiet."

"I can't. I want those to be the last words out of my mouth. I love you, Rivas."

"Do you still need the toilet?"

"Yes."

"Get dressed, go to the loo and come back down immediately."

--- oOo ---

This woman is a freak, thought Rivas. I threaten her with death and her response is, she has to go to the toilet. When she's finished, she'll come downstairs again and carry on negotiating. How could anyone kill *that*? He took a few drags of his cigarette and Catherine reappeared on the staircase.

--- oOo ---

"Must I take my clothes off again?"

"No."

"Must I kneel in front of the chair again?"

"No." He blew a last cloud of blue smoke into the cellar and put the cigarette out by stepping on it.

"May I have one please?"

He handed her a cigarette and gave her a light. No sooner had the nicotine taken effect, than she begged, "Rivas, I'm sorry, but I need the toilet again."

"Where on earth did I find you? Come, let's go."

"You won't kill me?"

"No."

"Why not?"

"Because you pulled the trigger."

"What do you mean? I don't understand."

"Neither do I."

Even though she walked away unscathed, happiness eluded her from this day on. Catherine's will had been irretrievably broken. She kept her promise not to resist anymore and she never again entered Rivas's room uninvited. She slept exclusively in her own bed.

If Rivas admired her for her single-mindedness at the pond, which at first she assumed he did, he didn't show it. Rivas often lost his temper, and he no longer showed her any of his previous courtesies. The sex continued, but it became increasingly brutal. Catherine let him do anything he liked. He demanded things from her which she simply couldn't cope with, no matter how hard she tried. He would then punish her by making disparaging remarks, or by giving her condescending looks, or worse, ignoring her altogether. Every form of attention, good or bad, was better than being dismissed by him. He never suggested a mutual outride anymore and he also terminated the riding lessons. She could ride unhindered whenever she wanted to, but always on her own. She threw herself into her love for Andalus, but completely lost interest in the other horses. Even Protestante, whom she loved so much, could no longer give her any pleasure. The men were also affected by the heavy atmosphere and carried on unhappily with their routine while the appointment in Paris dragged slowly nearer. Her appetite decreased again as her misery increased. It was no longer due to her wish for freedom, but because she was so hurt by Rivas's treatment. He'd become the center of her universe. Everything had revolved around him. And it still did, but to different effect. Was he angry? Was he pleased? Was he satisfied with her work, the way she looked, or did she disappoint him? She was just an empty shell, drained of any life force. Despite her weak disposition, she worked even harder to please him, wore his shirts to look sexy for him, did everything he asked of her, let him rule her completely.

Her despair had reached its absolute peak when Rivas overstepped her very last remaining boundary.

Part III

Rivas

"Not beauty decides
whom we love,
but love decides whom we
find beautiful."

Hermann Hesse

31.
Peru, September 10

For two full days there'd been no sign of Rivas. When he finally turned up, it was late on the third night. Catherine was still immersed in her work, despite the late hour. She shut down her computer and stared at him. "Where've you been? You haven't come to eat with us, even."

"I made my own arrangements."

His tone had an edge and Catherine despaired about his ongoing resentment towards her. She could find no reason for the ever-present antipathy. She'd kept her promise to conform but the more she tried to repair their relationship with hard work and obedience, the less pleased he seemed with her. "Have I annoyed you? Please tell me what I'm doing wrong. I do wish you'd be happy with me. I made a lot of progress this week. I think I've found an alternative prospect at last. Please don't be mad at me. What can I do to make things better?"

Catherine realized that she'd probably protested too much, but she was tired. Now she shivered as she waited for the predictable outburst. And sure enough, Rivas reacted explosively. "What's wrong with you? You're pathetic! Do you think your peevish mood swings entertain me? I beat you up so badly that you can hardly get to your feet and you ask me what *you're* doing wrong? You're crazy!" She was at a complete loss. She could think of no reply, and this provoked him anew. "Half the time you act like a spoilt brat on a pony camp and the other half, like the two of us are on honeymoon. Just because I'm sleeping with you doesn't mean I'm your lover. There's nothing between us, so stop pretending we're a couple. You're my prisoner. I keep you captive because I have a job to do, not because I like it. You're here because I force you, not because you're having so much fun that you don't want to leave. You do as you're told, Catherine, because it's your only chance of getting out of here. Stop denying reality and deal with it!"

"Where would I go? What would I do without you? Who would I be?" she interjected helplessly. Tears started to roll.

His reply was a smack in the face. "That's enough! At least be honest and stop rambling on about dinner and nonsense like that. You behave like a hypocritical martyr. Tell me what you want.

Tell me that you want to go to bed with me. That you like everything I do with you. That you like *everything*. I want to hear you say it now, dammit!"

"I don't like everything," she whimpered.

He hit her again. "I told you to be honest," he screamed.

He was now making no sense at all anymore, contradicting himself and flying into an uncontrollable rage. It seemed that there was nothing she could do. She placed her head in her hands and, breathing deeply, tried to control her sobs. Her evident pain, her grief, only seemed to provoke him further. He hit her again, so hard that she lost her balance. She rolled from her chair onto the floor, where she lay in the fetal position, shaking and sobbing uncontrollably. Her lack of resistance merely spurred on the sadist in him and he beat her even harder, unmoved by her submission, or perhaps even because of it. What did he want to hear? Curled up on the floor, she struggled to find an answer. Barely audible, she whispered "I want you."

He stopped hitting her. "Say it louder."

"I want you."

"What's the magic word?" Towering over her he pushed her with his foot. "Say 'please'. Come on. Say it."

The situation was already beyond control. If he started to kick her, he would seriously injure her, but she couldn't get the word "please" past her lips. She got up to her knees and clung to his legs to prevent him from kicking her. "Why are you torturing me like this? Is it not enough that you dominate me completely?" Tears were streaming down her face, her nose was blocked. She gasped for air. "You humiliate me, you're cruel beyond belief, you reject me in every way possible, but what do you still want to squeeze out of me? I am drained, Rivas! I'm empty! I have nothing left to give you! Your hungry ego can't feed on me anymore. I've got no resources left. You've stripped me of everything except my thoughts. And now I must let you into the last corner of my soul? I hold nothing back. I do only what you tell me to do. I love you without knowing why. When I try to be cheerful and brave you tell me I'm too lively and demand that I be quiet. When I keep quiet, you don't like it either. You force me into complete obedience and when I do as told, you become even more aggressive. You accuse me of martyrdom and that I'm trying to manipulate you, but you're looking at the product of your treatment. And the utter contempt which you continue to unleash on me, tells me how abysmally you despise me, or that you have no conscience whatsoever." Rivas's rage cleared as self-awareness set in. "Now I must beg you for sex on my knees. But," she panted, completely out of breath, "I won't do that. I won't let you extinguish my last spark of dignity. I'll never again allow myself to be humiliated like I've just done. I'd rather die. I'm not saying that lightly. I've come to the point of death before, I know what that's like, and I'm serious this time." She paused and drew breath quickly. "As of today you'll never touch me again, except by using force."

"You'd like that, wouldn't you?" Rivas responded, his anger flaring up again.

"I mean it. It's over."

"You're telling me it's *over*?"

"Yes. Over."

"Point one, Catherine: you can't end what never began in the first instance. That's just what I've been trying to tell you. And point two, the hostage doesn't determine when something's *over*, the kidnapper does. And third, you won't keep it up. You're impulsive and undisciplined."

"Just leave me alone, okay?" She let go of his legs and got up, while checking her body for bruises and cuts. "As far as our unavoidable proximity is concerned," she continued, "I'll cooperate. Give me a few minutes and I'll be fine again. I apologize for asking why you weren't having your meals with us. We don't have to eat together, not today. Not ever. I've learned an important lesson today, Rivas. You encouraged me to be true to my passion. In the kitchen, remember? On the floor. You advised me to let myself go and to give myself up to love. I trusted you and now you despise me for it. You're the most vile hypocrite this planet has ever produced. But that's over. I feel only one thing for you now: loathing." At this point she trembled, fully expecting further blows, but when nothing happened she steadied herself quickly. "And, Rivas, I am not undisciplined. I've exercised extreme self-control over the past months. How else would I have held up? Despite this utter misery, I'm ticking like a Swiss watch. You, on the other hand, are mistaken when you think you have yourself under control. Your composure is rooted in nothing more than your lack of conscience, your coldness. You are an egomaniac, a washed out despot from a bygone century. You suffer from severe megalomania, from the sick delusion that you can re-order the world at your own ridiculous dictate. Don't lecture me on discipline. It was *my discipline* that brought me through. I even managed to overcome lying with crushed limbs in the mud of the jungle!"

"Your limbs were not crushed, and you certainly didn't pull yourself up by your own bootstraps. We fixed you up immediately. What happened in Columbia is regrettable, but stuff happens when one goes amok the way you did. You broke the rules. What were you thinking? That you were taking a leisurely hike through the Black Forest?"

"You're justifying yourself? That's something new! Are you perhaps sorry after all?"

"Sorry for what? For kidnapping a fool?"

"Maybe for ripping this fool out of her world from one moment to the next? Without any explanation! Or perhaps you could feel sorry for handing a young woman over to a mob of perverts so they could drag her across a godforsaken jungle?"

"Do you have any idea how lonely I felt?" continued Catherine, "How scared I was every day? Of being shot, of snakes and poisonous plants? Every day I expected to be my last, that my strength would expire and that they'd leave me behind and I'd end up dying like an animal. I was in pain, I was hungry, I was thirsty. I could never go to the toilet without being watched and only when I begged and begged for it. More than once I peed in my pants, because they wouldn't let me go. I couldn't wash myself or comb my hair. I couldn't stand my own stench, let alone that of my abductors. I never knew when the tea merchant would attack me again with his rod."

"What tea merchant?"

"The squat, fat guy."

"Why 'tea merchant'?"

"It doesn't matter."

"You're right, he is a pig. I'll deal with him."

"He's not half as diabolical as you! Added to that was the fear of being raped by this unpredictable horde of forest inbreeds."

"What?"

"Have you seen what these men looked like?"

"The men who took you across Columbia were transporters. They may use limited force if circumstances dictate, but they may not sexually abuse hostages. They have clear orders and they follow them, otherwise they get neither their money nor new contracts. None of our transporters has ever raped a hostage. And neither have the kidnappers in charge. They may be tempted, but they're expected to stay rational and not to abuse the situation to satisfy their sexual urges."

"Really? How was I to know that the torture was all so beautifully and ethically laid on? From my perspective I was in a byzantine abyss, leaving me bewildered and frightened. Never did anyone encourage me or give me a clue as to what was happening and where I was being taken. You all bullied me, smiling coldly. Can you imagine what it's like to be so defenseless? Men have upper body strength. If they get into trouble they can at least try to defend themselves. They don't experience helplessness in all its horror, because they can act. God knows, I tried. You heard about the results. I didn't dare expose myself to further injuries. Not in that suffocating, overpowering forest. Even worse was the waiting. Waiting for the next atrocity, waiting for what might happen and then didn't. The fear of the fear because at the very next hour everything could change. I was as tense as a race horse at the stalls. I could hardly sleep, even though I was exhausted by the daily struggle through the forest.

"I had nobody to talk to, Rivas! I had to stay quiet even though I was screaming inside. I had nothing to offer; I couldn't speak their language; I had no means of trading favors. I could only hold on to the vague, miserable hope of any little gift of mercy and pity."

Rivas lit a cigarette and offered her one. She shook her head. "And then you allowed me a couple of idyllic days on the farm, followed by the degradation in the cellar. To this day, I'm uneasy about walking across the yard, from shame of encountering those that saw me in this wretched state. Stripped down to my underwear, my face covered, tied up in a bizarre position, strangulated, disgraced and helpless, near death. And then you exposed me to this inhumane room arrest. The bare room, the dog bowl, the bucket, no change of clothes, no toiletries, hardly any food, a single daily jug of water. My eyes were permanently pinned to the door in the hope of finally, finally, being released from my prison. Then, every time you opened the door, you dashed my hopes and unleashed further malice on me. Do you know how cruel that was? Then you confused me with sweet talk before making me suffer again. Think about how you beat me up with the curb bit without any provocation whatsoever, or how you dragged me to the paddock to plunge my head into the water-trough. You called me stupid and ugly. Then I was clever again, and beautiful. What *have* you done to me? Are you not ashamed at all?" All the while Catherine had not stopped crying. She continuously wiped her nose with the back of her hand. Apart from that, she was drenched in sweat and utterly exhausted. He body ached and her soul was torn to shreds.

Rivas handed her a tissue. He put his arms around her and placed his hand on the back of her head. She was too finished to ward him off. Using both hands, he stroked her hair out of her face. "Kill me now, Rivas," she responded. "You don't need me anymore. You're only keeping me alive because you enjoy seeing me suffer. We both know it. Everyone knows it."

"Catherine, I do need you. For a long time I didn't understand why. I realized it as you were speaking. What I asked from you earlier, and everything I've done, I regret. It's over now. You were right. It *is* over. Come, get some food and then lie down. I'll take you upstairs."

"No. I know you're only employing your tried and trusted tactics. I won't let you seduce me anymore, Rivas." She tore herself away.

"Please have your dinner before you go. I don't believe you're putting even forty kilos on the scale."

"I'll eat a big breakfast tomorrow, I promise. Good night, Rivas."

"Good night Catherine. Everything will work out. Don't give up now, my girl."

--- oOo ---

Rivas lingered in his study and reflected on what happened. He realized that he was much fonder of Catherine than he cared to admit. The trigger for her revolt today had been his excessive use of force. He'd broken the rules. Pedro had tried to warn him a few weeks ago. It was the last unmistakable sign that this kidnapping was drifting further and further off course. The vessel which was supposed to bring him to his destination, had started to leak. No matter how many times he mended the holes, new leaks sprang almost every day. How could he still keep this ship afloat? More than his hostage, it was he who was under pressure. Catherine showed herself to be far more robust and extreme than the norm. Rivas, on the other hand, could no longer come to grips with his feelings for his victim. He'd had a hunch ever since the incident with the curb bit, but today he became fully conscious of what was going on. He could no longer deny that Catherine had taken over the ship. Without either of them realizing, she'd started to dictate the tone – and he'd reacted to it by using excessive violence in order to regain control. But now he'd lost his taste for this cocktail of madness. It was at the pond where he fully grasped that he no longer wanted her to die. Shortly afterwards, in the cellar, he'd started to contemplate that he had to protect her from WICED. And now - he was sure.

He sat down at his desk and lit a cigarette. After a final moment of reflection, he decisively reached for the telephone. "Rivas?" answered Maria when she saw his name on her display.

"Yeah, it's me."

"Hello, my angel. How nice to hear from you. What's up?"

"Maria, we have to talk."

"Speak. I have time."

"Not on the phone."

"Where are you?"

"On the farm."

"Do you want me to come there?"

"No. I'll come to you. Where are you?"

"On the hacienda. I'll find out if one of the WICED planes is available to fetch you."

"I'll take a scheduled flight. My visit must stay between us."

"But that's much too complicated."

"I need the break. It'll give me a chance to think. Andalus will take me down to the valley and I'll spend the night with Bertoli. From there I'll take the car to Chachapoyas and I'll fly to Lima from there, and then on to Buenos Aires."

"What an unnecessary trip around the world. Then we'll only see each other the day after next. But okay, if that's what you want! I'll fetch you from the airport."

"Not necessary."

"As you wish. Rivas, whatever news you'll bring me, I love you. Remember that."

32.
Argentina, September 12

As soon as Rivas pulled up the driveway in his hired car, the housekeeper Sophia flung the front door open. She rushed out, smiling, to greet him: "*Buenas tardes Señor*! The Señora is expecting you, but she was needed down by the stables. Esperanza foaled last night and she's not doing well. Señor Veterinario is with her. I'll call Sancho, he'll take you down in the golf cart."

"Thanks Sophia, I can still find my way to the stables." Rivas dismissed her and put pedal to metal for about three hundred yards, across immaculately kept lawns. There he met Maria and the vet, in front of the block where the mares were stabled.

"Oh, Rivas! Come here, give me a hug!"

Rivas greeted Maria and then shook hands with the vet. "Hello Pablo. How's Esperanza?"

"*Mucho mejor*. She just gave us a little scare," replied the vet – a man whom Rivas had known for most of his life. "Well, I must be off."

"Take a look at the foal," said Maria. "I'll see Pablo off." Maria and the vet left in another golf cart, while Rivas went to examine the snow-white mare and her newborn. He was patting them both when Maria dashed back, eager to greet him properly. "Let me take a look at you!" she exclaimed. She was turned out as if she'd just stepped out of a Hollywood movie. The long-legged woman wore a pair of camel colored casual mock riding pants made of the finest calf leather, adorned with a thin leather belt that had a silver clasp in the shape of a snaffle bit. Her pants were elegantly tucked into high-heeled equestrian-style burgundy boots. These were complemented by a matching riding hat made of felt. She'd casually thrown a velour leather jacket over her shoulders, which partly covered her long-sleeved cotton sweater with a convoluted pattern in earthy colors. The entire outfit was by Hermès and a testament to her discerning fashion sense. This sense she now turned to Rivas, appraising him closely, but her immediate impression was "You look tired." She put great store on appearances, especially when it came to Rivas, but she was astute enough to detect his travel-weariness. He answered by embracing her once more, and then gesturing at the horses.

"Aren't they beautiful?" she said.

"A newborn foal is always a miracle," he agreed, and looked at Esperanza with kind eyes. "Clever girl." He gently patted her shoulder. "Do you have a name for her daughter yet?"

"You just gave it to me."

"Clever girl? I meant Esperanza."

"No. Maravilla."

"Miracle! Yes, that fits," he approved, gazing at the foal, tilting his head to get a look from another angle.

"Splendid. Maravilla it is! Come, we'll take a walk up to the house."

"I've got the car here."

"Yes I saw it. You know you're not supposed to jaunt across the lawn!"

He shrugged her protest away, laughing. "You've been telling me that ever since you bought me my first motorcycle."

"And you still don't listen!"

"Neither do you. I've been telling you for almost as long, that you need a driveway up to this stable block. That little bridle path is totally inadequate."

"I want to preserve this part of the hacienda for the mares and foals. But, if you insist! Next time you stay a bit longer, I'll let the workers come and you can take care of it yourself. You'll inherit everything one day anyway."

"Please don't start again," groaned Rivas. "With my current lifestyle you'll probably survive me by decades."

"Don't talk like that!" She quickly crossed her breast to ward off any evil spirits he may have invoked. "It's sinful to even think like that, never mind speak it aloud. Come, we'll walk anyway. Leave the key in the car. Sancho will fetch it presently."

They made their way to the stately mansion, which Maria occupied with her staff. They entered the drawing room, which was elegant and richly furnished. Heirlooms mainly, Rivas knew, including some highly valuable antiques that went back as far as the sixteenth century – the early years of Spanish colonial settlement. "Please, sit down."

Sophia, Maria's attentive housekeeper, hurried in. "Señora?"

"Sophia, please make us some tea," and turning to Rivas, "You will have some, won't you? Or would you like something else?"

"Tea sounds good, thank you."

"Are you hungry?"

"Later."

Sophia scurried away.

"What's on your mind? I can tell you're not in good shape. Is this about Catherine again?"

"Yes."

"You know, we actually don't need her anymore. She was right on target with her Ruckebier. We'll interview him ourselves and after that we would have taken over anyway. I'd like to have kept her on in case we need a back-up candidate, but I checked up on Ruckebier's background and I'm pretty sure he'll accept. His profile couldn't be more perfect. Rivas, you can dispose of her."

"Maria, do you sometimes have doubts about our mission?"

"Do you?"

"Can we still tell the difference between right and wrong? Why don't we look for alternative solutions? Why don't we even consider non-violent means? Rational negotiation, mutual respect, tolerance and consideration?"

"Good heavens, Rivas! What naïve thinking is this? What happened? Is this the latest bit of philosophy that the *Cat's* dragged home?"

"Maria, I'm going to disappoint you," Rivas replied. He ignored her dig at Catherine.

"How?"

"I can't control Catherine anymore."

"Whatever do you mean? Is she no longer tractable? Or are you saying that you don't have a grip on yourself anymore as far as she's concerned? There's a big difference."

"The latter. I don't want to brutalize her anymore. I don't want to deprive her anymore. I don't want to beat her, lock her up, confuse her and lie to her anymore. These past months she's had to endure just too much. One day I carry her in my hands like a goddess and the next I treat her like a slut, as if I want to take revenge on her for something. How can she even function anymore?"

Maria was puzzled. "But this is how it is, Rivas We *want* her confused!"

"Why does it have to be like this?"

"You're asking *me*?"

"She stopped resisting a long time ago. Why continue then with the usual program?"

"The 'usual program' has proven itself infallible. You of all people should know that."

"Not with her."

"I see. I'm sorry that she's causing you so much grief. That's why I said, get rid of her."

"Maria, what I'm really concerned about is that I seem even more unstrung than she is. The constant, unjustified punitive phases put me in an adrenalin and testosterone rush and switch off my brain. That's never happened to me before. It's as if, just because it's become so hard for me to hurt her, I'm even more heartless than intended. The boundaries are blurring. It's become virtually impossible for me to play this inhumane game with her. I manage only by imagining her to be some hapless victim. And then, once I get started, something abysmal in me takes over the rudder and I lose command over my own actions. The last time I was intimate with her, I almost choked her into unconsciousness. I only realized it when she stopped fighting for air. After that I avoided her completely, until the day before yesterday and then the moment I was with her, I became overwrought again. But at least I finally figured out why I behave the way I do. I avoid being close to her from fear that I'll kill her out of pure passion. It's hard to explain, but I suppose I resent the fact that she's with me only because we're forcing her to be. For me, Maria, she stopped being merely an instrument long ago."

"Oh no, Rivas! You've fallen in love? I always asked myself who'd come after Chand, but surely not this little red-head? How could she ever fill Chand's shoes? Chand is educated, has a perfect figure and a face as if chiseled by Michael Angelo himself. And she's a successful professional!"

Catherine, Rivas reflected, could not fill Chand's shoes because her own shoes were already the perfect fit. And not only could she keep up with his ex-girlfriend in every way, she was also a much stronger personality. But his thoughts went unexpressed because he didn't see the need to defend Catherine in front of Maria. Besides which, this line of argument was not factual enough for him, so he reasoned more objectively. "Catherine knows who I am, contrary to Chand, with whom I had to lead a double life. I introduced Chand to someone from WICED only once – apart from you, of course. To Miguel. And it didn't take long for him to let something slip and I spent the rest of the evening inventing excuses. Do you know how strenuous that is? Nobody can uphold a lasting relationship based on lies. I don't have to hide anything from Catherine. She knows what I'm up to. That's why" – Rivas returned to his original purpose - "I can hardly sleep at night. And if I do, I have this recurring dream: *I'm riding with her – she's tied up – into a forest. At a clearing, I help her off her horse, am undecided. Then I hear a shot being fired and she falls down. Dead.* When I wake up I feel dirty and weak. Sometimes I feel like I'm bursting. More and more often I have to leave the *finca*, because I either melt by merely looking at her or I half kill her from being so angry with myself. I can't carry on, Maria. The day before yesterday she was lying on the ground, completely crushed, and I didn't stop hitting her – simply because she refused to satisfy my perverted need for affirmation. I couldn't stop myself. She may not have survived, if she hadn't found the right words to bring me back to my senses. Luckily she managed to do that. I cannot dose my brutality anymore, and I'm no longer the right man for this job. I've decided to put an end to it. I've sworn to myself never to hurt her again. I merely want to protect her."

"Good-evil, addiction-restraint, passion-murder, love-hate exist in close proximity to each other. You love her?"

"More than my life."

"Does she make you happy?"

"To tell you the truth, it's more like she makes me unhappy."

"That is happiness, my boy. Believe me, I know what I'm talking about."

"You understand?"

"Very much so."

"Then you'll also know why this type of relationship doesn't satisfy me anymore. She fascinated me from the start, but I just couldn't categorize my feelings – I'd never felt like that before. Maria, I hate the fact that her affection towards me is merely the result of our psychological manipulation. She believes she loves me, but she's way too self-sacrificing. Although she drew the line and terminated our relationship, I know she won't be able to follow through on it."

"A hostage who draws the line? Are you insane?"

Rivas's face lit up briefly at the thought of his unconventional prisoner. He decided not to respond to her objection. "She doesn't know it, but she's desperately fighting for survival. Even her death wish is driven by nothing more than the will to survive, if you get the paradox. I know now that I want more from her. She interpreted my cadenza as sexual, and it was, but it was more than that. I want her to love me. Really. Not because I tricked her into it. Now it is I, who depends on *her* affection. That's my punishment. The proverbial irony of life. Maria, I've completely messed this up. I'm endangering all of you. If the mission is aborted because I…."

"Nothing will be aborted. We just have to rethink the whole thing."

"You forgive me?"

"There's nothing to forgive and you didn't disappoint me. Rivas, *it is, what it is*. No use arguing with reality. I'm surprised that you lasted this long. You know, Rivas, what happened between you and Catherine renders one powerless. We'll forge a new plan. Do you have the code, so that we can use the data in the future?"

"That's not the problem. She'll carry on decoding until the database is exhausted. She promised me."

"Her promises mean nothing."

"In her case they do." He told Maria about the events at the pond and Catherine's oath to cooperate, which she hadn't broken since.

Maria was incensed. "Rivas, how could you let her live? She wanted to kill you!" She took a deep breath. "Oh, I see. That's why you're so fond of her. Because she didn't, as was to be expected, lose her nerve at the last minute. This sort of thing has always impressed you. Just like César's stubbornness."

"Yes, she's unusual. The world needs decisive, courageous characters like her, instead of the millions of oxygen thieves without guts or purpose."

"My, you're really very angry with the world. And I would tend to agree with you, were it not for the fact that she and us are fighting on opposite sides. But that's not the real reason for your partiality."

"Oh yeah?"

"It runs much deeper than that. She's like you. By loving her, you're loving yourself. To kill her in the cellar would have been pure self-execution. That's why you spared her. By saving her, you saved yourself."

"An interesting analysis. But whatever my motive, I want her to regain her self-will and to start making her own decisions again, at least as far as possible under the circumstances."

"What about the sex?"

"What about it?"

"Well, as far as I can recall you mentioned a certain," she said haltingly, "insufficiency in this regard."

"Success is shy – it won't come out while you're watching."

"Huh?"

"Tennessee Williams."

"Still don't get it."

"You'll work it out."

"Well, I think it's time to meet this Catherine. I'll make the arrangements."

"No!"

"No?"

"Leave her alone, Maria. I'll kill every one of your men that even comes near her. There'll be no time for explanations."

"Don't threaten me. It's not necessary. Nobody will harm her."

"Promise me."

"I promise."

"Really? That's not our norm. We always dispose of hostages after a mission, or if they cause trouble. And believe me, with or without me, Catherine Zitgow is the epitome of trouble."

"Rivas, I swear. I can see how much she means to you. Have I ever lied to you?"

"Father Christmas, Easter Bunny, Stork."

"Touché!"

"No, you never seriously lied to me."

"She's an exception. Look, this woman has turned your worldview upside down. In a very short time she managed to plant seeds of doubt in a matter which has dominated your life for almost two decades. I want to meet her. She interests me. And, I have to gain a clearer picture of the situation, in order to reshuffle our plan."

"Deep down, I was expecting you to help me, but what about WICED? Carlos won't play along."

"Leave Carlos to me."

"And the sponsors? Maria, please help me to protect her."

"I've assured you twice. What is it? Do you want it signed in blood?"

"Sorry, but she's in a precarious position. Surely you understand that?"

"Yes, she's messing us around and that's dangerous, but everything will work out. Don't lose your nerve now."

"Maria, please tell Carlos she's done nothing wrong."

Maria was both moved and disconcerted to see Rivas beg for something for the first time in his adult life. She decided to set some boundaries. "Nobody's ever completely free of responsibility. Much of her dilemma, she's caused herself. Just think about these irritating escape attempts."

"You don't know her. She's got fighting spirit. Because her active resistance failed, she wrestles on with subconscious skill, even though her situation is in essence hopeless. She's structured her day in order to invent some state of normality. She pretends to be going to work every day and behaves as if we're a couple and the farm was our home. But she'll never sympathize with us. That will not happen." He shook his head. "In any case, she didn't destroy my world view. She brought me back to reality by forcing me to choose between right and wrong."

"It's called conscience, Rivas."

"Correct. She's activated my conscience and the courage to search for alternatives. She's motivated me to turn around. My world is not broken. It's in the process of being reshaped. But my security has vanished. I feel helpless and unsure of myself. I'm scared of the future, for her, for me, even for you. Breaking out and turnaround takes courage, but my 'courage' has an extremely frightening feel to it."

"You've told her already?"

"No. I wanted to talk to you first, but I'm getting her out of there, one way or another."

"You'll find a way and I'll be by your side whenever you need me."

"I need you now."

"There may be a way," she replied, contemplating various options.

"What are you thinking about?"

"Let me handle this. It'll all work out and you have my blessing. Is she ready for Paris?"

"Soon. We need passport photos and fingerprints."

"I'll organize the forger and the flights. It'll only take a couple of days and we're well within schedule. I'll meet her in Paris then. Oh, here comes our tea! Rivas, do what you think is right and prepare Catherine for her role in Paris. Does she look professional enough now? How is her weight? Her hair? Her complexion? How can I help?"

Rivas fended off Maria's interference. "She looks magnificent."

"Good. I'll take care of the Camargue."

"Maria, I won't let her anywhere near the Camargue."

"That's why I said I'll take care of it. Come on, trust me a little now. Let's change the topic. I do want to have a bit of you, after all. You're staying a few days, right?"

"I didn't plan to. I brought nothing with me. And anyway, Andalus is staying with Bertoli. I need to get him home."

"Don't worry about César. I'll call Bertoli and tell him you've been delayed. It'll do you good to have a civilized meal again and you've never had to worry about clothes to wear when you're with me, right?"

"Have you been shopping again?"

"And how!" Maria gushed and was about to call Sophia, who beat her to it when she appeared as if by magic. "And everything else you need, we'll organize, too."

"Señora?"

"Sophia, please get Señor's room ready."

"It's always ready, Señora," she interjected shyly.

"Nonsense! Change the sheets!"

"The bedding is always fresh, Señora," persisted Sophia, with a mild gesture of indignant pride.

"Do it anyway. Air the room, put flowers in the vase, freshen up the duvet and pillows, restock the bar, make sure there's ice. Do I have to list each task separately? And bring me the shopping from yesterday."

Maria tapped imperiously on the arm of her chair, Sophia let out a candid sigh, and Rivas squirmed – he felt as if he was regressing into the role of a child in the presence of a domineering mother. Yet again he pondered on his inability to set boundaries with her.

Sophia, recovering her dutiful expression, asked, "All of the parcels, Señora?"

"Only the bags from La Martina, Prada and Yves Saint Laurent. Oh yes, and the little box from Jaeger-LeCoultre. And the two parcels from Italy - they're in Señor's bedroom. Please fetch those as well." Sophia trudged away and Maria turned to Rivas. "I'm attending a polo match tomorrow. Do you feel like a chukka or two? You could take my place."

"Whom are you taking?"

"You don't know him. Chestnut thoroughbred, eight, brand new. Regalo. You'll like him. And Breva of course."

"Maybe. We'll see."

Sophia resurfaced with the parcels and a pair of scissors, and Maria eagerly unpacked the goods: a white tight T-shirt and an elegant black pair of pants with folds, casually cut. It came with a black leather belt. "You see, that's nice and comfortable," she announced in motherly fashion, while holding up the items. "Now you can have a shower and then you'll rest a bit and get changed. You must be completely exhausted. When are the Peruvians going to build some roads in the highlands?"

"That's why we're up there, Maria," he reminded her, and he reflected on Catherine's hard trek through the Amazon basin compared with the relatively decent roads of the Peruvian Andes which Maria had just criticized.

Maria didn't respond. She was preoccupied with the parcels. She pulled a pair of leather sneakers from the next bag and put them down on the couch next to Rivas. Then she reached for the scissors and opened the parcels from Italy. The first one was from A. Testoni, Milano, a famous supplier of made-to-order men's shirts and suits. She pulled out two handmade shirts. "I hope the measurements are still correct." She tilted her head and scrutinized Rivas's body.

"Maria, I've got more shirts than I could wear in a lifetime." Again, his thoughts wandered to Catherine and how cute she'd look in these two new ones.

"The likes of us have to be perfectly tailored. We don't want to look like *cartoneros* now, do we?" Then she sliced open the parcel from Alessandro Berlutti, also from Milano. This manufacturer's shoes were individually crafted to each customer's foot shape and size from the finest exotic leathers. She retrieved one such pair, together with a matching belt. "And here, you can wear this for your polo match tomorrow," she gloated. She tore impatiently at a compact little box which contained a reverso watch, especially constructed for polo players. This watch is reversible, with the display pointing inwards towards the wrist, protecting the glass against damage during sports events. Nowadays the glass was shatterproof, but the reversible polo watch was part of the game's tradition.

Rivas took off his watch and strapped on the Jaeger-LeCoultre. "Thanks, Maria." He'd long given up protesting against her generosity. It was, at times, overbearing – but his acquiescence to Maria wasn't about lack of self-assertion. He knew how much she loved shopping for him – in giving to him, she was giving to herself. The watch that he'd just taken off was one of the world's most expensive men's chronometers. Over the years, Maria had equipped him with a unique collection of Limited Edition Vacherin Constantin watches. Next she presented him with two polo shirts tailored by the undisputed leader among competitive polo outfitters, the Argentinian brand La Martina. And lastly, she handed him a gaucho belt. These belts, decorated with traditional Argentinian weave patterns, were worn for polo and gaucho matches.

Maria inspected the items on the couch and pronounced herself satisfied. "*Sí, muy elegante.*" She turned to Rivas for confirmation. "And, do you like the things?" She fished for his approval, while she stroked to one side the raven black hair that fell over his forehead. Looking at it critically, she now decreed: "We'll have to fix your hair while you're here. I know you like it like this, but I can't even see your eyes. This handsome face, all covered up!"

"The things are great, Maria, thank you." He bent forward to give her a kiss on the cheek while he rearranged his hair to its original look. Like most men, Rivas hated it when a woman fiddled with his hair, rearranging it.

"Are you going to wear the things?"

"Oh yes! They'll be worn at the very first opportunity." By Catherine, he thought mischievously. If Maria knew that he preferred Catherine in one of his men's shirts, instead of in something from Maria's glamorous lady's collection! But he couldn't resist teasing her. He said, "Especially that beige-pink one – it'll look very fetching on Catherine."

"Catherine? What do you mean?"

"Oh, she wears all my shirts. Didn't I mention that?"

"*Santa Maria!*" she exclaimed, as expected, crossing her breast again at the thought of a young lady in men's shirts, and five sizes too large at that. For Maria this was almost as big a sacrilege as conjuring up a premature death. Suddenly she put on an animated face. "Ah! If I'd known that! I'll have to ask Sancho to drive me to town. Chanel has have some truly exquisite pieces in a masculine style. The Mademoiselle Coco look from the nineteen thirties. Do you know what I mean?"

Now it was Rivas who frowned. "Please don't. How am I supposed to drag all that stuff over to France? She'll want to take everything with her."

"Very well!" she laughed. "You got me there. But seriously now, she wears your shirts?"

"Yes, she likes it. And so do I."

"Was it your idea? I mean, she wouldn't have dreamed this up herself, I hope?"

"At first it was part of the strategy and then we stayed with it."

"What will you think of next? Oh well. How is my *campeón*?" she enquired about Andalus. Is my little *galitto*, behaving himself?"

"Your little César thinks he's Catherine's hero as well now, the show-off."

"She rides Andalus? Maria gaped at Rivas and forgot for a moment that she refused to call César by his nickname as a matter of principle. She was of the opinion that pet names were unfitting for such a valuable stallion as him. "I knew that he was part of the plan to impress her and draw her in, but does she really ride him?"

"And not too shabbily," Rivas responded, not without pride.

"She wears your shirts! Rides your best horse! I'm starting to comprehend," remarked Maria, and she took a contemplative sip of tea.

Smokes my cigarettes, drinks my bourbon, sleeps in my bed, captures my heart, Rivas added to himself.

33.
Peru, September 12

While Rivas was away, Catherine's zest for life returned. First of all, her renewed optimism brought back her appetite. She made regular between-meals trips to the kitchen for snacks. Returning from one such snack, the house deserted, she felt the compulsion to snoop around on Rivas's desk.

Rivas had warned her that her work telephone was being tapped, and she assumed that all the numbers she dialed were being registered and that many of her calls were recorded. That's why she never considered calling for help this way. Neither did she dare send an SOS via the contact form of a random website. First, people would surely assume they were dealing with a crank and second, how would she explain why she'd called up the contact page of that particular site. By means of simple spyware WICED would be able to trace every one of her mouse clicks. Essentially, though, she'd promised to cause Rivas no more trouble – and she kept that promise. Her urge to flee had subsided in any case. Close now to the end of the mission, she was more concerned about facing the world without Rivas, than about running away from him. To have a quick look around his desk, however, felt okay to her. She justified her curiosity by telling herself that she wouldn't abuse whatever information she discovered, and thus fortified in her conscience she went about her clandestine mission. She rummaged through the shelves and drawers of his study but unearthed nothing of significance. Combing his bedroom would have been in vain – other than men's couture she'd found nothing the day she cleaned up there. Besides, if he wanted to hide something, he would lock his room. Thus she rationalized away this strong temptation.

Six days he'd been away, and she'd begun to seriously miss him. She felt completely lost without him. She confessed to herself that he'd been right when he predicted that her emotional boycott wouldn't last. After finishing her work for the day, she retired to her room and started a new book. *Berlin, Alexander Square* by Alfred Döblin. To her regret, only the English translation had been laid out for her.

At around half past eleven in the evening, she heard someone knock on her door. She jumped up in anticipation, but it was Joe, not Rivas who stood in front of her. "Rivas wants to see you downstairs."

"He's back? Why doesn't he come up?"

"Don't know."

She felt uneasy, because whenever Rivas summoned her, something unpleasant usually followed. Nevertheless, she looked forward to seeing him. Hurriedly, she slipped into a shiny blue Versace mini dress with a slit on the side, and into high-heeled sandals with sexy cross-over ankle thongs. She fixed her hair, refreshed her makeup and went downstairs.

Rivas, still dusty from the long journey, sat at his desk, making a phone call in French. She perched herself onto the corner of his desk, letting her legs dangle, and wondered who he was talking to by long-distance. She understood even less French than Spanish but she enjoyed listening to him, while observing with glee that the slit in her dress revealed her shapely leg, and how it briefly caught his eye.

"Hello," he said, after putting down the phone.

She couldn't read his mood. "Hello Rivas. Did you bring me something?" she asked, wired up. "I missed you. I've finished the list with all the other contacts. I can hardly believe it myself – I managed to untie all the knots and now you've got all my father's contacts at your disposal. Not just those concerning our case, but all of them, just like you wanted. There're only two left, which I just can't seem to crack, but I haven't given up yet." He didn't reply, so she asked, "Aren't you happy about that?" What she really wanted to know was where he'd been all this time, but she feared that this would be one question too many.

"No, that's great. Well done, Catherine!"

"What can I do for you? You wanted to see me?"

"Catherine, what were you doing at my desk?"

"What would I have done at your desk?"

"Didn't I just ask you that?"

"I don't know what you're talking about!"

"Are you trying to tell me you didn't dig around in my drawers?"

"Of course not! I know very well that you always lock everything away in your safe."

"Are you lying to me again, Catherine?"

"I'm not lying," she lied.

"Catherine!"

She sighed. It was, as always, hopeless. "How do you know?"

"That wasn't hard to figure out. I hope the loot is worth the consequences."

"I didn't look for anything specific. I was bored, that's all. What do you mean by 'consequences'? After all, no harm was done. Are you going to punish me for that?"

"Is that what you want?" Rivas sounded tired.

A red-hot fire, fuelled alternately by defiance and surrender, flickered in her eyes. How did he always know what was going on inside her, she wondered.

He heard her silent reply. "You're asking me to punish you?"

"It depends how."

"Whatever it is, it'll hurt."

"I know."

"You're seriously provoking people to hurt you?"

"Not people. You."

"Why do you want me to hurt you?"

Catherine held the situation by keeping up intense eye contact. Then she replied with a firm voice, "You know why, Rivas."

"Fill me in."

"May I take a detour?"

"Go ahead. I'm keen to know what's going through your pretty little head this time."

"On my bookshelf, there's a booklet with quotes by Hermann Hesse."

"I know. I was the one who had it put there for you."

"You selected the literature in my room specifically for me?" she asked, distracted from the topic. "I thought they came with the house. I mean, they're not exactly new."

"We tailored the selection specifically to your taste. Didn't you notice most of them were from German authors? And secondhand books are much more quaint than new ones, are they not?"

"You wanted me to be comfortable," she remarked, touched. Rivas took a deep breath but didn't answer. Catherine continued: "The little Hesse book is so valuable to me that I permit myself only one quote per day. This morning I read, 'Love does not exist in order to make us happy. I believe it exists to show us how strong we are through our suffering'. What I'm trying to say, is that it's through my suffering that I feel closest to you. Because it makes me realize how wholly I can love you. Without any expectation of receiving anything in return. Just love flowing from me to you." Catherine beamed at him. "If only you knew how much I adore you. You'll never feel closer to anyone than the closeness I feel to you when you hurt me."

"I can't imagine that Hermann Hesse meant we must create suffering on purpose to conjure up feelings of love."

"You don't understand me." She was disappointed.

He strode over to the green leather couch and patted the back of it. "Catherine, come, sit down." Expectantly, she sank into the upholstery, while he went to the door and bolted it. She thought it unnecessary to lock the door; nobody would have disturbed them at this late hour. It was now almost midnight. The ceiling fan, which was actually not needed on this cool evening, moaned peacefully and dispensed moving shadows across the room. "Catherine, I understand you very well. You're borrowing the quote in an attempt to master your situation somehow; but I won't hurt you anymore, at least not on purpose."

"Didn't I just tell you, I don't mind? I've accepted that there can be no relationship with Rivas, without pain. I can endure it, and I will."

"Now you're dressing up your pain as a virtue. That's not necessary. It's over, Catherine."

"You're letting me go? Why now?"

"Not yet."

Catherine tried to understand, but comprehended *nothing*. "You see! I'm still reeling from your last beating and already you tie me up in a new painful game. But very well then. I'll play along."

Rivas looked at her. Her confusion tugged at his conscience. "Whom do you love, Catherine? he asked, in a sudden change of direction.

"What do you mean? I just told you."

"Whom do you love?" he repeated. He'd asked her this question before. Then, he'd done so with manipulative intent. Now, the question surfaced out of an inexplicable wave of emotion, which engulfed him entirely. "This time I need to know. Whom do you love?"

"You. You, Rivas."

"Tell me again, whom you love. Tell me."

"You know I love you."

"Say it again," he demanded, his eyes screwed closed, hardly able to wait for confirmation.

"I love you."

"Again."

"I love you."

"What about the man in your fantasy?"

"What?"

"The man you fantasized about in the kitchen. You like him."

"He means nothing."

"I'll find him and kill him right before your eyes."

"He doesn't exist."

"Swear it."

"I swear."

I've forced her to commit perjury for the first time in her life, he noted - without regret.

"Rivas, I love only you. There's only you."

Rivas had no plan. The hunter had turned to prey. She'd struck him down like a stag - with a single bullet, aimed straight at the heart. He was overwhelmed by the intensity of his longing for her. He felt his blood pulsate. Passion welled up and whirled around his head until the aching desire pushed his blood into his groin – with such vehement force that he felt the urge to leave the room. Without saying a word he staggered to the door like a drunk, unbolted it and went outside. He hoped to come back to his senses in the fresh air of the cool night. Then his legs turned around and marched him back to Catherine. He put his arms under her and with great impetus he picked her up from the couch and carried her to his room. He put her down on his bed and sat down next to her. For a long time, nobody spoke.

Catherine lay there. Eyes closed. In love.

Not only in him. She also loved her deep love for him. Without words he'd erased her last skepticism. She was no longer a thing, but a woman and a friend. Shrouded in a pink cloud, she was gripped by a pan-galactic force that bundled up all her feelings and thoughts and carried her off into the land of euphoria.

Rivas popped her love bubble: "Catherine, I want to talk to you about what happened between us a few days ago."

She opened her eyes and sat up. "I'm so sorry. Really. I said terrible things. Please forgive me. Just forget them." The pink cloud drifted off.

"I don't want to forget it, because what you said was true. I've been treating you despicably. I found it hard to remain objective towards you, but that's over now."

"No! Please don't be objective." She saw herself morph back into a "thing". "Nothing must change." The remaining pink vapor of happiness was dissipating.

"Listen to me, Catherine. The real suffering I caused you, you cannot even fathom now, but it will catch up with you. I manipulated you the whole time, to get you give up your own will and to succumb to my plan."

"I know all that, but…"

"I navigated your emotions to and fro, left and right, wherever I wanted and needed them - at will. And used your confusion to my advantage. The destruction of your psyche is more serious than the physical damage, and much harder to heal. A lot of what I did to you is irreparable, but what I can make right, I will. You'll be happy again."

"But I am happy! More than ever."

"What you interpret as happiness, is dependency, a primal drive for safety and the known. What you prophesied the day I beat you up with Andalus's bit - that I would experience bitter regret and shame one day - has happened. I can't turn back time, but from now on you have nothing to fear. I'll never touch you again, unless you want me to. I'll never manipulate you, or try to retrain you, and I won't lie to you anymore."

Catherine began to sob. He took her face into his hands and wiped away her tears. "May I hold you?" She was too dissolved in tears to be able to answer. So he let go of her as promised. "Wait, I have something that belongs to you." He bent over and reached into his bedside drawer to retrieve her wrist watch, and he handed it to her. It had definitely not been in the drawer the day she cleaned up there.

"My Rolex!" Catherine briefly closed her eyes. She put one hand over her open mouth and the other on her cheek, before stroking the watch like it was a kitten. "Oh, Rivas! The doctor got it to you and you kept it for me? I thought I'd never see it again. They let me keep it for so long and when the man eventually took it away from me, the loss was all the more painful. It was a very emotional purchase, you know. I bought it years ago from my first commission check as a reward for my first really big placement. I actually didn't like it much at first because it always loses time. For a long time I couldn't accept that such an expensive watch could not keep accurate time and I kept taking it in to be adjusted, until I gave up on it. They told me that I don't move my wrists enough for the kinetic mechanism. I wore it mostly for travelling and riding as the glass is so robust. And look, it's not scratched at all, even though I scraped it against the wall of the shaft when I escaped from the compound."

Catherine's extensive description of her relationship with her watch moved him. "Tell me how you managed to escape through the well," he asked. Rivas longed for a shower and sleep, but he took her cue, helping her into the means to begin processing her abduction.

"Do you really want to know?"

"I do. Come on, I'll make us a *mate*, while I listen."

Already on their way to the kitchen, there was no holding her back. She drowned herself in her own torrent of words. "So one evening we arrived at this camp and I had to lie down immediately because they switched off the lights. The next morning I woke up on a thin, torn horsehair mattress. It was so comfortable after the jungle that I wasn't disgusted by it. They'd untied my hands and it was the first time I could sleep without being restricted. I had such a heavenly sleep. The next morning I was allowed outside. There were two long wooden tables with equally long benches on either side...."

"I know this camp, I've sat at these tables myself."

"I drank some weak black coffee and wolfed down some chewy white bread. Not bad actually. After breakfast one of the men gave me a change of clothes and also a small chunk of laundry soap, which I used for my body as well as my clothes. And they gave me a towel and a few sheets of newspaper, and showed me how to crunch up the newspaper to make it pliable for toilet use. I asked for a comb but that fell on deaf ears, because either the men didn't know what I meant or didn't want to know. Then they left me to roam around the inner court and the adjacent buildings. Well, that was my first day. Do you really want to know all these details?"

"Of course." While the water was boiling, Rivas placed the tea leaves into the pot and put out the cups.

"My Rolex," she eagerly continued, "they left untouched."

"We're not thieves."

"Oh yeah?" She intended to rebut but since his comment defied all logic, Catherine let it go. "Anyway, it was great to be able to tell the time. It felt comforting. I cannot describe how important the least little bit of information was to me. Perhaps there were one or two hours' time difference with Miami but the time on my watch seemed to correspond pretty much with routine in the camp. Still, I was very careful to always hide it under my sleeve. I didn't want to draw their attention to this valuable item by looking at it when they were watching me. They couldn't have missed Warner's engagement ring, but they didn't seem interested in it. The huge diamond was nothing but a bother in those primitive conditions, but I was glad to have an object with which to trade or bribe, in case I needed to. I was sure I'd be able to put it to good use, since I didn't know what this abduction was all about."

"That was smart."

"But in any case, they didn't pay much attention to me and I welcomed everything they gave me. The water, the soap, everything was a precious gift. I was grateful for every meal and I tried to always stay calm."

"Well done."

"There seemed to be a bit of friction going on among the men from time to time, though I never really understood what triggered it. I was just glad not to be treated like an animal anymore but I hadn't forgotten that you'd prepared me for an onward journey on foot. The meals were meagre and apart from the uncertainty, I was always hungry. The men, too, seemed under-catered for. I couldn't find another explanation for their volatile behavior. I guess there were about thirty of them. They were difficult to count as they were constantly moving around and somehow they all looked the same. They all wore military uniform and were armed with machine guns. Only in their private quarters, I occasionally saw them unarmed. It kept me in a state of permanent dread."

"I'm sure, it must have been frightening."

"One morning I started to speculate about how Germany, South Africa, the States or Columbia would try to free me. The mood in the camp was almost unbearable that day. Everyone seemed tense and nervous. The camaraderie among them often swung from one moment to the next. On this day they seemed particularly irritated and in conflict with one another."

"The conditions there are terrible. Everyone fights for survival. Everything's scarce and people start to fight for scraps. Everyone longs for home."

"Yes, that's the impression I got too. But there was one kind man, who shared his food with me and exchanged a few kind words with me every day. On this unsettling morning, he indirectly pointed out a means of escape. Will he get into trouble now?"

"No. Carry on."

"Really?"

"Catherine, I don't know who he is, besides – I can understand why he wanted to help you. You're really gorgeous."

"You're so sweet."

"Still, he shouldn't have endangered you. That was foolish of him."

"He wanted to help me!"

"*¡Está bien!* Carry on."

"He left me to myself, I think to facilitate my get-away, because at that moment, there was nobody nearby. I was at the well at the center of the courtyard. I was drawing up some water to do my laundry. They had tap water from a borehole inside the quarters, but I wasn't allowed to do my washing there. Anyway, I spotted a hole in the wall of the well, which was stuffed with what looked like loose bricks. This, I guessed, is what the man had been trying to show me before he left. I bent over the rim of the well to pull out the first brick. Because it was easy to remove, I carried on until they were too deep for me to be able to reach them. I climbed down a rusty steel ladder which was mounted to the inside wall of the well and peeped inside the shaft to gauge if I could get through it. It was so narrow that I was about to give up, and then my brain seemed to clear. For many days I'd been held captive, but now for the first time I saw an opportunity to regain my freedom. You know, if you want to reach a goal, you can't get there by being passive. You always have to plan, act, and drive forward. Only chaos happens by itself."

"You're preaching to the converted."

"I climbed into the shaft. It was difficult, but I got the entire length of my body inside it. I leopard-crawled deeper into the musty shaft and then backwards again with each new brick, which I threw into the water of the well. Then forward again up to the next brick. The further I progressed, the more suffocating the shaft became. I felt so trapped. But after a while, the shaft was free of obstacles and it wasn't long before I saw the proverbial light at the end of the tunnel." Rivas poured the tea and handed her a cup. "Thanks. So eventually I got to the exit of the shaft and looked with my face down into another well – and above me extended the blue sky. The sunlight hurt my eyes. I can feel it now!"

"In your eyes?"

"Yes. And the sense of freedom! Illusion, rather. I climbed up the iron ladder and I heaved myself over the rim only to find that I was still inside the compound, although this seemed to be an unoccupied part of the camp."

"I would have been surprised if it'd been that easy."

"Actually, it was easy, when I think about it now. But at the time, I was disappointed – there was no way out. I had to get back before they discovered my disappearance."

"You were very brave."

"What would they have done to me, if they caught me?"

"They would have called me."

"And then?"

"You know what happened. I mean, you did manage to escape but you didn't get very far."

"Yes, there was this short guy, the tea merchant, and he beat me 'til I was unconscious."

"He beat you 'til you were unconscious?"

"He punched me full in the face. Eventually I passed out. Did you hear about it?"

"Yes. I was annoyed about the complications, but I thought you were courageous."

"Actually it was my fear, not my courage that prevented me from going back in the end." She put the cup of steaming tea to her lips, but put it down immediately - it was too hot. "I was clueless about what to do. Forward? Back? I was stuck but I thought if I go back, they would torture me or execute me, or both."

"They wouldn't have, but carry on. What happened next?"

"I forced myself to get up and look for cover until I had a plan. I ran across the yard into one of the deserted buildings and hid there for a while. But knowing that they'd eventually catch up with me, I had no option but to get back into the shaft and carry on crawling into the unknown, from the other side of the well this time. But as I was squeezing myself through the tunnel, I faced another unexpected challenge. I got gripped by claustrophobia and I struggled to breathe. So I talked to myself like we talk to fearful horses. We drive them forward when they want to run out, or stop and turn around. It did the job, even for me.

"The next problem was that the bricks in this shaft were partly cemented in and not all of them were brittle. I used my bare hands and loose bricks as tools and worked myself through painfully slowly." Rivas took her left hand and stroked it. "The last brick was so tight that I almost couldn't get it loose. I tore open the palm of my left hand, but it was worth it. The shaft was free." Rivas turned her hand around and stroked her palm. "The tunnel then dragged on endlessly but I was convinced that it would lead me all the way out of the camp. I was starting to worry about how long it took when suddenly I got to the end of it. I climbed out, and I ran across meadows and fields, and then I spent the night under a tree. You know the rest."

"Are you hungry?"

"Yes, but it's late."

"I'll fix us something, okay?"

"You?"

"Why not? Sandwich or empanada?"

"Empanada."

Rivas took two from the fridge and put them into the microwave. "Would you like a special drink with it? The Peruvians have it before a festive meal."

Catherine was amused. "You're calling microwaved empanada a festive meal?"

"What's festive about it, is that *I'm* placing it in the microwave."

"What drink are you talking about?"

"*Pisco Sour.*"

"Yeess? And what is *Pisco Sour*?"

"As I said, every official dinner commences with this Peruvian national drink. *Pisco* is distilled from grapes and served with beaten egg-white, sugar and ice."

"Raw egg-white? That's awful."

"It tastes exquisite. Sip on it and if you don't like it, we'll pour it down the sink, alright?"

"I don't have to finish it if I don't like it?" With horror she recalled how Rivas had threatened to force-feed her like a goose not too long ago. "But you'd have to beat up the egg-white," she protested.

"Pedro can do that. I'll call him."

"Oh no, don't bother him, Rivas, please. I can do it," she offered and pointed out the late hour again, but Rivas insisted.

"I'm sure he's not sleeping yet. Even if he is, it's his job and he's partial to *Pisco Sour* himself."

"If you're sure he won't mind."

Rivas called Pedro on his mobile. Shortly afterwards he joined them in the kitchen and prepared the cocktails. "Catherine is busy talking about her abduction," Rivas explained, and turned to her. "Go on."

"I've told you everything."

"What happened next, when you got to the jungle? Pedro also wants to hear. Right Pedro?"

Pedro nodded, but he wondered what was motivating Rivas's friendliness this time. He didn't yet know about Rivas's change of heart.

"They took me into a tropical forest and made me march through it even though I was tied up," she continued. "It was really hard to make progress. I had to ask for permission for everything. Lying down, getting up, having a cat-wash with the water from the puddles, going to the toilet. I'd picked up some basic Spanish words at the camp and I tried those out, hoping the men would look more kindly on me. Sometimes I asked them, '*baño por favor*' and one of them would scream at me, '*No!*' Then I would ask, '*por qué?*' No answer. It made no difference if I tried in English,

Spanish or German. Everything was in vain. I was angry about their reaction to my minimal requests. I felt entitled to getting my basic needs met: eating, drinking, a couple of hours of rest and *baño*, the toilet. It wasn't much but these guys seemed to think I was after superfluous privileges. Not a hint of compassion from any of them!" Catherine started to become emotional, her words coming out in a rush.

Pedro handed Rivas and Catherine their drinks and joined them at the table, with a glass of *Pisco Sour* for himself. Catherine licked skeptically at the foam and pulled a face. "Take a small sip, Catherine. I'm sure you'll like it," Rivas encouraged her. She did so and found that it tasted fabulous. It reminded her of an extremely sour lemonade covered with a creamy foam. She emptied her glass and asked for another one. "Hey, careful! *Pisco Sour* goes down easily but it's got a very high alcohol content."

"You wouldn't say so."

"Exactly." Rivas stood up and put the empanadas, which he'd forgotten in the microwave, on plates. "Pedro, if you want one, you'll have to warm it up yourself."

Catherine jumped up. "I'll do it." As she heated up Pedro's meat pie, she asked, "Do you remember, Pedro? This is what you gave me to eat, on our way to the farm."

"Yup," Pedro replied.

"How delicious it tasted! In the jungle I only got to eat what I could carry myself. My rucksack was mainly packed with water containers and only a little bit of food: two packets of army biscuits, two raw green cabbages which were wrapped in newspaper, and some strange root vegetables. They looked like beetroot, except that they were long, not round, and white on the inside. They contained a lot of starch, which I could clearly taste. By that time I was missing the accommodation and supplies of the compound, which seemed like a five star hotel by comparison. On my first evening in the jungle I found a few strips of beef jerky in my rucksack, but I couldn't restrain myself and ate my entire protein ration on my first day. I never knew how much I could eat and how much I should keep. 'How long will the march take?' I asked the man who tied me against the tree, right in the beginning. No answer. 'I just want to know how to distribute my rations.' No answer. 'Please.' The answer was always nothing except the loud bird song from the trees." Catherine, already tipsy from the first glass of *Pisco Sour*, downed her second one and retold her adventures more and more graphically.

Even without the influence of alcohol, it was hardly surprising in the circumstances that her narrative should be so vividly told. The experience of abduction or being kidnapped is logically unfathomable, and therefore the brain often either suppresses the details or stores the information in picture form, and this is then how the victim re-lives the events. Rivas knew the syndrome well, and he listened to her patiently. He carefully observed how she was dealing with what had happened to her, hoping to help her as much as possible, when the time was right.

"In the end, I gave up talking altogether. I erected an imaginary fence between myself and my surroundings. When I got too lonely, I spoke to the trees. I, the notorious lone ranger, was craving for human contact like never before.

"Each day, we walked from dawn to dusk. The steaming stench was overpowering and the cobwebs that pulled across my face and the many insects were a plague. The mosquitoes were cruel and I had no means of fighting them off. Pure torture! Eventually, we arrived at the deserted FARC camp and there the situation escalated because I tried to run away again. Then the man fixed me up in the hut and kept me inside for a few days until we carried on fighting our way through the jungle – until Pedro and Andalus arrived to fetch me. I feel dizzy."

"Too much *Pisco Sour*. Didn't I warn you?"

"The room is spinning."

Rivas said to Pedro, "Wait here. I have to talk to you. I'm just taking Catherine upstairs."

He tucked Catherine into bed and returned to the kitchen where Pedro was clearing the dishes. With burning curiosity he awaited Rivas's explanation.

"I want to thank you, Pedro."

"For what?"

"For sticking up for her."

"Gave you a wakeup call, huh?"

"I was already awake, but you confirmed it for me. I want you to know that I'll look after her better from now on."

"Until next time."

"There won't be a next time. Do you still want to go home? You can leave now. I'll take it from here."

"Not necessary. I'll stay to the end as planned."

"I won't kill her, Pedro."

"What are you saying?"

"You heard me. Maria's been informed."

"Has she also lost her marbles now?"

Rivas's head jerked up in surprise. "What do you mean?"

"You can't let her survive. Are you crazy?"

"Pedro, it was you who fought for Catherine from the outset – fought for her like mad!"

"I asked you not to make her suffer *unnecessarily*, Rivas. To let her live is something entirely different. It's completely out of the question. She'll endanger us all."

"No need to worry."

"Is she defecting to us?"

"No. I *am* letting her go, but I've got her on the bit. Nothing will happen."

"You've got her on the bit, huh? Can't say that I've seen much of you having anything under control when it comes to this little wild mare."

Rivas laughed.

"You think this is funny?"

"*C'est la vie!*"

"What does Carlos say about all this?"

"Enough now! I've made my decision."

"You owe me an explanation, Rivas."

Rivas kept quiet.

"Are you in love with her?"

"Even if I wanted to, and I certainly don't, I couldn't kill her anymore. Could you, huh?"

"Of course not. She's been with us far too long, we have too many ties with her now. Let someone neutral take care of it. I just can't believe that Maria would go along with this - or Carlos." He shook his head.

"Maria will deal with Carlos."

"I see."

"What do you *see*?"

"What I see is that you've thought nothing through."

"That's true. I am clear about the 'what' but not yet about the 'how'."

Pedro pressed on, "Did you fall in love with her?"

"Yes, dammit."

"What about Chand?"

"What *about* Chand? How do you even know about her?"

"Our mutual friend Miguel filled me in. And I know enough to see that you're on the rebound."

"Stop it now."

"To deviate from the plan is dangerous. It'll have serious consequences. Not only for you."

"You just be careful that you don't deviate from *my* plan. That's the only consequence you have to worry about."

"She's got you big time!"

"You of all people, lecturing me about consequences! What a joke. I wasn't expecting this, Pedro."

"Because you can't think clearly anymore."

"My head is crystal clear. Perhaps for the first time in my entire life. I'm going through a change."

"You believe a man can change?"

"Don't you?"

"No."

"He can, Pedro."

"Why have I never seen it then?"

"When the gain of the change is greater than the gain of the status quo, it ignites the wish, which engages the will. And the will is ultimately what drives the actions to effect the change."

"'Men can do all things, if they will'. Leon Battista Alberti, 15th century," quoted Pedro, reconsidering.

"Well said. And, when undergoing change, a man needs friends. *I* need friends now, Pedro."

Pedro rose. "If it were possible to let her live... I would wish it on her. Let me know if I can help."

"You can help me by trusting me."

"I've always trusted you, otherwise I wouldn't be here. Good night, Rivas. If anyone can pull this off, it's you."

"Yeah, see you in the morning, Pedro."

34.
Peru, September 18

Catherine was keen to tie up the loose ends of her assignment and she got straight down to work the next day. Only two pieces of the puzzle were still missing, though the remainder of the database had been successfully unraveled. At the end of her day's work she asked Rivas to come to the library. He entered, and with a ceremonial air she handed him her Rolex. "What do you want me to do with your watch?" he asked, surprised.

"I've been mulling things over and I want you to have the watch. It's my gift to you. To remember me by. When I'm dead."

"Catherine, you're not going to die! At least, not at the hands of WICED."

She ignored his assurance and continued, "When the time comes for me to die, please don't hand me over to anyone else. I want you to be my executioner. And please tell me before you do it. I want to know when and how it will happen, I want to experience death consciously. And most importantly, tell me where. Please don't take me down to the cellar, but out into nature. Do you think you could that?"

"Aren't you listening? Nobody will murder you. Not I and not anyone else."

"Maria will feel differently about this."

"No she won't. And even if she did, I wouldn't allow it."

"You wouldn't be able to prevent it. Even I can see that she can't take the risk of letting me live."

"You underestimate me. And Maria. You pose no threat to her. She won't let anyone push her into a corner. The police forces of the entire world couldn't touch her. Her contacts would protect her and her mission under any circumstances. She decides case by case and, in this one, she'll spare the victim." He sincerely hoped not to have lied to her again.

"Did other hostages have to die before me?"

"For other reasons, yes."

"Why, if Maria is so untouchable?"

"It would be messy not to close all loopholes after an operation."

"I feel sick when I hear this."

"You're right. Too much information. But I did promise not to lie to you again."

"Why will she spare *me*? What makes me a special case?"

"Because I asked her to."

"That's why you were gone for so long? And she agreed?"

"Yes."

"What if she changes her mind?"

"She's never denied me anything if it was in her power. And that's been the case up to now."

"But what if it's the first time? What if she has no choice?"

"Then I'll take you to a safe place myself. I promise you."

"Take me to a safe place now."

"Here with me, you're in no danger."

"Rivas, why were you so nasty sometimes, and sometimes so kind?"

"I was always nasty, Catherine. The kindness was a façade – a tactic to move things along. I captured you not only physically, but also your soul. The kind of hostage drama which involves for instance a ransom payment or where there is political pressure, in other words where an external party plays the essential role, works differently. There the prisoner herself is merely a lever. You don't have to be nice to hostages like that. It's not necessary to influence them because they themselves can't bring about the direct result. They merely serve to pressurize the decision-makers at home. It's different when the purpose of the kidnapping is about information that the hostage alone can provide. In your case, there was the additional factor of needing your active participation. This is why our tolerance was so high. We couldn't have carried out our plan without your personal engagement, so we had to systematically build up your will to cooperate. Exposing a victim to foreign vegetation is an acknowledged form of torture and in your case was a kind of initiation process."

"Ha! I knew this jungle business wasn't just about getting me from A to B."

"After the first terrible experiences, the hostage is led to believe that there's hope by allowing her a few comforts. Shortly after, the victim is exposed to fresh traumata again, relieved by peaceful phases, again replaced by the next psychological shock – all this is carefully mapped out. The more harrowing the last experience, the stronger the longing to obtain affection from the caregiver, usually her kidnapper. The victim becomes so dependent on this one human being that she submits voluntarily. Then the second phase begins and so does the actual work."

"How easy I was to manipulate! I'm ashamed of my cowardice."

"What you call cowardice, is intuitive intelligence. It was your only chance of survival. The longer one stays alive, the greater the chance of freedom. The subconscious knows how to behave in an emergency situation."

"Did you feel sorry for me?"

"No."

"Not at all?"

"No."

"But Pedro did, right?"

"Yes he did, that's true. He twice threatened to walk out if I don't treat you better."

"Is this why he was packing the other day?"

"He told you?"

"No. I just happened to walk in while he was packing. He said it was a personal matter, that's why he had to leave."

"I sure hope so."

"He didn't spill the beans, Rivas, and I didn't draw any conclusions." Catherine was touched by Pedro's attempts to help her and moved away from this topic in order that her indiscretion should not get Pedro into trouble. "Does the next phase end in death?"

"Usually."

Catherine's chest contracted and her eyes ran with tears. "Would you have killed me, if something had gone wrong?"

"We have to consider all options."

"You didn't answer my question." A film covered her eyes and through her wall of tears she was seeing him double.

"Yes, I'm sure I would have, Catherine. I'm so sorry."

"How?"

"I would have sedated you, have you carried downstairs and shot you in the cellar."

"Why are you telling me this?"

"You wanted to know."

"When did you start caring about me? I don't mean mechanically, like looking after a hostage, but caring for me as a person?"

"I became fully aware of it after you fired at me at the pond, and probably subconsciously, before that, the day I beat you up with the bit."

"But when exactly did you care about what would happen to me?"

"Gradually, over time, Catherine. It'll be my undoing one day."

"What do you mean?" she enquired and pressed her palms hard against her eyes to curb the flow of tears.

"It's hard to explain. I just know it. To have sympathy with hostages is dangerous because it kills the objectivity needed to make level-headed decisions, and that leads to mistakes. Normally, we swop kidnappers when this happens."

"So why did you carry on?" Her tears rolled uncontrollably now and dripped onto her dress.

"Why are you crying so much?"

"I don't know. Please answer my question."

"Because we would have had to start from scratch. I'd already come a long way with tying you to me emotionally. And of course because I was too proud to face reality. Up until a few days ago I told myself I'd be able to pull this off regardless."

"Will there still be an exchange now?"

"I won't let anyone near you. I've already promised you that."

"Did you sleep with me because you had to?" Catherine managed to calm down a bit.

"I don't *have to* do anything. But we work with sexual manipulation when it aids the operation. It completes the dependency. It wasn't hard, believe me. It was harder to wait for the right time, with someone as attractive as you."

"You called me an ugly skeleton," Catherine sobbed again, drowning in self-pity.

"I said that, but never meant it." He noticed a faint smile flicker from behind the wall of tears. She's so enchanting, he thought. The mood was becoming less tense. He would have loved to have held her and was burning to gather her up in his arms and carry her upstairs. Catherine, however, was on a roll. He guessed her next question. "So now you want to know how I feel about you right now, if I consider it my duty to sleep with you now."

"Exactly."

"I'm mad about you, Catherine. The thought of someone even looking at you, makes me angry."

"If you like me so much, why do you beat me then?"

"I won't hurt you anymore. I don't expect you to ever trust me again, but it's the truth."

"You said, trust is the foundation of love and I've been loving you for a long time. You prophesied it on our first evening together. Why do you doubt my love for you?"

"Because I wasn't talking about love then, but about the consequences of the treatment that you were to receive. If you work systematically, you can predict the psychological development of a kidnapping victim with almost 100 % certainty. But true love? Think about it rationally. Should love hurt so much? True love is considered and kind. I gave you none of that."

"You also told me that love is irrational and that you can only gain access to it at that level. You talk about reason but the heart doesn't give a damn. I know what you mean. You're convinced I feel some kind of pseudo-love for you but you underestimate me. I've had plenty of time to deal with myself internally over the past few weeks and to get to know myself. You don't get this opportunity in the rush of everyday life but I had plenty of time to examine myself. When we first met, you told me that you would break my heart and I said that I'd never allow that. And I didn't. It was broken before I met you, I just didn't know it. Only, since I've known you, it's whole."

"Catherine, you don't have to reassure me because you feel bad for me. That's not necessary."

"Then why did I have to swear a thousand oaths the other day, that I love you?"

"Because I wanted it so much, I guess."

"I do love you." He smiled at her warmly. "Will you keep your promise not to lie to me anymore?"

"As long as I live."

"Rivas, may I speak freely?"

"I would be happy if you did."

"You won't get mad?"

"Definitely not."

"I really do love you, but I'm afraid that you're just maneuvering again - with your apologies and assurances. Phase 2b, so to speak."

"Catherine, everything I've said is true."

"My brain is interfering again. My heart believes you and I feel safe with you, but my head is making me unsure. It's not my love for you that it doubts, but your sudden turn."

Rivas dug up his packet of cigarettes, extracted one, lit it and handed it to her. Then he lit one for himself. "I know this will be hard to understand. But the way I can live with myself at all, has always been by separating the kidnapper from the man. What I did to you, I did as your kidnapper. I am no longer your kidnapper, Catherine."

"I know what you mean." She nodded. "Rivas, did you plan from the beginning to seduce me? I guess what I'm trying to find out is did you seduce me as the kidnapper or the man?"

"I did what I predicted I would do at our first encounter. Your seduction was premeditated."

"I remember how you made fun of me."

"You're really pretty and I enjoyed teasing you. I knew you only from the reports of the transporters and I admired you for trying to fight off three men at once. That wasn't very clever but it was a try. This hardly ever happens. The same with escape through the well. Who would dare? You were courageous. Followed by the ride with Pedro, without batting an eyelid! That meant you really could ride. It was all very unusual and impressive. I found you interesting, an unconventional hostage. And you really did look cute in that huge shirt, on our first evening together." Rivas tried in vain to lighten the robust discussion. Catherine stayed serious.

"The arrival of a new toy, delivered by Pedro and Andalus."

Rivas nodded, filled with consternation. "Forgive me. If you can."

"Did you merely carry out your plan to seduce me or did our intimate relationship develop naturally?"

"It was calculated."

"I didn't feel like you were seducing me in a calculated way in the shepherd's hut. Other men are not so indulgent - they get straight down to business. You were so considerate, and you talked to me and encouraged me. Why?"

"Because women respond well when you show interest in details that concern them. The fact that you didn't realize you were being seduced was the whole magic of it, after all. I had to work up your passion gradually. There were many opportunities, Catherine. Just think about the day in the barn when I pushed you into the hay stack, or the time before, just after the room arrest."

"Or straight after the first outride. Oh no, before that already, when you smiled at me, in front of Andalus's stall."

"You remember that?"

"I'll never forget it. You could have had me at that first smile."

Rivas laughed. "Practically, yes. But psychologically, it would have been too soon for my purposes."

"Have you ever raped a hostage?"

"Of course not, Catherine."

"Did you seduce them?"

"When it suited me and if I found her attractive."

"And when you didn't find her attractive?"

"If it was necessary I made her believe that she meant something to me until she confided in me with whatever I needed to know, but I didn't sleep with her."

"You didn't?"

"*Como una prostituta*? Do I look like I would sell myself at any price?"

Catherine swallowed hard. "The poor woman. What kind of a man are you?"

"A bad one, Catherine. What more can I say?"

Catherine exhaled deeply. "Why are you doing such terrible things?"

"It's what's done with hostages, if, as in your case, we're after information. It's more pleasant than torture - for all concerned. WICED's success rate with hostages is 100 %."

"And then you kill them anyway."

"We are going round in circles. I already told you. But yes, if we have no further use for a hostage, he or she is eliminated."

"Did you use the same tactics with the others? Except that you haven't killed me of course."

"Every situation is unique."

"Did you also feel affection for the others?"

"No."

"Did you have compassion with them?"

"No, Catherine."

"Not even when you killed them?"

"No."

"Why not? How is it possible to kill a helpless woman without any emotions whatsoever?"

"You need a certain disposition for it. If you have that disposition, you can train yourself to see a victim as an object. If this wasn't possible, there would be no assassinations. In order to remain committed to the task, you have to avoid building up a relationship. This way you stay distanced and the victim stays anonymous."

"But in my case you built a relationship."

"You did with me."

"I must confess, I did try to draw you in, but it never worked."

"No. As you can see, it did work."

"The others didn't try?"

"They did. Anyone who is half intelligent will consider this possibility. Some hostage takers, and I'm talking now about the perverted kind, who abduct a girl to sexually abuse her, even count on that. They like it when the victim believes that she has a chance to connect with the kidnapper, in order to influence him. Then they satisfy themselves with disappointing the victim by torturing her to death. That often happens."

"You're no different! You also kept disappointing me and tortured me almost to death."

Rivas was about to rebut, but then quietly conceded, "Yes, I did."

"Why did the other hostages not manage to influence you?"

"Because I wasn't interested in them. After all, this wasn't about sexual offences, but about missions with purpose. I have deep insight into the human psyche gained from professional training. This just doesn't happen to a professional."

"But now it's happened to you, because I am *interesting*." She couldn't help being pleased about that.

"Any man would be powerless against you. I comfort myself with the fact that this would have happened to everyone else who had to deal with you for this length of time. You're invincible." Catherine stayed silent now and Rivas exhaled, relieved. Finally, she'd stopped grilling him. This had been just too much truth all at once, for her and for himself. He closed his eyes briefly when he heard Catherine asking her next question. "Catherine, please. I'd like to stop now. I've confessed so much already and still it's only the tip of the iceberg. If you force me to carry on, I'm afraid you won't be able to take it. I don't want to lose you."

"Thank you for being so honest with me. I'll always respect you for that and I'll carry on doing what you tell me to. I love you so much. Will you tell me everything one day?"

"Yes. When the time is right."

"Okay, let's leave it at that."

He was amazed that she could let go now. What an incredibly sensible woman, she could be, he thought. So childlike one day and so mature the next. He loved this Catherine so much that it hurt. A mortal stab in the heart couldn't have hurt more than the love he felt for her. "Catherine, one more thing. If any doubts creep in over the next few days, please don't be afraid. From now on I'll protect you with my life. If you feel safer, you can sleep in my room again."

"I'm not afraid, Rivas. Don't worry about me. I'll sleep in my own room. I know how much your space means to you."

As they were leaving the library, he asked, "Do you still want to have dinner with me?"

"You know I do."

"Get ready early tomorrow morning. It'll be a long ride."

"We'll eat out? That'll be the first time. Oh, I feel like fresh fish and a huge bowl of green salad."

"If you want fresh fish, we'll have to fly to the coast, to Lima. They don't have fresh fish down in the valley."

"Then I'll eat whatever specialties they offer in the valley, no problem."

Rivas laughed. "You know Catherine, I don't think you'll enjoy the regional specialty. It's called *Cuy*. We'll fly to Lima."

"What's *Cuy*?"

"Grilled Guinea pig."

"I was so lupine in Columbia, I'm sure I would have wolfed it down then. But you're right, now I'm not so keen on that. I'll find something else on the menu. Fries with ketchup? The nice thing about this experience is that you learn to appreciate the simplest pleasures again."

"You don't have to eat potatoes when you want fish. I'll have a helicopter take us down to the valley and from there we'll take a light plane to Lima. We'll be back by nightfall. You can shop if you like, and eat whatever you want. This is a new beginning. If you give me the chance." Then he added "Please".

The trigger word, now the healing word. She noted it and smiled at him, knowingly. Then she asked, "A helicopter will come up here? Just for me?"

"I told you, nothing's too much trouble for my little headhunter. I said we'd make available whatever you need. It's no big deal."

"I'm impressed," she remarked, "but not by the helicopter." She granted him a last smile, before disappearing to have a bath.

Her world had become so bizarre that it didn't seem to bother her to finish a discussion about murder by making plans for dinner.

--- oOo ---

Rivas, however, was aware of this, and he understood what she meant by her last remark. Just as on Maria's hacienda, he was again gripped by uncertainty. Self-honesty can be a frightening experience. It was no different for Rivas. Facing up to his feelings and the consequences that would arise from this, and especially getting in touch with his own shadows was not easy for him. Where to from here? In a few days they would fly to Paris and shortly afterwards Catherine's job was done. Originally, they'd planned to take Catherine from Paris to a WICED hideout in the Camargue, in the south of France. This venue was disguised as a respectable country estate and equipped similarly to the *finca* in Peru. It was more luxurious. It also housed an enormous underground lab and a large amount of livestock, ready for the medical trials. In order not to draw attention to the mission, middlemen had been buying up at auction big amounts of slaughter horses from France, Germany, Austria, Italy and Poland. It was a convenient coincidence that Ruckebier happened to be in Paris towards the end of their mission. This simplified the logistics of a site visit to the Camargue, Ruckebier's first and Catherine's last stop. There, they'd planned to hold Catherine captive until she was no longer needed and then kill her. However, Rivas now hoped to be able to facilitate her return to her old life. For this she needed patience and faith, while Maria made the arrangements for her release. Maria would never trick him, but he needed a plan B in case the others didn't go along.

The excursion to Lima suited him well. He had suggested it spontaneously to make her happy, but now it would also serve as a trial run for Paris. He booked the chopper and, before turning in, he called Maria. He asked her to arrange a few appointments for the planned trip and for a WICED light aircraft which would fly them from the valley to Lima.

35.
Peru, September 20

Catherine slipped into a devilish, transparent silk bodice by La Perla, threw her favorite delicate purple Dior dress over it and pushed a chic pair of Dior cat-eye sunglasses into her hair. Her makeup, cigarettes and a lighter - a present from Joe - as well as a couple of tissues, she stuffed into her petite Lady Dior bag, seamed with orange tassels. She was tempted to take her work cell phone along, but she assumed that Rivas would object. The outfit came with a matching pair of eight inch plateau sandals, which threatened to cause immense problems for such a long excursion. She sacrificed her feet because she believed she owed it to Rivas to look smart for her first public appearance, since Rivas had once mentioned that this was important to him.

Punctually at 6.30 am she took her place at the breakfast table. Pedro had made coffee, but he disappeared to his room straight afterwards. She nibbled on a piece of toast but was too wound up to enjoy it. Rivas joined her. Seemingly without noticing her appearance, he pushed two tablets across the table. "Morning. Take these."

"Morning, Rivas. What are they for?"

"The helicopter and the light airplane will probably make you nauseous. They'll prevent things from getting out of hand."

"Tablets don't help."

"I'm hoping that these will," he replied tersely as he always did early in the morning.

She swallowed the pills and rushed to the stables to say goodbye to Andalus for the day. She was disappointed that Rivas didn't comment on how she looked, considering all the trouble she'd gone to. She clip-clopped across the dusty yard in her high heels and heard the chopper approaching. Andalus was kissed on the nose and promised a treat from Lima before she hurried back to the house. There, she grabbed her handbag and alongside Rivas made her way to the helicopter, which waited droning, blades rotating slowly. Rivas at this juncture finally commented on her clothing – or rather, her problematic choice of shoes. "I forgot to tell you that you'll be on your feet all day. The helicopter will wait for us. You're welcome to return to the house and put on a more comfortable pair."

She firmly declined. "These are perfect!"

The Eurocopter EC 120 took them down to the valley from where a Beech Duchess 76 aircraft was to fly them to the Peruvian capital.

The two flights combined removed two hours of time from their intended city tour of Lima, but there was no more speedy way of reaching the city from the remote ranch. Leaning against Rivas, Catherine admired the scenery and tried to absorb it as consciously as possible. She did feel sick during the flight but the pills prevented the worst of it. They approached the coast and when she saw the sea, she felt a happy freedom like never before. As if drunk with joy, she pressed herself against Rivas. He put his arm around her and said, "Catherine, in Lima we have to visit someone who'll take a biometric passport photo of you as well as your electronic finger prints. He would have come to the farm tomorrow but since we're here, we can take care of it today."

"Why?"

"We need fake passports for the flight to Paris."

"I see. Is that why we're flying to Lima?" she asked distrustfully.

"It's just good timing."

After this, they hardly spoke, because the cabin was noisy and both were deep in thought.

The approach to Lima offered a breathtaking view. At last! A city! But how run down it looked! And yet how reassuring it was to see that there were still *cities*! They landed at an airport for small aircraft where another helicopter was standing by to fly them to the roof of a highrise building in downtown Lima. From there, they took a cab out of the city center towards Miraflores, one of the capital's residential suburbs. The taxi waited while Rivas and Catherine stepped inside an apartment, which looked exactly like Catherine imagined the workshop of a forger: small, dark, messy. The man greeted Rivas, and they conversed in Spanish. He ignored Catherine until it was time to take the photo and the fingerprints, which only took a few minutes. After another short taxi ride through Miraflores, they entered a café. Rivas seemed to be well known there, because they were immediately ushered into a side room where a beautiful woman, about the same age as Catherine, brought them two *espressi*, without even taking down their order. The waitress almost forgot to put them down, staring brazenly at

Rivas instead. He took no notice of her. He was used to being stared at by women, Catherine deduced. She envied the girl for her hourglass figure and her long legs. Why had she been blessed with both? Legs and a tiny waist? Then she remembered a quote from her Hermann Hesse booklet: "What's not in us, doesn't bother us." The waitress had merely held up a mirror for Catherine's own soul.

Rivas handed Catherine a Chanel purse containing a huge amount of US dollars and a few Peruvian soles. "You don't have to exchange the US currency. The boutiques are happy to accept dollars. I'm calling you a taxi now. The driver will take you to a hairdresser whom Maria has organized for you. The salon is in a part of town that offers excellent shopping opportunities. Then you have the rest of the day free. Have fun in the city and buy what you like. Just remember, though, to choose items which are easy to take to Paris, otherwise you'll have to leave them behind, and that would be a shame." He grinned. He scribbled something onto a piece of paper. "This is the address of a bus station. It's easy to find - it's on the corner of Paseo de la Republica and Manuel Cuadros, directly between the Palace of Justice and the Sheraton Hotel. Meet me there at 4.30 pm. From there we'll take a city bus to a restaurant where we'll have the finest fish in Peru. To mingle with Peruvians on their public transport system will be an experience you won't forget for a long time."

Catherine was anything but pleased. "You're not coming with me to town?"

"I've got things to see to, and when a woman shops she doesn't want to drag a man around with her. I'll only be a bother, and in any case it's not my scene."

"But Rivas, you have to come with me! How can you let me run around Lima all by myself? What if I report my abduction?"

"Are you planning to do that?"

"What would you do if you were in my position and a cop suddenly crossed your path? Especially around the law court! The place must be crawling with police. Please don't ask me to make such a difficult decision. I don't want to disappoint you."

"Catherine, I'll be waiting for you near the bus stop of line 26 at 4.30 pm. Don't worry if you don't see me straight away. I'll walk towards you as soon as I've spotted you. If you don't show up, you'll be on your own from now on and there's nothing more I can do for you. You must choose whether you trust the police more than me. I can't drag you around town in handcuffs."

"But we could walk together. You can guard me without cuffs."

"Catherine, I don't want to degrade you anymore to the role of prisoner."

"Yes, but if I turn up at the bus stop with civilian cops in tow, you'd run straight into a trap." She couldn't believe her ears. He was actually taking the risk of letting her go off on her own.

"I won't walk into a police trap, and this business of guarding you is over. Now and forever. Either you trust me or you take your fate into your own hands. You're safe with me for now, Catherine, and then I'll officially let you go, once all the necessary precautions have been taken."

"I would also be safe with the police."

"Briefly at the station, and then?"

"Then the matter will take its course and they'll offer me a witness protection program."

Rivas laughed. "You're not an important enough witness to warrant that. You're reading too many novels, Catherine, but fine, take a chance. Just remember, I'm offering you the opportunity to return to your old life unharmed, if you don't lose your nerve now."

"Rivas please don't leave me behind in this big town, like an unwanted pet! I'm not worried about my safety. I can't live without you anymore, that's why! Please don't leave me."

"Catherine, later on we'll eat out like I promised you and then we'll fly back into the mountains. I won't desert you. Why would I do that when we haven't finished the job yet? Besides, I would never abandon you like this."

"You've abandoned hostages before!"

"What are you talking about?"

"When you were on the run with the FARC guys, in the jungle, remember?"

"That was different. I feel responsible for you."

"I'm a responsibility to you?"

"Much more than that. Don't you get how much danger you'd be in if I wasn't looking after you?"

"I don't want to shop and I don't want to eat! I want to go back to the ranch. Please let's fly back!"

"No. You're going to spend these couple of hours on your own. Besides which, it's not fitting for a lady to *want* things. A man *wants*. A woman *would like*."

"What outdated nonsense is that? Didn't you say you weren't going to retrain me anymore?"

"Where I come from, ladies have manners!"

"I believe in gender equality."

"I don't."

Catherine was so in love that she couldn't be mad at him. She laughed, and she relented, "So, I'm off to town on my own? Is this some sort of birdcage exercise? You let me fly off and if I return, you have proof that I love you?"

"If only it was that easy," he sighed. "Please let me call the cab now. Surely there must be something that you'll find nice to do, in this big city!"

"I'm scared."

"That doesn't surprise me and that's exactly why you need to do this."

"I'd rather come with you."

"No. You're going to take a cab to town now. Do I have to force you? Do I always have to get strong with you before you get it? I can't use you here now, so off you go." He got up.

"You said you wouldn't treat me badly anymore."

"Then give me a chance, Catherine. You're behaving like a child. It's completely unattractive."

That hit home, especially because the pretty waitress was still lurking around. "Promise me, this isn't going to be next edition of *Casablanca*."

"I promise. Will you do the same? After all, in *Casablanca* it was the woman who stood up the man."

"4.30 pm, line 26?" She studied his handwritten note.

"Yes."

"I'll be there. Without the cops."

He put Catherine in a taxi and instructed the driver where to take her.

--- oOo ---

Rivas went back inside the café. "Where's the car?" he asked the manager.

"Parked around the corner. Pepe got me out of bed at the crack of dawn this morning."

Rivas held out his hand for the smart key. "*Adiós*," he said, and he strode quickly to the WICED car, which had been made available for him for the day.

He was on his way to a very important person in his life.

He intended to surprise her – his gorgeous Chand.

36.
Peru, September 20

Pepe was in charge of sourcing vehicles for the WICED fleet. A WICED car had to be fast. A coupe, not a flashy soft top model. It needed a decent-sized bench seat at the back, but only two doors, to prevent victims escaping without having to remember to lock the doors. Reliable, lots of power with the engine mapping chipped, but not too ostentatious. Seven gear paddle shift, four wheel drive, preferably an S-tronic Quattro. That was the WICED standard. And there she stood: anthracite, metallic, stylish – the perfect understatement. Only an expert would spot the true signatures of her power – not the usual regalia, the badges and emblems of marque, but a handful of discreet details – the modified exhaust, discreetly enlarged air-intake scoops and a slightly modified grill at the front, as well as the polished aluminum covers of the side mirrors. These told the connoisseur that this car was a true wolf in sheep's clothing. Understated on the outside, yet undeniably cosmopolitan and elegant – and, beneath the bonnet, a brutal beast.

Against the passenger door of this elegant brute leaned the waitress, who'd served the *espressi*. "Why are you leaning against my car?" Rivas asked, sounding semi-interested.

"I'd like to test the back seat. I imagine the leather is very - hard."

"What about your job? Shouldn't you be serving customers?"

"Taking a break."

"Didn't you notice that I was with someone when you served us earlier?"

"That doesn't bother me."

"But it bothers me," mumbled Rivas barely audibly. "So you'd like to come for a spin, huh?"

"Mhm."

Rivas pressed the main button of the smart key. The indicators briefly lit up all around and with a smug click the Audi unlocked her doors. The interior lights faded in gently. "Get in." He opened his door and sank into the contoured Recaro seat. The woman opened her door also and was about to swing her flawless legs across the passenger seat. "In the back, Chica. Didn't you want to test the bench?" Obediently, she pulled the back of the seat forward and climbed into the rear. Rivas leant over the passenger seat, pushed back the backrest and pulled the door closed. The dashboard lit up and tinted the front console with mellow shades of red and blue. The display welcomed him personally – in Spanish. Routinely, he clicked himself through the complex electronic system, setting the driver recognition and motor mapping to "sport", the driving aids to "off". That car handled curves just as well without ESP – on the contrary, in fact. On his last assignment that damn ESP nearly took him out when the road-surface-based engine performance made it nearly impossible for him to get out of the line of fire on a dirt road. He pushed the ignition button to the left of the gear panel and with a discreet hiss more than 300 horses reared up and throbbed into life. Her six cylinders softly bubbled away in neutral. Rivas fastened his seat belt, adjusted the rear mirror and briefly looked at himself in the glass.

"The car suits you," flattered the waitress, who didn't let him out of her sight for a second. Rivas set the S-tronic to manual and engaged the first gear by using the gear paddle on the right of the steering wheel. He released the handbrake and the Audi smoothly rolled forwards, directly towards a black thunderstorm that approached the city from the Pacific coast.

Silently Rivas navigated his way through the heavy traffic, paying no attention to his attractive cargo. They covered several suburbs and made their way out of the city, along Lima's main coastal road, the Costa Verde. The thunderstorm caught up with them. A mighty power struggle erupted in the heavens, made personal, immediate, for Rivas by the contest between the drumming rain and the wiper blades.

"Where are we going?"

"We're almost there. How old are you?"

"Twenty two."

"What's your name?"

"Pureza."

"Tell me, Pureza, do you know what's likely to happen, when a girl just gets into a car with a stranger?"

"Well, I guess, with someone like you, she could have a little fun?"

"That's right. I could think of quite a few ways to have fun with you, but believe me, darling, you wouldn't enjoy it a bit." He rolled into a parking bay parallel to the road, leaned over the passenger seat, opened the door and pulled back the back rest. "Get out."

"But why? I thought..."

"I don't like your name."

"Excuse me?"

"Can you hear the thunder, Pureza? I am this damn thunderstorm. Out with you! I have to get going."

Pureza stayed seated, undecided, confused. "But I thought...."

He could have delivered any of a thousand retorts, but he stayed silent.

"How am I to get back? I don't have my cell phone with me and it's pouring with rain."

"There's a *playa* four hundred yards back. You'll find plenty of bus stops at this beach promenade."

"I didn't bring any money. At least give me a few soles for the bus ticket."

Rivas left the engine running, got out and walked around the car. He pulled the girl out of the rear and pinned her against the car. Then he slid his hand under the thin scrap of cloth that was supposed to serve as a miniskirt. Pulling his hand back, he gave her an ungallant look and hissed condescendingly, "Oh, never mind. Get lost!"

She stared at him helplessly.

"One look at your skirt and the bus driver will pick you up without a ticket. Beat it now, before I cut your delicate little throat."

He pushed her away from the car, neatly closed the passenger door, got back in and navigated the car in the direction of San Juan de Lurigancho.

He rolled the Audi into an empty parking bay (reserved for doctors) in front of the Clinica Maison de Santé, made his way directly to the back entrance of the pediatric ward and hurried to the reception area. "Good day. Is Chand Basu on duty this morning?"

"*Buenos días, Señor. ¡Lo siento!* I've never heard of the name Basu."

"Just check your roster, okay?"

"There's no Mr Basu here."

"*Ms* Dr Chandara Basu."

"I'm new here. Hang on."

The receptionist left briefly and returned with reinforcements. "Good day, Señor. You're looking for Dr Basu?"

"Hello Sister. Is she on duty today?"

"She doesn't work at our clinic anymore."

"Where can I find her?"

"I don't know."

"Find out please."

"I'm sorry, Señor." The senior administrative sister firmly shook her head.

"I get that you can't help me, Sister, so please call somebody who can answer my question."

"Even if one of my colleagues knew of her whereabouts, we wouldn't be at liberty to tell you."

Rivas weighed up his options: he could bully her or he could storm past her and try to find someone more informed and helpful. Or he could try to charm her. The latter seemed the most sensible way forward. There was always time to employ more drastic measures if necessary. "Please forgive me, I didn't mean to be impolite." He put on a sorry face and was about to launch into an invented story about some poor dying kid, when the sister melted away at the sight of the handsome "dejected" young man.

"I'll see what I can do." She disappeared down the corridor. While waiting, Rivas googled for Dr Chandara Basu on his smart phone. Evidently it wasn't so smart after all, because it only unearthed an outdated entry, still showing that she worked at this clinic in Lima. The sister scurried back, smiling and waving a piece of paper. "Here is the address she left with our HR department." Rivas glanced at it briefly. It was familiar to him. The drive there would take just under two hours. It was 11.55 am. He would barely manage, even if he didn't stay for long. Still undecided, he returned to his car and drove off.

At the next major intersection he turned, spontaneously, onto the Panamericana Norte en route to Barranca.

He parked in the street outside a run-down apartment block and dashed, two steps at a time, up the outside concrete flight of stairs. He rang the doorbell of apartment 17. An elderly lady opened the door as far as the safety chain allowed. The door closed again and then flew wide open. "Doctor!" shouted the woman, and embraced Rivas. "Come in, my son!" Rivas entered and the woman led him into a shabby and outmoded sitting room, which was decorated in what once were conspicuously bright colors. "Please! Sit down. How nice of you to pay me a visit!"

"Yeah, it's been a while. How are you, Mataji?"

"Oh my legs, you know! And my sugar!" She elaborated on various ailments. "But my legs are the worst. They can hardly carry me anymore. Chand always used to massage them for me, but since she's been gone…."

"Come, put your feet up. I'll do that."

She heaved her stiff body onto the sofa. Her legs were hidden chastely under a pair of old fashioned woolen pants tucked into thick medical stockings. Over these two layers, she also wore a heavy skirt. Rivas got up, sat down next to her on the couch and massaged her calves as best he could through the thick material. Mrs Basu saw in Rivas not only her daughter's ex-boyfriend, but also the "impressive" doctor. She was a simple pensioner who had no idea about forensic psychiatry, Rivas's field of expertise. To her, all doctors were the same – blessings or curses, depending on their personalities. If she hadn't believed him to be a medical professional she would have deemed it improper to let him touch her like that, but in her blissful ignorance she gratefully let him carry on.

"Where is she, Mataji? At the clinic, they told me she doesn't work there anymore."

Mrs Basu scratched her head. "Yes of course, you didn't just come to see me. She no longer lives in Peru, Rivas. I only have my nephew and his wife left. She didn't hear from you anymore. She moved away."

"Where?"

"A year ago she accepted a position at a children's hospital in Pakistan. She calls me once a week. I miss her, but my nephew's wife is very good to me. She works hard and she cooks well. She's a good woman."

"Where is Chand, Mataji? Where in Pakistan?"

"In Karachi – for five years to start with. Maybe she'll stay forever. It wouldn't surprise me."

"But why Pakistan?"

"Why is that important to you now? You haven't got in touch with her for over a year, Rivas. She said you didn't bother to call her even once!"

"Has she met someone?"

"She was tired of waiting, Rivas. She had to get on with her life."

"And how are you, Mataji? Is there anything you need? Can I do something for you?" Rivas bridled his curiosity for a moment. He didn't want to seem like he was merely squeezing her for information.

"You're helping me already, Rivas. The rubbing is so good for my circulation. Oh that reminds me, I'm out of my heart tablets. Almost."

"Give me your prescription. I'll drive to the pharmacy and get them for you."

"Please pass me my handbag. It's over there on the counter."

Rivas brought her the battered old bag. After digging around without success, she emptied out all its contents onto the couch. "Oh now I remember! My neighbor's son offered to get them for me after his shift today. Whenever I need an errand, he's very helpful and kind. I'm getting so forgetful." He shook her head in despair over her aging. Rivas helped her to repack the bag. "But other than that, I'm taken care of. Chand sends me an allowance every month. I have everything I need. Next spring she'll fly me over to be with her for good."

"But, Mataji, why expose yourself to an Islamic culture? As a Hindu? Pakistan and India aren't exactly on good terms. Why don't you return to India instead?"

"Religion has never concerned my Chand. She'll always help where she's needed the most."

"And you? Won't the trip be too strenuous for you? And you could be victimized."

"If you extend kindness, you receive kindness in return, irrespective of where you live or what your faith is. And even if it's hard at first, I'll have to adjust. I don't blame her. She must live her own life regardless of the needs of an old lady. It's bad enough that I'm like a millstone around her neck even here. She'll be thirty-five next year. I'm happy that she's finally starting a family, if it's not too late already. But the young people, they marry so late nowadays." Again, she shook her head. "I've been wanting grandchildren for so long. Did you expect her to sit around waiting for you forever?"

Rivas felt the urge to defend himself, but it seemed shallow to say how "busy" he'd been. Instead, he kept quiet.

"You were always gone. She didn't even know what you got up to half the time. She told me once that she's known you for so long but that there's nobody whom she comprehends less than you."

"I didn't make it easy for her," he conceded.

"But I know you. You're a good boy, Rivas. She also said she believed you'd been led astray somehow. But I assured her, she's imagining things."

Rivas felt guilty, was lost for words.

The old woman straightened up. "I didn't offer you anything to drink. I'm a bad hostess!"

"I'm good. How about you? Would you like me to make you some tea?" For the second time in a week, I'm making a woman tea! Rivas noted, irked.

"Yes please."

They went into the dated old kitchen. With a half-hidden grimace of distaste Rivas cleared the table's surface of lentil flour and a rolling pin, to make enough space for a cup of tea. He looked around. "Where's your kettle?"

"Use the enamel pot on the stove, Rivas".

While the water was boiling he asked, "Why didn't she say good-bye? She has my phone number."

"You also had her number and a good woman doesn't run after a man. That wouldn't be dignified. And she always believed, when she would hear from you eventually, it would only be to break things off for good. Is this why you came?"

Rivas, convicted, lowered his eyes. "Please give me her new number. I don't want to leave things open like this."

"It would be better if you left her alone, Rivas."

He took the bubbling water off the stove and poured it into a little pot in the shape of an elephant's head with the curled-up trunk serving as the handle. "With whom is she starting a family, Mataji?"

"With someone with whom she's worked for a long time. Dr Farad Sandali."

"Her previous boss? The chief of the pediatric ward?"

"You remember him?"

"Vaguely yes."

"He got an offer to run a clinic in his home town – in Karachi. He took her with him. Yes and then, a few months ago they decided to get married. Now then, as I said, Chand predicted that you may show up here one day and she left a letter for you. Would you like to see it?"

"She left a message for me? Of course, yes!"

Mrs Basu shuffled back to the lounge in her oversized slippers and scratched through a drawer, while Rivas poured tea into her cup. When she returned, she ceremoniously handed him the carefully folded piece of paper without an envelope. Rivas read: "Out beyond ideas of wrongdoing and rightdoing, there is a field. I'll meet you there. Rumi".

"And? I never read her note to you. Does she say where you can find her?"

"Yes Mataji, she's left me clear directions. I have to be off now. It's over a hundred miles back to Lima and I don't have to tell you how heavy the inward-bound traffic is." A concerned glance at his watch confirmed he'd spent far too much time with her already.

"Please stay a while longer."

"Alright. I'll probably be late anyway; doesn't make much difference now." He chatted another five minutes and then insisted, "I really have to leave now, Mataji. It was good seeing you again."

"You'll come visit me more often from now on, won't you? Now that I'm all alone?"

"Yes. Whenever I'm in the area, I'll look in on you."

"Until I move to Karachi."

"Yes, we'll do that, Mataji. Goodbye now."

"Do you have a message for Chand?"

"Yes. Tell her thank you for the note and that I'm on my way to the place she mentioned."

"Does this mean, you'll look for her there?"

"Yes - in the spirit of the message, Mataji."

The intuitive old lady understood and nodded. "Drive carefully, Rivas." In the corridor she called after him, "Oh Rivas, she left something else for you. I almost forgot." She trudged after him, a black little book in hand. Rivas recognized it straight away. It was Chand's collection of Arthur Schopenhauer quotes, sorted alphabetically according to topic. Whenever a quote spoke to her, and this was the case with almost all of Schopenhauer's immense wisdom, Chand used to write it into this booklet. Rivas and Chand had spent many nights philosophizing over just one of his sentences. She regarded Schopenhauer as a trove of richness, and Rivas enjoyed the debates with her.

He took the little book from her and was about to leave when the doorbell rang. "Are you expecting someone?"

"Not really, no."

Rivas was at the door and he opened it without hesitation. He found himself looking straight into the face of a young woman. A young woman who'd clearly escaped from an exotic picture book and landed on a magic carpet in front of this humble door. She stared at him for a few seconds, without saying a word, as though this was the first time ever that she'd seen a man of flesh and blood.

One, two, three, four. Rivas loved pauses. He'd grown fond of them; they served him as useful weapons for power games and demonstrations of his dominance, with which he could overwhelm anyone. It was just a matter of time. Whoever spoke first, lost. Five, six, seven.

"You're Rivas. You must be," whispered the mouth of the tigress.

"Do we know each other?"

"I know you. But you never met me."

"Please. Come in," he invited her, marveling at her feline, enticing demeanor. It also didn't escape his attention that, while she slinked past him like an exotic cat on the prowl, she rubbed against his body with her breasts.

"Who is it, Rivas?" The old lady stuck her head into the passage.

"It's me, Aunty."

"Oh! Hello my darling. Have you come to bring me back my watch?"

"That's right. Here you are, Aunty Lata." She handed her an old watch, with a wrist band that was shredded to tatters from wear.

"How much do I owe you?"

"Nothing. Sergio fixed it for free. He owed me a favor."

Rivas reflected on his own expensive watches and felt sorry for the old lady, whom he liked very, very much. He resolved to bring her a new watch on his next visit. He'd not lied when he promised to visit her again.

"Thank you. Have you introduced yourselves?" Mrs Basu turned to Rivas as she asked this, traditionally addressing the man.

Rivas explained, "Your visitor claims to know me already."

"No, Shanta! You're wrong. You've only been here for six months," Mrs Basu corrected her. She turned again to Rivas: "This is Shanta, one of Chand's cousins. She lives two floors up from me. But I see even less of her than I did of Chand. She never has time for me. She's very smart and ambitious. Managed to get a year's contract, didn't you Shanta?"

"What field?" enquired Rivas.

"Software development."

"What kind?"

"Embedded."

"My compliments! That's really hard core. Which language? C++?"

She pretended to smile shyly about the ambiguous wordplay on both their parts, and she looked down and slantwise before answering. "A little C++, too, yes."

"I know they've been manufacturing microprocessors in India for a few years now, but here in South America?"

"I'm working for a Silicon Valley enterprise from one of their bases here in Peru and I'm not writing code yet, well, application software yes, but not yet embedded. I work in a call center and I mainly do research for developers based in the US."

"I see." You little confidence trickster, you really are misleading your poor old aunt! mused Rivas to himself.

Shanta looked at him expectantly. Rivas knew she was waiting for him to greet her first, formally, because that was good etiquette in Indian Hindu culture. Her informal exclamation at the door must have slipped out from pure surprise, but he couldn't guess why.

"Hello Shanta," he said. "Nice to meet you. I'm Rivas." He didn't stretch out his hand. This would have been improper with a young Indian woman at a first introduction.

She folded her hands in front of her breast, bowed lightly and said "*Namaste.*" A glittering, alluring smile escaped from her eyes, negating the respect that she'd just paid him by means of the traditional greeting.

"*Namaskar,*" Rivas replied.

Chand's mother interjected, ending their ritual. "She also paints, you know. Why don't you show Rivas the portrait you painted of Chand?"

"You're good in math and you paint? An unusual combination."

"You have no idea how good it is for my logical thinking when I indulge myself in a few creative breaks here and there."

"Makes sense. Um, I was about to leave. It was good to meet you, Shanta."

"Don't you want to see it? My painting of Chand?"

"Next time, okay?"

"Please let me show you. Who knows how long it'll be before we cross paths again?"

The old lady withdrew to the kitchen and then called out to him from there.

"Yes Mataji, what is it? I really have to get going now."

She scolded him, "Don't be so rude to the girl. Look at her painting."

"I'd love to, but I'm out of time. Why is this so important? The whole time we talked, you never said a word about Shanta."

"I told you, I'm so forgetful these days. Rivas, it's such a beautiful picture of Chand. Shanta worked hard at it and she's always nice to me. Of course only when she can squeeze me in. She's a very successful career woman, you know. Be charitable, Rivas."

"Charitable? What makes you think I would do anything for the sake of charity?"

"I know you have a big heart. Thank you, Rivas."

He returned to the lounge. "Where's the painting?"

"In my apartment."

"Are you going to fetch it, or is it mounted?"

"Come upstairs with me please." She summoned another one of her beguiling smiles.

Why is she coming on to me like that? Rivas wondered. "How come you think you know me, Shanta?" he asked on the landing in front of her apartment.

She opened her front door and as soon as it closed behind them, she shed her Indian protocol and revealed, "I secretly read Chand's diary. She wrote down everything you two got up to together. In bed."

"I hope you were well entertained. When I consider how you get right down to business, I fear my sexual creativity would bore you to death."

"I've had many lovers but never did I experience anything nearly as exciting as Chand did with you. I was envious, even jealous of her. I still am. I've read the diary so many times that I know many passages off by heart. I recite them like a poem and then I imagine that you're doing with me what you did with Chand."

"You're not bad looking." That's an understatement, he thought to himself. "Don't you have a boyfriend with whom you can imitate those things? Or better still, invent your own together?"

"I want to do them with you."

"Enough now. Are you going to show me the picture or not? I'm in a hurry."

She threw herself around his neck and whispered, "What do you want? I'll do anything you want. You opened the door, stood there, and I knew that it's not a coincidence. Today I don't have to pull myself out of my dreams. You've come to pull me into them."

"Is that so? Don't kid yourself, Shanta. What I would do with you, you wouldn't be able to stand, not even in your dreams." He made the veiled threat to put her off, freed himself from her grip and turned to leave. Like a whirlwind she spun around and threw herself against the door, turned the key, pulled it out of the lock and made it vanish down between her breasts.

"Unlock the door!" he commanded, and he stepped towards the door, and thus closer to her. She pressed herself against him, slung her arms around him and buried her face in his neck. Rivas grabbed her perfect shoulders in order to free himself from his groupie. Touching her like this drew his attention directly towards the burnished, golden skin of her arms. He guessed her at around thirty. Her long, blueberry colored hair fell over her narrow shoulders like a fleece of silk. With her back pressed firmly against the door, she ran her hand under her dress. Then she retrieved it and gently touched his lips with her fingers. The fiery glow from her sparkling onyx eyes brought Rivas's blood to boiling point. He gave in to the pressure of her middle finger and sucked it into his mouth.

"How do I taste?"

He replied by nailing her to the door with a greedy look in his eyes.

She stroked down over her red dress, as if to smooth it around her hips and waited.

Rivas's head hammered. Yes or no? Pro or con? Or was the real question: now or later? A consenting, uninhibited, attractive woman. *Pro*. Not a victim with a history, like Catherine, who could be so strenuous when it came to love. Also not a cheap tart like Pureza. Even though Shanta also was literally throwing herself at him. *Con*. But her classical beauty excused this potential flaw. He rationalized it away with the argument that she knows what she wants. *Pro*. And she knew how to use herself to get it. *Pro*.

And what about him? He was curious. *Cure*. *Rigorous*. About this unexpected toybox, delivered to the door, unordered, and yet accepted.

"You can do with me what you like," breathed the enchanting packet of sex. "You won't frighten me."

Her offer was tempting.

Catherine came to mind again. The long time with her on the farm, during which she longed for him but he did not touch her. "Enough already of this silly coyness!" he'd often wanted to say, fling her down, flip her over and get some ass - good and proper. But because of Catherine's sexual passivity, it hadn't been too hard to restrain himself. These thoughts called him back to reality, and he let go of Shanta. "You don't know what you're talking about."

"You can do things with me that you wouldn't even have dared with Chand." Again she cast her net over him. Rivas took her by the arm, gently led her into the lounge and onto the couch. From there she let herself glide slowly down onto the carpet and as if by accident pulled up her dress to show off her long legs. "Come," she pleaded. "Come." Because he made no move, she pulled herself to her knees and crawled around him. Kneeling behind him, she slung her arms around his lower torso, sleek like a cobra. From this position she now tugged at him gently to get him to join her down on the floor. The unnatural writhing behind his back had an extremely erogenous effect. For a while Rivas didn't move, enjoying the growing throbbing sensation. But it became so strong, immediate and real that it awoke his scruples. He began to wrestle with his conscience. There wasn't only Catherine to consider, but also Chand - after all, this sex bomb was her cousin. Chand's mother also gnawed at his gallantry. But the covetous tugging at his jeans continued to flood his groin with a wave of lust.

Unbridled, unadulterated sex. With this Indian goddess.

Shanta had managed to open his belt from behind, using her long, slim arms, and now she loosened his waist band. Rivas put both hands on his head and gasped for air. Then he felt her warm tongue stroke over his lower back, directly underneath the belt area. He was about to turn around, toss her onto the carpet and throw himself onto this heavenly creature, when she crawled around him, looked at him as if transfigured, and suddenly got up. "Wait a moment," she sang cheerfully, and she ran to the CD player to put on some music. "I've fantasized about this moment so often. This is a song I always play when I'm with you in my imagination. Jail me anytime, Rivas." Because she believed she wasn't able to seduce him, she reckoned a bit of romantic music would move things along. How wrong she was – for him, this wasn't about romance. She disappeared briefly into her bedroom. That was her biggest mistake because while she was away the lyrics of the song made their way from his ears to his heart: 'You jail me, please jail me. You may jail me anytime'. Shanta had inadvertently called up *his* jailer: Catherine. Slowly, a strange wave of nausea rolled over him. It was as if the cobra had turned into a boa constrictor which now slung itself around his chest and cut off his air supply. Catherine's red-blond hair flickered up before his eyes. He recalled how she'd stood in front of his house for the first time – her scratched face, strewn with foxy freckles. Her hair untamed, her clothes filthy and tattered. Half child, half woman, spat out by the jungle, landing directly in front of his feet. "When you smiled at me the first time, in front of Andalus's stable, you could have had me then already", she'd confessed cheerfully a couple of days ago. With her life she trusted him. All the pain he caused her, she'd forgiven him – and what was he doing to her now? This would be too much to bear. She'd never forgive him for this. How could anyone endure that much betrayal? What man would do something like this? He! He was about to annihilate Catherine completely.

Shanta returned to the lounge. She'd changed into a beautiful royal-blue silk sari. It was embroidered with a pattern of golden elephants, which accentuated her flawless complexion. It must have cost her family a small fortune, he surmised. She beamed at him – in her festive attire. Rivas knew she was expecting a compliment. It was hard not to pay her one. "You really want me to give you some, don't you?" By now he was overcome with longing for Catherine.

"Yes, yes!" She noted his tone had an edge to it. She ignored it.

"But I don't want any from you! Don't come near me again. And if you ever touch me again, I'll kill you. Because that, Shanta, is the only thing I'd enjoy doing to a little slut like you!" Her eyes went glassy. He saw it. "Tears? Already? Why, that's not a fraction of what I'd have in store for you. Chand's diary games are way out of your league, Shanta."

"No, it's fine. I didn't realize…." She gulped and tried to smile bravely.

"Shanta, seriously now. You shouldn't try to turn your lounge into a sandpit and a strange man into your playschool buddy. Otherwise your dreams will turn into a horror movie with you in the lead role." He felt sorry for her but he believed that she needed to get a grip. And so did he! "Whatever you had in mind, it's not going happen. Not with me. Ever. Give me the key now, or I'll knock your damn door down."

She sank to the floor and crumbled, like a rapidly fading flower. Rivas knew she wasn't putting this on. And how hard it would be for her to come out of this clinical obsessive fixation. That was his quick diagnosis for her condition. He bent down and pulled her up gently. Her toned body now felt as limp as a rag doll. "Shanta, don't get involved with guys like me. If you just throw yourself away like this, you're nothing but a piece of meat. Good on the palate for a few minutes but spewed out straight afterwards." He reached into her bra and pulled the front door key from the cup.

"Please don't go. I don't mind if you call me names and take me by force."

"Force? You're throwing yourself at me like a bitch on heat."

"Please tell me what I can do for you."

"Nothing."

"I don't mind if you get violent."

"Why do you keep harping on about violence?"

"I thought you liked that. Since I've read Chand's diary I haven't stopped fantasizing about you. On the bus, while eating, while working. I imagined what you looked like, how you desire me, how I fight you off and you take me anyway. It's not my fault - I can't get these pictures out of my mind."

"I'm sorry that Chand's diary confused you. Those erotic games developed over years. We trusted each other and we experimented with our sexuality, gradually increasing the intensity. Those were role plays of symbolic character, nothing more. Stop going on about violence. You don't even know what that is."

"But you liked it. And I also liked it."

"You? Shanta! You weren't there!"

"Oh but I was. Chand's diary made me a witness. May I remind you?"

"Remind me of what?"

"I quote…" She looked at him triumphantly and started to recite.

Log – 57 Hours in the Mountains. Day 2

I'd slept for three hours when he shakes me up. "Fix me something to eat. There should be some eggs left in the refrigerator."

He permits me to slip on one of his shirts. I go to the kitchen and look for a clean pan, because I don't want to wash his dirty dishes. When I can't find one, I'm forced to wash the only frying pan anyway. I can't find any oil or butter. How am I supposed to fry these damn eggs? I ask myself. Not him. I'm afraid he might get angry. I pour some water into the pan and try it like this, hoping it'll work. I can't find any bread, potatoes, don't know what to serve him with the eggs. I' want to spit into the pan but daren't, in case he notices. I'm also hungry. I go to the living room. "I'm also hungry," I say. He doesn't answer. I take this as permission to also eat. Disgusted but hungry, I knock two more eggs into the pan. They're sticking to the bottom. I scramble them together and scrape the chaos onto two plates. I bring him his portion and a fork. I purposely forget the knife. I return to the kitchen and eat. He joins me with his plate and fork. After one bite he gets up to fetch salt.

"Why are you serving up such a mess? Can't you cook?"

"I couldn't find any oil."

"Why don't you ask then, if you're too lazy to open your eyes?"

I hear myself say "I'm sorry" and hate myself. And him. Especially him.

He rummages through the kitchen cupboards. When he doesn't find what he's looking for, he starts tossing things on the floor. His anger is growing, I'm scared he'll hit me, but he sits down again and carries on eating. Afterwards he orders me to clean up the kitchen. I have to wash up after all. I do it. Then I go to the toilet and lie down again, without asking him for permission. I'm so tired. He follows me, pulls off my shirt. He strokes my breasts and pays me a compliment. I feel flattered. I'm losing my mind.

"Did you clean up?"

"Yes."

"Go back in the kitchen and lie down on the table."

Comment: I'm angry with Rivas. We'd agreed on the following signals: If I can't go on, or don't want to, I say "Stop". If he can't go on, or doesn't want to, he'll say "Stop". If he wants to reassure himself that I'm still okay, he asks me "Claro?" and I answer "Sí" or "No". I want to call out "Stop", but I also want to conclude the experiment successfully. If I terminate prematurely, I'll feel like a failure and like I've let him down. But if he asked "Claro?", I'd shout "No". I'm sure of it. But this whole time he hasn't once asked me if I'm still okay. This is horrible. I want to go home.

I go to the kitchen and lie down on the table. He positions himself in front of me, spreads my legs and puts them on his shoulders....

"That's enough, Shanta." Rivas wasn't bothered by the narrative as such. The log had been agreed upon and he was familiar with its contents. He also knew about Chand's comments, because he'd of course wanted to know how she felt and they discussed it afterwards. This is why Chand recorded everything. But to have it all recited completely out of context, upset him. "I can't believe that you're rattling all this off by heart. And I really can't understand why you'd want to experience this."

"And everything else in the diary, not just what's in the log."

"You've just recited what went on in Chand during all this and still you persist?"

"Let me tell you about Day 3, then you'll know why."

"Enough of the recitations. Do you have any idea what you'd be in for if you carried on inviting strange guys to get nasty with you? I can promise you – what you read in Chand's diary will be a bed of roses in comparison."

"I *want* to know what that's like. I've always been, um, the adventurous type."

"Is that so? Alright, here's your adventure. Listen to me carefully now. You're going for a Sunday afternoon stroll down an idyllic country road. A man walks behind you for a while, overtakes you with big steps, turns around to face you, and in a fraction of a second he lunges towards you. He grabs your neck with both his hands and drags you into the bushes. Apart from not being able to breathe, the pain from the pressure on your throat alone is almost enough to make you pass out. There, in the cover of the bushes, he strangles you until you lose consciousness so he can take you to an isolated spot. It has to be close by, he doesn't have much time. He drags you to his car, which he parked not far away. On the way to his hide-out, he changes his chaotic mind and spontaneously diverts to a barren field. When you wake up you're not lying on a cozy carpet dressed in a blue sari but find yourself on an abandoned stretch of land in the dirt, with your nose bleeding, strangulation marks on your neck and a scratched face. Naked. You smell your blood, you're freezing and you're ashamed. You can't believe what's happening to you. The man is not the man of your dreams but a dirty, ugly bastard who's continuously slapping you in the face and pinning you to the ground with his immense body weight. With his free hand he tugs at your breasts as if he was milking a cow. You suppress the pain for fear that he'll smash your face with his fists. Your nose is already broken, your eyes are bruised. You can't even thrash about or kick him, or fight him off with your hands. You can do nothing at all. No matter how hard you try, you can't move your arms by even one inch. You're not experiencing sensual desire like in your dream. You're paralyzed by fear because you don't know what he'll do to you next, how often, or if he'll let you catch your breath for even a minute. And you continuously think about whether he'll strangle you to death with your own bra afterwards. Death is what concerns you most. The rest seems like a side act, but the worst is still to come. He towers over you, drools on you and blows his stinking breath up your broken nose. You're glad that he doesn't force you to lick his disgusting, sweaty body. Screaming is out of the question because he's gagged you with your panties, or if he didn't shove anything into your mouth, you still can't breathe because he's bearing down on your lungs with his two hundred pounds of flab, while holding your mouth closed with his huge, dirty hand. He grinds you down not only physically but also mentally by screaming and cussing at you in the most vile way. His revolting language and his stench flood you with disgust. You suppress the urge to throw up for fear of making him rant even more, or worse, because you may just choke to death on your own vomit while you're lying flat on your back. You pray that he is fully erect, because if he isn't, and that's often the case, he'll struggle to penetrate you and will demand that you stimulate him manually or orally, or that you stroke yourself or groan and play around to arouse him. Or he'll force you to whisper obscene words in his ear, or to shout them out loud. You recall having read somewhere, that when such a rapist does manage to gain an erection, and isn't under time pressure, feeling fairly safe, he penetrates his victim vaginally up to thirty times per hour. From all directions, in all imaginable and unimaginable positions because this is the part of his crime which he finds the most exciting. You're trapped, you don't even know what to pray for. If he can, it's dreadful for you, and if he can't, it's even worse. And when he eventually pokes around inside you, you won't think about how nice that feels, but wonder whether you'll ever be able to straighten up, that's how much your womb hurts. He'll scratch around in you, as if he was using a cheese grater and his thrusts hammer against your cervix with increasing brutality. You'll get so many internal injuries, that you almost pass out from the pain. But an inexplicable reservoir of mental strength keeps you from passing out again, because you know if, you do, he may kill you if you just lie there, useless and limp. And when he's finally, finally, finished with you and doesn't cut up your face and neck, or kill you with sixty stabs in your stomach before burying you, he leaves you lying in the dirt. His sperm runs into your butt and gums up your inner thighs. If you do manage to get up, his ejaculate drips down your legs. You feel as if you've just rolled in sewage and then as if you turned into sewage yourself. You want to get home to wash off this shame and injustice. You want to crawl into a cave and hide, but you don't know where you are. There's nobody around. You pray for someone to rescue you and at the same time you pray that nobody sees you in this abysmal state. You're thirsty, but you've got nothing to drink, you collapse from exhaustion and you shake from cold. As soon as you can, you struggle back up and if you're lucky, you find your clothes nearby and pick them up one by one. Suddenly you hear a car approach. Is he back?..."

"Enough! I get it. But what I don't get is how someone can invent such a dreadful story."

"No story! Factual account - I've heard and read many like it. These reports are from patients' files and court records. And from what I gleaned from survivors *and* perpetrators during personal interviews. In addition I've sat in on countless court cases, listening to rapists and victims being cross-examined. Why don't you attend such a hearing? Some of them are public. That'll cure you."

"But why did you and Chand get up to this stuff if it's all so terrible?"

"I told you – we kind of grew into it. With reference to the log – I invented an abduction scenario for research purposes to do with my studies. We locked ourselves away in the holiday cottage of a good friend from Thursday afternoon 'til Sunday lunch time. We purposely under-catered in terms of our provisions and pretended that I'd kidnapped her to abuse her. It was an experiment. We wanted to test human boundaries. How far would I go? How much could she take? But I was her boyfriend and she was in no real danger." Rivas sighed. It was unbelievable that he had to justify himself in front of a strange young woman, today, here in Barranca. But it was also good, because this gave him the strength to draw the final line under his relationship with Chand. Up until ten minutes ago he wasn't sure he was ready to let her go. Now it was over.

"I also want to explore myself."

"There's nothing wrong with that, Shanta, except that you'll have to find your own partner, a man whom you can trust, not the first stranger who comes along."

"You're not a stranger and you'd never seriously hurt me."

Rivas exhaled almost as hard as a snort by Andalus. He grabbed her by her shoulders and shook her so hard that she really got a fright. "How do you know that, huh? How do you know how far I'd go? You have no idea what I'm capable of. Perhaps you wouldn't be the first one I'd send to her grave? If you don't get a handle on this, you're predestined for what I've described. If you weren't Chand's cousin I'd knock you around so hard now that you'd never trust a man again. What I've just told you is no game, Shanta. It's the truth."

She looked at him. He couldn't read her. What was she thinking about now? Did she still not take him seriously?

"I don't want us to break up like this."

Of course – that!

"We're not breaking up because we've never been together."

"Do you despise me?"

"No."

"What now?"

"We forget the whole thing and pretend it never happened. Come, freshen up your face and let's go downstairs. Your aunt's probably wondering why we're taking so long."

"I'm embarrassed."

"Wash your face and change. I'll wait for you."

"Really?"

"Yes. Go now."

After a few minutes she returned. "This is so embarrassing."

"I've seen worse. And done worse. Nothing happened."

"I love you."

"Shanta, you don't even know me."

"I love you anyway."

"You don't love me. You love a phantom."

"No phantom. I love you!"

"You've really lost your mind, Shanta. You need help."

"I didn't lose my mind. You robbed me of it."

"I didn't rob you of anything because you've got nothing that I want. Are you coming now or not?"

"Please kiss me. Then I've got something to hold on to for the rest of my life. You'll never see me again after that."

"Fine! I'll kiss you and you'll stay away from bad guys in future, alright?"

--- oOo ---

You're not a bad guy, she decided. She nodded vigorously and clung to his neck again. He took his face in her hands and stroked the hair off her face. She held out her closed mouth, hoping he would shove his tongue through her lips, forcefully and egotistically. Despite Rivas's horror account, she wanted it so badly. But that's not what happened. He gently stroked her face and kissed her neck before he placed his lips upon hers, with inimitable tenderness. Many women love men to caress their necks and Shanta was no different. She tried to press her lips together but her appetite for his kiss rendered her powerless – stubbornly her mouth opened by itself. Her throat uttered a helpless animal sound. "Shhh," he calmed her down and then his tongue stroked over hers. The fraction of a second became an eternity. Eternity became a fraction of a second. Then it was over. This kiss was the kindest and most wicked thing he could have done to her.

--- oOo ---

"Let's go."

"Yes." She didn't move.

"Shanta!"

"Sorry." On the staircase she held him back again. "Why did you kiss me if you don't care for me?"

"I recently found out what it's like to want something that you can never have. Let's call it charity."

"With your charity, you've broken my heart for good."

"Maybe, but the pain in your heart will remind you that you're still alive. If you carry on like this, you'll meet the wrong guy sooner or later, Shanta. Don't sacrifice yourself on this altar of madness."

"How could Chand ever let you go?"

"Yeah, yeah, alright. Put on a happy face now and act normal in front of Chands' mom. Your frail old aunt would be appalled if she knew what went on two floors up. By the way, where is that diary now?"

"In my apartment."

"Burn it."

"I wanted to confess my indiscretion to Chand and give it back to her one day."

"Believe me Shanta, if she still needed or wanted it, she wouldn't have left it behind. She's through with it and you need to do the same. Get rid of it. It's done enough damage." As they reached Mrs Basu's front door, Rivas realized his error. "You know what? Go back upstairs and bring me that damn diary."

"I just want to read it one last time when you're gone." Without a further word he grabbed her by the arm and forced her upstairs again. She opened the door and he asked, "Where is it?"

She didn't reply.

"If you don't tell me, I'll find it anyway, but not without taking apart your entire apartment."

"I fastened it with tape under the kitchen table."

He shook his head, went to the kitchen and tore off the little booklet. He opened it briefly to ensure that it was indeed the ill-fated exhibit and shoved it in his pocket.

He hoped that this beautiful woman would not lose her way again. And he? He would also stop this madness.

Rivas was a seducer, not the kind of man who forced himself on women, though he enjoyed imagining that when his partner played along. But with Catherine all this was not possible anyhow, he thought. It wouldn't be hard to give up these morbid sex games. He didn't need them anymore.

Convinced that this part of his life was over, he sped back to Lima. Knowing he would be over an hour late for his appointment with Catherine.

37.
Peru, September 20

Having her hair done not only boosted Catherine's looks, but also soothed her soul. Highlighting and trimming her stressed hair had taken just over three hours. The rain had eased up and she spent the remainder of the time window shopping.

It was 4.15 pm when Catherine arrived at the bus stop. Up and down she paced - like a caged circus animal. She chain-smoked nervously, worried that she might never see Rivas again. By 4.30 pm there was still no sign of Rivas. Instead a strange man, who seemed to have appeared from nowhere, tapped her on the shoulder. "*Señorita Catarina?*"

She turned around. "*Sí. Por favor?*"

Unleashing agitated Spanish on her, the stranger tried to get her to accompany him. This much she understood, but she evaded his insistent attentions. He shoved his mobile under her nose and frenetically pointed to the display. She read, "Catherine, I've been delayed. This taxi driver has come to fetch you. I know, after your experience in M, you'll be reluctant to get into an unknown car, but you'll be safe with him until I arrive. R. 1248."

Catherine wanted the man to dial the number from which the SMS had been sent, but he didn't understand. So she pressed the green dial button herself. At this, the man promptly ripped the phone out of her hand. Why didn't Rivas just call her on this cab driver's phone, since she didn't have her own? But the number 1248 calmed her down. Only she and Rivas knew this code. She doubted that he'd have passed on this type of information. That was so unlike him, and who would have been interested? What had happened? Was he in trouble? She had to see him! She followed the man to his cab, which he'd parked at the taxi stand outside the Sheraton, across the road.

They cruised through the confusing town for what seemed like forever, until she recognized the suburb of Miraflores.

The taxi drew up and parked in front of what appeared like a very modest-looking restaurant.

She was taken inside, where this first impression was blown away.

The driver introduced her to the manager, who was clearly expecting her. He showed her to a quiet corner table. A polished waiter opened a bottle of water and poured some for her. Next to her table, in an ice bucket on a stand, he placed a bottle of Taittinger champagne. Her favorite! The table was laid with a classic white linen cloth and fine Rosenthal bone china. The cutlery felt so heavy that she guessed it was made of real silver. Two champagne glasses promised a romantic late afternoon dinner. Even though she hardly drank alcohol before she'd met Rivas, she could always drink Taittinger like lemonade. Not that it had no effect on her - she just really liked it, contrary to other champagnes, or, even worse, sparkling wine, which wasn't the same for Catherine at all. She had to laugh. How did he know that? She sipped at her water and inspected her sparse purchases: a CD, and biscuits for Andalus.

Suddenly he stood in front of her. The sight of him took her breath away. She felt like jumping up and hugging him but she was so taken aback that she could only stare. She remembered the woman who'd served the coffees - and Hesse. She couldn't blame the waitress.

That smile.

That charm.

And the body! He bent down and kissed her on the cheek before he sat down. "I'm so sorry. I should have been back long ago, but something - crept in."

"I love you," she stammered, blown away yet again by his looks.

How can anyone look this good? It's not fair!

Once again she became intensely aware of his immaculate appearance. It must have been the surroundings. His cosmopolitan flair suited the general picture that they painted, of the free, wide world.

"Have you had a look at the menu? May I order for you or would you like to choose something yourself? Then I'll translate for you. Unfortunately, we have to hurry up. It's not safe to fly in the mountains after dark. Please forgive me. The last thing I wanted was to spoil your day."

"My day is wonderful! Now that you're back. Yes, please order for me." She'd always wished that a man would order for her in a restaurant. She found the idea intensely romantic. The waiter poured the champagne and took Rivas's order. She didn't understand a word. "How do you know that I like Taittinger?"

"Catherine, I know everything about you."

"Everything? Surely not!"

"Yes, everything. Do you think you're the only person who can conduct a thorough background check?" She laughed happily. He changed the topic. "You look stunning. Not just because of your hair. I also like you shaggy, as you were on the day you arrived."

"Don't go there!"

"So? What did you buy? Let me see."

"You're so sweet. Does that really interest you?"

"Of course. Why don't I see any shopping bags? Are they keeping them at the back for you?" She pulled out her CD and a plastic packet with cheap biscuits, which she'd bought from a street vendor at the last minute. In her mental turmoil, she'd nearly forgotten her promise to Andalus. "That's all?"

"Yes. *Me and Mrs Jones* and cookies for Andalus."

"How do you relate to this song? Did you have an affair? How come I don't know about that?" he joked.

"I thought you know everything about me."

"Apparently not. Will you borrow Joe's CD player?"

"I'll play it on my laptop."

"Why didn't you just download the song if you like it so much? I told you, you have an unlimited budget for whatever you need. You can order anything you like. The same goes for shopping in Paris."

"That wouldn't be the same. The song is more like a symbol for me."

"For love?"

"For freedom. In Columbia the men had a radio and one evening this song came on. I was so taken with it. It connected me with home. I already told you how lonely I felt. It was painful to listen to the song and yet it was too short. It hurt even more when it was over. I resolved then that I would survive, no matter what. And that the first thing I would do, when I was free again, was to buy this CD. And, as of today, I am free."

"Let's drink to that."

They toasted cheerfully and she took such a big gulp of champagne that she emptied half the glass in one go. This tender sensation on her tongue! She felt alive again. "If I'd thought then that when I finally have the CD in my hands, I would drink to this together with my kidnapper, I really would have written myself off." He smiled at her, thoughtful, but didn't say anything. She continued, "I looked for another CD but couldn't find it. The song's called *Spanish Guitar*. Do you know it?"

"No, isn't that rather more suitable for Joe?"

"Well, it's more of a woman song, if you know what I mean. But I want to tell you something through it, even if it's not really your taste. Please don't download it. I want to surprise you."

"No problem. Did you really buy nothing else?"

"Yes. Nothing else." She reached into her bag to hand him back the purse.

"Give it to me later, then I'll change the dollars to euros. For Paris."

"You know, Rivas, if I'm really allowed to download something, I'd love to watch the movie *Marnie* again."

"That fossil?"

"Ha! That's something you didn't know I liked."

"You're wrong. I've got an entire Hitchcock collection for you at the ranch."

"What? Why did you keep it from me?"

"You never asked for entertainment. Your nose was always in your books. Besides, I would have dug it up sooner or later. As a reward."

"You're awful! Anyhow, give me *Marnie* as soon as we get back, please. I'll watch it on my laptop tonight. Or have you also kept a DVD player hidden from me?"

"We've got one somewhere."

"Will you watch it with me?"

"Catherine, it's a terribly old movie. It's corny."

"Yes, but Sean Connery and Tippy Hedren are so romantic together."

"Marnie reminds you of your own plight, right? Because Mark holds her against her will?"

"For someone who finds the movie kitschy, you sure know a lot about it."

"I told you I'm a thorough investigator."

"You even watched my favorite movies?"

"Sure did."

"It's true what you say about Marnie. The story does touch me personally. Her love for horses, her drive for independence, her sexual inhibitions…."

"Her childhood trauma?"

Catherine jerked her head up and deflected him: "Except that Mark impulsively marries her, that doesn't apply to me."

Rivas noted her sad expression. He'd also taken note of her shock when he brought up Marnie's past, but he decided to let that slide for now. "And you want me to also marry you spontaneously. Catherine, that won't happen. You must forget about that."

"You sure don't believe in subtlety, do you?"

"You don't strike me as someone who prefers beating about the bush. Am I wrong?"

"Rivas, I don't know how to go on without you. How will I ever be happy with some old bore? I'll always draw comparisons. I want to stay with you."

"Catherine, I cannot and will not marry you. I don't want to start a family with a kidnapping victim, who believes she's fallen in love with me because I manipulated her into it. That wouldn't work. Surely you can understand?"

"Now you're punishing me for the way I met you. I simply can't win!"

"Don't you see how unrealistic all this is? A few weeks ago you would have freaked out - justifiably so - at the thought of someone digging through your things at home. Now you feel flattered that I had you spied on."

"How did WICED get into my house, actually?"

"Your housekeeper," he said briefly. "You have your whole life in front of you. Once you're free, you won't miss me for long."

The food arrived.

Catherine chewed on a lettuce leaf and poked listlessly around in her fish. "Don't you like it? Would you like to order something else?"

"I've lost my appetite."

"What's wrong, Catherine?"

"You've been so loving. I thought we belong together, but you're just leading me on."

Rivas sighed, "Catherine, there's no way around it. You'll do as I say. That's it. Deal with it."

"You're neither my father, nor my boss. You gave up your kidnapper status voluntarily and you don't want to be my husband. You can't tell me what to do anymore."

"Must I remind you of what you promised me in the cellar?"

"That's unfair and inappropriate in this context."

"Must I?"

"No."

"Then eat now. Come."

"I feel sick when I think about you leaving me as soon as you don't need me anymore. Of course I want to be free. I mean, of course I'd *like* to be free – but I don't want to. I *wouldn't like* to be free." Her head spun from the champagne, and her tangled statement seemed to be the fine alcohol that spoke. "What?" she interrupted herself. "What's this trash about 'want to' and 'would like to'? I'm getting confused! Any case, I *don't* want to live without you."

"Catherine, I'm begging you. Please eat. This fish's got little enough calories, but it's fresh and you need the vitamins."

"I'll never eat again after you've deserted me."

"Stop being so childish!"

"Sorry. I think it's the champagne." She sat up straight and recovered her focus, although her next words again seemed to make little sense: "What's my name?"

"What do you mean, Catherine?"

"In the new passport," she explained.

"Ah! I don't know yet. We can't always choose. It depends which names are available. Do you have a particular request?"

"What name will you travel under?"

"I don't know yet. I've got several passports. I'll be told which one to use."

"Then I want my surname to be the same as yours, and my first name must be Catherine."

"Noted. I'll see what I can do, but only if you eat now."

"If that's not possible, then Jones."

"As you wish, Mrs Jones."

Her appetite returned and she ate the delicious meal while they carried on talking. "Rivas, was the thing with the cab driver a test?"

"I really couldn't get away earlier. Though I wasn't sure if you'd get in his car after the experience in Miami."

"Why didn't you call me on the driver's phone?"

"I thought 1248 would do it."

"It did, I suppose. But about Miami – I don't even want to think about how stupid I was! No, not stupid. Brazen! My father always warned me about being overconfident."

"You must have got a huge fright in Florida. Were you very scared?"

"That's the thing, Rivas. Not at all. I kept saying to myself that I'd be able to talk my way out of it. I wasn't even really afraid of the pistol."

"They pulled a gun on you?"

"Yes, briefly. In the car. Didn't you know that?"

"No. But it's nothing unusual, as long as they don't use it. Why the gun? Did you put up a fight in the car?" Amateurs! he hissed to himself.

"Actually, I think I stayed quite cool. I was just surprised about the strange set-up. Besides, at that stage, I found it all rather exciting."

"An abduction is not 'exciting'!"

"You're scolding me? For being kidnapped?"

"Do you know how many moral boundaries a man has overstepped by the time he's ready to pull a gun in order to achieve his end?"

"As well as someone who's pulled the trigger, and several times at that? No, can't say I do."

"Hey! You also pulled the trigger!"

"Out of self-defense. I kidnapped nobody! I didn't mistreat anyone for months on end!"

"Can you see now why we don't have a future together?"

"I'm sorry, Rivas. I don't know how that slipped out. Now that we are talking like a couple for the first time."

"Sooner or later, every intimate conversation between us would land up there. My past would always stand between us. But I want you to know that I never killed out of greed or bloodlust."

"But out of hatred and revenge."

"No. Neither out of hatred or revenge. There was always a rational reason behind my actions."

"Yes, yes, I know. You were only restoring the balance of good and bad in the world."

"Are you still defending yourself or is this a disinterested attack on my past?"

"It's not your past that concerns me, Rivas. It's your present and your future that I worry about. Besides, you started it because you're rebuking me for something I'm well aware of." Rivas studied Catherine's face. "What's wrong?"

"You're beautiful."

"We should've taken the passport photo after the hair appointment."

"And vain."

"How will we get across the borders with our false passports?"

"We'll separate briefly before and after the checkpoints, but if you don't wander off too far, and if you stay calm, it'll be no problem."

"Will you bribe someone?"

"No."

"At home, the bribe for a border crossing to a neighboring country is the equivalent of twenty-five US dollars. That's the official price. The border posts also like to take chickens as payment. They stuff them into their desk drawers and filing cabinets 'til they knock off work." She emptied her glass. "Rivas, I'm worried about this passport story. I'm not a seasoned liar. I could get you into trouble and you could end up in jail. An overcrowded South American one. How would a privileged individual like you cope in such a place?"

"I wouldn't even be able to manage a First World jail. Let's toast once more." He refilled their glasses. "Here's to your future, Catherine. I feel privileged to be able to spend time with you and to get to know you."

"We're always talking about me. Tell me something about yourself."

"Alright. I have a Spanish father and a French mother."

"What does she look like?"

"She's dead."

"I'm sorry. When did she pass away?"

"Twenty years ago."

"How did she die?"

"It's complicated."

"Do you have a picture of her?"

"Not on me, but I'll show you one day. She was exceptionally beautiful."

"I can believe that," she said, happy to have found another excuse to stare at him. "Did she work?"

"She worked in the textile department of an upmarket department store until she met Maria."

"How did they meet?"

"By coincidence. Maria is the only daughter of a wealthy Argentinian industrialist. She wasn't working at the time. She was a university student; she was focused on her graduate studies; and she travelled a lot. She was staying in Catalonia then, and on the day that she met my mother she was visiting family in Barcelona. Maria was shopping and it just so happened that my mother was helping out at the Yves Saint Laurent counter. The usual sale assistant was ill that day. My mother was so good looking that they always called on her when they needed an extra hand in cosmetics. My mother…"

"What was her name?"

"Tamaryn. So, on the day that Maria came to sample perfumes, she was working at that counter. My mother was four years older than Maria, and Maria was a very sensitive, caring woman, even in her early years."

"Forgive me if I burst into a fit of laughter."

"Do you want to hear what happened, or not?"

"Yes."

"Somehow she sensed that my mother was upset. She asked her what was wrong and my mother burst into tears. They arranged to meet at a café at the next tea break. My mother told her about her violent husband and that she couldn't get away from him, because he'd chase after her and find her wherever she went. She was four months pregnant – with me – and he'd again been violent the night before. She was afraid for her unborn child and herself. Maria had grown up in a very loving and protective home. She's an idealist. She's always felt a call to save the world." Catherine suppressed the sarcastic remark that was again about to jump off her tongue. "And of course Maria has a connoisseur's eye for physical beauty. That's why it was a matter of course for her to take my mother under her wing, and my mother was more than glad to accept Maria's help. She suffered from what we in psychological circles call 'learnt helplessness'."

"Seligman," Catherine interjected. She couldn't help wanting to impress Rivas.

"You know his work?" He was impressed indeed.

"Only since Peru. From your library."

"You read his theories on positive psychology?"

"Yes," she bragged, "and about the Psychology of Evil."

"Peck?"

"Yes."

"Well, Peck's more mainstream and very controversial."

Catherine quickly added, "And Fromm. And Jung."

"You're quite a bookworm!"

"Anything that interests you interests me."

"You're not only a bookworm, you're also a dream woman! Where've you been all these years?"

The smile, the smile!

"Are you trying to flatter me?"

"I mean it. So you'll understand a bit about my mother's problem. At least this is how I would diagnose her symptoms today. She let Maria take over completely. When you're with Maria, you believe there's nothing you can't master. She radiates immense power. She persuaded my mother not to wait for the end of her shift but to act straight away, while her husband was still at work. Instead of resuming her duties my mother marched, feeling hugely empowered, straight into the HR manager's office, and she resigned on the spot. They drove to my parents' apartment, packed my mother's things, and Maria took her in. Two days later they flew to South America. My mother became Maria's travel companion and later, when Maria took over the family business, she became her personal assistant. They lived mostly in Argentina. I was born on a business trip to Nicaragua. After this, they spent most of their time travelling between Spain and South America. Up to my mother's death, they were the best of friends."

"Was your father an alcoholic?"

"My mother denied that. She said he didn't smoke and was always sober, even when he became violent. He didn't do liquor, tobacco or drugs. But he always wanted his way, got on with nobody - an unpleasant character, as far as Maria described him, although my mother rarely talked about him."

"What do you think of him?"

"Nothing. I never met him. After I was born, my mother filed for divorce. With Maria's help, of course. And as far as I know, my parents never saw each other again after that. I assume Maria paid him off, although she never confirmed that. Maybe she also threatened him to agree to the divorce. I don't know."

"Hm. Always the same pattern."

"What do you mean?"

"Well, it's said that the man follows in his father's footsteps and the daughter turns out like her mother. If the father beats the mother, there's an increased likelihood that the son will also beat his wife. There seems to be a genetic propensity after all. Since he never lived it out in front of you directly."

"I would never hit my wife."

"Excuse me?"

"You're either for me or against me and if someone belongs to me, I would never hurt that person. I would protect her or him with my life. Have you ever seen me be mean to one of my horses? Or to Pedro or Joe or Sam?"

"Sorry, I forgot. I didn't make it into your inner circle. I don't belong to you." Catherine wasn't being sarcastic or cynical. She was simply and immeasurably sad.

"You'll always be part of me, Catherine. Even if you should ever turn against me, you'll be an exception. Your welfare is more important to me than anything else on earth."

"In one of the books from your shelves, I read about the effect of the absent protective figure in a child's life. When it's grown up, it compensates for this absence by drawing on the power capacity of an adult - in other words, such a person has an obsession with power. These people divide the world into two camps: friend or foe. Foes they mercilessly cut down, emotionally or even physically, and friends they protect."

Rivas laughed. "Yes, Doctor Zitgow, if you say so. Would you like to order anything else?"

"No, thank you."

Rivas gestured to the waiter, who served the remaining champagne. He then turned his attention back to Catherine. "I wouldn't be able to cite that as an excuse. I had more than enough love and attention from my mother and Maria. There can be no question of the absent protective figure. Maria fulfilled that role better than any man could have done. They took good care of me. If anything, Maria spoiled me too much. She loved me just the same as she'd been loved by her parents. Perhaps my environment was a little too matriarchal, but I can't say I suffered because of it. Everything revolved around me. Whatever I wanted I got. Just about."

"Until your mom died."

"After that, even more so. I think Maria tries to this day to compensate for the loss of my mother. I was at an awkward age when she died. At fourteen you experience loss consciously, but without real understanding. Therefore the child may subconsciously interpret the loss of the primary caregiver as rejection or betrayal." Catherine reflected briefly on her own family situation, while Rivas continued: "I think it was then that your friend/foe theory started to take hold. A second loss of a parent, a second rejection if you like, was probably too much even for me."

"Were your mom and Maria…? I mean, did they have an intimate relationship?"

"Were they lesbian? I doubt it. Maria is way too conservative for that. And if they did, I certainly knew nothing of it. My mother had a boyfriend from time to time, but never Maria. I think nobody was good enough for Maria, or she intimidated men and they didn't get close enough to get to know her."

"Does she intimidate you as well?"

"In some ways I suppose she does. Our relationship is complex."

"Is she lonely?"

"Undoubtedly. When I visit her, she goes completely over the top. She spoils me and I let her, even though it gets on my nerves."

"Do you love her?"

"Very much."

"You have a big heart, Rivas."

"Come on Catherine, that's not true, and you know it."

"Yes you do! *You* just don't know it." Rivas thought of Chand's mother who seemed to think similarly. He verbalized his reflection carefully: "What I do know is that people, women in particular, tend to project qualities into me that they desire of me." Like you, he thought to himself.

"Not I!" Catherine protested as if she could read his thoughts. "I know it! No man can treat a horse as tenderly as you treat Andalus. When I see you with him, I see your heart."

"Andalus is an unrivalled seducer! You can't help loving him, can you? He has this effect on everyone."

"I want to be like Andalus."

"You are."

"Rivas, what would you have done if I hadn't followed the cab driver? Wouldn't you have seen me as a traitor and foe after all?"

"No. I was prepared for that. I know this cab driver well. WICED often uses him when we're in Lima. I would have picked you up somewhere, no worries."

"And if I hadn't shown up at the bus stop?"

"Do you know the Pareto principle?"

"Yes, the 80/20 rule."

"That's right. Since nothing in life is completely predictable, there's a theory that says that any risk where the desired outcome has an 80 % probability, is worth taking. The remaining 20 % is referred to as residual risk and can never be eliminated."

"Are you saying you were 80 % sure that I'd show up?"

"I'm saying that an 80 % certainty can be viewed as 100 % since residual risk is a fact of life, unless we are omniscient."

"So you're saying that you were absolutely certain?"

"Correct."

"No observation? No surveillance? Maybe with the help of that cab driver?"

"No."

"Honestly?"

"Honestly. My only concern was that you might not have got into the cab, and I certainly wouldn't have forced you into a car a second time. But the fact that you showed up at the appointed time and place told me you that wanted to come back. If you hadn't, only then the taxi driver would have followed you. For your own safety – and to get you back to me in the end."

"If you'd found me then, what would you have done with me?" She felt relieved that he wouldn't have left her behind.

"I would have held you in my arms, Catherine."

"When I was choking to death in the cellar I motivated myself with the fantasy that you'd hold me in your arms. I was convinced that you'd rescue me." With remorse Rivas remembered the cruel show-executions. He knew that the consequences of such psychological torture would endure for years to come, and could even be fatal. He was lost for words. "Hold me," she demanded. He walked around the table, she got up, and he held her, paying no attention to the other guests. "Nothing else? You wouldn't have dragged me off to the water-trough again, or locked me up?"

"No. I would have brought you back to the farm for your own safety, but you're really free to go, Catherine. If you'd refused, I wouldn't have insisted. I would have found it unwise and I would have worried, but I wouldn't have put you under any pressure."

"And if I'd gone to the police?"

--- oOo ---

Rivas was moved about Catherine's anxiety, even if she wasn't aware of it. How would she be able to trust any man again? Would she ever stop blaming herself when a relationship got complicated? And for how long would she continue to fear the consequences? He pummeled his brain: to which therapist could he send her? There was only one in whom he would have entrusted Catherine's treatment. But he couldn't refer her to him without endangering himself. He held her closer.

--- oOo ---

Catherine withdrew from his hug and looked at Rivas, but he seemed to gaze right through her. "Rivas! I asked you something."

"Forgive me. What?"

"What would you have done if I'd called the police?"

"I would have kept it from WICED for as long as possible, to give you a head start. And in the meantime I would have closed down the operation at the farm as quickly as possible." Catherine giggled briefly at the thought of Rivas on the run from her. Then tears welled up, because she was so touched. Rivas had no taste for another emotional drama, this time in public. "Come," he said gently. "We must go." He quickly settled the bill, and ushered her from the table.

Catherine wondered at the Audi that took them to the chopper, but she didn't ask any questions. She assumed that it was another of Rivas's expansive gestures – a costly rental car. They were about to enter the multistory building on top of which was the helipad, when Rivas's phone rang. He saw Maria's name on his display and stepped aside so that Catherine, who spoke a little Spanish by now, could not follow their conversation.

"Hello Rivas! How was Lima? Are you back?"

"We're on our way to the chopper."

"It's late!"

"I know."

"Check into a hotel and fly back in the morning."

"It's fine, Maria. Why are you calling?"

"Catherine's colleague Tom Rivers has been in touch with the FBI. They haven't responded yet, but he's booked on a flight to Miami for the day after tomorrow, to take up the search from there. When was her last contact with him?"

"A couple of weeks ago, via e-mail."

"She must call this off as soon as you get to the *finca*."

"I'll deal with it."

"Otherwise it went well?"

"Yes, all sorted."

"Did Ricardo fix her hair?"

"Yes. About five inches shorter, but perfect."

"Make sure she'll at least dress decently in Europe!"

"Maria, please!"

"Alright, have a safe flight. I booked business class to Paris, nothing too flashy with your unpredictable child in tow. Is that fine with you?"

"Yes, makes sense."

"See you in Paris. Take care, Rivas."

"Maria, one more thing. Could you please arrange for Catherine's passport to be in the name of Catherine Jones?"

"Why?"

"It's what I want."

"You mean, it's what Catherine wants. Rivas, you know better than that."

"Yeah, I know, amateurs always choose the same first name or the initials of their real name for false papers."

"Well then?"

"Well, she is an amateur. isn't she?"

"Yes, but you're not! And that's not funny."

"It's important to me. Please."

"You're so besotted with this girl. Rivas, I'm getting worried. And why Jones? That's complicated. You know very well that it's much more complex to manufacture a passport with a fresh name instead of modifying existing data. It could cause a delay."

"Just do it!"

"Why didn't you ask Kiko this morning?"

"I only thought of it afterwards."

Maria sighed. "As you wish, Rivas. Catherine Jones it is."

"Thanks Maria. *Adiós*."

After the call, they took the elevator to the helipad in silent contemplation. Catherine noticed the change of mood. "What's wrong, Rivas?"

"Nothing that can't wait. Tonight, you're going to enjoy your evening with your movie and your song."

Back at the farm, Rivas handed her the Hitchcock DVD and sent her to her room. She was bitterly disappointed that they weren't to spend the rest of the evening together. In her room, as if in consolation, another bottle of Taittinger and a champagne glass awaited her, as well as a bunch of Peruvian meadow flowers, personally picked by Joe and Pedro. She seized the bottle, ran herself a bath, put on the CD, selected track 11 – *Me and Mrs Jones* and pressed "repeat". Just like it was in the jungle, she felt lonely and sentimental. This time, though, the trigger was not the wish for civilization but her yearning heart. Her disappointed heart. She no longer felt like Hitchcock after all – too much Mrs Jones and far too much champagne.

The next day she rose early and took a walk to the stables, biscuits in hand, to ride out with Andalus. When she got there, she found his stall empty, but she discovered him together with Rivas in the arena. She climbed up to sit on the wooden fence, legs dangling, and for twenty minutes she enjoyed another display of absolute riding perfection. When they were finished, Rivas and Andalus walked up to her. "I see we had the same idea. Do you want to grab Protestante? The *azabache* needs to cool off - we can ride together."

"You know what? I'll accompany you two on foot."

"You get on. I'll walk." Rivas dismounted, and helped her into Andalus's saddle. She let the stirrup leathers dangle while the three of them ambled down the path, cooling Andalus off on a long rein. Rivas asked, "How did you sleep after your Lima adventure?"

"Excellently, thank you. And thanks for the little surprise in my room. Although I had way too much champagne, there was something I kept mulling over last night. May I ask you a question?"

"Sure."

"Why can't I travel with my own passport? I'm not registered as a missing person."

"It's about the border controls. Your own passport doesn't have a visa for Peru and with 25 dollars instead of papers, or a couple of chickens, we won't get very far here, and certainly not in Paris. We could easily forge the visa, that's true, but a fresh identity is much safer. It's a standard precaution. You see, if something does go wrong, things usually happen fast. It's better this way..."

Catherine missed the rest of his rationale. She was tickled by the idea of her solemnly presenting a pair of Peruvian hens to the notoriously strict immigration officials at Charles de Gaulle. The silly image triggered off her pent up nerves, and she couldn't restrain her giggles. She broke into open laughter and she couldn't stop. Her stomach muscles ached so much that she had to halt her horse. Andalus turned his head. Horses have nearly all-round vision but whenever Andalus's rider did something unusual, he often turned his neck to get a really good look. At the sight of his baffled horse and the hysterically laughing Catherine, Rivas had no choice but to rein back and wait. "Sorry," she gasped, still shaking with mirth, "What did you say?" Andalus lost interest and started to nibble at the tip of her boot. "No, Andalus! That's naughty!"

"I said that it's merely a precaution."

She composed herself and rode on. "And you? Is it also a precaution in your case? Why do you have to travel with forged papers?"

"A few years ago I was on a job with a colleague in Marseille. He messed up. I've been on the Interpol list ever since."

Her laughter ceased instantly. "He endangered you?"

"We were both to blame. When two argue, the third party usually comes off the winner. And the third party in this case was the French police."

"What assignment was that?"

"You don't want to know. Anyway, I couldn't tell you if I wanted to. It would make you an accomplice."

"I see. You're on the run. That must be awful. Yesterday we talked about jails and all the while you're knocking at the gate, asking for entry."

"I'm not in any real danger. The world is big. I just have to travel under an assumed name and avoid certain places in France where I could be recognized. Other than that, life carries on as usual."

Back at the yard, they handed Andalus to Sam and strolled up to the house.

"Are you sure you don't want to ride further? You're dressed for it."

"I'm sure. I just wanted some fresh morning air. We won't have this good Andes air for much longer. I'll get changed now."

"Will you come to the library straight afterwards, please?"

"Rivas, if you have another headhunting assignment, then, then...."

"Then what?" Catherine smiled at him mysteriously. "It's not that, Catherine!"

"What do you want to talk to me about?"

"I'll tell you when you're back."

"Okay, see you just now."

When she stepped into Rivas's study, two cups of coffee in hand, he filled her in about Tom reporting her missing.

"Oh no! Is he also in danger now?"

"What does he know about your database?"

"Just about nothing."

"Then he's of no interest. If you call him now and tell him what I say, nothing will happen to him."

"If he doesn't answer?"

"I reckon at this stage he's sleeping with the phone glued to his ear."

"So that's why I needed the passport! I *have* been reported missing. You lied to me."

"No, Catherine. The passport was planned all along. I only found out about Tom yesterday, while we were in Lima."

"The call outside the building?" He nodded. "How do you know that Tom contacted the FBI?"

"Your home's under surveillance until this operation is finalized."

"But what can I do about this now? My disappearance has been reported. It'll take its course. WICED will kill him, to stop him testifying or something."

"Tom's no threat, as I said. Only the lower ranks of the FBI will look into this, if at all. If the investigation turns serious, they'll get instructions from the top to call off the search."

"Who *are* these people?"

"The less you know, the safer you are."

"Rivas, if there's never any chance of being investigated because WICED is supposedly so powerful, why are you on the run?"

"Because of the incident in Marseille. That's an ordinary police matter."

"I don't understand."

"You don't have to."

"What am I supposed to tell Tom? He's obviously no longer buying my story."

"You don't mention the FBI. You pretend that your assignment went well, and that it'll be finished in a week's time. You tell him you'll be flying from Washington to Johannesburg via Frankfurt on September 28. If he doesn't mention tipping off the FBI, you don't bring it up either. If he does raise it, you react with irritation and accuse him of sabotaging your assignment. You have to convince him to call off his trip and to inform the FBI that you've resurfaced and that they can put this thing to bed. Just a misunderstanding. They're used to that. Over 90 % of all missing people eventually turn up by themselves."

"And if he doesn't mention the FBI?"

"That means he'll call the whole thing off anyway."

"Good. I'll say that about the flight. But if I then don't show up at the airport, he'll be even more suspicious than before."

"You'll be on that plane. Because when we're finished in Paris, I'll take you back to the States and you'll board with your own passport and fly home. We've already taken care of your visa extension for the States. What's your usual fee?"

"33% of the project compensation." Catherine was not focusing. She was shocked to her core by the realization that she had so little time remaining with Rivas. Automatically, in a dull voice, she added: "Plus taxes."

"When you're back, you'll issue an official invoice for twelve million US dollars to Bahamas Resources Corporation, Box 1798, Nassau. You don't have to add tax because it's an international transaction. You won't send off the invoice. Instead, you'll destroy it. It's only for your books. I'll make sure that within one week of your departure from Washington the funds will be transferred to your business account. We have your account details."

"Absolutely not!"

"You earned your fee. It's no more than your standard, topped with an 'international bonus'."

"I don't want WICED's dirty money."

"Then donate it to a good cause or burn it. Whatever. How else do you want to explain your absence? Do you want to show up empty handed? If you tell nobody about your abduction, WICED will never bother you again. After your arrival in Johannesburg, you'll destroy your copy of the database and that will protect you against further enquiries."

"Anyway, 33% of eighteen million is six million, not twelve."

"I doubled it. I told you, 'plus international bonus'. Between us we'll call it damages."

"Rivas! I won't be able to breathe without you, let alone return to my old life. How can you expect me to resume business as usual, as if none of this happened? The pain of being separated from you has no relation at all to what I went through – even during my time in the jungle. That won't change, even if you offer me 'damages' a hundredfold."

"Everyday life will catch up with you before you know it. You'll be even more successful. You'll be wiser than your contemporaries, more serene. You'll radiate a very distinctive beauty. After a time of processing your experiences you'll reinvent yourself and blossom again - if you choose the right attitude. You'll need therapy and I'll provide you with a good contact once we've got to Paris. There are two ways out of your dilemma: to let it destroy you, or to let it work for you. Knowing you, my little survivor, you'll manage to profit from it."

"No!"

"You won't manage?"

"No, I won't leave you! I won't let you just deport me like this."

"Catherine, how many more times do we have to go over this? You've got out of it all alive, you'll be able to carry on without fearing anything from WICED. Make the best of it. There's nothing more I can do for you."

"So – now that you've got no further use for me, you're discarding me like an old mule. Don't you care about me at all?"

"Why do you think I'm doing all this?"

"Then let's stay together. There can be no life for me without you."

"Wait and see. I know what I'm talking about."

"No!"

"Alright, here's what we'll do: I'll get in touch with you in six months' time. By that time you'll have started your therapy, things will have cooled off between us, and you can think soberly again. If you still want to see me then, I'll come and visit you. Okay?"

"You're just saying that to keep me quiet. But I'm *not* leaving quietly!"

"No, I'll do that. Look. It's 9.15 am on September 21. Next year, on March 21 at exactly 9.15 am, your phone will ring and I'll be on the line."

"That's a public holiday for us. Human Rights Day. How fitting!"

"Great, then it'll be easier to remember."

"I'll remember that day without it having to be a public holiday. Do you promise to call me?"

"Yes."

"No Casablanca?"

"No."

"As soon as you meet someone else, you'll forget about me."

"I could meet a hundred women and I'll still keep the date. I give you my word, Catherine. I *will* call you. Please ring Tom now."

He handed Catherine her own cell phone. She dialed Tom's number. "Catherine! For goodness sake! Wherever have you been?"

"Tom, what's wrong? You know where I am."

"Catherine, I'm not buying that anymore. What's wrong? Are you in some kind of trouble? Or did you meet someone? I know something's not right. I should have acted sooner."

"Tom, get a grip! You think I've eloped with some dude?" How smart Tom was, Catherine thought, but she carried on making a show of being incensed. "What's the matter with you? What do you mean by 'acting sooner'?"

"I couldn't sit around anymore, waiting for your e-mails. Something's seriously amiss here. Even Trevor's worried! I started phoning around and I'm convinced that the Pentagon story is hogwash. Is someone pressurizing you?" He added in Afrikaans, one of the South African local languages, "Is someone listening in?"

"No, Tom. Why are you making such a scene? Where did you 'phone around'?"

"I was going to call the cops but Trevor was of the opinion that the authorities here are a waste of time in a case like this. He put me directly in touch with the FBI. I'm flying to the States tomorrow. We'll find you."

"Are you insane? Call the whole thing off! I'm almost done here. Just about to close the deal and now you're messing me around like this. If I don't finish the job properly, all my hard work will go down the drain. I told you everything was top secret, man! I'll be back on September 29. I'll text you my arrival time as soon as I know it. And you can fetch me from the airport - you wanted to anyway – and I'll fill you in then."

"Why didn't you answer my mails and voice mails?"

"I'll explain all that. In a couple of weeks this whole thing's over anyway. Now please go and cancel your flight and call off the FBI. My 2IC tips off the cops on my key client? What an embarrassment! I'm touched that you worried about me, but that was the wrong decision, Tom. It's still my company. If I want to dedicate myself to a long-term assignment abroad and withdraw from daily operations for a while, I have every right to do so. Just wait till I tell you about my huge fee! It'll blow you away!"

"Catherine, if that's the case, then I'm sorry. Really. I didn't want to cause you any trouble. I thought you might have been kidnapped."

"Kidnapped? From Washington? From the Pentagon? What utter nonsense! I kept in touch whenever I could. Enough about me. Let's talk business. How's it going?"

"Not great, Catherine."

"Are you saying you guys aren't making target?"

"You know how it is. When Cat's away, the mice…"

"Yeah, and Tom Cat who's supposed to look after things is purring around among his kittens."

"Hey! Are you suggesting that behind your back I do nothing but goof off and flirt with the staff?"

"I'm mad because the first thing I have to do when I get home is to clean up, as usual. You've got just over a week left. Make sure that productivity goes up. I don't feel like having to throw a tantrum as soon as I walk through the door. I always have to be the monster, and I'm sick of it!"

"You know what? Me too. Nobody talks to me like that. I've been worried sick about you, and all you do is go for me. What's become of you, Catherine?"

"I am who I am."

"Yeah, sounds like it. Find someone else to bully! I've had enough. I'll carry on here till you're back and then you can run things on your own. Morgan Search have been after me for months. I'm done here!"

"Morgan Search? I'll show them! They've got some nerve! But you should know better, you won't have a moment's peace from me. I'll personally snatch every client away from you just as soon as you think you've got one!"

"Oh yeah? Is that right? You're on, Catherine!"

"You can't do this to me, Tom! Everything you know about the headhunting business you've learned from me."

"Catherine, I'm sick of your moods. Your unpredictable behavior. It's over."

"Tom, please decline Morgan. Please don't you desert me as well!"

"Why? Who else has resigned?"

"I meant, I miss the team-work here. I *feel* deserted."

"Didn't you say you're working with a project team?"

"That's not the same." After her faux pas, Catherine back-peddled desperately. She changed her tune. "I know that you're doing your best, Tom. I know that you meant well. I'm sorry that I flew off the handle. It's been really strenuous here. I just want to come home, without having to dive into crises first thing after landing. Surely you understand? Please forgive me. I can't wait to see you all again. Please don't increase the pressure. I didn't mean that."

"Alright Catherine, we'll talk. But you'll tell me everything, okay?"

"Okay," lied Catherine. She hung up and burst into tears. Rivas wanted to hug her but she shook him off and turned abruptly, and ran out of the room. She yelled at him as she ran: "Was that convincing enough for you? It's insane! As if I care if Firm Commitments makes target or not! And all this rubbish I'm supposed to deal with as soon as I get home. Who cares about all that? No, Rivas – leave me alone! I want to be alone! Please!"

A search party! Getting home! Freedom! Everything for which she'd hoped for so long, was coming true. Why did she feel like a heap of misery? She ran to Andalus's paddock and wept into his coat. After a few minutes Rivas joined her there. He patted Andalus's shoulder. "Andalus will never forget you, Catherine." At that, she lifted her head and let out an uncontrolled sob. "And neither will I," Rivas added, sadly.

"I'll love you both forever, Rivas! I can't stand this good-bye. I don't want to think about Washington." She grew calmer and she let him take her into his arms, while Andalus gently caressed her hair with his lips.

Neither Catherine nor Rivas could know at this point that she would never get to Washington to board that plane.

38.
Peru, 22 September

While WICED's people worked on Catherine's passport, she – up at the mountain farm – lapsed into a state of sluggish apathy. The reality of parting with Rivas cast her down. The changing season's gray skies and chilling winds fed into Catherine's sense of ennui.

She decided to pick herself up, to get over this elegiac and irksome mood. She decided to be positive and do constructive things to pass the time. She went to the kitchen, and set herself on baking a cake. It was a flop – she had no experience at this, and no recipe book, and she threw out the dry result for the chickens to peck. They ran at it greedily, and she decided to recover a piece to give to Andalus. He took it trustingly, no doubt anticipating one of his beloved butter cookies – and then the shock! He tossed his head up and down in panic, stretched out his tongue in disgust, and ejected the thing onto the stable floor. "I should have known," she sighed, patted his neck and left the stable.

Dejected and bored, Catherine wandered around the house like a ghost. She was on the prowl for distraction or entertainment, and for this she needed Rivas. She couldn't find him anywhere, until she knocked on the door of his bedroom and – without waiting for an invitation – opened it. She saw him lying on his bed reading some sort of booklet.
"Come in."
She stayed on the threshold. "What are you reading?"
"Nothing." Rivas put Chand's diary aside. "Why don't you come in?"
She stepped over the threshold and stopped again, clearly unsure of herself. Then she said, completely out of context, "I feel like having sex." She pulled the door closed.
Rivas sat up in surprise. "*You're* initiating sex? What's going on in Peru these days? Is there something in the air?"
Catherine blushed. She wasn't in the mood for an analysis about the state of her sexuality. "I mean I want to, I'd like to, just have an ordinary…."
"Shhh. You said you want sex. I know what that means."

Catherine was embarrassed about her boldness. "Was it a mistake? I mean, you did say I should tell the man plainly... what I want."

"No mistake. I was just surprised, that's all. It's just not like you. But don't destroy the moment with talking."

"Or don't you know how?" Catherine recovered her courage and her humor.

"You don't have to come on so strongly. That won't work with me. Just be yourself. Now come here." She didn't move. "What now? Are you bailing out?"

"Now you're the one playing games."

"No more games. Say it again."

"You just told me to hush. Why must I say it again after all?"

"So that I can believe it."

Catherine gnawed at her thumb nail. "I'm not sure I'm in the mood anymore."

"Oh yes you are. Come here now." She still didn't move. "Catherine! Don't tease without dealing with the consequences."

Catherine asked playfully, "What consequences?" She tried to look blank and innocent.

"Do you want me to come and catch you?" She opened the door and sped into the hall. That was exactly what she wanted. Rivas rose with a sigh, caught up with her and dragged her down the passage. "You know I'm really too old for games like this. We're not teens anymore!"

"Not me! I'm not too old!" she retorted with spirit, relishing it as he tugged her into the narrow guest bathroom that opened off the passage.

"Yes, I can see that." He was already kissing her to prevent any more unpredictable silliness, and with his free hand he closed the door behind them.

She freed herself from his kisses and asked excitedly, "What are we doing in here?"

"You should ask, 'what are *you doing to me* in here?'" Rivas corrected. What followed was another bashful giggle. He picked her up, she clasped her legs around him and he took her standing up. He supported her by holding her by the butt, which impressed her. In her opinion this was really hot. Standing up. Toilet. Shameless. Indecent. Exciting. But then it all went too fast for her.

Before she even began to even think of having an orgasm, it was all over. It wouldn't have bothered her much. To mess around in a bathroom was thrilling enough. But the sudden end of the game surprised her. She was used to that from Warner, not from Rivas. "Sorry, my darling, that's what you get from having sex in a washroom." Rivas amplified the last word playfully.

"Yes, now I can see how much you've spoilt me. But I had fun anyway. No worries. You're so strong!" She thought that flattery was needed, to compensate for what was missing.

"You're as light as a feather. But who said we're finished? Just wait, we're going to do something different for a change. Something very different!"

--- oOo ---

Rivas knew well enough that his premature ejaculation was on account of the literature he'd been immersed in when Catherine entered the room. He was sorry to have disappointed her because of this.

--- oOo ---

He obviously doesn't need any encouragement from me, thought Catherine. But she was happy enough now about the attention that he again paid her. "What are you doing to me now?" she asked, correctly this time.

"Come outside."

Rivas headed towards the bushes behind the barn, while Catherine haltingly trailed behind him. He broke a twig off a bush and they went to the kitchen. Rivas put on the kettle and then stripped the leaves off the twig and placed them on a saucer. Then he took a root out of a tin which had been hidden right at the back of the kitchen cupboard, and he grated a small quantity of it into a cup. He poured hot water over it and let it draw. "What witches' brew is that?" she asked curiously.

"A Peruvian aphrodisiac. The root is black *maca*. It grows exclusively here in the highlands. It'll tickle your sexuality and it'll disinhibit you. The leaves and the bark of the twig that I got behind the barn are *borrachero*. It grows wild here in the Andes. It's an agent that'll make you completely acquiescent, no matter what I do with you," he announced ceremoniously, while taking some of the leaves from the saucer. He crumbled them up and put them into the cup with the root shavings. "Columbian thieves use it in high doses for nonviolent robberies. After ingestion the victim hands over his valuables voluntarily."

"Wonderful thought!" Catherine started to feel perturbed.

Next, he took a powder out of another tin and added a pinch of it to the cup. "This powder is *chushiwasi* extract. That's sexually stimulating."

"I won't drink this concoction, Rivas! You may as well pour it down the sink right now."

"You don't have to. I've got other plans for it."

"Is this brew for yourself?"

"No, for you. You'll like it." He stirred the mix together and poured the liquid into a shallow bowl. While these doubtful ingredients were drawing, he called Pedro on his cell phone. She didn't understand what he was saying, because he spoke rapidly in Spanish. Then both sat down at the table.

"If it's not for me to drink, am I supposed to inhale it?"

"Don't be so nosy. Let me surprise you."

"That's supposed to get me in the mood? Does this stuff really work?"

"Always."

"Nonsense! Maybe because of the placebo effect, but how is something like this supposed to affect the body?"

"You're not that far off. Most people believe it affects the physical organs, but all it does is animate the imagination. The circulation carries the substance to the brain, erotic thoughts are stimulated, and that causes the effect."

"But I won't hallucinate?"

"No."

"Okay, let's give it a try."

"Wait. Pedro's bringing us something from next door which we need for the ritual."

"The ritual?"

"Just come along and enjoy the ride, okay?" Pedro appeared with Joe's CD player. Catherine got up and headed for Rivas's bedroom but he stopped her. "No, we're going upstairs because afterwards you'll fall into a heavenly sleep and you'll have the best rest you've ever had."

So they went upstairs to Catherine's room, even though she objected. "But it's afternoon. I won't be able to go to sleep this early."

"You will. It'll do you good."

She lay down on her bed, fully dressed. He sat down beside her, took a pocket knife and carved a few lengthwise cuts into the twig. Then he took the tea prepared of roots, bark and leaves, rubbed the mixture into the notches that he'd cut, and let the twig lie for a short while in the broth.

"What *are* you doing?"

Rivas whispered, "Shhh" for the second time that afternoon. He got up and closed the shutters. An air of decadence crept across the shadowed room. It felt eerie to her. Unfamiliar. "Get up." He removed her hairband and her loose hair fell over her shoulders. "The loose hair will make for a brilliant effect." He put on the CD.

"What CD is this?"

"Carlos Santana. Do you know his music?"

"Heard of him, but can't say that I know any of his songs."

"You're too young. This is an older piece from his hippie times."

"I see! That's why the loose hair!"

"Exactly. Take off your shoes now and stand in the middle of the room." He pushed her gently away from him and pressed "play" and "repeat". Slowly Santana played in *Jin-Go-Lo-Ba*. "Imagine you're taking part in an Inca ritual. You've been travelling for days, weeks actually. You've crossed the Urubamba River, you're feeling exhausted, it's misty. After the long trek through the primal forest you had to manage the steep inclines up Machu Picchu. And now you've reached your goal: the center of the Temple of the Sun. You're standing in the middle of a circle of ritual participants. You give yourself up to the music. You're jerking your head, following the rhythm."

"Like at a rave?"

Rivas laughed. "I almost forgot your age again. But the clipped drumming causes an incredibly hypnotic effect, much more intense than Techno, and it builds up much faster."

"Did the Inca have drums?"

"Yes, drums and flutes. But this piece has African origins. Our little show isn't completely authentic, but it'll do."

"Do for what?"

Instead of answering, Rivas increased the volume and Catherine launched, hair flying, into her goddess dance. Hesitantly at first, she quickly let the music rip her up and away and after just a few beats she felt slightly intoxicated. After the song had played twice, he turned down the volume. "Get undressed and sit down on the bed. Do everything in tune with the music, stay united with it." He dunked his middle finger into the potion and stuck it in her mouth. She licked it off and asked, "Um, will it hurt? This ritual?" She fixed a gimlet eye on the branch.

"Yes."

"A lot?"

"No," he said, with a calming voice, and he kissed away her concerns. "Stretch out on your stomach." Catherine vacillated between wanting to comply and wanting to refuse. So she did nothing. "Turn on your stomach and close your eyes. Don't be scared, Catherine. If you don't want to go on, just say '1248', but only that, otherwise I won't know if you mean it. It's our code word, okay?"

"That sounds like a BDSM contract."

"It is."

"What's my role in this?"

"What role do you want it to be?"

"I'm not sure. Which role have you assigned to me? Is it the D/S or the B/M?"

"You have three guesses."

"I can't guess three times because there are only two options."

Rivas interpreted her prolonged need for dialogue as anxiety, and he wanted to make sure she wasn't too far out of her depth. "Do you want to go ahead?" He hoped that she'd find this game erotic but he didn't want to force it on her, merely because it was so easy for him to influence her.

"No, I'm scared," she heard herself sigh. She inhaled and thought, what on earth have I let myself in for now? Then she audibly blew the air out of her lungs. She was worried that Rivas would get annoyed, so she quickly asked, "Are you disappointed?"

"Of course not. It was meant for you to enjoy yourself. But I can see you're not comfortable with it." He flung the branch away and began to massage her body with the fluid.

"I want to feel you in me, Rivas," Catherine begged while pressing her thighs against each other and doubled over in order to get control over her twitching stomach muscles. She stretched out again, with Rivas on top of her.

He entered the red-hot femininity below him. For a moment he didn't move inside her, to prolong the comforting, warm feeling, but then Catherine's hips forced his pelvis into a rhythm and he followed it. "Deeper, stronger," she issued instructions. "Faster, harder." The effect of the *maca* root increased Catherine's ecstasy and her feverish commands drove him deeper and deeper into her innermost zones. "Now sideways and a little higher," she insisted breathlessly. Shortly afterwards Catherine uttered raw screams and dug her nails into his back with a force he never could have imagined from such a petite woman. Screaming and scratching in turns, she gradually subdued the movements of her pelvis. She managed a last convulsive rear, and then he heard her quietly whimper, "What was that? Oh my goodness, what was that?"

A bit of day 3, Rivas answered in his mind. On day 3 Chand and he had successfully completed their experiment and fell into a six-hour Tantric sex coma, followed by a blissful sleep. Still shaking from sensual exhaustion, Catherine clung to Rivas. There's a sex kitten lurking under the surface after all, Rivas remarked to himself, happy about Catherine's unexpected erotic naissance.

Her excitement ebbed. As if intoxicated and slumbering in a down of chick feathers, she cuddled up under her duvet – utterly content. The lively rhythm of the Inca music now had a drowsing effect on her, just as if she'd really trekked through the Amazon basin again and then still mastered the Andes on foot. When she yawned from the depths of her sweet tiredness, Rivas turned off the CD player, tucked her in and stroked her head. By the time he left her room she was fast asleep. She slept right through the night.

The next morning she felt stiff from her long slumber. Feeling hung-over she knocked on Rivas's door. He accompanied her to the kitchen where Pedro was making himself a cup of *Mate de Coca*. She lamented about how strange she felt, and, yawning, ambled over to the cupboard to fetch herself a cup. "Enough for two, Pedro?"

Rivas stepped in before Pedro could hand her the tea. "No *mate* for you today, Catherine. But it just so happens, we have the very thing for you."

"Not another one of your Peruvian potions please."

"I don't remember hearing you complain last night, but that's exactly why I don't want you to have any coca tea this morning."

She smiled contently. "True. Yesterday I had nothing to moan about. But what actually went on there?"

"I'll tell you later. Joe's brought us something delicious."

"Oh, that's right, he stocked up yesterday. Did he remember my pineapple?"

"Yes, and he also brought us *Ceviche*. He was really lucky to get some fresh stock yesterday."

"Is that also a tea of bark, leaves and roots?"

Pedro stared at Rivas in astonishment. Rivas winked at him.

"No, it's raw fish, marinated in salt and lemon juice. You'll have this for breakfast with thinly sliced onions and chilies and you'll feel better in no time."

"Ugh, that sounds horrid!"

"They're very delicate, piquant fish cubes. Try one and if you don't like it, leave it. But you'll see, *Ceviche* is delicious." To Pedro, he said, "Dish up a small portion for her please." Pedro nodded with a broad grin and prepared the exotic hangover cure.

"For me too, please." To Catherine he said, "Peruvian men believe that *Ceviche* increases male potency."

"And does it?"

"Of course not. That's nonsense. You believe anything, huh?"

Rivas was right. It tasted heavenly. She asked for more, explaining proudly that she wasn't unfamiliar with the concept of pickled fish as a cure for hangovers. Her father had been a staunch believer in sour herring to alleviate the effects of too much beer the night before.

In the early afternoon Catherine and Rivas took a walk along the paddocks. Catherine asked, "How did you do that Rivas? Yesterday. That was a completely new sensation for me."

Rivas smiled. "I didn't do anything, Catherine. I just followed your directions. For the first time you had the courage to actively participate, that's all."

"But it felt so different. Rivas, it was so intense, it was almost unbearable."

"I was under the impression that you bore it only too well."

"Yes, it felt good, but what I want to know is how you managed it. I can't believe that I'd ever experience something like that. It was like a cheap porn movie." Truth was, she spoke about how she imagined one to be. She'd never seen one.

"I told you, you brought it on yourself. You're simply coming out of your shell. And by the way, pornos are flat and boring. The sex scenes are empty, meaningless and completely dull, devoid of anything that could be regarded as even slightly interesting."

"Don't talk about movies now," she demanded, despite the fact that she'd brought the topic up herself. "I want you to fill me in on *my* sexuality."

"Catherine, why do you think that I always know everything?"

"Because you do."

"That's not true. In the study there're a few books on erogenous zones. Why don't you look them up? It'll be good for you to explore your body. Who knows what other surprises are in store for you?"

"You make me so happy. Thank you, Rivas."

"Catherine, you must really stop thanking me for sex. First, one doesn't have to say thank you at all, and second, it's not proper for a woman to do that. If anything, the man should thank her and even that's dumb."

"You find me dumb? Would you like a peppermint? Joe bought me some." She held out the tube to him.

He helped himself to one. "That's not what I said."

"Ha," she scoffed, "you're really old fashioned when it comes to male and female manners. I'm sure you'd never let me pay for a meal on a date."

"You can count on it. The tradition actually has a mean background. The man paid for the meal so that his date would feel obliged to return the favor, if you know what I mean. Still, I can't get how a man can degrade his date and himself to allow himself to be invited. It's different in business or within close family, but surely not on a date." He thought of Maria who traditionally always pulled out her purse when it came to paying the check at a restaurant.

Catherine's sentiments pushed aside the logical conclusion that Rivas hadn't hesitated, all these months, to degrade her in much worse ways. Instead, she remarked, "You're so romantic."

"What happened to your sense of gender equality?"

"I don't believe in that."

Rivas choked on his mint. He was profoundly amused at Catherine's sudden turnaround. Today like this, tomorrow like that, whatsoever she happened to feet at the time. "You're really cute, you know that?" Then he asked abruptly, "Catherine, what happened to you?"

"What do you mean?"

"Did someone molest you when you were a girl?"

"What makes you think that?"

"When you came into my room yesterday, asking to have sex, that was not exactly typical of you. And before the Inca game yesterday, I often had to work really hard to release your tension even the slightest bit. There must be a reason. Tell me what happened."

"I've never spoken about it to anyone."

"Speak about it to me. Perhaps I can help you."

"I need help? Excuse me for being too stiff for you. You're welcome to find a more pliable woman, who gives you more acrobatic sex than the housewife version you get from me."

"That's not the point. I don't want another woman. Come on now, don't get into a huff over nothing."

"I try really hard not to be like that, but I just can't let go. I'm different, that's all."

"I didn't ask for justification. I asked for background information." She remained silent so he changed his tactic and turned the closed question into an open one. "How old were you?"

"Eight."

It was working. "Who was he?"

"Our neighbor."

"Age?"

"Oh – I don't know. All adults seemed ancient to me. Maybe fifty, or older, I really don't know."

"What was his name?"

"Why do you want to know?"

"A name could help to resolve this."

"I can't remember. Something with 'mann'. Herr Kaufmann, Hoffmann, Bergmann."

"Describe him."

"I don't know, he was just... old."

"How tall was he?"

"Average. Maybe five seven."

"Hair color?"

"Brown."

"Full hair or thinning?"

"Full."

"Did he wear glasses?"

"Glasses? No."

"The color of his eyes?"

"No idea. I was too shy to look at him so closely. Is all this really important?"

"Did he have a family?"

"No, he lived alone. We had no close contact with him. We greeted him over the fence, or on the street, nothing more than that. Why all these details?"

"The end of the suppression is the beginning of the resolution. Where did you live at the time? In that suburb of Cologne?"

"Yes, in Frechen, in Malergasse."

"Where were your parents?"

"I lived alone with my dad. He was at work. I had a nanny. Her daughter was sick that day and I had to stay at home on my own for a few hours until my father could get away from work to be with me."

"Where did it happen?"

"In that neighbor's house. He'd seen me playing in the garden and said he had chocolates in the house and that I should come over to get some."

"And then?"

"He helped me to climb over the fence and I followed him into his lounge. It was sparsely furnished, disgusting really. Very dark and old fashioned and it smelled funny. Not at all clean and cozy like our house. There was a dark brown commode with marked, snake-like carvings on it. He opened one of its drawers, and it had a few cheap boiled sweets and loose pieces of chocolate. They looked unappetizing. The chocolate was unwrapped, just stale open pieces, going white, scattered around the bottom of the drawer. I expected a bar of chocolate, not these bits. They disgusted me but I took a piece and a sweet as well, so as not to appear impolite. I thanked him and I wanted to leave, but he said I must first lie down on the floor." She gasped for air. Rivas did likewise. "I sensed that something was wrong. I can't explain it, but I felt horribly uncomfortable."

"Were you scared?"

"Not really. I just found the house eerie. Awful. Gross. I knew nothing. I hadn't even been given the birds and bees talk yet. I hadn't even ever been slapped, not even after that incident, by the way. For that, I first had to meet you." She paused and Rivas nodded sadly. "Up to this point, I'd grown up completely protected. So I lay down, like he told me to. He was an adult - I did what he said."

"What happened next?"

"Rivas, this is so hard. I can't talk about it."

"What did he do then? Talking is a cure. It'll help you."

"Well. It was summer. I was wearing a light little dress and white stockings up to my knees. He lifted up my dress and pulled down my panties."

"Did you resist?"

"No, I didn't even protest, I just lay still."

"Did he touch you?"

"Yes. He fumbled around with his fingers and then poked around inside me. That already hurt so much and then he opened his pants and …you know."

"He penetrated you? And you were eight?"

"Yes, but only briefly, once. And as I see it today, not deeply. It happened really fast. I think the whole thing didn't take longer than a few seconds."

"Did you scream?"

"No, I just bit down."

"Did he get off?"

"I'm not sure. Everything felt wet, but I thought I needed to go to the toilet and I was ashamed."

"Did he wipe you?"

"Why is that important?"

"Cleaning up a victim after rape indicates remorse."

"No. He just pulled up my panties and helped me up. He put a few more sweets in my hand and told me that I could go."

"Unbelievable!" Catherine's account was in fact anything but unbelievable for Rivas. Through his studies he'd been exposed to countless cases of under-aged girls being abused, but the fact that this was about his own Catherine shook him up tremendously.

"What's really unbelievable is that he instructed me to return the next day." Of course I wouldn't have dreamed of it! I actually never played in the garden again. When I came from school I went straight into the house from then on. Until we moved away."

"What transpired after you left his house?"

"I took the sweets and staggered home. I already wanted to discard them on the street, but I didn't dare in case he was watching me. I held the sticky stuff in my hands until I was inside the house. I couldn't climb over the fence anymore. I left through his garden gate and walked down the street to our gate. It was only a distance of a few yards, but I really struggled to walk properly. I pulled myself together because I didn't want anyone to see me like this. Once inside, I tried to lessen the pain with hand cream and toilet paper but of course it didn't do any good. Don't ask! I've no idea how I could think that would help. I couldn't even wash myself, or didn't think of it. I really only remember my attempts to dab myself with the toilet paper and the cream."

"How did your father react?"

"I told you, I never spoke about it. You know Rivas, my dad had always drilled me not to accompany strangers. I believed I'd made a mistake and that the neighbor was a stranger after all and that this was my punishment. Besides, my father always claimed that I was so much trouble. He didn't mean it in a bad way. I was a strenuous child and I wanted to avoid 'making trouble' again. The worst was the shame. I can't explain it because it makes no sense, but the humiliation was even worse than the pain. As you can see, I'm still embarrassed about it."

"Didn't your father notice anything at all?"

"No. After I'd tried to wipe myself with that cream, I crawled into bed and fell asleep. Sure, that was unusual, but of course he didn't expect such a crime to happen right under his nose. When he got home, I woke up briefly. I told him I was tired and not hungry and wanted to carry on sleeping. I wasn't lying. I really did feel exhausted and I just wanted to hide away. The next day I felt better already."

"And as an adult? Did you never consider therapy?"

"Rivas, can't you guess how much I trust you to have confessed all this? I'll never talk to anyone else about this. I'm so sorry that you have such trouble with me in bed, but don't you think it's gotten a lot better lately? I feel safe with you and much freer. It's just that every now and then these inhibitions rise up again."

"That doesn't surprise me. And you're not making trouble for me in bed, Catherine. You're really sexy. That's not what I meant earlier. I love being with you. I just wanted to explore what was behind your symptoms."

"Symptoms? Do I have a disease?"

"On the contrary. You're completely healthy. Your resistance to intimacy is the result of that experience and nothing unusual. But the more openly you deal with it, the quicker you'll be able to process your trauma."

"Do you think you can help me?"

"Do you remember your desire for punishment the other day in the study? You connected it with Hesse and said that you consider suffering to be an expression of your deep love?"

"Yeah."

"This need for self-retribution could be rooted in this experience. You still believe what happened was your own fault because you didn't listen to your dad. You're ashamed, and you allow yourself to be abused because you're working off your guilt."

"Isn't that a bit of a premature diagnosis?"

"Perhaps. But it's worth considering. How do you experience the possibility? Do you feel resistance? That could indicate that it might apply. You made enormous progress today. Let it fade out again now. We'll take it slowly, okay? If you try to force healing too quickly, it only hinders it. The time it takes, is the time it takes. We'll talk some more another time."

"Will you hold me?"

"He took her in his arms and stroked her back. "Are you scared of men?"

"Not at all. I never associated him with *men*. He was a monster in a league of his own. Of course I was scared of the transporters and of you as well, but that's nothing to do with men per se."

"You don't have to be scared anymore, okay?"

"I'm not. I also don't hate men. I actually admire them."

"How so?"

"They think so clearly. So logically. I've often observed that in business. In my niche I work mostly with males and I've noticed that they quickly reach a conclusion and have the ability to react wisely quite spontaneously. They have a fascinating sense of the essential, and they're so strong. I don't just mean physically. Men can carry heavy mental loads."

"Every quality you've listed also applies to women."

"Sure, Rivas. There's constant talk about how strong women are and everything they achieve, but men are just as wonderful. For instance how they deal with disappointment and pain, without burdening their environment with their emotions. They process their concerns internally and don't scream or cry about. They restrain themselves physically and even though they could 'quickfix' many things they don't use their superior body strength. That impresses me. Men are controlled and they are very loving beings. You especially. You, I admire most of all."

"And that coming from *you*. About *me*!"

"Oh I'm a cry baby, you know that."

"I also admire you, Catherine."

"Really? You respect me also?"

"Yes. I think you're a strong woman. You have panache. You have tenacity. You're smart, you can master impossible difficulties and you're just as able to think clearly, as any man. And still you show a lot of feeling for every situation. You're not in any way inferior to men. No woman is, especially not you." To receive a compliment from Rivas was more precious to her than any material gift. He knew that and hoped it would help to rebuild her confidence.

Suddenly she remarked, "Just not physically."

"Huh?"

"I've realized that I can be pretty helpless at times. I'm definitely inferior to men in some ways. If I'm ever attacked again, they may as well kill me then and there. I'm not going through all that again."

"Don't say that. You should always try to fight back and call for help."

"But don't they always say that you shouldn't resist when someone attacks you physically, because it makes things worse?"

"That's true, if you're already in the hands of a perpetrator. Then it's best to stay calm and cooperate. But right in the beginning, even a woman has a good chance of getting away. He's still unsure of himself, doesn't know yet how things will turn out, or if he'll manage to overpower you. He's nervous, doesn't want to draw attention to his crime. If you're fairly fit, and if you quickly apply certain moves, you could fight him off, gain an advantage and use it to run away."

"Surely not. But I could try to talk to him, maybe?"

"Yeah, you could try, but statistically it hasn't proven very effective and it could make things worse. If you babble too much, he could knock you out or gag you."

"Can't you show me some defensive moves?"

"There's no quick fix, Catherine. You'd have to practice daily. You can't learn these things in an hour or two. OHLPA offers weeklong training courses, specifically geared for female members. They learn to free themselves from just about any fix, from all directions and with all sorts of methods, with only their bare hands and the use of their legs."

"I want to attend a course!"

"Impractical. You'd have to go back to Columbia, to a similar camp to the one you were at, but even more bleak. The training is exhausting. You need very strong inner motivation to get through it. If there's no immediate need to do it, you'd give up halfway through."

"I never give up halfway through."

"And eat the maize porridge that you hate so much - every day! The conditions are appalling. I've got video recordings of some of these sessions in my study. I'll see if I can dig them up. You can watch them if you're interested, but you should rather try to close off with your jungle experiences. You're safe now and soon you'll be home. Your life will normalize, you've got nothing to fear anymore. But I'll provide you with some telephone numbers of people who'll be there for you when you're gripped with anxiety attacks. You'll definitely experience some moments of panic, especially in the first few years. I'll see to all of this before we separate."

"I want *you* to protect me."

"I will, Catherine. Even from afar. I promise you, even from the furthest corners of the earth, I'll never be far away. I'll always be there for you when you need me."

"I'll always need you. Forever."

"Forever, then."

"You say that now but when you're in a new relationship, your partner won't be very understanding when you tend to some South African missy who's going through a crisis again."

"Catherine, you know me. This woman, who, by the way, doesn't exist except in your imagination, wouldn't have any say about my personal affairs."

"You could tell her I'm one of your patients," she gushed in her relief. "I love you."

"Do you feel like watching one of your Hitchcocks?"

"That'll be nice. I still haven't watched *Marnie*.

"Start so long, I'll be there just now."

"Really? You're going to watch it with me?"

"Yes, I just have to take care of something, I'll join you soon."

"Oh, wonderful!"

--- oOo ---

Back in his study, he retrieved Catherine's file from the safe, looked up her childhood address and switched on his computer. He opened Google Earth and surveyed Catherine's old house and its environs. Then he strode into the yard and took a deep breath. Out of earshot, he pulled out his cell phone and dialed a Spanish number. "Rivas! *Hola!* Where are you?" answered the party on seeing Rivas's name on his display.

"I'm on the farm – and you?"

"I'm in Amsterdam, visiting a friend. Nothing better to do right now."

"Excellent, Miguel. Amsterdam isn't far and you've got time on your hands. I need you to do something for me."

"Sure."

"I need you to be in a small town called Frechen, just outside Cologne in Germany. Malergasse, that's the name of the street. I want you to comb the immediate neighborhood and find an elderly man. Sixteen years ago he lived alone in one of the houses bordering Number 14."

"What's his name?"

"Something with 'mann'. He should be around sixty-five, average height, dark- or gray haired, probably not balding. If he's still alive, it's quite possible, that he still lives there. Elderly continental owners of suburban homes dislike change. Gain entry to the living rooms of the houses around number 14 - while nobody's home of course - and if you find one that's distastefully furnished, dark, dingy, disgusting, then dig around the drawers of the sitting room commode. Its wood is decorated with a swirly, snakelike carving. If you find loose pieces of chocolates and unappetizing sweets, wait for him to get home."

"And if I don't find anything in any of the houses around 14?"

"Then I'll have to try to find him another way."

"Don't you want to tell me what this is about? I mean, sweets in living room cupboards? What's going on?"

"I'm hunting down a pedophile."

"Maybe he's been locked away?"

"Then at least he's out of circulation, but I'll catch him wherever he is. It'll just take a bit more time. The only place where I can't get to him is the grave."

"What do you want me to do if the description fits and he comes home?"

"Then you'll break every single one of his dirty fingers and stuff that kiddies' bait from the drawer down his throat. And for good measure, shove something up his ass - whatever you find lying around."

"Do you want him to suffocate?"

"If it can't be avoided, but I'd prefer it if he got the opportunity to think. Handle it as you see fit. Call me after you're done."

"I'll leave tomorrow."

"Miguel, this isn't a WICED job. How much do I owe you for this?"

"*Nada, amigo.* It's no big deal. Besides, I can't wait to get my hands on one of these pigs."

"I have an old account to settle. I *want* to pay for it."

"Fine. We'll talk about it at our next meeting."

"Thanks."

He returned to the lounge to watch the movie with Catherine, but he found her in the kitchen instead, where she was preparing a huge portion of French toast.

"I felt like something sweet and fatty," she declared. "Want some?" Rivas was pleased to see her tackling the calories. He declined her offer, but when she started eating, he changed his mind. Together they ate the sliced bread - fried in egg batter - with plenty of syrup. They ate the sticky treat with their fingers, and she found that somehow comforting. "I'm so happy, Rivas. Much happier than Mark and Marnie."

"That's great, Catherine. But come on now, let's watch the film."

"Can't we rather watch it tomorrow?"

"Alright, what do you feel like doing instead?"

"Going upstairs."

"Again? You really are starved out. How am I going to keep up with you? I'll needing the Peruvian potion myself soon."

"I want to see what else you've got in store," she giggled.

I think not, thought Rivas, but he answered, "You know what? We'll grab a bottle of wine and read in bed."

"I don't like wine. I only drink beer. Or Taittinger!"

"Try some, okay?"

"What wine is it?"

"Bull's blood."

"What?"

Rivas elaborated, laughing, "Sangre de Toro, vintage 2009. Import from Catalonia. If you're a good girl I'll stay with you the whole night."

"The whole night? How tempting. But I never learned how to be 'good'."

"That's why I have to teach you."

"You'll really spend the night with me in my room? Really? Like a married couple?"

Rivas sighed. "Yes, like that."

The next evening, after another unbearably boring day, Catherine and Rivas had just settled down in the lounge to watch the movie when Rivas's phone rang. "Sorry, Catherine, I have to take this call. Start the DVD so long."

It was the return call from Miguel Fernandez. On the continent, it was just past midnight. "Mission accomplished! It was the first house. I didn't have to break in anywhere else. His name's Walter Hoffmann. There were no sweets in the cupboard but the wooden façade was just as you described it, as well as the whole character of the house. And I found plenty of sticky sweets in his jacket pockets in his bedroom cupboard."

"Did he survive?"

"Not sure. He was already blue in the face when I left him there. In any case I shoved the entire contents of his goddamned pockets down his throat, like you said."

"And the rest?"

"Fingers kaput. Oh yes and I found an old broom in the kitchen. You can google the result in the Cologne press."

"Too much effort. Thanks. By the way, who are you visiting in Amsterdam? Surely not our Benthe Petersen?"

"Yes, her. She called me a few days ago and wanted to know how I was. So we arranged a little reunion at her place."

"Seems like you didn't keep her waiting long. Send her my regards."

"Not on your life! Do you think I want to spoil those couple of days with her reminiscing about Rivas?"

"No worries, Miguel, I only have eyes for one girl now, and it's not Benthe Petersen."

"Chand?"

"No."

"Who? Man, talking to you is like pulling teeth!"

"You don't know her. Fairly young. Her name's Catherine."

"What does she look like?"

"Um - breathtaking would be an understatement."

"Hang on. A strikingly beautiful young woman? Is that perhaps your little hostage from Miami? With that funny Prussian name - Zitgow?"

"Yeah, right. How do you know about her?" Rivas's blood ran cold. Miguel was one of WICED's top assassins.

"Maria sent out a notification yesterday that a certain Catherine Zitgow, alias Jones, who'd been abducted from Miami a few months ago, was listed, but that it'd been an error. She sent a picture of her with the instruction that we were to inform her if any of us was assigned to the case, but that there must be no hit on the woman under any circumstances."

"That could only come from Carlos. In the event of a conflict, would you follow Maria's orders?"

"Sure. Maria's in charge of the finances at WICED. I know who butters my bread, but just in case, I'll let the others know, that Zitgow's your deal. Nobody's been officially assigned, Rivas. She's safe, you can count on it."

"Just as well I got in touch with you, otherwise I wouldn't know about this."

"Maria didn't mention it?"

"No. She just assured me that she'd take care of Catherine's safety."

"Well? Isn't that exactly what she's doing? But Carlos of course wouldn't indulge in such sentimentality. How could he?"

"You're right. I need to talk to him myself, urgently. Keep well now, and thanks for everything."

"No problem. Oh, hang on Rivas, about the payment…"

"Didn't we agree to handle that next time we see other?"

"I won't take any money from you, Rivas, that's why I've been thinking about how you could make it up to me."

"How?"

"Could you give me a few tips for Benthe?"

Rivas laughed. "Does she still have that chestnut warmblood gelding? What was his name? Matador or something like that."

"Torro Rosso. Yeah, she's still got him."

"Dreadful name. Pretend to show interest in him. Drive with her to the yard where he's stabled, get on and tickle a Piaffe out of the creature. That'll impress her so much that she'll throw herself on you right there in the riding hall."

"She's busy qualifying for Badmington with that 'creature'. She's just won an important three phase event. Belgium, I think. It's not a dressage horse, Rivas, and I can't ride that well. How am I supposed to get an eventer to piaffe? Are you crazy?"

"Shame on you, Miguel. You're a disgrace. A Spaniard who can't lead a horse into Piaffe. Every nag is capable of that - you just have to animate it to do it. Alright, if you're such a lousy rider, just ask her what she wants from you. You'll be surprised to hear what she has to say, I guarantee it."

"Do you always do that?"

With dismay Rivas thought of his shy little Catherine. "Miguel, *qua quaeque femina natura sit atque quantopere voluptatis cupida, haec omnia ex illius consuetudinibus investigentur.*"

"What the heck…? Is that Latin?"

"Yes. It means something like 'the nature of a woman and how much she wants it can be seen in her habits'."

"Who said that? Some ancient Roman?"

"The Verses of Desire."

"The Kamasutra?"

"You got it."

"Why Latin?"

"Antique translation from Sanskrit. Considered the closest to the original."

"Did you get that from Chand?"

"Yup. So, just ask Benthe. She'll tell you exactly what she wants. She'll even give you a manual, if you don't know enough about women. Heaven's sake, Miguel! No women, no riding, no Latin! How do you get through life? I have to go now. Have fun, you two."

Rivas felt the urge to confront Carlos right away, but thought it wiser to touch base with Maria first. He was about to call her when Catherine appeared at the door to his study. "Why aren't you coming? Marnie's already clearing out Mark's safe!"

Man, this woman can be a pain sometimes, Rivas thought. For the second time in two days the age difference between them was getting to him. "Catherine, here's the deal: I've assured you I won't lie to you anymore. Could you please return the favor and stop nagging me? I can't take it, especially not when I agree to watch a chick flick to make you happy. Can we agree on that? Fair's fair, wouldn't you say?"

His vexed impatience reaped a sullen answer. "No! I can't agree! I'm not able to do that. Besides, Hitchcock didn't make chick flicks!"

"How wonderful it must be to make life so simple. Okay, at least you're honest. Pause the movie and give me ten minutes. I have to call somebody. It can't wait."

"You're always on the phone," Catherine moaned.

Because I'm trying to ensure your safety, he thought, as Catherine dragged herself reluctantly away.

He dialed Maria's number.

"Maria! Why in hell is Catherine's name on the hit list?" Rivas put aside all courtesy.

"Hello, Rivas," Maria countered, "I'm very well thank you. How are you?"

"Why, Maria?"

"I told you I'd take care of it. Carlos has agreed to let her go but she'd already been put on the list. That's why I sent out a memo reversing his orders. Nobody's been assigned, Rivas."

"Is Carlos already in France?"

"Yes. On the estate."

"*Gracias, adiós.*"

"Rivas, what are you doing? Don't interfere!" she implored him, but he'd already hung up.

Carlos answered immediately.

"It's me, Rivas. I'll get straight to the point. Maria and I have an agreement that no harm will come to my hostage, Catherine Zitgow, but now I hear otherwise. She's my hostage. If anyone assassinates her, it'll be me. That's how it's always been, so what's this about?"

"Rumor has it that you want to release her. Since you've obviously lost your head, I have to think for you. But calm down, Rivas. Maria's recalled my directive. Didn't she tell you?"

"She did, but to tell you the truth I don't know what to believe anymore. One thing you can believe, Carlos, is what I'm going to tell you now. If you don't leave her alone, I'll take her away from here. To a place where even the Devil himself won't find her. Second, there'll be no more Ruckebier for you. With or without Catherine. Because I'll personally eliminate him and you'll have to start from scratch. And, should anything happen to me, I'll blow the whistle on the lot of you. That's all been prepared, so you'd better take good care of Catherine and me, if you want this operation to carry on as before."

"What's this all about? Why are you talking about us as though you're an innocent party? Look, Rivas, I won't be blackmailed - especially not by a greenhorn like you."

"You just make sure that nothing happens to either of us. Do you understand me?"

"Mind your attitude. You shouldn't talk to your family like that."

"You're not family. Maria is the only family I have, and now Catherine. Carlos, leave her alone. Please."

"Why didn't you tell me that you want to marry her? That's different."

"We're not getting married."

"You just claimed she's part of your family."

"Dammit, what's it got to do with all of you anyway?"

"It's got everything to do with us. WICED has principles, which we adhere to. For good reason."

"She's an exception. I'll fill you in soon."

"How kind of you."

"Will you be at the briefing in Paris when I give my feedback on Catherine's interview with Ruckebier?"

"Yes, I'll be there."

Rivas hung up. He needed a backup plan. He returned to his study and scoured Catherine's database, but he didn't find what he was looking for. Again, he reached for his phone.

"Hi Miguel, it's me again, Rivas. I need someone who can take on a long term surveillance."

"What about your own contacts?"

"Everyone I know is tied to WICED."

"Why don't you ask Maria?"

"It's personal."

"I see."

"So, whom do you know?"

"Rivas, I also only know WICED people. Who are we talking about?"

"Catherine."

"Do you want to know who she's seeing?"

"No. I'm concerned about her safety. And soon I won't be able to watch her anymore. I need someone from September 29 onwards."

"I'll ask around, but I can't promise you anything. Wait a minute. There's a Belgian guy, I think he also does body guarding. Underground I mean."

"Name?"

"On the tip of my tongue. Wait, wait…. Something with a B. Bertrand, Bernard. Nope. Sorry, it's not coming to me right now. When I remember, I'll call you."

"Is he based in Brussels?"

"No, in France. Toulouse, I think."

"Thanks. Call me if you think of anything else."

"Sure."

Rivas turned again to Catherine's source lists and found a Bertrand Lucien from Toulouse, but listed under a different profession: diamond smuggling. His industrious little hostage had diligently recorded all of the man's contact details. Rivas dialed his number and got through right away. "*Bon jour*, Monsieur Lucien. Miguel Fernandez referred me to you."

"Never heard of him. Who are you and who gave you this number?"

"Miguel," lied Rivas. He withheld his own identity.

"What do you want?"

"I need an observation."

"When?"

"In a week's time."

"Where?"

"South Africa."

"I know Southern Africa like the back of my hand. Namibia, Zambia, Zimbabwe, Botswana, RSA, one could say it's my second home."

"Even better."

"For how long?"

"Six months."

"Too long."

"Don't you have capacity?"

"I have time right now but if I commit for this long, I annoy my other clients and when your deal is through, I sit with a problem."

"I'll pay double."

"What's it about?"

"I want you to watch a young woman 24/7."

"Bodyguarding?"

"No direct access. You'd have to handle it discreetly."

"An observation? Not my thing. Too much paperwork. You want to know who she's seeing?"

"I don't want to spy on her. I just want to know that she's safe until I can take care of it myself."

"You don't need reports, photos?"

"Absolutely not."

"24/7 without access? That requires a team. Four or five people. I can't possibly be involved full-time solo, and that's a positive from my side. If I can do it with a team, I can make it happen. What's the danger to be averted?"

"I'm not sure. It's a precaution, but if – either kidnapping or murder."

"Who's targeting her?"

"That's not important."

"Sure it is. Single assailant or organized?"

"Organized."

"Is she prominent?"

"No."

"Wealthy?"

"No."

"Is this about revenge?"

"No."

"Then what's the motive?"

"I've got her into a pickle and until I've fixed this, she's in danger."

"Where are you?"

"In South America, but on my way to Paris."

"Alright. Come to Toulouse and we'll talk. I'll make a few calls so long."

"Who've you got in mind?"

"I know a Congolese couple. That would make three of us. I'll dig up one or two others."

"Africans?"

"Yeah."

"That would be great. Male and female's also good. Less conspicuous."

"*Exactement!*"

"Look, I won't be able to meet you in Toulouse. I have this woman with me and I can't bring her along. I also can't leave her too long on her own. Can we meet in Paris? I'll pay for your expenses of course."

"Where and when?"

"September 27. 2.30 pm. CdG Airport. At the taxi stand outside International Arrivals. I'll wait for you next to the first cab in the line. Here's my number. You can reach me anytime."

"What did you say was the name of the guy who referred you to me?"

"Miguel Fernandez. So, are we agreed?"

"I'll be there and we'll take it from there. What was your name again?"

"Rivas."

"Monsieur Rivas…"

Rivas had already hung up and was on his way to the sitting room where Catherine awaited him eagerly. "Everything sorted?"

"For now, yes."

"What was so urgent?"

"Your journey home and our stay in Paris," answered Rivas, evasively but truthfully.

"Is everything alright?"

"It is now."

"When are we leaving? Aren't we cutting it a bit fine? I mean, the appointment's just a few days from now."

"If all goes well, we'll be leaving the day after tomorrow."

Part IV

Catherine & Rivas

"Man is nothing else but he proposes a design;
he exists only in the measure by which he develops himself."

Jean Paul Sartre

39.
France, September 23

At Jorge Cháves Airport in Lima, a WICED employee handed Rivas Catherine's passport under the name of Catherine Jones. They took off punctually with Air France AF 441. The next day at 2.30 pm they arrived in Paris.

Catherine felt intoxicated on the drive from Charles de Gaulle to the center of the city. Filled with joie de vivre, she held her head out of the car window and drank in deeply the mild autumn air of Paris.

Despite her excitement, progress was slow. The early rush hour caused traffic jams in both directions, towards the city center as well as out of it. She pushed herself between driver and passenger seats to let Rivas know how much she enjoyed the timeless metropolis. "The traffic, the energy, the air, the language, the music on the radio! It's absolute heaven! Can't we stay in Paris forever?"

"You've only just arrived!"

"I already know that I belong here. Let's move to Paris for good."

"Why do you keep popping your head out of the window?"

"Because I get nauseous in the back of cars."

"Do you want to swap seats? It'll be a while before we reach our destination."

"No. As long as we're not driving fast, I'll be alright." She slid back into her seat and Rivas returned to his conversation in French with the driver. The car was not a cab and Catherine assumed from this and the animated discussion between the two that they knew each other. Probably another member of WICED, she suspected. She envisaged herself yet again caught up in a spider's web of conspirators. But – it's Paris after all! It's the city of affairs, of secret agents and secret lovers and intrigue!

They approached the Champs Élysées and headed for the Arc de Triomphe. Shortly thereafter they double parked in front of the entrance to the Heriton Hotel in the Rue de la Paix. Catherine wanted to dawdle, to revel in her first moment on a Paris sidewalk, but Rivas urged her forward into the lobby. He paid no attention to the driver, nor the car or their luggage. Nor did he do the usual thing on checking into a hotel – the arrangements at reception. Instead, he went straight to the elevators. He produced a key card, which he used to operate the lift and again to unlock 211 on the second floor. He stood back to let Catherine enter the suite. It consisted of a living area and two bedrooms. Each bedroom narrowed in hourglass fashion into a dressing room that opened up again into an understated but elegant bathroom. The bathrooms were done in plain marble and mahogany, in a statement of expensive minimalism. Each had a naturalistic rain shower and a whirlpool tub, and the romantic lighting combined with clever use of mirrors gave an illusion of space in what was actually a relatively small suite. Other wall spaces were decorated with shallow reliefs in bronze.

"Less is more," whispered Catherine, awed by the classic luxury, after months of Peruvian rural deprivation.

"What did you say?"

"I'm overwhelmed. Everything is so classy." She strolled to the windows and looked out onto a petite balcony garden. The chauffeur arrived with their luggage, and while Rivas saw him off, she seized the guest booklet and took it with her to the balcony. She dropped into a garden chair and from her unseen vantage point she observed the hustle and bustle of the Rue de la Paix below. She simply couldn't get enough. Freedom! Traffic! People! Shops! Delightful noise! She flipped through her booklet, and then – still in high spirits, unable to keep a single focus – she went back into a bedroom and threw herself onto the bed. She gently bounced on the mattress, and stretched. Rivas was on the phone in the living room, speaking in French. Restlessly she got off the bed and joined him. He was clearly in a jovial mood himself. He ended the call and lit up a cigarette. Catherine acted scandalized: "Rivas! How can you? Smoking's only permitted on the sixth floor!" As proof, she waved the booklet at him.

"We're in France. Here, anything goes."

"Don't you ever obey any rules?"

"I invent my own. It's much more fun. I'll demonstrate." He picked up the phone again and put through a request. Catherine understood the meaning of *"s'il vous plaît"*.

"What did you ask for? What was that about?"

"You'll see in a minute."

"Why didn't we have to check in?"

"WICED books this suite for a year at a time."

"Is it worth that much to WICED?"

"Yes. In fact the WICED administration's often hard put to avoid overlapping occupancies."

Five minutes later the doorbell rang. The suite had a bell, which surprised and impressed her. Rivas, however, showed no reaction. "Rivas, the *bell*!"

"Answer the door please, Catherine."

"Why don't you?"

"To avoid unnecessary contact."

It was a page boy. Grinning, he pressed an ashtray into her hand. Rivas turned to her with sardonic teasing: "Do I have permission to smoke now, in my suite, Mademoiselle Chef de Ville?"

"They're obviously making an exception for this suite."

"It's nothing to do with the suite. In every situation you should test the boundaries. You'll get much further in life that way than the masses ever do. What can go wrong? If you get rejected every now and then, you move on to plan B. And you can always give in, if you have to."

"By 'masses', do you mean people like myself, who conform? Charming!"

"It's up to each individual to work out and assert his or her personal preferences. I'm certainly never going to live the way every Tom, Dick and Harry tell me to."

"What an anarchistic philosophy!"

Rivas shrugged and smiled. He suggested that they go out, but Catherine insisted on staying in. Ruckebier had returned to her thoughts, and her euphoria over Paris was dampened as she began to fret about the first meeting with the man. It was to take place the very next day at ten in the morning. And she was starving – she hadn't eaten on the flight. She asked Rivas to ring up room service and order her a double portion of French fries, a diet coke and a vanilla ice cream. He looked at her: "A *diet* coke with fries and ice cream?"

"To balance out the calories."

"You're supposed to put on weight, not lose it. Besides, can't you find anything else on the menu? It's Paris, Catherine! You might as well go to McDonalds."

"No! Room service is totally romantic! And I want - I'm sorry - I would *like* fries and vanilla ice cream from *this hotel*."

"A double portion? How'll you manage that?"

"Just order them for me, okay?" At least she's eating, thought Rivas, and he indulged her craving. She nibbled for a while on the thin sticks of *pommes frites*, and then she asked him to place another order. "Now I feel like onion soup and beer – and strawberries with cream to follow!"

"What? Another crazy combination? Please won't you at least have something a little more refined to drink with your *soupe à l'oignon*? And there aren't any fresh strawberries at this time of year. If they've got strawberries they'll be imported or from the greenhouse."

"Of course. I forgot. At home it's strawberry season now. But it doesn't matter. In Columbia I would've gobbled down greenhouse strawberries like there's no tomorrow."

"But now you're in France."

She studied the menu again and came to the champagne page. "Here's a champagne that costs over two thousand dollars per bottle. Is that possible?"

"Which one?"

"It says 'Krug Clos du Mesnil'. She exaggerated her attempt to pronounce the words. Something in her wanted to remind him how foreign it all was, how difficult it was for her not knowing a word of French. She had always liked to think of herself as sophisticated – but Rivas outdid her on every score. She chose to defend herself by playing at Miss Contrary. Clumsier, more awkward, than she could possibly be.

"And that's the one you want to order?" Rivas responded with lazy indifference.

"No! That's much too expensive!" Catherine put on an air of consternation. "I told you I want a beer!"

"Hey, am I glad about that! Luckily we can afford a beer."

"And apple pie with cream, since I'm not *allowed* to have strawberries from abroad."

"Whatever. Order what you want. Just make sure you don't get sick on the upholstery."

"No! You must!"

"I must get sick?"

"No man! You must call room service."

"Why don't you do it yourself?"

"I don't speak French."

"They speak English."

"But I love listening to you when you speak French. Then I'll enjoy the order even more." Rivas sighed, but he did her the favor and shortly afterwards they brought her the soup, the pie and a bottle of "1664" – a local beer. She toyed at the thick topping of French bread and cheese that rested on the hot soup, but she did so without great appetite. While the second order was put through, she'd carried on tucking into the fries – and she wasn't hungry any more. "Rivas," she said, looking up.

"Yeah?"

"Who's financing this project? Where does WICED get so much money? For instance for Ruckebier and the lab and this expensive year-round suite. And, more specifically, how does our bill get settled? Do you yourself have to pay for our extras?"

"These Heriton suites are sponsored. I don't even get to see the bill."

"There are others too?"

"Yes. Apart from this one in Paris, we've got arrangements with Heriton in Washington, Madrid, Berlin, London, Tel Aviv and Rome. We've also got benefactors for a WICED jet and various helicopters and small aircraft. As well as for scheduled flights such as the one we took from Lima to Paris."

"What kind of sponsors are we talking about?"

"The hotels for instance are made available by a businessman."

"An American."

"What makes you think that?"

"Heriton's an American chain. US citizens usually prefer US brands. *Is* he an American?"

"Yes."

"What's his name?"

"Catherine!"

"I mean, is he famous? Would I recognize his name?"

"No doubt."

"Who is it?"

"Quit it now! Do you really think I'd disclose that? I wouldn't know his name myself, if Maria didn't fill me in on everything."

"You said you'd never lie to me again."

"That's why I won't give you the name."

"You're lying by omission!"

"To withhold information is not the same as distorting it. If you decide not to reveal something, and openly admit it, is that a lie in your opinion? Are you sure about that?"

Catherine was deeply irritated. If she couldn't match his sophistication, at least she could meet him blow by blow over matters of what she now regarded to be common interest. His patronizing tone annoyed her. "You don't trust me! Maria trusts you, I trust you, but you don't trust me. After everything I've done for you."

"Catherine, it's a pointless discussion. Let's drop it. Okay, Baby?"

"Baby"! Catherine's pulse quickened. "Darling" would have been sufficient to delight her, but "Baby"! *Baby. He called me Baby!* She dropped her need to reassert the ego. *It's all right! He called me Baby!*

The jet lag now began to hit her, and she kissed Rivas on the cheek and went to lie down for an afternoon sleep. And yet her mind kept turning round and round, asking questions, raising new issues to fret over. She tried to calm it by reading a few pages of *The Gambler* by Dostoevsky. She was too restless, though, and she couldn't focus on the novel. She regretted not having packed a lighter read. At last she dropped off, fitfully.

At 8 pm the doorbell rang. Catherine was up and refreshed, and Rivas sent her again to answer the door. She opened it and stared straight into the face of Venus. Catherine's eyes were still riveted on the vision in the doorway when Rivas came up behind her. Without acknowledging Catherine, the gorgeous woman flew past her into Rivas's arms, and let him whirl her through the air. She was a few years older than Catherine - perhaps three to four. Her long hair was a natural jet black – not so much combed as burnished back on one side and falling forward on the other, and beneath it flashed a perfectly tanned shoulder. The woman was tall and slim and everything about her was impeccably proportioned. A completely natural woman with no hint of makeup. Her heedless indifference accentuated her distinguished and elegant looks. Without the woman having said one word, Catherine put her in the box "self-confident woman". As only a

French woman could be. She wore a simple skin-colored shift dress, apparently with no regard to its effect on the beholder. Catherine could only hazard a guess at its immense price tag. The seam of the sleek outfit played casually with her knees and drew attention to her impeccable legs. These at some distant point finally ended in exquisite leather pumps. The red soles and the thin metal heels were the distinct signature of Christian Louboutin. A matching tote bag crafted from hand-woven lamb nappa hung casually around her right wrist which was otherwise unadorned. The eight inches annoyed Catherine. Why, she asked herself, do tall women find it necessary to wear such high heels? She felt dwarflike and bland alongside this apparition that had seemingly stepped straight from *Vogue*. Even though (it hit her) the only splashes of color on the woman were the red soles of her shoes. Catherine's self-confidence plunged into the abyss. To make matters worse the visitor seemed to ignore Catherine completely, not necessarily from lack of manners. It was perfectly evident that she had eyes for Rivas alone. The sable-haired Venus was now back on her own two feet, but she continued to hold Rivas in a tight clasp and she pressed her face against his shoulder. Then she looked at him and he spoke to her in Spanish - much too fast for Catherine to understand. Great! They also had the language in common!

Catherine felt hopelessly excluded. She mustered up her fiery spirit and, in an attempt at self-assertion, pointedly positioned herself next to Rivas. Rivas freed himself from the arms of his fan, who still didn't want to let him go. He made an inviting gesture to include Catherine and he said, in English, "Sandrine, this is Catherine. We're working together on an assignment. Catherine, this is Sandrine. She's a special friend."

The women shook hands. "I'm Daria, Catherine," said the beauty in fluent English. "I'm Sandrine only for him! It's nice to meet you." Catherine, gripped with envy, thought, Oh! Does she have to be charming, too? And she glanced at her distrustfully.

"No, no, she's Sandrine! *Toujours ma petite* Sandrine!" insisted Rivas boisterously. They both laughed at the private joke and Catherine didn't know what to say. Totally out of her depth, she didn't utter a sound while Rivas showed his visitor to a chair. "Come, join us Catherine," he said in an appeasing tone. "I'm sure Sandrine doesn't have much time." He looked at Daria-Sandrine quizzically. She nodded, understanding.

Catherine sat down warily, but got up again straight away. "I'll leave you two alone. I won't understand anything anyway."

"Please stay. We'll speak English."

"No, no, you two catch up," countered Catherine, and she went into the room next door. After ten minutes, though, she returned and sat down with them anyway. Rivas changed back to English and Daria-Sandrine followed his example. But after only a few words of small-talk his guest said she need to leave and got up. On the way out she intimately hooked her arm under his and said goodbye with a hearty hug and a double kiss on the cheeks.

"See you on the estate on Sunday."

Rivas answered regretfully, "I have to leave for the States day after next. I would love to have been there, but it won't work out."

"But we all agreed to celebrate grandpa's birthday together! I was so looking forward to spending time with you again."

"Me too, Sandrine, but I've had a change of plans. I'll fly to the States with Catherine, run a few errands in Washington and be back in Paris by Wednesday. And from here, as soon as I can, I'll come down to the Camargue. We'll definitely see each other there. Just a little later than planned. I'll call you."

"Au revoir, Rivas."

"Yeah, see you next week."

She shouted in a friendly way, "Goodbye, Catherine."

"All the best," Catherine replied. Rivas closed the door and lit a cigarette. Catherine, meanwhile, was in freefall. It wasn't just the familiarity between Rivas and his visitor that bothered her. To hear how Rivas was making plans, with such nonchalance, without including her, was bitter. She didn't want him to see the emotional crisis that was trailblazing its way into her soul, and she resolved to stay calm. But her resolution didn't work. She found herself expostulating: "So this is this why you've been floating on top of the world the whole day! You could have told me that you're expecting a VIP. I would have got changed into something a little more formal." She underlined "VIP" with bitter sarcasm.

"Catherine, I wasn't expecting anyone. You know I wanted to go out with you." He imagined what must have been going on inside her and he felt sorry for her. He didn't want her to have to speculate about Sandrine's relationship with him, so he addressed her concerns head on. "Sandrine and I are not involved, Catherine.

She's Carlos's granddaughter. Carlos is Maria's cousin and partner at WICED. As children we often spent our vacations together. Nowadays we hardly see each another. That's why it's good to get together once in a while."

"Such a stunning woman! And how she adores you! And you don't have a thing with her? You expect me to believe that? Just tell me the truth. Everyone has a past - that's nothing I can't handle. And it's perfectly clear, too, that you'll be just fine without me from here on. I won't make a scene, Rivas. It's simply not worth it to me."

"I told you that I wouldn't lie to you again. Of course I'll miss you. I won't be 'just fine'. And as far as Sandrine's concerned, there's never been anything between us but friendship. She's eight years younger than I am. She was still a child when we used to vacation together, and she always saw me as her hero. I took her on outrides on her pony. I invented things with which she could tease her teachers when she was back at school. I taught her card tricks. I scared her with ghost stories."

"I'm eleven years younger than you and that didn't seem to be a problem. You obviously can't wait to return to your old life without your bothersome hostage around your neck."

"I thought you weren't going to make a scene?"

"I'm not. I'm going to bed now."

"It's ten to nine!"

"I'm still tired from the flight and all the excitement here, and tomorrow's going to be a hard day for me."

"Of course. Sleep well, Catherine. You really don't have to worry about Sandrine. Okay?"

"Okay," she said, and disappeared.

After a couple of minutes she popped her head back in the room. "By the way, what was all that song and dance about her name? Is she Daria or Sandrine?"

"Daria. But when she was a little girl, I rechristened her in a secret ceremony just between the two us, because I thought a French name suited her better. She was such a sweet little thing and the 'adult' name she'd been given sounded so serious. I didn't like it, so I've called her Sandrine ever since."

"*Ma petite* Sandrine, my little Sandrine," she mocked him. "How silly is that? You constantly disregard 'what is' and make up your own stuff and everyone lets you get away with it. Oh, what am I saying? They love you and admire you for it!"

"You know what I think?"

"What?"

"You're jealous! And you want me to invent a name for you, too!"

"Yeah, you're probably not too far off. Everything you like, you rename. Andalus you also made up yourself even though his name is César. So, what'll my name be from now on?"

"Catherine's a strong name already, and I like it."

"Is that the truth?"

"Think about it. Cathe*rine*, Sand*rine*. She laughed and threw a couch pillow at him, while Rivas carried on. "But seriously, why should we accept everything that the world dishes up? Rules are there to serve us, not for us to serve the rules. If they no longer suit us, we invent new ones. What's wrong with that?"

"Because you're not God and also not the president! Rules are there for a reason. And didn't you demand that I keep to yours and god-help-me if I resisted even the slightest one!"

"Because they were my rules, not what society imposed, but even my rules are free to be broken, as long as one deals with the consequences. To create your own limits, to keep to them, to break them and to draw new ones, if necessary, is true liberty, Catherine. If one has the courage."

"This is exactly what your plan to 'liberate' the world is about."

"Don't you do the same in your world, too? I'm sure, in your company everyone has to dance to your tune!"

"That's true. I dictate the tone and pace. But after all, I'm the one saddled with all the responsibility."

"There you are. You've got your justification. I've got mine."

"In a way we're really not that dissimilar, you're right. Only that you go further. You live out your extreme ways, which secretly I wish I could, but I don't have the courage. I don't think I'd be up to the conflicts that would arise from this way of life. That would mean," she philosophized carefully, "that by loving your unbridled character, I'm actually loving myself. It also means that the traits I dislike in you, I also dislike for the very reason that they mirror the challenges in my own soul."

"Hmm. A psychological theory states that some people 'marry' their own weaknesses (which are also in the partner in an even more pronounced form) but they don't recognize them as their own. In other words what's in you is also in me, but more distinctly evident."

"That's exactly what I mean! But what should I, or anyone for that matter, do to develop beyond that?"

"Actively, we can do nothing. We have to increase our self-awareness. Self-honesty is strenuous and takes courage. It's not possible for a human to do more at this point, because any forced change will merely result in strengthening those traits as soon as an event triggers stress again. It's not about those facile mantras like 'today I will only think positively' or 'from now on, I'll be a better human being'. People who try this might have the best intentions but they're doomed to fail. That's why the man who abuses his woman and then showers her with roses will keep on resorting to violence as soon as the first serious conflict arises. Nothing changes until one day he *hears* his own alarm clock and wakes up to *himself*. In the beginning this works through a reflection mechanism, in other words it only happens after the deed is done, but as self-awareness increases, he manages to counter the automated reactions and to explore his full repertoire of resources. Sooner or later he'll find alternative means of handling problems and he'll increase his choices."

"That makes sense. It would be a great blessing to unite with someone who increases your awareness of your reactiveness and sharpens your consciousness, which leads to your emotional and mental development."

"Precisely."

"It's exciting to get to know yourself!"

"Yes. It's like a balm for the soul. But the initial routine responses are important because they deliver the necessary energy to manage the early phases of building a career and life, which can be so hard. Each state is important. None should be dismissed."

"Rivas, if you know so much about this stuff, why don't you apply it to yourself? I mean, just look at the hamster wheel you're caught in! With this terrible WICED story. Think about that!"

"I am, Catherine. I've been thinking about little else lately."

"What conclusion have you reached?"

"I'm still processing. I can't change so drastically from one day to the next."

"But you've started to have doubts about your mission?"

"Sure." Rivas reflected on Chand and her future husband.

"Just break the rules, like you always do."

"It's not that simple, Catherine. I haven't got there yet."

"Is there any way I can help?"

"Yes. By giving me time."

"Rivas, one more thing. How did Sandrine get up to our floor? You need a card to get up here."

"We all have access to this suite. Are you starting that again?"

"Is she also part of all this?"

"Not actively, but of course she interrelates with us."

"And her 'interrelation' with you is limited to friendship?"

"I told you that already. You're really overtired. Go and lie down now."

"Are you still going out tonight?"

"No, I'm staying here with you."

"I love you."

"Good night, Catherine."

40.
France, September 25

The next morning they ordered up coffee and croissants to the room. While Rivas smoked, Catherine nervously nibbled on the crumbly pastry and neither of them mentioned the junoesque visitor from the night before.

After breakfast, Catherine changed twice. First she put on a red Guy Laroche dress, and then a black Lanvin dress with white polka dots, both from Maria's suitcase. She took off the Lanvin and put the red dress back on. Rivas observed her feeling of despair. "You look stunning in both outfits, Catherine. Just choose the one in which you feel the most comfortable."

"I'll only feel comfortable when I'm dressed strongly. I need a power outfit, with power colors, with a jacket in power style. It's because I'm so young, Rivas. People don't take me seriously otherwise."

"Then either way it's solved. Red and black are both powerful colors. Besides, this nonsense about power outfits is below you. From the moment you open your mouth, Ruckebier will know that you're power personified."

"That's helpful."

"It's true." She settled on the fire-red dress with a matching red latex leather belt and scarlet patent leather pumps. Then she prepared herself mentally for her meeting with Ruckebier. The interview was to take place at his hotel. She'd wanted to conduct it at the Heriton, so that the candidate came to her, not she to him, but Rivas felt that this was unwise. "Are you clear on everything?"

"Yes. I have to land him, otherwise I'll have to start from scratch and I'm all out of options. You can count on me. If he's right for the job, I'll deliver him to your doorstep ready for negotiations. Will you take over from there?"

"I'm only responsible for your kidnapping. The rest will be handled by other members of WICED." He handed Catherine her real passport. "Take it along to your meeting."

"Why?"

"He'll want to see some ID."

"Rivas," she waved him off, "nobody asks a headhunter for identification at an interview."

"Take it."

When it was time, she got into a taxi and drove to Ruckebier's hotel in the Rue de Courcelles, approximately ten minutes from the Heriton. As arranged, when she got to his hotel she sat down in a quiet alcove in an area that was called the Andalusian Garden, and she waited for her candidate. The name of the venue made her think, with a sudden pang, of Andalus. She mused on the coincidence of names. She had described to Ruckebier what she looked like. Actually, she'd wanted to SMS him a photo, but Rivas stopped her. He said it would be too risky if anything went wrong. She was still thinking about Andalus when a man approached her in confident, long strides. She got up and walked a few steps towards him. Surprised at how tall Bernhard Ruckebier was, she stretched out her hand, which he shook with the strong grip of an artisan. "Dr Ruckebier! How good to meet you at last. Catherine Zitgow."

"Good morning, Ms Zitgow."

"Please, sit down!" She stretched her arm out to the chair.

"How was your journey?" he enquired while sitting down.

A waiter appeared. "What may I order for you?"

"Earl Grey please."

"Excellent idea. Two Earl Grey teas please," Catherine placed the order. "The flight was pleasant, thank you, and Paris is such a beautiful city. This's the perfect opportunity for me to visit it at last."

"Do you have other business here?"

"No. I came especially for you," Catherine replied with a charming smile and paused for effect. She'd never had much time for the game of "I'm-sooo-busy". She found that ordinary and silly.

"I'm flattered that you made the trip. It's a long way from Argentina. Don't you live in South Africa anymore? That was where your father operated from, was it not?"

"I'm still based there. My stay in Argentina is connected specifically with this assignment."

"Where are you staying there?"

Dammit, she thought, who's conducting this interview? She was completely unfamiliar with urban Argentina. Thankfully, "Buenos Aires" came to mind.

"A stunning city!"

"Yes, charming. And, how did your talks go?"

"So far so good. It's one of my last official tasks. After this I'm afraid it's nothing but boring admin for me."

"What's your visit in Paris about?"

"I accepted an invitation by Constance Pharma, in return for a fundraiser for our research institute."

"And how does it look?"

"Good. The finances are secured. In the next couple of days there'll be a few more talks and I'm hoping to also close a deal for a new multi-million dollar project for my successor." He sounded pleased with himself, but justifiably so.

The waiter brought the English tea. They let it draw. "I'm happy that we could meet here today. My client's keen to meet you. I've already made it clear to him how intricate this search has been, but the shortlist hasn't been finalized. If you don't mind I'd like to explore your background a little and then I'll tell you more about the task that you'd be facing."

"That's why I'm here."

"Good. Let's start chronologically, since I don't have your resumé. Is that okay with you?"

"Go ahead."

"You were born in Cologne?"

"Correct." He also stated his birthdate.

"Hometown and vintage of my father, too." Catherine eyed up her hoary candidate. His hair was almost white, and his full beard was gray. He was a shade over six ft. with huge, rough hands. They looked like a bear's great claws, covered with elephant hide - not at all "scientific". They betrayed a slight tremor which didn't gel with his confident appearance. She was sure, though, that it wasn't from nerves. Rather, it pointed to an illness or the side effects of some medication or even an illegal drug. "Please tell me a little about how you grew up. What did your parents do professionally?" She enjoyed being able to ask questions without the constriction of labor-regulations protocol. One little advantage of this cloak-and-dagger procedure. Her own nervousness had dissipated and her savoir faire had returned.

"My mother was a home maker," said the man, "and my father was a coal miner. They made immense sacrifices to allow me to study. It was important for them that their only son should make for himself a significant career."

"The medical or law degree, that so many parents wish on their children?" He laughed affirmatively. "And, did you meet their expectations? Did you get far enough for them?" she challenged him, as was her custom.

"I must have. Why else would you and I be sitting here today?"

"Are you parents still alive?"

"My mother is. She's just turned eighty-eight. She still lives in our old house in Weinstrasse in Cologne. She refuses to even discuss moving into a retirement home and she still takes care of her own household - even her own shopping."

"Does your wife visit her? I mean when you're in Appleton and your mother's not well, who looks after her?"

"My ex-wife had no problem with that. She's patient with the elderly, including her ex-mother-in-law, who can be really stubborn. Unfortunately we got divorced a few years ago. My ex-wife lives in Cologne. She'd gladly have carried on tending to her, but since our divorce my mother wants nothing to do with her. Clearly she projects the blame for our failed marriage onto my ex-wife."

"Do you have children?"

"A daughter and a son. We haven't been in contact for years."

Catherine dug around in his domestic situation in order to explore possible family commitments that might influence his mobility. She couldn't dwell on this too long, though, and soon she'd have to get to the professional aspects. "May I pour your tea?"

"Thank you."

"Please tell me about your studies. Do you take milk or lemon?"

I wonder if he knows that lemon doesn't go with Earl Grey. Why do they even serve it like that?

"Milk please. Lemon doesn't go with Earl Grey. Why do they even serve it?"

"I was just thinking that myself. Sugar?" This Ruckebier was growing on her.

"No sugar, thanks."

"There you go." She handed him his cup and poured for herself.

"Thanks. It wasn't easy but it wasn't that difficult either. I had brilliant professors and the university had an excellent reputation. I specialized in trauma and war medicine. I took up an opportunity to practice in the Congo, which was reeling from the aftermath of the Shaba invasion. There we encountered an unexpectedly high amount of viral infections. Every day we watched how these destructive little bandits annihilated our patients from the inside out. Compared to that, stab and bullet wounds and even amputated limbs were relatively merciful ailments. The suffering of the people whose bodies were covered in painful boils and open sores was horrendous. Many could hardly breathe. Most couldn't take in nutrition and were beyond saving. All they could do was hope for a quick death. This prompted me to go into research and development after my three-year contract was up. I wanted to research antidotes and develop vaccines that would put a stop to all this horror. That was thirty-five years ago, Ms Zitgow. And to be honest, as one of the world's leading viral scientists, I must confess that we're not one step further today than we were then. How naïve we were! We managed neither to eradicate the diseases of those times, nor are we on top of all the new challenges that the viral world throws at us daily."

"But smallpox has been eliminated, hasn't it? And polio can be prevented. There *was* progress!"

"Pox?" the disillusioned scientist scoffed a little too loudly, "yes, pox kept us more than busy in the seventies and we believed we'd conquered that vicious brood. However, in 1995 pox resurfaced in a small village at the border between Siberia and Mongolia. Only, this time we weren't permitted to report on it. Pox is just waiting for an opportunity to attack humankind. The epicenter's moved from the African continent to Asia and dictatorial regimes simply deny its existence."

Catherine found herself in the company of a deeply disillusioned man. A man who'd set out to change the world and believed, decades later, that he'd failed. This reminded her of something her father had once told her: "A cynic is a passionate person who doesn't want to be disappointed anymore". Ruckebier seemed to be such a man. "And now? How do you see your role and your goals in terms of being of service to mankind in the field of viral science?"

"Viruses that we have eradicated tend to resurface under a new disguise. I try to uncover their latest camouflages and develop suitable remedies to try to wipe them out. It's a little bit like the criminals always being ahead of the authorities. We're always a step or two behind them. The virus acts; we react. But with the limited means available to me I'm caught in this vicious circle."

"You consider the 'means made available to you' as insufficient?"

"Certainly. Any scientist will confirm that. Not only is viral science not sufficiently promoted in educational circles, but as a top caliber scientist you spend most of your time travelling the world cap in hand, begging for grants and aid."

"If you could link up with an organization that would grant you unlimited funding, would you then be in a position to focus on the essence of your profession?"

"There's no such organization in the world, Ms Zitgow."

"Dr Ruckebier, if there *was* an association with unlimited financial possibilities, under whose auspices you could dedicate yourself to your research without ever having to worry about finances, would that foster your goals?"

"Of course yes."

"If, in addition, this organization lets you get on with the job independently with no outside interference whatsoever – would you be interested in cooperation with them?"

Ruckebier became suspicious. "That would depend on the type of project."

Catherine ignored this, carried on "selling" instead. "You would be given a state of the art laboratory and the assurance that you can work without being bogged down by administrative or financial distractions, and operational matters would be kept to the minimum that you yourself determine. Should you require additional equipment, it wouldn't present a problem. You could achieve a scientific breakthrough of significant magnitude. To retire on the back of such success - how would that be for you, Dr Ruckebier?"

"For whom are you recruiting?"

"My client is particularly interested in your skills in the field of Venezuelan Equine Encaphilitis or a virus like it, as well as your genetic knowhow."

"You haven't answered my question."

"I'm not at liberty to disclose the identity of my client at this stage. I hope you understand."

"Your father always spoke openly."

"Even my father could only reveal this information with the permission of his client. In this case, I don't have it."

"Ms Zitgow, forgive me, but could you please identify yourself?"

For a moment she didn't know what he meant.

He repeated, "Do you have ID on you?"

"Oh I see. Of course." She reached into her handbag and retrieved her passport.

Ruckebier slowly leafed through it. "I see no Argentinian visa?"

"That's in my South African passport. In Europe I prefer to travel on my European passport."

He handed it back to her. "Why VEE and genetics? What does the one have to do with the other?"

"Dr Ruckebier, my client's aim is to keep the use of biological weapons within comprehensible limits and to prevent terror attacks."

"So this is about developing biological weapons for counter attacks?"

"No, only to prevent the enemy from posing a threat."

"Yes. I think I understand." Ruckebier started to connect the dots. He viewed Catherine as a naïve young recruiter who hadn't been filled in completely. "There's nobody who knows more about VEE than I do. VEE is an interesting choice." While Ruckebier was mulling things over, Catherine glowed. She had on her own initiative identified VEE as a possible viral link between human and equine physiologies. Ruckebier now warmed to the theme: "Before the US government terminated its biological warfare program in 1969, the VEE virus was one of the States' seven standardized weapons. For good reason – it offers many possibilities. But because you get fairly close to the virus during trials, your client will need the very best VEE specialist for his endeavor, and there are further complications. Since the formation of environmental protective initiatives in 2003 - in response to the anthracite attacks in 2001 and 2002 - chemical terrorists have had a hard time getting round the regular air particle readings that are taken in most major cities in the developed world. However, the interesting thing about VEE in the context of warfare is that it's hard to recognize, and this can lead investigators in the wrong direction and mislead their defense mechanisms. What's more, you can go the vascular route if you aim the virus at a certain target group, or via the respiratory organs for attacks of a widely spread nature."

"I don't understand?"

"For thinly populated areas, where no particle measurements are conducted, one could spread the causative agent via a spray fog, and for more densely populated areas one could choose the distribution via insects. One would have to develop a mutation to limit spreading of the virus to a genetically defined target group, because I assume this is where the connection to genetics comes in. This is about a certain ethnic group, is it not?"

Catherine took a deep breath. Her silly moment of pride had turned to deep shame and she didn't know what to say.

He noticed this and decided to spare her the reply for now. "Tell your client, I'm listening. Where do we go from here? When, where, for how long and on which terms?"

Catherine had hooked him but she'd lost control over the conversation. Ruckebier had taken the lead. That wasn't an unusual interview situation with someone of his caliber and it didn't intimidate her, because she knew she had him. She'd succeeded in baiting him with her statements about unlimited financial possibilities and creative freedom and she had no doubt that he'd remain cooperative. She now retracted her offer slightly in order to get her hand back on the rudder. "We're a long way from that, Dr Ruckebier. We'll have to talk about your background a little more. Let's return to your studies. When did you get your PHD?"

"Just a sec, Ms Zitgow," Ruckebier took over again. "You must know that I'm a virologist and a geneticist, but I've never gone anywhere near racial science. This would be a serious breach of ethics in terms of human rights conventions, apart from the fact that it's illegal."

Smart, Catherine remarked to herself. He knew…. "If I could provide you with a competent specialist who would assist you in any area that is not directly linked to your own sphere of expertise, would you then consider tackling such a project, Dr Ruckebier?" Catherine contemplated digging up Van Wyk for this role, even though Rivas had been opposed to her previous suggestions in this regard. But now she had to fast-track in order to prevent a premature turn-down by Ruckebier. Rivas would surely be creative enough to help her solve this problem later.

Ruckebier, however, didn't let her dismiss his objection this easily. She does know what game is being played here after all, he surmised. He continued to mine for details. "What area of expertise exactly are you alluding to when you say 'competent specialist'?"

"Genetic anthropology" miraculously shot out of Catherine's mouth. She breathed a noticeable sigh of relief, and Ruckebier who was impressed by how skillfully the young woman had once again evaded him, decided to torture her no more.

"1980."

"1980 what?"

"You asked for the year in which I obtained my doctorate."

This is how quickly he's extrapolated himself from his ethical dilemma, observed Catherine. Ruckebier wasn't on her father's database for nothing. "What was the topic of your thesis?"

"I presented a paper about Central African viral hemorrhagic fevers with respiratory or cutaneous impact. After that, I immediately turned to the clinical application of my findings."

"One thing at a time please, otherwise I can't follow."

"Perhaps it would help you to use pen and paper?" There was the sarcastic touch of the pedant in his voice.

"I'm not a messenger," she countered. "I'm a decision maker." Like Rivas, she thrived on pushing the envelope – on laying down a challenge.

Apparently Ruckebier did, too. He wasn't in the least offended. He continued, smiling. With every one of her quick retorts, his confidence in Catherine's competence grew. "Hm," he smiled, "even without ID I can see whose daughter you are. Alright. As I said, I practiced in a rural hospital in the Congo, attending mainly to patients suffering from hemorrhagic viral diseases. Working with humans as opposed to lab rats was a disturbing experience. I decided to abandon my career path as a clinical physician and dedicated my life to science instead. In 1983 I took on my first independent role as a researcher at the Center for Viral Diseases in Hamburg. I believed that the prevention of further epidemics would be the most meaningful way of employing my talents. I focused on cutaneous diseases as well as melioidosis and declared war on the devil we call Virus." They traced his career during the nineteen eighties and early nineties at which point Catherine's interest peaked. "In 1996 I founded my first lab in South America. Its establishment was as a direct consequence of the outbreak of Venezuelan Equine Encephalitis in Columbia at the time. The move had been initiated by the institute in Hamburg and was financed by the German government as well as CDC Institutes around the world."

"Forgive me – what does CDC mean?"

"Center for Disease Control"

"Of course! Please continue."

"As I said, it was a reaction to the epidemic of 1995, which was the third outbreak of VEE. There'd been two previous occurrences: 1962 and 1967. These three epidemics infected every horse, every donkey and every mule in Venezuela, Columbia and Peru." Catherine was startled – another mysterious coincidence – the three countries of her abduction. "The perishing of the equine population brought great suffering to these three countries. Over and above this, three hundred thousand humans were infected - with around two thousand recorded fatalities. Especially children and elderly villagers fell prey to the virus."

Catherine felt sick at hearing this. She couldn't believe what she was about to set in motion. However, completely helpless as she was, still trapped in her status as a hostage, she saw no way out. She quickly repressed her guilt. She listened intently while Ruckebier continued: "VEE is difficult to diagnose, as I mentioned earlier, and that's what fostered the unbridled outbreak of the disease. If the symptoms had been categorized more efficiently, the virus could never have spread this easily."

"What do you consider to be the biggest challenge of your career to date?"

"Even though my research was moving along well, I've always had difficulty mastering the responsibilities that go hand in hand with every leadership function: finances, and operational politics."

"Yes, I can understand that."

"Irregularities in terms of the financial resources started to surface and I was exposed to countless intrigues and troubled with huge staff turnover. Without the support of a competent team of scientists, our VEE center was shut down. I lost my post with the Hamburg headquarters but I then found employment as the acting head of a viral research center in Vienna. After six months I lost this job, too, no doubt due to the poor interpersonal relationships that prevailed at this institute. I'm not entirely blameless here. I focused exclusively on my own research and hated having to entertain the illogical rules and regulations, not to mention the foolish colleagues that were imposed on me."

"Of course, that couldn't have been easy." Catherine feigned objectivity and understanding. Behind the scenes she evaluated him as a choleric. However, she conceded that he was at least honest enough to hint at the true source of the problem – his own personality. That was refreshing and a sign of confidence.

"I was offered a position as lab scientist at the CDC in Brussels and at first I thrived on working with petri dishes and test tubes again, but the limits of authority got to me eventually. Furthermore, I was irked by the hordes of dilettantish students who knew nothing, but thought otherwise. Luckily I went straight on to run the State Lab in Sarajevo. There I could again run things the way I saw fit, but this post had a negative effect on my family life, not to mention the huge salary cut. It was then, that I received an unexpected call from your father. He placed me with the Secret Service of a small but significant independent state. It was a lucrative appointment and it was my entry into genetics." Catherine couldn't fathom just how accurately she'd hit the bulls eye with this candidate. She believed she knew exactly what type of genetics Ruckebier had been exposed to. His denial of any involvement in race science had clearly been a lie. "This operation took four years. It was camouflaged by using a commercial manufacturing enterprise as a front. You wouldn't be able to run a background check on it."

"Please send me some evidence of your work during this period by e-mail. I take it you don't have that kind of documentation with you today?"

"I'll gladly furnish any proof your client requires and give them insight into my previous projects, as far as the confidentiality agreements allow. However, I'll only do that when I know more about the matter."

"I completely understand." Ruckebier had to remain guarded. He had to voice this objection at this stage. She didn't dwell on it. "Did you move straight to Appleton from there?"

"Yes, I've been based in Appleton for the last six years now."

"How did you get the position?"

"I was approached."

"By a headhunter?"

"By the CIA."

"Thanks for the overview. May we now return to the beginning of your career and discuss your appointments in more detail?"

"What else do you want to know?"

After the informal phase had been concluded, Catherine went over all the stages of his career again. This time she asked targeted competency-based questions, asking him for concrete examples concerning his attitude, his work processes and the results of his various decisions and actions. This review of his practical daily operations and project processes gave her insight into principal behavioral and thinking patterns. Past behavior was considered the most effective way of predicting the success or failure of future ventures. When Ruckebier protested against the interrogative questioning technique, Catherine replied politely, "Every detail of your career development is important to my client and me. With a project of this magnitude it's imperative to thoroughly investigate the competencies of potential candidates. If it wasn't important, Dr Ruckebier, believe me, I would spare us both the time and trouble." Satisfied with her rationale, he continued to cooperate. The bait she'd laid out right in the beginning was yet again proving effective.

After a further hour she had enough information to be able to leave it there. The next phase would have been to telephonically check references with his former employers, followed by a secondary discussion with Ruckebier with discreet reference to any weaknesses she would have uncovered, but Rivas had told her not to go there. This is why she didn't even ask him for any referees. "Thank you very much, Dr Ruckebier. It's been a truly informative meeting. I'd like to conclude at this point. At the next meeting, project content and compensation will be fully disclosed. There's a possibility that I will not attend this meeting personally, but everything we've discussed today, I will pass on to my client, along with my recommendation. Your information will be handled with the utmost confidentiality. Will you find time to continue talks with my client before your departure to the States?"

"I'd be happy to."

"Then I will call you later today or tomorrow to set up the next appointment. This will include a lab visit here in France."

"The position is in France? I thought it was in Argentina?"

"I never said that. Does this pose a problem for you?"

Damn, how could I have overlooked this?

"Not at all. I'm not tied down in any way and I love Western Europe."

"You'll need at least half a day for a site visit. Can you arrange that?"

"I'll make the time."

"Good! I'll make the arrangements and get in touch with you. Agreed?"

"Yes, I look forward to it."

Catherine was satisfied. She'd managed to reel him in without once having to resort to the huge amount of money that was on the table. And she'd even got away with only the merest hint at the dark nature of the project while letting him know that it wasn't exactly a reputable organisation that sought his talents.

Ruckebier wanted to charge the tea to his room but Catherine insisted on paying cash for it, as Rivas had drilled her. Ruckebier gave in and said goodbye.

Back at the Heriton she gave Rivas a detailed run down of Ruckebier's past experience before offering her evaluation. "Ruckebier is an excellent scientific tinkerer. Had he been satisfied with growing cultures in the back of a lab, he may have made a ground-breaking discovery. But I suspect he was in debt, maybe due to substance abuse, probably cocaine. Something went wrong at the Hamburg institute and his career took a nose dive. This was turned around when my father recruited him into the underground where he rebuilt his career. In reputable scientific circles he'd landed up in a vicious circle, which almost ended in long-term unemployment despite his undoubted genius. His track record points to ongoing conflicts with superiors and he openly admitted to frequent personality clashes with colleagues and twice indicated his lack of respect for juniors. Someone in his position is expected to groom and mentor future generations and he couldn't get a foot in the door of any respectable organization once his lack of social competency was evident. Anyway, this semi-political appointment, facilitated by my father, opened up his chances to gain re-entry into an exciting venture. In that milieu they probably had to tolerate whatever came with the 'package Ruckebier'. That's how he entered the world of secret services. I think he was working for a supplier to a defense ministry, but I can only assume this. He didn't confide in me much here, and I didn't pursue it. That wouldn't be wise at this stage. I'm sure at the next meeting he'll put his cards on the table. I'm surprised he was even this forthcoming - I gave him practically nothing in return.

"Like many scientists he has a generative motive: to be able to leave something significant behind, after retiring. I also believe he can be blackmailed. You just have to look a bit further into his background. The reference to 'financial irregularities' under his leadership points to something. Debts, I assume. You'd need to check this out. Bribery could also work – he's after money. Why would he turn down a remunerative offer and scrape by on his pension instead? But you sure don't have to go to eighteen million with him. And, to disguise greed as humanitarianism will be right up his street. I haven't got the slightest doubt about his professional competence, but you'll have to check this out yourself since you won't let me check his references. I'm really good at this, Rivas. There are certain techniques that I use to extract information that wouldn't be openly declared to anyone else. My father was the best teacher! Let me do this - let me go on to close the deal. I'd feel better." Rivas was moved by her dedication. She must have known from experience that the deeper she dug, the higher the chance that something could backfire. The fact that she did it anyway really touched him. When he asked her about it, she explained: "Rivas, a problem doesn't go away by ignoring it. In recruitment, a candidate's past always comes back to haunt the headhunter if he or she didn't do a thorough job. I'd rather deal with it now. Are you sure I shouldn't just close this loop?"

"I'm sure. So, in conclusion?"

"In conclusion, I believe he's a substance abuser of some sort, could be 'just' alcohol, but there's definitely something wrong. Check it out. And he lacks social competence. Most importantly, I believe he'll have no qualms about working for WICED. And he finishes what he starts. In my opinion, he can do the job. He wants the job and he'll do it. Is it over now?"

"Is what over?"

"The reason for kidnapping me!"

"Is the list you compiled complete?"

"Yes, Rivas."

"You've decoded the entire database? You didn't invent information – it's all genuine?"

"There are two clues which I couldn't decipher but the rest is complete and real. You can check it out. Rivas, I'd never dare to deceive you on that. Please tell me this is over! Even if you killed me, I wouldn't be able to crack the last two entries. I wouldn't hold anything back, you know that. What would I still have to lose?"

"Delete these two entries and I'll do the same on my copy."

"Really, Rivas? You'd do that for me?"

"We have to, Catherine. Only when WICED believes they've got the entire contents of the database, will they leave you alone."

"It's like I told you. I've disclosed everything I know. I also don't have any other databases. I don't know why my father only captured candidate information and never made any reference to clients."

"He protected the sources that provided his income and assumed the clients would find you in any case and, in time, you'd find them."

"Yeah, that's probably it. But really, Rivas. Everything I know after decoding the database, you know, too. That's the truth." She stretched out on the couch and sighed.

"Let's go for a drink."

They chose to avoid the hotel bar. They went out, and walked to a small jazz club, which was in full swing even at lunch time. They sat down at a small table and ordered two Cokes. "Where to from here?" asked Catherine. "What'll happen next?"

Rivas replied, "You'll call him about the next appointment. I'll give you the details later. That's it. You were fantastic, Catherine. You wrapped this up with one single candidate."

"Did you have doubts?"

"I would have felt more comfortable with a few other prospects lined up."

"I told you how headhunting works. The headhunter's source list is very long, while the client's shortlist very short." Catherine smiled at her phrasing. "The client doesn't need to draw the usual comparisons precisely because the candidates have been so carefully selected. Headhunters don't fish in an ocean of willing applicants but in a small pond of the best professionals in their field. The less candidates, the better the recruiter."

"Yes, yes, you did very well." Rivas again reassured Catherine, who was clearly hungry for praise. "It's over now."

"I don't have to wait 'til he signs up?"

"I'll make sure of it."

"What if he turns it down?"

"WICED will secure him. They've got lots of tricks up their sleeve."

"Force?"

"That won't be necessary, especially if it's true that he's got generative ideals." Rivas leaned across to Catherine and whispered, "I want to be inside you now."

Catherine pulled her head away. "Rivas – I'm drained out from the interview. I'm utterly exhausted."

"Yesterday you didn't feel like it because of Sandrine; today you don't feel like it because of Ruckebier. Before that, the flight. Soon I won't even remember how, if you never let me sleep with you."

"You? Not remembering how to make love? Because of three days of abstinence?" She laughed and then said seriously, "I really had to concentrate this morning. I just want to relax now."

"First I tense your strings, then I release them and hey presto - you're relaxed."

"You're begging?"

"Have I ever forced you?"

"I must confess, I sometimes wished you had."

"After the room arrest in the kitchen... in the feed room."

"And a hundred times before and after. But you knew? How embarrassing. Apropos tensing the strings, I just remembered I haven't bought you the CD about the Spanish guitar."

"You see, that's why there'll be no more begging. We'll catch up a hundred times with what you wished for, and I get what's due to me."

"Due to you? What exactly is due to you?"

"You forgot to buy me the CD and now you have to pay!"

"Oh yeah? How exactly?"

"We'll go back to the suite, I'll drag you into the bedroom, rip off your pretty dress, toss you onto the bed and do terribly indecent things to you."

"I already know them all."

"No you don't, darling. There's a lot more on offer."

"Alright, I'll take you up on it and don't you dare promise too much, or else you're the one who'll have to pay. With a ring!"

"Catherine I'm not buying you a ring!"

"Why not?"

"Because a ring is a symbol for a relationship."

"You want sex with me but no relationship? Do you think that's fair?"

"Completely fair. See it as honesty." Rivas put the money for the drinks on the table.

"Okay, I give in. But not up!"

Back at the hotel, Rivas said, "Let's play a new game. Come, sit down on the bed."

"Okay?"

"We're going to play 'What if'."

"I don't know that game."

"I've just invented it. Listen carefully. I open with 'what if…' and you continue, again with the question, 'what if…' *Claro Señorita?*"

"I'm ready."

"What if I could read your thoughts?"

"What if you couldn't?"

"What if I couldn't read them, but felt them?" He used his index finger to stroke over her stomach. Catherine, like many women, loved that.

"What if I didn't let you feel them?"

"What if I tricked you into letting me feel them?"

"What if I disguised them?"

"What if I kissed you so that you could no longer disguise them?" He kissed her neck. Catherine, like many women, loved that, too.

"What if I escaped your kisses?" she asked and half-heartedly pulled away.

"What if you escaped but I caught you again?" He pressed her back on the bed and held her down by her wrists. Catherine, like many women, loved that even more.

"What if I resisted?"

"What if I were stronger?"

"What if I found that irresistible?" she laughed. "Okay, you've won."

"You give up too easily. Carry on."

"Alright then. What if I screamed for help?"

"What if I kissed you so you couldn't scream for help?" he asked and kissed her already. He let her wrists go and turned her face down, to open the zip of her dress. Catherine felt her brain switch off and her heart announced itself with loud beating inside her chest. Like a boiler, it built up steam in the direction of her loins. She turned her head to look at him but he pushed it down, face first into the pillow. "Spread your legs, Catherine," he demanded. There was nothing she would have rather done but the steam descended deeper and caused a yearning ache, which she could only salve by pressing her inner thighs against each other and pulling the throbbing affliction in and up. "Come, open your legs for me. Now, Catherine!"

She felt his controlling weight and noticed how her voluptuous lust robbed her of the strength to comply. "I can't," she panted weakly, surprised by her disobedient limbs, which just cramped up more to increase the pressure on the inside. Rivas gently forced her legs apart. Without further resistance her deceitful legs obeyed and made space for him. The strange sensation from behind and above made her even more receptive to his touch. Her legs trembled from the tension and pushed down her pelvis, which arched up her butt into the palms of his hands. One hand now slid between her legs. The tingling arousal caused by her helpless position made her break out in goose bumps. "Don't stop, please," Catherine begged, worrying at the same time that she wouldn't be able to stand much more of what he was doing to her.

What is he doing? He can't do that. Not with me. I can't cope with that.

She stiffened.

Will he go further with this?

When he did, the tape played back again.

I can't do more. I won't cope with more.

"Please, no more. More's impossible," she whimpered, while her body twitched treacherously. Rivas slowly removed his hand and Catherine regretted her resistance. She lifted her head to see what he was up to now and groaned again, "Don't...."

Don't stop, don't stop, she now wanted to shout. Rivas knew that, but he spontaneously changed his plans. He grabbed her hair, wrapped a bunch of it around his fist and pressed her face into the pillow. She blubbered a few unintelligible words into the feathers, until she gasped for air so badly that she thought she'd suffocate. Rivas tugged at the hair that was gathered around his wrist. The pain at the roots shot spasmodic impulses into her burning body. She wanted to turn over but Rivas continued to pin her firmly to the bed. Faceless and speechless she lay beneath him with no chance to protest, express her wishes or look him in the eyes. He was so rough with her. Why was she not scared?

"You like that?" he presided over her. How could she reply? For a brief moment he lifted her head. "Tell me. Tell me that you like it."

"Yes," she whimpered, using the chance to get some air.

"Talk properly to me!"

"I like it." Again, she caved in under his pressure, her head plunging into the pillow. I like it, I like it, hammered her oxygen-starved senses. Rivas continued to torture her. It became unbearable for Catherine. The French phrase *la petit mort*, the little death, took on meaning. Tears shot into her eyes but they had nowhere to go. The pillow even robbed her of the chance to cry. Suffocated in feathers, drowned by tears, squashed by his weight, martyred by her own lust. Loved almost to death by Rivas. Surely he'll release me soon, she hoped with all her heart.

Don't let me die, please don't let me die.

Like an animal, driven by raw urges, Rivas satisfied his lust on her. He used her, oppressed her, held her captive under him. She was his prisoner again – wanted to stay that way forever. Overcome by these visuals the lust inside her exploded and the painful tension gave way to several cloudlike contractions, followed by one final orgasmic spasm which dissolved into a sweet weakness, causing her muscles to tremble. She shook uncontrollably. Rivas in her, above her. He'd completely faded away but now she became aware of him again. Only when she felt Rivas withdraw from her, let go of her neck and roll himself off her, did she return to the present. In deep, irregular gasps she sucked the air back into her tortured lungs and slowly came round. She blushed as she realized what had happened and that she had no idea how and when he'd come. Had she really drifted off this far? How is it possible to switch off like this? He! He made it possible. "I love you," she stammered.

Rivas smiled at her. Not a sound crossed his lips.

He loves me, too. He must love me!

Instead of the desired declaration of love, she heard him say, "I'm thirsty. Will you fetch me a Coke from the minibar?" Catherine giggled. "What's funny?"

"Shouldn't the man get the woman a drink? You're obviously still in a dominant mood."

Rivas tilted his head to the side and asked, "Are we still talking about a Coke?"

"Do I *have to* fetch it?"

"You don't *have to* anything."

"You nearly killed me."

Rivas took her head in his hands and stroked her face. "Do you really believe that?" Catherine shook her head. "Then don't say things like that. Don't even think it. Nobody will take better care of you than I. No harm will come to you when you're with me, Catherine, okay?"

"Okay."

"Do you feel safe with me?"

"Yes."

"Really?"

"Yes, Rivas."

"Will you get me a drink now?"

Rivas laughed and Catherine returned a self-conscious giggle. She handed him the Coke, which he drank from the bottle, while looking at her, clearly amused. "Why are you looking at me like this?"

"I'm happy that you turned me down three times in a row."

"Why does that make you happy?"

"Because you're regaining your independence."

"And because this is a new experience for you. That's never happened to you, hey?"

"Of course it has. That happens to every man."

Catherine didn't believe him. "You're not allowed to lie to me anymore. Remember your promise." Her forehead crinkled and her tone was husky. All that was missing now was a threateningly raised index finger. Her body language didn't have the desired effect - it made her look cute instead.

"I'm not lying and you shouldn't be so in awe of me. I don't like that." Catherine got a fright. Displeasing Rivas was as good as a death sentence for her, still coming out of her abduction experience. But then he gave her a captivating smile and completed the sentence. "...anymore."

Encouraged, she continued investigating. "How do you do it then? I mean, how do you get her to come round?"

"Didn't you just witness that?"

"I don't count. I'm already head over heels in love with you. With another girl, I mean."

"There's no one else to bring round. You're strenuous enough."

"And in the past?"

"Same way."

"With rhetoric?" Rivas looked at her, not understanding. "Like the 'what-if-game' you invented today?"

"With words, yes."

"Does that always work?"

"Often, but not always, as I said."

"Do you enjoy it? The hunt?"

"Sure."

"I'm a sad case."

"What?"

"Because I want to win you all for myself and I'll never achieve that."

"You have won, Catherine. I already confessed as much on the ranch."

Now or never.

"Do you love me?"

"I can't afford to love anyone, Catherine. Not you. Not any woman."

"Why not?"

"You know why."

Catherine sensed this conversation was going nowhere. To spare herself further sorrow, she returned to the original topic.

"But how do you manage to always get me in the mood, without even touching me? I was exhausted, I didn't feel like sex and then you started with the word game and wrote history for me, once again."

"Have you heard of the Kamasutra?"

"Sure."

"It says, 'a man, no matter how much he loves a girl, will never win her over without many words'."

"Hm. It says things like that? Perhaps I should read it some time. I saw it in a bookshop once but I found the drawings so embarrassing that I pushed it right back deep into the shelf."

"That's cute."

"What's cute? The Kamasutra with its graphic illustrations – or that I'm once again so bashful that I can't even look at a book?"

"You're cute. The Kamasutra also says, 'he who gives up on a girl because she seems shy to him, will be despised by her as a monster who knows nothing about the female nature'."

"If you carry on knocking out clever verses, I'll feel like sex again and then, Señor, you'll have a serious problem."

"Such a problem is easily solved."

"Oh yeah?"

"Have you forgotten how well I know my way around inside you?"

"That's vulgar."

"Vulgar or not, you'd like it anyway. We just proved that, didn't we?"

"Yes, I'll give you that," called Catherine over her shoulder. She was on her way to the bathroom where she wanted to experience the spectacular whirlpool that the hotel brochure spoke of. Rivas didn't hear her – he was on the phone again. While she descended into the bubbles, Rivas came in and announced that he was going out that evening. She insisted on accompanying him.

"Alright," he agreed reluctantly, "but I'm meeting with a few WICED people. You'll have to stay out of the way. Pedro will keep you company and afterwards I'll introduce you to the Paris nightlife, okay?"

"Pedro's here?"

"He arrived this morning."

"And the ranch?"

"He's not needed there anymore. Joe and Sam are still there, but Joe will leave soon, too. Only Sam will stay behind to look after the livestock. The farm's available for WICED projects throughout the year. That's why you saw so many people coming and going. And the guys need the horses to get around, besides which they're our cover and they alleviate the boredom."

"So the horses stay there?"

"Most of them, yes."

"And Andalus?"

"For now, yes."

"And later?"

"That depends on where my next assignment takes me. He's a good traveler and WICED speeds up the cross-border quarantine regulations."

"What will you do after me? Will you kidnap another woman?"

"Nothing's planned."

"But if and when you do, will you treat her the same as me?"

"Every case is unique. Only the principles remain the same."

"That would be?"

"You see, when we plan to integrate a victim into our group, we use certain rhetorical techniques which are specifically tailored to each individual. It's not just the choice of vocabulary which we use to achieve our aims, but we alternate tone and emphasis and we use well-placed speaking pauses."

"You're mocking me!"

"Look, you can wear down a fifty-year-old politician as quickly as an eighteen-year-old backpacker or a thirty-year-old school teacher. But in each case you employ different means of persuasion. See it as a sale. Surely you also approach each client differently and put on a show if you want to close a deal? There are few professions where you don't have to adjust to a certain degree to meet the needs of the target person."

"I wouldn't exactly call what you do, a profession." He didn't answer. "If the next victim happens to be a woman," she started again, "will you also alternately intimidate her and spoil her with affection, and offer her Andalus to ride?"

"I've answered this question several times now, Catherine, so for the last time, nobody but you, Maria and I, and Pedro (that one time only), has ever ridden Andalus – and that won't change."

"What about Sandrine?"

"Not even Sandrine." Catherine confessed her jealousy and he replied, "Yes, I can see that but there's no need. WICED abductions are devoid of any emotion. We simply lead the victim into behavioral patterns, which are motivated out of their human survival instinct. You, my dear, turned out to be a particularly hardheaded case."

"I don't want you to work so intensively with your next hardheaded case."

"Catherine, first, there's no abduction on the cards for a long time now and second, the hostages mean nothing to me."

"But what if? You said you were considering giving up this lifestyle."

"I never said that. I merely stated that I was thinking about my life and that I was having some misgivings about certain aspects of it."

"I don't want you to carry on with it."

"What must I do? Must I withdraw to the ranch and let WICED pay me to ride Andalus all day while I reminisce about you?" Catherine shrouded herself in sad silence while Rivas continued trying to talk his version of sense into her. "If you insist on loving me, you've got to accept who I am. You don't have to agree with my lifestyle, and every person can change, but like everyone I come with baggage. In any relationship you have to accept the whole package, otherwise the nagging starts. And the nagging is what breaks down the relationship. And if you can't live with the package, you have to walk away. Sooner or later."

Despite their intimacy there were boundaries which she dared not cross, and she really didn't want to engage in a full-blown argument with Rivas. He'd never tolerated her excessive argumentation but now she couldn't hold back. "You don't love me. You see me as stupid and cheap. And totally predictable! I half killed myself for you. Voluntarily, without a gun to my head. I would prefer physical pain to this unjust powerlessness which you've sentenced me to."

"Catherine, it's important for you to start understanding how much you were manipulated. Do you see now why we could never have a future together? But I can also tell you that you really made me sweat with your constant escapades. There can be no talk of voluntary cooperation. You used every possible means available to you to keep up your resistance." She burst out laughing and he pounced on the opportunity. "And your abduction wasn't exactly 'cheap'. Apart from the cost of the trek and the fuss at the farm, the stuff that Maria organized for you she didn't exactly pick up at a flea market. But seriously, Catherine. You're not to blame for any of this. Don't torture yourself with guilt and shame. Yes, it will be part of the healing process, but go easy on yourself."

"Please spare me another one of your psychology lessons!"

"Okay. What do you feel like doing? We've got a bit of time. Would you like to go to the movies? There's an art cinema not far from here which shows really unconventional films. Would you like that?"

"I don't speak French," she muttered, as if it was his fault.

"We'll watch one with English subtitles."

"I can barely follow demanding art movies even in my own language."

"Alright. What can I do for you then?" His question was on the level, and gentle.

Catherine was touched. She'd always been the one asking this question. She knew what it was like to look for something that would make the other person happy. "You can tell me about your time in Paris and show me the places that mean something to you."

"Where do you want me to start?"

"With your studies."

"I told you about that in Peru."

"Not everything. What exactly did you specialize in?"

"First year social psychology, as you know. It was an obvious choice - Argentinians are fascinated with psychology. There are more psychological practices in Buenos Aires than in New York. There's suburb called Alto Palermo, which is densely populated with psychologists. The main shopping center there is called 'Villa Freud'. But like I told you the other day, it wasn't enough for me, so I changed over to basic medicine in preparation for moving on to psychiatry. I had to complete a compulsory year in neurology and after that I specialized in forensic psychiatry. I focused on scientific explanations for the pathological relationships that are formed between long-term kidnappers and their victims."

"You're a real medical doctor? That's why you had no trouble stitching up my face! Or giving me first aid after my suicide attempt! And you always knew what went on my head."

"What's going on in *your* head can't be learned from a textbook!"

"What does that actually mean? 'Explanations for pathological relationships'."

"Why kidnapping and abduction victims identify with their captors."

"Is there a distinction between kidnapping and abduction?"

"There are several, some of which are defined by the penalties imposed by law:

"1. When deception is used to get the victim to the hideout, it's referred to as an abduction. An abduction may include force, but a kidnapping never involves deception.

"2. Erroneously, kidnapping is the preferred term when minors are involved even if it's an abduction. Kidnappings often carry a lighter sentence than abductions. This definition stems from a 'kid' being 'napped' but the correct differentiation has nothing to do with age. The real difference lies in the fact that the kidnapper discloses his crime in order to make his demands known, whereas an abduction is shrouded in secrecy. A kidnapper gets his demands met by a third party whereas an abductor takes what he wants directly from his victim.

"3. In both cases, kidnapping and abduction, the location of the victim is unknown, as opposed to a hostage taking. If the hideout is discovered but the perpetrator continues to hold his victim captive, the abduction or kidnapping becomes a hostage situation."

"So I was abducted not kidnapped? Because you wanted something from me personally, at the location where I was held captive."

"Correct."

"So what did you find out about the identification of victims with their abductors?"

"The longer a victim is in the hands of the perpetrator, the greater the mental suffering and the more extreme is her helplessness. In time, her physical dependency leads to an emotional bond with the captor. She strives for his benevolence and her physical dependence extends to the psychological realm. That means, the victim starts to feel fairly secure with her kidnapper and starts to believe he wouldn't harm her. More than that, she 'transfers' her desire for protection into the perpetrator himself."

"I get it. She not only thinks he won't hurt her, but that he'll protect her against being harmed by anyone else, because he manipulates her into being afraid of others."

"He doesn't even have to actively drive this. It kind of happens naturally over time due to the vulnerability aspect. As her gratitude for his 'protection' grows, so does her overall trust. She begins to care for him and develops an interest in his needs and ideologies"

"Are you talking about male/female relationships?"

"I'm referring to the victim as female and the abductor as male just for the sake of an example - gender plays no big role here. The principles apply equally to male and female and they still apply if there's more than one abductor or victim involved. It makes no difference. So, she starts to support him and craves for his attention. Gradually, she switches allegiance and actively sabotages rescue efforts, or at least takes those amiss. And the more the victim sees things from the kidnapper's vantage point, the more she loses her own identity and merges with the character of the abductor. The gradual loss of her own values leads to a distorted appreciation of her abductor. The victim starts to evaluate 'good' treatment as generosity and the fact that he's letting her live is viewed as 'kindness'. And in the end, the hostage rejects freedom, preferring instead to stay with her captor. This means the captive doesn't seize opportunities to escape even when they present themselves, because she no longer wants to live without him."

"She actually makes a conscious decision to stay?"

"It may or may not be conscious. She may tell herself it's too dangerous even when the coast is clear. In any case, at this stage it takes huge courage and strength to flee."

"That's unbelievable! That sounds like my own story!"

"Do you remember the helicopter flying overhead when you were hanging up your laundry?"

"That's why I didn't wave them down! But how can anyone be this foolish? I mean, why did this happen to me, too? Am I also this stupid?"

"There are several reasons for this and none has to do with stupidity. A human being under duress is anything but stupid. She subconsciously develops a survival strategy and out of necessity kidnapper and victim form a community. Just think about our life at the *finca*. Didn't we also live commune-like to make life more pleasant? We rode together, we played cards, ate our meals together."

"We even barbecued!"

"Don't remind me!" Rivas laughed. "Another aspect is that the hostage falls back into infantile behavioral patterns due to the lack of control over her life. She becomes helpless like a child who needs at least one adult to ensure her survival. The kidnapper takes on a superior role, and the hostage turns into the needy child. Didn't you notice how immaturely you acted up at times?"

"Now that you say it," Catherine replied, thoughtful.

"If the abductor feels this process is taking too long, because he has time issues or becomes impatient, he increases the pressure by treating the victim like an animal. This accelerates the feeling of inferiority and drives the victim faster into deeper dependence. The more submissive a being is – man or beast - the more obedient and easier to control it becomes."

"I once read that during the Iraq war, prisoners were forced to crawl around on all fours and to bark like dogs."

"Yes. What seems like the absurd conduct of wayward soldiers is in fact rooted in war psychology and often premeditated. Third, the victim develops tunnel vision and loses sight of her long-term goals. She can only think hours ahead, days at the most, and evaluates her situation subjectively. From this childlike subjectivity she starts to increasingly tolerate and even buy into the worldview of the perpetrator. She begins inferring humane traits and motives. Paradoxically, less communication leads to more mental freedom, because bonding increases exponentially with the amount of verbal exchange between them. Via the communication strategy, a gang of hostage takers can even determine with whom the bond should be formed, like a game of good cop/bad cop. Do you want to hear more?"

"Yes!"

"What you called carrot and stick, sugar and whip is officially referred to as positive and negative reinforcement. This is a strategic game which alternates between penalty and reward. You'll know a little about it from the conventional way of training horses. This tactic tightens the emotional knots. What also plays a role is that the hostage cannot direct her emotions about the injustice she is subjected to towards the perpetrator. She selects a substitute enemy, usually society, or even family members who are trying to get her released."

"Does what you outlined apply to all kidnappings, abductions and hostage takings?"

"Not all, but it's not uncommon. However, all victims sooner or later try to align themselves in some way with their kidnappers and adjust to their circumstances. Wherever possible they form some kind of amenable relationship. It's just the intensity that varies. There are only a few documented exceptions among OHLPA member organizations. A case which stands out for me concerned three Israeli tourists. They absolutely refused to subject themselves to their captors and mentally resisted 'til the day they were freed. They managed this because they'd been trained accordingly during their compulsory military service. Bad luck for the South American terrorists! Ongoing mental resistance is always bad news for the kidnapper because it increases risk and effort. WICED hasn't had to deal with this though."

"What do you put your success down to?"

"The selection of hostages. We never deal with incidental victims. And the detailed preparation and the individual treatment strategy that we develop for each case."

"And that's what you studied?"

"Yeah."

"I can't believe this!"

"It's the obvious choice of studies for a career path as a court expert or counsellor who deals with victims and abusers."

"Did you acquire your academic qualifications specifically to apply it to this dark practice?"

"It worked out that way," he replied curtly. He abruptly changed the topic: "I think you should go shopping and buy yourself something nice for tonight."

"I've got plenty of things to wear from Maria's suitcase. I'd rather you filled me in some more."

"Enough for today, Catherine. Don't you think? Do you want to go sightseeing? It's still early."

"I don't want to wander around town by myself. I'd rather stay with my abductor."

"I'll come with you."

"Really? We can do tourist stuff?"

"Yes we can. Get changed. I'll get us a cab."

"We didn't get to the bus ride in Lima. That would have been so nice. Can't we rather take the Metro?"

"Metro's fine. Where do you want to go?"

"Louvre, Notre Dame, Eiffel Tower, Seine, Versailles."

Rivas smiled, knowing that they would never be able to cram all this in. The Louvre alone would take a whole day. The same applied to Versailles, which was located way outside Paris. The queues at the Eiffel Tower were too long, but Notre Dame and the bank of the Seine were a feasible combination.

They took the Metro to the Bastille and continued on foot along the Seine towards Notre Dame. Rivas slipped into the role of tour guide and bought her crêpes and souvenirs. On entering the imposing cathedral, he said softly, "1163."

"We have so much in common," she whispered back. "Who will ever understand me the way you do? No one could ever replace you. I'll die without you."

"If you wanted to die, you could have done it long ago in the jungle. Pull yourself together and see your future as a new beginning."

"But only for six months!"

"Come, we have to get back."

They rode back on the Metro which was bursting with pushy commuters eager to get home after a hard day's work. Catherine envied their fellow passengers for their ordinary lifestyles. "I'd so love to also come home from work now, open the door to our apartment, put my things down and start cooking. I'd make us dinner and then we could watch a thriller on TV while I iron. We would be just like an ordinary couple."

Rivas laughed at the thought of citizen Catherine, ironing and cooking up a storm. "You know, Catherine, I'm not cut out for a life like that. And as for you - do you even know how to iron?"

"Not well enough for your exquisite shirts, that's for sure. Oh! But how romantic it would be!"

"You could have cooked on the farm every now and then, but not once did you volunteer to relieve Pedro and Joe."

"Rivas, that was different. I didn't dare to get too familiar. I never knew what I was up against from one moment to the next. Just imagine - if you didn't like my cooking – then what?" In a nostalgic tone she added, "Besides, I did cook twice, remember? Toasted cheese sandwiches, the evening we hit on Cologne Cathedral. And the second time when I made the French toast."

"Yeah, cheese toast and French toast. Two variations of sliced bread. Very culinary!" After this, reality caught up with them and they remained silent for the rest of the journey back to the hotel.

Shortly afterwards Rivas had to leave. He said goodbye, promising to show her a good time as soon as he was done with his meetings.

41.
France, September 25

Catherine showered, made herself up again - envying Sandrine who apparently had no need for this perpetual procedure. She put on a black, low-cut Dolce & Gabbana dress, adorned herself with Chanel jewelry and perfume and was still busy with her hair when Pedro rang the doorbell to fetch her. He drove with her to Quartier Latin, the Parisian student quarter with its countless restaurants, cafés and bars. When they entered the Café de Jerez at 10 pm, she looked around for Rivas but couldn't spot him. They made their way past the many tables and chairs of the half-empty establishment until they reached an inconspicuous backdoor. From there they proceeded along a dimly lit corridor before being stopped by a second door. Pedro knocked and had a brief conversation in Spanish before they were allowed entry. This room was filled to the brim with patrons. It was so smoky and sparsely lit that you could barely make anyone out. How was she supposed to find Rivas in that haze? Catherine and Pedro fought their way through the tobacco smoke up to the front towards a small stage where a man played a love song on a Spanish guitar. In the center of the venue was a small sunken dance floor in the shape of a square. Miraculously, a tiny round table for two was becoming free - directly between the parquet and the stage. Pedro dashed towards it and pulled up a chair for Catherine. She sat down. "Don't move, I'll be back in a sec," he ordered her and headed for the bar. Again her eyes scanned the room for Rivas. She lit a cigarette and Pedro returned with two beers in thin glasses.

"Where's Rivas?"

"He'll come for you as soon as he's done." Nervously she took a big drag of her cigarette followed by an impressive gulp of beer. "Hey Catherine! Not all at once!"

"I'm German," she lectured. "My father taught me how to drink beer. If you sip it like 'a lady', it tastes bitter. You have to drink it like 'a man'. Beer has to pass the tongue quickly and proceed straight down the throat."

"Still! Go easy! This is strong stuff, I'm supposed to look after you and not hand you over to Rivas completely drunk." More than Rivas's reproach, Pedro feared Catherine becoming unruly, causing one of her scenes.

"This beer does taste funny. What is it?"

"It's a French beer called Kingston."

Catherine giggled and remarked: "In Kingston they drink this weak Red Stripe and here they drink this strong Kingston." Pedro was right, even this first gulp had made her slightly tipsy. "But what's that strange aftertaste?"

"It's aromatized with rum."

"I get it! That's why they call it Kingston. But why beer with rum?"

"No idea, Catherine. They also serve a very smoky beer here, which is laced with whiskey flavor. There seem to be many variations. Ask Rivas, he may know. After all, he lived here for a few years."

The crowd made her restless. Where was Rivas? The guitar player took a break and a CD blared from the amplifiers. An interesting song came on. "Listen, listen! What song is that?"

"No idea," repeated Pedro.

"They play such phenomenal songs here in Paris. This vocalist's voice reminds me of Rivas's." She sounded dreamy. "Why are you grinning?"

"You're really crazy about your Rivas. Can't you think about anything else?"

"Apparently not."

"Just how does he do this? Kidnapping psychology aside, I mean, he's also just a guy. What do women see in him?" Catherine winked at him, followed by a mysterious smile. Pedro sighed. "Do you want me to find out the title and artist?"

"Oh yes please!"

"You'll stay here. Don't move!"

"*Si Señor.*"

Pedro wasn't gone for long. "Old song from the eighties."

"Do you think you can get the CD for me tomorrow?"

"Nice try but you'll have to do your own shopping from now on. I heard you're here out of your own volition now. This schlepping stuff around for Catherine is over."

"He said that?"

"He told me he's not holding you captive anymore."

Catherine smiled, satisfied. Then she became thoughtful. "Pedro, do you remember the evening when we cleaned up the pieces of broken glass in the library?"

"Yeah."

"You said that if I just do what he says, I would soon be home, safe and sound. Did you really believe then that he'd let me live?"

"Yes," lied Pedro keeping a straight face.

"Do you still want to know what makes Rivas so attractive to women? I mean to-die-for attractive, not because of good looks or psychological trickery?"

"Tell me."

"He wouldn't have lied to me now. He's by no means 'just a guy'. He has class. For me there is no man more attractive than one who has the courage to tell the truth, even if it's hard. That's what distinguishes him from others." Pedro pulled a reproachful face. "Sorry, Pedro, but just like errands for Catherine are done with, so are your hostage games. I won't let you take me for a fool anymore like I did in my desperate situation. Rivas has come to terms with it and you'll have to do the same. Alright?"

"You're right, Catherine. That was cowardly."

"Oh now I feel bad, especially because you always stuck up for me."

"How do you know that?"

"Rivas told me. Are we good again?"

"Sure we are. I asked you a question and you answered."

"You see, now you also have class. I'll miss you, Pedro. All of you from the ranch."

"We'll miss you, too, Catherine."

"Will you give Sam and Joe a message from me?"

"What would you like me to tell them?"

"Every day they must give Andalus at least one butter cookie or a handful of molasses and tell him it's from me. Will you do that for me?"

"*Sí, claro.*"

She turned away again, looking for Rivas. She spotted him at one of the tables sitting with an intriguing looking woman. They were together with a few other men at a table directly beneath the steps to the stage at the other side of the room. The woman was wearing an extremely stylish strapless cocktail dress in tones of jungle green and black. It snuggly hugged her feminine figure and a glamorous broche accentuated her waist. Dark green evening gloves made of silk reached up to her upper arms. They were of the kind worn at red carpet events. Catherine also noted her black high heeled patent leather sandals and as far as she could make out she was wearing a low hanging collier put together from black diamonds, onyx stones and emeralds. Her blackberry hair was smoothly combed back, like a tango dancer's. Despite the distance and the dim lighting she saw that the woman was dramatically made up. Particularly her ember lipstick glowed through the plumes of smoke. Catherine guessed her age at around sixty. She reminded her of the queen of the fairy tale "Snow White and the Seven Dwarfs". The "queen" held Rivas's full attention with what seemed to be sad conversation. No, an intimate one! Then the woman gently stroked Rivas's hair out of his forehead. Why was she allowed to do that? Rivas didn't like people messing with his hair. Who was she? And which role did she play in his life? Catherine's heart was ablaze with jealousy and passion. Was Rivas her lover? Catherine fixed her gaze on him but he didn't seem to notice her. Instead, he leaned closer to the woman and whispered something in her ear, followed by an affectionate look. He must have felt Catherine's eyes on him after all because he turned towards her and their eyes met, but his face stayed expressionless - as if she wasn't important or even in the room. He left the table and Catherine saw that the woman was now also looking directly at her, also without any expression. Rivas didn't move towards her as she'd expected but made off in the opposite direction, where he was soon swallowed up by the haze. Now the alluring woman also stood up and followed him. As soon as Catherine lost sight of her, she jumped up, but Pedro pulled her back. "You're staying right here."

"I've spotted Rivas, I have to go and see him."

"He's busy. Just be patient. Would you like another Kingston?" She nodded. "You don't move from here, you hear? I don't want any trouble with Rivas. Got it?"

"Yes."

As soon as Pedro turned his back, she shot up and pushed her way past the many tables and people in the direction in which she'd seen Rivas and the woman going. At the door, a bouncer stopped her. "*¡No pase!*" he said, and pointed towards another door - the one which she had come through with Pedro earlier.

"They're waiting for me. Let me through!"

She heard Pedro behind her and felt him put his arm around her. "Here you are, darling. Come, we have to go this way," he said sweetly and then to the bouncer, "Excuse us. She's lost." Without drawing any further attention to themselves, they returned to their table which was just about to be occupied by another couple. Pedro chased them away rudely and then turned to Catherine. "It's easier to guard a sack of fleas than to visit a bar with you Catherine! Why do you make things so hard for me?"

"Yeah, okay, I'm sorry, Pedro. Who's that woman?"

"A friend of his mother."

"I thought his mother was dead."

"She is. Sad story. She died during a bomb attack. Both women were attending a soccer match. The tickets were actually meant for Rivas but he was unexpectedly invited to Sweden to spend the summer vacation with a family who were friends with that woman. Since they'd bought the tickets already, they decided to attend the match without him. After the game, several bombs went off at some of the exits as the spectators were leaving the stadium.

"When was that?"

"Twenty years ago."

"Where?"

"Barcelona."

"Who was playing?"

"Barcelona against St Germaine. Did you hear about it?"

"No, that was before my time. This woman survived?"

"Only by a miracle. But she was badly hurt, spent eight weeks in a coma and after that she was in rehab for almost a year."

"Rivas took care of her?"

"No, he was only fourteen at the time and had trouble dealing with his mother's death himself. As the only relative, he even had to identify her himself. He was put in a home but as soon as this woman had recovered, she took him in and gave his life meaning again."

"Rivas was in a foster home?"

"No, an orphanage, for about twelve months."

"And then?"

"And then, and then. Enough now. I told you too much already."

"Is she part of your group?" Catherine was now sure the woman was Maria Santa Cruz, but didn't want to let on.

"Yes."

"Who claimed responsibility for the bombing?"

"Religious extremists."

"Which religion? Which faction?"

"Which, which! What difference does it make? Here's Rivas. Be quiet now and don't question him about this. He doesn't like talking about it, at least not to us. Got it?"

"Mhm. One last question, Pedro. Please. What's the name of that woman?"

"Maria Santa Cruz. The woman who supplied your wardrobe and cosmetics. You obviously couldn't do much with the things I'd laid out for you."

"The toothbrush and the nail file were from you?" Despite the macabre context, Catherine couldn't help laughing. "Please try a bit harder next time!"

"I told you, your 'visit' caused an unprecedented runaround! Besides, there'll be no next time for me."

"Why not?"

Pedro couldn't reply. Rivas had joined them and said, "Let's go. I promised you the Parisian nightlife." He nodded to Pedro to leave. Rivas briefly sat down.

"What were you doing for so long?"

"I was negotiating your release."

Catherine was irritated. "You had to negotiate? And, were your negotiations successful?"

"Yes, we're all clear. Tomorrow we'll spend the day together any way you like and the day after we'll fly to Washington, Mrs Jones."

"I want to go back to the hotel," she demanded pettishly.

"Goodness gracious! What sort of a spoilsport are you? There's nothing doing with you."

"Excuse me, if I'm not exactly in a party mood under the circumstances."

"Don't you look forward to going home at all?"

"Can we at least go somewhere where we can talk, if you don't want to go back to the hotel?"

"What do you want to talk about, Catherine?"

"About you. I want to make the most of the little time left, surely you can understand that."

"Catherine, what else can I tell you?"

"We can carry on from where we left off yesterday. We'd got as far as your studies and then ended up talking about kidnappings."

"I moved to London and worked in the practice of a leading authority in forensic psychiatry as his assistant. When I got my license to practice I went straight to WICED. Did Pedro pay for your drinks?"

"I think so, he fetched them from the bar." They left the venue and carried on talking in the street outside. "Do you have siblings?"

"You know that I don't."

"I mean a stepsister or –brother. Any children on Maria's side with whom you grew up?"

"My mother never re-married and had no more children and Maria never married and had no children either. But Catherine, how was your family life? I've gleaned that your mother didn't play a big role in your upbringing. Why?"

"I don't have a mother."

"Everyone has a mother."

"I don't."

"What happened?"

"We had a swing in our garden. It happened one sunny day in spring. I was five. I jumped on the swing and my mother pushed me. While I was swinging back and forth she suddenly said, she had to get a few groceries, but that I had to stay home. I never saw her again. She ran off with some other guy, my dad told me years later. He said he was a foreigner, an asylum seeker, and that she'd gone abroad with him eventually."

"She just left you sitting on the swing?"

"Yes. Perhaps she did want to see me again and my father prevented her from visiting me, I don't know. All I know is he took good care of me. Did you have girlfriends while you lived in Paris?"

"One."

"What was her name?" Catherine froze. She would have preferred more than one.

"I'll tell you some day. Let's not talk about her now."

"What did you do in your spare time?"

"Maria organized for me to get accepted as a riding student at the Cadre Noir. I spent all of my vacations there."

"What? You studied riding at the French National Riding School?" Catherine exclaimed, overcome with admiration. "Did you qualify?"

"Yes."

"Oh my goodness. That's incredible! I thought you only ride Iberian?"

"I do now. But at the time I was keen on combining the lightness of the French school with the classical elements of the Spanish school."

"Do you prefer Selle-Français horses to Andalusians?"

"I like them a lot. They're light off the leg, they're fresh going forward and airy in their movements, but Andalusians are Andalusians. Once you've discovered them, you're hooked."

"I agree." They walked for about fifteen minutes and Rivas persuaded her to visit a club after all. Even from afar Catherine couldn't miss the soft sounds of reggae and came alive. "You know that I like reggae?"

Rivas smiled. "The reggae here is the best in the world."

"No, the one at Rick's Café in Negril is the best."

"That tourist trap?"

"Okay Strawberry Hills then."

"Wait and see." As they sat down at a table in the reggae club, Rivas answered his phone. Catherine hadn't even heard it ring. "Catherine, I'm sorry, but I have to go. I'll call Pedro, he'll take you back to the hotel."

"How long will you be?"

"I'll see you at the hotel in about an hour."

"Can't I wait for you here? I'm having such a good time."

Rivas, glad about Catherine's happy mood, replied, "I'll ask him to keep you company here."

"Rivas, don't bother him. It's not necessary and you said you wouldn't be long."

"Fine. If you need anything ask François, that's the club owner, to call me."

"He has your number?"

"Yes. May I order you a drink?"

"I'll manage, thanks."

Rivas left and Catherine enjoyed the syrupy rhythms of the reggae band while sipping a Montego Bay rum cocktail. A handsome man in his early thirties with long, tied back dreads came up to her table and addressed her in French.

"Sorry, I don't understand you," she apologized in English.

"May I sit down?" he now asked in English with a Jamaican accent.

"Why?"

"Because I want to get to know you."

"I'm Catherine."

"Benji." He sat down. "I haven't seen you here before."

"It's my first time."

"May I show you something?"

"What could you possibly want to show me, Benji?"

"I want to teach you how to jam."

"Thanks, I already know how to jam."

"Where would you have learned that?" he asked, unconvinced.

"In Jamaica," she bragged.

"No kidding! That's my home country. I'm from Kingston."

"Don't take this the wrong way, but you don't look much like a Jamaican to me."

"Seriously? I thought I looked exactly like one would imagine a Jamaican to look. Only better!"

"Replica!" she scoffed to tease him.

"Excuse me?"

"Your accent sounds authentic, but you're no Jamaican."

"Explain."

"Where I come from, young men have taken to dreads, real Jamaicans, however, are ahead of the pack and short cropped hair has long taken over from dreads on the island."

"You're right, but I'm a real Rastafari and my dreads are real. Replica!" He shook his head.

"Respect," Catherine consoled him in Rasta fashion. She spread the first three fingers of her right hand and twice tapped her chest with them.

"A miracle!" he exclaimed. He replied with the same hand movement and ended the ritual by giving her the "brotherly fist" as a sign of recognition and acceptance. "You said, where you come from people wear dreads. Where might that be?"

"I'm from Africa."

"Oh princess! You're from the mother land. Today is the best day of my life!"

"Benji, relax. You say your dreads are real?"

"Yeah mon, Princess." Catherine glowed about this term of endearment. "Princess" was the Rasta term for a really desirable woman or one who was dearly loved. It was a big compliment.

"How long have you been growing them?"

"For twelve long years."

"They turned out great."

"How come you know so much about Jam-Down?"

"I love Jamaica. Been there four times. Three times with my dad and once on my own."

"Dad? Alone? That's no good! Next time you're coming with me. So, how about it?"

"Yeah, yeah, next time, I'll come to Jamaica with you. No proooblem. Soon come."

"Soon come? You speak Patois? I've just met my dream woman. But what I meant was, how about a jam?"

"I can't jam to Sizzla or Luciano. I would need Bob for that. The original sound!"

"Soon come," he said and vanished. Shortly afterwards the band took a break, Benji returned to her table and stretched out his hand just as Bob Marley's seductive drum opened "Jammin'". Catherine couldn't resist. She slipped off her shoes and accompanied Benji to the dance floor. She leaned her upper body slightly forward, bent her arms at her elbows and loosely clenched her fists. She bent her knees softly and put her weight onto her thighs, while making sure she kept her heels firmly on the ground. Benji positioned himself behind her, held her by her waist and pulled her hips into a soft rhythm, which she followed skilfully, just like an African woman. The song was much too short. They took their seats again and while Catherine slipped back into her shoes, Benji remarked once more, "Yeah mon. You're my dream woman, Princess!"

"You made it easy for me. When dancing with Jamaicans you just have to let go. It's so easy to flow along."

"But you have the strength to keep your upper and lower body steady and to let the movement spring from your core. Non-African women don't know how to do that."

"Yeah, the old cliché. Only Africans can sing. Only Africans can dance. But there's some truth to what you say. I did need years of training. I've been practicing since my tenth birthday, much to the dismay of my late father. And horseback riding helps, too."

"Come Princess! Once more. You're so much fun. Beenie Man's on."

"I told you I can only jam to Marley. Really. Otherwise I can't sustain the 'square' motion."

"No proooblem. They'll play it again."

"Are you saying, the band will stop once more and the DJ's going to play 'Jammin' again?"

"Sure he will! All I have to do is point to my princess and Winston will play the song a hundred times."

"Yes and chase away all the other patrons. Later, okay? Where did you celebrate your independence and emancipation days last month? Here in Paris?"

"You know about those, too?"

"Sure. August 01 is emancipation day and on August 06, 1962 Jamaica became independent, right? They're immensely important days for Jamaicans."

"Yeah mon. Get up, we're leaving."

"Leaving?"

"I'm taking you home with me to lock you into a cage, so that this rare bird can never fly away again."

Catherine laughed. "This rare bird already has a cage."

They talked a while until Benji managed to persuade her to another dance. When they returned to the table, Rivas was already sitting there.

"Hello. You're back," Catherine greeted him exuberantly.

Benji stretched out his hand. "One love," he said. Another friendly Rasta greeting.

"One love," Rivas replied correctly without – not correct – shaking Benji's outstretched hand. Catherine sat down and Benji, sociable and outgoing like most Jamaicans wanted to sit down, too. Rivas growled, "Your little performance on the dance floor was really cute, but beat it now, okay?"

Suddenly Benji shouted: "Kiss me neck! Rivas?"

"Benji?"

"Respect, mon." Benji used his three fingers to tap against his chest to signal "we're one of a kind". This honor was not bestowed on just anyone.

"What are you doing here, you old bandalu?"

"Client canvassing." Benji winked at him.

"I'm already a client and this princess is mine. We'll talk soon, okay? Will you leave us now, please?"

"Pity," replied Benji, sounding good natured and then he said, "Cool runnin's mon."

"Exodus," said Catherine. It was the Rasta way of saying good bye.

"Exodus, Princess."

"How do you know each other?" Catherine enquired after Benji had vanished in the crowd. "Don't tell me he's also part of WICED? I feel like I'm in a science fiction movie, surrounded by aliens."

"Benji is not part of WICED. Do you remember your journey on the fast boat?"

"How could I forget it? I almost died from thirst. That idiot never gave me anything to drink. I'm sure he drank every time I fell asleep. And the whole time I was sea sick!"

Rivas comforted her by gently stroking her cheek with the back of his hand. "That was a drug route. Benji puts them together for us, not for drugs in our case, but 'passengers'."

"Benji is a drug dealer?"

"No, he's one of the route planners we hire from time to time. He organizes the cigar boats and the skippers and tells them how to navigate on that particular day. He knows when and where the patrol boats are lurking and how to avoid them."

"Benji made the arrangements for my transport?"

"He planned it but of course didn't know who was involved. Only that it was a single young female."

Catherine was so astounded, she dived right into a cliché. "The world is a village."

"Not really. After all, you're with me, in our circles. Of course we run into each other here and there."

"Did you see me on the dance floor?"

"Yeah, towards the end."

"Didn't it upset you?"

"No."

"I wouldn't like it if I saw you dancing with a Jamaican woman."

"I didn't say I liked it, just that it doesn't upset me. I'm happy that you're integrating into society again. You can flirt and dance and whatever else you feel like doing with whomever you like, Catherine. I'm not going to stand in your way anymore."

Catherine was disappointed and impressed at the same time. It was just impossible to put Rivas into any kind of box. "Can we go? I want to go back to the hotel now."

They paid the check and left.

On the way back Catherine said, "One thing I can't get out of my head. Real body contact with Benji doesn't bother you but about the fictitious man on the farm you said, you'd kill him if he touches me."

"Come on Catherine. How can I take that little flirt with Benji seriously? I choose my battles carefully. Or are you having visions of what Benji would do with you on the kitchen floor?"

"Of course not!" she protested and immediately launched into a request. "Rivas, you said, I can decide how to spend the day tomorrow. I want to visit the Cadre Noir. Is that far from here? Can we?"

"The Cadre Noir is in Saumur on the Loire river. That's a beautiful region situated about two hundred miles from Paris. Of course we can do that. Unfortunately there aren't many performances and they're usually booked out well in advance. I'll see what I can do, okay?"

"Oh that would be wonderful. Thank your Rivas."

--- oOo ---

After Catherine had retired to bed, Rivas took care of the tickets for the Cadre Noir. He was lucky that there was a performance scheduled for the next day and that he could get two tickets. He called Maria again to make sure that everything was on track concerning Catherine's release. Maria had called him back to the Café de Jerez earlier that evening as Carlos had had second thoughts. He was not to be convinced that Catherine was trustworthy despite the fact that she refused to switch allegiances. Carlos had initially agreed to let her go, but after Rivas had left the meeting, ordered a surveillance. It was to commence as soon as

Catherine would be separated from Rivas. That was the issue being discussed while Catherine had been chatting to Benji. "Maria, I've decided to agree to the surveillance, but only for six months and only a telephonic and e-mail observation and only if the info goes directly to you. You'll let me know if there's any cause for concern and let me handle it with her. And after six months of this, Carlos will hopefully be convinced that she won't blow the whistle on us."

"You're setting one condition after the next. Can't you at least compromise on this? It'll give Carlos peace of mind and it's completely harmless. I mean, what could happen to her if we keep her on our radar a little longer? Do you have any idea how much inconvenience your little romance is causing?"

"Maria, I'm warning you. If Carlos doesn't stop stirring, he'll be the one needing guarding."

"I didn't hear that."

"All the better."

He filled her in about his plans for the next day. She was beside herself. "Rivas, some of the old riding masters may still be working there. They could recognize you. You're wanted in France. You can't just turn up at your old riding school. There are enough sights for her to see in Paris. Be sensible now!"

"Are you forbidding me to go?"

"Of course not. I'm asking you, Rivas. Please be reasonable, don't drive to Saumur. If she must go, let Pedro take her."

"She wants to go there with me, not with a babysitter. Don't worry, I'll be fine."

"Wow, will I be glad, when this little terror is back in Africa where she belongs. Your judgment is completely clouded by this little hussy." Maria sounded utterly saturnine.

"It's very unfair of you to call her that."

"You won't even introduce me to her. I have to look at her from a distance, through clouds of smoke. Such a performance over this little hostage. What am I supposed to think, huh?"

"There's no need for you to meet her. I want to keep her completely away from WICED. It's bad enough that Sandrine turned up unexpectedly last night."

"Daria paid you a visit? How nice of her!"

"It wasn't exactly a nice experience for Catherine. I'm trying to avoid anything that could hurt her. Now that she'll be leaving shortly. That's painful enough for her."

"And for you, too, I suppose."

"Yes, but there's nothing I can do about that."

"How are you dealing with it?"

"I have to accept it. What can I do? It's my punishment."

"What nonsense, Rivas. Since when do you believe in Yin and Yang? What's next? Feng Shui for Andalus' stable? You've done nothing wrong, only your duty in terms of a higher goal."

"It's easy for you to talk. You weren't there! You're *never* there, Maria! Maybe you should check things out for yourself one day. I'll gladly take you to the Rio Putamayo. You wouldn't even manage the boat ride, never mind everything else this girl's been through."

"Don't be so mean to me. You do your job and I do mine. What you do with your hostages, which route you expose them to, and how much force you use is up to you alone."

"You're right."

"I told you I'd think about a solution and I think I've found one. If you married her instead of sending her home, she'd be officially in your care. Nobody from WICED would dare put any pressure on her if she was your wife. Marriage is holy, thank God! At least in our circles! We would even defend her collectively against any danger from the outside."

"She would never join WICED. Every attempt I made to discuss the aims of WICED with her has failed. And even if she would, I don't want a wife who has to marry me, lest she be killed! That's completely absurd!"

"Why don't you test the waters in the next couple of days?"

"Will you please stop pushing me to get married! First you went on and on about Chand and now suddenly I must marry Catherine?"

"I can see that Chand is history but I also see you need to settle down."

"Catherine's constantly going on about getting married, but she doesn't know what she's talking about."

"She won't know about your reason for your decision and you wouldn't only marry her for her own safety. Or don't you want her for a wife?"

"I would wish a better husband on her than one that constantly reminds her of her trauma."

"You're dodging the question."

"I would want nothing more than to spend the rest of my life with her but I don't deserve her. You can't imagine what I did to her."

"Yes, so you keep saying, but leave the decision to her."

"Look, I also want to forget this whole thing and not spend the rest of my life being riddled with guilt."

"Aha! So this is about you!"

"Yeah, it's about me, too. I need time. I arranged to get in touch with her in six months' time. Of course I didn't mention anything about marriage, but if she still wants me then, I'll seriously consider it. And then I'm out, Maria – whatever it takes."

"You, too?"

"Why? Who else quit?"

"Pedro asked to be excused from any further abductions. Didn't he tell you?"

"No. When did he let you know?"

"Shortly before he left Lima. Why don't you do the same? It's not necessary to throw in the towel completely. And we'll take Catherine in, too."

"How many times do I have to tell you that Catherine doesn't share our ideology? She'll never buy in! Besides, I would never drag her into the underground. How could I do that to her? That would be a lifelong hostage drama and violence would surround her constantly. She couldn't hurt a fly. Even if she agreed, it would be like killing her softly. If one of us has to give in, it'll be me, not her. And Maria, do you honestly think I could ever be part of an abduction again? Even from afar? The thought alone makes my blood go cold. I get what's going on in Pedro, but any job within WICED is out of the question for me. I'm done, Maria."

"What will you do?"

"Sooner or later I'll run out of money. Maybe I'll get a new medical license under a false identity and eventually start practicing. I'm sure I'd make an excellent therapist for victims or perpetrators of crime," he said lightheartedly. "Or I'll do something with horses. I'm not bad with horses."

She laughed. "Yes, you've got many talents, my boy. Horses, psychiatry, women anyway. Rivas can I really not persuade you not to drive to Saumur tomorrow? Letting your guard down for even a minute could be the end of you."

"Don't worry. I'll be careful. I'll call you as soon as we're back. Good night, Maria."

He was looking forward to visiting the Cadre Noir. He loved spoiling Catherine. Her innocence and good faith touched him and revived him. In his conversation with Maria, he'd played down the danger of his decision, but he knew full well that this move went against any common sense. Nevertheless, he wanted to do that for Catherine. She'd done her job with Ruckebier. To the bitter end. On their last day together he would have done anything for her.

Anything at all.

42.
France, September 26

It was 6 am, one day before their planned departure to Washington. Catherine lazed around on her bed, tired from the late night before. Rivas sat, smoking, at the side of her bed. "Rivas," Catherine remarked while observing the plume of blue smoke, "that sounds like a cigarette brand."

"That's not exactly a compliment Catherine. How would you like it if I said that Catherine sounds like a cake? Mm, Catherine cake with cream!"

Catherine giggled. "Why doesn't WICED just occupy a smoking suite? I mean, just think of the other guests!"

"Catherine this suite is exclusively for WICED members, I told you."

"Do they all smoke?"

"Are you starting that again? Are you looking for a fight or does my smoking really bother you this much all of a sudden?"

"Non-smoking regulations seem to be programed into me I suppose. Kind of hard to turn off."

"That's because your generation grew up with those rules. We used to be able to smoke just about everywhere, especially in Spain." Rivas put out his cigarette.

"Thanks. Rivas, what's your surname? Will you tell me?"

"Romero."

Catherine sat up. "Romero? Isn't that the name of the bullfighting family from Ronda?"

"Yes, but we're not related. How do you know about the Romeros? Ronda is a very small town."

"When I turned eleven, my father gave me a birthday cake in the shape of a horse's head and said I could make a wish before blowing out the candles. I wished for all the animal suffering to stop. It was then that I solemnly resolved never to travel to Spain until they abolished bullfighting. I'm familiar with the name Romero because I'm an anti-bullfighting activist!" She pronounced the word "activist" so dramatically that Rivas had trouble holding back a spluttering laugh.

"You do know that this riding that you like so much was almost exclusively developed for cattle work, including the maneuvers in the bull fighting arena. I'm not just talking about

Doma Vaquera but also the non-military elements of the Classical High School. The dramatic full halts for instance. And the turns on the haunches are necessary to protect the horse from charging bulls."

"Are you defending this detestable practice? You probably enjoy it? Those poor bulls."

"Catherine, they have a wonderful life, in contrast to the majority of commercially raised cattle." Catherine had many rebuttals on call but decided against a debate. Time with Rivas was passing too quickly. "Besides, they also practice bull fighting in the South of France and you even wanted to live in France."

"Hm," Catherine reflected. "You're right about my double standards. I'm no better with my VEE virus. It's all so terrible. Why can't we lead an ordinary life?"

"Why do you keep going on about being ordinary?"

"With you, nothing would make me happier."

"Come, this conversation is too gloomy for this time of day. Get ready." He pulled her duvet away. "We're late already."

Catherine went to the bathroom and Rivas turned on the radio. They were playing Aretha Franklin's "I say a little prayer". Catherine burst into the living room, tooth brush in hand. "Do you hear that? Man, do they have great radio in France."

"You like it?"

"Yes, please always remember me when you hear this song and I'll pray for you every day from now on. I'll pray that you'll be safe and healthy and that you stay alert. In the past years I only prayed once. That was the day when Andalus fell and I sat by the wayside. I prayed something like 'Dear God, if you exist, please let me survive this.' I did survive. Since then I believe that he exists. Do you also believe that?"

"You survived because *I* let you!"

Catherine realized she'd stepped onto a minefield and quickly fled the scene. "Never mind. Let's just listen to the song." Aretha sang her heart out. As the song faded from the stage, tears arrived on the set. Tell me that you love me, pleaded her glassy eyes.

You've not once told me that you loved me. Why not? Please tell me that you love me.

Rivas remained silent, just took her in his arms again. She tore herself away, her tears flowing like rivers now. "I can't take this anymore! I feel so miserable. I've never been unhappier in my entire life!" She stormed back into the bathroom.

Rivas had no idea how to ease her pain. He didn't even want to think about the drama that awaited them in Washington. How was he to cope with Catherine's dark moods when he could hardly manage his own emotions? He still had to get the whole tragedy of her departure behind them. Telling her that he loved her would only make things worse.

Of course Catherine had lost her appetite for breakfast, and so they listlessly took the elevator down to the small parking garage of the hotel. There, a similar edition of the car that Rivas had driven days earlier in Lima awaited them. The car was unlocked and the key had been deposited under the driver's seat. A WICED employee had delivered it at 5 am that morning. Rivas navigated the car onto the street and headed southwest in the direction of Rue Danielle Casanova. After four miles through the city center he took the turnpike onto the A6 Périphérique. Paris was beautiful. Despite the increasing traffic, it was peaceful and controlled, in contrast to the wild confusion of Lima. World class cities could appear pensive in the early hours of the morning. Paris even more so. Rivas thought about how his days on the *finca* had so often begun idyllically - with outrides on Andalus for instance. But the beautiful sunrises were soon swallowed up the day's terror, once it had begun. He saw scenes of the past months flash before his eyes. Terrifying scenes full of fear, pleading and tears. Many of Catherine's tears. It had to stop. Not just for Catherine. Also for him. The incidents with Pureza and Shanta showed him just how strongly his notions of unlimited power were still anchored to his lifestyle. To decide on the life or death of others was becoming more and more foreign to him. Life outside WICED would bring new challenges. How was he supposed to fit into this kind of life? He needed the six months to prove to himself that he would manage to say good-bye to his old habits. And even if he managed, what was he leaving behind? He thought about Chand and her planned family in a Pakistan infested with VEE. Chand's planned child would be unprotected due to its father's genes and Chand would expend herself in vain in her children's hospital, trying to repair the damage that he had caused. Chand, this wonderful free spirit, reduced to collateral damage – because of him. First Catherine had opened up a new perspective for him and now the news about Chand's liaison with the Islamic world. That was no coincidence. This was synchronicity - and an urgent warning signal to rethink his future. As soon as Catherine was home, he would use all his energy to extrapolate himself from WICED. At the same time he aimed to also convince Maria to reconsider her values.

Catherine's mood had lightened. She was enjoying watching Rivas drive through the light morning mist. "This car is Andalus on wheels," she remarked cheerfully.

"Hm, there are over three hundred Andaluses taking us to Saumur, Catherine."

"May I drive?"

"You may do anything you like."

"Except be with you."

"Do you want me to pull over?"

"Hm? Driving on the right? Maybe later, when the fog has cleared." Catherine marveled at the lush green scenery. It reminded her of her early childhood in Germany. After this they hardly spoke. Sometimes Catherine glanced at Rivas and he would respond by putting his hand on her thigh, and smiling. Catherine turned on the car radio. As a teenager, she'd twice been to the south of France with her father and loved listening to French radio stations. Even the morning's traffic updates sounded to her like marriage proposals. Rivas turned off at an intersection and Catherine saw a sign to Les Mans pass them by. "Tom would be green with envy if he knew that I'm driving past Les Mans," she commented.

"I'm glad you're thinking of home."

Peacefully they continued their sedate journey into the awaking day. The French country side turned the sad morning into a romantic one. Even the rain, which had started to set in, could not dampen her high spirits. Rivas interrupted the idyllic atmosphere. "You wanted to drive, how about it now?"

"Maybe later, Rivas. It's so cozy." She nestled back into her seat, yawned heartily and dozed off.

Rivas watched her sleeping and turned off the radio, so he could hear her breathe. He would miss her. She's a unique woman, he thought, she would get far in life. He thought about who would take his place in it. The thought of her childlike body and innocent trust in him caused a knot in his stomach. He didn't want another man to touch her and yet, he wouldn't be able to prevent it. He looked at her petite frame, her narrow hips, the beautiful waist in her tight denims. She'd curled up into a ball, looking uncomfortable and as if she was cold. He reflected on the early days on the ranch in Peru, how feminine and vulnerable she'd been when he undressed her the first time. He found her attractive from the start even though she wasn't really his type. Too childlike-cute, too petite, much too young. He'd never been into that. Till he met her. Back then, he'd felt so invincible and "strong". Now, several weeks later, the opposite applied. Her release was imminent and he was the one who was trapped. The time of indecision was over. He would change his life, that was clear, but how? And without Catherine? It rained harder and the windscreen wipers fell into a hypnotizing cadence. The road was quiet, promising another hour's peaceful drive. He thought again about the new man by her side. He just could not imagine that they would really see other again after Washington. He would call her to keep his promise, but held no expectations in terms of a physical, lasting reunion.

He spotted a quiet side road and pulled off spontaneously. By now it was pouring down and dark clouds covered the firmament. Catherine, awoken by the sound of the engine being switched off, asked sleepily, "Are we there?"

"Not yet."

"Is there a problem with the car?" She sat up and pulled the backrest upright.

"Catherine, I love you."

For a while one could have heard a pin drop in the car, then Catherine snuggled up to Rivas and said, "At last! At last you tell me!" She closed her eyes and took a deep breath. "I love you, too, Rivas, more than my life. For days now I've been trying to prepare myself for the day you leave me."

Rivas was already regretting it. Her renewed talkativeness forebode more drama.

"This morning I secretly wished that we wouldn't fly to Washington but back to Peru and that you would take me down to the cellar and shoot me. The only thing that would scare me about that, is not to be with you anymore, but a quick death in the cellar would be more merciful than to carry on living without you. So many months I fought for survival but now the fear of losing you is greater than the fear of dying and now you tell me that you love me. Why then can we not stay together?"

"We can't, Catherine," he groaned. She was full of false hope again, and he was angry with himself for causing it.

"But why not? Why don't you want to be with me, even though you love me?"

"I already told you. I don't want you to carry on suffering."

"And I already told you that I prefer suffering to separation. Like Terry Scott once said, 'the resolve in my heart is stronger than the pain in my body'."

"Now you're ripping a quote out of context again. Terry Scott spoke about sports performance. You can't just tailor everything to suit your needs."

"You also do that!"

"Catherine what's happening here is not my first choice either, but there's no other way. I've gone over this a hundred times. Be reasonable!"

"You always find a solution for everything."

"This is a solution."

"A free man never limits himself to this or that, but makes use of both options, or chooses neither and invents his own alternatives."

"A free man. But we're not free, Catherine. I'm caught up in a lot of issues and you can only be free if you follow your own path from here."

"Life is cruel."

"Life is good. We humans make it cruel."

"That's not helpful."

"It's the way it is."

"Alright then. If I can't stop you from breaking things off with WICED, then I'll stay with you anyway."

"How would that work?"

"I could do a job similar to Pedro's. Next time you kidnap a female victim, it would be easier for her if there was another woman in the house."

"Oh right! While I'm banging her upstairs or beating the hell out of her, you'll cook us a paella with fresh seafood from Lima, or what?"

"You're horrible!"

"I'm realistic and you've lost your mind." Rivas was angry. Out of his sentimental love declaration sprung a fierce argument.

"I'm not leaving quietly, Rivas."

Her voice had a threatening edge to it. This irked him immensely. "Do you want to know one of the reasons why WICED kills its hostages after an operation?"

"No."

"Because they won't have to put up with this sort of drama if they do."

"So kill me then. I already suggested as much. If you can't think of anything else. As far as your other solution is concerned, it is hereby officially declined."

"Quit it now. You're going to do exactly as I say."

"The hell I will. I'm free now and won't take orders from you no more!"

"Anymore! Catherine, listen to me. You're right in the middle of processing your trauma. This refusal to let go is nothing but fear of change. You'll need therapy, but you'll get over it, I promise you."

"You're the one needing therapy. I'm just trying to make the best of a bad situation."

"Catherine, you're all mixed up. You don't mean what you're saying. Let's quit fighting, okay?"

"First you tell me that you love me and then you abandon me."

"Catherine, we have to stop trotting round in circles."

"Well then. Close the loop and kill me. Otherwise I'll do it myself."

Rivas considered this possibility for a moment. A quick end may indeed be better for her than the psychological hell that awaited her, he pondered. The only alternative left was to stall Catherine for those six months while he made arrangements to leave the organisation. But there was no way he could have let her in on this, because should he fail, he would expose her to further disappointment. He decided to use good old sales psychology - the negative sale: "Catherine, I promised to contact you in six months' time. I hoped that you would come to your senses during this time, because the state you're in would make any relationship completely unfeasible. But I realize now, you won't manage. With or without therapy."

"I'll make it, Rivas!"

Catherine reacted exactly as predicted. And so quickly! "I'm experienced with things like this and I'm telling you, you won't make it. It's hopeless."

"I've overcome far worse challenges. I'll get through these six months."

"Okay, we'll carry on as planned but only if you promise to see the specialist I'm sending you to."

"I can see that this is the only way for me to ever see you again."

"Exactly. So we're agreed?"

"Yes, agreed. Six months!"

Rivas steered the Audi back onto the road to Saumur and put his foot down on the accelerator, pressing Catherine back into her seat. Even the permanent four wheel drive couldn't prevent the brute force of the engine from making the car drift briefly, since he'd turned off the ESP as always. In a skillful power slide he drifted over the road markings back into the lane and as soon as grip was restored, the car catapulted forward with such vehemence that Rivas couldn't help smiling for a second. Okay, enough now, he called himself to reason. He changed up to sixth gear and drove on steadily now, keeping to the French speed limit. Due to the unplanned stop they'd lost even more time, but he dared not risk a confrontation with speed cops, not in France, not even with false papers.

After this, both were silent as neither of them wanted to spoil what was meant to be a happy excursion. Half an hour later they turned into the entrance of the famous riding school. The facility looked promising, even without any horses in sight. Rivas reversed into a parking bay, facing the exit – as prescribed by WICED's regulations – always ready for a speedy escape. In the shade of the many chestnut and oak trees they strolled hand in hand towards the main building where the performance was to commence at 10.30 am. Catherine couldn't wait to feel the atmosphere, to smell the fragrant chips of wood, covering the floor of the riding hall and to see fresh and boisterous horses strutting their stuff. Since they were early after all, they bought some coffee and snacks and killed time exploring the grounds, while the spectators were rolling in by the bus load. On the way to the hall they passed a souvenir shop and Catherine spotted a pendant in the shape of a horse performing a courbette, which she insisted on buying. "Catherine, that's much too kitschy, come, I'll get you something prettier and much more valuable when we get to Paris."

"No, this amulet is more precious than any other piece of jewelry in the world." He followed her reluctantly into the shop and she insisted on paying for it herself. "It's your money anyway," she reasoned so he would agree. She took some euros out of her Chanel purse and clumsily fussed with the unfamiliar currency.

Next they took a tour of the stables gazing at the Prestige horses. Those were the horses, which were schooled well enough to participate in these performances. One hundred and seventy employees took care of the four hundred horses at this traditional facility. Rivas excused himself briefly to take a phone call while Catherine proceeded to the outside arenas. She watched two young men who were being tutored by an instructor in Cadre Noir uniform. These riders were eighteen to nineteen years old at the most. Both wore T-shirts with the word "Emirates" printed on them. Rivas came back and they went into the lobby of the main hall where Rivas showed her the brass plated names of all the school masters dating back to the year 1815. According to tradition, only soldiers could qualify as school masters of the Cadre Noir. Rivas pointed out the name of the Colonel who ran the school during Rivas's time as a student here. Catherine became sentimental. "Why couldn't we have met then? Everything would have turned out differently."

"Catherine, you were barely thirteen then!"

"Oh right! But I would have fallen in love with you anyway."

"Come, let's go in."

It was 10.20 am when they took their seats and punctually at 10.30 am the first in-hand horses, all side-reined, were lead in. Catherine felt dizzy at so much grace and beauty all at once. She grabbed Rivas's arm and whispered, "Amazing, hey?" Rivas nodded in agreement.

The horses spread out on the 115 by 300 ft. rectangle, performing their first courbettes and croupades. While the riders still showed their horses in-hand, the first rider and bay combination trotted in and began to work on a circle in working trot. As the in-hand group left the hall, eight horses cantered in, accompanied by march music, led into a formation by the bay horse that had entered earlier. The riders looked very smart in their cavalry uniforms and their traditional *Képis*. The two female riders didn't wear *Képis*, but round hats and they were turned out no less impressively. The choreography of their performance at those swift paces was of the highest standard. All horses were bay or black in accordance with the dark tones of the Cadre Noir. They looked altogether beautiful; slender, athletic and extremely well groomed. The riders' seats were flawless and the horses attentive. When something did go wrong every now and then, the riders corrected them laughingly, much to the amusement of the audience. The atmosphere was generally light and jovial. There was no sign of tension or forced compulsion as was sometimes the case with performances of this nature. One of the female riders was experiencing considerable trouble with her bay stallion and Catherine observed how she discreetly positioned him left and right alternately while continuing to canter in formation, until she'd regained his attention. It was so subtly done, a novice wouldn't have noticed it, but Catherine bumped Rivas with her elbow who acknowledged that he hadn't missed it either. This troop was relieved by the next group of riders who sat in cream colored saddles and now performed mounted croupades and courbettes. The danger of a fall was high, which is why the saddles were equipped with extra high cantles and pommels but were without stirrups. A further pair rode in. This black horse was so beautifully on the aids that Catherine gasped. His extreme obedience did not prevent him from showing off his energy and joie de vivre in any way. Each of his paces was bursting with optimism and controlled power. The rider calmly and skillfully pushed out the energy from the hind quarters to the front through the horse's back and poll. The animal was under the spell of its rider, perfectly united and working willingly, with no hint of compulsion whatsoever. When the rider asked his horse for an extension, Catherine observed how the muscles of the horse braced causing his steps to lengthen energetically, but calmly with no sign of rushing at all. His movements stayed light and subtle throughout, they were not theatrical like with the Iberian horses. Catherine was happy to be able to tell the difference, having learnt so much about horses under Rivas's guidance over the past months. Perfectly cadenced, horse and rider floated across the diagonal. The horse's mouth was in full contact with the rider's hands and he rolled up his neck further, but never came behind the bit by even as much as half an inch. It was high in the poll and chewed on the bit industriously, the resulting foam being the telltale sign that it was working correctly through the back. The rider led his horse into a circle on the left rein and reduced it to a volte which he kept up for a while. Eventually he returned to trot, went large and then changed rein while extending the trot from F to H. Catherine was overwhelmed by a further extension of such dramatic proportions. She wondered what it must feel like to sit to that and if she would manage.

A fifth rider entered on a chestnut. Catherine noticed that not only did this horse break with the bay and black tradition but also that its rider cantered in light seat. With great anticipation she awaited what the pair was about to show them. An announcer said something in French, and repeated his words in barely intelligible English while a table and chairs were being carried in. Some of the officers laid the table with a cloth and crockery while others stood around it, chatting. The chestnut then headed directly towards the display and jumped clean over the laid table between the chatting men. Rivas explained that this was a reenactment of a true story which had occurred a hundred years ago. The chestnut mastered many more unconventional obstacles and after clearing a row of chairs, the rider allowed his horse a short break to catch his breath. A new obstacle was being built while the rider walked around the arena on a long rein. Underneath the spectator's area the rider briefly looked up and directly at Rivas.

Rivas recognized him immediately. He was one of his former instructors. He didn't know if the man had recognized him but he sure didn't want to let him take a second peep. He took Catherine by the arm and they hurriedly left the facility.

Catherine was disappointed. She'd been looking forward to watching the tempi changes which were invariably part of any High School demonstration. Rivas offered no explanation about their abrupt departure and she was dying to find out what happened but refrained from questioning him, thinking he may have spotted his old girl friend in the crowd. Instead, she satisfied her curiosity regarding another matter. "Rivas while you were on the phone, I was watching two riding pupils having a lesson. They seemed to be from the Emirates. Can non-nationals have lessons here?"

"Probably sons of sheiks. You have to audition but you can become a pupil at this institution not just with talent but also with money and connections."

"Like you!"

"Hey! I had talent!" he protested.

"Are you trying to tell me that you would have managed to get accepted without Maria's money or connections? Just on the basis of your talent? And, furthermore, that these boys have no talent?"

Rivas showed himself teachable. "You're right, that was an arrogant thing to say."

"Were there sons of sheiks here at the time you rode here?"

"And daughters, yes."

"How did you get along with them?"

"Fine. Why do you ask?"

"Just asking. What connected you with each other?"

"Our love for horses of course."

"Love for horses is exactly what will soon seal the fate of these riding pupils that I saw training so exhaustively today."

Rivas changed the subject. "Do you feel like visiting an underground facility where they produce sparkling wine?"

"A champagne cellar? Oh yes."

"No, a sparkling wine cellar. We're not in the Champagne."

"Oh, right, but actually I don't like sparkling wine. I only drink Taittinger."

"Yes, I know, but it's not about drinking. It's about visiting a *cave*." Rivas wanted to compensate for having disappointed Catherine by prematurely leaving the Cadre Noir and was trying to think up other ways of entertaining her in this beautiful region. So they drove to one of the many Chablis manufacturers in Saumur. While he was parking the car, Catherine spotted a sign in French and English, which said that there would be no further guided tours to the cave for the day. She pointed to the sign but he said, "Stay here. I've got this." Rivas disappeared behind the reception door and remerged five minutes later with a young woman. He fetched Catherine from the car while the woman unlocked a gigantic wooden door to an underground vault.

The cave was moist, the walls covered in mold, it was cold and it smelled penetratingly of yeast and wine. The woman and Rivas were having an animated conversation in French and Rivas translated glimpses for Catherine. He explained to her about the history and this particular wine manufacturing process. It almost seemed to Catherine as if the two of them were flirting. But surely it couldn't be that Rivas would chat up another woman right in front of her, so she put it down to her imagination. She did learn quite a bit about making Chablis but what fascinated her the most was the dungeon-like facility. It was thirty ft. below the city of Saumur and the many corridors even had street names. It reminded her of the story of the Count of Monte Christo.

Back in the car, Catherine asked, "How did you manage to persuade the woman to give us a private tour? Did you bribe her?"

"Sort of."

"How much did you pay her?"

"Good grief, Catherine, do you always have to know everything?"

"Now I really do!"

"I told her I would kiss her."

"You what? Are you crazy? That was completely uncalled for. The cave wasn't that great, you know. Don't think for one moment that I'll ever let you kiss me again. Bah! What on earth were you thinking?"

"Calm down. I teased her by saying I would kiss her if she opens up the cave for us. Nobody kissed anybody. It was a joke and her sense of humor prompted her to do me the favor, nothing more. Am I not allowed to negotiate anymore?"

Catherine was still sulking when she was distracted by a romantic looking castle. "Look over there! What kind of fairy tale castle is that?"

"That's Château de Saumur. It's six hundred years old."

"Can we drive up there?"

"We can drive into town and walk up, if you like."

"Yes please." They crossed the Loire river, drove into the center of Saumur and parked the car at the foot of the hills of the castle, which could only be reached by foot or with a delivery permit for public events at the castle. On this day it was deserted, which added to the romantic allure. To get to the castle they had to cross two wooden draw bridges. Catherine remarked, "That reminds me of the bridges in the jungle. They were so scary. It was okay when there were ropes to hold on to, but most didn't. Some were not broader than wooden planks with just enough space for both feet. The transporters always untied me so I could balance myself better, but it was terrifying nevertheless. You know, in front of me and behind me were the heavy men and the board jumped up and down from their weight and underneath me was nothing but brown, croc infested water. I don't even want to think about it."

"I know the bridges, but with some practice it gets easier, don't you think?"

"That's true, yes. You do get used to them. In the end I could cross quite quickly." They arrived at the castle grounds and crossed a small vineyard. Behind the vines extended a mowed meadow which offered a view of the entire region. The imposing castle rose up behind them and beneath them the Loire flowed at leisurely pace. Their view extended over the roof tops of Saumur far into the distance to the hills, forests and fields of the fertile Loire valley. No other person was in sight and so they sat on the lawn together, smoking and looking into the distance taking in the view. "Do you remember the last time we sat on the grass together? Before we rode to the shepherds' hut?"

"Mhm."

"Everything changed after that. At least for me. And in a few days everything will change again."

Rivas who didn't want to be drawn into yet another debate about separating, stayed quiet. Catherine sensed this and also stopped talking. Because of the dreamy look in her eyes Rivas felt compelled to ask, "What are you thinking about Catherine?"

"I just made up a fairy tale in my head."

"What's it about?"

"It's about a princess from ancient Germania."

"Tell me the story."

"No, it's silly."

"Not any sillier than telling a wine merchant some story about kisses. Come now, I want to hear it."

"Haha, you're right. Alright then. Once upon a time there was a princess. She lived in her father's castle on the banks of the Rhine river and was the pride and joy of her father, but she had neither mother nor siblings. She was very young."

"How young?"

"Mm, seventeen," Catherine invented spontaneously.

Rivas continued, "She was the most beautiful girl in the land. She had ember-red hair, emerald-green eyes and was dainty and delicately built. Her valuable jewels and her wardrobe were the envy of all the neighboring princesses."

"Rivas, it's *my* fairy tale!"

"Sorry. Go on."

"One day her father passed away unexpectedly and from that day on she lived alone in the castle, with only her servants for company. She also had a few knights for her protection, but they were lazy and stupid. She had no friends except one Arabian prince who was the same age as her. Since his fourteenth birthday he travelled from the Orient once a year to take riding lessons on one of the princess' two white miracle stallions. He and the princess were very fond of each other.

"In the land over the Rhine lived a plundering knight. Everything about him was pitch black. His hair, his armor, his horse and especially his heart. He owned the Château de Saumur and also had it painted black inside and outside. He didn't tolerate people whose views differed from his. He declared such people to be his enemies in order that he may have a justification for killing them. He was eager to become even more powerful and rich and one by one he conquered the entire region along the Loire, annexing every province and declaring them as part of his territory.

"One day he heard about the beautiful, lonely princess and her wealth in neighboring Germania. He set off on his black stallion and rode to the land over the Rhine while thinking up how he could ensnare the princess in order to abduct her. As he spied out her land, he came across the Arabian prince and killed him and the noble white horse with his sword.

"The princess grieved for her riding companion and for her white miracle horse. She loved horses above all and found comfort in taking long outrides through one of her many forests along the Rhine valley on her remaining white horse. One day she carelessly rode off into the forest without her guards. At a crossing she saw a beautiful black horse lying on its side on the path. She dismounted to help the animal but as she bent over the black horse, it jumped up. The princess fell to the ground from fright. The black knight came out from hiding, scared away the white horse, jumped on his stallion and scooped up the princess with his powerful right arm. He galloped with her over a bridge across the Rhine and then they rode and rode and rode. At last they crossed the Loire and from there, he took her to his castle.

"When they entered the draw bridge to the Château, the princess felt sick from grief but half way across the bridge she fell in love with the black knight. But his bad heart was as black as the coat of his black horse. He loved nobody but his black horse and himself, because a wicked witch had cast a spell on him.

"In the castle, he locked her in a cold, damp dungeon that smelled of mold, wine and yeast. Every day he brought her water, apples, cheese and bread in a dog bowl, except when he was on one of his raids, then a servant attended to her. The girl cried bitter tears every day but the knight showed no mercy for the poor princess. He was too busy grabbing the princess' land and possessions and killing her allies. One day the girl fell ill from grief. She couldn't eat or drink anything and became thinner and thinner. Then the knight carried her from the dungeon high up into the tower of the castle and locked her in there instead. Because it was not so wet and cold, her health recovered but she stayed immeasurably sad. On her eighteenth birthday, when bringing her her daily ration of food and water, the knight kissed her. And from this day on he kissed her once every day."

"That's all? He only kissed her?"

"Rivas, this is a fairy tale. There's no sex!"

433

"I'll take it from here."

"No! She's an innocent princess, there definitely won't be any sex. First he has to marry her."

"Oh goodness. Okay, carry on."

"One day a fairy flew past the window of the tower and heard someone crying bitterly. She flew inside and the princess told her about her fate. The kind fairy promised to return the next day and encouraged her to stay strong.

"The next day, the fairy brought the princess some medicine from the far country of the Inca. She instructed the princess to dab a little of it on her lips every day, just before the knight came to kiss her. She told her, this potion would make the bad heart of the knight turn good and his black hair white. The princess did as told and whenever the knight kissed her a little bit of the concoction went from her lips onto his. She noticed that each time he visited her, he had another white streak in his black hair, because his heart warmed towards the princess more and more. He shared his royal meals with her and although he still held her captive, his love towards her grew." She stopped.

"And then?"

"Nothing. They were in love and they lived happily ever after."

"No! That's too easy. I'll carry on."

"Okay."

"One day the black knight rode into the forest on his black stallion. What was his name?"

"Le Noir."

"So, he was riding through the forest on Le Noir, when he crossed paths with the treacherous witch who'd cast a spell on him. The witch saw the white streaks in the knight's black hair and this told her that his heart had softened. She immediately saw through the fairy's trick and she egged him on to punish the princess for it. Ablaze with fury he galloped home and banned her back into the dungeon and again only gave her water, apples, cheese and bread to eat. And he no longer came to kiss her. The princess wept so loudly every night that the fairy heard her cries again. When she found out what had happened, she brought the princess a golden bowl. She told her, instead of wasting her tears, she should catch them in the bowl. Every evening, she promised, she would collect the bowl from the dungeon window, carry it into the royal stable and pour the contents of the golden bowl into the drinking water of the black stallion. That would soften the horse's heart and it would free her.

"And so it happened that one day when the evil knight was plundering a village, the black stallion's softened heart became angry about the injustice. On their way home through the forest, he threw his rider off. The black knight fell headlong into a tree and was impaled through the heart."

"No good! We need a happy end."

"The bad knight is dead, that's the happy end. But okay, if you say so. Le Noir galloped back to the castle, freed the princess and took her back over the Rhine to her country and there they lived, together with her white horse, happily ever after."

"No man! Let me finish the tale. So the knight fell head on into a tree and was impaled by the branch when the witch came by. She was doubled over from schadenfreude when she saw the dying knight. He begged her to help him but she just laughed, got on her broom and flew away, because she was really evil.

"It so happened, that shortly afterwards the fairy flew past and saw the knight in his agony. She felt sorry for him and held him upright. He asked her to pull the branch out of his heart but she explained that if she did, he would die instantly. Only a person who loved him unconditionally could pull the branch out, without him bleeding to death. She asked him whether there was a person like this whom she could fetch for him. The knight sadly replied that there was no person in the whole world who would do this for him. 'Not even Le Noir loves me anymore because I have such a wicked heart,' he confessed. The fairy replied that she knew of the captured princess and suggested asking her. The knight became even sadder and objected that he could definitely not ask the princess because he'd been very mean to her and she could only hate him. Le Noir saw that his rider was nearing the end of his life and his soft heart regretted having thrown him off, because he still loved his owner very much. While his tender heart grieved for his rider, his coat turned snow white, he grew a unicorn and gripped by valor he galloped back to the castle. He trotted down the stairs to the dungeon and positioned his hind quarters in front of the solid door. Then, with a massive croupade, he kicked it open. The fairy had flown alongside and told the princess of the knight's fate. Hurriedly the girl swung herself onto Le Noir and he galloped back into the forest with her. The black knight was taking his last breath when the princess leaned over him and pulled the branch out of his heart. The hair of the knight turned white as snow and the wound in his heart closed up before her very eyes. The good fairy jumped up and down with joy and clapped her hands. Le Noir whinnied and happily pushed the rider up with his muzzle. The princess meanwhile had disappeared into the forest on her way back to her country because she believed the knight didn't love her. At least, he'll let me go, she thought, because I saved his life. But she was wrong. The knight and Le Noir searched for the princess the whole night and finally found her sleeping under a tree in front of a well. The rider got off and knelt in the mud in front of the princess, to ask her for forgiveness. Then he pulled out an emerald ring from far away Columbia. It was the ring of his late mother. He put the ring on her finger and took her to be his wife."

"Does she have no say? What if she doesn't want to marry him?"

"Of course she'd say yes."

"And what if the wicked witch casts another spell on him and he locks the princess up again?"

"Oh? Right. Okay, so when the witch heard how the knight was saved and learned about his wedding plans, she was foaming with anger. She disguised herself as a medicine woman and set off for Saumur on foot in order to poison the princess with a horrible virus concoction. But on this day, Le Noir was grazing right next to the draw bridge over the moat and spotted the old woman. His horse sense was not fooled – he instantly recognized the witch by her foul smell. He took a run up and jumped over the fence directly onto the sorceress. Then he squashed her with his hooves even before she could step onto the bridge. He flicked her into the moat with a toss of his head, and the witch drowned. The princess and the knight married and he returned all the counties and everything else he'd robbed, to their rightful owners. He became a good and wise monarch who was respected by all peoples, irrespective of their ethnic origin. All his subjects loved him, especially his queen. The lord mayor of Saumur awarded Le Noir a medal, which he proudly wore around his chest. And every morning the royal baker of Saumur baked him a tray of crispy butter cookies. And they all lived happily ever after."

After Catherine finished her fairy tale they set off for Paris. In the car Catherine asked, "Rivas, are you upset with me because of the tale?"

"Not at all. You're very smart, Catherine. Don't think that I don't appreciate that."

"What do you mean?"

"Earlier you wanted to convey something about the riding pupils from the Emirates but you know that I can't stand being nagged, so you found another communication route and got my attention after all."

"To tell you the truth, it just happened."

"It doesn't matter how a strategy develops. What's important is *that* it develops."

"If that's the case, will you do me a favor?"

"What?"

"After you've banned your princess to far away Africa and see Maria the next time, will you please tell her the tale?"

"You little strategist you! You're not so innocent after all!" Rivas laughed.

Catherine giggled happily. Not because she'd planned the story but because she liked it that Rivas thought of her as smarter than she actually was, or believed she was.

"Which role does Maria play in the fairy tale? The good fairy or the wicked witch?"

"That's up to her to decide, Rivas."

"I see, my Rhine princess is not only the most beautiful and wisest in the land, but also the most just."

An hour later they pulled up at a wine estate. Rivas ordered *Beuchelle Tourangelle* and explained this was fried calves' sweetbreads with calves' kidneys. This variety was prepared with truffles instead of morels and covered with parmesan, which gave the dish a more piquant taste. He told her it was a traditional dish from the region Pays-de-la-Loire.

"I'm sorry, Rivas, but I don't eat veal or offal."

"Did you also turn into a calf *activist* on your eleventh birthday?"

Catherine launched into a lengthy lecture about the evils of veal mass production but as always, Rivas convinced her to try some, which she did. They drank a regional Chablis and Rivas explained its origins. "These grapes are from the Bourgogne and what distinguishes this Chablis is its mineral note which plays together with hints of apple, hey and other sweet aromas."

Despite the explicit explanation about the menu, he didn't waste a syllable on the abrupt departure from the Cadre Noir. She knew he was keeping a secret from her but didn't want to compel him into having to lie since he took this promise to her so seriously. Again she put it down to an old girlfriend and that he didn't want to be embarrassed again - like with the scene about his 'little' Sandrine.

At 1.30 pm they were on their way back to Paris and Rivas selected a different radio station. Chopin's "Prelude No 4 in E Minor" came on and Rivas noticed Catherine freeze up. "Would you like to change stations? Not in the mood for classical music?"

This music was the epitome of grief for Catherine. "That piece is a bad omen, Rivas."

"You believe in foreboding?"

"I believe in fore*warning*."

"And this music constitutes a warning for you?"

"Chopin composed this piece for a sad good-bye."

"Oh Catherine, I'm sorry. This is bringing up Washington again?"

"A terminal good-bye, Rivas."

"We'll see each other again, if you like. I promised you."

"Chopin tells me otherwise."

Rivas didn't answer. He didn't belittle her. Her didn't calm her down, but drove on in silence while the short piece was playing. Then he switched off the radio and for the second time that day, pulled over at the side of the road. He wiped Catherine's tears away and held her in his arms.

--- oOo ---

At the same time in Saumur, Cadre Noir riding master Maurice Du Toit slowly made his way home from his shift. He was deep, deep in thought. He didn't even remember how he'd covered the two miles home when he arrived at his door step. As always, his wife greeted him with a glass of *Chinon Domaine de la Colline*. He sank into his living room chair and slowly drank his wine. However, today he didn't read *Le Courrier de l'Quest* and *Le Figaro*, the two newspapers that his wife had put out for him while she was preparing ratatouille in the kitchen, but he ruminated on what he'd seen a few hours earlier. He got up and wandered into the kitchen, the empty glass in hand, lost in thought. He leaned against the door frame and watched her cut up onions.

"Claire, do you remember the Commissaire who paid us a visit a few years ago because of that murdered politician in Marseille? He asked me about this Rivas Romero bloke."

"Yes, that nice police officer from Paris! You couldn't help him and after that they put up warrant posters all over town."

"Do you still have his card? He did say, I should call him if I remember or hear anything."

"The question is, can I still find it? Do you remember something now? After all these years?"

"No, but I could have sworn I saw Romero in the crowd at the performance this morning."

"Why would he attend a Cadre Noir performance?"

"I have no idea, Claire. When I rode past the stands the second time, his seat and the one next to him were empty. He left in the middle of the show. He must have noticed that I recognized him. I'm pretty sure it was him."

"Then call the Commissaire. I'll find his number."

"It's probably better if I just leave it."

"No, call him. I'll look for his card." Madame du Toit put down her sharp knife, washed her hands and marched into the room next door. She dug around in a shoe box and came into the lounge a few minutes later – empty handed. Her husband was now reading the newspaper. "I can't find the card, but just call the Gendarmerie in Saumur. They'll pass on the information."

"Oh, that's too much trouble, I probably made a mistake, let's just forget about it."

"Then I'll call them! Monsieur le Commissaire said that his crime was probably of a political nature and that this man was a threat to State Security. Unthinkable that he would be roaming around in our town again!" Defiantly she picked up the heavy receiver of their ancient dial phone. A gendarme took down her information and promised to send a patrol car over.

Twenty minutes later it pulled up their drive way. Two officers took down a statement and asked Monsieur Du Toit to come down to the station in the next twenty four hours in order to file an official report. They also told him to expect a further enquiry in the next few days. But not long after the policemen had left, the Du Toit couple received a call from Commissaire Moreau from Paris. He was the investigating officer who'd interviewed the Du Toits four years ago. The cop in charge of the case was based in Marseille and he had mobilized the Saumur police to identify all the instructors and fellow pupils of the suspect. The case had then been escalated to the Sûreté, the French equivalent of the American FBI. Moreau kept his call brief. He simply ensured that the Du Toits would be home. He intended to pay them a visit later that evening in order to question them personally. He planned to be there by 8 pm. Du Toit regretted having made a fuss, fearing that he would disappoint the officer.

It was 9 pm when Sylvester Moreau finally knocked on their door. Du Toit relayed the morning's events and on Moreau's insistence gave him the name of the administrator who handled the bookings. He drove to his house, five miles from the Du Toits. This man couldn't help him at this late hour. Because the reservations were usually made long in advance and as there was no box-office ticket facility at the Cadre Noir, Moreau demanded a complete list of registered ticket sales points and the respective ticket numbers to be sent to him the next day. The man suggested asking the doorman by the entrance of the hall who tore each spectator's ticket and the souvenir sales lady who'd been on duty that morning. Moreau wasted no time in doing just that. He showed the elderly lady an old warrant poster of Rivas.

"Yes, he was in the shop this morning. Such a handsome young man. He was in the company of a petite young lady, also very beautiful. He didn't speak one word with me, but *she* was definitely a foreigner, because they spoke English to each other and she struggled to identify the notes and coins when she paid for her memento."

"Two gendarmes will take you to Paris tomorrow morning. We need an identikit of the female companion of the suspect." Moreau said good-bye and drove to the doorman's house but he couldn't remember the various spectators.

It was well past midnight when Moreau – tired from his long day - arrived back in Paris.

43.
France, September 27

Catherine only got up at 10 am. Rivas insisted on going shopping so Catherine could choose a "decent" memento from Paris, as he'd promised. He suggested purchasing a new watch at the Rolex shop near the Heriton but Catherine maintained that her own Rolex which he'd "given" her a few days ago was much more precious. She also never wore Maria's 20 000 Dollar Chanel watch again, after she'd got her old Rolex back. If anything, she was even more attached to it now.

"If you want to buy me something, buy me a ring."

"I'm not buying you a ring."

"Are you insinuating that I'm trying to swindle an engagement ring out of you?"

"I told you, rings are symbolic. I don't want you to misinterpret a gift like that." No more love declarations, Rivas resolved quietly to himself.

"Rivas I get it. You've expressed often enough that you're not going to propose. This ring here," she pointed at Warner's engagement ring, "accompanied me all the way through the jungle. I want to take off this hostage ring now. I feel I deserve a freedom ring from you. That's the only symbolism that you have to worry about."

"You can use Maria's ring for that. Rings don't get better than that anyway."

"That's not the point. I don't want a ring from Maria."

"Alright. Take the money I gave you in Peru and buy the damn ring with that money."

"No, that's WICED's money. I only use it for purchases of very little value, like the pendant from Saumur or the CD and cookies from Lima."

"So that's why you've been so reluctant with your spending."

"Yes."

"But Catherine, what other means would you have? We took everything away from you. See it as your money."

"Exactly. That's why you have to buy me the ring! Because I have no money of my own! I'll give you back the purse and then you can pay with your money and replace it with the euros from the purse. What you do with WICED's money is none of my business."

"Do you think I can't afford it or that you're not worth it to me?"

"Either I get my ring or we don't buy anything at all."

"Do you always have to get your own way? You're impossible! Do you know that?"

"I have a lot of catching up to do with regards to asserting myself."

"Yes, I can see that. Alright, if you find something you like, we'll buy it, irrespective of what it is. With my money, okay?"

"Including a ring?"

"Yes, Catherine, whatever you say. Am I really condemned to give in for the rest of my life?"

Catherine beamed.

"Now you're happy, right? When I concede and you win?"

"Rivas, Sigmund Freud just spoke through you, that's why I'm happy."

"What was the slip? I didn't notice."

"You said, 'condemned to give in for the *rest of my life*', that means you really plan to see me again."

"Doctor Zitgow is listening very attentively again."

"Doctor Zitgow had a good professor."

After this she marched straight to Cartier, which was also just around the corner, Rivas in tow. There she selected a plain platinum ring without a stone. In consideration of Rivas, Catherine purposely refrained from any piece which even slightly resembled an engagement ring. On their way back to the hotel she was tempted by a golden colored silk scarf in the window of a Hermès outlet. Rivas gave her the money for it but waited outside the shop. The receipt she stuffed loosely into her handbag. After this they went back to the hotel and packed.

"Catherine, I have to talk to you. Is now a good time?"

"Strange question. Why wouldn't it be?"

"Would you stop packing for a moment and sit down? I want to discuss a few things with you. They can't wait till Washington."

"What's wrong Rivas?" She sat down next to him.

"Catherine, I can only tell you, if you promise to stay calm."

"You're scaring me."

"It's to do with that piece of music by Chopin. Catherine, I've been thinking. I have to take precautions to make sure everything runs according to plan, even if the situation changes temporarily."

"What's changed?"

"Someone may have recognized me in Saumur yesterday."

"During the show! That's why we left early!"

"Yes."

"Oh no! It's all my fault. I dragged you off there."

"It's nothing to do with you and please don't panic. Nothing happened."

"I'm so stupid and egotistical! Besides, something could have happened or could still happen."

"That's the reason for this talk."

"Talk? We have to get out of here immediately. I can't bear the thought of anything happening to you. You always know what to do. Why are we hanging around here? And now you want to leave for the airport? Of all places? That place is crawling with cops. You have to do something, please don't be so stupid."

"The stubborn pursuit of a goal is the opposite of intelligence. And, to know when something is over, Catherine, is the opposite of giving up. To pursue the real goal behind the goal means to bring a matter to the conclusion for which it's meant, even if it pans out differently."

"Rivas, excuse me, I feel sick." She briefly disappeared in the bathroom and re-emerged shortly afterwards. "Sorry. Go on."

"Is everything okay?"

"Yes, carry on."

"Even if it was wrong of me to drive to Saumur, I am still of the opinion that it was necessary. If I try to run away from what is due to me, it will pursue me relentlessly, because the time for your freedom has come. Really free, physically and mentally. We may never see each other again, Catherine, I don't want to deceive you."

Catherine paled to ash grey. He who has no hope for tomorrow, dies today, she thought.

"When I said I'd call you in six months' time, I meant it, but since yesterday I fear, it'll never get to that. I can see clearly, you were never meant for my oh so grand master plan and also not for our new, mutual goals. Fate has mapped out a better future for you. That's why I want to tell you a few things, because things may happen very fast now and who knows if I'll get the chance again. If what I expect to happen does transpire, our paths will lead in separate directions for good."

"Rivas, I want to be free. I can't say that I'd really rather side with WICED but you're scaring me. Let's not drive to the airport. Let's hide somewhere in France until things cool down. I'll be free a little later, what difference does it make?"

"Catherine, first, you're really expected back home now and second, I'm not planning to hand myself in, just that we have to be prepared for the worst. What I mean is, whatever life holds in store for us, we have to be able to deal with it. Do you understand?"

"I understand. But what will happen to me if you don't protect me anymore? WICED will kill me because despite your 'negotiations' I'll remain a key witness."

"I'll speak to Maria. With or without the approval of WICED, she'll make sure you'll always be safe. She'll do this for me, because she knows how much you mean to me. If anything should happen to me, the police will put you under pressure to testify…"

"I'll never betray you."

"Just listen to me. They'll grill you, there's no question, and you'll tell them everything you know. It doesn't matter either way. They won't be able to crack WICED whatever they try. Don't worry about Ruckebier either. He's shrewd enough and they have nothing on him, it would be your word against his, they wouldn't get very far. He would deny everything and Maria's untouchable anyway. You've been through enough, I don't want to burden you with having to lie on top of everything. Catherine, you're not experienced enough to dodge an interrogation like that. Therefore, this is my first instruction: you'll disclose everything they want to know. Then they'll leave you alone. If you don't stick with the truth, they'll see right through that and suspect you of collaborating.

"The second thing is that you must visit an orthopedic surgeon to see to your hip. It may not trouble you for years but the tiniest hairline crack could become a problem when you get older. Do you know someone to go to? You must insist on an MRI, not just x-rays, okay?"

"No problem. South Africa has some of the best medical specialists in the world. I'll say I fell off my horse. It won't be my first time in the MRI tunnel," she added flippantly.

"Talking about doctors. The contraceptive we gave you will lose its effect in less than three months' time. You'll have to see to this yourself again."

"Until I see you again, I'll have no reason to do so."

"Third, you'll need psychological support. If I don't get to organize this anymore, don't let just any police psychologist treat you. Or some other quack! Look up a doctor by the name of Lammingcourt. I'm not sure if he's still practicing or where, or even if he's still alive. If he's passed on, get in touch with his successor. He'll have left his practice in the hands of the best. If he's still alive and practicing himself, call him up. If he doesn't take your calls, write him a letter or e-mail and tell him you have his name from me and that you were my hostage."

"I'll find him. Have you forgotten with whom you're dealing here?"

"In your sessions, tell him everything that happened to you. Leave nothing out. What may seem trivial to you, may be essential to him. He'll put together a therapy specifically for your needs. After the first few conversations he may continue remotely or refer you to a colleague. There's nothing wrong with that."

"I don't need therapy."

They sized each other up like a snake and a mongoose, each wondering who would strike first. "Catherine please! Yesterday you agreed to therapy."

Irritated, she shook off his gaze and lowered her eyes. "Yeah, I'll do it for you, I just meant that I don't need one."

"That's what you think now because we're still together but believe me, you won't settle into normal life without professional help. You'll hide behind a façade, but sooner or later your experiences will catch up with you and by then Dr Lammingcourt may indeed be dead. Think of it like your database. Could one crack it without knowing the code? Maybe, but it could take years. Knowing the code will yield faster results. Will you contact him?"

"Yes, if I need him, I mean yes, for you."

Rivas put his hand on his forehead in exasperation. She was taxing him of all his patience. "You will need him. You can confide in him fully. You don't have to be ashamed of anything, there's nothing he hasn't heard before."

"I'm not ashamed. Why should I be?"

"Shame and guilt will come, you can count on it and then I don't want you to be without a support structure. Your emotions will drown out all judgment, you'll hate me, you'll hate yourself. You'll be ashamed for me, then you'll be ashamed of yourself. You'll alternately become aggressive and depressive. These are normal symptoms after an abduction. Lammingcourt will put all this in context and help you to regain control over your life.

"The last thing I want from you is that you fly to Jerez de la Frontera and visit a stud farm called El Aduoa. Forget your anger about bull fighting for a few days and do it for me. Ask for Alberto Aduoa and tell him I sent you to buy a stallion with the same temperament as César VIII. The money for the horse is in this envelope." He pointed to the golden Heriton stationery on the coffee table. "Give him the entire contents. Trust him. Don't try to get smart and negotiate. Most of his horses are white. Classical PREs used to always be white. He's kept with this tradition, experimenting with only a few exceptions, Andalus being one. But color doesn't matter."

"Like they say, 'a good horse knows no color'."

"Exactly. However, insist on a male horse that hasn't been gelded, and older rather than younger. Andalusians mature slowly and PRE stallions are relatively gentle. Take the horse he recommends. Believe in the magic of intuitive selection; the first, spontaneous choice is often the right one. Don't get advice from anyone else and don't even try him out so you don't start getting side-tracked by too many doubts. Alberto knows what he's doing. Bring the horse home and before getting on him the first time, tell him what you expect from him and what he absolutely may not do. It'll only take a few seconds and he'll understand. Take him to a meadow or a big open arena where he has lots of space and ride him on slowly. Don't restrict him in any way. Don't pull on the reins. Don't clamp with your legs. Give him space to move and stay in walk until you're used to each other. Become his pupil. If you trust him, he'll teach you everything you need to know about Iberian riding. Don't get an instructor for a while, especially not one who's unfamiliar with the classical school. The horse will be fully trained and together with what you've learned on Andalus, he's all you need for starters. He'll take you to a heaven, which Andalus won't be able to show you anymore, unfortunately."

"Andalus showed me riding heaven already."

"Believe me, what you've tasted so far is a nibble of chocolate, I'm talking about a whole bar. I promised you that you can learn to ride classically and this horse will take you there. With the help of this horse and Dr Lammingcourt, Catherine, you'll recover from your ordeal."

"Rivas, for heaven's sake, what are you saying?"

He handed her the envelope. "Here is the money for the PRE. It's my own money and I didn't earn it working for WICED. It's part of my mother's inheritance. I've never touched it before and fetched it from one of WICED's lockers at Gare du Nord station while you were sleeping in this morning. My mother would approve. I can't give you a letter for Alberto. I want to commit as little as possible to paper because the cops may find it. The money is the only lie I can't spare you. Say that it's always been your money in US currency. It's a big sum of cash but to have it on you is no crime. I know you have a safe at home, WICED discovered it when they searched your house. If they check your bank accounts, say you'd kept it in your safe and exchanged it at the airport before you left for the States."

"I can't do that because at home they register all currency transactions due to the foreign exchange restrictions."

"Then say that you exchanged it in Miami."

"Okay."

"Tell them that I took your money from you in dollars and returned it to you in euros in Paris. You don't know why. Keep telling them the same story and don't deviate an inch to the left or to the right from it. Keep repeating the same sentence, a hundred times, if you have to, and don't invent any additional stories. Will you manage that?"

"Rivas, I don't need this money. I'll fly to Jerez and buy the stallion with my own money. I'll just save up for a few months."

"You'd have to save for a long time and…" He hesitated, sounding sad and factual at the same time. "…Things change. You'll meet someone, go on vacation together and gone will be the dream of Spanish riding. Please take it for me."

She leafed through the notes briefly without taking them out of the envelope. "First, I can see already that this is enough money for at least fifty vacations and second, the only one I'll go with on vacation is you, Rivas - when we eventually meet up again." She stroked the back of his hand. "And anyway, this sum exceeds the amount permitted for border crossings, but go on."

"That's true, but for this transgression, they'd only fine you. **If** this *préfecture* even pursues this - goodness knows, they have other problems. Lying about the money is a worst case scenario in the event they search through your effects. That reminds me - we'll have to dispose of your cell phone."

"Why?"

"Because if they do search you, they'll trace back your calls from Peru to Tom in no time. If they don't find the mobile, they would check the numbers only if they launched an official investigation. It's not really important, but we don't have to hand it to them on a silver platter now, do we?"

"Rivas, let me at least keep my SIM card. I need my contacts."

"Don't you have them in your PC or on a backup SIM?"

"No, I'd have to start from scratch. That's so complicated."

"Come on. Let's throw the phone and the SIM into the Seine. We'll make it a ceremonious occasion to baptize you into your new life."

"No!"

"Okay, but if anything happens, discard it immediately! But the other things are important to me. Will you do them?"

"If I do, will you also do something for me?"

"Anything."

"Have you ever heard of the US preacher Billy Graham?"

"Not my scene, but who hasn't? What about him?"

"He was married to Ruth for sixty four years before she died at the age of eighty seven. During the final years of her life, Ruth suffered from dementia and was in frail care. I heard that she didn't recognize her husband anymore but despite this, he visited her several times a day."

"So?"

"Reporters asked him why he bothered, seeing that she didn't even know who he was anymore."

"What did he reply?"

"I know who she is," she explained with a hefty dose of drama in her voice.

"That's a touching story," Rivas said with a puzzled look on his face, "but rather inappropriate. Are you asking me to visit you in frail care in sixty three years' time? Then I would be almost a hundred. I've heard that Germans like to think long term but this is going a bit far, don't you think?"

"This is a serious story. Don't ridicule it."

"Forgive me. What did you want to tell me? What can I do for you?"

"You must believe that I will always be there for you, no matter where you are, whatever becomes of you. If you let me swear to this, I will do all those things you asked me to."

"Catherine your romanticism is clouding your judgment. Remember in the past, every time you put emotions before rationality, you ended up disappointed. It's not necessary to swear to something like this, you'll only end up letting yourself down."

"I swear anyway."

--- oOo ---

Early that same morning Moreau handed his assistant the file on Romero and the list of ticket sales points which had issued the *billets* for the performance in question. The man from Saumur had sent it through at 8 am per email. The lieutenant grabbed his phone and launched the investigation while Moreau disappeared into his office and dialed a number in Marseille. He asked for Bayard Rousseau. "Bayard, good morning!"

"Oh, my friend Sylvester! How's Paris? How may I help you today?"

"Bayard, I have some information which I believe may help *you*. I have a lead in the Romero case. He was allegedly spotted in Saumur yesterday morning. I can't shake off the notion that there's something to it, even though the witness has some doubts. However, there is an additional positive ID from a souvenir shop assistant. Is there anything new regarding this case on your side?"

"No, after our initial investigation four years ago, Romero vanished like the Scarlett Pimpernel. We suspect he's somewhere in South America. Other than the murder in Marseille he's wanted for no other crime in France. Our Spanish counterparts suspect there is a connection between him and a bombing in Málaga from roughly the same time period but the last I heard, they had no concrete evidence to substantiate this. I'll get in touch with them right away."

"Do that. In the meantime I'll follow up on the leads from Saumur. Could you please let me have the updated file on Romero. I want to familiarize myself with the whole case again."

"Will do. I can't get away from here right now, but let me know if you find anything."

"No problem. If I have any more questions after studying the file, I'll be in touch."

"*Merci beaucoup. Bonne chance.* Oh one more thing: what was Romero doing in Saumur?"

"That's the strange thing. He was watching a Cadre Noir show."

"Impossible! That makes no sense. He's much too shrewd. We're dealing with a professional here, he would never endanger himself just to follow a sentimental notion. And a souvenir purchase! Looks like a wild goose chase to me. Who reported him?"

"One of the riders we questioned at the time: Du Toit. He believed he spotted him in the audience. Maybe his visit has something to do with the female subject who was seen with him."

"Well, it would be nice, if our efforts from four years ago paid off. Thanks for following this up, even though there's little hope."

"No trouble, Bayard. We spent so much time on this back then, we've got nothing to lose. *Adieu.*"

"*Adieu*, Sylvester."

"Monsieur le Commissaire," shouted the assistant shortly afterwards, "I'm done. Most tickets originated from block bookings by travel agents or singles via the internet and a few tickets from tourist class hotels. But there was one last minute purchase from a five star hotel concierge. The Heriton at the Place de la Opéra. Should I send an officer?"

"No, I'll handle the Heriton, that sounds the most promising, especially the last minute thing. Re-issue the warrant photo across Paris for now and dispatch some officers to visit the other hotels. Has the souvenir woman arrived? For the identikit of the female suspect?"

"Not yet, but I'm expecting her any moment."

Fifteen minutes later Moreau entered the lobby of the Heriton. He looked around. It had an anonymous feel about it. It was unusually designed in that the reception area was situated way clear of the elevators. He made a mental note of this and proceeded to the front desk.

Because Rivas and Catherine never had to pass the reception area, and had had no contact with any of the staff, other than obtaining the tickets – which Rivas had not ordered personally but by telephone (and had insisted on paying for in cash) - nobody could identify him. And of course there was no entry by the name of Romero. Moreau requested a copy of the register for closer inspection back at the station. Next he interviewed the doormen and porters. There only remained one female concierge who'd been on duty at the time of the purchase but who was now off duty. Neither the porters, nor room service, nor the cleaning staff could identify Rivas. Moreau planned to return with the identikit of the woman as soon as it was done. In the meantime he paid the concierge a visit at home. He was in luck – she was in.

She looked at the picture and nodded. "*Oui!* I definitely handed this guest two *billets* for the Cadre Noir a few days ago."

"Madame, are you sure?"

"Monsieur le Commissaire! How could any woman forget an encounter with this charming gentleman? Can't you see how good looking he is?"

"Madame - when I look at this picture, all I see is a criminal," Moreau retorted, sounding cranky.

"Oh you already know he's *criminel?* Silly me always thought whether someone is a suspect or a convict can only be decided by a judge." Moreau wasn't thrown – after three decades in the police force, nothing surprised him anymore. "*Alors,*" she added, winking at him, "if you ever need me for an ID parade - for a *mec cool* like this, I'll cancel all my other commitments."

Moreau shook his head in disgust and grunted, "Cool guys, Madame, don't pose for mug shots. *Au revoir*!"

"See you again, Monsieur Moreau."

Moreau was no longer listening. He was on the phone to his assistant. "I need you to go through the complete list of Heriton guests. Investigate everyone currently residing there, starting with couples, plus all departures from the last two days. You'll have the list of names shortly. In the meantime, send a team to survey the entrance 24/7. He's probably still hoofing around with that woman."

"Yes, blond, very slim, attractive, a touch above 5 ft. The description is out, but we're still busy with the phantom photo."

"What's taking so long?"

The lieutenant cleared his throat. "Um, the witness… she's… elderly, Monsieur le Commissaire, she, um, insists we're not getting the subject's attractive features right, um, as she puts it."

"What? Are we at a fashion shoot? Who's on duty in the *département grahique*? Do I have to do everything myself? *Merde alors*!"

"They're getting there, Monsieur Moreau."

"Okay, send it through to me the minute it's done. I have to meet Monsieur le Préfét before his media briefing on the Montavon affair now."

"Yes, sir, I'll take care of everything."

"Make sure you check out each guest personally. I want the names and addresses of the occupants of every room, every suite and every broom cupboard!"

"Shall I have them block the access key cards, so that each guest has to report to reception?"

"No, Lieutenant!" Moreau again rebuked his eager but inexperienced colleague. "All the innocent guests would crowd the reception while this rascal would get suspicious and get away even faster. You need to be discreet. In addition, put out the word among our patrol cars, at luxury restaurants, hotels and cafés, also at all train stations, airports and car rentals in France and our neighboring countries. Oh and check the register of the cars that have been parking in the garage. I want each registration traced and matched to the respective guest. Put a search out for any unidentified vehicle to be located.

"He's definitely on the continent, maybe still in Paris. Dammit, this time he's not getting away!"

--- oOo ---

At 11.45 pm Catherine and Rivas left the hotel without checking out. They were still in possession of the Audi S5 which Rivas would leave behind at the airport from where it would be collected by a WICED employee for its next "assignment". Flight AF 039 was to take them to Washington at 4.25 that afternoon. Before their departure Rivas planned to take Catherine to lunch at a country-style estate on the outskirts of Paris.

Catherine trudged somberly next to Rivas as they went down to the parking garage. The charismatic Audi surged up the ramp into the Rue de la Paix and headed towards the Place de la Opéra. They turned into the Avenue de l'Opéra, passed the Louvre on the left and turned right in the direction of Rive Gauche. From there Rivas drove four miles along the Seine and then took the circular highway around Paris. Rivas clicked through the on-board computer's menu, checking the engine sensors' data feeds: the Gran Turismo was at optimum operating temperature. Let's see what you got, he whispered to his car and steered it towards the Boulevard Périphérique. Once on it, he pulled the left lever behind the steering wheel twice in rapid succession, changing down from fifth to third gear. The rev counter shot up to five thousand revs, the exhaust flaps opened and the sonorous growl of the six cylinders gave way to the aggressive hiss of the turbo waste gate. He was mindful of speed traps but the acceleration rush was too intoxicating to resist. As a result, he drove much too fast. They reached the St Germain sur Ecole at the edge of the nature park, south of Paris. He proceeded onto the off-ramp at a more moderate tempo and then turned off towards the Cély golf course. The sun had conceded to the clouds of an upcoming rain front. A few minutes later a cranky downpour drummed down on the Audi, which automatically activated its headlights and windscreen wipers. When Rivas turned into his destination at the back of the golf course, loose gravel and sand were thrown up by the broad low-profile tires. The pounding sound in the wheel arches reminded Rivas of his rally driving training at WICED. He proceeded up a private path lined with poplar trees. At 12.10 they disappeared into the restaurant. At 13.20 they came out again, setting off for the airport.

Instead of taking her seat, Catherine cumbersomely crawled over the passenger seat into the back, to look for her Hermès scarf. "I think I left my scarf at the restaurant."

"Wait in the car, I'll get it for you," offered Rivas who was standing by the driver's door.

"Oh here it is!" Catherine exclaimed and looked up at him.

Rivas stood motionless for a fraction of a second and then shouted, "Down, Catherine! On the floor! Get down!"

She didn't react, so he pushed her down onto the backseat. Now Catherine also heard the police sirens. Rivas jumped into the driver's seat, stabbed the start button and put his foot down, closing his door as he drove off. The gravel again ricocheted around in the wheel arches as the S5 bolted down the small path. The four wheel drive scrabbled momentarily for grip for about three hundred yards until it pounced onto the country road in a wide drift. Normally, he would have driven far more inconspicuously but his sixth sense told him that these sirens were on account of him. There was no time to vacillate.

The Audi streaked along. Blue lights filled the rear view mirror. Rivas changed the S-tronic to "automatic" and tramped down on accelerator pedal. The windy road actually helped because of his car's superior road holding. In principle, losing the Flics would have posed no problem – the sheer acceleration would have catapulted them out of sight within seconds, but he was certain that he would encounter a barricade at any time. Catherine cowered on the floor between the rows of seats. "Stay down, Catherine, don't move."

"Rivas, please stop the car," she pleaded, "it's hopeless."

"Stay down and keep calm, Catherine. I drove over the speed limit earlier, that's how they must have got onto us, but it's just a patrol car. Don't worry, I'll lose it." Rivas tried to calm her, without mentioning the anticipated road block. He pulled a pair of handcuffs from the cubby hole and dropped them over his shoulder. "Put these on. Don't attach them to the car, just put your wrists together and let them click," he told her calmly.

"What?"

"Come on now."

Rivas seemed so composed to Catherine. He didn't scream at her, he didn't swear. For the first time she became aware that during her entire captivity, not even during his most diabolic phases, did he even once cuss at her. Even now in this extremely stressful situation - he didn't raise his voice. That's why she still managed to stay relatively calm. Her trust in Rivas was almost inexhaustible and she felt safe. For now.

A high speed car chase ensued with a number of cars on their tail now. The penetrating howl of the sirens drilled into her ears and while the velocity kept her pinned to the floor, she put the handcuffs on with trembling hands.

"Hit your head against the neck rest, Catherine."

"What?" she asked again.

"Give yourself a bloody nose, come on."

She considered his suggestion even though she had no idea what his intentions were. However, she lacked the courage and the strength to follow his instruction.

Meanwhile Rivas fingered around on a tiny radio and selected the police frequency. There was a lot going on: all turnpikes were being closed off, a police helicopter had been dispatched and they were dead right about his suspected position. The rain had turned into a massive thunder storm; flashes of lightning sliced through the sky. Rivas opened the sun roof to stay alert about the arrival of the chopper. His eyes scanned the sky. Clear so far. The rain pelted through the open sunroof, drenched the interior, the two occupants, the console. Then some good news: the weather conditions were too poor, croaked the radio, the chopper had to turn back. Rivas closed the sun roof and drove like a demon. The wipers were working at full force and with every curve Catherine, dripping wet, was being flung around the floor.

Rivas realized that Catherine wouldn't be able to hurt herself. "Hold out your head, Catherine. I have to do this, baby, come." He stretched out his right arm and she held up her head towards him. He grabbed her neck and was about to knock her head against the neck rest when the curvy road straightened up. Although it was hard to see through the torrent, Rivas could just make out some blue lights up ahead. There it was: the road block. He let Catherine go and turned his focus back to navigating the car. "Hit your head against the neck rest, Catherine," he encouraged her a last time, but instead she withdrew back onto the floor, rolled up into a ball and lay there frozen with fear.

At this point she no longer believed she'd escape this trap alive. Not even with Rivas behind the wheel.

Lieutenant Decouvert was the first one to spot the approaching car. "Down! Get down!" he shouted to his colleagues. "I think that's him." They pulled out their firearms and aimed at the oncoming headlights.

"Don't shoot!" Commandant Nevère shouted. He couldn't risk his team discharging their weapons without establishing if it was indeed the getaway car. When it didn't appear to make any attempt to slow down, and Nevère recognized the car to be an Audi, he felt he'd seen enough. "Aim at the tires," he shouted and opened fire.

Rivas saw the flashes from the muzzles of firearms. A bullet hit the left headlight. The onboard computer audibly reported the defect, which amused Rivas briefly. He pulled in his head and headed directly for the squad car, which was parked diagonally across the road as part of the barricade. Two officers saved themselves by diving into a ditch just before the Audi tipped the Peugeot's rear. The patrol car spun around. The front spoiler of the Audi dislodged and the left fender was ripped off the chassis. But they were through. Rivas accelerated again. Half a dozen airbags had been deployed. Apart from the one in the steering wheel, one each directly on either side of his head from the roof, as well as from the driver's door. The propellant of the airbags had made a deafening noise causing Rivas's ears to ring. Therefore he didn't hear the shots that were to follow.

Commandant Nevère was standing to the left of the road when the Audi powered its way clean through their barricade. He turned around quickly, steadied his weapon on the roof of his car, took time to aim and fired. Twice.

Seconds before: Catherine clambered up and paddled through the slack airbags. Their gas smoked up the interior, causing Catherine to assume the car was on fire. "Rivas, stop the car," she screamed.

"Get down *now*!" For the first time, he shouted at her.

She ducked. "Rivas, the car! It's burning! We have to get out."

Rivas was about to reply when the rear window burst and Rivas's shoulder was hit by Nevère's first bullet. A fraction of a second later, another bullet blasted through the head rest and lodged in Rivas's head. His body went limb. Although the acceleration decreased markedly, the S5 was still going at around ninety miles per hour. Catherine scrabbled through the gap between the front seats on her knees and elbows, her hands restricted by the cuffs, and grabbed the steering wheel with both hands. The brake pedal was way out of reach, so with the unfathomable presence of a mind bent on survival, she instinctively concentrated on keeping the car on the road. The impact had damaged the front left suspension strut and as a result, the Audi was pulling strongly to the left. She barely managed to avoid colliding with a small delivery van and now started to panic. Suddenly a police car appeared next to the naturally decelerating Audi. Commandant Nevère hung outside the back window, his weapon at the ready. When he saw the collapsed body of the driver and the handcuffed woman stretched over the seat and hanging over the wheel, he was quick to react. "Get in front of the car! Quickly! Get it to stop!" he called to his driver. The officer pulled in front of the Audi, let it run carefully into his rear and got it to come to a halt.

Catherine crawled all the way over the mid console to the front and discovered that Rivas was no longer conscious. Without even a chance to call for help, the officers of an elite unit who had arrived, pulled her out backwards through the rear. At the same time others opened the driver's door and Rivas slumped onto the wet tarmac. The shooting and sirens had ceased ushering in an eerie silence despite the fact that more and more cops rushed towards the Audi. They dived onto Rivas's body while Catherine hollered: "Why did you shoot? He's not armed! You just shot at us!" And then to Rivas, while someone was pulling her away from the accident site: "Rivas, Rivas! Please wake up!" She saw his blood on the street. "Rivas, please, please don't leave me, please don't die." She looked around and again shouted like a madwoman: "Why did you shoot? Why did you just shoot?" She thrashed around at the officer holding her until he forced her down on the ground. "Leave me! I've done nothing wrong! Let me go!" Someone dragged her to a patrol car and slammed the doors shut. She observed several ambulances parked at the scene; the storm raged on. Then it got very quiet around Catherine while the outside world faded away. One officer sat next to her, another one behind the wheel but they didn't drive off. They waited for instructions. She stared at the raindrops, which chased each other down the window until one would catch the other, forming bizarre patterns, similar to a river delta. For a few minutes, what happened out on the street passed her by. Her brain was paralyzed, she couldn't protest anymore, she couldn't cry. And what would happen to her didn't concern her.

She became present again and watched how numerous paramedics and two ER doctors were attending to Rivas who was still lying on the road. The police frequency spat out unintelligible announcements in regular intervals, but Catherine's ears only heard the melody of Chopin's piano strumming. Eventually an emergency doctor approached the car and she had to get out again. "I'm fine," she objected, "Leave me!" Ignoring her protests they put her down on a stretcher, a cop took off her handcuffs and they fastened her to the stretcher where the doctor checked for injuries. From the stretcher Catherine had a better view of Rivas. He was still lying on the street. A paramedic was holding his head up, another attached a drip. The storm calmed and the first sunrays pushed their way through the rain clouds. The doctor measured her blood pressure, took her pulse and listened to her lung function looking for signs of obstructions in her respiratory tract. She watched a brief exchange between the other ER doctor and the police. Shortly afterwards, this doctor came up to her and took over from his colleague after a brief exchange about her vital signs.

"*Comment allez-vous, Mademoiselle?*"

Catherine asked, "Do you speak English?"

The doctor repeated in English, "How are you feeling?"

"I'm good."

"What's your name?"

"Catherine Zitgow." Catherine Jones didn't even enter her mind at this point.

"Mademoiselle, we're taking you to a hospital now, but before we leave, the police will arrest you and read you your rights. Do you understand?"

"Yes."

"Are you sure that you understand everything? I can delay your arrest by saying that you're not well enough and that I first have to examine you thoroughly at the clinic."

"Not necessary. And I don't need to go to emergency. I'm fine."

"Do you know the driver of the car?"

"Yes."

"If you want to postpone an interrogation until you're calm and lucid, come with me to the hospital. Let me help you."

"I'm really alright. How is he?"

"It's too early to tell."

"Is he dead?"

"No, he's alive. Very well then, if you don't want to come to the clinic voluntarily, I won't force you. The initial examination confirms that you are physically in good shape. But consider that you're probably under shock. Shock can mask injuries. Can I really not persuade you?"

"Could I stay with him if I came with you?"

"Of course not. You'd be taken to a suburban hospital nearby."

"Then I don't want to come. Please leave me now."

"As you wish. They will cuff you again now and then drive you directly to the Département de la Sûreté in Paris."

"Where will you take him?"

"You'll have to ask the investigator in chief. He may tell you, if he thinks it's relevant."

"Please."

"They'll probably take him to the Hôpital de la Salpêtrière. I have to go now, Mademoiselle Catherine. If you're in trouble, refuse to make a statement for now. You could definitely still be in shock. Would you like my number? Just in case?"

She nodded. He handed her his card. She glanced at the name. "Thank you Dr Fournier. Why are they not leaving? With him, I mean?"

"We're waiting for a helicopter. There's been a delay due to the bad weather. Going by road would expose his head injury to too much jarring and also take too long. But a chopper is on the way now. It'll be here soon. Do you have an attorney? Or relatives? Would you like me to call someone for you?"

"I have no family and I don't need legal counsel. I did nothing wrong."

"Why were you in the getaway car?"

"The driver was my kidnapper." She had no sooner said that, when Julius Caesar's words spooked in her head: "Et tu, Brute?" "I'll never betray you," she'd assured Rivas, even though he didn't ask her for that. At the very first opportunity she'd done it!

I will always be there for you.

She was ashamed of the ridiculous comparisons she'd drawn with the story of the Grahams. She'd accused Pedro of a weak character and what had she just done? She hated herself and the treacherous Brutus in her.

"Catherine, if you were kidnapped, I'm obliged to take you in for an examination - even against your will."

"He didn't hurt me. Please just leave me. I want to get all this behind me and go home as quickly as possible."

"What caused that scar above your eye? It looks recent."

"I slipped in the mud and hit my head against a well."

"Why are you protecting this man?"

"I don't know what you're talking about. I told you, I fell."

"What's the name of the man you were with?"

She didn't reply.

"Tell me his first name. That's all I need."

"To make him come round?"

"There's no chance of that now but a name is helpful. You wouldn't be revealing much. I can get his name from the police."

"Then ask the police."

"*Au revouir*, Catherine."

"Will he make it?"

"I don't know." After hesitating briefly he added, "He was hit by two bullets, one in the shoulder and in the head, as you know. Catherine, headshot injuries are mostly fatal, but as long as the patient's breathing, there's hope. We won't give up on him."

"Why wasn't he killed instantly?"

"Do you believe in guardian angels?"

"Not really."

"He had one – the headrest. It appeared to have buffered the impact somewhat. But you're right, ordinarily he should have been dead."

"Rivas. His name is Rivas."

"Thank you Catherine."

"How do you know that I care about him?"

"You asked if you may stay with him."

"Oh right. Will our conversation stay between us?"

"*Naturellement.*"

"Dr Fournier?"

"Yes?"

"If you see that he, I mean that he's not fighting anymore, please let him die. He wouldn't want to go to prison or live with any permanent physical or mental damage. I know that for sure."

"Catherine, I won't treat him personally. I'm not a surgeon. I'm an internist on ER duty at the local clinic today. Since you don't need me, I'll stay with him until we get to the helipad at the hospital. But a colleague will take over from me as soon as we arrive. I wish you all the best. Good-bye Catherine."

"Good bye."

A fresh chance. The doctor wouldn't disclose anything and there would be no further betrayals. She firmly resolved not to pay heed to Rivas's first instructions to testify.

Dr Fournier called an officer who cuffed her again and took her back to the car. Before the helicopter arrived, they raced her - under the howl of sirens and flashing blue lights - to the Direction central de la police judiciarie, directly to the office of Commissaire Moreau. En route to Paris she saw a helicopter approach from the opposite direction. She thought of Lima and the cheerful day which had begun and ended with a helicopter flight. Her first day of freedom. It seemed so long ago. Now their mutual plans had burst like balloons. Her future, her whole life had been erased. Rivas's life in any case. In less than half an hour. And, Catherine concluded, it was all her fault.

Part V

Catherine & Maria

"You still have to have chaos in you to give birth to a dancing star."

Friedrich Nietzsche
Zarathustra's Prologue

44.
France, September 27

Commissaire Moreau was in his mid-fifties, with a potato nose, cauliflower ears and carrot fingers. At first Catherine misjudged this harmless looking "veggie man" to be a paper shuffling bureaucrat, but he turned out to be a robust and tireless interrogator, and fluent in English.

Catherine persisted with her story that she'd been kidnapped in Miami and taken to Columbia via Venezuela. In Florida, she maintained, she'd been pulled into a car by four masked men outside her hotel's entrance on her departure day. She described the transporters, in particular the squat "tea merchant", and the skipper and his fast boat, hoping to add credibility to her story by means of these vivid descriptions. She mentioned nothing about the Pentagon trap or about Peru. She hoped they hadn't been able to get in touch with Tom, and if they had, that he wouldn't have mentioned the Pentagon "assignment". Catherine was no seasoned liar, even the fibs she'd told Tom had cost her enormous strength and her experience with the police was limited to traffic fines and routine license checks. So she dealt with the interrogation in the way that Rivas had told her to: Questions such as how, who, where and when she answered by repeating, "*Je ne sais pas* – I don't know." This was one of the few French phrases Catherine knew and she made a meal of it.

Moreau didn't believe a word of it.

"Why don't you believe me?"
"You have to admit that your appearance – your wardrobe and your jewelry – raises questions about your kidnapping story. What you're carrying around in your suitcase amounts to hundreds of thousands of euros. No hostage travels the world like this. Is the jewelry stolen?"
"No."
"It's yours?"
"Yes."
"Do you have receipts at home?"
"The jewelry were gifts from him. As were the clothes."

"Why?"

"*Je ne sais pas.*"

"Fine, if he didn't tell you, do you at least have a hunch as to why he would've done that?"

"Maybe a way of making things up to me?"

"You're kidding, right? Okay, let's set your valuables aside for now. Let's get back to the masked men. What time did you say this happened?"

"At exactly 10.30 am."

"Please give me the name of your hotel in Miami."

"Why?"

"Because we'll question witnesses."

"I can't remember."

"Ms Zitgow, this isn't going to work."

"I'm so confused. Right now, I really can't recall the name."

"Everything else you've recalled with vivid attention to detail."

Catherine went the passive-aggressive route and studied her finger nails.

"Never mind. We'll find out another way. Then there is the large amount of cash you have on you. Where did you get this money?"

"It was my travel cash. They'd taken it away from me and then he gave it back to me in Paris."

"Sorry, but this doesn't gel."

"He got me out of Columbia, he treated me well and he assured me he was taking me home via Paris."

Moreau already knew about the flight to Washington but withheld this information for now. "Yes, I can see he treated you well. Very well. Then we have this here." Triumphantly he waved two passports around, holding up each one alternately before pulling his next card: "This one is real. This one is a forgery. Why did you enter France under an assumed identity?"

"He didn't tell me."

"Where was the passport photo taken? It looks recent."

"In Columbia."

"In the jungle?"

"Yes."

"All dolled up?"

"That's how he wanted it."

"Stop talking bull! We also found this cell phone on him. It's yours, as we found out while you were being brought here. In the last four months this phone was used to make two calls to South Africa. From Peru. We are trying to get in touch with the party, a certain" – he glanced at his notes – "Tom Rivers. Who's that?"

"One of my employees."

"He's not answering his phone but our counter parts in South Africa are on it. It won't be long now. What was being discussed on these two occasions?"

"I don't remember." Damn! thought Catherine. I should have listened to Rivas and let him throw that wretched phone into the Seine. After the accident everything happened so fast. The handcuffs would have made it difficult to dispose of the phone, but in the end, in all that excitement, she'd simply forgotten about it anyway.

"Who made the calls?"

"I don't know. I'm seeing the cell phone for the first time since they took it away from me in Miami."

"Do you think it's possible that this Tom Rivers is in cahoots with your abductors?"

"Certainly not!"

"That brings us to motive. The mobile could provide insights into the background of your alleged abduction. Maybe a ransom demand was made after all?"

"*Je ne sais pas.*"

"But either way, if your kidnapping story is true, why would Romero have let you go without getting his hands on the money? We're busy checking out your financial position. Are you wealthy?"

"I'm not exactly poor, but not rich enough to justify a ransom demand."

"I have another question concerning your alleged stay in Columbia. How long did you say, they held you there?"

"About four months."

"Tell me about the climatic conditions there."

"You want me to describe the weather to you?"

"Yes, in particular the climatic changes during the four months. For instance how did the vegetation change? From your first to your last month?"

"As far as I know primary forest vegetation stays constant throughout the year."

"As far as you know? I didn't ask you what you know, but what you remember from personal experience. Stop constructing answers and just recall what you experienced."

"I can't remember."

"What do you mean, you can't remember? Was it cold, hot, dry, rainy? How could one forget something like this?"

"Wet and hot."

"The whole time?"

"Yes."

"It was not rainy season then."

"But it did rain the whole time. After all, I was there!"

"We'll check out the precipitation levels."

"Be my guest."

"Why did you travel to France from Peru?"

"I don't know why we flew via Peru. Isn't that normal?"

"No, that's not normal. For how long were you in Peru?"

"Peru? I wasn't in Peru, I told you."

"Ms Zitgow, that's not true. First, nobody takes a detour via Lima to get from Columbia to France and second, you wouldn't get an exit stamp if you were in transit from Columbia because you wouldn't have passed Peru emigration."

Shucks, thought Catherine. It was starting to dawn on her why Rivas had insisted she tell the police the truth. "Hm? Yes, that's true, actually. But we were really only in the international part of the airport. The kidnapper had my passport with him the whole time. He only handed it back to me when we got to passport control in France and then took it away from me again. I really can't explain how this stamp got into my passport. But Monsieur, if you say there is an exit stamp, there must also be an entry stamp, not so?"

"There isn't."

"You see! Because we didn't stay in Peru. I told you."

"That's irrelevant. We're aware of several informal entry points at the Columbia-Peru-Brazil triangle. He could have slipped you over the border there and the immigration officer at departures may simply have overlooked the absence of an entry stamp when you exited. Or he was bribed. Probably the latter."

"Señor Romero didn't bribe anyone."

"How do you know that?"

"I know it because there was no need to bribe anyone. We weren't in Peru. Only inside the airport terminal. Like I said."

Moreau used the back of his hand to wipe away the film of perspiration that had formed on his forehead. "Ms Zitgow, I have a daughter your age. I'm trying to imagine how she would have acted under the circumstances. May I call you Catherine?"

"Sure."

"*Alors,* Catherine, speaking as someone old enough to be your father, I comprehend what you must have gone through. It's clear that you've been briefed on what to say, you may even have been threatened. Nevertheless, I can't accept your story. If you were truly abducted, you're no longer in danger."

"Nobody threatened me. I just want to go home. Can't you understand that? I've told you everything I know."

"Catherine, we know that there was a flight booked for you from Charles de Gaulle to Washington under the name of Catherine Jones. For this afternoon." Moreau glanced demonstratively at his watch. "Your plane left exactly two hours ago. We're busy checking out further bookings under the names of Zitgow and Jones, worldwide, but it'll take a while. Why did you want to go to Washington when you were supposed to be en route to Johannesburg and halfway home already?"

"I don't know why they booked the flight to Washington under this false name. He just said he'd make sure I'll get home."

"They? Whom do you mean when you say '*they* booked a flight'?"

"He. I meant he!"

"At 3 pm there was a call from a public phone booth at one of the taxi stands at the airport to Romero's phone." Moreau pointed ostentatiously to Rivas's phone on his desk.

"Who called?"

"I was rather hoping, you'd tell me. When my colleague answered, the caller briefly identified himself as Bertrand, then hung up abruptly. Who is Bertrand?"

"I don't know," said Catherine, truthfully this time. "Do you really think he informed me about what calls he was expecting?"

"You know, I've been an investigator for three decades now. No true story can faze me anymore but I definitely won't let anyone lead me up the garden path. Not a hardened criminal and certainly not a novice such as you. Because this is what you're trying to do right now, Catherine. Even if this was my very first day at police college, I wouldn't believe one word of what you're dishing me up here. So, you'll either start working with me a little now, or I'll make sure you won't get home at all, at least not for a good few years."

"I don't know what else I can tell you. You don't believe me anyway. You're unfair. I'm the victim here! I can make trouble for you. Your people just shot at unarmed people. I mean I could have also been hurt, or killed. After all, I was helplessly handcuffed and just sitting in the back of the car."

"Yeah, yeah, the cuffs! Nice try but what on earth was that supposed to be? You go on a shopping spree through Paris, have a leisurely lunch, and in the car you're wearing cuffs."

"He always cuffed me when we were alone. Obviously he couldn't keep me tied up in public! But why are you assuming I went shopping?"

He showed her the receipt for the Hermès scarf. "Why are you covering up for this suspected murderer? And if it's true what you've been telling me, he'll also be charged with abduction. If you're not under any kind of threat as you say, did you have an intimate relationship with the suspect?"

"You can save your abduction charges for the four masked men. Señor Romero helped me by getting me out of the jungle. I already told you he was nice to me, he treated me well. He didn't hurt me and all things considered, he was in the process of releasing me by taking me to Washington and probably home from there. Until you interfered and now I'm being held against my will again."

"This man is not 'nice', Catherine. Now. I asked you if you were intimate with him. I'm waiting for your answer," Moreau demanded, sounding near the end of his tether.

"Not that it's any of your business, but no."

"I'm investigating a murder case and your relationship with the suspect is very much my business. Everything about you and him is my business from now on. In the next few days, I'll take you apart so badly that you'll have trouble remembering your own name. And I haven't even introduced you to the prosecutor yet."

"Stop trying to intimidate me. You're not scaring me. Do you honestly think I can respect you if you carry on like this? Or that I would shrivel up in fear? After everything I've been through? Not on your life!"

"Catherine, I grant you one thing: it's clear that you're new to criminal circles. You have no previous convictions, you're tying yourself up in dilettantish lies. You're not familiar with, nor are you cut out for this milieu. Whatever brainwashing this Romero subjected you to, you won't be able to withstand the pressure that awaits you. Just tell me the truth." Catherine remind silent. "What are you scared of, Catherine?"

"I'm scared of not getting home. I want to go home. Can't you understand that? Wouldn't you wish for your daughter to get home after such a terrible experience? If *my* father was still alive, he would get me out of here. But since I have no relatives I have to face this by myself. But Monsieur le Commissaire, no matter how many times you bombard me with your threats and questions, I can't tell you more than what I already said. What do you expect of me? That I invent answers to the questions which I'm unable to answer? Should I do that? Will you be satisfied then?"

Moreau sighed, got up and opened the door to his office. He called out something in French and to Catherine he said, "We'll carry on tomorrow."

It was just past 8 pm when Moreau released Catherine into an overnight holding cell. Not for one moment did Catherine believe Moreau's threats that she would end up in jail. They had nothing on her, except her false testimony and they would have to prove this while having no other statements to test hers against. Neither was she concerned about Moreau's tactic of jumping from topic to topic. As a seasoned headhunter, she conducted interviews in a similar manner. Candidates hoping to deceive recruiters were able to keep track of their lies and exaggerations by reporting sequences of events chronologically. The human brain could recall true facts in any order, but struggled to remember constructed facts when they were out of sequence. Similar to a child only being able to remember the lines of a poem in the order of the paragraphs. The fact that she tripped up every now and then was to be expected but she put that down to her exhaustion of the day's events and vowed to focus better the following day. Her only real worry (apart from Rivas) was that the police would get hold of

Tom sooner or later. It was unusual for him not to answer his phone. However, she was sure, even when he eventually did take the call, he would use caution when conversing with the police about his boss. He was extremely loyal, besides, headhunters preferred asking questions to answering them. Candidates were constantly trying to extract information and recruiters were skilled and trained in evading them to protect their client's confidentiality. Once the police had revealed that they were tracing one of her calls, it would alert him that she may be in trouble and he would probably dodge them and call Trevor, her trusted attorney before engaging with them.

Comforted by these rationalizations, she lay down fairly optimistically. However, as the night progressed, the prison cell turned into hell. Until dawn announced the new day, she lay awake, thinking of Rivas, who was facing a long jail sentence - should he even survive. Only when it got light, did she briefly fall asleep.

And then - she had to face Moreau again. This time they took her into an interrogation room, not his office. Moreau and two strangers - a man and a woman - were sitting at the table in the center of the windowless, but surprisingly well aired room. Moreau motioned Catherine to sit down

"Good morning Catherine. This is Monsieur Rossouw from Marseille and this is Dr Wernier." He pointed with his head to the lady. "Dr Wernier is our psychologist on duty. Would you like a cup of coffee?"

"No thank you," Catherine was inimical and poised for a fight. She let them know by the tone of her voice, her body language, piercing eye contact and by not greeting them back.

"Let's start by exploring the possible motive again," Moreau announced, not wasting any time, and ignoring her antagonistic stance.

Catherine resolved not to depart from her version in any way. She replied, "Sure."

"We were delayed this morning because we were waiting for your personal and business banking records, which we received a few minutes ago. No significant transfers or withdrawals were made from them. There have been no demands made recently to the Columbian authorities, nor to the German or South African governments in terms of any hostage takings. What reason did your abductors give you for your kidnapping?"

"None."

"In four months of captivity nobody gave you the slightest hint as to why you were being held?"

"They hardly spoke to me at all. Our conversations were limited to topics around food, water or visits to the toilet. Why don't you let yourself be kidnapped, then you'll know what goes down?"

The police officer from Marseille spoke up for the first time. "Ms Zitgow, I'm mostly interested in what you can tell us about the murder suspect Rivas Romero. Are you aware that we're dealing with an alleged coldblooded assassin whose motives are completely unknown? If you could provide us with information about his motives or any observations around his associates, it may even be helpful to him."

"We didn't chat."

"No matter how trivial it may seem to you…"

"Do you think that we were having cozy tea parties where he casually mentioned stuff about supposedly killing people and who was involved? Do you have any idea what it's like to be a hostage?"

"My colleague was not referring to tea and cake, but to pillow talk," Moreau interjected, adding to the provocation by using a condescending tone.

"How impertinent! Do you treat all victims of crime with such contempt? If you'd done your job properly in the first place and caught your murderer when you should have, you wouldn't have to resort to badgering me now!"

"The smallest clue could be immensely helpful," Rossouw mediated.

"He really didn't confide in me, Monsieur Rossouw."

"Would you agree to a routine lie detector test?"

"You're kidding!"

"Do I look like I'm in the mood for jokes?"

"Do I look like *I'm* in the mood for jokes? Certainly not!"

"Why not?"

"Because I know this drill. In my father's company we had a series of thefts a few years ago. Every employee underwent this procedure. Voluntarily of course. We all agreed. Naturally, I wasn't a suspect, but out of fairness to the rest of the team my father asked me to participate as well. I agreed that I should not get special treatment but mainly I was curious about the process so I went along. A grimy guy arrived with his equipment. He looked like a bouncer. He confused me so much that in the end I didn't know myself any more if I'd stolen anything or not. Of course I wasn't the thief, but the pressure was so massive that I remember coming out of the room completely muddled up. Polygraphs are totally untrustworthy investigative tools. I'm not going through that again."

"Was the thief identified?"

"Yes."

"By means of the polygraph?"

"Yes. The woman confessed afterwards."

"Case in point."

"My answer is no."

"Our officers are not 'grimy guys'. We don't outsource our polygraph testing to private security companies"

"No!"

They went back and forth.

"How is he?" asked Catherine during a short break.

The psychologist, who'd listened quietly the whole time answered, "There's no change. He's unconscious but alive. Everything humanly possible is being done to save his life. Are you worried about his condition?"

"Yes. I told you he was very nice to me."

"How nice, Ms Zitgow?"

"Just nice. He didn't hurt me and he assured me he would release me."

"Did you have an intimate relationship with him?"

"No. I already testified to that yesterday and earlier today. I've told you everything several times!"

"We can conduct tests to verify your statement."

"What?"

"Your relationship with the suspect."

"How?"

"Believe me, we can. Why don't you stop this charade and tell us what happened?"

She's bluffing, Catherine thought and replied, "Just because you may find a few of his hairs on my clothes doesn't mean that we had an intimate relationship."

"Catherine, we have many possibilities at our disposal."

"Go ahead. You won't find anything."

"A positive result would not come as a surprise to us. Nobody would think badly of you. Many abduction victims have sexual intercourse with their kidnappers. They do it out of fear, or love. The kidnapper acts as a proxy for other human relationships to which the victim is denied access due to her circumstances. In addition, some kidnappers invent a pack of lies which create a false sense of security and earn them affection. That makes keeping a hostage easier than restraint by gadgetry or torture. This is particularly common if the victim has to be moved around in public. If this happened to you the law would not view this as a crime on your part."

"None of this applies to me."

"Would you prefer to speak with me privately?"

Definitely not with you, thought Catherine. "No."

"Where did you get that injury to your face?"

"I knocked my head against a well."

"Where was the well?"

"In Columbia."

"How did it happen?"

"I slipped in the mud."

"I don't believe you."

"Okay, I've had enough now. I won't say another word. You are all against me!"

"Ms Zitgow, as a witness you have to testify in full. If you don't, you would not only make yourself a suspect but also open yourself up for prosecution for obstruction of justice. Only as a suspect or if you are a close relative or have an intimate relationship with the suspect, may you withhold information during a criminal investigation."

"I can tell from your questions that you already suspect me. Besides, I was arrested at the accident site, handcuffed and rushed to the police station, so please don't pretend that I'm a *witness*. And anyway, even if you drag all your witnesses off in handcuffs and I'm really only being questioned as a witness, why did I have to have my photo and finger prints taken and spend the night in a prison cell?" Catherine mutated into the role of innocent victim and gasped for air in indignation. "Are you even allowed to keep me here this long? Either you tell me now of what crime you are accusing me and take me to a magistrate or you let me go. And anyway - now I want to speak to my legal counsel." Catherine got sentimental when she remembered Rivas's lecture about female manners but decided that "I *would like* to speak to my legal counsel" was completely inappropriate here.

"Do you see a need for requesting legal support?"

"Yes. Because clearly I won't get out of here without help from outside."

"Fine," intervened Moreau. "Would you like your cell phone? For the number."

"I know it off by heart."

"You've memorized your attorney's number?" Rossouw wanted to know.

"Does this also contravene some French law?"

"I'm just interested."

"Just give me a phone," she snapped.

The investigators connected a phone and left the room.

She got through straight away. After ensuring that they weren't listening in ("They're not allowed to do that", Trevor explained), she briefed him and he promised to get on the next plane. She told him that she'd been kidnapped and that she'd had a relationship with her kidnapper which is why she was now suspected of being his accomplice but that she'd denied everything. When she asked Trevor to instruct Tom to do likewise and not to mention the Pentagon assignment, he said, "Already taken care of. The South African police already paid him a visit but when he heard you'd been taken in, he said you were on a business trip and that he couldn't recall any telephone calls from you. He said he'd think about it and get in touch with them. Then he called me. He assumed you got yourself tangled up in some or other criminal action with your weird assignment. We were just trying to find out your whereabouts when you called me now. Why didn't you ring sooner?"

"I was embarrassed, Trevor. And I thought I'd manage this on my own. Please tell Tom to erase all my e-mails and also to delete all my correspondence from the server. I mean all those he got from me after I left for the States. He must also keep quiet about the two calls he had from me."

"That's no problem for now, Catherine, but they'll be able to restore the deleted data eventually. I'll get in touch with a colleague, who specializes in European criminal law in the meantime. His practice is in Frankfurt. Say you're traumatized and that you need medical attention. Also tell them I've instructed you not to make any statements until I've arrived. How long have they been holding you?"

"About eighteen hours now."

"What's the charge?"

"They haven't charged me yet and won't really tell me what's going on. They're saying they're questioning me as a witness because I was in a getaway car with a murder suspect."

"Let me talk to the chief investigator. What's his name?"

"Not necessary. But thanks for coming, Trevor. See you tomorrow."

"My attorney in Johannesburg says I may not give you any more information until his colleague from Frankfurt and he have arrived," she announced freshly spirited.

"That'll take too long. We're in the middle of a murder investigation. We can't wait till your legal team has travelled through world history to get here."

"I don't see how you have a choice if you want me to open my mouth at all anymore."

Moreau sighed. "Fine. We'll take you for a medical checkup now. That's long overdue."

"I refuse that."

"You can't."

"But what do you want to check?"

"A doctor will test you for substance abuse and signs of physical mistreatment as well your general state of health."

"I wasn't mistreated," she flared up but then she added sheepishly, "actually, that's not a bad idea. My lawyer said I sound traumatized and needed medical attention in any case."

Moreau raised one of his thick eyebrows.

The psychologist rolled her eyes and exchanged a few words in French with Roussow while Moreau picked up his phone.

Stupid cow, thought Catherine. Dr Wernier had no chance with Catherine. According to Rivas all police psychologists were quacks and for Catherine, Rivas's opinions had become as binding as divine commandments.

The same afternoon the attorney from Frankfurt paid her a visit – Manfred Merensky. After his arrival she didn't have to speak to the police at all anymore but was still kept in her cell. The next morning at 11 am Trevor arrived. She fell into his arms and told him her story. Not everything, and nothing about WICED and very little about the Pentagon trap, but enough about her relationship to Rivas so that her legal team could understand the context. Shortly afterwards both lawyers spoke with Moreau again and came back after fifteen minutes. This time to fetch her. "I may go?" she asked disbelievingly. "I don't have to give a statement while you're present?"

"They waived further interviews. Come, we'll sort out the paper work now, collect your belongings, have some lunch and then we'll drive to Manfred's hotel. There we'll work on your case for the rest of the day and then we'll go directly to the airport. Everything's alright, Catherine, don't worry about anything." He comforted her in his arms and thought, the poor confused child. With no family – oh if Rainer was still alive – but then none of this would have happened in any case.

"We're leaving the country? Surely I have to stay on in Paris?"

"No. Our flight leaves tonight at 11.20 – AF 990, direct to Johannesburg. Tomorrow morning at 9.50 you'll be home, Catherine."

"Really? They released my passport?"

"Yes, your real one. It's over. The case will go on for a while but Manfred and I will take care of anything concerning you. They'll have to convict their murderer without your help."

"And I? Won't I be prosecuted? I mean the false passport, the contradictions."

"They'll try but with what exactly would they charge you? If they could, they would have done it already. The passport photo was taken by a murder suspect who forced you to pose for it, and the contradictions are common symptoms of post abduction trauma. Most significantly, Catherine, the crime being investigated here is a murder committed in Marseille four years ago and they certainly can't accuse you of being an accomplice to that. And the kidnapping story makes no sense to them anyway. To prosecute you under these circumstances is pretty hopeless, no prosecutor would take this on."

Merensky affirmed: "Trevor is right, Catherine. In criminal defense law, there's an important principle: eliminate motive and establish an alibi."

"What do you mean?"

"It'll be hard to get a prosecution going in the absence of a reason for the suspect to have committed the crime and if you were not at the crime scene at the time."

"What does that have to do with me? I mean I was part of the car chase."

"What Manfred is saying, is that they need both. You don't have a motive. Even if they think you're as guilty as hell, they'll have to drop it. In the French justice system a crime consists of two elements: the physical event and the intention to bring it about. When the will to commit the crime meets the event, prosecution is possible. If either element is missing, there is no basis for a prosecution. In your case they cannot substantiate your intention, nor can they link you to the physical event in Marseille. "

"Trevor and I will still develop our defense strategy in detail but at first glance, it seems like this is the route we will go," said Merensky.

"And a lot went wrong at your arrest, Catherine. You were under shock and that's not even a lie! Nevertheless, they went ahead and interviewed a highly traumatized accident victim. It's not illegal for them to do this, but it's not wise, because we'll use this to our advantage. Apart from this, they held you for far too long without taking you to a magistrate or pointing out your right to legal support."

"They did that at the accident site."

"Yes, but then at the station they pretended you were a witness and confused you. A suspect may not legally be interrogated as an ordinary witness. No, you don't have to worry. From now on we'll say that you can't talk about your dreadful experiences. We'll send them a medical testimony to the fact that it's psychologically too stressful for you. And if they should pursue it nevertheless, we'll pull our trump card."

"We have a trump card?"

"Yes. We would press counter charges and they know it."

"You mean a civil suit?"

"Civil and criminal! They opened fire without ascertaining who, other than the suspect, was in the car. Despite the serious road block misdemeanor they may not just fire at the driver - maybe at the tires – but certainly not several bullets at the occupants when fire is not returned."

"Rivas didn't even have a gun. I've never seen him with one," Catherine confirmed eagerly.

"That's not true. Manfred and I read the police report and there was a firearm stowed under the driver's seat in the car, but without prints and previously unused."

"See! I told you! That wasn't his, it was probably delivered with the car." She hesitated when she realized that she'd given something away again.

"What do you mean? Who delivered the car and hid a weapon in the car?"

"Oh nothing, I think the car belonged to a friend."

"Never mind. It's not important. Manfred and I will work on a strategy on how we'll present our case, if it even comes to that. This pig probably won't live to have his day in court in any case. I don't understand why they don't just let bastards like him die."

Catherine burst into tears for the first time since the Aretha Franklin song. "He's not a pig, Trevor. How can you as an attorney say a thing like that? He's such a wonderful person. He just wanted to make the world better a better place."

"Alright, Catherine, alright. I'm sorry. As soon as we're home, we'll talk about everything and you'll get well again, my poor little girl." Her late father's dear friend held her in his arms and comforted her as though she was his own daughter.

But after returning to South Africa Catherine didn't speak about the incident anymore, not with Trevor or Tom, nor with Manfred or anyone else. She only enquired once how Rivas was and what punishment would await him should he survive. The tears in Paris were the last that she shed for Rivas.

Until one summer day in Johannesburg – it was November 11, five weeks after her return, a mysterious envelope was delivered to her office.

45.
South Africa, November 11

Catherine had rapidly begun experiencing all the emotions Rivas had predicted: Guilt, shame, hatred, depression, the whole pallet. Her combative attitude isolated her socially. She submersed herself in her work like her office was a submarine.

She followed none of Rivas's instructions. She didn't contact Lammingcourt, nor did she look for an orthopedic surgeon and she also didn't buy herself a PRE. She didn't destroy the database but took it out of her safe and buried it in a money box in her garden.

She gave Maria's clothes to her new housekeeper. Catherine wasn't gracious enough to forgive Christina, her previous helper, for letting strangers dig around in her house. Christina vehemently denied all allegations. Had she confessed, Catherine may have softened and let her stay on but instead the sumptuous wardrobe went to Neo, her new helper. The clothes were too small for her but she gladly accepted them anyway saving she would give them to her daughters. The value of the clothes was higher than Neo would probably earn in the her entire life time but of course she knew nothing about that. Only the night-blue Armani Black Label satin cocktail dress that she'd never worn she couldn't part with. She didn't know why. She folded it in tissue paper and stored it on the top shelf of her bedroom cupboard. She didn't give away the fateful Hermès scarf either, but burnt it one evening in her barbeque unit. While observing the dance of the flames she – despite her non-superstitious nature – wondered, whether her curse on Rivas on the day he beat her with the curb bit had triggered this tragedy.

Rivas's money for the PRE and Maria's jewelry she intended to donate to an animal shelter. While she vacillated about which organisation to choose, she kept the valuables in her safe at home. Catherine wanted to wipe out everything that connected her to Rivas. Her memories seemed like a bad dream and she shooed away any thoughts of Rivas as soon as they surfaced. Even the memory of what Rivas looked like, faded - until on this day, November 11, she was ripped out of her mental shutdown.

"Catherine, this letter arrived for you," Gaby said parenthetically, handing it to her.

Catherine recognized the stationery. She sat down slowly, took a deep breath and opened the envelope. Gaby stood curiously by while she read its contents. Catherine glanced at her watch: 3.45 pm. "Who brought this?"

"I don't know. It was handed in at reception."

"When?"

"This morning."

"It says 'urgent' on the envelope. Why do I get this letter only now?"

"Are you serious? Everything's always urgent. Must I interrupt your meetings now every time someone says something's urgent?"

"Never mind. I have to go." Catherine grabbed her bag and turned to leave.

"Wait! You have a 4 o'clock with the new marketing people."

"Cancel the presentation."

"I can't. They'd be on their way already."

"Cancel it anyway."

"Is everything okay?"

"Yes, everything's fine. See you later."

At the next red traffic light, she read the card again:

Catherine, please meet me today at 4 pm in the garden of the Johannesburg Heriton Hotel. Go all the way to the end and wait for me in the arbor. It's important.
Maria Santa Cruz

Catherine hurried to the venue at the back of the little garden where she was already expected by Maria, since she was ten minutes late. Maria was taking a great risk to come here - and to travel such a long distance for a meeting! She must have wanted to see her badly.

They recognized each other immediately. "Good afternoon, Catherine. Thank you for coming." Maria wanted to embrace her but Catherine stayed stiff, didn't even answer her greeting. Maria had a completely extravagant appearance. Her black hair was combed back and shone like satin. She wore a classical elegant Yves Saint Laurent tuxedo made of white silk with a plunging neckline. Her open shoes were silver with a wedge heel from Mary Jane and her clutch bag was made of white lamb's leather with a silver clasp, also from Laurent.

"Why are you taking the risk of meeting me here?" asked Catherine after she'd recovered from the overwhelming sight.

The venue had been prudently selected. It was always quiet here and there were rarely any guests or staff around in the far end of the garden of this business hotel.

"The risk is minimal and I'm well protected," said Maria while inspecting Catherine's – in her opinion – insufficient wardrobe. "On the contrary, I'm surprised that you accepted my invitation. I could have lured you into a trap to have you killed or to force you into cooperation again. Our mission will be completed one day, the world will have changed but there will always be reasons for further interventions. You're not even under police guard." They sat down at one of the garden tables and Maria calmly extracted a cigarette from a valuable looking etui. With an effortless click she ignited a matching lighter and lit her cigarette. Catherine stared at the flame prompting Maria to offer her a cigarette. She declined because she'd stopped smoking again. "You're right, but tell me Maria, why *am* I still alive? I gave you the decoded database. I'm of no use to you now, only a threat."

"Rivas asked me to make sure no harm came to you. And you? Why did you decline police protection? Surely they offered you this?"

"Rivas assured me that I had nothing to fear. I trusted him. But don't think that your 'generosity' impresses me. I can report you to the authorities at any time. So, before I call the cops now, what do you want from me?"

"I want to know what you will testify and what you have already revealed to the police."

"Why should I tell you this?"

"Please. It's important. Help me."

"Why is this important when you are so well 'protected'?"

"It's not about me, it's about Rivas. Even if you've given up on him, we haven't. I'm also not worried that they could use your statements against him. For this we have other plans. I'm concerned that he doesn't feel betrayed by you, that he can continue believing in you."

"He's alive?"

"Yes."

"You have a plan? What is it?"

"It's not the right time to discuss this."

"You always have a plan for others, don't you Maria? You also had a plan for me, and Rivas's whole life was mapped out by you. Apparently you haven't stopped making plans for people."

"I've always only wanted what's best for him."

"Yeah, keep telling yourself that. But I can tell you that you raised a puppet, you indoctrinated him and then used him as your trump card for your dirty work whenever he was useful to you. You used his terrible childhood experience to satisfy your lust for revenge. He lost his mother, but there would have been better ways of helping him to cope with that. As soon as he's better, you should have him prescribe something for you, before they take his license away from him – some strong medication against hatred and madness, because you're sick! You're lucky that I didn't send the police in the first place. Please go now. I want to stay on here a little while."

"My relationship with Rivas is complex. I don't expect you to understand it – not from your perspective, but you haven't been listening. I'm not here for myself. Actually, that's not entirely true," Maria added thoughtfully.

"What do you mean?"

"It's not true that my visit is completely unselfish. I love him and I want him to be happy."

"Yeah right. You love him like your own child, I know. Please spare me your pathos."

"Catherine, I don't know what it feels like to love one's own child, but I know that I love him in a very special way. Nobody is closer to me."

"Yes, you're a fine couple. Even though, frankly, you look positively prehistoric compared to him."

The lady in Maria bore Catherine's nasty dig with equanimity. "We're not a couple. Rivas has only loved one woman in his life – in the way you mean - and because of her, he's now in hospital and we are sitting here together."

"If it was up to you, it would be I who would be lying in hospital. The morgue actually."

"Every mistreatment was carried out according to medical standards and the boundaries were never crossed, and," she said haltingly, "he prevented your execution."

"Why do you remind me of a concentration camp nurse?"

"Things escalated between you and Rivas personally. That was never how it was meant to be. He fought on all fronts to keep you under his protection."

"Protection! Wow. That's a really creative interpretation!"

Maria continued unflustered, "First because you were 'his' hostage and he didn't tolerate any other players who could have endangered his plan and in the end he risked his life for you and almost lost it. You really don't seem to know how much you mean to him and how much fuss was made about your release. Your bitterness towards him is written on your face but I cannot understand it. You've suppressed your feelings for him but I want to invite you to search your heart again as soon as you're able to. In any case, he took your relationship seriously and was prepared to give up everything for it. And indeed, he did just that by deviating from his plan and driving to Saumur with you. He would have even married you. Don't let him down now. When he's fully recovered, you'll have ample opportunity to rethink everything again."

Catherine was annoyed about Maria's reproach but reflected on one particular sentence. "You say, he wanted to marry me? That's not true. I offered more than once to stay with him forever, I actually importuned him to the point of irking him."

"It's a massive task to leave WICED. He didn't want to disappoint you, in case he failed."

"He told you about it?"

"Yes. Do you trust me a little now? Rivas trusts me completely. He didn't want to hurt you, but please see it in context. He is, was, a key player in our projects. Many kidnappings are never made public by the respective governments – at least when it can be avoided. They don't want to expose their vulnerability and of course want to avoid the media hyping up these incidents and scaring the population..."

Catherine interrupted, "The *context* Maria, is that Rivas is a common criminal - a kidnapper and murderer. No matter how nobly you are trying to dress him up, he remains a thug, so stop this now. I don't want to hear any more of your ridiculous justifications about this killer."

"He did it with ... feeling. They didn't suffer painful deaths."

"Right. They only had to kneel on plastic drop sheets in his cellar and wait for death while he was leisurely finishing his cigarette."

"What are you talking about, Catherine?"

Catherine briefly explained about her ordeals in the cellar. Maria was not moved. "That was probably after one of your numerous escape efforts? Or after your attempt to shoot Rivas?"

"You know about that, too?"

"Of course I do. Surely you're also informed about everything that happens in your organisation? But he didn't tell me about torturing you in the cellar. Nevertheless, I can assure with 100 % certainty, that he never killed anyone like *that*. This is a known execution method by some of the OHLPA members, but we don't do that. He probably wanted to give you a fright. You can count yourself lucky that you didn't manage to kill him. If he'd died, they would have caught up with you immediately and without his protection you wouldn't have survived another day. I personally would have ensured that you would have been executed without delay. Our way." Maria gave Catherine, who was as white as a sheet, a moment to compose herself. "He made many sacrifices for our anti-terror-organisation. But he was about to exit. After Ruckebier, he would have been done."

"I can't believe what I'm hearing." Catherine felt a bout of nausea coming on. Rivas had confessed the murders to her already but the time with him seemed so surreal, as if none of this had really happened. Maria's visit ripped her scars open again but now Catherine's perspective had changed completely. "He really believed all this trash about making sacrifices?"

"It's true."

"It's not true. You hammered this theory into him."

"Rivas never let anyone hammer anything into him. He always made his own conscious decisions. But whatever, he needs you now."

"Where is he?"

"Three weeks ago they moved him from Paris to a clinic in Berlin. They have a team of eleven head injury specialists practicing there. He was operated on two weeks ago and they managed to remove the bullet. He's doing well. There are no signs of any permanent damage at this stage and for four days now he's been conscious but not yet in a position to be questioned by the police."

"How do you know all that?"

"I have contacts, Catherine. The authorities will leave nothing to chance in order to save his life. They haven't had an opportunity to interrogate him. They have a political murder to solve which caused a lot of public uproar and they are completely in the dark. He's of no use to them dead. Only, before they get anywhere near interrogation stage, we will have freed him."

"He's really recovering? He'll get through this?"

"Yes. This is why they could move him to the specialist clinic. They're about to operate again and then once more, but the worst is behind him. He'll survive. For you. He needs closure as far as you're concerned, because he intends to keep his appointment with you, on your 'human rights day'."

"He even told you about that?"

"Yes."

"Maria, I asked Rivas once how he found out about me and my database and he told me that this was your doing. How do you select your target people?"

"It varies. In your case, Carlos beat me to it. He'd worked with your father during the Bosnian war of 1992." Catherine remembered the mysterious assignment with which her father had saved the company from bankruptcy. "Carlos drew your father's attention to a lucrative business idea. He built up a central database and in the beginning specialized in the placement of war experts, terrorists and mercenaries. He acquired significant wealth and his little agency – now yours, Catherine – was nothing but a front from then on." That was a hard blow for Catherine but she found Maria's explanation plausible. "In the planning phase for this project, Carlos remembered your father and wanted to assign him to identify an unscrupulous bio terror expert, who was also a specialist in equine virology and human genetics. An impossible goal. Who still fights a war with horses in this day and age? And, the one area of specialization excludes the other. You know this too well. However, we didn't want to deviate from our requirements and on top of that wanted to secure the best in the world. Too much was at stake – we knew, that if there was anyone who could fulfil these requirements, it would be Rainer Zitgow. When Carlos heard of your father's death he hoped he may have passed the database onto his successors. We first checked out his former business partner Trevor Torrente, but instead we found the data in your possession. Your father's collection is unique and comprehensive. He'd built it up over twenty years. But he endangered your life with it. Nevertheless, he clearly wanted to secure your financial future, it would have been a shame to let this lucrative source dry up. So he encrypted it for your safety. He must have hoped that you would grope your way through the contacts piece by piece. His plan worked, at first, because you had indeed started to use the data, without comprehending the enormity of this treasure chest. In your ignorance, you could not really identify the big potential deals without his guidance. In any case, we learned about the location of the database and gained access."

"Alex!" Catherine realized audibly.

Maria nodded. "This is where I came in. But we could do nothing with the information without the code and there were two further complications. First, your father's contacts trusted him. The target group would have been extremely skeptical about being approached by an unknown, if at all. Most experts don't work on these sorts of assignments full time. On the surface, they are 'ordinary citizens' employed at institutions with unblemished track records. That was the second problem. We didn't know which of his contacts would identify with our ideals, or at least would have no qualms about engaging with us. Your father had a good feel for this. We needed you for the decoding but also for the approach. The name Zitgow would break down the natural barriers. We had to assume that your identity would be checked out before a candidate would talk to us. Therefore we couldn't have someone else pretend to be his daughter. We needed the real Zitgow. That's when I appointed my preferred kidnapping expert, Rivas. From then on we had you on 24 hour surveillance. We read your mails with the help of one of your employees, that Alex you mentioned, who also gave us a glimpse into the database. He'd declined our first offer for the sale of the entire database when you found out about his breach and fired him. The last time we heard from him was when he told us that you were leaving for the States and that he assumed you would take the information with you.

"Via your CIT unit we listened in on your calls and followed you everywhere. After a few months we knew everything about you. From your dress size and your eating habits to all your opinions and your life style. Your enthusiasm for horses was a bonus for us. For Rivas especially, because he could use your passion for horses to manipulate you, apart from his staggering charm," Maria added dreamily. "So he brought César into the picture and planned to use him right from the beginning so that you would identify with him as an ally from the start, subconsciously of course. I mean, he is irresistible - is he not? Our little César? This way Rivas developed an effective triangle relationship. He began with the psychological preparation work and researched your business practices, your childhood, your love life – everything that had formed your character. Now we had to simply choose the place and time and before long we had our chance. Due to your greed for success and wealth you had nothing with which to withstand the appeal of the database and even carried it around with you. Almost all the way to our front door in Miami! Things couldn't have run more smoothly because now we didn't even have to worry about remote access. Yes, and the lure of 'being important' and having something unique in your possession you also could not resist. We laid out a simple trap and you fell for it." Catherine blushed from shame. Maria appeased her, "Don't feel bad, child. Pride is a common vice. At your age, I probably would have done the same."

"Has Ruckebier accepted?"

"Yes."

"Why are you telling me all this?"

"Because Rivas would want me to. Like you, I respect his wishes."

"Oh no I don't! Not anymore!"

"Don't kid yourself. If he were here now, you would melt like wax." Again Catherine felt herself blush.

"Catherine, when he is stable again, he will ask about you. He'll want to know if you are well. What should I tell him?"

"When he is 'stable' again dear Maria, they will take him from Berlin to France or Spain or some other place - who knows where else he committed crimes. And then they'll lock him up for thirty years. I *have* thought about it and I don't believe a word of your story about getting him out. If he's lucky he'll get out after eighteen, then he'll be fifty three and you? Eighty five?"

"You're cruel."

"Oh, you know, I've just completed four months' intensive training at WICED Institute. I had a superb instructor in the subject of 'Cruelty'."

"Don't neglect to mention the subjects of love and remorse, Catherine! Anyway, I assure you he will not even see the inside of a prison cell. Preparations for his breakout are already in progress. We would never abandon him, our organisation sticks together, we are idealists in every way. And we need him. And you need him, too. Don't bother to inform the police of our intentions. They can't stop us, even if they know." Catherine was flabbergasted. Maria carried on talking. "I have access to people with power and infinite financial resources. For the true movers and shakers of the Western world, freeing Rivas is nothing more than half a day's work."

"Who controls WICED?"

"Do you remember Mr Brower?"

"He exists?"

"Yes, he does. And many like him."

"So the Pentagon after all?"

"Oh no! On its own every organisation is merely a tooth in the gear. We have many mighty patrons."

"An association of organizations?"

"Yes, made up of peace loving people, who are prepared to do everything necessary to stop their compatriots from being terrorized any longer."

"Of course. You love peace so much that you want to extinguish all those that don't suit your own aims and ideas, and millions of innocent people at that. It's better if you leave now, Maria."

"What about your statement now? What did you tell the police? Ruckebier was never questioned, so you couldn't have said much."

"Rivas told me it didn't matter what I'd tell the police."

"I said as much myself earlier, do you believe me now? It's really not about the court case, only about what you mean to him.

Of course he would be angry if he knew that I came to influence you."

"To *try* to influence me! But if you don't want him to know that you were here, how do you intend passing on a message?"

"I just don't want him to know that I pressed you regarding an official statement."

"Maria, if I don't blow the whistle, will you abandon your plans to infect half the world with a deadly virus?"

"Catherine, I'm not going to engage with you on your exaggerations and generalizations but I assure that this plan will be carried out, if not by us, then by someone else."

"Yeah, this part I can believe. Anyway I won't testify against Rivas. I never intended to. It has nothing to do with you coming here."

"What are you going to say in court?"

"Why is this important? If you'll bust him out as you say, there never will be a court case."

"It's the what-if-principle. With a project of this magnitude we have to consider all eventualities. You're a manager, surely you're familiar with this principle."

When Maria mentioned "what-if" Catherine started to feel weepy as she remembered their cheerful "what-if" game but she managed to restrain herself from crying for now. "I will testify only to that which I have been saying all along, only the minimum and that I didn't know what it was all about. I couldn't really identify the location and neither could I describe the perpetrators and overall I have suppressed most details due to post traumatic stress. The latter's not even a lie."

"Under cross examination, the prosecution would expose you to immense pressure."

"Immense pressure? Have you lost your mind? Have you forgotten that I've just come out of four months captivity and isolation? You want to talk to me about pressure? Nobody will ever force me into anything again. Do you think I'm scared of being cross examined by pompous officials in antiquated robes in an air conditioned court room? Or that a prison cell can scare me? Believe me I know what it's like to be scared and this child stuff sure doesn't. Don't think they haven't already tried to intimidate me. Without my statement they'll convict him anyway, it'll just be a bit harder. In any case, I won't do a bit to help. Every psychologist in the world will confirm that I'm too traumatized to speak about my experiences and if not, how would they force me?"

"Thank you Catherine. May I ask what your motive is? You said you planned it all along like this."

"I don't owe you any explanations."

"This is true. Tell me anyway, please."

"Because I only do and say what I want to. From now on, I *would like nothing*, I only *want!*" Maria had no idea what she meant by this, but didn't ask. "I'll consider nobody but myself anymore. And do you really want to know why? It's not about what you've done to me. The real reason is that torture and death couldn't have been worse than losing Rivas. To see him lying bleeding in the street, to not be able to hold him for even one moment to say good-bye – this experience was spared you, but I had to live through it. That, Maria, is my true prison. Yes, I loved him but also hate him. I hate him for letting me distract him, I hate him for loving me. That's what caused my true suffering. Not the kidnapping. If I was still his prisoner, I could carry on loving him. How I wish it was so! I hate this supposed freedom, my meaningless life. Eating. Not eating. Success. Failure. Who cares? And riding without Rivas is the worst thing I can do to myself. I can't look at a horse anymore without thinking of Rivas and Andalus. If I stand in front of one of my horses, and want to love it, I only hate it instead, for not being Andalus. I see him in front of me: his strong neck, his mane, his round back, his soft mouth, oh my goodness – how I miss him! If you knew what a desperate state I'm in. I would so love to apply what the two of them taught me, but I can't." Tears were pouring now. "On the day of his arrest, Rivas gave me money to buy an Iberian stallion. I was supposed to fly to Jerez…"

"To Alberto Auodo." Maria handed her a fine, embroidered handkerchief. Catherine took it and, in unladylike fashion, blew her nose hard with it and energetically wiped away her tears.

"Yes, but I didn't. Instead I gave up riding. It was unbearable. My former riding instructor's taking care of my horses now."

"Claudia," confirmed Maria.

"You're incredible! Are you still observing me?" Maria remained silent, because Catherine was indeed still being observed around the clock, just as ordered by Carlos. "Then you'll also know how much I loved riding. But now the shortest hack is more traumatic than if Andalus was throwing me off at a stretch gallop. And as far as Rivas is concerned: every day 'in peace' is worse than the most horrendous time with him on the farm or even in the hands of the transporters in Columbia. Before my abduction I didn't know what it meant to be lonely. I believed myself to be independent and loved my freedom. Rivas still holds me captive. But today it's not my body that is his hostage, but my heart. And it's in a pitiful state. He could tie me up again anytime. I would stretch my arms out." She'd lost control over her crying and wildly wiped away her tears. Maria reached into her chic bag and pulled out another noble hanky. "Thanks."

"Rivas tied you up?" Maria enquired distractedly. "I can't imagine why. At the most, he would have someone else do it. I'm sure he wouldn't lower himself to tie someone like you up."

Catherine thought about for a moment. It was true, he really had never tied her up, but she didn't bother to correct herself. Instead, for some unknown reason, she continued to pour her heart out to this strange woman before concluding: "That, Maria, is the reason why I'm not telling my story. Who, other than you, would understand it? But you, I feel sorry for. You lead an even more miserable life, tied up in intrigues and blinded by the illusion of a power which soon will find an abrupt ending."

"Catherine, here is a key to a locker at the Paris train station Gare du Nord. If you want to get in touch with him, or me, place a note into this locker and my people will notify me. The locker is safe. It's guarded day and night by WICED. Here is the locker number." Maria took out a diamond studded Mont Blanc pen and wrote something into a handy note book. She tore out the page, folded it and handed it to Catherine.

Both got up, Catherine took the piece of paper and tore it up without reading its contents. "I won't need the locker number, because I'll never seek contact with you. But the key here, I'll keep, if you don't mind. As a memento. Whenever I fall into a state of self-pity, it'll remind me that there's someone worse off than me – you."

"Catherine, if you don't use this locker opportunity now, you'll never have a chance to see Rivas or Andalus again if you should change your mind. Are you sure that you want to break off all contact?" Catherine nodded sadly. "At least give me a final word for him. Please."

Catherine asked, "What became of Andalus?"

Maria smiled warmly. "He's at home with me. On my estate. He's doing well."

"Do you have a picture of him?"

"I will send you one."

"That would be nice. Look after him well – for Rivas. They will need each other."

"That's what I intend to do."

"Maria, would you do something for me?"

"Whatever you want."

Catherine took out a simple notepad and less glamorous pen and scribbled 'Spanish Guitar' on it. She handed it to Maria with the words, "Buy this and when you have him back, give it to him."

"What is it?"

"It's a song. I'm giving you what you asked me for – a message for Rivas."

"May I tell him anything else?"

"The song will speak."

"As you wish. Keep well, Catherine." Maria turned to leave.

"Maria?" Catherine called her back.

"Yes?"

"What I said about your age, I said out of jealousy. I have envied you for your bond with Rivas since I saw you the first time in the Café de Jerez in Paris. You are beautiful. Outside and inside, just shaken up by fate and terribly confused. Your love for Rivas is admirable. I hope you will soon find your way out of your labyrinth and return to who you really are – a sensitive and smart woman. This is how Rivas described you, and now I see it, too."

Maria turned to the door without replying. Two tears ran down her cheeks. The first in twenty years. For Maria Santa Cruz, too, a life-chapter closed and made way for a new one.

That afternoon Catherine didn't return to the office. Instead she telephoned Trevor and Tom and asked them to spend the evening with her. She now suspected her own house was bugged, that's why she suggested meeting at Tom's house.

Catherine had a plan and needed help.

46.
South Africa, November 11

Trevor set off immediately after Catherine's call and Tom quickly tidied up the living area of his condo while his visitors were on their way. Trevor and Tom both assumed that her request for a meeting had to do with her abduction, particularly since Gaby had informed Tom of Catherine's unusual behavior after receiving the mysterious letter.

At around 6 pm they were assembled in Tom's living room. An unusually hot day was nearing its end and a typical Johannesburg afternoon thunder storm shook the Highveld. Despite the heavy rain Tom left the glass door to the swimming pool area wide open to allow the room to cool. In anticipation of the power cut which usually accompanied a lightning storm of this magnitude, he put out a few candles. Trevor opened a bottle of Meerlust Pinot Noir. He poured two glasses of wine when Catherine interjected, "For me, too, please." Trevor and Tom exchanged "doubting Thomas looks", before Tom fetched a third glass. "I'll get straight to the point. I had a visit from Maria Santa Cruz today. She is part of the group that kidnapped me." Tom wanted to interrupt but Catherine put her index finger on her lips. "In a minute, Tom. I decided to fill you in on my abduction. You know some of what happened, barely a little more than the official version, but the most critical pieces of information I've withheld up to now. I said I don't remember anything else but this is not entirely true. Today, I had occasion to reflect on everything again and I *want* to talk about everything that happened to me now. Please don't interrupt me. When I'm done, I'll give you ample opportunity to ask questions. I promise, I will not leave anything out. And you must promise me never to reveal any of what I told you to anyone. Even if you have to testify in court someday. Can you agree to that?"

"I promise," said Trevor.

"So do I," said Tom.

"Are you sure, Tom? As my attorney, Trevor doesn't have to reveal anything, but for you it'll be different."

"Very sure."

"I have a further condition. I don't want you to evaluate my actions or judge me in any way. I don't even want to know your personal opinions on the matter. My decision is my business alone."

"If you're not interested in what we have to say, why are we assembled here?" objected Tom.

"Because it's not about you, but I need your help. Can you two handle that? Yes or No?"

Trevor answered for both: "Of course we'll help you."

"Great. How much time do you both have?"

"As long as it takes," both replied in unison.

She took a sip of wine, even though she'd stopped drinking alcohol again after her return. Without a hint of emotion Catherine reported on the events in South America and France. She relayed explicit facts and circumstances and also didn't hold back on her sexual affinities towards Rivas, because she felt it important to be understood as much as possible in order to win them over for her plan. At some point, Tom filled the generator with petrol in the storeroom next door, because it had got dark and the storm raged on. While he was busy there, he tried to listen through the open door because Catherine didn't stop talking. After two hours she terminated her monologue. "Do you have any questions?"

Both shook their heads. The storm had moved on, the door had been closed by now and the expected power cut had not happened. She went to Tom's kitchen and put a few snacks, which she'd brought with her, on platters, while Tom and Trevor talked among themselves. She returned and put the finger food on the coffee table. Then she announced her plan: "I have to prevent this terror attack, but I won't do it by going to the cops because I believe it's not possible to destroy WICED from the outside. I don't need the authorities anyway, because I have a better idea."

Violent protests ensued. "Didn't you learn anything Catherine?" Tom attacked first. "Now you're back to where you started with your delusions of grandeur and your imagined invincibility."

Catherine, hands on hips, looked at Tom and scolded back, "Tom! Consider whom you are dealing with here. I have overcome the 'unovercomeable'! I'm alive! I'm free! I'm home! If you two had been in my position, I guarantee you, you'd both be dead as mice."

"You have to give her that, Tom," she heard Trevor come to her defense. "We wouldn't have defeated this killer. Let her finish."

"Thanks Trevor. So, we won't start with WICED, but one level higher. We also won't blow the whistle on anyone as long as they do what we ask. This way we keep control."

"You want to blackmail these people?" asked Trevor.

"If she knew whom to blackmail!" Tom interjected sarcastically.

Catherine ignored Tom and explained, "Yes, by threatening to go public. They're not scared of authority but the media could harm them greatly. Their plan has to stay secret. At this stage the public is their biggest threat. I could stop them in their tracks, at least for now, I'm sure of it. Rivas's arrest was a big blow to them even if Maria denies this. And if I now appear on the scene, things could start getting too hot. Of course I have to arrange it so that nothing will happen to me."

"Even if they abandon this operation, they'll work out a new strategy."

"That'll no longer be my responsibility, but this VEE-business definitely is. I can't save the whole world. Whatever happens next I may not be able to avoid but in this matter I'll leave no stone unturned to upset their plans. If they come up with a new tactic I'll deal with that when it happens. And we're gaining time. In addition, I'll dig up the best negotiator the world has to offer and introduce him or her at the right time to mediate in the conflict hot spots."

"World peace is a piece of cake for a Catherine Zitgow candidate," laughed Tom.

"Exactly," she confirmed with the same immodest smile she always wore, after she'd just closed a deal. "So, will you help me?"

"What can we do?"

"We'll start with the usual suspects when it comes to conspiracies – the secret services. I'm sure there's a connection, but they are not the puppet masters. Maria mentioned that behind WICED are Western governments, and that WICED has no financial limitations. In her own words she spoke about the 'true movers and shakers' and those are never the politicians but people with money. Governments can release significant funds that's true, but never 'unlimited' amounts. There have to be private financiers. Rivas alluded to this, too. Maria also specifically mentioned this Mr Brower. Of course that's not his real name, but we'll go to the Forbes List and for starters and check out the richest of the rich and examine their ideals."

Tom burst into scornful laughter. "Great! Agent Zitgow starts with the secret services and the Forbes List. A walk in the park! The Fantastic Three against the mightiest of the world."

"Tom, from now you're working exclusively on this research. Make all calls from a separate cell phone and mail only over a free-mail address. Leave the company out of it because they may still have us under surveillance. I'll talk to Jan tomorrow. He'll look into this for us."

She saw Tom go a shade paler before he asked, "And where do you expect me to start?"

"I told you! With the Forbes List and the secret services."

"I need something a little more concrete."

"That's Trevor's job." She looked at her lawyer, who, when he heard his name being brought in, had also gone as white as a sheet. "Can you organize me a prison visit?"

"Which country?"

"Local."

"Grade?"

"The highest. C Max, Pretoria."

"Oh Catherine! That'll be hard. With whom?"

"Willem Van der Sonsen."

"Good grief, Catherine, that'll get political."

"Trevor, what I'm planning *is* political."

"What are you getting out of it?"

"Van der Sonsen knew my father. He's not on the database – I assume the two of them had an agreement not to capture his details – but they worked together, I'm sure of it. Up to this day, he's the biggest Apartheid criminal our old regime produced. I want to get to others like him, in other countries. I'm hoping they'll lead me to 'clients'. I'll use the ruse of wanting to present candidates. And to be able to do that I'll trick Van der Sonsen into giving me a few names or even set up appointments. Her eyes went to Tom again. "I'll get us these names and we'll work through them telephonically. In the meantime I'll get in touch with Dr Lindenbaum."

"Who's that?"

"An American proponent of the 'non-violent society' and a superb mediator. I once had four weeks group training with him in Norway. My father was of the opinion I needed to improve my diplomacy skills. He'll remember me. Fourteen of us, all from various nations, ages and genders were locked away for thirty days in a loft and I was his most uncooperative student. Trevor, will you manage the paper work in the next few days? The appointment with Van der Sonsen is urgent. Millions of lives are at stake."

"You don't have to remind me, and I'll try, but I'll need money for bribes. This won't be cheap."

"Do it!"

"Hey! Weren't you always against this sort of thing? I remember I once wanted to give a telephone technician a bottle of Whiskey to get a bit of priority, and you threw a huge tantrum."

"That was different and I don't care about that now. The 'system' demands bribes, so we'll just have to pay."

"And your principles?"

"Sometimes it takes more courage to change your mind than to stay true to your principles. And rules are there to be broken or to be re-invented."

"Oh is this another one of your kidnapper's truisms? Or should I call it a rivasism?"

"We're trying to save lives," she repeated, deflecting attention away from Rivas.

"It's irrelevant anyway. It won't work," Trevor tried to avoid an argument. "Van der Sonsen is a big number and you want to meet him soon. Where do you want to get so much money? The company's finances went into free fall while you were away and you haven't had enough time to recover the losses."

Tom raised an eyebrow but let it go. Catherine sighed at the thought of the twelve million dollar fee that Rivas had offered her before his plans were thwarted by his arrest. She was sure she would have stayed resolute but was glad that she didn't have to face the temptation in the end. For this purpose, however, she wouldn't have hesitated for a moment, to use the money. "Hm. I have pretty valuable jewelry in my safe at home." She spontaneously decided to sacrifice Maria's valuables. For Rivas's cash, however, she now had other plans. "With it I can also finance some of the rest of the operation, at least get started. If it's not enough, can you lend me some money Trevor? I'll turn twenty five in January. Then I can get to dad's money. This way I can fix what I started. He would agree, if he was here now, wouldn't he?" She glanced in Trevor's direction.

"Yes, he would."

While Trevor affirmed Catherine's plans, Tom paled again. "What's wrong, Tom?"

"Oh goodness, Catherine…"

"What? What's going on?"

"Last month there was a money transfer from the Caribbean. Dora couldn't assign it, because we'd sent out no such invoice. I told her to send the money back, thinking it was a mistake…"

Catherine interrupted. "Tom! Why didn't you mention this earlier when I was talking about the fee."

"Which fee?"

"I think Tom was busy with the generator when you mentioned that, Catherine," Trevor mediated again.

"Did Dora send the money back?"

"Yes of course. Why wouldn't she have?"

"Why didn't you tell me that we received such a large sum of money?"

"Exactly because of that. Such an astronomical amount made no sense to me. Especially coming from the Caribbean! And without an invoice! It had to be a bank error. Look at it from my perspective, Catherine."

"Damn! We could have put the money to such good use. To fight WICED with its own money! Call Dora, Tom. Perhaps she hasn't got to it yet or we're lucky in some other way. Come, call her."

Reluctantly Tom grabbed his phone. He spoke to Dora, listened to her for a long time and then said, "No, that was right, Dora. You did nothing wrong. We'll talk tomorrow, don't do anything until we've spoken again."

"What, what?" Catherine urged.

"She reversed the payment but the day before yesterday the same amount landed back in the account. This time from a Financiero Del Caribe from Caracas, Venezuela. She wanted to talk to you about it personally, but couldn't find the courage yet to go over my head."

"Oh Dora and her submissive cowardice! Oh I could kiss her. Trevor, is Commissaire Moreau still allowed to access my bank account information?"

"Not without a court order."

"Hang on," Tom intervened. "You're calling Dora submissive and cowardly? After everything you've told us, you of all people shouldn't say things like that."

"You think I'm a coward? I was brave! Rivas explained to me that I only adjusted to my emergency situation."

"Yeah, body and soul!"

"Stop it!" Trevor said in untypical impatience.

"No, I want us to thrash this out. Rivas said that my actions were a subconscious survival tactic."

"Sure whatever the great master says!"

"What would you have done, Tom? Huh? Come on, let's hear it."

"Tom, she's right, it's not your place to judge," interjected Trevor.

"But it's okay for you guys to judge! Dora for not speaking up, me for supposedly not running the company properly!"

"I never said that!"

"Trevor did. But let's leave it. It just kills me to see how this nasty piece of work is clearly still in control of your life, Catherine."

Catherine said, "Tom, you are right about one thing. It probably is also Dora's survival strategy not to speak up. One really shouldn't judge others, especially not without knowing the full background. I shouldn't judge Dora, Trevor shouldn't judge you and you shouldn't judge Rivas or me. Back to the topic. You, Trevor will handle Van der Sonsen. Thanks. I need something else from you, Trevor."

"Yes?"

"I need visitation rights for Rivas as soon as he's physically able. Yes, I know he's being guarded but I have to get to him before WICED gets their hands on him."

"Catherine, how do you think this works? I'll see what I can do with Van der Sonsen, but visiting Rivas in Berlin, that's just out of the question."

"In the European justice system the victim has the right to become a side plaintiff, and the victim's legal team works alongside with the public prosecution. You could bring yourself in because of the kidnapping story and insist on a victim-perpetrator meeting. If both parties agree, there's nothing that can stop it. Just say I need it for my psychological healing."

"Catherine, first, thanks for the lecture on the legal aspects but second, you must be kidding! You didn't even have psychological therapy, you absolutely refused to go, even though Tom found such a brilliant psychologist for you."

"Excuse me, but you really can't expect me to have sessions with this bimbo!"

Tom protested, "She's an excellent psychologist. Don't talk like that."

"Yeah, probably blond and long legged. Just right for you. Tom, for four months I experienced firsthand, the most ingenious psychology possible. Do you honestly think that she can get even close to Rivas or that I could gain any kind of insights from her at all?"

"Are you crazy? Her job isn't to keep up with that criminal bastard but to fix what he broke."

"Rivas was seduced into ideals that weren't his. Please believe me that this part of his life is over. He's changed. What else can I do to convince you?" Tom sent a desperate look into Trevor's direction. Trevor in turn looked quizzically at Catherine. "Yeah alright. I'll go to therapy. But not to her. Tom could you please find a therapist for me by the name of Lammingcourt? I'm not sure where to start but please research that for me."

"I don't have to. He lives in Edinburgh, he has a practice there, but doesn't take on new patients except very special cases."

Catherine was taken aback. "You know of him?"

"Yes, he specializes in abduction and torture trauma. After you came back from France I worked through the internet looking for ways of helping you and that's how I came across him. There's no way of missing him, he's the most renowned expert in this field. How do you know of him?"

"Rivas told me about him, I think Rivas was his student or even his assistant. I forgot to mention that earlier. So I'll start a therapy with him, because I am such a 'special case' and as soon as Rivas and I are reunited, I promise you both, I'll do the best therapy with the best in the world. Rivas himself!"

"That'll be the therapy of the century, no doubt." Even Trevor succumbed to a condescending remark. He was starting to get concerned about Catherine's emotional state. Clearly there was something wrong. She needed help and he was sorry that he'd not insisted on her getting help earlier.

"If you two don't stop being judgmental, I'll carry on without you. Is that clear?"

"All clear," sighed Tom.

"Is he even present enough to receive visitors?" asked Trevor.

"I don't know, but we're pressed for time. I have to try. Are you going to get me the private meeting with him?"

"What? A *private* meeting? I'll never get permission for that."

"Why not? I'm the victim. I have, well, victim rights. Don't I?"

"I can go this route, closure etcetera, but it'll be no private meeting, that's for sure. If they agree, they'll do so to further their case. They'll try to trap you and use it against you. And him."

"Alright, if they'll be present, I'll talk cryptically - in such a way that only he'll get me. Then he'll go back to Maria until he can bring Andalus to a place of safety and the three of us can be together again. Somewhere where nobody will find us. That's the plan. Tom, you'll help me with your headhunting techniques to save the world from WICED, WICED will save Rivas from the justice system and I'll save Rivas from WICED, eventually."

"And the people who finance WICED, whom, if I may remind you, you want to blackmail? There's no place on earth where they won't find you," said Trevor.

"I have two answers for this. First, the danger that I contact the media will never go away, even if they plan further attacks. This I can achieve even if they kill me. Especially then. Trevor, we'll draft a letter to Moreau and if anything should happen to me you'll get this letter to him and at the same time a copy to the press. To let me live was WICED's biggest mistake. Now it's too late, I've got them!"

"And second?"

"Rivas and I will hide out in the mountains at first. He knows about things like this. We'll need new identities."

"Exactly."

"I have my little database for that."

"You still have it?"

"A copy, yes."

"Alright, that's it!" shouted Tom. "Do you honestly think that I'll help you to humiliate yourself by running halfway across the globe after this sadist pig so that you can hand yourself over to him again? Voluntarily? And to an unknown location in some mountain range where he can beat you up every day, just because 'he feels like it'? I don't even want to think about what he'll do to you."

"He won't hurt me."

"At least consider the other victims."

"Without WICED, he'll have no reason to carry on. And just for the sake of it? That's not his style."

"Oh he's got *style*? Sorry, I didn't realize! You know what? You've completely lost your mind."

"He loves me."

"Catherine! He's a bad guy, a mean, violent criminal. Even if he feels love for you, or whatever his bizarre perception of this may be, sooner or later his true character will come out. You're the one that's always preached that you can't squeeze mayonnaise out of a toothpaste tube. Why do you want to hook up with him again? I get that he's a real stud, and that he satisfies you like no other man ever could, and all that trash, but I won't let you expose yourself to this danger again."

"Don't speak so condescendingly of him. It's not about sex. Don't you get any of what I confided in you? What's wrong with you? Are you jealous or what?"

"No thanks, I'm not into crazy chicks."

"Tom, listen to me. It's true I lose my head when it comes to him, I know you're right about that. But there are other forms of intelligence. My gut tells me, and every cell of my body confirms that my plan will work. It's too crazy to fail. Everything great begins with an unconventional idea but everything new originates from chaos and is ordered bit by bit from there. Every civilization began at the point when someone dreamed up an incredible plan. Think about God. He had the imagination to create this incredible world. Just think about making a single star. If he had to ask one of us, we would all have said, he's lost his head."

"Oh of course! You're God. Sorry, I forgot. Please Catherine, get a grip and come back to earth now. You're totally irrational."

"George Bernard Shaw once said, that progress depends on the irrational man. Here, my motto." She pointed at a quote on her cell phone display: "The reasonable man conforms to the world; the unreasonable man tries to make the world conform to him. Therefore all progress depends on the unreasonable man". "And then there is the intelligence of my heart and it tells me that I can only be happy when Rivas and Andalus and I are together again."

"He'll hurt you, Catherine, or kill you. Probably both."

"He'll never hurt me again, Tom. He swore to it."

"That means nothing."

"It does to me. You see, the wicked witch is dead and black hair of the knight has turned white."

"Huh?"

"Never mind."

"Let's presume you return to him and he mistreats you, do you promise to leave him immediately when it happens for the first time?"

"I can promise you that easily, because I would do that anyway."

"One strike, one end?"

"Yes, one strike, one end. Promise."

"And if he locks you up?"

"Tom, if he does that, I was a fool and made a huge mistake. But to take this risk is my fate. Tom, will you pour some more wine for us, please? I have to call Gaby." She reached for her phone and dialed Gaby's shortcut. While waiting for her to answer, she addressed Tom again, "Could you take over the company for a few days again?"

Gaby answered, "Hello Catherine. What can I do for you?"

Catherine looked at Tom; he nodded.

"Gaby, sorry I'm calling so late, but I won't be in the office tomorrow. Could you please move my appointments for tomorrow and the day after to Tom's calendar and book me the first flight to Málaga. I'll also need a rental car. Give me the reservation numbers as soon as you have them."

"Return flight?"

"Same evening as my arrival day. It'll be tight, but I'll have to manage."

"Alright, you'll hear from me in the morning."

"Another thing. Please call Dr Jefferson and ask her for a referral to an orthopedic surgeon. Make me an appointment for the day after I get back from Spain."

"Will do. What must I tell her is your problem, so she'll do the referral telephonically?"

"Riding accident. Hip. MRI."

"Did you have a fall?"

"Old injury. Gaby, one last thing. Please find out if Alex has found a new job. If not, give him an appointment for when I'm back. I want to re-employ him if he's still interested." To Gaby's stunned silence, Catherine answered, "A good fairy flew past and showed me that I was heartless and that I have something to make up. I know now how quickly one can mess up and how important it is to get a second chance when one is remorseful about having made a bad decision." Catherine put the phone down. "Don't say a word about Alex, Tom!" she warned him.

"I didn't say anything."

Trevor, however, was now most concerned. "Catherine, what's this nonsense about good fairies and Alexander? You don't owe this traitor anything."

"Without Alex I would have never met Rivas."

"Now I've heard everything."

"Enough now. I can employ whomever I want!"

Tom changed the subject. "You want to fly to Málaga?"

"No to Jerez de la Frontera, via Málaga."

"Do you want to visit the Royal High School of Riding?"

"No Tom, I'm going to a stud farm. A Spaniard awaits me there."

Tom looked at Trevor and raised his eyes. Trevor returned the look and asked, "Who?"

"A magnificent white Andalusian stallion. Very valuable," she enthused.

Tom asked, "What's his name?"

"As of today, Machu Picchu."

"And you're going to buy this Machu Picchu?"

"Yes, Rivas gave me the money for him. It's not WICED's money," she explained quickly after a look at Tom's facial expression.

But she'd misread it. Tom was glad that Catherine was doing something nice for herself. "You want to bring him here?"

"No Tom, I don't know his destination yet."

Both now fully comprehended how serious Catherine was about her intentions. Trevor got up and embraced her. "I hope you'll be happy, my dear little Catherine."

They said good-bye.

"Tom, do you have any cash on you?"

"For what?"

She grabbed her car keys and handbag. I have to get a packet of cigarettes."

Trevor said, "But you don't smoke anymore."

"I do again now."

Tom suggested, "Wait, I've got some of Barbara's in the car. I'll get them for you."

"Thanks Tom. But I only smoke one brand."

Epilogue
Jamaica, March 21

"Did I pack the right clothes? I mean what does one wear on a yacht for so long? I don't think I brought enough sweaters. I'll get cold."

"Benji will take care of everything."

"Where's he anyway? Maybe there's a problem?" She threw a concerned glance at her old Rolex: 9.10 am.

"Soon come. Jamaica time," Rivas laughed.

The little Montego Bay harbor café where they were waiting for Benji was not chic but charming and warm - the Jamaican way. Gentle reggae waved across to them. Rivas had insisted on a champagne breakfast. "I don't like champagne for breakfast, and anyway, I only drink Taittinger," she'd reminded him and then Rivas had produced a bottle of Taittinger as if by magic anyway. Still, she was not in a mood to party. She was annoyed because Rivas refused to tell her where the yacht would be taking them. Up until half an hour ago, she didn't even know that they were going on a cruise.

"Excuse me please, I have to make a call."

"Are you calling Benji?" Rivas disappeared around the corner without answering. Catherine drummed her fingers impatiently on the table top and finished her last sip of Blue Mountain coffee. Her cell phone rang. Before taking the call she looked at the display. "*¡Hola! Rivas?*" she said quizzically as she answered.

"Yes, it's me, Catherine."

"What's going on? Has something gone wrong?"

"Please look at the date and time of your phone."

"March 21, 9.15 am," she read and saw Rivas returning to their table. "I don't believe it! I completely forgot. Everything turned out so differently."

"I didn't forget."

"I can see that!" Rivas sat down and handed her a white box. "What's that?" Catherine lifted the lid and saw a picture of Machu Picchu, her Andalusian. She took out the photo and saw a ring underneath it. It was made of white gold with a multiple carat diamond in the center. On the left and right of the diamond were three emeralds each. "For me?"

Stupid question, Catherine thought immediately afterwards, but Rivas surprised her with his answer. "No."

"For whom then?"

"For the white miracle horse and its princess from the Rhineland."

Catherine waited. When he didn't add anything she asked impatiently, "Is this supposed to be a marriage proposal?"

"Yes."

"Then ask me."

"I can't."

"Why not?"

"Because I wouldn't bear it if you said no, that's why the ring is for the princess in you."

"I don't get it."

"You said it wasn't necessary to ask her. Of course she would say yes."

"She's saying yes right now."

"I love you Catherine."

"One love. *Me redi arredi*," someone cheerfully announced in Patois next to them.

"One love, Benji," replied Catherine and wiped away her tears with trembling hands while Rivas got up and this time shook Benji's hand. Benji grabbed Catherine's suitcase and Rivas took his own. Catherine followed and they strolled towards the pier while Benji talked nonstop.

His words faded into the background and Catherine heard the cry of the seagulls who circled hungrily above them. In the distance she saw several ocean liners – huge like skyscrapers - slowly slicing the horizon. The smell of diesel and stale sea water went up her nose. She briefly looked up to the bright blue Caribbean sky while the men helped her onto the yacht. Not an easy undertaking with her high heels and her short, night blue Armani Black Label satin dress, that she wore for the first time.

"It's just as well I put out some more suitable gear for you," Benji remarked, "robust, comfortable clothes and shoes, exactly your size. Army issue, strong and warm."

"Never again!" said Rivas.

"I agree, I'd rather freeze," confirmed Catherine and took his hand.

Another exciting title in this series

This sequel to *On the Bit. Catherine* is due for release in 2015.

What happened between November and March to bring Catherine and Rivas together again?
Can Catherine's ambitious plan succeed?
Or will it merely propel her into another dangerous adventure?
Will she fully recover from her ordeal?
How will Rivas escape the justice system? For how long?
And, can he really change?

Near the coast of Tanzania pirates kidnap Charlotte, the teenage daughter of a US diplomat, and sell her on to traders.

Why would a Ugandan mountain gorilla impact on her fate?

How are Catherine Zitgow and her former kidnapper, the darkly handsome Rivas Romero, involved in this?

And why is Romero's stallion, the magnificent Andalus, being held in the stables of Washington's FBI?

"If you read the first book you will fall back into Rivas and Catherine's world with ease. If you have not, you will still find this book one that you cannot bear to put down."
www.equimondi.de - review of the German original.

www.on-the-bit-thriller.com

A darkly passionate romantic thriller, with the power to captivate even as it shocks.

On the bit - Charlotte

Other titles by Annette Kinnear

Annette Kinnear hat Personalverantwortliche, Headhunter und deren Kunden Arbeitgeber und Arbeitnehmer interviewt und ihre prägendsten Erfahrungen in 16 spannenden Fallstudien zusammengefasst. An jedes Kapitel schließt sich zudem eine Analyse mit hilfreichen Tipps für die eigene Karriere an.

In Headhunting gewährt die Autorin exklusive Einblicke in eine Branche, die für ihre Diskretion berühmt ist. Die lehrreichen Fallbeispiele aus dem In- und Ausland machen dieses unterhaltsam geschriebene Buch zu einem Muss für alle, die sich für den globalisierten Arbeitsmarkt fit machen wollen.

Headhunting. Bitte husten Sie, falls Ihr Chef gerade mithört. Insiderberichte von der geheimen Jagd auf dem Arbeitsmarkt.

www.annettekinnear.de

ISBN: 978-3862652143

16 true and entertaining insider stories from the lives of headhunters. Available as a paperback and e-book in German from Schwarzkopf & Schwarzkopf, Berlin.

Headhunting

ABOUT THE AUTHOR

Annette Kinnear was born in Southern Germany and currently resides in Johannesburg, South Africa.

inspiration@irie.co.za
www.on-the-bit-thriller.com
www.facebook.com/Thriller.Onthebit.Rappenschwarz
www.twitter.com/AnnetteKinnear

Volume 3 - the sequel to 'On the Bit. Charlotte' is due for release in 2016:

(Picture of the German original cover)

On the Bit. Shanta

Catherine, Rivas and Andalus are busy settling into their new home when the doorbell rings.
It appears as though there are people out there intent on taking revenge on Rivas. Among them is the seductive Shanta.
She has a wicked plan which threatens to destroy the idyllic setting of Rivas' stud farm.
Reluctantly, Catherine and Rivas dive into another adventure.